Calypso's Heart

An Orion's Order Novel

M.C. SOLARIS

Calypso's Heart by M.C. Solaris
Edited/Formatted by Marchesa Schroeder
Cover by Mayhem Cover Creations

Copyright © 2020 M.C. Solaris LLC
All rights reserved.

ISBN: 978-1-952655-00-5 (Paperback)
ISBN: 978-1-952655-01-2 (Ebook)

Library of Congress Control Number: 2020906583

This is a work of fiction. All of the characters, organizations, and events portrayed in this story are either products of the author's imagination or are used fictitiously, and any resemblance to actual events, business establishments, locales, or persons, living or dead, is entirely coincidental.

First printing edition 2020

M.C. Solaris
Huntington Beach, CA
For bulk order inquiries contact:
mcsolarisauthor@gmail.com
www.mcsolaris.com

Acknowledgments

Thank you so very much to my extraordinary imaginary friends. Oh, and that crazy super blood moon eclipse the day we met.

To the book crew: Marchesa Schroeder and the badass beta readers (you know who you goddesses are).

To the mentors: Steven Farmer, Nicole Jardim, and the Universe.
With love to my friends and family (shout out to the Schroeder Clan!)

Name Pronunciation

Aetius
Pronunciation: ae-tee-us

Aleia Reaux
Pronunciation: uh-lee-uh r-oh

Alexina Astéri Diamánti
Pronunciation: aa-lehksiy-naa aa-steh-ree dia-ma-n-tee

Anguis
Pronunciation: an-️wis

Azaeleia
Pronunciation: uh-zay-lee-uh

Deloreia
Pronunciation: de-lor-ee-uh

Eliades
Pronunciation: ee-lie-ah-deez

Caly
Pronunciation: kal-ee

Riordan
Pronunciation: reer-dun

Table of Contents

Calypso's Heart

An Orion's Order Novel

M.C. SOLARIS

Chapter 1

Midnight darkness. It was that inky darkness where there's no difference whether your eyes are open or closed.

Where am I?

While desperately trying to focus her eyes to see a glimmer of... well, anything, a single pinprick of light appeared in front of her. Her eyes were glued to the speck of light which seemed to be growing. All the while, darkness remained all around her.

Wait... It's not getting bigger. I'm getting closer to it.

Yes, it actually felt like she was traveling in a dark, underground train tunnel and she saw the light.

Wow... I see the light at the end of the tunnel. Really, Caly?

Judging by how quickly the light grew, she realized she must be traveling incredibly fast. As the end of the tunnel sped closer with every second, she saw that the light looked like a shimmering, translucent barrier.

Shit!

She realized she was about to smash into this light barrier and she couldn't stop the momentum.

Three... Two...

Preparing for impact, she closed her eyes and exhaled. There was a moment of silky warmth all around her and then a gentle yet immediate slowing down.

What...?

As she opened her eyes, her thoughts of the tunnel immediately dissipated. In front of her was a breathtakingly beautiful garden full of wild and exotic looking flowers, trees, and plants. She had never seen anything like it before. *This can't be real.* Her gaze followed what appeared to be a glimmering butterfly. But before she could take a closer look, something else caught her eye in the magical yet serene scene.

She wasn't alone.

There appeared to be a silhouette of a person sitting on a bench overlooking a nearby lake. She couldn't see what the person looked like because the bench was facing away from her. Already forgetting the strange butterfly creature, she curiously carried her feet forward toward the person...

Man? Yes, it was a man sitting on the bench. With her newfound wonderment for whatever this entire experience was, she approached him and curiously gazed upon the man's profile.

He looked to be in his early thirties—that age where the eagerness of the twenties has faded and the maturity of life's lessons has set in. And there certainly was something that felt mature about this man, despite his rather sophisticated and strapping appearance. His medium-length, light brown hair was naturally highlighted with golden-auburn and effortlessly styled away from his classically handsome face. He had light skin with a hint of tan, a strong, clean-shaven jaw and a natural pout of his lips. He was wearing dark blue slacks paired with a crisp, white button-up which was casually styled with the sleeves rolled up, revealing strong arms.

God, did I just walk into a Harry Potter-themed GQ modeling photoshoot?

Without taking his gaze off of the lake, he made a slight hand gesture indicating for her to sit next to him. It was casual and felt as if they had been friends for centuries. Yet, this man was a complete stranger.

As she sat down, something in the lake flashed in her peripheral view and her gaze naturally turned to see what it was. Reflecting off of the water, the sunlight was glimmering impossible shades of blue, green, and even hints of purple.

"*Wow,*" she exhaled in breathy awe.

The man's lips warmly curved and his face softened a touch at her reaction. She was mesmerized by the magical body of water and the colorful light show that was dancing across the glass-like surface.

"It's time..." the man said in a gentle and welcoming Irish accent that seemed to wrap around her and give her a warm hug.

At the sound of his voice, she turned her head to look at the man and saw that he was handing her something.

Is that...?

It was a paper, coffee-to-go cup from The Drip (her local coffee shop) with her name written below the logo along with the scribbled words of her newest drink obsession—a mocha latte.

Confused, she stood for a moment, holding the piping hot cup of her current favorite beverage. One of the things she loved about mornings was her morning drink ritual, which was subject to change based on the seasons... and her moods. Before mocha lattes, it was peppermint tea lattes. After all, the same drink every single morning would be too boring and she already had enough boring in her life. Come to think of it, her morning drink ritual was the one thing she could count on. Well that and her best fur-iend, Felix.

"Meow."

She blinked her eyes open only to see a pair of bright, wide eyes staring back at her. Glimmering gold with a hint of viper green in the middle, these eyes were as familiar to her as the back of her own hand.

"Morning, Felix. Let me guess, breakfast?" she said with a sleepy smile, still coming out of the strange dream with the man at the magical lake.

Felix, now purring with delight from her voice, gave her a lick on the hand that she was using to scratch behind his ears. Confident she was awake and had received his breakfast order, he triumphantly padded off to the kitchen with silent feline grace.

Rolling over in her warm, soft cloud of a bed, she took a deep breath in and a glorious good-morning stretch of her arms and legs, as she shook off that weird dream with the man and the breathtakingly impossible scenery.

I know I always have weird dreams but that one certainly takes the cake.

Before rolling out of bed, she checked the time. She was a morning person and more often than not, she woke up before her alarm. Today was no exception, especially because she was looking forward to her morning drink ritual.

Speaking of which, I better get a move on because now all I can think about is a mocha latte from The Drip. Her thoughts flipped back to the strange dream with the man and her beloved hot beverage. *I mean, the GQ photoshoot vibes aside, I guess it's really not that surprising I dream about my favorite part of my day.*

Swinging her feet off the bed, she slowly pressed her feet onto the ground as the cold, cream-colored carpet slid in between her toes. She definitely appreciated that her light carpet had flecks of darker colors naturally weaved into it because it helped to forgive the occasional "oopsie" that occurred from time to time—well, except for the infamous smokey-eyeshadow incident that happened only a few weeks after moving in. But other than that, it was great. Reaching over to the cup of water that took up permanent residence on the nightstand next to her bed, she took a quick drink. The cool liquid slid down her throat. Oh, how there was almost nothing like that first drink of water after a deep sleep.

She made her home in a small one-bedroom apartment with a basic layout composed of a bedroom, kitchen/living space, and a bathroom. It was LA after all and with the income as a paralegal, she was not made of money. The walls were a simple white and intentionally left blank—she was never really into the whole interior decorating thing. Of course, she wouldn't argue if a home decorating fairy swooped in one night and spruced up her place. But she was good with what she had. It was simple, clean, and easy to maintain. That didn't mean she was living like she was eighteen again—thankfully, that chapter of her life was closed. So, she invested her money in practical yet simple things... from IKEA. Okay, so maybe she hadn't fully grown out of that phase of her life. But, hey, IKEA still had nice looking things and that was all her budget allowed for after her ridiculous rent that cost an arm and a leg. She still didn't even know how she lucked out with her apartment in the safer and relatively nicer part of LA because the prices were usually way outside of her budget.

Getting out of the shower, she looked at herself in the bathroom mirror. Stormy, gray eyes, pale complexion, and lips on the fuller side—naturally full, not like all of the purchased, botoxy, fake, duck lips she was surrounded by in LA. Her thick, long, straight, dark-brown (almost black) hair cascaded down past her slim waist on her curvy body. Toweling off her hair, her thoughts took a sudden sharp turn down a road she tried to never go down. It could hardly be helped; any number of thoughts (conscious or unconscious), could trigger the automatic lights in the driveway of the house at the end of that proverbial road, with the bold yellow "DO NOT ENTER" sign. Her parents passed away four years ago in a freak car accident. This triggered the sudden avalanche of her life in a direction that she never could have imagined. Growing up, she was always kind of a loaner and preferred to stay at home and read or watch movies rather than "people-ing." She guessed that went with the territory of being an extroverted introvert at heart. Curling up on the couch with a romance novel, her drink flavor of the week, and Felix purring on her lap, brought such peace and joy to her soul. Okay, so maybe she was a total sap and hopeless romantic. She grew apart from the few friends she did have because they were all about guys and going out. There was nothing wrong with that but she was always on the fringe of that party phase of her friends' lives, especially being a bit socially shy. It was fun every once in a while to dress up, talk about guys, and go out dancing. But the night she got *the call*, she retreated to the cave: the inner safe space of her mind.

Slamming the door shut on those thoughts, she finished getting ready quickly with her go-to look of black mascara, rose-colored tinted lip gloss, and a dash of light-pink blush with a hint of gold shimmer. She threw on a pair of gray slacks and a white blouse, gave a goodbye pet to Felix, and was out the door.

Opening the door to The Drip, she paused for a brief moment, shocked to see the line was double what it usually was.

Oh, hell.

She didn't exactly want to wait in line, but damn it, she was already there—it was like that weird dream sparked this irresistible craving for her mocha latte. Besides, she definitely needed it today to set her day off on the right foot in preparation for her big client meeting at the firm. Waiting for her order, she noticed the barista's frazzled "deer in the headlights" expression.

It must be her first day.

She couldn't imagine how crazy all of the orders were. *Sub coconut milk for dairy, add collagen, swap out the plastic straw for a paper one, and most importantly sugar-free because—Duh! Sugar is public enemy number one!* She rolled her eyes at the thought.

"Kaylee! Large mocha latte!" The male barista pronounced her name incorrectly.

Caly waited a few moments to make certain there actually wasn't a Kaylee in the building who just so happened to order the same thing as her. There wasn't. Not bothering to correct the barista, Caly got up, grabbed her drink from the counter, and continued out the door.

Flipping through her playlists, she was onto her next order of business: the hunt for a song that perfectly complimented her mocha latte and, of course, the infamous, wonderfully unwonderful: LA traffic.

Hmmm. What sounds good? Nope. Not that. Definitely not that. Never that! Why is that even on here? She paused on a possible contender. *Yeah, no. Not feeling that right now.* She kept scrolling. *Oh, maybe this.*

"Lights Down Low" by Max started playing. Her eyes closed and her head swayed side to side for a moment before she began to sing along with the music playing on the speakers of her very practical white Toyota Corolla.

Probably cooled off enough by now, she thought, a

few songs later, as she reached for the mocha latte in the cupholder. With the cup lid pressed against her lips, the anticipation built with thoughts of that first, sweet sip of silky mocha. Just as the first taste touched her tongue, out of nowhere, a car swerved in front of her and cut her off forcing her to slam on her breaks.

"Shit!" she blurted out with echoes of car horns speeding by. She looked down to see that the mocha latte had spilled all over her.

"Damn it! I just had to wear the white shirt and gray pants today, didn't I?"

She inwardly cringed as she felt the warm coffee wetness dripping between her breasts creating a mini pool in her lap. On an exhale, she looked down to see just how bad the damage was.

"Great. Just fucking great. I can't go to the office like this. Especially today with my client meeting with the Fergusons. Well, soon-to-be client."

BAM!

She looked up to see that she accidentally tapped the bumper of the car in front of her.

"Oh my god! Are you serious right now?"

Thank God she wasn't driving too fast because of the traffic. She pulled over to the side of the road behind a non-descript black sedan and got out of her car to look at the damage.

Oh god. Please don't be bad... Please don't be bad... she internally chanted, walking up to a man who was a real-life giant at well over six-feet tall. He had dark hair, tanned, olive skin and was sporting blue jeans, a white T-shirt, and a leather jacket with Aviator sunglasses.

He's definitely gotta be an actor.

"Hi..." She tried to speak in a friendly voice, presenting

a smile. Meanwhile, internally, she was trying not to freak out.

And he is kinda good looking... but in a cold, metal freezer sorta way, she thought, shuddering slightly.

"*Umm... I'm Caly.*"

Okay. Mr. Intense.

"I'm so sorry about this. I didn't even see you... well... because..." She looked down at the multiple fresh coffee stains on her white shirt and gray pants. "I only looked down for one second..."

She trailed off and recoiled inside slightly when she looked at the bumper that had a visible small dent. She mustered up the courage to look back at the intense man and saw he was no longer wearing his glasses. It revealed the coldest, dark brown eyes with hints of a golden yellow. A wave of goosebumps rushed over her.

Mr. Intense is staring at you, she thought in a sing-song voice. *Probably because you look like a frazzled hot-mess complete with coffee stains. Oh, and you just dented his fucking car for crying out loud.*

"Hi, Caly." His voice was deep and matched his giant frame.

There was a pause for the longest moment as his brown and gold eyes remained on her. She could've sworn she felt a palpable wave of cool intensity.

Breaking the gaze, he pointed to his bumper and said, "There's no damage really." His intense eyes flicked back on her. "We're good." There was another pause. "Where are you headed?"

What?! No damage? Clearly there is a dent. Whatever, don't argue with him. Hurry up and answer his question before he changes his mind. Besides, a car insurance claim with increased premiums is the last thing you need right now.

"Really? Thanks! And, umm, I'm on my way to work. I'm a paralegal for Geoffrey and Laird."

Okay, he is staring at you again. Politely finish the conversation before he changes his mind.

"Speaking of which, I do actually need to get going especially because..." She pointed down at her coffee-stained clothes. "I need to take care of this now too. Anyways, thanks again!"

Maybe he is just a good person and you've become jaded by living in LA. At that very moment, someone honked at another car as they sped by. *See? Case and point.*

With those intense eyes locked on her, he flashed her a cool smile. She walked back to her car and got in. As she pulled away, she saw that he was still staring at her.

That was... her thoughts trailed off with a strange feeling that drifted away almost as fast as it came.

* * *

The wind shifted directions slightly and Caly's scent drifted over to him on a gentle breeze.

Interesting, he thought, inhaling and immediately sharpening his senses. With focused intent, he took another deep breath to confirm and sift out the odors assaulting his senses, like car exhaust and the other smells of the streets and passing pedestrians. Removing his glasses, he completed a quick assessment of this female. Something about her seemed familiar.

Heartbeat is a little fast but that's nothing abnormal considering the circumstances. Her pupils and scent are not giving away any lies or hints of deceit. Although, she could be well trained... There was something about her scent that he couldn't quite place.

"Hi, Caly," he said while still appraising her and the

situation but playing along... for now. "There's no damage really... We're good... Where are you headed?"

With cool calculation, he decided to keep a close eye on this female who was not as she appeared to be. He couldn't be too careful, especially right now. No one should have been able to find him. Yet...

What are you hiding, Caly?

And he should know when one was hiding after all. It wouldn't take him long to sniff out the truth.

* * *

Shifting her eyes away from the strange man's gaze in her rearview mirror, Caly let out a big exhale she didn't even know she was holding. Her thoughts shifted back to the present moment and flicked to the clock.

Shit... Okay, I have just enough time to swing back home really quick and change.

She was going to be a little late but oh well. She couldn't look like a slob, especially with the client meeting today. With her favorite playlist on shuffle, she replayed her thoughts about the events of the morning, starting with the vivid dream of the GQ model and the breathtakingly beautiful lake.

At least there is a little mocha latte left. Probably cold by now but whatever.

Resisting the temptation to look down at the coffee stains on her clothing (obviously she was not going to make the same mistake twice), she thought about the weird interaction with... *Wait, what was his name? Oh well. Whatever. It's not like you'll see him again.* Her thoughts trailed off with the change of the song on the car speakers.

She finally got settled in at her desk and took a breath. At least she knew she was about to work with the Ferguson's. They were going to sign off on the contract today. She had been working hard to get a sign-off on this client. Yesterday when they called, things ended on a really good note and they made the appointment to come in today.

Anita, one of the older office assistants, approached her desk.

"Good Morning, Caly."

Is she really throwing shade at how late I strolled into the office? Caly thought, analyzing Anita's judgy expression and tone of voice. Internally, Caly rolled her eyes annoyed at all of the office drama. And, of course, it would start not five minutes after she sat down.

"Good Morning, Anita," Caly said, sliding her professional fake smile into place.

"Burgess wants to see you," Anita smugly announced, walking off as though she knew something Caly didn't. Clearly, there must've been some juicy office gossip that Caly missed.

Great, Caly thought on a sarcastic beat.

Burgess was her boss. He was a nice guy but she didn't really have time for a visit to the principal's office. But it also wasn't like she could ignore the summons. So, she decided she would just stop by quickly to see if it was urgent. And if it wasn't, then she would just tell Burgess she would stop by later.

"The Fergusons came in early this morning and wanted to sign the deal," Burgess announced.

"Wait... What?" Caly cut him off. "The Fergusons came in this morning already? Their appointment isn't until..." She checked the clock on her cell phone. "An hour from now."

"Well, they decided to come in early due to something that came up last minute for them. And Anita let them know you weren't here. But they happened to see Brett walk in and, well, it turns out Brett knows the Fergusons' son from college and… Shit, well, they signed with Brett."

There was silence for a moment as her world did a flip flop.

"Wait, hold on. The Fergusons signed with Brett?! This morning?!"

Caly vaguely heard Burgess' voice in response but in reality, she was too wrapped up in her own thoughts to follow along.

Fucking Brett… of course it was Brett. He probably jumped at the chance to get back at me because I turned him down (nicely mind you) when he wanted to "get drinks." No one turns down Brett, the office hottie with an ego as wide as his perfect smile, that has surely gotten him several clients before. Smug-ass player acting like I didn't notice him all over Brittnie the week before. God, I am so over all of the dumb dating games. Hence why I have sworn off guys right now. Especially considering my track record— however short and pathetic it may be. Not to mention the fact that the last date I went on was with Eric, AKA Mr. Stick Shift. Why was he so obsessed with his manual transmission car anyways? I guess the one and only time I tried online dating could have gone worse though. Which reminds me not to listen to my neighbor, Megan, no matter how much her friend swears by online dating.

"Caly?" Burgess' voice broke into her inner monologue but the conversation was cut off by a sudden phone ringing. He answered before the first ring was over and signaled for her to close the door on her way out.

As she sank into her desk chair, Caly let out an exhale that seemed like it lasted an entire minute, as if it was making up for the unconscious holding pattern it seemed to be in during that cheery chat with her boss.

Well, now what? My whole day was planned around the Fergusons. And no it was not just because that was the only client I really had going for me right now either. Really! ...okay, who are you lying to Caly? Oh well, everything happens for a reason, right? It's not like you love this job anyways. It pays the bills and does have its perks but it's just a job.

Chapter 2

"That's a load of bullshit, Rhy!"

A deep chuckle filled the room as Rhyland walked to the fridge to grab a beer.

"It was worth a try. I mean, Nico looked like he was about to believe me."

With a teasing glint in their eyes, Rhyker and Rhyland looked over at Nico who was standing stalk still by the window. A pair of stone-cold, light-hazel eyes, perhaps with a hint of amusement under the icy layer, was staring back at them.

"Yeahhh. Hey, throw me one," Rhyker said to Rhyland, as he lazily lounged on the leather couch he loved so much. It was *his* couch and everyone knew it. Possessive? Yeah. But damn, he didn't care about claiming some territory in a house full of dominant males. Besides, he had spent hours one day testing out couches and it was hard finding a good couch that not only fit him but was comfortable.

Rhyker caught the beer with feline grace just as Blake strode across the room in his usual white T and blue jeans combo. It was simple and practical. He'd never been one to fuss over clothes. The same went with his dark brown hair that was shorter on the sides with a little length on top, holding a slight wave. The color complimented his light skin that naturally held a year-round summer tan. His strong jaw was framed with the perfect amount of stubble that was neat and trimmed yet, somehow, it simultaneously gave off a relaxed vibe. Despite his casual appearance, it only took one moment in his presence to realize he was a strong and intelligent alpha male. That paired with his incandescent golden eyes. And if that wasn't enough, his well-built body stood at 6'6," giving away the fact that he was a shifter and an alpha wolf. Predatory shifter males with larger animals were notoriously tall—it was just how they were built. They also had abilities associated with characteristics from their animal. Wolf shifters were highly instinctive with super-human strength, night vision, and a keen sense of smell.

Not missing a beat, Blake shot a quick glance around the room. "Where's D?"

"He's on his way. Was just finishing up following up on a lead," Rhyland said, sitting down in one of the leather chairs.

"Good. I hope he's got something. Speaking of, does anyone have... *anything*?"

"No," Rhyker and Rhyland echoed in unison.

And silence from Nico, unsurprisingly.

Nicolás was a three-hundred-year-old vampire. The centuries of immortality, mixed with his past, had brought a layer of ice and distance. But his loyalty to Blake and the others was unbreakable. Nico's 6'3," muscled body was in his usual attire of dark jeans, snug black T-shirt, and black combat boots. Strands of his medium-length, coffee brown hair fell astray, tantalizing his eyebrows and framing his light hazel eyes. He had a strong jaw and chiseled cheeks with barely a hint of stubble.

"Well, shit," Blake said, rubbing the scruff of his jaw. "Let's review what we have so far. James Barker, AKA The

Ghost, has managed to evade SILE for decades but they finally have a lead due to the recent murder of Marie Chan, the SILE investigator, who was deep undercover on the hunt for The Mastermind. Marie was apparently getting close to a possible lead, which would be the first time in centuries, and then, she was presumably taken out by The Ghost. This is assumed because of how she was chained, drugged, and tortured with broken bones and calculated cuts along the body to inflict pain without inducing death, all before the bastard was ready for that final act of his sick game—which fits Barker's MO with his past victims to a T. He was last seen heading into the human world presumably to lay low after taking out Marie."

The human world was on the other side of The Barrier, a magical barrier that separated the human world from the world of species. According to legend, it was created as a final solution to bring peace to the world, ending the ancient territorial world war, where humans turned on the other species out of fear.

SILE was the Species Intelligence and Law Enforcement and had been on the hunt for one of the biggest threats to the species, The Mastermind. The Mastermind was a mentalist, a rare subset of mind healers with gifted abilities that were all on the mental plane. He was said to be one of the most powerful of his kind in history but went mad in his immortality and was seduced by the darkness and power. The Mastermind had been in hiding since The Great Clash, where he battled the last ancient mentalist. It was said that when he was so close to death during the end of the battle, he struck an evil bargain with the darkness and retreated into a dark sleep. There were whispers in the wind that his power was waking and his ancient dark slumber was stirring.

"Deacon's here," Rhyland and Rhyker echoed at the same time.

It was a twin thing.

Blake and Nico were accustomed to Rhyland's eerily sensitive sense of smell and Rhyker's ridiculously acute hearing. Being identical twin black jaguar shifters, they were just shy of seven feet tall with hefty, muscled frames. They both had strong jaws, light skin with cool undertones, and obsidian black hair that contrasted their piercing, electric blue eyes. However, it was easy to tell them apart at a simple glance. Rhyker had detailed tattoos weaving up his right arm and teasing above the neckline of his tight, black T-shirt, all the way to his jawline. Completing his look, his black jeans, combat boots, and signature black diamond stud earrings tied everything together. *"You know I gotta highlight my best features somehow,"* Rhyker playfully announced to his brother when he first got them pierced. In contrast, Rhyland was tattoo-free and more casual in his faded blue T-shirt and jeans. His trademark look was complete with his hair brushed out of his face and a baseball cap worn backward. However, even a blind man could tell the difference between the two with Rhyland's slightly more casual and youthful demeanor. Whereas Rhyker had a bit more of a hard edge as if something had caused him to be more closed off than his twin. Regardless, they were both cats to the core—curious and almost couldn't help the urge to paw with anything that crossed their paths... which was usually Nico.

A minute later, the door opened and Deacon entered the room. Deacon, shorter than the shifters but still somewhat tall at 6'2," was wearing his deceptively casual, form-fitting black slacks and a light-gray sweater with the sleeves pulled up to the elbows, revealing his light complexion that naturally held a light, golden tan. Somehow, he made it look like the perfect blend of business and casual. His sandy blonde hair was somewhat similarly styled to Blake's, except cut shorter. Upon the bridge of his straight nose were square, black-framed glasses which seemed to enhance his baby blue eyes. The bold, large frames only added to his debonair demeanor.

"Tell me you have something," Blake demanded.

"Oh, he has something." Rhyland's playful grin widened at the opportunity to paw at Deacon. "Because is that...?" He took a theatrically long, audible sniff. "Oh, yes it is." He playfully smirked and waggled his brows. "Starr's scent."

Rhyker and Rhyland exchanged twin grins with a mischievous gleam in their eyes.

"Was Starr the *lead* you were following up on?" Rhyker pounced into the play, his smirk spreading a fraction wider.

Nico shifted his icy gaze to Deacon and, for a fleeting moment, there was a flicker of amusement behind the layer of ice.

"Alright..." Blake said, glancing at Rhyker and Rhyland with a look that said, "*No more.*"

Rhyker took the cue and lit up a smoke, keeping his mouth busy to ensure his silence. Rhyker smoked indigo, a plant with blue flowers that was said to have evolved from the tobacco plant species after The Barrier was put in place. It now only grew on the magical side of The Barrier. Species were more relaxed about smoking than humans because they were not susceptible to the negative side effects of smoking, like cancer. And the blue-gray smoke didn't bother anyone because of its lightly floral, somewhat incense-like, aroma.

"I have something," Deacon said, sending a sideways glare at Rhyker and Rhyland. "Starr's contact was able to pick up a whisper of what she believes was The Ghost crossing into the LA territory."

"How much truth does this *whisper* have? Blake spoke without missing a beat on a possible lead.

"It's nothing concrete... You know how seers are—always cryptic and on the knife-edge of crazy. But Starr trusts this contact and says The Whisper has not led her astray yet. So, it's worth checking out. And let's face it, we don't have anything else."

"Great. LA. Land of the big egos and even bigger pockets. Oh, and let's not forget all the humans. So many damn humans," Rhyland added with a whoop-de-fucking-doo type of voice.

"Yeah. More humans means more cover," Rhyker followed up, taking a drag on his indie.

"It's a shot in the dark but, D, hack into the human security camera systems around the LA border crossing of The Barrier and see if you can pick up on anything," Blake ordered.

There were various entry points into the human world across The Barrier. Unless accompanied by species, humans were unable to cross over. Otherwise, before they could even get near the entrance, their memory was wiped and replaced with memories as if the area was nothing special and easily forgettable. And well before the memory wipe was triggered, human technology would conveniently malfunction in some form or another, effectively rendering the area a technological dead zone.

Deacon was a steorrian with a special ability in computer languages. Steorrians, or *Keeper of the Stars*, were those born with the ability to read and translate the long lost, ancient language of the stars. This ability was said to be passed down through the genes, where some had the rare ability to speak and translate all languages—ancient and modern. It was theorized that all languages originated, in some form, from the stars. So steorrian minds held the key to language translation of the old and new. Although Deacon did not have the ability with language translation, he said that he could still sometimes see "stories" in the stars.

"Already on it. And Starr will contact me if her *whisper*—" Deacon paused, unamused after noticing the suggestive duplicate grins that flashed in his direction. "... sees anything else."

"Good." Blake spoke, moving his gaze to the twins. "Do a perimeter sweep around that area to see if you can pick up on a trail." He shifted his gaze from Rhyland to Rhyker. "Or hear any *whispers* of your own."

Being jaguar shifters, the twins both had shifter strength and heightened senses of smell, hearing, and eyesight. However, Rhyland was born with an incredibly sensitive sense of smell that far exceeded the standards for shifters and the same went for Rhyker's acute hearing. Together they made some of the world's most lethal hunters.

Chapter 3

From the shadows of two buildings across the street, the male watched Caly enter her apartment. He knew it was where she lived because he followed her after they met that morning when she hit his car. He saw her walk in with the coffee-stained clothing and a few minutes later, walk out with a new change of clothes. He then followed her to work, again, keeping a few car lengths of distance the entire time. Besides, who would think twice about a black nondescript sedan in LA? This was the reason he chose that car specifically. Still not convinced of this female, he decided to continue to keep a close eye on her.

She will slip up. Because they always do.

His thoughts momentarily glided to a memory of another female *they* sent to him. He was brought back to the present when Caly's apartment lights turned on. And he had all the time in the world to watch and wait.

* * *

Midnight darkness with the pinprick of light ahead.

Tunnel traveling adventures part two, Caly thought with a mix of sarcasm and curiosity.

As the light grew, she saw the Harry Potter GQ model next to her.

Naturally, my mind just couldn't let that man go away with the last dream.

In the next blink of an eye, they were about to breach the wall of light. She tried to keep her eyes open this time but the light was so bright her eyes closed in a natural re-flex. There was a moment of warmth around her and then a slowing down motion. She blinked open her eyes. It was dark... again. But not like the pure darkness of the tunnel. She was standing in what looked like a simple shallow rock cave and she was looking out at a white sand beach with blue crystal waves melodically ebbing and flowing as they kissed the shore. The sound of the waves was amplified by the cave, creating a relaxing, meditative effect. Up ahead, she saw a man on the shoreline with his back to her wearing blue jeans and a white T. It wasn't the Harry Potter GQ model. And on that realization, she suddenly recognized that she no longer saw GQ anywhere. The man on the beach turned around at almost the same instant she saw him. His otherworldly, golden eyes locked onto her.

He had dark brown hair that was shorter on the sides with a little length on top complimenting a slight wave. His jaw was framed with the perfect amount of stubble that was neat and trimmed. He gave off a relaxed yet very much alert vibe.

Okay, maybe I need to lay off the romance novels right before bed. But those eyes...

This man with impossibly beautiful, golden eyes pene-trated deep into her soul. His intense gaze was slightly ter-rifying but she couldn't seem to look away. They stayed in silent stillness as the waves continued their courtship with the shoreline.

"Meow... Meow..."

Waking back to reality, she pet Felix and sighed deeply with the vivid dream of the man with the golden eyes on the beach still fresh in her mind.

"Oh, Felix. I've sworn off men and yet I just dreamed of a gorgeously mysterious man in what could easily be one of my favorite places in the world—though, I've never been there. And don't get me wrong, GQ is good looking but there was something so dreamy about..." She paused, thinking of what to call the gorgeous golden-eyed man. "Mr. Mysterious. I mean, what does that say about me, Felix? I bet Freudian psychologists would just have a field day with me." On that lovely note, Caly lazily rolled out of bed and fed Felix breakfast.

"Meow."

"You're welcome."

Shuffling to her bathroom, she reached into the shower and adjusted the knobs until it was the perfect temperature. A little on the hot side but not scalding. She slipped under the warm spray and sighed. Nothing like a good hot shower to start the day off. She squeezed a generous amount of shampoo in her palm (because no one ever used just a little shampoo) and massaged it into her scalp. Her thoughts drifted to her dream of the beach and the gorgeous male with the mesmerizingly beautiful golden eyes.

"Ow!"

While she was off in La-La Land dreaming of Mr. Mysterious, soap dripped into her eye. She used the warm spray to help flush out what she could. But, damn, it burned. She quickly finished her shower, not daring to daydream again. Wrapping the towel around her, she looked at her eye in the mirror. Yup. Just as she thought: red and irritated. Maybe she could use this to her advantage and say she had pink eye and not go to work today. She let that thought play out in her mind and then decided she was going to have to face Brett, the client stealer, at some point. Yeah. She was so stopping by The Drip and getting a mocha latte again today. As she cycled through her thoughts, the weird dream she had yesterday with GQ popped into her mind. Then her thoughts coasted to the mini fender bender with Mr. Intense. Shaking off those thoughts, she finished getting ready.

Just leaving The Drip and driving to work, she took that first, sweet sip of mocha latte and sighed with pure caffeine pleasure.

Mocha lattes and music. Yup. Good ol' M&M. Hey, that's a thought.

She decided to put on some Eminem. Flipping through her playlists, she stopped on "Not Afraid" by Eminem. Fitting. And a little inspirational angry Eminem was exactly what she needed to let out some frustration with the whole Brett stealing her client thing.

In a pretty good mood, thank you M&M, she walked by Brett's office and his office door was closed.

Thank God he is on the phone. Probably with the Fergusons. Nope. So not going there.

She took a sip of her latte reminding her of her therapeutic car music sesh and made her way to her desk. She logged into her computer and decided to use the universal sign for "Do Not Talk To Me." Headphones. Despite her mind's internal battle of whether or not to continue with the (very enticing) angry DGAF therapeutic music theme, her logical side won. She put on her new playlist obsession which would hopefully allow her a temporary escape while at work today.

She pushed shuffle. "R.A.N." by Miguel started playing. Okay, so maybe it was a little emo but whatever. She was not exactly feeling the Katy Perry upbeat pop right now. And she hadn't been feeling that type of music since like forever. And who was she kidding anyway? She knew her emo music playlist was a direct reflection of how truly unhappy she was. Unhappy with her job. Unhappy because she had always felt different. Unhappy because it felt like there was something missing in her life. Unhappy with all of the fake LA ego dating games. So, yeah, when Miguel sang about slicing heartstrings and skipping broken records, as emo as it was, it hit home.

She tried to switch her thoughts back to the positive. She was grateful for her job and the pay was good. It allowed her to live with reasonable comfort in LA. Granted, there was nothing left over for savings but oh well. It would all work out one day, right?

As if the Universe was in a funny mood, Brett walked up to her desk with his winning player smile.

Gross.

His smile made her internally gag. It was perfect on the outside but she didn't trust it. Also, of course he wouldn't heed the universal headphones sign. Because it was Brett and, god, what woman wouldn't want to talk to him?

"Hey, Caly," he said in his slick, silky male voice that he definitely used to his advantage. Again, gross—she saw right through that privileged facade.

"Hi, Brett," she said in her I-will-play-nice voice, giving a convincing, fake office smile like nothing was wrong at all. Maybe she should be an actress because she had really sharpened her method acting skills while working in LA and pretending to fit in.

"Sorry about the Fergusons."

No you're not, she thought with a bit of a snippy edge.

"It turns out their son and I go way back to our college days."

You mean your frat days where you and the Fergusons' son probably were competing with how many girls you could fuck? Okay, so maybe she was in an extra spicy mood right now. Whatever.

"They wanted to support Matt's brother. You know, Phi Psi. Go Trojans!" He flashed his winning smile.

Here he goes again. Living in the past. She internally rolled her eyes but externally, her acting character was on fleek. "Yeah, totally!" She smiled and even let out a convincing laugh. Yup. She definitely was going to quit and become an actress.

"See, I knew you would understand, Caly. That's why you're my favorite girl in the office." He flashed another smile, this time, paired with a wink of his blue eyes.

Gag. And Girl? I am a full-grown woman. Continuing with her smile she responded,

"Of course! We're good, Brett."

He ran his hand through his golden blonde hair and said, "I have to go to a client meeting now but I wanted to talk with you. We have to do lunch sometime."

"Definitely!" Okay, maybe she needed to tone it down on the fake enthusiasm.

He flashed another smile and strode out.

And the Academy Award goes to...

Putting her earbuds back in, she got with the emo music program again. With her thoughts like the looping broken records Miguel sang about, she started to daydream about moving. LA was not for her. It was never for her. She was just trying to escape after the accident. Now she could say she actually tried the big city thing and that it wasn't for her. LA had too many people and she didn't belong.

Where do I belong?

Maybe somewhere with trees and nature. Somewhere peaceful. Somewhere without big, fake egos and constant traffic. Her thoughts trailed off until she landed on a thought she went back to often.

There has to be something more to life than this, right?

Cue the song "More To Life" by Stacy Orrico. Yup. That pretty much summed it up perfectly.

❊ ❊ ❊

Blinking slowly, Blake awakened from the strange, vivid dream. The female (yes, his wolf had sensed that she was female) was somehow blocking his night vision, so he couldn't see her because she was shadowed in the darkness of the cave. Except, her eyes. All he could see of her was her soft yet curious gray eyes, the color of a swirling storm. No matter how intriguing this female was and how she made his wolf stir with intense focus, he needed to make a call.

"Blake, what a pleasant surprise." Alexina greeted him with a welcoming smile on the communication screen but it was as if he could feel her warm embrace.

At first glance, she appeared young, around thirty years old, but ancients just had this aura about them. They had an old flame of knowledge in their eyes. She looked as she always did, sporting a clean face as her natural beauty illuminated her sun-kissed and light-gold complexion. She had her thick hair in a loose bun (with some rebel hairs straying free of the bun), which was secured with an old-fashioned pencil. Her hair was chestnut-brown with strands of golden shimmer. She had always used a pencil, moonlighting as her hairpin, and she never saw a reason to switch to more modern elastic bands or clips. Besides, it meant she would never be without a pencil and that could be quite useful for an ancient steorrian who spent her days curled up with the old texts. Her thick yet perfectly groomed female brows framed her big brown eyes with a splash of hazel around

29

the irises, which were ever swirling with ancient knowledge of the stars.

With an appraising look and without missing a beat, she said, "Ahh... So what is the question that I see in your eyes?"

Chuckling warmly, Blake replied, "Sharp as ever, Alexina."

Her gaze softened slightly with a hint of fondness for Blake in her smile as she simply waited for the question.

He shared the dream and asked, "What do you make of this?"

She tapped the eraser side of a wooden pencil on her full lips, an indication that she was in thought—no doubt sifting through all the memories and knowledge in the library of her mind. Her earrings caught a glint of light and he focused on them. Five diamond studs that resembled a shooting star up the curve of her ear.

"In a single glance, it reminds me of our beautiful origins and the infinite stories of the stars." That was her response when he asked her about her earrings once.

When she finally spoke, she simply said, "Intriguing..." And it was clear her thoughts were still filtering and formulating.

"Dreamers, or rather travelers in this case, do have the ability to visit others or a place in the dream space." There was a pause. "Yet, in your dream, she stays hidden. Except for the eyes. As you know, travelers—rather, any subspecies that we know of—do not have the ability to... block... to use the word you used (and I do think that word fits here). Anyways, travelers can't block abilities." She paused again as if she was sorting through additional thoughts that surfed by on the waves of her mind. "Curious that she was also able to pull you into that dream space. Only powerful travelers have that rare ability. Hmmm... Yes. This is indeed curious

30

and intriguing."

"What should I do?"

A soft, playful smile formed on her lips. "What *can* you do? Hmm? Trust your instincts and stay alert."

With shared goodbyes, he ended the call with more questions than when it started. His thoughts were interrupted when he sensed Deacon approaching. A moment later, Deacon appeared in the door, and the two exchanged typical acknowledging male head nods. Skipping any verbal greetings, Deacon sat in his usual spot on the sofa.

"Anything from security cameras?" Blake asked.

"No. Nothing. Still scanning."

"Good. Hey D?"

"Yeah."

"You and Starr. Do I need to know?" However unconventional a pack it may be, as alpha of Orion's Order, it was Blake's job (and natural instinct) to make sure his pack mates were healthy, happy and thriving—well, as much as they could be. He didn't know what was going on between Deacon and Starr but everyone knew there was something, at least on Deacon's side, despite how much he tried to deny it. And Deacon had been a little distant since getting back from seeing Starr yesterday.

"There's nothing to know."

Blake gave Deacon an appraising alpha stare for a long moment. Satisfied (for now), he looked at the pool table and back at Deacon. "You in?"

"Yeah."

With The Ghost being the highest priority not only for SILE but for all species due to his possible connection with The Mastermind, they did not take on any other cases. So, he knew to take advantage of the time that presented itself during the lulls of the hunt by spending bonding time with his pack mates. Right now, both he and his wolf knew

Deacon needed him—even if Deacon didn't want it. A good game of pool could be a good distraction... for both of them. Because damn if he couldn't stop thinking about those stormy gray eyes. They were captivating. His wolf stirred at the memory.

No. He tried to command a cease and desist order to both his own and his wolf's fascination with those eyes. It didn't work. So he tried reasoning. *This female... No. This powerful traveler pulled you into her dreams and was watching you... blocked.* The reasoning helped... a little.

Nico stalked into the room and halted at his spot next to the window. While Blake and Deacon were distracted with their game of pool, he thought about sitting on Rhyker's couch just to start shit. Of course, there were plenty of other places to sit but he was in an icy mood. Then again, when was he not? He was also going a little stir crazy from all of the dead ends surrounding The Ghost's trail, in addition to not having another assignment to distract him. That was one thing he liked about The Order. There was always something to investigate or someone to track. *Fuck it.* Nico decided to sit on Rhyker's couch. It would be fun. Especially because he knew the twins were due back soon with a report of their hunt.

As if on cue, the twins strolled in. Rhyland beelined to the fridge and Rhyker had planned to do the same until he saw Nico on his couch giving him an antagonizing look.

Fucker, Rhyker thought with narrowed eyes honed in on Nico.

Rhyker knew Nico was trying to start shit. But little did Nico know, he was also wanting a good fight after the hunt they just had. He abruptly changed course and plotted a direct route to Nico.

Nico grinned a cool smile, taunting him.

That was all it took.

His fist hit home with Nico's jaw and a loud crack echoed in the air like a whip. Nico's jaw was no doubt broken but that didn't stop him from swinging a blow to Rhyker's gut. Rhyker tackled Nico an instant later. Punches were spearing through the air. Hands were connecting with muscles, bones, tendons—anything and everything was fair game. The fists were flying while their bodies wrestled. Nico managed to get enough room to generate a momentous hit that sent Rhyker smashing into something.

Oh, hello, Rhyker thought, grabbing the side table that was next to him, as if placed there by an angel, and smashing it over Nico's body.

In a bolt of strength, Nico shot up in a tackling bear hug that sent them both sailing through the air. They smashed into something with a deafening boom.

"ENOUGH!" Blake commanded in his most powerful alpha voice.

They stopped moving but their chests were pumping hard to suck in air. Rhyker caught a glimpse of Rhyland munching on a bag of chips with a feline grin on his puss. Christ, if his brother's smug face didn't almost set him off again. Blake interrupted his thoughts, anticipating Rhyker's desire for round two, this time with Rhyland.

"Clean. It. Up." Blake's three-word order delivered a verbal punch to Rhyker's head, clearing some sense into him. Blake gave one final warning glare to everyone and then marched out of the room.

Rhyker lit up a hand-rolled indie and assessed the damage. First, he did an internal check of his injuries. Yup. Things were definitely broken and bruised. But with his fast shifter healing rate, he was already healing and would be fine soon. Same with Nico... *unfortunately*. Then his eyes settled on a broken pile.

Damn it. His couch was smashed. "You owe me a couch," he growled at Nico.

Nico shot him a frosty glare, out of his already healing busted eye, that glimmered with a hint of satisfaction. His eyes narrowed in response.

Asshole. Oh, Nico was going down. He wouldn't know what hit him.

* * *

Blake knew that everyone was on edge with the case progressing at a painfully slow pace. They were already so used to plenty of fistfights and wrestling between all of the hot-blooded males in the house but, Jesus, that was why they converted the back living space into a makeshift gym, known as the "fight room." It was specifically designed for them to spar and let out their aggression. After Rhy vs. Rhy, the twin brother match of the century, it was their supposed solution to not having to replace furniture every goddamn week with brawls breaking out in the house. It seemed to have been working... up until this point. On that thought, Blake ran his hand through his hair and decided he needed to go for a run to clear his mind. Between The Ghost, Deacon, the dream with gray eyes, and everything else, both he and his wolf needed some fresh air. He walked out of the house and was welcomed by the embrace of the clean and crisp fresh air, the warmth of the sun, and the trees surrounding their house. He stripped down and called forth his wolf. In an instant, the most excruciating combination of pleasure and pain ripped through his body. With his four paws digging into the earth, he took a deep inhale, one glance back at the house, and ran into the forest.

Just getting back from his run, Blake walked into the living room and saw that it was put back together with some very noticeable gaps. It was also cleared out of all the debris from the aftermath. Good. There were more important things to discuss. Although, he had an idea that the twins didn't find any leads or clues on The Ghost's whereabouts, considering Rhyker's volatile mood earlier.

As Blake walked toward the kitchen, he saw Rhyland and Rhyker shoving food into their faces, naturally. Even for shifters who burned a lot of calories shifting forms, those two had bottomless pits as stomachs. He grabbed a bottle of water out of the fridge and twisted off the cap. He took a long pull. Nothing like a cool, refreshing drink of water after a good run.

"Meeting in ten," he told the twins. "Round up the others."

With a synchronized nod of their heads, the twins agreed as Blake made his way down the hall toward his room. Despite being the master suite and largest bedroom in the house, Blake's room had a simple and efficient setup. His massive bed was facing the sliding glass wall to the forested scenery. The only other things in the room were a dark leather couch, wooden coffee table, and a large TV. To complete the room, there was a walk-in closet and an en suite. Casual. Practical. Blake.

He stripped out of his clothes and turned on the shower. Getting under the warm spray and soaping up, his thoughts drifted to the female with eyes of rain clouds. There was something about this female that had both his own and his wolf's attention. Alexina was right, there was something very intriguing about this female. Setting those thoughts aside, for now, he rinsed and toweled off.

He walked into the living room and everyone was in their usual spots—well kind of. Nico was standing by the window and it looked like one of the couches survived the massacre, which was where Deacon and Rhyland were sitting. Rhyker was sitting in one of the kitchen chairs in the exact spot where his couch used to be. Nice. Rhyker with the quiet act of defiance. Okay, Rosa Parks. Oh, and it looked like he was nice enough to bring in one of the chairs for Blake too. Blake sat down in the chair and turned his attention to the twins.

"Update," Blake ordered.

"Couldn't catch a trail," Rhyker announced, suddenly back to his edgy mood.

"Too many people. Too many scents. If I knew his scent, it might be a different story," Rhyland continued.

"And depends on the timeline. We don't know how long it's been since he crossed over."

"From what we know, he is a shifter," Rhyker started.

"So he is also probably messing up his scent trail with the usual things like chemical disruptors and water," Rhyland finished.

"I didn't hear anyone talking about someone who could be described as him either." Rhyker continued with the verbal twin tennis match.

"Then again it probably isn't too alarming to see large males in LA because people probably think they are actors, basketball players, or even just some important LA douche." Rhyland sent the verbal tennis ball back to Rhyker.

"LA was a good move on his end. Un-fucking-fortunately."

Blake nodded and looked at Deacon.

"No. Nothing as of yet," Deacon said with a slight shake of his head. "Like Rhy said, the computers aren't likely to pick up anything because he can blend in there."

With a round of grim, frustrated male looks and low cursing, they went back to the drawing board to see if there was anything they could drum up. There wasn't.

Chapter 4

With the sound of waves crashing in the distance, Caly's eyes slowly opened and began to come into focus. She was back at the beach, standing in the dark cave with her eyes locked on the impossibly beautiful golden eyes of Mr. Mysterious. Kissing the shoreline in the distance, the crystal blue waves highlighted his eyes, which were like two suns shining on her. God, his eyes. They were intensely beautiful and captivating. And also a little terrifying, as if he was a predator sizing up his prey. Yet, she didn't feel threatened by this man. She was a little wary because, well, duh, he had the gaze of a lethal predator. But he wasn't aggressive, threatening to attack her or anything. And underneath the wariness, she actually felt a little calm. It could be the rhythmic ocean waves giving her a false sense of calmness. But, no. There was definitely something about this man's presence that made her feel... kind of... dare she say, safe?

Let's not forget that this is a dream and nothing about this is normal. Besides, this has got to be one of the strangest dreams ever. Well, this and the dream with GQ.

"Meow. Meow."

Sleep faded away and she lazily blinked her eyes open to

Felix, the kitty alarm clock, letting her know it was time for breakfast.

"Morning Felix." Scratching behind his ears, Caly continued the conversation with her cat. After all, conversations between her and Felix were a normal occurrence. "Guess what? Yup. I had another dream of Mr. Mysterious."

She exhaled on a dreamy sigh. It had been two weeks straight that Caly had dreamed of the gorgeous male with the golden eyes every night. And it was always the same dream.

"Felix, I wish you could see him because you are always a good judge of character. Like, remember Jimmy, AKA McMaca? God, as if his strong fetish with maca wasn't my first clue. LA men." She rolled her eyes. "And thank you, Jimmy, for also being the reason my morning drink is no longer a hot chocolate maca latte, which I was totally vibin' with. But then again, that's how I discovered the peppermint tea latte phase of my life. So one good thing came out of it. Anyways, remember how you hissed at McMaca the instant you met him when he picked me up for a date? Well, turns out he was seeing another woman at the same time as me. I mean, we never explicitly said we were exclusive but you know I'm not like that and I even kinda mentioned it briefly in light conversation. Whatever. It still hurt."

"Meow." Those golden cat eyes with a hint of viper green paused on her for a moment before Felix gracefully jumped off the bed, feet silently padding off to the kitchen.

"Yes, you're right. Breakfast."

In the groove of her morning routine and on her way to The Drip, she pushed shuffle on her playlist. "Can't Take My Eyes Off You" by Cary Brothers started playing on her car speakers. She thought of the dream with Mr. Mysterious and how they couldn't take their eyes off of each other. Coincidence? Obviously. Except she was someone who didn't really believe in coincidences. And what was up with this dream anyway? They just stared in silence. This gorgeous man, this figment of her imagination, who was a little terrifying (yet somehow not), with an intense golden gaze watching her as if he could devour her. Well, what would he say to her anyway? And, again, what the hell did it say about her that she dreamed of a handsome man who was apparently mute? Then again, the same thing could be said about her because she didn't speak either. God, maybe she should see a psychologist.

On that thought, she found a parking spot at The Drip and walked inside. There was a small line but nothing unusual for this time of the morning. A moment later, she heard the door open and she glanced up to see a few feminine gazes flick behind her in interest. It was probably some slick LA ego, like Brett. Oh god. What if Brett was behind her? She wasn't going to turn around and she was half expecting to hear his voice say, "Caly! I knew my *favorite girl* in the office would also—" Before she could finish the thought, a low deep voice was a welcomed interruption.

"Hey. Caly, right?"

She slowly turned around, not recognizing the voice at first.

Oh my god. Mr. Intense?

God, she forgot just how big and intense he really was. She had to tilt her head up slightly just to make eye contact. Just then, he took off his shades and revealed his cold, dark brown eyes with hints of gold. Except what was she thinking? They weren't cold. *Come on, Caly. Stop being ridiculous.*

"Oh! Hi... I, umm, actually don't think I ever got your name?"

"Nick." He stuck out his hand and gave her a cool smile.

And she swore she heard a female sigh in the corner. She

had to admit, he did have a nice smile.

"Hi, Nick." She shook his giant, warm hand. It probably just felt really warm in comparison to her cold hands. "Sorry, my hands are cold."

"I didn't notice."

There was silence for a moment as he gave her a calculating look with his eyes that had hints of gold.

Oh my god. He has gold in his eyes.

This had to be how her subconscious mind conjured up the man with the golden eyes in her dreams. Was it really a wonder that she started having these dreams *after* she met Nick? Mystery solved.

"Next!"

Startled, Caly jumped from the female barista's loud and slightly annoyed tone as it broke the silence. He chuckled at her response.

"Oh, sorry! I, umm, I will have a large mocha latte and a coffee cake."

"Okay..." The barista's voice trailed off as her fake nails clipped on the computer screen while she entered in Caly's order.

As Caly reached in her purse to get her wallet, Nick looked at the barista and said, "I'm paying. And I'll have a large regular coffee and the coffee cake too."

Okay, that was unexpected and nice of him.

While the barista was inputting his order, Caly looked at Nick and said, "Nick, this is really nice of you but if anything, I owe you for the... whole car incident."

"Let me be a gentleman, Caly," he said with a cool smile and handed the barista cash. "Keep the change."

They walked to the other end of the counter and waited for their orders.

"Nick, thank you. That was really nice of you. But like I said, if anything I probably owe you."

"How about you accept my offer to take you out, when I ask in a moment, and we call it even?"

Okay, that was also unexpected. She laughed a little. And, yeah, so this guy was smooth. Besides, he had been nothing but nice so far. And remember that he didn't even bother to file an insurance claim or anything? And it wasn't like she didn't notice the other LA fake females glossing up their lips waiting for a chance to pounce on their prey.

I know I swore off guys right now. But one date won't harm anything.

"Okay. Deal."

He smiled but didn't say anything.

"I thought you were going to ask me out?"

He chuckled. "Demanding are we?"

She laughed a little. Okay, so maybe he wasn't so intense or cold after all. She probably misread the entire situation and was just frazzled from the whole hitting his car thing. Really, who was she to judge someone by how they looked? That wasn't fair of her.

"So, do you get coffee here often?" she asked.

"I have seen this place for a while now and have been wanting to stop in to try it. You?"

"Yeah, I probably pay most of their rent here." She gave a guilty laugh.

"That good, huh?"

"They're good and convenient. It's on my way to work."

"Where do you work?"

Caly could've sworn she mentioned this that morning she hit his bumper. But she didn't fault him for not remembering that minute detail of her life. "I'm a paralegal for Geoffrey and Laird."

"A paralegal. Sounds fancy."

She laughed a little. God, if he only knew the drama in a legal office.

41

"It's not really that fancy or anything."

"You don't like it?"

How could he tell? Maybe her acting skills weren't all that great after all.

"It's okay. I mean, I never thought I would grow up to be a paralegal." She smiled and shrugged her shoulders a little. She opted for honesty because why not? That was one reason she really didn't fit in LA and another reason why she wanted to work in law originally. The truth will set you free, right? Except, when snakes like the Bretts of the world were playing for money.

"And what did you think you would grow up to be?"

"I… umm… Wow. You're asking really hard questions. Especially before I have even had my coffee."

He chuckled. "Good point. I'm just interested in learning about you, Caly."

"No, it's okay. I just… I guess I'm not sure."

"Fair enough." He paused and then spoke once more. "I'm sure you hear this a lot but… you have beautiful eyes."

"Thanks." She smiled and tucked her hair behind her ear, as she looked down at the ground, a bit shy. She had always been a little uncomfortable with accepting compliments. Switching subjects, she said, "So, what do you do? You know, for work."

"Bodyguard. And I do a little acting on the side."

Actor. Called that. Bodyguard? Makes sense. "Cool! And I could totally see that."

"See what? Bodyguard or acting?"

"Both really. I mean, who would dare to mess with someone as big and, umm, strong as you? They would probably have a death wish. And I could also see acting because I mean, I would imagine, there are not too many people with your size and strength. Especially with all these superhero movies being so popular nowadays. I wouldn't be surprised if I see you as the next lead in one of those," she joked and he smiled.

"Order for Kaylee! Order for Nick!" the male barista called out.

"It's Caly," Nick corrected the barista as he grabbed their orders.

"Order for Caly," the barista said with the correct pronunciation in an unamused tone. And it didn't take a mind reader to know he was internally rolling his eyes.

Okay, that was nice of him to stick up for your name, Caly thought as they walked toward the door.

"I'll walk you to your car. Where are you parked?" Nick prompted while holding the door open for her. Again, continuing with the whole gentleman thing.

"Thanks. Just right here." She pointed to her car with her hand, holding the brown bag of coffee cake. It was only two spaces away.

He smiled. "So, Caly, would you like to go on a date with me sometime?"

"Wow. This is really unexpected," she quipped with a smile on her face. "Yes, Nick, I would love to go out with you." She set her coffee on the roof of her car in order to open her car door.

"Allow me," he said as he opened the door for her, fulfilling act three of the gentleman routine.

"Thanks." She set her coffee in the cup holder and her coffee cake on the passenger seat. She reached into her purse to grab her phone so they could exchange numbers.

"Caly, I am really glad I ran into you. I'll call you to set up our date."

"Me too, Nick. I'm looking forward to it."

On that note, he made sure she was settled in her seat and shut the door for her. Sealing the deal with the final act of the "let me be a gentleman" play.

Smiling. She was smiling ear to ear.

Okay, so maybe this day was turning out pretty damn good so far. Dream of gorgeous golden eyes? Check. Breakfast paid for by gentleman? Check. Get asked out by said gentleman? Check. I feel like nothing can stop me today. Speaking of which…

She scrolled through her music and put on "I'm All The Way Up" by Fat Joe. The remix, obviously.

* * *

Nick watched Caly park her car in The Drip parking lot. This female was so predictable with her routine. Except maybe that was what she wanted him or everyone to think. He had been watching her for two weeks and nothing seemed out of the ordinary. From a distance, she appeared to be just another unassumingly dumb human. But he couldn't be too careful especially right now because it couldn't be a coincidence that she just happened to hit his car like that. Regardless of her plans, that was her mistake and they always made mistakes. Because if he didn't scent her up close, then he might not have thought twice. And her scent didn't lie, which proved that this female was not who she appeared to be. So, why was she living here? Why was her life apparently so deeply integrated in LA? Was she deep undercover like the other one they sent after him? He would sniff her out eventually too. Besides, her evasion of the truth from him had captured his attention.

You can run but you can't hide, Caly.

* * *

"Nothing," Deacon shared with the group. It had been two weeks and they did not have any updates or leads on The Ghost at all.

"This is such bullshit!" Rhyland uttered in frustration.

"Such bullshit," Rhyker echoed.

They were all gathered in the living room which moon-lighted as their meeting room. Nico was standing by his window. Deacon and Rhyland were sitting on the only sur-viving couch since the recent Nico vs. Rhyker smackdown. Blake and Rhyker were sitting on the kitchen chairs. Yes, Rhyker's chair was still making a silent point, positioned in the spot where his couch used to be. Rhyker was also the one tasked with getting new furniture but he was dragging it out because, as it stood, Nico didn't have anywhere to sit. Unless Nico also grabbed a kitchen chair. Okay, so it was not like Nico chose to sit for meetings that often anyway. But to Rhyker, the simple fact that Nico now didn't even have the option to comfortably sit was satisfying. Sure, Rhyker was antagonizing Nico in his own way and thor-oughly enjoyed knowing that he was just buttering Nico up for the revenge entrée.

"Starr said that "The Whisper," since we are all now calling her that apparently, doesn't have anything. We know that The Ghost is somehow blocking or evading seeing abil-ities. Although, no one knows how because that shouldn't be possible. Regardless, The Whisper told Star, it's like she's trying to see through a dark foggy window."

"Damn." Blake, just like everyone else, was seriously frustrated with how the hell The Ghost was able to essen-tially disappear. Then again, his name was "The Ghost" and disappearing was what they did.

"Starr will let me know if she hears any updates from The Whisper at all."

"And will you let her know what you would like to *whisper* in her ear?" Rhyland teased.

Rhyker laughed and fist-bumped his twin. Deacon nar-rowed his eyes at the twins. Deacon was in a bit of a mood after speaking with Starr earlier. Everyone knew that but then again, everyone was in a bit of a mood and just trying to let off steam from this case going nowhere fast.

"And when was the last time you whispered in a female's ear, Rhy?" Deacon retaliated.

"Ouchhhh." Rhyker laughed.

"I am choosy with my females. I do have standards. Besides, I got bored a long time ago with all the females throwing themselves at me," Rhyland retorted as low laughter filled the room.

Deacon decided to continue with the shit-talking. "And, Rhyker, when was the last time you actually could remember the females who whispered in your ear?"

"Ouchhhh," Rhyland echoed back to his brother, inspiring round two of laughter.

"The females I fuck don't whisper. They're moaners and screamers." Rhyker gave a wicked smile and lit up a hand-rolled.

"Alright. We're all on edge and a little trigger happy because of the case." Blake tried to stop this from escalating too far because he knew it could happen in an instant with these caged stallions.

"I bet Nico is trigger happy with the females," Rhyland quipped.

A third round of laughter rolled through the room. They all knew that Nico was one kinky son of a bitch and probably would use some sort of triggers in his erotic endeavors.

"I'll show you just how trigger happy I am," Nico shot back with a frosty smile.

"Save it for the females. Remember, I'm choosy and you don't make the cut," Rhyland drawled.

A fourth and final round of laughter filled the room.

"Okay. I did set you up for that didn't I, Rhy?" Blake's laughter subsided.

"Yeah. T'd up perfectly. There was no way I could pass it up."

"You pass up on the thing that matters though," Rhyker teased his twin.

"Touché." They bumped fists with twin grins.

They all talked shit but it was all in good fun and everyone knew that.

"Alright. No more or this'll end in a brawl. Speaking of, Rhyker, enough with the furniture boycott. Get the new damn furniture," Blake ordered.

"Roger that," Rhyker said and took a drag on his hand-rolled.

Okay, so maybe Blake was right because he was in the middle of the warzone by default, AKA sitting on a kitchen chair too. No big deal. Rhyker would just have to implement his revenge plan sooner than expected. It was time to go shopping.

Chapter 5

Caly didn't hear from Nick yesterday at all.

Well, he probably didn't want to text too soon because it would make him look desperate. Isn't there like some sort of "you have to wait three days" rule to dating or something? Hell, he probably has been busy too. Slow your roll, Caly. Remember, you've sworn off guys anyways. On that thought, she opened the door to The Drip and walked up to the counter. *Oh good. It's Sam. She always makes really good drinks.*

"Hi, Caly. Your usual?"

"Hey, Sam. Yes, please. Thanks." Caly reached in her purse for her wallet but Sam chimed in.

"It's already taken care of by..." Sam said and paused dramatically with a wicked smile. "Nick."

Okay. So, that's really nice of him. Points to Nick. While she waited for her order, Caly texted Nick.

> **Caly:** *Hi.* She inserted a smiley emoji. *Thank you for breakfast again! That was really thoughtful.*

Nick responded almost instantaneously and Caly thought, *That's nice that he's a fast responder and not doing the whole dumb dominant texting games thing.*

> **Nick:** *My pleasure, Caly.* He inserted a smiley emoji. *Besides, it's my apology to you because I didn't text you yesterday. I had a long shift and then went to a last-minute audition. I didn't get home until late and I didn't want to wake you in case you were already sleeping... You have been on my mind though.* He inserted a winky emoji.

See? Caly thought. *He is not playing games with you, Caly. He was at work. He has not one but two jobs. And he even admitted he was thinking of you. Clearly, because he paid for your breakfast... again. Stop overreacting. He seems like a nice guy.*

> **Caly:** *No apology is needed! I get it. Besides, you more than made it up to me with buying my break-fast again (thanks!)... And I have been thinking of you too.* She inserted another smiley emoji, because, hey, you can never go wrong with a smiley emoji.

> **Nick:** *Are you free for dinner tonight? 7 pm?*
> **Caly:** *Yes.* She added another smiley emoji.
> **Nick:** He also sent a smiley emoji. *Do you know that place Faith's Edge?*

Do I know of that place? Caly thought. *It only has like one of the most jaw-dropping interiors in LA and is the go-to date night spot.*

> **Caly:** *Yes I know that place. It's really nice!*
> **Nick:** *Great! I'll make us reservations.* He inserted a smiley emoji.

Nick: *Would you like me to pick you up or do you want to meet there?*

Caly: *I can meet you there. It's not far from my place actually.*

Nick: *Great! I'm at work and it's hard to text but have a beautiful day and see you tonight.* He inserted a smiley emoji.

Caly: *You too!* She inserted a smiley emoji.

See? Totally overreacting. He can't text at work because... Duh! How can you guard someone if your face is glued to your phone? Caly internally reasoned with herself and won the inner debate.

The day went by at a turtle's pace but finally, Caly was at home. She needed to get ready for her date. So the first thing in the date night pampering ritual was: music. Duh.

Hmmm, she thought, as she scrolled through her playlists. *Oh yeah. This!*

She put on "This Is How We Roll" the remix by Florida Georgia Line. Yeah, it was country. She didn't discriminate. She danced out of her work clothes and tush-pushed her way into the shower. Maybe this date was a good idea.

"Regardless of what happens, it will be nice to get dressed up and do something different and exciting. No offense, Felix." She gave a little scratch to Felix's head and it looked like he forgave her for ditching him tonight.

With a towel wrapped around her body and another in her hair, she perused through her closet.

Nope... No... Yeah, no... Definitely not... Oh! Where is...? She frantically flipped through hangers. *Yes!*

It was a simple black dress that positioned itself just above her knees. It wasn't too revealing but also not Catholic Church status. It hugged her hourglass curves in just the right way. She would pair it with a black clutch, a pair of black pumps, and accessorize with a bracelet, and small diamond stud earrings. She wasn't much of a jewelry person and liked to keep it simple.

With her outfit all picked out, she finished getting ready. She went with her usual black mascara, rose-colored, tinted lip gloss, and a dash of light pink (with a hint of gold shimmer) blush. But she decided to add a little eyeliner and eyeshadow to complete the date night look. She kept her hair casual and let it spill down to her waist. She slipped into the dress and gave herself an appraising look in the mirror. Okay, so maybe she cleaned up pretty darn well. She looked at the time. *Shit!* It was already 6:50 pm. She had to leave. Good thing the place was within walking distance.

Caly approached the restaurant and spotted Nick a mile away. There was no way to mistake a giant man in dark jeans, a leather jacket, and Aviators. It was no wonder he was a bodyguard. People would literally have to be crazy to take him on.

"Hi, Nick!"

"Hey, Caly! You look beautiful, as always." He flashed his cool smile.

"Thanks." She smiled and blushed a little. She wasn't used to such focused male attention and it made her a little nervous.

He made reservations just as he said he would. They only had to wait a moment before being brought to their table.

"Can I get you both started with some drinks?" the young brunette waitress said with her attention primarily on Nick.

Okay, so he does look like he could be an Avenger but come on! Clearly he is on a date... with me, Caly thought but politely ordered a glass of wine and Nick ordered a beer along with some appetizers.

"How was your day today?" Nick said, casually starting the conversation.

"Well, it started off pretty great." She smiled. "Thanks again for breakfast. It was really thoughtful."

He smirked. "You're welcome. I'm glad it started your day off great."

"Yeah. And then work was kinda boring today. I have just been doing legal admin work lately."

The rest of the dinner was filled with the standard first date casual conversation. You know, the typical getting to know someone questions: "What do you do? How did you get into that? What do you like to do for fun?" They eased in with the surface-level questions and nothing intense or too vulnerable for a first date. He seemed genuinely interested in her and kept the conversation going without any awkward pauses. He also didn't have any red flags that she noticed as of yet.

Let's not forget how McMaca was basically a walking red flag though.

Nick was a total gentleman. He paid for the meal with no expectations or awkwardness of who was going to pay. And when he found out that she walked to the restaurant, he insisted on taking her home because he wanted to make sure she got home safe. It made sense, especially because he was probably protective by nature being a bodyguard and all. So she let him. Besides, it actually was nice to be cared for like that. He also didn't even make some creep move to go up into her apartment to "continue the date." Hell, he didn't even make a first move for a kiss. But it was clear he was interested in her and asked her if she would go out with him again.

So, yeah, the date went well and she had a good time with a few laughs too. He checked all the boxes. Nice guy? Check. Sense of humor? Check. Gentleman? Check. Has his shit together? Check. Good looking? Bonus check. But there were no sparks on her end. Then again, it was only the first date.

It's not fair to judge our sole compatibility based on the first date, right? Maybe we just needed to get the first date wiggles out of the way.

Then again, maybe she just had unrealistic expectations of the whole chemistry and fireworks thing because let's face it, she was comparing it with her romance novels. Which was completely crazy. Overall, he seemed like a really nice guy who was genuinely interested in her and she enjoyed the company. Verdict? Yes, she would go out with him again.

Even after the first date with Caly, Nick still hadn't sniffed out any lies or deceit. But he needed to do some further digging into her background. There was nothing that set off his senses directly and nothing seemed out of the ordinary. Yet, her scent didn't lie and told him there was more to Caly then she was letting on. Plus, the fact that he couldn't quite get an exact read on her? That was intriguing to him even more so now. In his eyes, it was only a matter of time before she slipped up. And he all but craved the patient predator stalking his prey part of a hunt... almost more than the fun games he played when they were caught.

Chapter 6

Now that they finally had furniture again, the males of The Order dispersed from their usual spots in the living room. It had been another week and they just had another frustrating meeting full of a-whole-lotta-nothing. The Ghost was good and lived up to his name, unfortunately. But it was only a matter of time before they had something. They just had to keep working all angles and stay on top of it. This male was bound to slip up eventually. And when he did, they would be ready.

Nico just got back from an all-nighter to chase down a possible lead on The Ghost that ended up being a complete dead end. Despite that, he still had a lot of pent up frustration from this Ghost case going nowhere. So, he beelined to his room to change into his gym clothes. The gym would be a good way to work out his frustration. The last time he felt like this was when he picked a fight with Rhyker. Blake might skin all of them if he initiated a repeat match so close to the last one. Not like he wouldn't mind a brawl with Blake because Blake had this alpha strength and intelligence when he fought that kept Nico's skills sharp. But they might have to move after the brawl because the house would be demolished. So, yeah, the gym was the better option. He opened his bedroom door and stilled.

What the fuck?!

Pink.

There was pink everywhere.

It was like a pink Care Bear threw up in his room. Pink bed set. Pink pillows. Pink lamp. Pink pajamas with a pink bathrobe and slippers. Even strands of pink hearts were hanging from the ceiling.

"RHYKER!" Nico roared.

As if nothing was unusual, the twins sauntered up with the biggest cat-like grins on their faces. Hearing the commotion, Deacon and Blake appeared in the doorway as well.

"Holy shit, Nico. What in the Pink Panther is going on in here?" Rhyland teased.

"Is there something you've been hiding from us?" Rhyker tacked on, taking a puff of his hand-rolled.

"Who knew you were so extra?" Rhyland quipped.

The twins continued with the Nico bash fest. It was technically Rhyker's turn but Rhyland couldn't help himself. "Yeah, no wonder you have to use your vamp charm on the ladies. They take one look at this room and run for the hills."

"No parting the *pink* seas for you," Rhyker jumped in.

"Haven't you heard, Nico? Real males don't wear pink, they eat it."

The twin tennis match of a conversation was on a roll and Rhyland passed the ball back to Rhyker.

"Oh, and the answer is no. Pink does not go with everything."

Rhyker and Rhyland couldn't keep it together for any more jokes and they both busted up in uncontrollable laughter. Deacon and Blake joined in on the laughter too because, no, they were not above this by any means. Soon the hallway was filled with the sound of deep, rolling male laughter. Well, except for Nico, who was shooting icicles at the twins. Nico was seeing red and was fuming out of his ears. Maybe he did deserve this after the couch incident. Regardless, right now, all he could think about was pounding Rhyker's face in.

With the laughter subsiding, Blake caught a glimpse of Nico's expression.

"Alright..." Blake said, shifting his focus to Nico. "Any fighting is taken out in the fight room. You know the rules."

"Rhyker. Fight room. Now," Nico gritted out and his eyes went permafrost with cool blackness in preparation for some serious ass-kicking: Nico vs. Rhyker round two.

"No fuckin' way! Not when you're in one of your moods." Rhyker shook his head, smirking in amusement.

"But when is he not Mr. Freeze?" Okay, so Nico really was approaching arctic levels right now but Rhyland couldn't help but slip that in.

Nico shot frosty daggers at everyone and then stormed toward the gym. *Fuck changing.* It didn't matter all of a sudden. *Payback is a bitch, Rhyker... and Rhy. I know he had his hands in this too.*

Blake turned to the twins. "Nice timing," he said sarcastically.

"Hey, how were we supposed to know Nico was going to be in vamp kill mode?" Rhyland retorted.

"Everyone keep your distance until he cools down," Blake addressed the males.

"Like you even gotta tell us that. We're headed for the bar. We will be back later or until you give us the 'all clear' text. Unless you both wanna join us?" Rhyland offered.

"I'm in," Deacon said.

"Blake?" Rhyland prompted.

"Yeah, me too," Blake accepted.

Blake figured it was a good idea to get away from the

house for Nico to cool off. But also it would be nice to take their minds off of the aggravating Ghost case and hang out with his pack mates. And if he was being honest with himself, it would also help distract him from the strange fact that the dreams of "gray eyes" abruptly stopped about a week ago. He should be glad that the powerful traveler was no longer pulling him into her dreams. Yet, both he and his wolf were intrigued and wanted to see the female again. Even if only to solve the mystery of why she was pulling him into her dreams while blocking herself from view. So, yeah, hanging out at the bar would do everyone some good.

* * *

"I'm glad we did this." Nick flashed his cool smile at Caly.

"Me too, Nick. I had a really nice time," she responded with her own smile.

Nick looked at her lips. "I'm going to kiss you now, Caly."

He cupped her face in his massive warm hands and leaned in for the kiss. She closed her eyes and followed his lead. It was a textbook first kiss. Not too demanding. Not too slobbery. And he had nice soft lips. But that was it. There were no sparks or fireworks... or anything really.

Breaking the kiss, he smiled and said, "I'll call you."

"Okay. And thanks again for dinner." She smiled in return and walked off to her apartment.

Again, Nick checked all the boxes and Caly enjoyed spending time with him. She reflected back on the week leading up to their second date. Her week was back to her usual routine. Except she and Nick texted almost every day. Honestly, she thought it was nice to have someone to text with and it did help her workweek pass by faster. Also, the conversation with Nick was easy and she still didn't see any red flags about him. The memory of their kiss replayed in her mind. But her body didn't react to him at all. The kiss was nice but it was like her body was in a coma.

Maybe something's wrong with me and I am just broken? she thought on a sigh.

"Meow."

"Hi, Felix." She bent down and pet Felix who was now swerving between her legs like a figure eight.

"Meow."

"The date was good. But..." She sighed again. "I don't know... There were no sparks."

With those thoughts swirling in her mind, she changed into her sleep clothes, washed her face, brushed her teeth, and slipped into bed with Felix curled up next to her. As she was drifting off to sleep, she thought about how she was starting to miss those dreams of Mr. Mysterious with the impossibly beautiful golden eyes. For the past week, she had another recurring dream where she was with GQ back at the Harry Potter-themed set. When she sat next to GQ on the bench, all he would say was, *"Tell the male with the cold, dark eyes: 'Blake Orion's Order.'"*

What the hell did that mean anyways? She didn't know. Her dreams were just getting weirder and weirder. *Then again, everyone's dreams are weird, right?*

But there was something about her recent dreams she couldn't quite shake. On those thoughts, sleep finally claimed her.

Chapter 7

From the shadows of two buildings across the street, Nick watched Caly in her apartment. They had their second date last night and he still hadn't been able to sniff out anything concrete about Caly. But he knew she was hiding something. The background checks he did on her showed that she had extensive human records (which could have been doctored, of course). Her records were really detailed. Someone did a really good job of making her life look real. To the untrained eye, she was a completely ordinary human. Yet, her scent told him otherwise. So far, that was her biggest mistake: not masking her scent.

The fact that she had been able to evade the truth from him for this long, intrigued him, peaking his attention. So, he had decided to claim her as his and he was going to have some fun with her while he was laying low. Besides, how do you think he broke Marie Chan? An evil, calculated smile dominated his face with the thought of Marie.

If this is another Marie, why would they send another female undercover? It just shows how stupid SILE really is. Then again, SILE has always been stupid.

If he didn't know that about SILE, he might've taken it as an insult to his intelligence and expertise that they would think it would be at all successful to send amateur females like Marie. But he made his point crystal clear with how he last left Marie. On that thought, he took out his phone and sent a text.

> **Nick:** *Hi. How was your day?*
> **Caly:** *Hi!* She inserted a smiley emoji. *It was good... it was boring at work but TGIF. I am at home just relaxing.*

I know. I'm watching you, he thought.

> **Caly:** *How was yours?*
> **Nick:** *Good. Still working but wanted to let you know I was thinking of you while I had a quick moment.*
> **Caly:** She responded with just a smiley emoji.

Without warning, Nick felt the subtle signature vibration all over his body and humming in his ears that denoted he was being summoned. Most likely for his next assignment.

> **Nick:** *I was just called in for another job and will probably be away for a few days... It's a VIP client so I won't have access to my phone.*
> **Nick:** *Want to go out on Monday night when I get back? I can pick you up at 7 pm?*
> **Caly:** *Yes.* She inserted a smiley emoji. *And 7 pm on Monday sounds great! Hopefully this job goes well and I'll see you soon.* She added another smiley emoji. Okay, so sue her for being trigger happy with the smiley emojis.
> **Nick:** *Thanks, I look forward to it.* He ended with a smiley emoji.

He took a few more minutes to watch Caly from the shadows before he took off. He needed to find a dark alley.

* * *

"Hi, Deacon." Starr smiled and opened her front door to let him in.

At a first glance, Starr looked like a male fantasy, with an exotic heritage blended between Disney's Pocahontas and a Hawaiian goddess. Her sun-kissed skin was a perfect contrast to her long and thick, obsidian blanket of straight silk hair that pooled down to her hips. Her dark brown eyes had flecks of light gold that glinted when in their element of the sun. She was a fire elemental after all.

Underneath the exotic goddess layer, she was a badass bounty hunter who was damn good at her job. Her 5'10" frame was long and lean and subtly wrapped in pure muscle. The ultimate "miss independent," Lara Croft meets Ms. America (minus the fake boob job). Starr often used her beauty to her advantage on her hunts because, as far as she was concerned, it was another tool at her disposal for her targets.

Today, she was wearing her usual non-hunt casual clothes of tight jeans and a form-fitting white tank top.

Damn if this female didn't do things to him. And that smile.

Be cool, Deacon ordered himself.

"Hey, Starr." He smiled in return.

"Wanna drink?"

"Yeah, thanks."

"Your usual?"

"You know me too well." He looked into her fiery eyes for a long moment before she turned away.

"Oh, is that so?" She looked over her shoulder and gave him a playful smile. "And do you know what my usual drink is?"

"Vodka soda on the rocks," he said casually as if he didn't make it a point to memorize it. He wasn't enthralled with this female or anything. Nope.

"Maybe you know me too well." She winked.

"Not well enough."

She responded with a flirty smile.

Be cool. She's just playing with you. It's what she does.

She walked over to him and handed him his drink. He could've sworn for a split second that they had a moment but before he could act on it, she broke the silence.

"My contact, The Whisper... By the way, I told her we're now calling her that and she finds it amusing. Anyways, she has something... and that's why I invited you over."

She could have called you to give you the update over the phone. But she wanted to see you. She just won't admit it.

"And here I thought you just wanted to see me." Deacon shot her a smirk before pressing the glass to his lips and taking a drink.

She laughed a little. "Maybe I like your company... I haven't decided yet," she quipped.

He watched her lips kiss the glass as she took a sip of her own drink. He saw her eyes follow his gaze to her lips. The chemistry between them was palpable. Suddenly, the room got ten degrees hotter. She broke the eye contact to grab a piece of paper with her handwriting on it. He knew it was her handwriting because, yeah, he was a sap and made it a point to learn anything he could about this female. Apparently, that included her handwriting. Yup. He had a problem when it came to Starr.

"I had to take notes because sometimes she just starts downloading and I wanted to make sure I captured it all."

She looked at his eyes once more for a brief moment and he gave her a casual smile. This time, her eyes flicked down to his lips for a hot second before she refocused on the paper.

He smiled internally. *Oh yeah. She wants you.*

"We have no idea how it happened but it was just like the LA vision she had. Where, and these are her words, the "dark fog" clears a little just for a split second, just long enough for her to get a vision." She looked up at Deacon and then back down at the paper. "She saw an image of The Ghost standing on a street corner. There was a liquor store in the background and, incredibly enough, the store posted some sort of lottery numbers, or whatever the humans gamble with, and it had the date and time. So we know when this is going to take place. And, again, lucky for us, this is in the future, not the past."

"I didn't know The Whisper had that ability. Impressive."

Seers with the ability to see the past were very rare.

"I told you she's a powerful seer. And yeah, she really is…"

"So I finally know who my competition is," he drawled, taking another drink. She laughed. Damn if her laugh wasn't a sirens song to his soul.

"Anyways…" she said in a sultry sing-song voice. "She saw The Ghost wearing all black with Aviators. He was standing on the street corner of this liquor store that had a sign out front: 'LA Liquor'…I know. Super original." She rolled her eyes. "It's tomorrow at 8:13 p.m."

"Shit. *Tomorrow?*"

"Exactly. That's why I asked you to hurry up… and *come.*" She gave a side smile as she took another sip of her drink.

Was that a double entendre? Focus. She just gave you the lead of the century.

"I need to call Blake. I'll be right back." He excused himself and walked outside to make the call. The phone rang once and Blake answered.

"Yeah."

"Blake, we know where The Ghost is going to be tomorrow night."

"Speak."

Deacon filled Blake in.

"Shit..." Blake drew out the word as if processing the information. Then Deacon heard rustling sounds and Blake's muffled voice. It sounded as if he was covering the phone speaker in an attempt to protect it from a blowout as a result of his booming alpha voice. "Rhy! Meeting. Now. Get the others." There was some more rustling until Blake's voice was back on the phone. "Get home. We're meeting."

"Understood. I'm leaving now."

Damn it. He didn't want to leave the apex of his desires but obviously the case was more important than the infinite dick-tease that was Starr. He walked back inside the house.

"I have to go. Blake's called a meeting and we need to plan."

They both looked into each other's eyes for another long moment before Deacon broke the silence.

"Starr—"

"Deacon," she cut him off before he could finish. "I'll call you if The Whisper gets anything else. Let me know how the hunt goes?"

Damn it, Starr! He internally grumbled at her deflection.

"Thanks. You know I will." He tilted his head back in a familiar motion to down the rest of the drink and then set the empty glass on the table. "Thanks for the drink." He gave her one last appraising look with a smile and then headed out the door.

* * *

"Wake now." Caly heard GQ's commanding voice abruptly cut into her dreams. Suddenly, she jolted awake out of a dead sleep and froze. She saw a large male wearing all black on the far side of her bedroom, staring at her with cold, dark eyes. Her heart was kicking and a wave of panic shot through her. In the blink of an eye, before she could even think, let alone scream, the man appeared suddenly right in front of her. His cold gaze silenced her body and mind. She swallowed. So this was how she was going to die.

Cold... Solid black, cold eyes...

In a fear-panicked flash, the words from her recurring dream crashed through her mind: *"Tell the male with the cold, dark eyes 'Blake Orion's Order.'"*

She somehow managed to stutter in a frightened rasp, "B-Blake Orion's-s Or-Order."

The male's gaze, or rather, her killer's gaze, sharpened to knife blades.

"What?" he lashed out in a cutting tone that matched his cold stare.

"B-Blake..." She swallowed. God, it was suddenly the Sahara desert in her mouth. She managed to rasp out the rest "...Orion's-s ...Or-Order."

This is it. The last thing she was going to see before she died were those cold, dark eyes. Darkness fell all around her before she could even blink.

Chapter 8

Sounds. No, voices. Caly was hearing deep male voices.
Am I dead?

It was pitch black everywhere as her mind tried to move through a hazy fog. It felt like she was sun drunk and had just woken up from one of those long naps in the heat of the summer sun.

Dream. It was a dream. No. This is a dream. Just another weird dream.

The masculine voices were starting to become a little more clear.

"Let me get this straight. This human female suddenly woke up from a dead sleep, took one look at you, and then said, 'Blake Orion's Order'?" a deep male voice said, as it strangely caressed her hazy mind.

"Yes." It was another male voice but this one seemed familiar. And it also gave her the chills.

"And let's not forget my favorite part," a different, amused, male voice playfully interjected. "He mesmerizes the human female back—"

Her thoughts were swiftly interrupted. Words. They were speaking words. But only a single word stuck out in the cloudy haze that was her mind.

H-human...?

Suddenly, all of the voices stopped and it was dead quiet. That, or she was dead. She didn't know.

Weird... dreams...

She tried to command her mind to work, damn it. But that was the thing with dreams, right? You could try to command your mind to do something but it won't listen. So, yeah. That was all this was... a dream. This was all just a weird dream and she seriously couldn't wait to wake up and continue on with her life.

Giving up on her brain, because clearly it was doing its own damn thing, she tried to open her eyes because that was a good place to start, right? It took her three coaxing tries before her eyelids started to respond.

God. Maybe I need to lay off the Sleepytime tea... It probably has some weird herb in it that explains all of this. Her eyelashes fluttered open a sliver. *Why is it so bright? How late did I sleep in?*

Yup. Definitely need to throw out the Sleepytime tea. She internally cursed her neighbor Megan. Come to think of it, why the hell would she listen to her after the exceptionally bad advice (resulting in epic failure) to try online dating? Her eyes were slowly focusing and adjusting to the light.

In an instant, she froze and her eyes shot open wide.

Her stare was locked on the impossibly incandescent golden eyes that belonged to the man in her dreams... Mr. Mysterious.

* * *

Blake's wolf suddenly came to attention. There was a new scent in the air that wasn't there a moment ago. A scent he had never smelled before. A second later, with vampire speed, Nico appeared in the room with a *female* in his arms.

"Shit, Nico. Couldn't get a female on your own so you had to use your vamp charm on her? We told you, pink scares off the ladies," Rhyland drawled with a mischievous grin.

Walking to the smaller side room, an offshoot of the living room, Blake indicated for Nico to put her down on the couch.

"Beautiful female... I'll give you that," Rhyland said.

Both he and his wolf agreed with Rhyland. She was a beautiful female and there was something about the way she smelled that had both him and his wolf's attention. Looking over her, he noticed she was wearing a thin, tight black sleep tank and shorts. His wolf stirred and he suddenly felt protective.

"Rhy, get a blanket," Blake ordered. Rhyland was about to walk into his room, which was the closest, but Blake blurted out, "From *my* room."

Why did it matter? He didn't know.

Rhyland paused for a brief moment, no doubt taken aback by the alpha tone in his voice with that last command. And, hell, he didn't even know why it came out like an alpha command. Rhyland came back a moment later and Blake threw his blanket over the female to cover her legs.

"Explain," he said in his direct commanding voice, without taking his eyes off the female.

"The Ghost was at the liquor store. I couldn't get to him without causing a scene. Too many humans. Too many unknowns. So, I followed him." Nico paused to look at Blake and then back at the female. "He watched the human in her apartment for about an hour. Then I followed him down the street. He turned down a dark alley. As soon as I stepped into the shadows of the building to fade down the alley, he was gone... without a trace." His gaze was met with furrowed brows.

Vampires had the ability to fade. This was how they could move even faster than shifters in pure darkness and hide in the shadows undetected. Vampires were in their true element in the darkness where they could become one with the shadows.

"Everything we know about him tells us that he is a predatory shifter. Yet, you just described something that would be like fading. Or, hell, a teleporter," Blake said with a frustrated breath.

Teleportation abilities were among the rarest of the species world and only showed up in an already scarce subset of species, to begin with.

"Exactly. With how intensely he was watching her, I went back to check it out. Nothing. I was about to fade, then she jolted awake. And right before I mesmerized her, she said, 'Blake Orion's Order.' "

Blake's wolf stirred and was completely focused on the female. Something had his wolf riled up. He hadn't felt his wolf like this before. There was something about her scent... There was a thought on the tip of his tongue but before it could formulate, it disappeared. "Let me get this straight. This human female suddenly woke up from a dead sleep, took one look at you, and then said, 'Blake Orion's Order'?"

"Yes."

"And let's not forget my favorite part," Rhyland playfully interjected with one of his charming grins. "He mesmerizes the human female back to sleep and brings her straight here—across The-fucking-Barrier—in nothing but her sleep tank and shorts. Nice creep touch by the way. We know you're kinky but this takes your kink to creep level status," Rhyland quipped.

"Fuck you," Nico said his two favorite words and shot lethal icicles at Rhyland.

"Wait until Rhyker and D hear about this…"

Blake sent Rhyland a look that said, *"Enough."*

"Wh—"

They all fell silent. Their conversation was cut short at the sound of the faintest rustle of the blanket.

A light, slightly groggy, feminine voice uttered, "H-human…?"

Blake, Rhyland, and Nico lethally shifted their bodies, forming a wall, with their focus completely on the human female.

"Weird… dreams…" the groggy feminine voice broke through the silence.

There was a slight flutter in her eyelids and a moment later, her eyes cracked open a sliver. Before she even blinked, her eyes shot wide open and Blake's eyes were locked on the female with the storm gray eyes from his dream.

Nico caught the flicker of recognition in her eyes. Without taking his eyes off her, Nico's gaze narrowed and he sharpened his peripheral vision to glance at Blake. Before he could question Blake about the flicker of recognition, his thoughts here interrupted.

"Outside," Blake said in his commanding alpha voice with his eyes still locked on the female.

A slight hint of fear rose in the air but Blake also caught a whiff of her scent. It was so beautifully feminine and there was something about it that had his wolf's rapt attention. But before he could take in her scent further, the sharp bite of fear filled his nose.

Rhyland took one quick look at Blake (as though his alpha tone didn't already say enough), just to be sure that he wasn't budging on this, before he walked out. Nico lingered a moment longer. Nico focused directly on Blake with a stone-cold expression. Yet, Nico's eyes said everything that needed to be said (including his complete disagreement).

Once they were alone, Blake and Caly were exactly as they were in the dreams—silent with unbreaking eye contact. His wolf's attention was utterly fixed in predatory silence and his senses were on high alert.

Remember, she pulled you into those dreams and was blocking herself for a reason, Blake thought, internally setting the stage for the conversation.

"The silent staring is over. What do you want?" His voice and stare were dominating as he stood there with his arms crossed against his broad chest. He was intrigued but his guard was up nonetheless.

Caly was a little terrified of him, shocked at the strange demanding turn that this dream had taken. She couldn't seem to find her voice. *God, those beautiful golden eyes.*

"H-h—" She tried to speak but a rasp was caught in her throat.

She broke the gaze and looked over at the bedside table to grab the cup of water she always kept by her bed. Except, she realized she was not in her bed... she wasn't even in her room. He twisted the lid off a bottle of water and handed it to her. The cold wetness of the bottle sent a reality shock to her system and a panicked terror flowed over her body as she realized this was not a dream. Her eyes widened and she froze.

Fight. Flight. Freeze. She was apparently the queen of freeze. Maybe she was a deer in her past life. And great. She couldn't think because even her brain was on board with the freeze response.

Fear continued to sting Blake's senses. Her heart rate had sped up, her stormy eyes dilated, and she had a slight tremor in her soft hands. His wolf did not have his teeth bared in fight instinct. Instead, he was intensely focused and hanging on her every breath, as if enthralled. Underneath the fear, there was something else about her scent but the thought floated off almost as soon as it came. With his wolf instincts telling him she was no threat, he softened his alpha power and presence just a fraction.

"Let's start over. Who are you?"

The cool liquid that washed down her throat, paired with his gentler tone, helped douse the fear enough for Caly to find her voice. "C-Caly Smith." *God, is that my voice?*

"How do you know me?"

"F-from my dream..." So many questions. She had so many damn questions. Yet, her brain was still in freeze mode.

He watched her lips as she brought the water bottle up to her mouth for another clarifying drink. A cool drop of water dripped down her chin and slipped in between her breasts. She watched his eyes follow the drop down. Just then, she looked down and became mortified as she realized she was still in her black sleep tank top. *Thank God for this blanket,* Caly thought while concluding that it was no doubt covering her sleep shorts.

Stop staring at her breasts—her nice breasts—you creep, Blake chided himself as if he was a horny teenage pup. "Why did you pull me into the dream, Caly?" His gaze was back on hers.

"I... What?... I didn't?" *Pulled him into the dream? What in the actual fuck is he talking about?* Caly thought.

He took a deep inhale and got a strong whiff of fear and confusion. But he didn't smell any lies or deceit. Then again, the scent of fear was so strong and pungent that it muddied up the scent waters. "You did."

Silence. They were back to the silent staring game.

"Who are you?" she inquired, as her brain finally thawed out enough to verbally form a question.

"You already know who I am."

And just like that, confusion sent her brain back into

freeze mode. Her brows furrowed. "I don't know you... I mean, except in my dreams."

Blake took another audible sniff. Her confusion was clear. "I am Blake from Orion's Order."

Everything came back to Caly in a flash. The dream with GQ who said, "*Tell the male with the cold, dark eyes 'Blake Orion's Order.'* " As her memory came flooding in, she thought about how the male with cold, dark eyes was not only in her bedroom but also, moved across the room impossibly fast.

Another wave of fear punched Blake in the gut and he saw a flicker of recognition in her eyes. "Tell me what you just thought."

"I... I had dreams of a man... he told me, 'Tell the male with the cold, dark eyes: Blake Orion's Order.' The dream has always been the same... Suddenly, I'm awake and I see the male with the cold, dark eyes." *Nope. I don't sound crazy at all,* Caly thought sarcastically, with a little internal facepalm action.

"What else?"

"That's it..." she said in a confused voice.

"What about the beach?"

"I... I don't really know or understand. It's a recurring dream." Her hand naturally reflexed to comb through her hair. Except rats had apparently taken up residence there so her hand was immediately greeted with a million knots and tangles.

Waiting for her to elaborate, he kept up with the silent staring.

In desperate confusion, she said, "I don't know you. I don't even know what you're talking about. And I don't know how you were in my dream! ...God. I can't believe I'm even having this conversation. I must be going crazy. No. Wait! I must still be dreaming. Yes. Felix will wake me up at any moment..." *Felix, any day now,* Caly's sing-song thought drifted through her mind. *And what the hell is up with his deep breathing?*

Felix? Of course she is already claimed. Why did Blake's thought suddenly have his wolf snarling? He didn't know.

"Who's Felix?"

"My cat."

He was relieved at that response. Again, why did it matter?

"Why were you on the other side?"

"What? The other side of what?"

He narrowed his eyes slightly and responded in a did-you-hit-your-head kind of tone. "The Barrier."

"The Barrier? What..." She cut off that thought. "No. Wait. Where am I? And why did you take me?" Finally, her brain was getting with the program.

"You asked for me."

Touché. Although, it's not like I knew that at the time. "Okay... Now, I'm asking you to take me home." Where her sudden boldness came from, she didn't know. But she clung to that shit like a desperate date.

"Why do you live in LA?" he asked, knowing that the only species who lived on the other side were usually hiding from something or someone.

I was running away. "Because I wanted to."

He scented she was holding something back. So, he stayed silent, narrowing his eyes slightly, and waiting for her to explain.

"I... err... I moved to LA after my..." Her voice cracked. *Oh god. Do NOT think about your parents right now,* Caly silently commanded herself.

A fresh wave of heartbreak and sorrow punched Blake in the gut and he saw tears form in those captivating stormy eyes. He knew that scent well. She lost someone. His wolf was now pacing back and forth from this female being in distress—caused by him no less.

"I want to go home. Please... Please take me home," she said in a broken voice, as a tear rolled down her cheek.

His wolf was now clawing to get out and comfort this female. Of course, he didn't like to see females in distress or upset but his wolf usually didn't react this strongly and with such determination. He inhaled. Fear. Confusion. Heartbreak. No lies or deceit. On the exhale breath, he made a decision.

"We'll take you home. But... Caly, we're not leaving your home until we have the answers we need."

After all, they weren't kidnappers. But they also weren't going to let this newfound lead on The Ghost, their only lead, walk away. Besides, Blake also needed to know why this female pulled him into the dreams and why she was living on the other side.

He walked out of the room a step and signaled for Nico to come back in. The moment Caly saw Nico, she tensed up, immediately recognizing him as the man with the cold, dark eyes... except now his eyes were light hazel? Confused and scared, Caly went ghost white. She didn't realize how much she had relaxed until then.

Seeing her reaction to Nico, Blake assured her, explaining, "It's okay. He's not going to hurt you. You have my word. He's going to mesmerize you and then we're taking you home."

She couldn't be conscious outside of this room because they still didn't know anything about her and they didn't want her to know where they lived. It's not like they kept their place a secret or anything. But there was something about her that wasn't adding up, including her connection to The Ghost and the fact that she lived on the other side of The Barrier. All of this supported Blake's decision to mesmerize Caly for her return trip home, which seemed like the best course of action. They couldn't be too careful after all.

Mesmerize? Caly thought, completely confused.

A fresh wave of panic laced fear surged through her as the man's eyes suddenly turned solid black. In an instant, he appeared in front of her and everything went dark.

"Damn it, Nico. That was uncalled for," Blake growled.

Nico shrugged. "It was efficient. Explain," Nico echoed Blake's previous order.

"We are taking her home. How did you get her here exactly?"

Nico paused with a calculating look on Blake. "Ground floor unit. Carried her to the SUV. It was dark. I was quiet. No one saw."

A thought crossed Blake's mind about how he didn't like her living on the ground floor because that was not safe at all. Shaking the disapproving thought off, Blake checked the time on his cell phone.

"Get the SUV ready. Brief Rhyland. I got her," Blake ordered.

Nico's appraising look flipped between Blake and Caly. He paused for a moment and then left the room.

Prompted by his inexplicable concern for Caly's comfort, Blake walked to his bedroom and grabbed one of his white T-shirts to cover her with. It wasn't the best option but he figured it was better than nothing. Besides, she would be warm enough in his arms. Shifters' body temperatures ran very warm after all.

He leaned forward to slide his shirt over her head and her scent filled him. His wolf was clawing to get out and rub his nose all over her. Hell, who was he kidding? He wanted to do that too. He took a deep inhale.

Definitely not human, Blake thought.

Even though he detected confusion and fear, the moment he recognized her as the traveler from the dreams, he was confident that she wasn't human and her scent just confirmed it. Wolf shifters, and other shifters with a keen sense of smell, can scent the difference between humans and species. Although everyone had their own unique scent, there was an overarching scent that differentiated the various subspecies. As if compelled to memorize her sweet scent, he inhaled again. His brows furrowed slightly. There was something about her scent that was... different. There was this subtle, easily missed, background note that seemed to differentiate her from the seer/traveler classification. And, yet, that was technically the closest scent category she fit into. Which made sense, considering she was the traveler who pulled him into her dreams.

Getting into the SUV with Caly in Blake's lap, Nico looked at Caly in the white T-shirt and then shot a glance back at Blake.

Glaring at Nico, Blake silently dared Nico to say something. He didn't. Good. Maybe Nico decided against getting a punch to the face. Smart.

"Drive."

Chapter 9

"Understand?"The voice was hypnotic yet haunting. Charismatic yet chilling. Natural yet unnatural.

"Yes."

"Good. Leave." The voice was dismissive and held the slightest lilt of an English accent.

The Ghost left with his new assignment and plans were already formulating in his mind.

* * *

"Do it." Blake looked at Nico and nodded.

Shaking Caly gently awake, Nico locked eyes with her before she could panic... again. They had to get it right this time because the first time Nico and Blake woke Caly up, she panicked and screamed. Jesus. What was it about females being able to shatter glass with their screams? As a matter of fact, she may be a siren because her scream summoned a neighbor to make sure she was okay. Megan. It was inconvenient but not the worst thing in the world to deal with. Nico mesmerized Megan and then continued on. Vampires had the ability to mesmerize, which could range from inducing a trance-like state to full-on hypnosis. The strength and degree of the ability varied from vampire to vampire based on a number of factors, including age, since abilities often grew and evolved over time.

Nico looked at Blake with a single head nod. He put Caly in a semi-trance state that she would naturally wake from. It was as if that space between sleep and awake had been extended. She would feel totally relaxed and a little dreamlike.

"How long?" Blake asked.

"Every mind is different but about an hour give or take."

Blake noticed that Caly seemed to have a strong fear reaction to Nico. It wasn't surprising since, on top of the fact he was one scary fucker, he did kidnap her with full-on vamp eyes. So, he ordered Nico to leave the room this time.

Caly was slowly coming to consciousness from yet another strange dream. Maybe she should see a psychologist about why, all of a sudden, she was having these terrifying dreams of being kidnapped by huge men. But it didn't matter right now because she felt like she was floating on a cloud of relaxation. God. This was the most relaxed she had felt in a while.

Her eyelids were heavy and she saw no reason to lift her lids. She lingered in this dreamy relaxed state and smiled. She vaguely heard Felix purring up a storm.

"Mmmmm..." she mumbled as the laziest morning stretch washed over her body. She may have even given Felix a run for his money with that stretch.

Damn if that female's sound and her stretching didn't have Blake and his wolf fantasizing about the nose nuzzling thing again, yearning to fill up with her scent.

"Morning Felix..." she said in a groggy and relaxed voice. With her eyes still closed, she rolled over toward the sound of his purrs. "I had another dream about Mr. Mysterious. You know, with the gorgeous golden eyes..." She exhaled out a dreamy sigh. "Except..." Her thoughts trailed off as she recalled just how strange the dream ended up. She lazily reached her hand toward the sound of Felix's purrs, as if they were a homing beacon. Her hand landed on what felt like jean fabric on something solid and warm. The instant contact was made, it flexed.

Muscle? she silently questioned and her brows furrowed slightly. She coaxed her heavy eyelids open and she was met with a pair of impossibly golden eyes... the eyes belonging to the handsome man in her dreams... who just happened to be sitting on her bed next to her.

"Nevermind Felix... I'm still dreaming," Caly said with a relaxed half-smile. *God. This man is taking over my dreams...* But she wasn't complaining.

"Mr. Mysterious?" Blake teased with a slight curve of his lips.

She sleepily laughed. "You're not supposed to know your own nickname." She looked down and saw that Felix was curled up in his lap purring in utter bliss. Damn if that wasn't cute. And damn if he wasn't even more gorgeous this close up. She scratched Felix behind the ears in just the spot he loved. "Even if this is a dream, if Felix likes you, then you can't be that bad," she admitted with another lazy chuckle. "He hissed at the last guy I brought home. And it turned out Felix was right. That guy was an ass."

Blake steered his thoughts away from the sudden desire to go find whoever this guy was and teach him a lesson. *Jesus. Stay focused.*

"Caly, this is not a dream."

"Yes it is. How else is the most handsome man with the gorgeous golden eyes from my dreams here, in my bed?" Her body was reacting in a very feminine way to his masculine presence. She wanted him and her body knew that.

There was another curve of his lips and his chest puffed

out a little more than necessary. What was this female doing to him? *Focus*, he repeated the silent order.

"You know that I'm Blake from Orion's Order. But what I don't know is how you know that."

Scenting the slightest hint of her arousal in the air, his body began to react in response. *Jesus. Her scent is like a drug*, Blake thought on an internal groan.

Hell, this is a dream, Caly thought. So, who was she to deny herself? Besides, with all that eye gazing in the other dreams, okay minus the kidnapping one, it felt like she knew him on some level. Still utterly relaxed and now a little sinfully playful, she closed the distance between them and curled up against his body—his very warm and muscled body. With a graceful leap, Felix padded off the bed to his favorite sun spot on the window sill, hidden behind the curtain where it trapped the most heat.

Wow. He smells so good. It was a dark, musky, masculine scent. Natural though—not some artificial store-bought scent. She sighed deeply. This was turning out to be a very good dream. She curled up next to him. She fit perfectly as if her body was meant to be at his side.

Blake went to put his arm around her shoulder and stopped midway. What was he doing? *Focus damn it.* Since when had a female had him reacting like this?

"Caly."

"Hmmm...?" *Maybe it was better when he didn't speak... Wow. Okay, if only the Freudian psychologists heard me think that.*

But with the sound of her name on his oh-so-kissable lips, her body bloomed even more. She wanted him. Never had her body reacted in such a primal manner to a man. Chemistry. This must be the chemistry that everyone talked about. Even if this was fake dream chemistry, she didn't care.

"This isn't a dream."

Jesus. Her scent. Her arousal filled the air and Blake's body started to harden, with his wolf at full attention. *No.* Yeah, as if he could command his body to not react to this beautiful female with her scent like a drug. He couldn't.

Maybe he's right because damn this dream feels so real, she thought. But with his scent in her nose and his warm body next to hers, she didn't care. For whatever reason, she felt safe with Mr. Mysterious and she wanted him. With all other thoughts drifting away, she did the boldest thing she had ever done before with a man. She straddled him, without pause, as if he was hers.

He hissed out a breath and his cock was impossibly hard.

Then they were back in their MO: silent eye gazing. Except, this time, she swore she saw a slight glow of his beautiful golden eyes.

"Shhhh... No more talking," she said, having no idea where this confident Caly suddenly came from.

Did she just shush me? No one shushes me. But Blake's hands locked onto her waist in silent rebellion of his thought.

God, Caly internally moaned at his very male hands that were so warm and possessive. She placed her hands on his solid chest and they stayed like that for another heartbeat. She bent down to kiss him but hovered just before their lips touched.

Am I really doing this? she silently questioned through the desire that was pooling inside her. *He's right. This can't be a dream because this feels so real... and so good. But his eyes are glowing, so this has to be a dream, right? Fuck it.*

Damn if she didn't care at this point. She felt so relaxed and safe. And so ready for him. She wanted him and she could feel her body readying herself for him now, with an aching tightness in her most feminine of places. *Listen to your own command and shhh.*

Blake needed to stop this. But this was only a light trance so all of this she was doing of her own volition. This was just her without the paralyzing fear. This was her releasing her inhibitions and giving in to her deepest desires. He wanted her and clearly she wanted him.

Her female musk was like a drug to him. It was filling his senses and adding fuel to the passionate fire.

Focus, he repeated the silent command. But that was when her full soft lips brushed his and pulled back slightly. His nerve endings were tingling from the tease. His grip tightened on her waist and this time, her lips crushed his in a hard demanding caress. Her long, silky hair blanketed him and trapped in the scent of her feminine arousal, which was now thick in the air. She lightly moaned and the feminine sound had him teasing her lips with his tongue coaxing them to open for him. When they parted slightly, his mouth took control and playfully nipped at her full lower lip. Their mouths devoured each other.

Needing air, Caly broke the kiss and his lips landed on her neck, licking and teasing over her pulse. She locked her lips back on his. They were battling in the most sensual of games. With another feminine moan, she started to move her hips against his cock. Her thin, cotton sleep shorts were a joke of a barrier. She felt everything. His erection was bulging from his jeans and straining to get free.

Using what felt like the last of his alpha control, Blake broke the kiss, trying to unscramble his thoughts. She protested and went in to seal their lips once more. He held her shoulders back, keeping them at a length from one another while he tried to think.

"Don't stop... Please."

Blake had alpha control but this female did things to that control, especially when she begged like that. In an instant, he flipped her on her back and settled between her legs claiming her mouth once again. He pinned her wrists above her head with one hand, while his other went under both layers of shirts she was wearing. He shuddered when he found bare soft skin. His hand slowly traced the curve of her hip, on a journey across her lower belly to the other hip. His warm, rough hand ascended upwards, brushing the underside of her breasts.

Her skin was so soft. Not to mention her biteable plump lips. His wolf was clawing to get out to touch and taste. In an impossibly swift motion, he used a claw to cut both shirts she was wearing straight down the center. Of course, he was careful not to scrape even one skin cell off of her body. She gasped in sinful delight at the sudden exposure of her breasts. He broke the kiss and released her wrists to look at her plump peaks.

"Beautiful," he said in a deep husky voice with hooded eyes. He saw a blush kiss her cheeks. Cupping her breast with one hand, he slid his thumb over her nipple. She shuddered while gripping his forearm in a coaxing squeeze and then let out a moan.

"Off," she demanded, pulling at his white T-shirt.

With a wicked grin, his shirt flew off in one fluid motion. Her gray eyes wandered down his torso, admiring his bare chest and chiseled abs. He bent down and took the neglected nipple into his mouth. Licking, sucking, and teasing moans out of her. Meanwhile, he was gently squeezing and rolling her other nipple with his forefinger and thumb. Her seductive arousal wrapped around his senses and his cock throbbed with the need to take this female. *Not yet.*

Wanting to please this female in every way possible, he kissed down her belly and teased the edge of her shorts with his tongue.

"Yes. God, yes," Caly moaned, urging him to continue. Her brain was in a deep sensual haze, thick with desire and need. Any fear and hesitation were completely gone and all she wanted was him inside her.

Even with her plea, Blake looked up into her eyes with his mouth still teasing her lower belly. He needed to make sure that she was sure. Her look gave him the confirmation he needed. He slid her shorts down her legs in a slow tease, revealing her simple black panties. He kissed a trail down her thighs as her shorts made their descent. With the shorts off, he kissed his way back up her legs, this time, parting her legs wider with each ascending kiss making room for him. She shuddered in response.

He was so close to her sex and her scent was intoxicating. He had to taste her. The need was impossible to resist. He needed to caress her with his mouth and feel her orgasm on his lips. With hooded eyes, he glanced up to look at her once more and teasingly flicked his tongue on her inner thigh. She moaned in response.

God, he was so close to her throbbing center, dripping with wet anticipation. At a pause in the kissing, Caly opened her eyes to see he was looking at her as if he wanted her confirmation. He flicked his wicked tongue on her inner thigh as if in question.

"Yes," she said with a breathy moan and closed her eyes. His fingers teased the edge of her panties as his breath caressed her in hot anticipation. She closed her eyes and let her head sink back into the pillow.

All patience gone, Blake used a claw to tear through her panties in another inhumanly fast motion. Her sex was now bared to him for his viewing pleasure. Jesus, she was so beautiful and glistening wet. She lifted her head to look at him and then closed her eyes as if she was a little shy.

"Beautiful," he said with hooded eyes and a deep groan.

Taste. He needed to taste. But with her sudden shyness, he kissed his way back up her belly and over one breast, lingering at her nipple for a teasing lick. He continued kissing upwards until their lips met in a hot, wet kiss. This time, his hand made the sensual journey down her body and his fingers slid over her wet heat. He groaned. She was so hot and wet. He was a knife-edge away from shredding his jeans and slamming his cock into her, balls deep. *Not yet.*

Caressing her slick wet heat with his fingers, she broke the kiss on a throaty moan. Blake was licking her pulse and stroking her core when she moaned again. He slid one finger inside her and this time he groaned. She was so tight and wet. He thrust in and out of her while teasing her sensitive spot with his thumb.

"Oh god," she said with a breathy moan.

Blake had to force his mouth away from her neck because he wanted to watch her.

"Come for me, Caly," he commanded.

And two strokes later she shattered. He groaned as her core tightened around his finger in pulsing pleasure.

He stroked her through the waves and when they subsided, he pulled his finger out. It was glistening with her hot honey. He locked eyes with her and sucked the honey from his finger in a slow, seductive motion. He groaned with pleasure from her intoxicating taste in his mouth. He needed more. He kissed his way back down her body, lingering on her nipple for a moment until his hot breath was on her sex in sweet anticipation. Locking eyes with her, he stroked his tongue slowly in a single ascent. Her head threw back while she quivered and moaned. His eyes closed with a groan as he tasted her slick, sweet honey. He wanted to know everything about how to pleasure this female. With her throaty moans guiding him, he slowly... oh so very slowly... continued licking, sucking, and tasting every inch of her core.

"Oh god! Blake."

That was the first time Blake heard her say his name. It just about pushed him over the edge, especially in that sexed-up female moan. His erection was throbbing in his jeans and was about to release with the act of pleasuring this female. Gritting back his last reserves of control with his cock, his tongue made a final ascent swirling over her sensitive point and he felt her release on his lips.

"Blake... I'm coming..." Caly's head threw back into the pillows as ecstasy ripped through her entire body for the second time. His hot wet tongue kept coaxing every last wave of pleasure out of her.

Licking the sweet nectar from his lips, Blake's patience was completely gone. He needed to be inside her. Right now. He swiftly removed his jeans and boxers and rose back over her, claiming her mouth once more as he settled back between her thighs.

Caly moaned, feeling his hard length between her thighs. With her eyes rolling back in her head, she widened her legs even further to welcome his massive body. He groaned as he slid a finger inside her again to make sure she was ready for him.

"You're so wet for me, Caly," he groaned out. He slowly thrust and then slipped another finger inside her, widening her to prepare her for him.

She was moving her hips and riding his fingers.

He growled.

But she was so caught up in the moment that the inhuman growl did not register.

Convinced she was ready (well, as ready as she was going to be—he was well-endowed), he rose over her once more because he wanted to watch her as he entered. He gripped himself and slowly pushed his tip inside her. She moaned and he growled in response. He lasted two shallow coaxing thrusts with his tip when his control finally snapped. He gripped her hips and slammed into her balls deep. She cried out a gasp and he froze.

Shit! You bastard, he chided himself. "Did I hurt you?" He recoiled at the thought.

"No... Oh god. Don't stop."

That was all he needed to hear. He pulled out with his tip still just barely inside her and then thrust deep, back into her fully. Growling and thrusting, her headboard was slamming against the wall in an erotic rhythm. With one hand gripping her waist, he reached down with his other hand and teased her sensitive spot.

"Blake!"

A moment later, he felt her shatter and her sex was gloriously milking him. With straining muscles, he growled out, "Caly!" in a deep voice as the pleasure shot through him. He spilled into her with wave after wave of pleasure. They both were breathing heavily and the pleasure was still pulsing through them. They laid there in stillness with him still inside her, semi-hard.

Coming back to consciousness with each heavy breath, Caly laid there, stunned. Yes, stunned at the fact that she just had sex with Mr. Mysterious. But more stunned at the fact that it was hands down the hottest sex she had ever experienced in her life. It's not like she had a lot of experience to compare it with.

Chemistry. This must be the "chemistry" everyone talks about. She echoed her thoughts that catapulted this sensual experience.

"Wow..." she pleasurably exhaled out, still in the haze of bliss. She heard a very satisfied, masculine chuckle vibrate over her breasts as his body was still very much on top of her.

Sensual memories of the past—ten minutes? Thirty minutes? Hours?—passed through her mind and she was growing wet once more. Then, she recalled a sound.

Did he growl? she silently wondered as he kissed her slow and deep before rolling off of her. She thought maybe he was about to get up and go... *Yes, go where exactly? And where did he come from?*

Instead of leaving, he just tucked her alongside him with her back to his warm chest and pushed his leg in between hers with his hand possessively draped over her chest. *God. How can this feel so right? Yet, who is this man?* With that last thought and the pleasure simmering away, reality started to crash into her.

Blake felt her slightly tense and suddenly he wanted to punch himself at the thought of possibly hurting this female. "Did I... hurt you?"

"What? No."

"Then what is it?"

"I... I don't do this." She motioned between them. "Random hook-ups. I mean, I don't even know you. Well, I know you from my dreams but this isn't a dream. Who are you?" *And why am I not running for the hills? Have I completely lost it?* Caly pondered her sanity.

Shit. This was not supposed to happen, Blake thought. Then a sobering thought hit him, washing over a little truth of his own. *Nico.* Nico was just outside that door in the living room. *Jesus. What is wrong with you?*

Trying not to spook her, he kissed the curve of her neck and gently hugged her before saying, "Let's talk."

"Okay... But not like this." She was referring to their hot, naked, and tangled bodies.

Chuckling, he rolled off the bed and slid his jeans and shirt back on. Suddenly, with his body heat gone, another cool dose of reality hit her. Yet, she wanted him to come back to bed and lay next to her.

Stockholm syndrome. This must be Stockholm syndrome

at its finest. Fuck the Freudian psychologists because, hell, I might as well be the case study for the modern-day Stockholm. No. Actually, I'm going to have my own syndrome named after me for this when I'm dead because surely I was in bed with a killer kidnapper. Crazy Caly Condition. The three deadly C's. Yup. On that lovely thought, Caly suddenly got shy and blushed.

He noticed. Of course he did with those intense golden eyes. She swore his eyes were glowing in the heat of the moment, but that was obviously not right—not to mention impossible. And, god. That was how this whole thing got started in the first place: his impossibly beautiful golden eyes.

With a wolfish grin, he closed his eyes and said, "I won't peek."

Wrapping the sheet around her, she saw her... his... Well, both of their shirts on the ground.

Sliced... Why does it look like it was sliced? Caly swallowed on that note. Apparently, at this point, she was all out of fear because the *kidnapping* must have milked her dry.

I need a shower. This—whatever this is—can wait until I do something normal. She grabbed a change of clothes and quickly shuffled toward the bedroom door.

"Wait!" She heard him say as she opened her door.

She suddenly became a statue as Felix padded out of the bedroom toward a man... No, *the* man... with the cold, dark eyes. Except his eyes were not dark any longer. So, yup. That was how she became a Greek statue dressed in a toga with sex hair.

And what was that you were saying about the kidnapping milking you dry of all fear? Guess there was a little left in your reserves after all. But not enough to change her mission. Operation: take the hottest shower ever and hope

93

she woke up. She looked at Blake and then back at dark eyes.

"I..."

Speechless. She was completely speechless. This was just too much crazy and she was officially milked dry. Whatever. If she was going to be kidnapped and killed then so be it. But damn it, she was going to enjoy a nice hot shower regardless.

Chapter 10

Caly plopped down in her favorite reading chair in a clean pair of clothes. Her skin was still a little pink from the hot shower. Felix usually joined her on the couch but... Her eyes flicked over to the sofa where Blake was sitting comfortably, laid back with his knees casually open. And Felix was currently taking up permanent residence at the cross streets of purr storm and bliss on Blake's lap.

Felix apparently has Crazy Caly Condition as well. It must be contagious. Ah, another "C" word. How fitting. But damn if he didn't look sexy as hell.

"Who are you, Caly?" Blake broke the silence.

Now, isn't that the fucking question of the hour, Caly thought.

"I... I don't even know how to answer that. What do you mean who am I? I think the more appropriate questions are: Who are *you*? Why are you here? And how were you in my dreams?"

Blake paused with a calculating look. "I am Blake with Orion's Or—"

Caly cut him off, "Yeah. I got that much." Okay. So apparently, she was Ms. Sassy all of a sudden.

One corner of Blake's mouth twitched in amusement of

her sassy side.

"I am here because you asked for me and you pulled me into your dreams."

What is this? Groundhog's Day Kidnapper Edition? Caly thought, a bit exasperated. *Yeah, technically he wasn't a kidnapper because I did unknowingly ask to be taken to him. Semantics.* She was confused and wasn't sure how to get out of this looping broken record stuck on repeat... And yeah, how was that for the Miguel song irony of the century?

"You have a lot of really *weird* dreams, right?" Blake prompted.

"So, what? Everyone does."

"But yours are vivid. Like real life."

"Again, lots of people have vivid dreams."

"It's pitch black and then you travel to places by the dream tunnel." Blake wasn't a traveler but he had heard about the basics of dream-traveling from others.

So, that is a little weird that he knows that, Caly thought. "How—"

"You have conversations and talk with others in your dreams. And they are too coincidental to be, well, a coincidence. Like us for example. I was in your dream for two weeks every single night. We were at the beach and you were in the cave. We didn't speak at all. Then the dreams stopped for about a week now."

Okay. You have my attention, Caly thought.

"How do you know all of this?" She narrowed her eyes suspiciously.

"Because I know what you are." *Well, sort of*, Blake internally corrected. He knew she was species but there was something unique about her scent that didn't specifically denote seer or traveler. Regardless, the fact that she could pull him into her dreams confirmed that she was a traveler.

"But what I don't know is who you are and why you pulled me into your dreams?"

Oh god. There he goes with the "pulled him into my dreams" thing. She closed her eyes and let out a long exasperated sigh.

"Look, I don't know where you're going with all of this. Okay, I have weird dreams. Again, so what? Everyone has weird dreams. I am just so confused… and exhausted."

He smirked at that last comment.

"That's not what I meant," she said with a blush.

She froze with wide eyes. *Oh my god! We didn't even use protection!*

When Caly was younger and her friends started to get their periods, her mom had the "girl talk" with her. Her mom explained that there was a genetic flaw for the women in her family which caused her to only be fertile every couple of years. She said that when Caly would first start cycling, it could be even more irregular until it naturally evened out. Her mom also assured her that she could still have children. Caly didn't mind because, hello, fewer periods! As far as she was concerned, she hit the female jackpot. To top it off, her mom said that she was infertile the entire time outside of the three "fertile days" of each cycle. So, taking birth control never made sense for the women in her family. Besides, she always knew when she was fertile because she would get intense cravings that were undeniable—sexual cravings. Apparently, it had to do with hormones and genetics or something. Caly didn't ask a lot of questions because, duh. She wanted to get the conversation over with as soon as possible and pretend it never happened. Fewer periods? Check. Infertile except for three days? Check. Still able to have kids? Check. Conversation over.

Shit! Maybe that's what this "chemistry" I felt—no, I feel—for Blake is all about?

And damn her body, because even right now, despite everything, she was undeniably attracted to him and wanted him. She had never felt like this with anyone else before. This… was different. There were the undeniable, fertility-induced, sexual cravings… and then there was this. Something different. She looked over at him and he was looking all sexy on the sofa with Felix. She noticed his chest expand as he inhaled deeply.

"What is it?" His voice shifted her focus back to the topic at hand.

"Ummm… We didn't… You know… Use protection." She blushed. God, why was she Ms. Red Cheeks all of a sudden? It was just sex. Okay, seriously steamy hot sex. And her body may have started to heat ten degrees hotter just thinking about it again. Because apparently, that was what this man, this sexy man, did to her. *Yup. Crazy. Caly. Condition.*

He chuckled a little and was about to say something but she cut him off and fired, "You think this is funny?! What if I'm pregnant?!"

"You're not fertile," he said with an amused smile.

"Oh really?! And how the fuck would you know that?!" Okay, so maybe she cussed a little when she was sassy. She didn't care.

"I can smell it," he said matter of factly.

She paused for a second, almost not believing this guy's answer. "You can *smell* it?"

"Yeah."

"Wait, let me get this straight." Her hand went up in the universal stop motion. "You think you can smell if I am fertile or not?"

"I *know* I can smell when you're fertile or not."

Red flag alert. Yeah, as if everything else wasn't a giant red flag slapping her in the face.

"Look, I have no idea what you're talking abou—"

"Caly, I'm a wolf."

"Is that some gang?"

Oh god, she thought. *Am I in a gang by sex default now?* She swallowed the thought of being featured in the next season of *Mob Wives.*

"No, I'm not in a gang. I'm a shifter. A wolf shifter."

Wolf shifter? She looked into his eyes and could see that he was dead serious. *He can't be seriously saying he is a werewolf?!* A laugh escaped her at the sheer absurdity.

"Oh really?" Her tone was sarcastically amused and she almost wanted to look around to see if she'd been Ashton Kutcher's next victim on *Punk'd.*

But his eyes somehow started to subtly glow deeper shades of gold, as if that was even possible, and his stare suddenly seemed... predatory. She swallowed. And damn it because his eyes had always been captivatingly beautiful to her and her body wanted him. And then he did something that she would have never, in a thousand years, guessed.

He threw his head back and howled.

She froze. Chills cascaded down her body in a wave of primal instinct. The sound was hauntingly beautiful. *Could this be real? No! Stop it! Don't believe this. He's an actor. Yeah, that's it. It is LA.*

"You know, you almost had me until you took it that step too far with the sci-fi werewolf thing. Look, we may have sexual chemistry..."

Sexual chemistry that is off the charts. And maybe she was kinky in a freaky sci-fi way because damn if that wasn't hot.

"And..." She let out a defeated breath. "Okay, I'm ashamed to admit I'm attracted to you despite everything and my better judgment. And, fine, I admit that was hot... and sounded so real. So, yeah. The whole werewolf thing is sexy as hell. I mean, *Twilight*, duh. Plus, I was always team Jacob. But look—you know, without me being in on the sex fantasy game, it's just weird. You should have told me before because apparently, I do have some weird sci-fi wolf sex kinky side."

His mouth turned up at the corners as if all too satisfied at her response. And, god, if that smile also wasn't sexy as hell. Caly was all of a sudden jealous of Felix. Because, damn, she wanted to be on his lap. *Stop! How can I still be thinking about sleeping with this man? Crazy. Caly. Condition.*

Her thoughts were interrupted by a knock on her door and she jumped a little. God, why was she so jumpy all of a sudden? Blake was at the door so fast that she blinked a few times to process what she had just witnessed. He opened the door and she saw Mr. Dark Eyes.

Oh god. That's right. He was right outside playing bodyguard. Oh my god, bodyguard! What if Nick sent them to keep watch over her while he was gone? He was protective but this obviously crossed the line. No, because then why the weird sci-fi kinky sex fantasy? Unless Nick was into this stuff too? Oh god. Of course he was. How could I be so stupid?

It looked like Blake was about to send him away but then she blurted out, "No. You come in here too." She needed to clear this up once and for all and tell these two men to leave.

"Did Nick send you guys to play bodyguard?"

"Who's Nick?" Blake asked with suspicious eyes.

She narrowed her eyes in response but it honestly seemed like he had no idea who she was talking about. Okay, so maybe she was wrong about the Nick thing. Throwing that wasted epiphany into the wastebasket, she focused on Mr. Dark Eyes, whose eyes weren't dark anymore.

"Are you in on the weird sci-fi sex fantasy thing too?" she accused. There was a brief pause before she laughingly said, "Oh my god. Don't tell me you're a 'vampire' with some kink fetish to complete this weird *Twilight* love triangle fantasy? That's why your eyes were black. Contacts, right?"

Nico, who already had no patience whatsoever, was done with the charade from this female and he was even more done with Blake only thinking with his dick.

Caly saw his eyes narrow to lethal slits and he appeared in front of her before she could blink. His eyes were suddenly black once again. She froze.

Okay, that looked real. Real freaky. Remember, it's not real. Just freaky sci-fi acting effects. But how was he in front of you before you saw him move? Okay, maybe she was a little frightened all of a sudden.

"L-look." She swallowed. "You both need to lea—"

"Nico, wait—" Blake blurted out as Caly's world went dark.

"Damn it, Nico!" Blake growled. Both he and his wolf were snarling at Nico's rash decision.

Nico narrowed his frosty eyes at Blake. "Blake, we don't have time for this. You're thinking with your dick. Her memory may have been tampered with. We need to get the info and leave."

Blake narrowed his eyes at Nico but stayed silent. He ran his hand over his jaw in a desperate act to think. Okay, so maybe Nico had a point. He knew he was being way out of character and completely irrational when it came to this female. He slept with her for Christ's sake. And this female was so confused. A vampire with strong mesmerizing abilities could have altered her memory on such a deep level that she forgot who she was. With that thought, Blake closed his eyes for a moment and pinched the bridge of his nose.

Nico was a much needed ice-cold bucket of water over his head. Jesus, what was it about this female that had him and his wolf not thinking straight? Their priority was The Ghost. And, fine, he also admitted to himself that now he had his own personal agenda to find out who this female belonged to so he could make sure that she was safe with her species family. Because, yeah, she couldn't be left in the human world in this condition. Besides, how could she not know about species when she was species?

"Alright. But we leave her memories as they are," Blake said.

"Agreed."

Nico may be a cold bastard but he didn't cross that ethical line, especially with females. Blake knew that was one of the reasons he was sought after as a Dom. He could read the submissives so well and knew their edges like his own. However, Blake, or anyone else for that matter, didn't know just how highly desired and notorious a Dom he really was. Yeah, maybe he had a different moral line in the sand than most others. But Blake still trusted Nico with his life.

As they both turned to the female who was sitting there in a hypnotic state, Blake started the questioning. "Who are you?"

"Calypso Smith," Caly said in a monotone voice.

"What species are you?"

"Human."

Both Nico and Blake looked at each other with that answer.

How can this female think she is human? Blake wondered. "Shit. Can you see if her memories have been altered?"

Nico took a moment to look deep into her eyes. When he broke eye contact and looked at Blake, he concluded, "No. Not that I can see."

"So, she thinks she is human? How can this be?"

Nico was silent because there was no need to reply—he was equally stumped.

Blake refocused on Caly and asked, "Do you know of the species world?"

"No."

"Who are your parents?"

"Aaron and Irene Smith."

"Where are they now?"

"Passed away."

"How?"

"Car accident."

"When?"

"Four years ago."

"Have you always lived in California?"

"Yes."

That was something at least. Because the only species who lived on the other side were the ones who were hiding from something. Then he asked something that had him and his wolf snarling since she mentioned it.

"Who is Nick?"

Nico gave him the side-eye with that question. Okay, so maybe it wasn't relevant but he needed to know.

"A man I've gone out with twice."

His wolf snarled at the thought and he agreed. *No. She is not yours.* He needed to switch subjects before this got out of hand.

"Why did you pull me into your dreams?"

"I didn't."

"Do you know that you're a traveler?"

"No."

Blake let out a frustrated sigh before continuing. "Why is The Ghost watching you?"

When Caly was silent, Blake looked at Nico with a questioning glance.

Nico asked Caly, "Do you know who The Ghost is?"

"No."

"Do you know who James Barker is?" Blake tacked on.

"No."

"Did you know that someone was watching you from outside your apartment?"

"No."

"Shit." Out of questions, Blake turned back to Nico. "We need to look into her background, parents, and records to see if we can find something." *Could it be that she was kept in the dark?* Cutting that thought off he continued, "Bring her back around but only in a slight trance state so she will see us leave."

Nico agreed and a moment later Caly was slowly blinking her gray eyes.

God, what just happened? Caly thought, blinking her eyes and shaking her head slightly.

"We are leaving just like you asked," Blake prompted.

She blinked again and refocused on the two men. She recalled that she did tell them they needed to leave. Yes, because they are playing some weird sci-fi sex fetish games with her. Her brain was starting to come back online.

"Good." She cleared her throat which was suddenly dry.

Blake and Mr. Dark Eyes got up and walked toward the door. All she could do was stare at Blake. Some part of her didn't want him to go. Okay, so she was ashamed to admit that but it was the truth. He turned around and looked at her in the eyes for a long moment. Damn, if that wasn't how this whole thing started.

"Lock the door when we leave," Blake ordered.

He was right. She needed to lock the door.

As the door clicked shut, she got up and slid the deadbolt into place. She was really exhausted and there was just too much to process. Her brain was a complete scramble and she was trying to understand what in the ever-loving hell just happened. Did she really just sleep with a complete stranger? Who was she? Nope. She couldn't go there right now. She decided to eat something and then take a nap. She was just suddenly so exhausted.

Blake waited outside Caly's door until he heard her deadbolt lock into place.

"Take first watch. I'll fill the others in and send Rhyker to relieve you. Keep your phone on," Blake ordered. With Nico's nod, Blake took off.

Blake's thoughts were on overdrive the entire trip back home. *How can it be that she doesn't know she is species? That she is a traveler? And her parents are gone?* He felt a sudden sting in his own heart at that thought. *And most importantly, how is she connected to The Ghost? And that she is dating someone. No. Been on two dates with. That doesn't mean anything.* Why did it matter? So they slept together. And both he and his wolf wanted more. But she wasn't his.

As he pulled up to the house, his thoughts were suddenly cut off.

What the...?

Standing on the porch were Rhyker, Rhyland, and Deacon. It was like they were some kind of fucking greeting party. No doubt, Rhyker heard him coming from a mile away.

"Meeting. Now," Blake ordered all of them as he got out of the SUV.

"We sure as hell are having a meeting. I have popcorn. This is gonna be good," Rhyland quipped. He took a deep inhale with his gifted nose and his mischievous smile widened. "Oh yeah. This is going to be real good." Rhyland fist-bumped Rhyker who was also grinning as he exhaled out smoke from a hand-rolled.

Damn it, Blake internally grumbled. Of course, Rhyland wouldn't miss the fact that Caly's scent was all over him. He marched past them and into the house.

Everyone beelined to their usual spots and the twins were acting as if they were getting settled into a movie theater. Rhyker sprawled out on his new leather sofa and shoved a handful of gummy bears into his pie hole. To him? Any color of gummy was fine. He didn't discriminate. Rhyland was on the new matching leather seat with a bag of popcorn. He fisted a handful of popcorn and stuffed it into his mouth.

Christ. These two. Blake gave them an unamused look. They were suddenly sporting their iconic twin feline grins.

"Here's what we know." Blake brought everyone up to speed. Well, minus the part about him and Caly having mind-blowing sex that left him wanting more.

"Shit..." Rhyland drew out the word. "And I was so distracted by Nico being a creep kidnapper so it wasn't until after you all left that her scent finally registered that she isn't human. And there's something about her scent that is... Well, I can't quite place it." Rhyland's voice trailed off.

"Agreed." Blake nodded, not surprised in the least that Rhyland's sensitive nose picked up on that, despite the distracted and brief interaction. "But she still fits into the seer and traveler umbrella." Although he said it as a statement, he was looking for Rhyland's confirmation of his assessment.

"Yeah... Close enough," Rhyland confirmed, words muffled by the cheekfuls of crunching popcorn.

"D," Blake began and took out his phone to send a quick text. "I just sent you a picture of her human ID. See what you can find out about her: human records, species records, parents... everything."

"Calypso," Rhyland purred. "Beautiful name for a beautiful female." He waggled his brows.

"Which reminds me. Paws off. Everyone," Blake said, looking directly at the twins.

"Like any of us would be crazy enough to make a move with her scent all over you. And it is *all* over you," Rhyland suggestively teased, exchanging a broad grin with his twin.

There was a sudden interest in Deacon's eyes at that comment.

Blake shot everyone a look that dared them to continue down that road. No one took the dare. Good. Maybe they were all on the same page as Nico in deciding against brawling with the alpha right now. Smart.

"We're keeping an eye on her in case The Ghost comes back and if anything else shows up as unusual. Nico took first watch." Blake looked at Rhyker. "You'll have second shift."

Chapter 11

"Report," Blake ordered Nico, who just got back from his watch and was perched by his window.

"Nothing. Didn't leave her apartment. No one stopped by. Except for pizza delivery. No sign of The Ghost."

He was relieved to hear that Nick didn't make an appearance because both he and his wolf adamantly rejected the thought of another male being alone with her. Especially when his thoughts were consumed with her—her scent, her taste, her touch. Damn. He wanted to feel her body beneath his once more.

Stop. Stay focused, he ordered himself.

"D, what did you find out?" He looked at Deacon who was sitting in his usual spot.

"Calypso Smith has extensive human records that are incredibly well-integrated into the human world. This was no 'quick job' by an amateur and the degree of details of her 'human life' are, frankly, impressive for an undercover op. If I didn't know any better, I would say SILE themselves were behind it and she has been deep undercover living with the humans as one of them for decades in the making. But we know that we are the only ones working the case. And I even checked their classified files and there are no records of setting up this undercover op."

He paused and everyone's brows furrowed in confusion.

"Her parents have the same type of work and detail in the human records. The human records show that they died in a car accident four years ago. If they were, in fact, 'real' then it was as if they all lived together for decades leading unassuming human lives."

Blake remembered Caly's sudden heartbreak the first time they spoke. "I scented her sudden heartbreak and sorrow when we first spoke. It was pure and undeniable. My instincts tell me her parents were real... at least in her mind. You can't fake a scent that pure, no matter how well you're trained."

Rhyland chimed in between chip crunching mouthfuls, "Yeah. Agreed."

Deacon nodded, taking that information in and then continued, "Starr also got back to me. The Whisper said that she is blocked from seeing anything about Caly."

"Damn it. How the hell is everyone blocking seers all of a sudden?" Blake let out a frustrated growl.

"She said it is different than The Ghost though. The Ghost is described as being concealed by a cloud of dark fog or smoke but she knows he is there. Caly's is as if she doesn't exist. None of us have heard anything like it."

"Can we try another seer?" Rhyland suggested.

"We can. But everything that I know about The Whisper is that she's one of the most, if not *the most*, powerful seers. If she can't get a read then it's highly doubtful anyone can." There was a pause and then Deacon continued, "The big questions still remain. Who is she? Who are her parents? Why is she living among the humans? How was she un-knowingly using her traveling abilities? And how is she connected with The Ghost?"

And why can't I stop thinking about her? Blake internally

added onto Deacon's good points. Then something suddenly clicked in Blake's mind. *Blocking.*

"You said The Whisper said she was *blocked*, right?" Blake said and Deacon nodded in agreement. "She was blocking herself when she pulled me into her dreams. I even asked Alexina about this and she didn't know. I'll reach back out to her with this new information."

This was good. It would give him something to do. Because right now, all he could think about was this female and how he wanted to be guarding her. Which was not a good idea considering he wanted to do more than just guard her. And damn his wolf because he had been pacing almost the whole time since he left her. He needed to keep his distance because this female was doing things to him that was testing his self-control.

✻ ✻ ✻

Caly laid in her bed staring at the ceiling. Her thoughts were swirling with the unexpected sharp turn of her life, given recent events.

"Who are you, Caly?" She heard Blake's voice repeat that question in her mind.

Yes. Who am I?

She was still trying to process her dream of GQ along with the fact that the man with the cold, dark eyes was in her room who took her to see "Blake from Orion's Order." Not to mention the fact that Blake was a real person... or rather, the sexiest man she had ever seen. This man that she could not stop thinking about.

And let's not forget the fact you were dreaming about him for weeks before you ever met him. Oh, and also, how both him and Mr. Dark Eyes were into weird Twilight sex fantasies. Oh, and you know, no big deal or anything but it was just the hottest sex of your life. That's all. What is wrong with you? Then a thought popped into her mind. *Yes. I must've seen Blake somewhere before. Maybe at the coffee shop? Client at the office? TV show?* That would explain how she dreamed about him. And, okay, yeah so what hot-blooded woman wouldn't dream about a man like that? He was gorgeous and his eyes were dreamy. *Stop. Stop thinking about him.*

Caly laid in bed for what seemed like forever with the constant congestion of thoughts and emotions until sleep finally claimed her.

There was darkness all around her with a pinprick of light ahead. *Oh good.* This was just what she needed. More tunnel adventures to have her life continue on the crazy train. Next stop, 72-hour psych hold.

Surprise, not surprise, she was standing in the cave with the beach and, yup, Blake was there and they were in their usual staring contest. For the first time, she walked out of the cave and straight up to Blake. God, even in her dreams this male had her body responding. Then again, this must just be residual dream chemistry as a result of what happened between them.

"Caly, why am I here?"

Oh god, now he talks? Caly thought, giving her subconscious mind a little side-eye.

"Oh, I don't know. Maybe it's because all I can do is think about you and the best sex I've ever had."

The best sex she's ever had? Blake thought, suddenly sporting a sly smile at her confession.

Damn, Blake's smile was sexy as hell. And damn, if being near him didn't put Caly under some sort of weird spell. Despite everything, she wanted him.

"What is wrong with me? Even with everything that happened, I still want you. And I'm completely ashamed about that. I need to let all of this go and pretend like it never happened. But clearly I can't because here you are in my dreams." She let out an exhausted sigh.

He went to say something but she cut him off. "No, I swear if in my dreams you say, '*Caly, this isn't a dream*,' " she said in a low male voice like Blake's. "...I will... Well, I don't know what I'll do but just don't."

"Caly, this *is* a dream. Your dream."

It looked like he was about to say something else but she cut him off again. "No. No more. If this is a dream then I'm done talking."

Hell, am I really about to do this... again? Whatever. This time, it was a dream, right? So no one would know but her. No harm. No foul. She would scratch the itch and then wake up and move on with her merry life. Her *normal* life.

She looked into his impossibly golden eyes and took a step closer. Yup. She was spellbound. She pulled his face down to hers and kissed him, hot and wet. One of his muscled arms wrapped around her waist to pull her closer into his warm body. His mouth was possessively taking hers and his tongue licked across her lips coaxing them to open for him. And she did. Their tongues were in the most sensual of dances when his free hand caressed up her neck and through her hair and gently tugged. She moaned and then bit his lower lip to entice him to continue. His big rough hands cupped her breasts through her thin, black sleep tank. His thumbs were brushing over her nipples and she moaned. He growled and she liked it. So what if in her dreams she was playing out the wolf fantasy?

"Howl for me, Blake," she pleaded in a husky voice.

With his lips still on hers, she felt him smile and growl in approval of her request. He tilted his head back and howled for her. It was just as hauntingly beautiful as the first time she heard it. It sent a shiver down her spine and she shuddered.

"Wow," she whispered on a fascinated breath.

He gave her a sexy, wolfish smile and then claimed her mouth once more, playfully growling a little. Suddenly, his strong arms lifted her off the ground and she was straddling his waist. With their lips still locked, she wrapped her arms around his neck and her hands were in his hair. She moaned in pleasure. From one second to the next, she felt the cave wall against her back and his hard body pressed to her front. He broke the kiss and started sucking on her pulse while he rocked into her core through her thin, black sleep shorts.

"Blake!" His name came out as a breathy moan full of need.

His mouth licked and sucked its way back to her soft lips to claim them once more. He only broke the kiss to lock gazes. He wanted her to watch as he used a claw to cut her shirt down the middle in a quick swipe. She let out an excited, pleasured sound at the sudden movement which had her plump breasts exposed to him.

"You're so beautiful," he growled out, taking in the view of her peaks.

She smiled and blushed. He took one of her breasts with his hot mouth and she arched her chest into him. He swirled his tongue around her nipple and used his teeth in a gentle tease. She closed her eyes and allowed her head to fall back against the cave wall in pleasure. His other hand was teasing her neglected nipple. He pulled his mouth away a couple of inches and then blew a hot breath over the wet nipple in a new pleasurable sensation. She moaned.

"Off," she echoed and tugged at his shirt, reminiscent of their first time together. She wanted skin on skin.

He smiled and tugged at her shorts. "Off," he commanded.

"Off," she said, giving him a sinful smile. She continued the playful tease by pulling on the belt loop of his jeans.

Smile widening, he set her down. Their eyes were locked as he slowly pulled his shirt over his head. Her body was responding to the sight of his large muscled body and chiseled abs. She let her ripped tank fall from her shoulders onto the cave floor. His gaze slowly made its descent down until it settled on her shorts, in a silent command for her to strip them off. With a slow shimmy of her hips, her shorts pooled at the cave floor. She stood bare to him for his viewing pleasure and he let out a low growl. She shot him a wicked smile and cupped her breasts. His growl grew louder in response. She returned to the game and stared at his jeans, echoing his silent demand. He smiled and slid out of his jeans. She made the descent with her eyes, taking him in for her viewing pleasure. He was so sexy and his hard length protruded out from his hips, commanding her body to respond by tightening in the lowest of feminine places. They stood there for a moment bare to each other with their eyes locked. It was one of the hottest moments of her life.

With shifter speed, he had her back up against the cave wall and she could feel his hard length between them. With their mouths once again in the sensual duel, his hand slid down in between their bodies to her sex.

"Blake!" she moaned out in pleasure.

His fingers were stroking her wet heat in a way that was driving her wild. She bit his lower lip hard this time and he growled in approval. She broke the kiss and turned her neck toward his mouth, silently demanding for him to suck on her pulse once more. And he did.

"Oh god, Blake! I need you inside me."

His fingers kept up with their erotic teasing around her sensitive spot.

"Blake, inside me. Please!"

He broke the kiss to look into her eyes and he got the confirmation he needed. The next moment he thrust into her wet core to the hilt. She let out a cry of passion at the sensation and he grunted.

"You're so tight and wet for me, Caly."

He filled her completely and she could feel herself stretching to adjust to him. Her legs were now propped up by his arms which were pinned on either side of her. She was spread so wide for him to thrust deep. He was slowly rocking into her, allowing her body to adjust to his size. The rocking was rubbing her sensitive spot in just the right way and pleasure was rippling through her body with each rock of his hips.

"Blake..." she moaned. "Oh god, that feels so good."

He kept the slow rocking until her body wanted more and she tried moving her hips in rhythm but she was pinned to the cave wall by his strong, muscled body. He must've understood what her body was saying because he pulled out to the tip and then thrust back in slowly. Yes, that was exactly what she needed. She let out a throaty moan and he groaned. His body was dominating hers in every way and she loved it. He repeated the slow, teasing thrusts until she couldn't take it anymore.

"Faster," she whispered the demand in his ear. Pleasure licked through her body as the pace quickened.

She felt herself tightening around him as her body prepared for a release.

"Oh god. Yes!"

He was pumping hard and it sent her into a wild, pleasure-filled haze.

"Come for me, Caly," he commanded on a growl.

As if waiting for his command, the orgasm ripped through her entire body and she let out a cry of pleasure. He kept rocking inside her to ride out the waves of pleasure.

When she came back down from the pleasured high, she took his mouth—hot and wet. He was still hard inside her and rocking. In a blink of an eye, he was on the cave floor with her straddled on top.

"Ride me, Caly," he commanded in a low growl. He gripped her hips with his big hands and together they found a slow erotic rhythm. She moaned and he growled in response.

"You're so beautiful." He pulled her torso down and took one of her pink nipples in his mouth.

She moaned.

She broke his kiss with her breast so she could claim his mouth with hers. Her hips were grinding in a sensual rhythm and erotic tightness was coiling inside her once more. She pulled back from their demanding kiss so she could pick up the pace and ride him harder and faster. His hands moved back to her hips in erotic possessiveness.

"Caly, come with me."

"Blake!" she moaned, riding him hard and fast.

"Come with me, Caly," he commanded again.

A moment later they fell together with waves of ecstasy rolling through their bodies. Their chests were heaving as they were coming back to consciousness slowly. She was laying on top of his warm body and didn't have any desire to move. She felt so complete in this moment.

As if reading her thoughts, he wrapped his warm arms around her to hold her. He gently whispered in his rough, sexed-up voice, "Stay."

And she did.

Chapter 12

Blake awoke to consciousness with the sensation of holding Caly's naked body over his—except, she wasn't there. But what was there was his raging hard-on. Shit, he really desired for her to be on top of him right now so he could take her all over again… and again.

"The best sex I've ever had." Caly's voice repeated that thought in his mind.

He had never experienced sex like he had with her before either. This female did things to him and his wolf that drove the pleasure through the roof.

Clearly she wanted you too because she pulled you into her dreams and then took you. Shit. You bastard.

She thought that was a dream. But when he tried to explain that it was a dream but at the same time that it was still really "him" (not like that would have gone over well anyway, considering their past conversations), she told him to stop talking and then took his mouth. Both he and his wolf liked when she let that dominant side out to play erotic games with him.

Maybe I will go see her—

The thought was cut off by his cell phone ringing. He picked it up by the second ring.

119

"Yeah." His voice was a deep, morning gravel.

"Blake. I know it's early but you'll want to hear this."

It was detective Bartell with SILE. That got Blake's attention. He sat up in bed and took a drink of water from the bottle next to his bed.

"What happened?"

"Another murder. MO appears to be The Ghost."

Blake internally cursed.

"He was one of ours. He was Marie's partner on The Ghost investigation. He took a severe blow to the head that night she was taken and lost some of his memory. The healers said he should have died that night and it was a miracle that he was alive with only a lapse in memory. We think either his memory started to come back or he must've known or saw something where The Ghost had to make sure he stayed silent."

"Shit. Sorry."

"Thanks. Greg. He was one of the good ones." There was a brief pause. "It just happened a few hours ago at most. We've blocked off the immediate and surrounding area. No entry, as to not tamper with the scene and scents any further. I'll send you the location."

"Good. We're on our way."

The call ended without any other words exchanged and Blake immediately made another call which was answered on the first ring.

"No updates. She's still slee—"

Blake cut Rhyland off. "There's been another murder. Get home now. We need to investigate."

"Shit. I'm on my way." There was a brief pause as if he was taking in the news. "What about Caly?"

Blake exhaled. He didn't want to leave her unprotected but he needed everyone there at the crime scene because everyone brought their own strengths and abilities that would be needed. Besides, it was Monday so Caly would be at work all day and she would be safe at the office. And it was likely The Ghost was still in the area of the murder because that sick arrogant fuck would probably revel in watching, which was what Blake was banking on. Between the twins and Nico, they might actually have a chance to take down the bastard. And the chances that The Ghost would act again so soon would be out of character for him. So, this was their best shot.

"She'll be at work today," Blake answered. "We'll have someone back on watch when we get back."

And that someone is going to be me, Blake thought to himself. He needed to see her and perhaps see if he could talk with her without setting her off.

"Roger that."

* * *

Caly blinked her eyes open, half expecting to feel Blake's warm muscled body under hers. But it was just a dream. The sexiest dream of her life with the hottest man that was consuming her thoughts.

Damn. Even the dream was tied for the number one spot of the most erotic experience of her life. The tie-breaker? Duh. The other time with Blake. At least that was in real life. Yup. She was seriously screwed, pun intended.

She let out an exhale and felt the damp hot wetness between her legs. God, she wanted him.

Stop. Scratch the itch and move on with your merry life, remember? Except clearly that was not going to be the case. She let out another exhale. *Yup. screwed.* This man may have ruined her for any other man in the future. *Shit! Nick! I have a date with Nick tonight.*

God, what was wrong with her? She not only slept with

the sexy, role-playing wolf but had also been fantasizing about him ever since. And damn if that kinky wolf thing did not play out to orgasmic levels in her dream. Did she really ask him to howl? Yup. Did she dream of him growling and cutting her shirt away with his wolf claws? Yup. Did she dream of his impossibly fast wolf speed? Yup. And was it really one of the sexiest things she had ever experienced? Yup. Okay, clearly she did have some hidden, kinky, *Twilight* fetishes she needed to work through before she could date anyone. *Speaking of dating... Let's circle back to how you have a date with Nick tonight. Nick is normal. Normal is good.*

But she knew this wasn't fair to him. She had been in his shoes before, where the other person was hung up on someone else and just not that into her. She wasn't going to string him along and do what was done to her because it hurts and it wasn't right for both of them. She would just be using Nick to try and forget about Blake. And clearly she was not attracted to Nick nor did she have any chemistry with him. Yeah, so, she needed to forget about Blake... but dating Nick was not the answer. She already committed to the date so she would go out with him tonight and let him know she was sorry because he was a nice guy but she was hung up on someone else and she needed time to be alone. And possibly make an appointment with a therapist.

Caly imagined herself laying on a therapist's couch and confessing, *I've become obsessed with a sexy man that is into kinky sci-fi werewolf role play. I don't even know him and had unprotected sex with him. It was the best sex of my life and my subconscious mind decided for round two in my dreams, which, by the way, I asked him to howl for me. So, yeah. That's it really.*

Yup. Crazy Caly Condition.

She tried to tell herself that she needed to forget about

Blake and get back to normal. It was one wild weekend of craziness. No big deal. People did that all the time.

I mean, hello, Vegas. But that's how this would work, isn't it? Have off the charts chemistry, paired with the best sex of my life, with an impossibly gorgeous man who just turns out to be crazy. But hey, clearly I'm crazy too because I can't stop thinking about him. With those thoughts, she got ready for work and then rushed out the door.

Caly heard a knock at her front door.

Shit! It's Nick, Caly thought with one last look in the mirror.

She decided to keep it casual for the date. She was wearing her favorite pair of dark-wash, skin-tight jeans and a simple, black tank top. She loved this outfit because it was simple, hugged her curves perfectly, and could be styled up or down depending on the occasion. She went for her go-to date makeup look, with the added touch of eyeshadow and eyeliner that was smoky enough to bring out her gray eyes. She opted to give her long hair relaxed curls. So what if she was going to break it off with Nick? Who said she couldn't get dressed up and look good while doing it?

Caly opened the door and said, "Hi, Nick."

She noted he was wearing his usual outfit including the Aviators.

"Hey, Caly. You look very nice."

"Thanks. You do too."

The way he said her name sent a shiver down her spine and not in the sexual chemistry kind of way. It actually reminded her of when they first met. He was like a giant statue of cool steel.

He took a deep, audible inhale.

She suddenly got a flash of memory of Blake doing the same type of deep breathing but she shook that thought off.

It's probably Felix's stinky, fishy wet food.

"Ummm sorry about the smell. I just fed Felix this fishy, wet cat food and I know it smells but it's his favorite." She offered a sheepish smile.

"Don't worry about it," he said, lips curving in one of his cool smiles.

She suddenly got the chills. "Thanks. Umm, hold on a sec. Let me grab a jacket real quick."

She indicated for him to come inside because she couldn't leave the door open with Felix and she couldn't just leave Nick outside and then shut the door in his face. He stepped in and she closed the door. She ran into the other room to grab her black jacket and came back a moment later.

"Okay. I'm ready," she said and turned toward the kitchen to say goodbye to Felix. Her brow furrowed slightly when she noticed Felix was nowhere near his completely full food dish.

Odd, she thought as she scanned the room. She saw Felix under the coffee table with his ears back, hissing, as the fur on his tail puffed out as if he had been electrocuted. She slowly went to turn her head to follow the trajectory of where Felix's gaze was transfixed. She already knew what set him off but she continued the swivel of her head anyway. Yup. It was Nick.

Don't worry Felix. It's over with Nick anyways. We won't see him again, she sent Felix the telepathic message as if he could understand her.

"Sorry about that. He doesn't like... ummm... strangers. Let's go." She opened the door and flashed a smile to try and not make this more awkward than it was becoming.

We'll go to dinner, have a nice time like the last two dates, and then I'll break it off with him gently, she internally recited the plan.

"It's fine. It's probably just my size that scares him."

124

But Blake is about the same size—bigger actually (impossibly enough)—and Felix was basically my competition for Blake's attention. With that thought, they were out the door. Why was her heart racing all of a sudden?

It's just nerves. It's always awkward and uncomfortable when you have to end it with someone, she reasoned.

"So," she tried to say in a casually light tone. "How was your VIP job? Hopefully it went well?"

"Yeah. The job was smooth and went as planned. You never know how VIP clients are gonna go. I'm sure you can relate with high priority clients at the law office."

"That's good. Oh, yeah, totally understand. The whole office has to put on their best behavior and we pull out all the stops with VIP clients."

"How was your weekend, Caly?" He sent her one of his cool smiles as they approached his car.

"Oh, good. You know… Just hung out and stayed home really."

Change subjects! she thought in a nervous sing-song voice.

"So, where are we going tonight?"

"It's a surprise. I hope you're hungry though."

See? A normal surprise about where they are going for dinner. Unlike kinky wolf sex fetish surprises. Stop. Don't go there.

"Yes, I am." And she actually really was hungry and looking forward to a normal dinner.

He opened the car door for her before walking around and getting in the car himself. Driving onto the street, he turned on the radio and flipped to 104.3 MYFM, one of the top LA radio stations.

"What kind of music do you like?" he asked.

"I guess it depends on what kind of mood I am in really."

"And what kind of mood are you in right now?" he drawled.

"MYFM is good right now."

"Well, feel free to change it if your mood changes too. I am not like one of those guys who are dominant about their radio in their car."

See? Nick is not only normal but totally nice. He may look like a macho dominant seriously intense guy but I bet you he is probably just a big old softy underneath that.

Despite her awkwardness, Nick kept the casual conversation going.

Hmmm… We have been driving for a while. Caly's stomach growled in agreement. Thank God the music was on and hopefully, he didn't hear that.

"So, I'm guessing this must be a really good place?" she said with a smile. She didn't want to be rude but she was really curious about where they were going and she was starving.

He exhaled a defeated breath. "Shoot. I'm sorry, Caly. I guess I didn't really plan this out too well. I can tell you're hungry. I heard your stomach growl."

Way to go, Caly. Now you've made him feel bad even before you've stabbed him in the heart tonight. He was just trying to surprise you and do something nice for you.

"Oh, no it's okay! I find it sweet that you went through all this trouble. Seriously, thank you."

"No, it's not okay. I planned to surprise you by cooking for you. And I just realized I actually forgot one of the ingredients. I was kind of in a rush once I got back from the VIP job earlier. So, we have to make a quick pit stop at the grocery store on the way. I feel like an ass. I'm sorry for messing this up so bad."

He planned to cook? Okay, so that is actually really

nice. Too bad we don't have chemistry because a man who cooks? Yeah, bonus points.

"Nick, it's totally okay. And you haven't messed it up. Believe me, I have been on *way* worse dates... like so bad it doesn't even compare." She let out a little laugh to try and hopefully help him not feel so bad. "And I'm sorry I have been a little awkward. I just had some personal stuff come up this weekend and I am still processing it all. But I don't really want to talk about it. I just thought you should know that you haven't done anything wrong."

"You've been nothing but nice and patient with me Caly." He looked over at her and smiled in apology.

God, he looked like a guilty puppy that knows he shouldn't have "chewed those shoes." He returned his focus back to the road. Well, if she didn't look like a total bitch now.

"Nick, honestly this isn't bad *at all*. So, like the last guy I went on a date with before you for instance. The entire date all he could talk about was his manual transmission car." She laughed a little. "And I mean, the *entire time.* Literally, everything somehow went back to his stick shift car in some way." She paused, smiled, and then in an imitation male voice, she said, "This green salad reminds me of Black Beauty." She switched back to her real voice. "That was his car's name by the way." Smiling, she continued with her male impression, "Her dash buttons light up green at night."

Nick laughed.

"See? Nick, you're honestly really great company and are nice to talk with."

But I am going to have to break your heart later, she internally added. *Yeah, so not looking forward to that.*

"I wonder what your impression of me is?" he joked with a half-smile.

She cleared her voice and tried to speak in the lowest register available to her vocal cords, "Hey, Caly. I'm a really thoughtful guy and we will have some great conversations and laughs."

God. Why was she buttering him up like this? This is going to be next level awkward at the end of the date when her words come back to bite her in the ass.

He chuckled and she smiled.

At least his whole "puppy in trouble" vibe is gone and he doesn't look like he's beating himself up anymore about the miscalculation with the dinner timing. And honestly, it's not that big of a deal.

On that note, he pulled into a dark and deserted parking lot. Okay, so it was a little scary but she wasn't alone. *I mean, no one in their right mind would dare step a toe out of line with Nick around.* He was a serious deterrent for anyone with the wrong idea. Again, it made sense why he was a bodyguard.

"I'm just going to run in really quick."

He got out of the car and she was about to say that she'll go in with him but then he said, "Again, sorry about this. I'll make it up to you." Then, as if he spoke his thoughts out loud, he continued, "Oh, my bags are in the trunk... almost forgot to bring them..."

And, see, he also cares about the environment by bringing his own bags. Why couldn't you have chemistry with Nick? But no. It had to be with a kinky sex wolf. Stop. Don't go there.

She flipped down the car visor so she could do a quick check of her makeup in the mirror. She threw on a little more lip gloss as she heard the trunk open and shut. She was about to get out and go in with him anyway but then his car door opened again and he casually slid back into the driver's seat.

In an apologetic voice, he said, "I'm all over the place tonight. I forgot my wallet in the center console. I swear I am not usually this forgetful. I think the VIP job just really wiped me out."

He was reaching for the center console but before she could blink, Nick's hand was at her throat emptying the contents of a syringe into her neck. Then his hand was over her mouth muffling any screams she attempted.

A shock of fear spiked through her body at lightning speed and her eyes went wide in horror.

RUN! GET OUT!

Before her body could respond to her mental command, her limbs were heavy and her vision was fading. Then the world went black.

* * *

Nick approached Caly's apartment and knocked. She opened her door and a mix of scents breezed over to him with the motion of the door opening. He sharpened his senses. Internally, his smile was pure evil.

"Hi, Nick."

"Hey, Caly. You look very nice."

"Thanks. You do too."

He took a deep inhale, filling his senses just to make sure. His internal dark smile widened a fraction more.

I caught you, he thought in a psychotic sing-song voice. *I knew it was only a matter of time before you made a mistake. Just like Marie. Now it's time for the fun and games.*

Chapter 13

"Fuck!" Blake growled and echoed what everyone else was no doubt thinking. He pulled open the door to the house, almost pulling it off of the hinges.

Everyone was just getting back from the hunt at the crime scene and they didn't manage to get any new leads. The Ghost was an experienced and calculating mother fucker that covered his tracks to a T. Rhyland couldn't even pick up on any solid scent trails because the body was dumped in some sort of chemical scent disruptor fluid and the surrounding area was covered with the stuff. There was also a local stream that was frustrating as hell because water and scent trails do not go well together. On top of that, Rhyker didn't hear anything that was a hair's breadth out of place. Although, it was difficult to narrow down how many beings were in the area because of the natural forest creatures that were curious to the scene but kept their distance. Since the body was dumped deep in the woods, there were no security cameras or technology that Deacon could work his magic. Even Nico faded into the darkness of the forest and Blake sharpened his own shifter senses to no avail. They all then went back to the last known location of the victim and picked up the victim's trail. But then the scent trail just suddenly disappeared, as if the victim just vanished into thin air—which was a part of The Ghost's signature characteristics. This really was the remaining confirming factor to rule out any possible copycats because of the victim's connection to Marie in combination with how everything was so precisely executed per The Ghost's calculated MO.

Blake really should join the twins for a run to clear his frustrated mind. But both he and his wolf couldn't stop thinking about Caly and he needed to make sure she was safe at home. Because they spent way more time than he anticipated searching both locations, Caly may already be asleep by the time he gets to her apartment. Although he wanted to talk with her, he also thought that it was probably a good thing she would be asleep because it probably wasn't a good idea to try and explain things to her when he was in this kind of mood.

"I'm going for next watch on Caly. My phone is on."

Everyone nodded.

Blake quickly showered, changed, and was out the door.

Blake arrived to guard Caly's apartment and something had his wolf stirring. He agreed that something felt... *off*. He decided to get a little closer and check on her just to be sure. As soon as he was a few feet away from her apartment, he stilled and his wolf growled with teeth bared. He inhaled deeply.

Shifter.

His wolf was snarling, growling and clawing to get out. He turned her door handle with his shifter strength and it broke effortlessly. The shifter's smell was even stronger inside. In a blink, he was in her bedroom but she was not there. He wanted to roar but he had to keep it under control. He couldn't attract human attention. He had to take a breath before he grabbed his phone so he didn't crush it in his hands. His wolf was clawing relentlessly to get out and he knew his eyes were going full-on, predatory wolf. He was only a trigger away from losing control.

Breathe.

The phone rang once before Nico picked up.

"She's gone. You and twins here *now*. D stays back to check security footage," he growled out, barely keeping it together enough to not alarm any of the human neighbors.

Hanging up the phone, he closed his eyes and took in a deep inhale. The shifter's scent never made it any farther than a few steps into the living room. He followed both Caly and the shifter's scent to the street where it started to fade.

NO! he internally roared.

She must've gotten in a car with him and then drove off. With the massive amounts of people, cars, and restaurants in constant flux, their scent trails would be gone and damn near impossible to pick up. He went back to the apartment and retraced every inch of the place over and over again to see if he missed anything. He didn't. He came up with the same infuriating results.

By the time Nico and the twins arrived, Blake had already been up and down as many streets as possible to try and pick up a scent or any clues as to her whereabouts. They all kept searching until each of them showed up at Caly's apartment, one by one, with nothing except lethal looks that were out for blood. They needed to leave soon before the sun threatened to rise. Just as they finished covering up any evidence indicating that they were ever in her apartment, including Deacon removing any images of them caught on security cameras, Felix cautiously peered around the corner. The distress in Felix's demeanor lessened a fraction when he recognized Blake and Nico.

"Shit. We can't leave him," Blake said.

"Agreed," the twins echoed.

"I'll mesmerize him," Nico added.

"Grab his food," Blake ordered the twins as he walked over to Felix. "Hey, buddy. You're comin' home with us." He picked up Felix and was petting him to try and comfort him. "We'll find her," he vowed.

Whoever took what is mine is dead. And with that thought, he finally realized what his wolf knew the whole time. She was *his*.

Chapter 14

"Caly... Caly..." The Ghost taunted Caly with his dark, psychotic, sing-song voice that broke the eerie silence.

Caly had a pounding headache and her mind was not working right. It felt as if her mind was in a dark haze and her thoughts were trying to move through black sludge. She tried to command her eyelids to open but they were not receiving the signals from her brain. She attempted to move fingers, toes, and any body part she could, but she came up with the same immovable result.

N-n-nightmare... Jussst a nightmare... she thought.

"Caly... Caly..." The Ghost repeated his dark psychotic taunts in an evil melody.

A fresh wave of terror flowed through her veins at the low tone she heard through the filter of foggy haze that warped her hearing. Again she tried to command her mind and body to no effect. Caly was stuck in an infinite loop of a horrific nightmare of evil taunting darkness where time didn't seem to exist.

* * *

"FUCK!" Blake roared after Deacon reported there wasn't

anything on the human security camera systems as of yet. It was impossible to know what to look for when they didn't have anything to go off of, including a description of the vehicle. Also, even with Caly's picture, there were still no hits from facial recognition. Which was a long shot anyway because a security camera would have to randomly get a clear enough image of Caly's face while she was presumably in the passenger seat of a vehicle.

All of the males were in the living room but the only one in his usual spot was Nico, stalk still, at his window with eyes of obsidian. The twins looked like lethal warrior statues about to go to battle. Deacon was standing with a semicircle of projected imaging screens around him, midair, as if by magic. Images were scrolling by impossibly fast on computer screens. His hands were flying through codes, images, and things no one else even pretended to try to understand. It was his genius invention that only he knew how to operate and understand because of his special abilities with computer languages. Blake was pacing back and forth to try and keep his wolf caged as he fought to keep control.

Chapter 15

Caly's head still felt as if it was split into two and her thoughts were like trying to sift through black sludge. Her eyelids felt as if they were being held down by invisible hundred-pound weights. But this time, when she commanded her eyelids to open, they fluttered slightly. She tried again and they fluttered a fraction more. On the third try, she thought she opened her lids but all she saw was inky darkness. Trying to focus on her other senses, she thought she smelled dank mustiness. She also thought she heard a faint rhythmic clattering sound of... metal? And she felt something heavy and cold around her neck.

Shivering. She realized she was shivering and the rhythmic clattering sound was caused by her body shaking. Time still felt warped and everything was impossibly slow and heavy. The feeling in her body was barely registering but it felt like she was glued to the floor. There was a cloth gag tied tight around her mouth. She tried to move her fingertips and they miraculously responded. Her fingertips felt something like cool rough cement under her. Eventually, her entire hand responded and she did a quick assessment of her body, only to find that she was practically naked in just her bra and underwear.

"She wakes..." The Ghost's dark voice broke the eerie silence.

Caly heard a flick and then a woosh, as a flash of light stung her eyes. When her eyes adjusted, she saw the room was lit up by a torch. She found herself chained and on the ground of what appeared to be a giant cement block of a chamber, that had one single doorway on the opposite side of where she was. She followed the light given off by the flames and saw Nick standing there with cool, dark brown eyes and an expression of pure evil on his face.

Her heart suddenly kicked with terror as her memory came back online. She remembered Nick sticking a syringe in her neck and covering her mouth before the world went dark. Coming back to the present moment, she noticed Nick's sinister smile. It was as if he could read her thoughts and knew that she remembered.

"You've been lying, Caly... If that's your real name even. No, wait, don't tell me. " Caly heard a malicious laugh as he looked at her gagged mouth. "I want to tease it out of you myself. It's more fun that way."

Revealing a large hunting knife in his hand, he put the tip of the knife on the cement wall and slowly walked over to her, step by slow step, sliding it across the wall to create a haunting noise of scraping metal.

"How you've been able to evade the truth from me this, long does show that SILE wasn't completely stupid this time. Marie was an insult and I had to kill her on principle." He let out a vile chuckle and clapped three times with a calculated pause in between each clap. "Bravo, Caly. You're the first real challenge I've had in a while. As such, I've decided to keep you... until I get bored at least. So, I hope you're as intriguing as you appear to be."

Caly's brain was trying to process what Nick was even talking about. And now that her eyes were adjusting, she could see that Nick's cold, dark eyes had an inhuman glow.

Oh god. She trembled in fear.

He noticed her looking at his eyes and inhaled. "You didn't know?" He quirked a brow and laughed as if amused. "Maybe you're stupider than I thought. That would be unfortunate for you."

He scraped the tip of the knife over the cement floor right in front of where she laid. She flinched and his grin widened at her reaction. He walked back to the doorway and placed the knife down so it was out of her reach. With the knife at a safe distance, he made his way back toward her and peeled off his shirt. Caly stilled.

R-rape... He is going to rape you.

He laughed at her reaction. "Oh, that part is not coming until later. I like a lot of... foreplay." His cold smile sent shivers of fear through her. And she noticed a tattoo of a strange set of symbols in a spiral on his chest. He unbuttoned his jeans and stripped out of them. He took a deep inhale and she could see his chest expand wide.

"Oh, how I do love that sweet fresh smell of fear. And your scent is particularly appealing... It has this subtle unique flavor I find intriguing."

Her eyes widened as he walked even closer to her. He didn't stop until his face was an inch away from hers.

"Boo."

She jumped and he let out an evil laugh.

"Yes, I am going to enjoy this. You have no idea how good I've been. Well, except for this past weekend."

He is going to rape and then kill you, Caly thought.

With his malignant gaze still on hers, he took a calculated step back. Before she could blink, a massive wolf stood before her. The wolf was as tall as a horse and his fur was marbled with shades of brown and black. His eyes were the same cold, dark brown with hints of dull, yellow gold.

Her eyes widened at what she just witnessed.

The wolf bared his teeth, revealing dagger-like incisors as if amused to be playing with his prey.

N-n-no... Impossible... she thought, utterly terrified.

An image of Blake's eyes and him howling flashed through her mind.

This can't be real. She swallowed. Except on some level, she knew it was real. This nightmare was real and she was going to die.

He growled as if to incite a fearful reaction out of her. And it worked. She had pure, icy fear pumping through her body and mind. In the next instant, he was back to a man and casually slid back into his clothes.

"I know you're hungry and I did say I planned to cook for you." He walked over to the entrance and grabbed a tray from just outside the door. "This is going to be your only food for a while, so let's see if you're smart and eat it." He paused. "Otherwise, I will just have to force it down your throat... And I usually reserve that for the second part of foreplay." His chilling laugh filled the room. He set the tray down in front of her. "I will be back later to see if you ate or if I am going to have to punish you."

She looked down at the tray and saw a small piece of bread, a cup of soup broth and water. The water looked like murky tap water and even had her hesitate—which was something, considering LA tap water was not known for being pristine Fiji Water or anything. He walked away and picked up his shirt and the knife before lifting the torch out of the wall holster. She saw his face with the evil expression in the light of the flickering flames as he walked out.

In his absence, there was a slow scraping sound, like cement on cement. He was closing the only way out. When the scraping sound ceased, the exit was sealed and pitch blackness consumed the room once more. She swallowed.

She knew the food was probably drugged but clearly he wanted to keep her alive, at least for now. She also didn't want to get punished for not eating. So, she slowly reached her hand out in the direction where the food was and her fingertips touched the tray. She let her fingers be her eyes to guide her to the cup of soup and she grasped it. She brought it to her lips and slowly drank. It was only slightly warm, which thankfully did help with her shivering body. It tasted very bland. She didn't want to eat the bread but again, she didn't want to get punished. So, she washed it down with the soup broth. When she finished the soup and bread, she found the water cup and drank that as well. It certainly had that slightly nose-wrinkling tap water taste, but nothing that triggered "toxic" alarm bells going off in her brain. Within a few minutes, she was feeling extremely groggy, confirming that the food and drink were laced with drugs. Although, she wasn't sure if it was the soup or the water or both.

"Why did you pull me into your dreams, Caly?... I'm a wolf..." She heard Blake's voice in her hazy mind and darkness came over her once more.

Caly started to rise back to consciousness from the drug-induced coma. She had a splitting headache and still felt as if her mind was moving through molasses. She had no idea how long she had been kept in that room of darkness or how long it had been since she ate the soup broth laced with drugs, of which was clearly still affecting her.

"Why did you pull me into your dreams, Caly?... I'm a wolf..." She heard Blake's voice repeating in her foggy mind.

Somehow Blake thought she was able to pull him into her dreams. But how? And she couldn't dream if she was drugged, right? Again, even if she could dream and hypothetically pull Blake into her dreams, she still didn't know how. Thoughts were hard to grasp as her mind fought the drugging haze. Her eyes closed once more and the last thing she remembered was Blake's voice.

"Why did you pull me into your dreams, Caly?... I'm a wolf..."

* * *

"DAMN IT!" Blake roared out his anger, as he aggressively pounded his fist into the table, sending out a ripple of impact on the floor.

The twins let out resounding growls and Nico looked as glacial as ever. Even Deacon had a frustrated scowl on his face in his own silent echo of Blake and the twins. It was now approaching midnight of Tuesday night. They had all been awake for over twenty-four hours and had nothing. No leads. No new information. Nothing.

Time was not on their side. Everyone knew that the first three days after someone was abducted were extremely important. Statistically, the chances of finding the victim alive diminish significantly after the first seventy-two hours. They were doing everything in their power to try and find her. But it was impossible to know what to look for when they didn't have anything to go off of. They still did not have a description of the vehicle but at this point, that vehicle was probably ditched. Deacon was still searching anything and everything for potential facial recognition but human technology, including their security systems, were subpar in comparison to species. They also had a BOLO (be on the lookout for) with SILE.

Everyone was exhausted but no one could even think about sleep. Even though they were just going in circle after frustrating circle, like some sort of twisted Groundhog's

Day. Blake knew they couldn't keep this up for much longer and it was not the best move because they all needed to keep up their strength for when they hunted for Caly. And it was just a matter of *when* they did go hunting because he couldn't think of the alternative.

"I'm calling it. We all need to rest in order to hunt. There's nothing else we can do right now. Everyone keep your phones on. D, keep up the searches. If anyone hears anything, then wake the rest of us," Blake said with a defeated breath.

No one wanted to follow Blake's order, including Blake himself, but everyone knew it was the right call. Blake took a quick shower and exhaled as he laid in bed staring at the ceiling. Both he and his wolf were consumed with thoughts of Caly. He didn't know how long he laid there before exhaustion demanded that sleep finally take a hold of him.

✻ ✻ ✻

There was a loud, melodic crashing sound. Caly's mind was filled with the ebb and flow of the ocean tide. She tried to open her eyes but her lids were so heavy.

"B-Blake..." she whispered out on a whimpering cry. Her mind was hazy and speech was slurred because of the drugs.

She heard Blake's voice, "Caly!" And suddenly felt the warmth of his body holding hers. She willed her eyes to open for a moment and she saw Blake's beautiful golden eyes staring down at her. She wanted to keep looking into his eyes but she was so tired and felt so weak. Her eyes grew heavy and closed.

"Blake... Help me... Please... Help me..." she managed to get out between exhausted breaths.

"Caly, where are you?!"

"Nick... He took me... Not human... He's a wolf..." She

felt warm wetness flow down her cheeks. Crying. She was crying. "I'm sorry... I didn't believe you... I'm sorry... I'm sorry..." Her mind clung to that phrase as it tried to process the shock and trauma of the situation in the midst of the hazy drug-induced state of her mind.

"Shhhh. It's okay, Caly. I'm coming to find you. Where are you?"

"I don't know... A room... It's so dark... Always dark. He's drugged me. Blake, I'm s-scared. I don't want to die. Blake..."

The dream was starting to fade as the drugs dug their claws into her brain and pulled her back into the dark coma.

"No! Caly! Keep fighting! I will find you! Caly, I will find you!"

Those were the last words she heard when she slipped out of the dream and back into the darkness.

Chapter 16

Blake woke in his bed and he roared with anger and desperation so loud that it shook his room like a rolling earthquake. The twins, Nico, and Deacon all heard the roar and, within a moment, they were all gathered in the living room. Blake told everyone about the dream of Caly and how she was being tortured and drugged. Everyone was out for blood, The Ghost's blood. Silence fell in the room, other than the twins deep resounding murderous growls.

Blake's cell phone suddenly rang. He didn't answer. No one dared to make a move with everyone so close to losing control. The damn thing rang again... and again. And it kept ringing. Everyone froze, not sure what to do. Even Rhyker paused on taking any more drags of his hand-rolled. Blake was always the level-headed one but he was an inch away from losing control of his wolf and succumbing completely to the wild ferocious beast inside him.

When the phone kept ringing, Nico, who was the only one crazy enough to move, was about to answer the phone. But Blake suddenly grabbed the phone, saw an unknown number and roared, "WHAT?!"

"I saw where she is held," a male with an Irish accent

said in a surprisingly collected voice, considering Blake's alpha outburst.

Blake froze. Before his thoughts could catch up, the male continued.

"I'm a seer. I just had a vision of Caly."

Blake put the phone on speakerphone not only so he didn't inadvertently crush the phone but also so everyone could hear. Well, the twins and Nico were already probably listening in with their heightened hearing.

"Where is she?" Blake gritted out.

"There's a dirt road along a forest. Then a sudden turnoff that can easily be missed. It goes through the forest on a hidden path. At the end of the path there is a small clearing just big enough for a log cabin in the woods. She is kept in a room of darkness in there."

"How do you know Caly?"

"I've seen her. I'm the one who sent her to you."

Caly's voice flashed across Blake's mind. *I had dreams of a man. He told me, 'Tell the male with the cold, dark eyes: Blake Orion's Order.'*

"Who are you?"

"Riordan Knight."

"Did you see any landmarks or anything that we can go off of?" Deacon cut in.

The phone was silent for a moment. If this was a powerful seer, which Blake's wolf instincts told him he was, then the seer was probably replaying the vision step by step.

"Yes... On the road, there is a large rock that has something carved into it..." Riordan paused once more as if trying to make out the carvings. "Dormiens Silvae..."

"The Sleeping Forest." Both Deacon and Riordan translated for everyone at the same time.

Even though Deacon's ability was not with languages, he was still raised as a steorrian child, studying languages and the ancient texts. With Deacon's aristocratic bloodline, his education was thorough and robust. So, although computer language was his specialty, he still had a solid foundation for language translation to a certain degree.

"So, this is on the species side," Deacon continued his thoughts out loud and immediately fired up his semicircle of projected imaging screens around him. His hands were moving through the air and his brain was quickly processing the data.

"Is there anything else? What do the trees look like? Any other landmarks?" Deacon prompted and there was another pregnant pause.

"If my memory serves me correct, it is either in or near the Terra Gigantum, Land of The Giants," Riordan stated.

Deacon's hands were moving impossibly fast through the air, sifting through data.

"The log cabin appears to be small with a single chimney. From the dark room I saw, my guess is that there is a basement she is kept in," Riordan finished.

"D?" Blake demanded.

"This is going to take me a while to sift through the data, including our records," Deacon answered.

"Blake, I saw that I am to be there helping in the search and I'm to bring my healer. We are already making preparations and should be at the local SILE station shortly. I got your number from Detective Bartell and he has set up a room for us nearby. I will let you know when we arrive. This is my direct line."

Damn seers, Blake thought. They were always two steps ahead... and one step away from crazy.

"See you at the station." Blake ended the call and without missing a beat, he dialed detective Bartell and put him on speaker. There was no time or need to reiterate the phone call to his pack.

"Was waitin' for this call," Bartell answered.

"Riordan Knight?" Blake asked, cutting through all of the bullshit even more than usual.

"He is an ancient and a seer. I've known him for a long time and trust him. He's a well-respected male amongst the ancients. Rumor has it that he turned down a seat on the Seer Council. I don't know if it's true but it would be in his character because he's not after power or status." He paused briefly. "Frankly, he already has those things without the political titles and my guess is that was strategic on his part. Anyways, he called me a few minutes ago and said he saw something that involved you and I gave him your number. He didn't divulge any details... Blake, I know you'll do your own evaluation of the male but for now, I set him up with a room here at the station under an alias until he coordinates otherwise. My guess is that he wanted to keep a low profile with this trip."

Blake paused to soak in the information. Blake had worked with Detective Bartell on various cases over the years and trusted him. Just as Bartell said, he was still going to assess Riordan for himself as well as have Deacon look into it too.

"Understood. Thanks," Blake said and hung up the phone. "D, do a search on Riordan Knight," he ordered.

"Already on it. Since he gave us his name. Preliminary data is already available."

He should've known Deacon would be on top of it.

"Riordan Knight appears to be who he says he is and the information I've found corroborates with what detective Bartell said, including the rumor of turning down the council position," Deacon confirmed.

"Let me know what else you find," Blake said and Deacon gave a nod of his head while continuing to sift through data on the screens.

The sky had a faint kiss of yellow, denoting the sun was about to rise.

"Nico, we leave in five for the station."

Chapter 17

"Caly, Caly, Caly," The Ghost said in an evil taunt. "Since the moment we met on that day of the fateful car accident... or rather, it wasn't an *accident* at all, was it Caly?" Nick's smile felt like ice picks down Caly's spine. "You staged the whole thing... Clever female, aren't we? But not clever enough. There's something about you that I haven't quite been able to place." There was a calculated pause. "What species are you, Caly?" He dragged the cool steel of the knife down her leg but not enough to draw blood. She knew he was just playing with his prey.

"Keep fighting! I will find you! Caly, I will find you!" Blake's voice resounded in her head over and over again. It was the one thing she clung to whenever she woke out of the dark coma. She didn't know how long it had been since she was taken but she remembered eating the drug-laced soup twice at this point. At least, she thought it had only been twice. The drugs were really messing with her mind and tampering with her memories. Blake's voice, vowing that he was coming for her, was the only thing keeping her somewhat sane.

"Caly, answer me before I lose my patience. What species are you?"

Species? Does he think I'm a shifter too?

"H-human."

He laughed. "That may work on others but not me. Co-incidentally, that was also your first mistake that day you ran into my car. Your scent gives you away."

My scent? she thought, thoroughly confused.

"I'm gonna ask one more time. What species are you, Caly?"

"I'm... h-human," she whimpered out.

He raised his hand as if to hit her.

"Please! I'm telling you the truth. I'm human." A fresh wave of tears rolled down her cheeks.

He took an audible inhale. Paused. And breathed again.

"Intriguing... I've never had someone lie so well that I cannot detect it even with the sweet sting of fear in the air. You have secrets that I can't wait to *break...*" She saw a sudden spark and heard a scraping sound as the knife dramatically made contact with the cement. "...from your mind."

When he raised his free hand, she curled into a ball and closed her eyes tightly in anticipation of being struck

"Keep fighting! I will find you! Caly, I will find you!"

A moment later, she heard a boom and a subtle vibration as his fist hit... *something.* She didn't feel any contact or pain but maybe it was just her body shutting down and unable to process the pain.

"Oh, Caly." She could hear the wicked glee in his voice. "You've been hiding something else. You truly are keeping my attention and I might just keep you after all. You make me want to break tradition and skip some of the foreplay."

She dared a peek and saw his face in pure evil fascination with a dark glint in his eyes as his fist went to strike again. She flinched in reflex and clung to Blake's voice in her mind.

"Keep fighting! I will find you! Caly, I will find you!"

The next moment she heard the same noise and felt a subtle vibration. He punched again with the same result. For the next punch, she dared another peek and willed herself to keep her eyes open. His fist hit some sort of energetic force field around her but it looked as if it cracked when his fist made contact. She suddenly felt even more exhausted and weak.

"Keep fighting! I will find you! Caly, I will find you!"

With Blake's voice, a repeating mantra in her mind, darkness claimed her once more.

* * *

"Riordan." Blake pounded his dominant fist over his opposite pectoral muscle to formally greet Riordan in the way species males did. In this case, it was also a gesture of good faith and a sign of respect, warrior to warrior.

For many reasons, species did not freely touch one another as humans did. Greetings certainly did not occur with handshakes. You never knew what kind of abilities the other subspecies had and some were dependent on touch. So, you didn't want to give your opponent the advantage or set them off inadvertently by touching them. Also, culturally, species had a much larger personal boundary in social situations than humans. Unless, of course, you were granted otherwise, either with familial or intimate touch privileges. One may have a death wish to approach and touch a predatory animal in the wild without clear consent. The same principle applied to species. Because in the species world, everyone understood the wild, primal nature of the soul was never too far from the surface, especially for shifters—let alone hot-blooded alpha male shifters.

"Blake." Riordan echoed the same motion.

Riordan was about 6'3" and looked to be in his early

thirties. Although, one glance at his jade-green eyes gave away the fact that he was an ancient. They just had that aura about them and you could almost see the wisdom swirling in their eyes. He had medium-length, light brown hair with natural highlights of golden auburn. It was effortlessly styled back away from his face, which looked aristocratic and strong. He had light skin with a hint of tan, a clean-shaven jaw and a natural, slight pout of his lips. He was wearing black slacks paired with a crisp, dark blue button-up complete with a dark blue jacket. No doubt the females found this male attractive.

This is the male Caly saw in her dreams?

Blake suddenly wanted to know if Caly had intimate moments with this male in her dreams like they shared. He wanted to rip this male's head off all of a sudden. He knew his eyes were going wolf. He didn't care. He was already on the razor-thin edge of losing himself to the wolf's instincts completely because of Caly. His alpha control was just about the only thing keeping it together.

"The best sex I've ever had..." He heard Caly's voice in his mind which calmed both him and his wolf with that reminder. Besides, Riordan was here to help find Caly not take her. And fat chance he would let Riordan take her anyway.

Riordan smirked with a hint of amusement in his ancient green eyes that said he knew too much, including that he probably knew that Blake was sizing him up and ready to fight to the death for Caly.

"I have no interest in Caly in that way. Remember, I sent her to you." Riordan spoke calmly as if there was not a male alpha wolf about to kill for the thought of him trespassing on his female.

Okay. So, he knew exactly what Blake was thinking. And it reminded him that Riordan knew more than he had shared so far.

Damn seers.

"Good. I see you both met each other." Detective Bartell's voice was the cold bucket of water Blake needed to wake him up and remind him that they needed to work together to find Caly.

Detective Bartell looked more like a sexy actor casted for the character of head detective—instead of actually being the head detective who happened to have the model-like looks that turned female heads as he walked by. He was wearing dark blue jeans paired with his gun strapped to his hip and a deep gray, tight-fitting T-shirt that had a slight V-Neck at the collar where his Aviators hung. His mocha skin held warm undertones, highlighting his dark brown eyes and dark hair that was stylishly cut close to his skin. At first glance, it looked as if he hadn't bothered doing away with his five o'clock shadow. But with a closer observation, it became apparent that was a calculated grooming choice which suited him quite well.

"Your room is ready and you know the code to program for entry," Bartell told Riordan, who nodded with a *"Thank you"* in return. It is common for secured rooms to have a one-time code to program the specian's unique fingerprints and/or eye signature for entry and exit.

"Don't mention it. My cell is on," Bartell indicated to both Blake and Riordan as he walked off.

Riordan looked over on the far side of the station to see Nico staring him down. Then, raised an eyebrow at Blake.

"Yeah. He's with me."

Riordan nodded.

"Blake, there are things we need to discuss. And I would prefer if this is done in private without the prying eyes and ears of the station."

"Agreed. We'll go back to my place."

Riordan nodded. Blake didn't know or trust this male

but he extended the invite in a continued gesture of good faith and a sign of respect. Plus, it would mean they would be on their turf and had the advantage with the support of his pack if anything went down. Aside from that, so far, it appeared that Riordan had been helping Caly and he was here to help them find her. Besides, it was not like their house was a secret or anything. They were just cautious when it came to inviting unknown species over.

"Is your healer still coming?" Blake asked Riordan.

"Yes, she is on her way. She got stuck with a client. Should I tell her to meet us here or at your place?" Riordan inquired.

"My place is fine. I'll give you the address to send to her."

They walked over to the exit where Nico was leaning up against the wall with his arms crossed over his broad chest and one leg bent at the knee.

"Nico, this is Riordan."

Nico didn't say anything, naturally. Instead, he was sporting his signature icy glare with a thick layer of mistrust and a whole lotta *"I dare you to fuck with me."* That was Nico's default though. And if anyone remotely knew why, it was Blake. Blake was probably the closest anyone got to Nico, and by "close" it really meant he was allowed past the first couple layers of frost. The twins and Deacon also had some defrost privileges but not like Blake. It took a lot to earn Nico's trust and loyalty and even then, it was kept at a distance.

Riordan held Nico's gaze the entire time and gave a single nod. Not many males could do that with Nico without getting frostbite. Good. It appeared Riordan wasn't just an ancient aristocrat seer after all.

Chapter 18

Although the brief rest and unexpected turn of events provided a much needed second wind, the tension was still palpable as Blake, Nico, and Riordan walked into the living room. Caly's safe rescue and return was mission-critical for everyone. Nico stalked over to his spot at the window. Deacon was sitting on the sofa looking somewhat crazed with his semicircle of projected imaging screens around him. His hands were moving through the air as his brain quickly processed the data streaming across the screens. Deacon's short blonde hair looked like his fingers had frustratingly been through it so many times that it was sticking in all sorts of directions, completing the "mad technology scientist" look. The twins both held permanent, predatory, scowled expressions as they let out their aggression on their own bulk-sized bag of chips.

The crunching of chips cracked like bones.

Shifter males, especially predatory shifters, were so innately protective of females that the twins were very close to going completely cat and losing control to their predatory instincts. Felix was also in the midst of the testosterone fury fest going on in the living room. Even though Felix was distressed at Caly's disappearance, it was obvious he took a liking to the males in the house by the way he was curled up on the couch next to his feline cousin of sorts, the chip-crunching Rhyker.

Rhyker, Rhyland, and Felix all looked up at Blake and Riordan as they entered the room. Deacon was deep in the data world and didn't even notice the new arrivals. He was on a current trajectory to total burnout but he knew his pack brothers would make sure that didn't happen and they would pull him out in time. Rhyland followed Riordan's gaze to Deacon, who was obviously stealing the introduction show because of the computer mad scientist vibe he had going on.

"That's Deacon. He spoke with you on the phone." Blake broke the chip-crunching pseudo silence.

"Or Deac the Geek as we like to call him." Thankfully, Rhyland's feline playful sense of humor tended to rise above all else.

Rhyland and Rhyker flashed twin grins before fisting more chips down their pie holes.

"And that's Rhyland and Rhyker," Blake continued with the introductions and gestured to the giant twins. The twins gave an acknowledging head nod to Riordan. Blake paused slightly and then said, "And that's Felix." A pair of bright yellow and viper green feline eyes, surrounded by midnight fur, gave Riordan an appraising look. Curious for a closer evaluation, Felix jumped off the sofa, paused for a lazy feline stretch, and then strutted right up to Riordan. The twins grinned before shoveling more chips into their mouths. They understood this feline's behavior and approved of it. Riordan had a slight smirk at the unexpected greeting of a curious house cat who took residence in this unorthodox pack of males.

"He's Caly's," Blake explained, interrupting the silence of Felix's sniffing interrogation. Understanding bloomed in Riordan's ancient eyes with another slight glimmer of amusement.

"Where's the healer?" Rhyland asked as Felix, satisfied with Riordan, strolled toward his spot on what had quickly become *his* couch.

"He's got good taste," Rhyker playfully responded earlier when everyone saw that Felix was staking his claim on Rhyker's couch. As it turned out, Rhyker didn't mind sharing... but only with Felix.

"On her way," Blake responded. "Nico, pull D out so we can all meet."

"Oh, Nico has experience pulling the D out alright," Rhyland quipped and Rhyker chuckled. They both were back to sporting their twin grins.

Blake gave an unamused look at the twins. Before Blake could continue, he noticed a slight hint of amusement in Riordan's eyes and a subtle smirk.

Okay. Another reason why Riordan may not be some pansy aristocrat ancient after all, Blake thought.

It was common for ancients to lose touch with themselves and think they were better than everyone else. Thereby, they often became uptight, power-obsessed dickwads.

"We like to keep it casual around here. Sit wherever you like," Blake said to Riordan. If that statement had been said to just about any other ancient aristocrat, they would've lifted their nose high in the air with disgust, and called their personal driver to save them from this undignified pack of unconventional hot-blooded males. Blake wasn't in the business of impressing anyone, ancient or not. Also, it was clear that Riordan wasn't any standard for his class by any means and Blake found himself wanting to know more about Riordan. Blake was also starting to see why Bartell had a friendship with this male.

Finding an open leather chair, Riordan shrugged out of

his dark blue jacket and draped it over the back of the chair. He proceeded to roll his sleeves up partway, revealing his strong arms.

Again, who the hell was this male? Blake thought as he sat in an identical leather seat on the opposite side of Riordan. All of the males formed a somewhat casual circle.

Rhyland picked that moment to get up, walk into the kitchen, and open the fridge for some water.

"Hey, grab me one," Rhyker called out to Rhyland as he lit up a hand-rolled. In a motion that looked like second nature to the twins, Rhyland tossed a bottle of water over his head without even sparing a glance and Rhyker caught it with feline grace.

"Grab me one too," Blake called out to Rhyland and then looked at Riordan. "Do you want one?"

"Yes. Thank you." Riordan paused and then added, "Toss me one."

Several pairs of eyes fell on Riordan with his request, staring at him as though he had just grown a second head. Rhyland turned around to appraise the situation, wondering if Riordan was being serious or not. His curious appraisal was quickly replaced with a playful grin. Cats were playful by nature and the twins very much lived up to that trait. Rhyland tossed a bottle of water to Riordan who caught it perfectly as if he were modeling for an Aquafina photoshoot.

Blake's brow raised at Riordan's modelesque display. "Throw me one too, Rhy. Can't let you show me up in my own house," Blake said with a smirk.

Another bottle sailed through the air and Blake caught it midair adding to the male model Aquafina scene. Both he and his wolf reveled in satisfaction with his retaliatory display.

"Think fast!" Rhyland blurted out as a water bottle shot

across the room with impossible speed straight towards Nico's head. In a blur of movement, Nico, who wasn't looking because he was focused on Deacon, turned and caught it just before it hit it's intended target. Nico sent a frosty look to Rhyland, who was grinning from ear to ear.

"Careful, Mr. Freeze, or you may need to wait until the bottle thaws out in order to drink it," Rhyland joked. He was all too familiar with fucking with Nico and right now, he enjoyed the much-needed distraction.

Blake swore he caught a slight smirk on Riordan's face accompanied by a split second of what must be a memory that Riordan was recalling. Blake was more curious than ever to know more about Riordan because he had never met another ancient who appeared to be still amused with playing just for the fun of it without any potential power, political or financial gain. Well, except perhaps Alexina and it was no wonder why she mostly kept to herself.

"Shit D. You look like hell," Rhyland said with a hint of humor. It was Rhyland's way to check in on Deacon to see just how bad of shape Deacon actually was in. They were all trying to cope with the Caly situation in their own way.

"Fuck you," Deacon responded while closing the semi-circle of projected imaging screens and adjusting his bold black frames that outlined his baby blues. Deacon may have been raised as an aristocrat, but hey, so were the twins. And that didn't do anything to curb their fluency in cursing. Rhyland was satisfied because a "fuck you" was a good sign that Deacon was, in fact, alright.

"Riordan." Deacon gave an acknowledging head nod to Riordan and then took a sip of the water Rhyland handed him.

"Deacon." Riordan returned the gesture. "Impressive. I've never seen anything like it."

"Thank you." Deacon knew that a compliment from an

ancient held weight, not to mention the part about how he had never seen anything like it? Yeah, that may have had his heart swell with a little pride.

"She's called ICIS." Rhyland pronounced it just like the Egyptian goddess, Isis. "AKA Deacon's first girlfriend who's clingy as fuck and never left," he quipped as Deacon shot him a sideways glare.

"Intelligent Computer Information System. She is the first computer I built and she has evolved as I have over the years," Deacon explained. Although Deacon didn't go around advertising his skills, his genius-level computer abilities were a bit of a low key legend among certain species crowds, particularly the aristocratic classes because of Deacon's family. So, there was no need for him to hide who he or ICIS was with Riordan. Being an ancient, Riordan probably already knew.

"Deacon has a way with the ladies... As long as they are in the form of megabytes," Rhyland tacked on with a cheeky grin.

"Alright." Blake stepped in before it escalated any further. Although the tension lessened a fraction from when they first walked in, they couldn't waste any more time. They needed to continue the search for Caly because with every passing second, her life hung on the line.

"Riordan, how do you know Caly?" Blake prompted.

Riordan blew out a breath before answering. "About a month ago, I had the first vision of Caly." Riordan paused as the vision replayed through his memory.

There was an image of a female about thirty years old with light skin, gray eyes and long, dark brown hair. In a flash, the image changed and the female closed her eyes. In the next flash, the vision showed her traveling through the dream tunnel and pulling a male into the dream. There was another flash and the female was standing with her legs hip-width distance apart, arms outstretched to the sky, eyes glowing gray, hair floating around and defying gravity. There was also some sort of shimmering vibration gathering all around her. This shimmering vibration also concentrated in her hands and was expanding.

"Riordan, you must protect her. Protect Caly," a distant angelic female voice whispered in his mind before the vision faded completely.

Noticing Riordan's distant expression and recognizing the similarity to how Alexina looked when she was sifting through her vast memory bank, Blake waited for Riordan to explain.

Riordan had not shared the vision of Caly with anyone and he chose to maintain that level of secrecy now. But it wasn't because he didn't necessarily mistrust this group of males. No. It was because it was not his place to share Caly's powers and abilities, if that was indeed what he saw.

In the species world, abilities were personal and kept private unless they were shared publicly by the individual themselves. Some abilities and subspecies were easy to spot, like predatory shifter males with large animals. And then there were those who were more free with making their sub-species and abilities public knowledge. But there were also subspecies who were more guarded for various reasons. In most cases, it was for a political power play or strategic advantage but not always. Some abilities were kept secret because it could be a means of survival. Rare or unique abilities that were known by the public, somehow always had eyes on them and those eyes did not always hold the best interest of the individual.

Again, Riordan didn't believe this was the case for any of these males he was sitting with, especially because of what he knew of these males. Deacon was one of those individuals with several pairs of eyes on his computer language abilities. And Riordan could certainly see why, now that he had witnessed a glimpse of Deacon's genius firsthand. There were also watchful eyes with hidden agendas on the twins for their heightened abilities. As a pair, their combined hunting skills were unparalleled. Plus, he knew that Blake and The Order had a few opportunities to further their power and position in the species world but they turned each of those down. Which was something that Riordan could relate to as well. So, even though this eclectic group of males was quite unconventional and often went against the social grain, Riordan's decision to keep the details of his vision a secret had nothing to do with mistrust or fear that these males would take advantage.

All of that aside, Riordan was still trying to understand what he saw in the final image of Caly. In the third image of that vision, Caly appeared to be a traveler and everything he knew thus far supported that. However, the final image of Caly didn't support that. In fact, that final image of Caly was what had been puzzling Riordan since he saw it. Despite his extensive knowledge and experience from his long existence, he had not seen or heard of anything like what he saw in that final image. Since the vision, he had been discreetly searching species databases and texts for any abilities that may fit with that final image but nothing lined up. He figured if the time came, then Deacon may just be the male to continue the search, under the radar and undetected.

"I have never met or seen Caly other than in visions or dreams," Riordan announced, breaking out of his churning thoughts. He was met with a round of furrowed brows.

"How are you able to see Caly? Our seer is blocked," Blake asked. And, okay. The Whisper wasn't *their* seer by any means but there was no need to go into that whole Deacon-Starr-Seer daytime soap opera right now.

"Ah, yes. When I attempt to see her, it's as if she doesn't exist. My guess is that's the same result as your seer?"

Blake nodded.

"The visions that I've had of Caly are spontaneous and come of their own volition. For seers, visions like this are not taken lightly. Especially spontaneous foretelling visions." He paused briefly. "There is a children's bedtime story shared to small seer children that says these types of visions are fate or destiny. But, again, it's a children's story."

Or is there some truth behind the story? Riordan trailed off with that thought and let the others come to their own conclusions and beliefs. Much like in the human mythologies, species had their own history and stories. Some species believed that these stories had truth to their origins.

"Are these visions how you knew to send her to me?" Blake continued.

Riordan paused and calculated how much to share exactly. He continued with the truth but didn't necessarily divulge every single detail. "Yes. Everything I have guided Caly to do is because I was counseled to do as such in one of the few visions I've had."

"Counseled? By who?" Blake probed.

Riordan paused again with calculation and continued, "That I do not know."

Riordan had been mulling over a possible theory since the first vision of Caly but, again, his undercover research had not yielded any proof. Not to mention that his theory would be impossible. But if he knew anything in his ancient existence, it was that nothing was truly impossible in the species world. When the magic and mystery of life was involved, even the seemingly impossible became possible.

"Is there anything else you know that can help us find

Caly?" Blake phrased that question strategically because he knew that Riordan knew more than he was sharing. But what seer didn't? Although Blake was continuing with the gesture of good faith, he still didn't trust Riordan. But there was no need to make it awkward and potentially lose their only connection to a seer that, for whatever reason, was being "counseled" to help Caly.

"I have shared everything I know of where she is being held and that could help find her." Riordan gave a nod of acknowledgment to Blake. He knew what Blake just did with that question.

Blake nodded and then looked at Deacon with a questioning glance to see if Deacon found anything.

"Nothing yet. I have all the possible searches going and will be alerted with any hits. But here is what I have confirmed so far. The Sleeping Forest expands over so much land that it would be illogical and unrealistic to search the forest section by section, even with shifter speed and Nico fading."

"Not to mention the usual bullshit with species forests," Rhyker mumbled, referring to the fact that species forests of this magnitude and age were full of secrets and had too many unknowns, including creatures and other species who may be hiding, like The Ghost.

"I am working on narrowing down a search radius by using what Riordan gave us in the vision," Deacon continued. "Speaking of which, are you able to draw the symbols that you saw in the rock? And I want to go through some other details with you to see if I can tweak my searches."

"Yes," Riordan agreed.

"Good. We'll leave you both to it." Blake was about to end the meeting but needed one more thing clarified. "When will your healer be here?"

Riordan looked at his watch. "About two to three hours."

"Be on alert and greet our guest. I have some things that I need to take care of," Blake ordered the twins. "Nico." Blake gestured with his head to walk with him down the hall.

When they were in his bedroom he closed the door. "Mesmerize me to sleep in case Caly tries to pull me into her dreams again. She may be able to give us more information. Stay in your room to casually guard the hall. No one is allowed in my room. Wake me if there are any new updates or when the healer gets here. Riordan doesn't need to know."

"Understood." Nico nodded in understanding. They don't really know or fully trust Riordan so he agreed that it was the right move to keep this under wraps for now.

Blake sent a quick text to the twins and Deacon clueing them in on the plan and then looked at Nico. "Do it."

Chapter 19

The twins were sprawled out on the extra-large, leather sofas, stuffing food into their bottomless pits and flipping between action movies and sports on the giant TV. Felix was catching a quick cat nap, curled up in his spot on the couch next to Rhyker. At first, the twins paced around the room while listening in on Deacon and Riordan, who were vetting out the details of Riordan's vision. They listened in hopes that they might be able to offer something, anything, to help the search with Caly. But they quickly realized there wasn't anything they could do to help. And the more they paced, the more frustrated they became. So, round and round they went. As much as it did nothing to calm them down, they were now in a waiting game. They felt like hot-blooded stallions pacing back and forth in the starting gates just minutes before the gun fired and the gates swung open. So, no. They were not apathetic about Caly's situation at all. It was quite the opposite. They were just trying not to lose it and go into full-on Godzilla mode, destroying everything in sight. So TV was their form of distraction. But they knew their part would come later with the physical hunt. This would be the release they needed where they could blast open the gates and let their animals loose.

Rhyland's nose suddenly twitched as he caught the faintest hint of a new subtle scent layer in the air. It was still too faint to distinguish but it was there. At the same exact time, Rhyker halted, mid-chew of his sandwich, as he caught the slightest new sound in the distance. They stayed like that for a few more moments, sharpening their senses.

"She's here," they announced at the same time. Satisfied with their announcement, they annihilated the remaining few bites of their second turkey, bacon and avocado sandwiches, stuffed with chips—for extra flavor and crunch. Rhyland preferred BBQ chips and Rhyker, Cool Ranch.

Deacon was so used to the early, twin-alarm system that it didn't faze him. In fact, he grew to expect it.

Riordan looked up at the twins, whose attention was back on their sandwich prey, and then raised his right eyebrow slightly in an impressed inquiry.

"It's a good place for a break anyways," Deacon interjected into the momentary silence.

"Agreed." Riordan took a drink of water and then got up from his place at the table.

Chewing the last bite of his sandwich, Rhyland strode down the hall to let Nico know that their guest was almost here and it was time to wake Blake.

A car pulled into the driveway just as Nico and Blake walked into the living room. With their cat-like curiosity, the twins took a quick peek out of the window and saw a black, nondescript SUV vehicle with tinted windows. They figured it was a loaner vehicle from SILE. With shifter speed, the twins were at the door just as a knock sounded. Not waiting for the others, they swung the door open and were met with something unexpected.

A female, about 5'9" with naturally long, light blonde hair, stood in the doorway, sporting a professional yet cordial smile. She slid off her large black designer sunglasses and revealed striking cobalt blue eyes of the deepest sea, mixed with flashes of silvery moonlight. She came off as sweet, innocent, ordinary, and caring. She had a casual, simple style with a touch of elegance. She wore a slightly roomy, white sweater–that hid her hourglass figure–with a solid black tank top underneath. Paired with the sweater were dark-wash skinny jeans and stylish black motorcycle boots that positioned themselves above her ankles. On her shoulder was a large, sleek, black tote that served as her purse and healer's bag. She completed her simple and elegant "girl next door" look with just a hint of natural makeup and mascara, light pink blush and lip gloss to highlight her features.

Her focus shifted to the massive twin towers with the piercing electric blue eyes and jet black hair. One of the males, who seemed to have a serious bad boy vibe going on, lit up what she presumed was a hand-rolled indie. The other tower was a bit more laid back with his backward-facing, baseball cap. Looking past the twins, she noticed the casually elegant style of the blonde-haired, blue-eyed male with bold black frames. Next to him, she recognized Riordan and on the other side of Riordan was a hefty male with bright golden eyes in blue jeans and a white T-shirt. He was tall but not quite as tall as the twin towers. To the left of him, her gaze landed on a male who was the epitome of dark and dangerous. Her pulse did a quickstep. He looked lethal in all black with his light hazel eyes that, she swore, had a layer of frost. He might as well have been walking around with a sign that said, "Do Not Enter." He was dark and mysterious with muscled arms crossed over his broad chest. Her gaze lingered on this male a moment longer than it probably should have but she found herself not wanting to look away from his gaze. She told herself it was only because he looked to be the most dangerous of the males and it was just natural instinct to keep an eye on those types.

But there was something intriguing about him.

"Welcome. I'm Blake of The Order." Blake broke the silent staring contest between the female and Nico. He knew he wasn't alone in wondering why Riordan would bring this sweet, innocent looking female to this type of a case.

"Hello, Blake. I'm Aleia." She smiled professionally while internally palming her forehead at her unprofessional reaction to the captivatingly dangerous male standing next to Blake.

Her mini embarrassment was subsided at the thought of how her parents would have thrown up their high-class noses with such a "disgrace" of an introduction of her name. If she was with them, she would have been forced to wait for them to introduce her before she could speak. *"This is Dr. Aleia Reaux of the Reaux Healer bloodline."* Aleia internally eye-rolled at that reminder of her parents. Although she never really got along with her parents, she still loved them in their own way—even if they didn't react so fondly when she let them know that she didn't want to follow in the bloodline's tradition of stuck-up, ungrateful aristocratic clientele. Okay, so maybe she didn't put it in those exact words but that summed it up pretty well. Aleia was truly grateful for all of the training and schooling she received which was all paid for by her parents but she wanted to help those in need and really make a difference.

"Aleia." Riordan had a fond look in his eye and gave her a welcoming smile. "Thank you for coming on short notice."

"Of course, Riordan. Sorry I'm so late. I got here as fast as I could."

They exchanged a warm-hearted smile that said more than words ever could. Aleia would do almost anything for this respectable and honorable male standing in front of her. After Aleia let her parents know about not wanting to continue in the bloodline healer tradition, her parents basically put her on lockdown. They wouldn't allow her to ruin her future and their family's proud legacy of respectable healers by serving nothing but the high class. *"It is an honor, Aleia, to serve the elite class of species as a healer. One should be so lucky. You're just being foolish and we won't allow you to throw away your future and dishonor our bloodline—a bloodline that our ancestors dedicated their lives so we could have these opportunities."* She recalled her father saying to her, as her mother stood by his side in silent agreement.

At the time, it was Riordan who went to her parents and made an offer for Aleia to be his personal healer. Since Riordan was a respected ancient and part of the aristocratic Knight bloodline, they were blinded by what Riordan was actually offering Aleia: her freedom. Outside of her responsibilities as his personal healer, Riordan not only allowed but encouraged Aleia to pursue her dreams of using her healing abilities to help those in need. So, in the eyes of her parents, she upheld the healer traditions of the Reaux bloodline by being Riordan's healer, while at the same time, she was able to uphold what she felt was her soul's calling. It was a total win/win. So, yeah, she would do anything for Riordan, including drop everything when he said it was urgent. Although it was technically a part of the personal healer job description, she did it out of her own free will.

"This is Deacon," Blake said, indicating to Deacon standing to his left.

"Aleia, pleasure to meet you." Deacon gave a welcoming aristocratic smile and slight bow of his head.

"And these are Rhyker and Rhyland." Blake continued with the introductions.

"Hey, Aleia," they both said in unison with identical, deep voices.

"And this is Nico." Blake motioned to the male ice sculpture that she previously had a mini staring contest.

"Hi," she said as she chanced another look at the stand-offish male. He stayed silent with his arms crossed over his broad chest in a way that pushed out his muscled biceps.

Okay. So, those two literally were twin towers, emphasis on the twin and tower. Clearly Blake is a shifter and the leader. Maybe alpha? Not sure what the geeky nerd is doing hanging out with all these other males. And, yeah, now might be a good time to stop staring at dark and dangerous, who looks like he wants to tie you up. Recap: I am suddenly standing in some sort of strange, macho bachelor pad with an eclectic bunch of hot-blooded males. This just got really interesting.

She cleared her throat and was about to say something, anything, to break her staring contest with Nico, when an unexpected noise broke the silence.

"Meow."

It was as if Felix was saying, "*Ummm, Blake, you forgot to introduce me.*" Felix strode up to Aleia as if he owned the place and did round two of the sniff interrogation.

Aleia's face immediately lit up and her gorgeous smile didn't go unnoticed. She knelt down and gingerly stuck her hand out for Felix to sniff. Her brows furrowed slightly.

Well, that can't be right, she thought, as she felt a ripple of something coming from Felix... She shook it off.

"Hi, you handsome male," she crooned in that pet voice that everyone had. She scratched behind his ears and felt his soft, raven black fur.

He approved and started purring.

All of the males were struck still with the sudden energetic bubbly response from Aleia with Felix's grand entrance. Well, except for Riordan, who kept that fond look in his wise eyes.

"Oh well, aren't you just the cutest cat ever," Aleia said in an adoring voice.

Pulling out all the stops now, Felix rubbed his head and body on her hand and leg and his purr-motor shifted into high gear.

The twins' smiles were so wide and all of the males knew Rhyland was holding back a joke.

"I just love cats," she openly confessed, disregarding what the males must've thought. Aleia always wanted to care for a cat growing up but her parents wouldn't allow it. They said it would distract her studies. One day, they caught her healing and taking care of a stray on the property and they stopped that immediately. They did allow her to find a nice, loving home for it, but nothing more. Her parents were strict and set in their ways but they weren't cruel. They were healers after all.

Aleia's feline love proclamation made the twins' eyes light up with mischief.

Blake shot Rhyland a look that said, "*No.*" Because he knew that was too good of an opening for Rhyland not to make some sort of comment like, "*Is that so?*" with his playful big cat drawl.

Nico internally rolled his icy eyes at the silent conversation. Outwardly, his focus was on Aleia.

She picked up Felix and then her brow furrowed in concern once again.

Shit. I wasn't wrong.

She cleared her throat, not sure how to broach the subject. She looked directly into Blake's eyes.

"As you know, I'm a healer. And I'm picking up a subtle layer of distress with Felix."

All of the males, except Riordan of course, again became statues as they took in the fact that this female healer was a little more skilled than they initially thought. Because an average strength healer would have needed to be in a full healing session to observe Felix's underlying distress. But then again, why would Riordan call an average strength healer? Hell, did an ancient like Riordan even know of any average strength healers?

"I'm not a mind healer but I think I can ease his distress a bit by relaxing his physical body. May I?" she asked tentatively.

Blake nodded.

"Hey..." She paused and before she could ask, Blake said, "Felix."

"Hey, Felix. You're going to feel some warmth, okay?"

Her fingertips started to have the faintest tint of pale, red glow for a few seconds. Felix visibly relaxed almost instantaneously.

"Ahhh. There you go, handsome." She kept petting Felix and looked up at a wall of male statues who were staring at her with approving looks in their eyes.

Okay. Yeah. This is not unusual at all. Nope.

Then her eyes landed back on Nico's hazel eyes. And, of course, her gaze lingered too long, again.

She cleared her throat.

"So, where's the patient?"

Good, she thought, getting back to the healer program. *You know, the reason why I'm here. Not to stare at hazel eyes and pet cats.*

Blake and Riordan exchanged a look that suddenly had Aleia's full attention.

"Let's all have a seat. We'll fill you in." Blake paused a beat before continuing. "And that's the... *patient's...* cat, which is why he's distressed. So, thank you for that."

Aleia nodded, understanding that Felix was uneasy because his beloved owner needed a healer. What Aleia didn't understand yet, was just how bad the situation really was.

When Aleia sat down on the couch next to Rhyland, Felix jumped out of her arms and made his way to his spot next to Rhyker. Rhyker gave a comforting scratch behind Felix's ears and then they both settled into the couch in a very feline way. Aleia suddenly wondered if she was in a house full of felines. It would make sense given the way all of the males looked at her when she lit up at Felix's purring introduction. She took a quick look around and reassessed that thought.

No. Only three of the males are shifters.

Her thoughts were cut off at Blake's voice.

"Aleia, would you like a drink?"

"Water would be great. Thank you."

Blake gave an inquiring look to Riordan.

"Water for me as well," Riordan answered.

Rhyland got up from his seat ready for round two of the water bottle throwing game. He was playfully curious and wanted to test Aleia's hand to eye coordination for no reason other than to appease his feline nature.

Blake shot Rhyland a look that said, "*No.*"

Rhyland shot back a slightly displeased look at Blake's silent command as if he reluctantly replied with, "*Fine.*"

Definitely an alpha. But maybe not a cat, Aleia thought, catching the silent exchange between Blake and Rhyland.

"Her name is Caly and she was kidnapped Monday night." Blake broke into Aleia's thoughts and her healer's brain kicked into gear with that one hell of an opening line.

* * *

"Caly, I'm only gonna ask one more time." The Ghost had a cold psychopathic flare in his eyes as he gave Caly a final warning. "What species are you?"

Caly tried to swallow but the thick metal collar around

177

her neck suddenly felt more constricting as a new wave of terror rushed to the surface.

"I... I don't know," she let out a whimpering, defeated cry. And it was the truth. She didn't know what was real and what wasn't anymore. The combination of fear mixed with a thick layer of the drug-induced smog was making it feel like she was stuck in a never-ending horrific nightmare.

There was a loud smack that echoed in her cement hell room as he backhanded her face. Her cheek split from the impact and she felt the warm crimson liquid flowing down her face mixing with her salty tears.

"Keep fighting! I will find you! Caly, I will find you!" Blake's voice reeled through her mind.

She didn't know if Blake was actually coming for her or if her mind made that up as a defense mechanism to the horrific nightmare she was in. She also was questioning if Blake was even real or if her mind constructed Blake out of her imagination as another coping mechanism. But whenever she was on the edge of succumbing to the feeling of death, his voice would appear in her mind like a lifesaver being thrown out in a turbulent sea storm. She clung onto the mental lifesaver because it was the only thing she had, real or not.

"Caly, you're making me lose my patience." He gripped her chin firmly with his free hand as his other tightly grasped the large hunting knife.

She felt the cool blade on her skin as he leaned closer. Her heart was kicking in her chest and he took a deep inhale as he examined her split cheek. He flashed her an evil grin with a maniacal look in his eye.

"Caly, love, how your evasion skills fascinate me," he said as if he was back to his non-psychotic self. "How about we work up to the species question?"

He slid the tip of the knife up her arm toward her throat.

Then he pursed his lips as he put the knife tip on his chin as if in thought. There was a gleam in his eyes as his lips curved. The knife was suddenly back at her throat and she felt a twinge of pain as he nicked her skin. A trickle of blood slid down the cool blade.

"Now, tell me. How were you able to block my punches?—Oh, and before you answer, think wisely because if you say—" he quickly switched his tone of voice to mock the shaky female whimper, "I-I don't know." His tone turned lethal once more. "Then I'll be forced to punish you. The choice is yours, Caly."

Caly didn't know how to answer. She was silent for a moment and tried to steady her voice but it was useless.

"Please... Nick, I'm telling you the truth."

"Ah ah ah," he chided as if reprimanding a child. "What have I told you? Hmmm? Don't insult me by calling me Nick. You know that's not my name. And as convincing as you appear to be, you leave me with no choice."

She caught a glint of the knife blade in the firelight as it tore into her leg. She winced at the stinging pain. At this point, she knew he was careful not to nick any major arteries so she wouldn't bleed out.

"Now let's try this again, shall we?"

"Keep fighting! I will find you! Caly, I will find you!"

The Ghost continued with the torturing interrogation. Before Caly was claimed by the thick, drug-induced fog once more, she suffered several knife wounds, causing fresh blood to pool under her skin and form dark bruises. With a black eye, split lip, and torn cheek, Caly's consciousness threatened to take her under as she writhed in pain on the cold cement floor. The instant he broke her ankle, a lightning bolt of pain speared through her nerves and surged well beyond her threshold. Her vision tunneled and narrowed as she blacked out.

Chapter 20

The sky was showing off its vivid display of gold, orange, and pink as the sun began its final descent on the horizon of the forest trees surrounding The Order's property.

"I've narrowed down a search radius," Deacon announced once everyone, including Riordan and Aleia, was present. All eyes were on Deacon's large, projected imaging screen with a map of The Sleeping Forest and a red outline signifying the search area.

"It's still a rather large area but doable. Especially considering the fact that we don't have a lot of options or time." His hand slid through his hair in a quick motion before continuing, "I believe I've located the stone with the old carvings of the rock from Riordan's vision. Actually, I located three different large rocks." The screen suddenly displayed the three stone images with carvings. "My theory is they are used to denote various entrances to the forest." The screen then showed where each of the three rocks was located in reference to the forest map. "However, Riordan was able to eliminate one of them based on his vision." A red X marked one of the images. "The other two, as you can see, look similar but are in total opposite sides of the forest. But presuming Riordan is correct in his assessment that it is in or near the Land of The Giants," pointing to a highlighted section of the forest map to indicate where that is, Deacon continued, "We were able to narrow it down to this location due to the proximity." Another red X marked the second image, leaving the one remaining. "From there, I extrapolated an estimated search radius based on Riordan's vision. Although, there was not much to go off of so I added a significant buffer."

"Good." Blake looked outside and saw the sun setting. "We hunt tonight."

Even though species forests like this one were unpredictable and dangerous at night, they didn't have time on their side to wait. Fortunately, night hunts were The Order's main element. Nico had the vampire ability to fade into the shadows and the twins were black jaguars that hunted as one with the night. By nature, Blake's wolf primarily hunted at dawn or dusk but he was also lethally skilled at night hunts. He could stay hidden in the shadows too but the others appeared to be specifically created for night hunts.

Everyone nodded and Blake continued, "D, split the search radius into two. And identify the best place for us to have a home base for the hunt."

Deacon worked his magic and a few moments later, he displayed the updates on the map.

"Here is search area one." The area had a blue outline on the map. "And here is two." This area had an orange outline on the map. "This is where home base will be." A large white H showed up on the map at the point of their entry and where the two search areas intersected. "It's just outside the forest tree line and gives us the closest access to the main road for a quick escape route."

Blake nodded and looked at Riordan and then Aleia. Blake was the alpha and leader on this hunt but he would be a fool not to heed the advice of the seer or healer. Riordan and Aleia nodded in agreement. With that, Blake continued,

"Nico. Rhyker. You're unit one, in search area one."

Both males nodded.

"Rhy, you're with me. We're unit two, in search area two."

Rhyland nodded.

When they hunted, the twins were often, but not always, paired up together. For this hunt, it made sense to split the twins up. This way, each unit pairing could benefit from the twins' heightened abilities.

"D, you stay at home base and see if you can pick up on anything."

Deacon nodded. Although Deacon went on hunts, he usually held up their base of operations for the hunt with ICIS monitoring from a distance so he could feed the males updates. In this case, that strategy held in place.

Blake looked at Riordan and Aleia. Again, he wasn't their alpha but spoke as the leader of the hunt. "I am unaware of what either of you possess as hunting skills." He didn't want to be an arrogant ass and assume that just because Riordan was a seer and Aleia a healer, they were not hunters. Although unusual, he had run across some unexpectedly skilled hunters in his life.

"None." Aleia wasn't ashamed to admit that at all. She knew her strengths and weaknesses and accepted them. "I'll stay at home base on standby for immediate healing intervention."

Blake nodded in agreement and then looked at Riordan.

"I'll do the same and let Deacon know if I see any more information for the hunt." Few knew just how skilled Riordan was in hand-to-hand combat but in this case, without speed or some sort of agility, he would just slow the hunt down. Besides, both him and Deacon could protect Aleia in hand-to-hand if anything happened while they waited.

Blake agreed with a nod. "Unit one and two. We go in

animal form. Nico keep your cell on silent. Rhyker, keep an ear out for my signal. D, keep track."

Blake's signal was a single distinct howl that each of them knew well, as it was Blake's designated distress signal on missions. When Blake told Deacon to "keep track," he was referencing Deacon's specialized microscopic GPS chip invention that bonded to each of their animal's fur. This enabled Deacon to monitor their locations from a distance with ICIS. It was the standard operating procedure for their hunts but it still had some shortcomings, one major one being that the chips wouldn't survive a full shift. Deacon was still working through that complicated mind fuck of a puzzle. So for now, it was all they had on the technology front for this type of a hunt.

"We search our entire area and once complete, we report back to home base. It should not take longer than three hours. If, for some reason, you don't report back by the fourth hour then the other unit will come looking for you."

The males grunted in approval and both Aleia and Riordan nodded.

"D, where's the nearest SILE station from our home base?"

Through quick maneuvering with his fingers on the projected imaging screen, Deacon expanded the map to show the nearest SILE station.

"We're in luck. There's a small mountain SILE station only about a forty-minute drive to home base."

"Good. I'll contact Detective Bartell to arrange standby teleport and two mountain terrain vehicles waiting for our arrival," Blake said, pulling out his phone.

In the species world, the fastest way to travel was by teleport via teleportation stations. Molecular elementals, which were a rare subspecies of elementals, had the ability to manipulate molecules, like telekinesis. Then, there were the even more rare subset of MEs that were either born with or evolved to have the ability of teleportation. MEs were typically the genius inventors and physicists of species that were a hair's breadth away from being mad scientists. Over the centuries, the MEs unlocked the secret to teleportation as a mode of transportation. So, there were teleportation stations allowing for travel from one station to another. Every SILE station had its own private teleportation station set up as a part of standard SILE protocol.

"Will one of the vehicles be large enough to either take out or put down the back seats in case we need to lay the patient out? Also, can you arrange for the vehicles to have two standard medical emergency supply kits and to be stocked with spare loose-fitting clothes and emergency blankets?" Aleia chimed in.

"Good point," Blake acknowledged. "I'll arrange for it. Do you need anything else?"

She furrowed her brows and bit her bottom lip slightly in thought. "I can't think of anything else right now. But I'll let you know if there is."

Blake nodded and looked at the time. "Everyone gear up. We meet back here in fifteen minutes for a final touch base before we head out."

And with that, everyone dispersed, sporting their game faces and running through their mental checklists.

* * *

Caly slowly blinked her heavy eyes, rising back to consciousness. It almost felt normal at this point for her mind to be navigating through a thick drug-induced fog. Except there was a new layer to the fog: pain. Her nerve endings sent an immense shock of pain through the fog as they registered the broken ankle in combination with the various cuts and bruises. Caly wanted to scream from the pain but she was too scared he would return. Although, she knew it wouldn't matter. It was never long after the drugs began to fade enough for her to wake that the ominous cement on cement scraping sound signaled his return.

As if on cue, she heard the terrifyingly slow scraping sound, which never failed to send a chill down her spine. Her heart pounded in her chest and pumped fear into her entire body. She wasn't sure how much more she could take and thought that this might be it.

"Keep fighting! I will find you! Caly, I will find you!"

The cement scraping sound echoed in her torture chamber as if announcing her eventual death. It was like the repetitive clicking of a cart climbing the peak of a roller coaster. The scraping sound ceased and it brought the briefest moment of complete silence, just as a roller coaster pauses at the top before it sails through the air on its final descent. Caly didn't see the flicker of light from the fire Nick always carried. He told her he didn't need it to see but he wanted for her to watch. When she heard heavy footsteps approach, her natural instinct had her curling up into a ball in the fetal position and sealing her eyes tightly shut.

"Keep fighting! I will find you! Caly, I will find you!"

* * *

They all arrived at their designated home base with their two black SILE vehicles, which were military-grade mountain terrain SUVs. With the advanced technology of species, the vehicles were specially made to maneuver through the mountains swiftly without damaging the forest terrain. Their semi-hover wheels, invented by two tech-savvy molecular elemental brothers, would only leave a trail with the equivalent impact of someone walking through the forest on foot. The species world was extremely mindful of protecting the natural world and habitats as much as possible. They respected the world they lived in and because some subspecies abilities were so attuned to the Earth and nature, they understood the delicate balance of nature very well. They also understood that these places were home to so many different subspecies and creatures that sustained the natural balance of life. So, protecting the environment was just the way of species.

Upon arrival, they all had a secondary mini-meeting, settling the last-minute fine details. Because they were in the middle of a species forest in the dark of night, Deacon, Riordan and Aleia were to stay in the SUV tank with the doors locked until given the agreed-upon signal. As a last resort, they had the escape option of fleeing in the vehicle. Also, Deacon and Riordan were trained in hand-to-hand combat and if it came down to it, they were prepared to call upon their training.

Deacon and Riordan helped Aleia prepare the back of their vehicle for a makeshift emergency/healing triage station by laying down the seats and ensuring the emergency kit supplies were ready. They finished the preparations by laying down a bedsheet and stacking the blanket and extra clothes nearby. Aleia went through a final double-check of the emergency medical supplies in the vehicle, as well as, in her own medical bag.

Satisfied, she shut the trunk and intended to walk around to get into the single open seat in the back of the SUV. However, her gaze fell on Nico, who was also at the trunk of the other vehicle, gearing up and doing a last-minute weapons check. From what she could see, he was in an all-black, tactical, modern, military type of uniform, complete with combat boots. It looked like he had some sort of weapons strapped to his chest and belt. She didn't even pretend to know or understand what all the weapons were but one of them looked like a black-bladed knife. Suddenly, Nico turned his head and looked directly at her.

Great, she thought sarcastically, as he caught her staring at him once again.

"Nico," Blake called out from the other side of the SUV.

Nico's gaze stayed locked on hers for a split second before he turned toward Blake.

"Need anything else?"

Aleia jumped at Deacon's voice to her left. "Sorry." She smiled a little. "I'm not used to being in the field like this. Guess I'm a little jumpy."

Liar. You know that mini staring contest with dark and dangerous is what made you jumpy.

"No worries. Do you need anything else?" Deacon offered her a comforting smile.

"No. I was just about to get back in the SUV..." Aleia trailed off, suddenly realizing she had to pee.

Are you serious right now?! It's just nerves. Hold it. Then it dawned on her that she would be holding it for several hours. Plus the potential for all healing hell to break loose depending on her patient's condition. *Better to go now.* Her cheeks heated a little.

"Ummm... Deacon?"

"Yes, Aleia."

"I'm sorry to pull the iconic female card but I actually have to pee," she admitted with a slightly embarrassed look on her face.

He chuckled. "No worries. Most of us, actually all of us, just relieved ourselves as well. It's standard before a long hunt. Let me get Blake." Deacon walked away toward the other vehicle.

That was nice of him, she thought. He could've been a

total ass and made fun of her but instead, he tried to make her feel better.

Nico stalked around the SUV, straight toward her. She swallowed. He stopped directly in front of her. It was the closest she had ever been to the lethal-looking male and it was the first time she saw his light hazel eyes up close.

"I'm your escort," he said in a low, slightly rough voice that came as a surprise to her feminine eardrums.

"Thanks." She smiled.

Okay. So, this isn't weird at all. Nope.

He took her just out of sight of the others behind the closest trees. He gave her just enough privacy so it wasn't uncomfortable but she knew he was close by. She did her business and pulled up her black medical scrub pants.

"Thanks again." She looked over at him for a moment as they walked back to the SUVs.

His facial expression didn't change but he nodded. She made herself keep her gaze forward because she found herself wanting to take in his profile as he walked beside her. As they approached the vehicle, she could have sworn she almost caught a slight movement in his arm to open the door for her but in a flash, his hand was back by his side. He gave her a slight nod and stalked off as she got settled in the SUV.

Her eyes focused on Deacon's projected imaging screen in the front of the vehicle. This time, he shrunk the size to float comfortably above the dash. It displayed the map of the two search areas, home base, and four blinking green lights.

Just then, she saw two giant black jaguars, a massive grey wolf, and Nico move into focus through the SUV's windshield. She did guess they were felines but predatory black jaguars? That was a surprise. And an alpha wolf? It made sense in hindsight, as she thought back to both the twins and Blake's mannerisms. She swore she saw Nico look at her once more before fading and literally disappearing into the shadows. Quickly joining Nico, the other males melted into the darkness of the forest. Of course, Aleia knew of species and their abilities but she had never seen males quite like these with such deadly grace. It was new for her to witness lethally trained hunters like these vanish into the dark of night.

"I think I had that same reaction the first time I saw them too. There are hunters and then there are *hunters*." Deacon smiled at Aleia, who smiled back, realizing she must've been gawking at the forest.

"It's impressive to witness." She refocused on the map and then on Deacon. "Just as with your skills. You probably caught me with the same expression when I saw you in action earlier," she teased a little as she indicated to the imaging screen.

Deacon's smile softened.

"Speaking of. I'm going to go out on a limb here and say the four blinking green lights are them?" she asked.

"Correct," Deacon answered.

"Can you tell which one is which?"

"Yes." With a swift motion, he split the screen and pulled up details of the first blinking dot.

"Wow," she said, taking in the unexpected information. "I thought these were just GPS. I had no idea it would keep track of things like their speed and vital signs too. Don't mind me gaping at the impressiveness again," she quipped.

Both Deacon and Riordan chuckled.

"The dots will turn yellow when their vital signs are less than optimal and red when there is a serious physical issue, like a vital injury. If it turns black... then that signifies death. The dot may disappear completely which denotes that one of them shifted and destroyed the chip."

"Why is it that Nico's chip doesn't get destroyed while fading but the other's chips do when they shift?" Aleia inquired.

Deacon smirked and let out an exasperated sigh. Wasn't that the mind-boggling question of the century? "That is the question, isn't it? How is it that vampires can fade with physical items and then reappear with those same physical items intact? Very similar to teleportation and, at the same time, vastly different. It's one of the many mysterious conundrums that MEs have been pondering for centuries."

Both Aleia and Riordan nodded because it truly was an unexplainable phenomenon.

Switching topics slightly, Deacon continued, "Tonight, I was also testing out a newly upgraded functionality to detect heat signatures within close proximity. However, looks like that is also a bust. I'm running into some issues with size and range. You see, it's difficult to have something that microscopic be capable of detecting at such a wide range, in relation to its size." Deacon explained his recent experiment.

"Impressive." Riordan looked at Aleia with slight amusement as he echoed her earlier word and then refocused on Deacon. His look let Deacon know he really was impressed and that didn't happen too often. Yet, here was this male who had managed to impress him twice within one day. Riordan continued, "I don't believe I've ever heard of anything quite like this to that microscopic of a degree and to such accuracy. Is this your invention?"

"Thank you. Yes. I call it MMG. Microscopic Multifunctional GPS. It's completely undetectable unless you're specifically looking for it. ICIS and I keep fine-tuning it and, apparently, it's back to the drawing board," Deacon said, pushing his bold black frames up the bridge of his nose.

"Honestly, it's brilliant," Aleia commented.

With that, they all watched the four blinking dots scan their respective search areas.

* * *

Nothing. There was nothing. No scent trails. No tracks. No sign of Caly or The Ghost. They had been hunting for almost two hours and there was only a small section left to search. The cool midnight air was heavy with moisture and the only light was the occasional silver rays of the moon slipping through the thick trees. More than once, Blake had to push away the terrible fear of this hunt being unsuccessful. He couldn't go there. He couldn't bear the thought. He couldn't be distracted.

From one heartbeat to the next, Rhyland suddenly stilled and Blake halted in his tracks. Rhyland was taking in puffs of air with his jaguar's nose and his feline mouth parted to taste the scents in the air.

Recognizing Rhyland must've caught a scent, Blake tilted his wolf's snout in the air and sharpened his senses. Pine trees, dirt, and various other forest scents and sounds. But no Caly or The Ghost. Without warning, Rhyland flew off into the trees to the right. Blake matched Rhyland, stride for stride. He guessed whoever's scent trail Rhyland picked up on was strong and undeniable.

Rhyland's incredible sense of smell was truly unparalleled. And combined with his other skills? Yeah. He was one lethal tracker. If Rhyland had someone's scent and was hunting for them then it was only a matter of time before he caught his prey. And, sure, Blake would have picked up on the scent eventually, because there was no way he was leaving the forest without any shred of doubt that Caly was not there. But it would have taken him more time. And time was not what Caly had.

Then there it was. Caly's scent. It was so faint but it called to him. A few moments later, Rhyland's speed slowed down and his midnight fur melted into the shadows with deadly stealth. It was as if Rhyland's obsidian coat was specifically created for the camouflage of night hunts. Even though Blake didn't have that natural midnight fur advantage, over the decades of hunting killers, he perfected how to hide in the shadows.

Rhyland abruptly halted. Blake had hunted with Rhyland long enough to know that he must've pinpointed the location. And with the slight breeze through his fur, he trusted Rhyland would make sure that they were downwind as to not announce their presence.

From one breath to the next, Rhyland shifted back to his two-legged form with silent fluidity. He pointed his finger just ahead and a few ticks to the right. Blake knew that meant that was where Caly was or at least where her scent trail was leading. Rhyland then held up two fingers, indicating that there were two scent trails. Blake nodded his wolf head once, knowing there was a good chance the other scent trail belonged to The Ghost.

Fan-fucking-tastic.

Not only was Blake out for that fucker's blood but also, this meant that Rhyland now had his scent. Which meant that the Grim Reaper would be visiting his door very soon no matter what.

Rhyland pointed to himself and then back toward the scent trail that he initially pointed out, indicating that he would take the path a little to the right of that location. Then, he pointed to Blake and back toward the scent trail that was slightly to the left of the location. Blake nodded and then Rhyland shifted back into his jaguar. They made final eye contact which promised, *"We'll find her and kill him."* A split second later, they silently bolted off into the shadows.

With his wolf's night vision in full effect, Blake slowed the pace in his muted advance, seeing the outline of a small building up ahead. Caly's scent was now strong and Rhyland was right, there was another scent in the air. Apparently, The Ghost didn't bother covering his scent here because he was arrogant in thinking no one would find him. His mistake would cost him his life. With a deep inhale, Blake stored The Ghost's scent in his memory banks. He continued the careful and calculated approach, step by slow step, as the building became more and more clear.

It was just as Riordan described. A small, nondescript, single chimney, cabin, sandwiched in the middle of a small clearing of trees. He agreed with Riordan's assumption that there must be some sort of small underground space because it just looked too small for both The Ghost and a prisoner.

Although he couldn't see Rhyland, Blake knew that he was just on the other side of the clearing, hidden in the forest waiting for Blake's approach. Rhyland may have the upper hand with his super scent but Blake was still an alpha and Blake's own keen shifter scent abilities were sharp and perfect for this closer target range. Blake did a sweep with his senses and examined the area. There was no light in the cabin but the two scents were strong. If Caly and The Ghost weren't in there now, then they were there very recently.

No. He couldn't think like that. He had to believe Caly was still in there and alive.

In a blur of movement, Blake bolted toward the cabin. This was an ambush. He had to go in hard and fast in order to use the element of surprise to their advantage because they both knew that as soon as he broke the clearing, their presence would be known if The Ghost happened to be keeping watch somehow. So, the risk was too great to try and approach slowly and quietly. However, they didn't give all of their cards away. Rhyland stayed in the shadows to keep a second surprise waiting depending on what met Blake on the other side of the door. They used this strategy often in their hunts and it worked to their advantage. Most of the time, their targets were so arrogant in thinking their hunter would be pursuing them alone in order to get their claim to fame. Or the target would miscalculate and think their hunter would go in, guns blazing, because of their inflated egos and abilities. So, they didn't anticipate a second wave of the surprise attack. Again, that was their deadly, arrogant mistake.

In another burst of movement, a wolf flew out of the cabin and charged directly at Blake. Blake's razor-sharp teeth were bared and he roared out a blood thirsty growl. The other wolf responded with his own snarling growl. Blake was visibly bigger than the other wolf and he was sure as hell going to use his size and strength to his advantage. They both leaped at the same time, aiming at each other's throats. Their mid-air collision was a deafening boom in the silence of midnight. Their massive bodies landed with a roll that sent a thunderous earthquake to the forest floor. Blake recovered a split second quicker than the other wolf and went in for a throat-tearing kill. The other wolf dodged the attack at the last second but Blake still managed to sink his dagger-like fangs into his opponent's flesh, sending warm blood gushing into his mouth.

Continuing on, the other wolf slammed Blake into a large boulder, which caused Blake to loosen his grip just enough for the other wolf to get free. They were in a standoff, circling each other and once again growling with their gleaming knife blade teeth shining in the moonlight.

In another streak of movement, they were at each other's throats. Jaws snapped ferociously. Growls ripped through the midnight air. They were a blur of lethal fur as their bodies rolled, trying to gain the upper hand. Powerful hind legs kicked out with bone-cracking blows. Blake knew he had to get into the forest to give Rhyland a straight shot into the cabin undetected. Channeling all of his alpha power, Blake sent the other wolf's body tumbling into the forest with a powerful kick.

In a flash of movement, Blake bolted toward the wolf and, in his peripheral vision, he caught Rhyland's jaguar shooting out like a black bullet toward the cabin. Blake charged his attacker and went for the throat. The wolf maneuvered his body at the last moment and instead of Blake's razor-sharp fangs slicing through the throat, they sank into the wolf's shoulder. With the sudden burst of red hot crimson into his mouth, he knew it was a damaging blow. He locked his jaw tightly around the flesh and forced both of their bodies to tumble deeper into the forest in order to give Rhyland the best chance to rescue Caly.

Rhyland shot into the cabin and halted in front of a thick giant cement slab. Caly's scent was so strong around it that he knew she was behind it. He shifted into his human form and gripped the side. Even with his shifter strength and being trained to peak condition, the slab took effort to move aside. There was no way anyone with less strength than him, let alone a non-shifter like Caly, would be able to move this by themselves. As the seal broke, a fresh wave of Caly's scent hit his senses and the sting of complete terror gave him a sudden burst of strength. He needed to get her out. He slid the cement slab away just enough for him to enter. A fresh wave of terror filled his nose and stung his eyes as he walked toward Caly. She was shivering in the fetal position. She was broken, bloodied, and bruised. He could see her because of his feline night vision but he knew she couldn't see.

Fuck.

"Caly, you're safe. I'm Rhyland. Blake and I are here for you."

"B-Blake?" Tears were flooding her face in complete terrified confusion.

"Yes. Blake. I'm going to pick you up and we're leaving. But you have to be quiet. Okay?"

"H-he... He will kill us..."

"No. You're safe. I'm picking you up now."

He bent down as she turned her body toward him. He sucked in a sharp breath as he examined the chain around her neck and the many cuts and bruises that covered her.

Fucking bastard.

"I'm going to break this chain. Okay?"

"O-k-kay..."

He gripped the metal collar and in a swift movement of strength, broke it in half being careful not to hurt her.

"Hold onto me, Caly. You're safe."

He bent down, scooped her up, and flew out of the cabin as fast as he could go. The cabin was deep in the forest and he wasn't familiar with the forest so he had to haul ass and head back in the general direction, hoping to pick up a scent once he got close enough.

He scented Rhyker on the wind. No doubt Rhyker was already well on his way considering the sheer noise of Rhyland's booming footsteps in the dead of night while he made a break for it with Caly in his arms. Rhyland wasn't trying to mute his presence because as soon as he got close enough to the meeting point, they would have the advantage of his brother and the others in case anyone or anything tried to come after him and Caly.

"Rhyker, I have Caly. She needs medical attention. Blake is battling The Ghost. Alert the others and send Nico to Blake. Come back to watch my flank."

Rhyland didn't have to speak very loud in order for his brother to hear and he knew Rhyker heard him because his scent was starting to fade. Rhyland shifted his course slightly so he could follow it like a homing beacon. Caly felt so cold and limp in his arms.

She must've passed out, he concluded. Holding her closer, he pushed on.

When he scented and heard Rhyker matching his own pace, knowing his brother was on high alert for any attacks, Rhyland took a small breath of relief. He knew he wasn't able to run Caly to safety and fight against any possible attacks at the same time. So with his brother nearby, he could complete his mission.

A loud wolf howl sliced the midnight forest air in two.

It was Blake.

Rhyland immediately knew it was not Blake's signal that he was in trouble. Rather, the howl was full of anger and frustration. Which was confirmed by his second howl. The signal for help is a single distinct howl—not two.

Shit. He couldn't think about what that even meant and he didn't want to believe The Ghost somehow got away. No. He couldn't go there right now.

Almost immediately, a chorus of wild wolf howls filled the forest like a choir of angels, creating a hauntingly beautiful song. Wild or not, wolves responded to strong alphas and Blake was a very strong alpha. Rhyland knew that right now, these wolves would most likely already be on their way to investigate and, if their alpha deemed so, they would offer assistance to Blake.

Rhyland caught the scent of the others on the breeze. He was so close. *Just a little farther. Hang in there, Caly.*

Finally, he shot out of the trees and halted in front of the vehicles.

"Bring her here!" Aleia commanded in an unexpectedly

dominant voice, as she tucked the emergency blanket under one arm. They had a makeshift patient bed ready in the back of one vehicle by laying down the back seats.

Before he could lay her down all the way, he saw Aleia's healing energy already starting to flow into Caly. It was glowing impossibly bright white with flashes of colors.

Okay, he thought, drawing out the word. He had never seen such potent power from a healer before. Usually, they had to touch the body they were healing. And the flashes of bright, vivid rainbow colors also indicated the potency of her healing ability. The colors of healing abilities varied depending on the ailment but, in this case, Rhyland guessed that Aleia was flowing a magic potion of everything she fucking had, which was kind of amazing to witness.

He could see Aleia's healing energy flow into Caly when Aleia physically moved her hands away from the body to palpate and check Caly's body. He knew she was more than an average healer with the Felix stunt but he should've known that anyone who hung out with an ancient like Riordan was not just above average but straight-up badass. As if the mid-air energy transfer wasn't a testament to her powers, Caly's eyes started to flicker and she moaned on a pained breath.

With the quick initial triage assessment complete, Aleia covered Caly's practically naked, broken, and bloodied body with the blanket as Rhyland quickly slipped into a pair of sweatpants and a T-shirt.

Species, especially shifters, were not like humans when it came to nudity. That's not to say everyone was a nudist walking around naked all of the time for kicks and giggles. No. Not even close. Rather, it was simply a natural part of shifting and it was handled in a cavalier and mature way. The way of species was to give the adult male or female privacy by turning or looking away as they cover up or shift.

So, even though Rhyland was naked, no one paid it any mind. It was commonplace and, at this moment, everyone was so intently focused on Caly and her current condition.

"Caly, I'm Aleia. I'm a healer. You're safe. Rest."

Again, with the surprisingly dominant clipped commands.

Okay, so maybe Rhyland's first assessment of this female was a little off. And by "a little," he meant "on the other side of the spectrum." From the look on Rhyker and Deacon's faces, they may have had the same epiphanies about this female.

Too bad Blake and Nico weren't here to witness this, he thought. Rhyland went to pull away from Caly to let Aleia do her work but Caly gripped his arm impossibly tighter with what little strength she had left.

"Stay," Aleia commanded when she saw Caly's reaction. "She feels safe with you." As a powerful healer, Aleia had the ability to detect hints of energetic "disturbances" when treating a patient. When Rhyland went to pull away, not only did she see Caly's grip tighten but she also felt a negative ripple in Caly's energy.

"I'm here Caly. I'm not going anywhere. You're safe," Rhyland assured Caly. Caly's grip eased a little with that confirmation and then her body went limp once more as she passed out.

"Shit... She's still mortal!" Aleia exclaimed on a frustrated exhale.

The tension tightened to constricting levels.

"Mortal?! As in she hasn't gone through her change?!" Rhyland bit out.

There was a round of curses on that new piece of information, especially knowing that Caly was still so young.

"Can you still...?" Rhyland asked, breaking the shocked silence. He knew Aleia was powerful but he didn't know how things went with someone who was in this condition and hadn't gone through their change yet.

"This makes it more difficult. She's heavily drugged. Trauma, shock, fear, broken bones... A goddamn fucking cocktail!" Aleia gritted out in complete anger for the bastard who did this to Caly.

Okay. So apparently, the innocent blonde was not only a badass healer but also cursed like a sailor. Yeah. Rhyland was way off on his initial assessment of Aleia.

Aleia's brows furrowed as beads of sweat started to form. "She's retreated into her mind. It's her body's defense mechanism. I'm not a mind healer but my guess is that's a good place for her right now, being a traveler and all."

Nico and Blake finally breached the forest tree line and sped toward the SUV. Blake was still in his wolf form since he had sustained injuries and the shift would be a waste of energy. His first priority was Caly and the scent of her blood was thick in the air.

One look. All it took was one look at Caly and the condition she was in and Blake lost control to his wolf. His consciousness was fading as the pure wolf instinct took over. The last thing he remembered was tilting his head back as a deafeningly haunting howl ripped through the dark of night.

There was a round of low cursing when everyone realized what was happening to Blake.

"Close us in," Aleia ordered, eyeing Blake's wolf.

Caly's eyes suddenly fluttered, as if in response to the wolf howl.

"Rhy—" Nico's command was cut off by a faint female voice.

"B-Blake..." Caly desperately called out for Blake.

Everyone refocused on Caly. Even Aleia paused at Caly's sudden rise to consciousness, appearing to be prompted by the sound of Blake's howl. With one look at Blake's wolf, Rhyland's survival instinct kicked in and it only took a moment for him to scramble out of the SUV and out of the way of the alpha wolf. With shifter speed, Blake's wolf was protectively lying next to Caly's body. She curled into him and gripped his fur.

"Blake," Aleia said, cautious but firm. "I'm going to continue the healing." She let the healing power flow out of her once more and into Caly.

Blake growled and peeled his lip back in a snarl, revealing his red-tinted fangs. When Caly let out a relieved exhale, Blake's wolf understood Aleia was helping Caly and allowed Aleia to continue the healing.

Aleia attempted to flow healing energy to Blake but he growled and nuzzled Caly. It was clear, even without words, his wolf said, *"Caly first."*

Without hesitation, Aleia listened. Once a shifter surrendered completely to the animal instinct, there was no logic or reason. You were facing a wild animal and, in this case, this wild animal was in complete protective alpha mode. Even with all of the fucked up cases The Order had worked, Nico, Deacon and the twins had never witnessed Blake lose control of his wolf. Usually, the twins were closer to the edge than Blake. Being an alpha, Blake had never fully lost control. Until now.

"We need to leave." Nico broke the silence but his eyes were still locked on Blake's wolf, who was acting as a blanket covering Caly. "Twins in the other car—"

"No." Aleia cut off Nico and challenged his command in her dominant, doctor voice.

No? Did she just say no to me?

Everyone froze because no one challenged Nico like that. Especially because he was technically second in command and, since Blake was a-wol(f), it left Nico in charge.

Aleia flicked her eyes up to Nico's and met his obsidian gaze. "We don't have time for this. He stays in this car. She's attached to him and feels safe with him."

Nico narrowed his eyes slightly calculating what she just said. He wasn't an arrogant ass who loved getting off on dominant power trips. Okay, well, not unless he was in a kink scene. There was a time and a place. And this was not the time nor the place. Although, he wondered what it would be like to be in that sort of time and place with this female.

Stop, he internally commanded his kink side to get with the fucking program. She was clearly a strong healer and her dominance was only because of this trauma triage environment... not anything else.

"Agreed," he said while keeping eye contact with Aleia for the longest moment.

Okay, Aleia thought, drawing out the word. She was expecting a full-on battle with this vampire. And he definitely was a vampire at that moment with his full-on obsidian eyes. She was *not* expecting him to accept her dominance, even with being a healer. Nico looked like the type to always be in control and get off on shit like that. *Little did he know...* She cut that thought off immediately because, no, she didn't bow down to just any dominant male. She was just exercising her right as the healer and, in that case, it was the right call. He wasn't there when Caly clung to Rhyland.

Witnessing the strange power play between Nico and Aleia, everyone remained still. And they were all unsure about what the fuck was about to happen next.

"Move out!" Nico commanded in a tone that said the dominance peep show was over. Nico caught the faintest glint of amusement in Riordan's eyes before he went to the other car. Nico shot icicles at Riordan's back.

Fucking seers, Nico thought with a growl.

Everyone knew that seers knew too much for their own damn good.

Both vehicles took off at the fastest possible speed down the road. The twins were no doubt channeling their twin bond (even though that was technically a myth), indicated by the matching speed and rhythm of the SUVs. Nico wanted to be piled in the other vehicle with Aleia, Blake, Caly, and Rhy. But Blake's wolf took up the entire back of the SUV with Caly, so there was no fucking way that Tetris game would have worked out. So, Nico was with Deacon, Riordan, and Rhyker.

Aleia assessed the situation while her healing energy continued to flow into Caly. Blake was licking Caly's face and nuzzling her neck as if to reassure her that he was there and she was safe.

"I'm going to start to flow to Blake now." Aleia gave a warning to Rhyland in case shit started to go down in the back while Rhyland was driving.

"Roger that," Rhyland called out over the loud noise caused by the speed of the SUV on the terrain.

Aleia allowed her healing powers to flow into Blake. She didn't dare touch him but she made sure her hands were visible to Blake's wolf, who was watching her like a hawk since the healing started.

He appraised the situation and when it looked like he was about to growl, Aleia said, "She's still getting healing too. This won't take away from her healing at this point."

Aleia wasn't sure if Blake's wolf understood any language other than body language at this point but she tried to use a calm and reassuring tone. He backed off on the growling and accepted the healing while keeping a close eye on both Caly and Aleia.

Aleia got several good minutes of healing into Blake

when the unexpected happened. Her bright healing light suddenly shot in another direction, as if it ricocheted off of something, and bounced around the inside of the car, in a flash of light.

Blake was growling as Rhyland called out, "What the fuck was that?!"

"I don't know!" Aleia was perplexed and examined Caly closer. She tried to send her healing light into Caly and it bounced off and flew around the car in another flash of light.

"Jesus Christ!" Rhyland shouted. "That hit me." He laughed a little. "And holy shit, Aleia, you pack a healing punch." He sent her a cheeky grin in the rearview mirror.

She smirked and then got refocused. She decided to put her hand on Caly to transfer the healing energy to her directly.

"Ow!" Aleia snapped her hand back in a fast knee-jerk reaction. Her fingertips felt like she had been slightly shocked. It actually didn't really hurt and kind of just felt like static electricity, like when clothes come out of the dryer and you can hear the static more than feel it, but the act itself was a surprise. So, her reaction was more of a natural, instinctive reaction rather than actual pain.

At this point, Blake's wolf had been at full attention since the first ricocheting flash of light. He kept eyeing Caly and then Aleia.

"Talk to me, Aleia. What the fuck is going on?!" Rhyland called out.

"There's some sort of force field around Caly. I can't get through it to heal her."

She paused at that because she was not believing what she was seeing, or rather, not seeing but experiencing. It was like an invisible force field. She cautiously reached out with her fingertips to attempt to touch the force field. She prepared for a static shock but this time, there was none. Instead, she met an energetic barrier and, where her hand touched, it sent a ripple through the force field like a drop of water in a pond. What she felt initially must have just been static electricity from the dry air.

"What?! What do you mean *'force field'*?!"

"I don't know! I've never seen or heard anything like this before," Aleia said and looked at Blake, who held a concerned expression, appearing as though he was about to growl again. *Great*, she thought. That was just what they needed: Blake's wolf to lose it in this confined space. She tried to give Blake a *"calm down, everything's okay"* look. It seemed to work so she kept it up despite having no idea what was going on. Her species healer training kicked in, guiding her to use reassuring gestures despite underlying feelings of slight panic and utter scientific curiosity.

"Blake appears to be unaffected somehow," she said, leaning in for a closer examination. She saw the faintest blur of the barrier around Blake. "In fact, he's surrounded by it too." There was a sudden cacophony of noise that broke into the car.

What in the...? Aleia thought. The ringtone was "Ice Box" by Omarion. *First of all, who even uses ringtones anymore? Second of all, what in the actual fuck? Third of all, Omarion?*

"Yeah," Rhyland answered the phone with dead seriousness as if that ringtone wasn't unusual at all. "We're fine. Right, Aleia? Everyone's fine still?"

She paused, shaking herself back into the reality of the moment.

"Yes. As far as I can see," Aleia answered.

"Yeah. As far as we can tell everyone's fine," he repeated and paused again. "She's not sure—" He was clearly cut off and then he growled out, "Hell, Nico, I don't fucking know if she doesn't know. We're fine and we'll meet you back at the house so we can all discuss it then." He hung up and shoved the phone in the cup holder.

She did a final check of Blake and Caly and then made her way carefully to the passenger seat. Without being able to heal or touch Caly or Blake, there was nothing further she could do right now. Even though Blake wasn't healed all of the way, his fast shifter healing abilities were more than capable of taking care of the rest. Plus, she didn't want to inadvertently set off Blake's wolf.

Even with the semi-hover wheels of the SUV, they were hauling ass and she was bouncing around a little by the mountainous terrain as she carefully made her way to the front passenger seat. As she got settled in, she did a quick mental check of herself. She was breathing a bit heavy, as though she had just run for some miles, and had a light sheen of sweat on her brow. Intense healing required a lot of energy and effort from a healer. Much like shifting required a lot of energy by shifting forms. Even though healers had healing energy flowing through their veins, they didn't have an infinite supply of energy and as such, they were still prone to burnout just like everyone else.

Rhyland took a quick glance at her. "You okay?"

"I'll be fine. Just need a little recovery time... and some food," she said, reaching into her jacket pocket and grabbing the energy bar that was specially formulated for energy depletion. She put this bar in her pocket earlier because she had no idea what kind of shape Caly was going to be in. Also, it was possible there was more than one patient because either one of the males could've been hurt in the rescue or they could've rescued more than just Caly. Aleia always kept some in her healers bag just in case. It was her standard protocol. But she was glad that she stashed an extra one in her pocket because her bag was still in the back of the SUV with who knew what, in the Star-Wars-force-field fuck, was going on. She peeled the wrapping off the energy bar and looked at Rhyland.

"I have this... but I know I am going to need something more to help me recover. Do you guys have food at the house?"

He gave her a look like he couldn't believe she thought they might not have food and then smiled.

"Female, the first thing you should know about Rhyker and I is that we *always* have food at the house. It would be a complete nightmare to wake up without any food." He shuddered at the thought. "You never have to worry about going hungry at our place. Besides, I'm hungry too." He gave her one of his winning wink and grin combos.

"Thanks." She smiled.

Rhyland's nose twitched and he glanced in the rearview at Blake and Caly. On an inhale, he sharpened his senses and his nostrils flared as he picked up what he swore was...

"Omarion?" Aleia's joking tone cut off his thoughts.

He suddenly burst out laughing. He had one of those infectious laughs and she laughed as a result. Blake's wolf growled a little at the sudden laughing outburst but it was just because he was startled. Rhyland checked the rearview while Aleia looked back just to make sure that was the only reason for Blake's growl. It was.

"Nico, AKA Mr. Freeze," he drawled. "Where to begin with that cold fucker?" He smirked and gave her a quick wink. "Don't you think the song is fitting? His heart is basically an ice chest and his body runs at arctic levels. Besides, Nico just *loves* it. And he's the only one special enough to have his own ringtone. Because, yeah, no one has fucking ringtones anymore."

"But if it's only programmed for his number, he'll never hear it?" Aleia questioned.

"Au contraire. We have our ways." He gave her one of his playful grins. "Our favorite is for Rhyker to swipe his phone and call me from it when we're all in the same room. The sudden outburst of "Ice Box" never gets old." He laughed. "Yeah, good times."

Aleia couldn't help but laugh a little. So maybe her first judgments (and yeah, they were judgments) were wrong. She was starting to see how cohesive this group of males were and how they were like brothers and cared for each other in their own unconventional way. Despite his cold outer shell, she could see there was definitely more than meets than eye when it came to Nico. That started to become apparent from the single interaction back at the forest. Again, her of all people should know that because she took full advantage of how she appeared to others at first glance: dumb blonde that was unassumingly sweet and innocent. She was nice and well-mannered, of course... okay, minus the occasional cussing. But she knew that was only the layer of her outer shell that she allowed people to see. So, believe it or not, she could relate to Nico in a sense. And she was really warming up to Deacon and Rhyland. She could immediately tell that they were aristocrats because that's where she came from too. However, unlike most, they weren't arrogant asses who only cared about bloodlines and money. They were actually rather pleasant and easygoing. Rhyland was clearly the joker of the group but he was also really charming. They may be a bunch of bachelors but clearly there was more than meets the eye for all of these males. She turned to look back at Caly and Blake's wolf. Caly was curled into his fur and looked to be in a very deep sleep.

* * *

"What happened?!" The hauntingly hypnotic voice, now

with a bone-chillingly deep and unnatural echo, lashed out with a venomous sting of fury.

"I—" The Ghost coughed up blood and his chest was heaving and straining to get air. "...was ambushed. At the mountain safe house. Two shifters. Alpha wolf and jaguar."

A loud crack echoed as The Ghost was struck across his face. It was not meant to be a lethal blow but rather, punishment for his stupidity. He was already severely injured but he would eventually heal from this.

"You let yourself be found?!" The hypnotic lull was almost completely overpowered by a deep and disturbing register, something reserved for horrific nightmares. There was a deathly silence for a brief moment. And when he spoke again, the demonic edge was replaced by the slight English lilt. "Even after showing you your true potential and all of the gifts I graciously bestowed upon you, for you know how I am generous and only have you in *mind*, this is how you repay me?"

Without warning, short clips of memories began playing rapidly in The Ghost's mind as if triggered by some unknown switch. Secret memories as he watched females and thought about his darkest desires to hunt and... *play* with females. Of course, others did not understand his urges and he knew he would be hunted if he acted on them, which was why he kept his thoughts hidden. A memory of a suave male with an English accent approaching him and offering him an existence where he was free to act on his desires and even gifted with an ability for a traceless escape. A memory of the male providing practically anything The Ghost desired, including his *playspace* in the woods and the various *toys*. A memory of the male encouraging him to follow his desires, affirming that it was part of his wolf's nature to hunt and play. And that it would be unnatural for him to go against the very essence of his being as the predatory hunter.

When the flashbacks ceased, The Ghost blinked back into the present. "I was careful as always. I don't know how they found me." His voice was frantic to explain despite his shallow strained breaths. "But... There's more." He paused to see if he was granted permission to speak.

"Continue before I lose patience," the other presence snapped back.

"There was a female... with some sort of energetic force field. It was strong even though she was weakened."

There was a silent pause. The Ghost chanced a glimpse up into the glowing, blood-red orbs that burned with the fiery depths of hell. Each ruby eye contained two serpent-like, black, vertical pupils that seemed as if two creatures were watching its prey. And if you stared too long, it felt like you would be sucked into hell itself. The Ghost was met with a look of pure evil fascination before averting his eyes.

"With this information, you have redeemed yourself." The male's voice was back to its chillingly compelling charm. "Now, tell me more about this female."

The Ghost felt the memories of the female being summoned in response.

Chapter 21

They arrived back at the house just before sunrise. It was a long night and felt like an even longer trip back. Everyone wanted to get Caly home safe for Aleia to continue healing and they all were eager to debrief what the fuck happened with not only The Ghost but also the force field. Once they all arrived at the mountain SILE station, Blake was out of the wild wolf instinct and shifted back to human form. He slipped on a loose shirt and pants and then wrapped Caly in a sheet, making sure to cover up her body and preserve her modesty. He held her close to his chest the entire time, even during the teleport and switching of vehicles. Everyone noticed that Caly's protective force field was gone but they kept the observation silent until they were back at the house. This was a private matter and there was no way to know the eyes and ears on them at the mountain SILE station, even if it was unintentional and just standard SILE station security protocol.

With Caly in his warm arms, Blake took the final steps toward the house and everyone followed suit. He was on a mission to gently lay Caly in his bed and have Aleia do a full assessment and healing. Blake's spacious room suddenly felt small with everyone piled in it. Aleia immediately flipped into full healer mode checking over Caly. Blake was right next to Aleia but giving her enough space to work. Nico was stalk-still in the shadowy corner next to the front right of the bed on the other side of the nightstand with a perfect sightline of Caly and Aleia. His face was covered in his layer of dark ice and his arms were crossed over his broad chest with one leg bent at the knee so his heavy combat boot could be propped against the base of the wall. Rhyker and Rhyland were positioned at the foot of the bed as twin towers. Deacon and Riordan filled the space on the remaining side of the bed. Even Felix was there at the foot of the bed, sitting at Caly's feet in between the twins. Everyone had uninterrupted focus on Caly. Aleia's potent healing power of iridescent white with flashes of rainbow colors once more flowed into Caly's fragile and frail body.

Time was passing in silence and the only movement was Aleia scanning Caly's body with her hands. Caly's major injuries were already experiencing expedited healing. It was as if weeks of healing had passed and there were just faint bruises now. With a renewed flowing of Aleia's healing energy into Caly, some of the minor cuts and bruises were starting to close before their eyes. When the body took in healing energy, it would naturally flow to where it needed it the most—starting with life-threatening injuries. Once those were under control, the healing energy would then work its way to minor injuries.

Breathing heavily from this second round of intense healing, Aleia wiped the glistening sweat from her brow.

"Okay," she said with a breath.

Rhyland handed her a bottle of water with the cap already twisted off.

She took a few long gulps. "Thanks," she said to Rhyland before continuing. "She will be fine and I suspect she will be back to a full recovery in the next day or two. Contact me immediately if she does not appear to be making a full recovery. The additional healing time is due to her still being mortal and the state she was in."

Everyone's faces darkened with renewed rage directed at The Ghost.

"Physically, she had a severely damaged and broken ankle, fractured cheekbone, bruised trachea and larynx, and several calculated cuts, scrapes, and bruises in various places on her body. I am not a mind healer but my opinion is that there is, most likely, psychological trauma that may need to be addressed as well. With Caly's consent, I will bring in Dr. Oliver, the mind healer I work collaboratively with on cases where the patient requires both physical and mind-healing. That can wait for now. The most important thing is for Caly to continue to rest and take it very easy in a safe and comfortable environment. She is currently in a deep sleep and I will be here for the next couple of hours, which is my guess as to when she will wake. I want to monitor her until then and make sure she is progressing as expected." There was a quiet stillness. "This female is a *fighter*. And I don't say that about all my patients. I felt something in her that was... strong. I can't quite place it. And then, there is the force field..." Her voice trailed off momentarily before continuing. "Speaking of which, if there aren't any questions about Caly's current state, then I would like to discuss the force field." Aleia looked at Blake and Riordan for confirmation.

"Agreed," Blake said as Riordan nodded.

"We were heading down the mountain and the healing was going as expected... Until it wasn't. Out of nowhere some sort of energetic force field, at least that's what I'm calling it, surrounded not only Caly but also you." She looked at Blake. "I've never seen or heard anything like it before. It deflected my healing energy and my guess is that it could deflect a lot more than that. In fact, I couldn't even touch her. It was like this invisible barrier."

Everyone's brows furrowed in concentration, curiosity, and confusion. Blake's hand scratched the scruff of his face and Deacon slid his glasses up the bridge of his nose as they took in the information.

"Is it even possible to have a new unknown ability?" Rhyland broke the silence and voiced the thought that ran through everyone's mind. There had not been any known, new abilities documented for at least a millennium. So, naturally, everyone looked at Riordan for answers. If anyone knew the answer to that it would be the ancient.

"It's possible..." Riordan began, his voice as an afterthought. He was recalling the vision of Caly. "I will need to sit with this."

"D." Blake refocused on Deacon.

"Consider it done," Deacon responded almost as soon as Blake asked the unspoken question. Deacon was already working out the various search algorithms in his head to check against the species archives about this potential unknown ability.

"It could explain her scent too," Rhyland added, naturally taking the scent angle of things.

The males that were gifted in the scent department nodded in agreement.

"The Ghost." Blake abruptly switched subjects and the room went stalk still with those two words. "Did The Ghost know of Caly's... ability? Is that why she was targeted?" Blake spoke his thoughts out loud.

Everyone let that thought sink in, inspiring a slew of new questions.

"How would he have known though?" Rhyland interjected.

"And, if that is the case, why would he have waited to

take her?" Rhyker added.

Another pondering moment went by.

"I'm with Blake. We have to assume he knows. It would make the most sense with the information we have now," Deacon said.

A round of curses filled the room. Because if Caly did have a new unknown ability and that information was in the hands of The Ghost, it put a huge target on her back. Additionally, if SILE investigators, like Marie Chan, were correct, then The Ghost had a connection with The Mastermind. And if The Mastermind found out about Caly's unknown ability (if that is what it was), then all bets would be off as to what might happen.

"What happened after I got Caly out of the cabin?" Rhyland asked, refocusing his attention on Blake.

Blake ran his hand through his hair in frustration and took a breath. "It was a fight to the death... and I was winning. He got in a few good blows but the moment I sunk my teeth into his shoulder and tore something, I knew it would soon be over. It wasn't until I unleashed another damaging blow to his chest, that I believe he came to the same conclusion. I was so focused on him that I didn't see it until it was too late." Blake paused with a killing scowl on his face. "That dishonorable piece of shit ran from a fight the moment he knew he would lose." Another brief pause. "I was about to strike a final blow that would incapacitate him and, believe me, I wanted to kill the fucker but I knew we needed him alive for questioning. Anyways, I was about to strike when a flash of dark black light suddenly appeared to my right and I was staring at a giant arched doorway of liquid black. The Ghost was counting on my stunned reaction and he kicked out with his hind legs into me, leveraging me as a springboard to propel himself into the black liquid. The kick sent me just far enough away for him to escape into the black liquid doorway before I could get there, and it disappeared the instant he was swallowed by it." Blake looked directly at Riordan who froze, meeting Blake's golden eyes with grim shadows. Dead silence filled the room as everyone tried to comprehend what Blake said.

"Blocking seers, force fields, and now black... portals?! What in the actual fuck is going on?!" Rhyland exclaimed.

Rhyker lit up not one but two hand-rolled indies at that mind fuck of a thought.

"Riordan, what do you know of this?" Blake's attention was still focused on Riordan and he caught the grim look on the seer's face.

Riordan hesitated for a long moment. Then on an exhale breath, he broke the silence. "When I was younger, I heard whispers from a young boy who said his bloodline battled in The Great Clash. He spoke of when The Mastermind was at the brink of death and made a deal with the darkness." Riordan paused and looked around. "He shared a secret with me that The Mastermind escaped without a trace because black liquid appeared under his body and consumed him."

The room fell completely silent for a split second before another round of curses.

"Fuck. We all know the story. He was seduced by the darkness and power," Rhyland began.

"And just before he died, he struck an evil bargain with the darkness and retreated into a dark sleep," Rhyker continued without pause.

"But how is it that no one knows just how *literal* that really is?!" Rhyland finished.

"So, is it possible that the whispers regarding his stirring slumber could be true?" Deacon thought out loud.

"I have thoroughly researched the ancient texts but none explicitly corroborate the black liquid. Until this moment, I concluded it was mistranslated in the boy's bloodline after generations of telling the story. But now I wonder..." Riordan added.

"How could such a thing not be spoken of or known about? Or, hell, *warn* us about?" It was the first time Aleia spoke since the change of subject.

Riordan was silent as he knew he had to choose his words carefully. "There are those who would wish to keep such powers a secret."

"Fucking council," Rhyker gritted out and Rhyland growled in agreement.

Everyone knew there was corruption and greed for power in the Species Council, the council that supervised all of the subspecies councils and consisted of representation from all known subspecies.

"They have too much fucking power and would keep this a secret from all of us who have a right to know. Why? Because they want the power for themselves. Or better yet, to cover up their fucking mistakes. Because how the hell would The Mastermind know about black liquid portals otherwise? He was the protégé being groomed for the Species Council after all." Rhyland finished his rant because both he and his brother knew too well about the council wanting to groom them. Who knew how they would have turned out if things didn't take a tragically unexpected sharp turn years ago.

"Alright," Blake cut in. "This is all speculation. We have no proof and nothing to go off of. But this doesn't mean it's not the truth." He paused before continuing, "We do finally know how The Ghost has been able to disappear though." There was another pregnant pause as that thought sunk in. "Regardless, no one can know about this, as of yet, including SILE. In fact, what we have discussed and witnessed tonight stays between only us in this room," Blake commanded in his alpha voice.

"Agreed," each of them said in accordance as they made an oath to protect Caly's secret and the mysterious dark liquid. All of the males pounded their dominant hand over their chest when they spoke the word, signifying their most sacred verbal oath, warrior to warrior, while Aleia placed her dominant healer hand over her heart.

Whatever all of this was, they didn't know. But they did know that they didn't have enough information to share as of yet. They also knew it was completely unethical to share another's ability, or, in this case, "speculated ability," without explicit consent from that individual. Unfortunately, ethics alone wouldn't stop some malicious beings. Fortunately, no one in that room was a part of that poisonous pack of evil. Morality aside, each of them had their own secrets they kept hidden and they all closely understood what it was like to either have or help protect someone who had an ability that was watched with ill-intent. So, this pact struck a deep chord at the soul and was taken very seriously.

Blake turned to Riordan and Aleia. "Due to the circumstances, you both are welcome to stay here until Caly wakes and is cleared by you." He focused on Aleia.

Blake still didn't fully trust either of them because they barely knew each other. However, so far neither of them had given any reason for him to distrust them thus far. In fact, his wolf instincts were telling him these two were trustworthy. Sometimes, all you had to go with was gut instincts.

"Thank you. I would very much appreciate that. I actually do need to rest and refuel." Aleia spoke candidly.

Blake nodded as Rhyland spoke. "Got you covered on the refuel." He winked and Aleia smiled.

At that interaction, Nico's gaze flicked between Aleia and Rhyland. Nico, who was a shadowy ice sculpture the entire time, suddenly felt compelled to stalk over to Rhyland and punch him square in the face in an effort to stop the playful banter.

"You can take the spare room to rest," Blake added, looking at Riordan.

"Thank you for opening up your home to us. I also find myself in need of the same," Riordan stated.

"Of course. And I think we all are in need of the same." Blake looked at the twins.

"On it," they both said in unison.

They weren't the designated cooks of the house or anything, far from it actually. And, hell, they were just okay with the cooking basics. But their love for food designated them as the kings of the kitchen in a sense. So they would be able to put together at least something.

With that, the twins strolled out. Deacon was closely in tow, halfway consumed by the single, projected imaging screen he pulled up in front of him. Over the decades, he had become quite good with the whole "autopilot" thing while his mind was at work. He first learned about this phenomenon long ago, while researching a case for SILE. He had been listening in on a conversation where two coworkers discussed autopilot. *"I was so consumed by my thoughts yesterday... Jessica, I actually found myself parked in my driveway with no recollection of driving home. Like, I was just sitting there, exhausted from work, mind swirling, wondering how I managed to drive myself home."*

This was Deacon's version of that.

"If you want to get cleaned up, Nico will show you the bathroom." Blake was going to offer for her to use the bathroom in his room but there was no way in hell he was leaving Caly's side and thought that might be awkward for Aleia with him just outside the door.

Aleia looked down at herself and realized that she definitely did need to clean up. Even though her medical scrubs were black, she still could see blood and dirt stains.

"Thank you," she said to Blake before daring a look at the male blending in with the shadowy corner. She couldn't help herself. It felt like his frosty eyes were on her the entire time. Yup. She was right. He was staring at her with his frosty eyes. Okay. She knew she probably made it on his hit list by openly challenging his order in front of everyone but, whatever, she was right.

Is he ever going to get over it? she thought, refocusing back on Blake. "Let me know if anything changes." She knew that Blake was not going to leave Caly's side.

Blake gave her a nod and then turned to Riordan. They waited until Aleia and Nico closed the door behind them. A wooden door technically could not stop shifter or vampire hearing but everyone knew to respect each other's privacy and not to eavesdrop. It was something instilled in them from a young age.

"You need to speak with Caly alone," Blake said, not being one for beating around the bush.

"Yes," Riordan responded.

They exchanged respectful looks, indicating an acknowledgment that they were both leaders in their own rights. Riordan appreciated the refreshing directness of Blake. So many aristocrats and ancients liked to dance around conversations and show off at any chance they got.

Blake nodded, knowing there was no doubt that Riordan knew more than he had shared so far. But seers were bound by confidentiality ethics just like healers and thus far, Riordan had lived up to his honorable and respectable reputation.

Riordan knew it would be known soon enough but she needed to be the one to make the call. At that, they both looked at Caly who was sleeping.

Aleia walked into the kitchen in the same clothes she wore

when she first arrived. Her hair was wet from the shower and she re-applied her mascara, blush, and lip gloss. It was her five-minute, go-to look. She saw the twins were still in their hunting clothes and making what she guessed was probably their third sandwich by the looks of the crumbs on their plates.

"Help yourself," Rhyker started.

"Eat as much as you'd like. There's plenty," Rhyland finished.

They both shot her a quick smile before taking a bite of their sandwiches almost in unison.

She smiled and, for whatever reason, she wondered what they must've been like as young males growing up. Twin troublemakers no doubt.

"Thank you," she said, still smirking a little at the thought.

She grabbed a plate and looked at the food options. They set out the fixings for sandwiches. So what if the sun was just barely rising? She could care less right now because she was starving and any food would do. Hell, the sandwich idea, with disposable plates and utensils, was smart of them because it was quick, efficient, and required virtually no cleanup. They also looked like they had it down to a science with an assembly line of sorts.

Clearly, this was not their first time with the post-hunt, fast food fix. Just as she was done making her sandwich, the twins were finishing their sandwiches with a chip crunching finale because they, naturally, stuffed their sandwiches with chips. She looked over at the couch and noticed Deacon was still on autopilot mode with his projected imaging screens. She gave a pointed look to his plate to make sure he ate.

Good, she thought, noticing his plate was empty with the evidence of crumbs to prove it. *But he still needs to rest.* She was a healer and nurturer at heart and couldn't help it even when she felt exhausted.

As if he knew what she was thinking, the screens disappeared and he rubbed his weary eyes a little before pushing his black frames into place. She walked over to him and stacked her full plate on top of his.

"I got your plate. Go rest," she said.

Deacon's tired eyes had slight bags under them but they softened as he said, "Thank you." Deacon got up and left the room.

Aleia looked over at the twins who looked like they were about to leave as well. "Do you know what kind of sandwich Blake likes? He needs to eat."

"Already on it," Rhyland said as Rhyker held up a plate that she didn't initially see behind the assembly line of food.

"Eat," Rhyker added.

"We got this," Rhyland assured.

Yes, it would appear you do, she thought to herself as she gave them a quick smile before taking a bite of her sandwich.

Satisfied with her eating, the twins both walked down the hall to give Blake his sandwich and then get cleaned up and crash. After all, it was the feline way to hunt, eat, clean, sleep, and then repeat.

Showered, cleaned up, and in a fresh change of clothes, Nico walked into the kitchen. His focus fell on Aleia, who was passed out on the couch. His eyes flicked to the mostly empty plate next to her. It only had two bites of sandwich left and a couple of chips. He looked back at Aleia and then left the room in silent stealth.

Turning the knob, he opened the door to the spare room. He didn't even bother turning on the lights because he could see perfectly fine in the dark. He approached the bed and snatched something quickly. He stilled. Listening to make sure no one knew what he was doing. With nothing but the sweet caress of silence in his ears, he slid out of the room and closed the door behind him on a muted beat.

He stalked back into the kitchen and straight up to Aleia who was still sleeping. He loomed over her like the dark tower he was and looked down. He hesitated for a moment before reaching his thick arm down toward her head. His hand slid to the nape of her neck and lifted it. In a fluid motion, he slipped the pillow he snatched from the spare room under her head and carefully lowered her head. Then, he draped the blanket he had also taken from the room over her. Nico grabbed her plate of food and appeared back in the kitchen, tossing it in the trash. No one was the wiser.

Chapter 22

Aleia blinked her eyes open and, god, she was exhausted. She was staring at a ceiling that wasn't her own and it took her a moment to remember where she was. Then, as if someone opened the floodgates of her mind, it all came back. It was no wonder why she was so tired and her body felt like it weighed a thousand pounds. On top of pulling an all-nighter, the healing energy cocktail she gave Caly was the strongest she had and, well, to give it twice in such a short time? She knew she was going to need some more R&R than just a sandwich and a quick nap. Good thing Riordan already advised her to clear the next couple of days. She learned very early on to listen to him for things like this. One would be a fool not to heed the advice of a trusted and powerful seer. Although in actuality, she really just needed some good nourishing meals and a solid night's sleep and she would be back on her feet. Being a healer, she was all too familiar with the warning bells of burnout. So, although she did exert a lot of energy for Caly's healings, she hadn't crossed that line into the overextended territory yet.

How long have I been asleep? She looked at the time on her phone. *Almost an hour.* She needed to check on Caly. Willing her body to get up, her brow furrowed slightly upon realizing there was a blanket over her and a pillow under her head. *Okay. That's a nice and unexpected touch,* she thought, neatly folding the blanket. That was when she noticed that her plate of food was gone too. *Must've been Rhyland or Riordan. Because who else would it be?*

She made a pit stop in the restroom and, upon her look in the mirror, she decided to quickly run a brush through her hair and touch up her makeup. She wasn't trying to impress anyone but she didn't want to look like a rundown slob. Okay, fine. Maybe she also didn't want to look like a slob for other "reasons." Reasons that were kind of ridiculous. Reasons that came with a frostbite warning. Reasons that were tall, intense, and handsome. Reasons that were nice to look at but obviously nothing more. Reasons that may or may not already be upset with her for her "healer's order" that directly challenged his authority in front of everyone.

Stop. Remember you're here for Caly.

Getting back with the program, she took a breath and did a final check in the mirror. Satisfied, she made her way to Caly.

Walking into Blake's room, she saw just what she was expecting: Blake sitting in a chair next to the bed with his undivided attention on Caly. Without words, Aleia approached the bed and gestured to Blake that she was going to complete a scan. He nodded in agreement. Her mouth slightly curved up at the corners when she noticed Blake must've wiped Caly down with a washcloth because most of the dirt was gone. And she knew it was him because there was no way in hell Blake's wolf would let any of the other males wash her.

Blake had originally planned to give Caly a full-on bath to clean her off but, after he thought about it, he revised that plan. Even if he had already seen Caly naked, this was a completely different situation entirely and he erred on the side of modesty because he didn't know how she would feel waking up to know he washed her naked body while she was unconscious. He also didn't know what The Ghost did to her and he didn't want to cause any additional trauma or stress. Blake had to bite back a low growl at the reminder of The Ghost mistreating Caly.

Aleia broke the silence with a gentle tone. "Everything is looking good from a physical standpoint. My guess is that she will wake within the hour." During the scan, she felt slight ripples of Caly's consciousness. It was different than an hour ago before her nap.

Blake nodded and refocused back on Caly.

Aleia quickly glanced at Blake. Although she wanted to scan him too, she knew that with the short healing energy she gave him, plus his fast shifter healing ability, that he was fine by now. "I can watch her if you want to get cleaned up?" She offered.

He almost immediately dismissed it but then glanced down at himself and saw the dirt and dried blood that stained the loose-fitting clothes he wore. Deciding it was probably best not to scare Caly with his appearance, he nodded in agreement.

Two minutes. That was how long it took him to wash off the dirt and blood and change into a fresh pair of jeans and a clean white T.

"Thank you," Blake said, taking up his post next to Caly's side.

"You're welcome." Aleia smiled. "Let me know as soon as she wakes. Otherwise, I'll be back to check on her in a little bit. She should be waking up soon." With that, Aleia left the room.

Silence stretched through the room once more while Blake watched and waited.

About forty-five minutes later, Blake sharpened his senses

at Caly's inhale. Yes, Caly's breathing pattern had just changed. She was waking up.

His wolf stirred.

Apparently, he wasn't the only one who noticed because Felix started purring and was looking at Caly expectantly.

In an unconscious motion, he reached his hand to hold hers but halted halfway and pulled back. He didn't know how she felt about him or how she would react to holding hands. And he didn't want to cause her any further distress. With her eyes still closed, he noticed her full lips smile slightly but it was instantly replaced with a wince and a furrow of her brow. A split second later, the acrid sting of pure fear flooded his senses. Both he and his wolf's fangs thirsted for The Ghost's blood and to end that fucker's existence once and for all. He needed to bring justice for what was done to Caly and all of the others who were hurt or killed at the hands of The Ghost.

* * *

Sounds. Caly was hearing sounds.

No, not plural sounds... but a singular sound. It seemed familiar. Some sort of muffled melodic rhythm. As the moments passed, the cloudiness from the deepest sleep of her life was slowly drifting away as if blown by a gentle breeze.

Purring. She was hearing Felix's purr. She smiled at the purring alarm clock. She winced and sucked in a quick breath. There was a faint twinge in her cheek and it felt sore. Her brows furrowed slightly as she tried to remember why.

In a flash, a wave of panic flooded her veins as the horror flooded back to her conscious mind. She shot open her panicked eyes and... locked onto Blake's impossibly golden eyes.

"I'm here. You're safe."

To hear Blake's voice *outside* of her mind pulled at something deep in her soul and the last word he spoke replayed in her mind.

Safe.

She was safe. It wasn't a dream. Blake really came for her. Staring into the depths of his golden eyes, she felt tears pool in her eyes only to fall like twin waterfalls down her cheeks. She felt Felix's rough feline tongue lick her hand as if he could feel her emotions and wanted to comfort her.

Blake gently sat on the bed next to her and held her close to his chest.

No other words were spoken as she tried to convince her slightly shaking body this was real and she was truly safe. Her streams of silent tears cleansed away the nightmare with each passing moment.

She didn't know how long she stayed like that, clinging to his promise of safety with his body wrapped around her like the warmest security blanket. When the waterfalls ran dry, she knew this was real and she was safe in Blake's arms. On that realization, her chest expanded as she took the deepest breath she had since being taken. That breath was inexplicably liberating. She took another. And then a third.

She stiffened slightly on her third exhale, realizing three things. First, and most embarrassing, she smelled like she hadn't showered in days... because she hadn't showered in days. Second, Blake's white shirt was completely soaked with tears where her face rested. Third, she must still be covered in dirt and soot from the dark room where she was kept.

Oh. My. God. I must look and smell like a rotting corpse resurrected as a zombie.

"Caly?" Blake cautiously checked in.

With her head on his chest, she felt the vibrations of

Blake's deep voice. She slowly peeled herself away from Blake's body to examine herself. Her brows furrowed slightly. It looked as if the dirt was somewhat wiped off her arms. Also, that was when she had a fourth realization. She was wrapped in what looked like a generic white hospital blanket that had some dirt stains, probably from her. She was fairly certain she was still only wearing the bra and underwear underneath the blanket. He cleared his throat a little and she looked up into his golden eyes once more.

"I tried to clean you up as much as I could," he confessed and then quickly added, "Without invading your privacy."

She smiled at his kindness and for protecting her modesty. Then, she realized that was the second time she was only wrapped in a sheet in his presence. She shook off that thought and went to say, *"Thank you"* but she coughed a little instead. God, she really needed some water.

As if he could read her mind, he reached over to the bedside table, grabbed a water bottle, twisted off the cap, and handed it to her. She closed her eyes and took sweet long sips of pure clean water. She could feel the cool liquid travel down her throat and drank almost the entire thing. Similar to the deep breaths, this water tasted like the freedom that birds must feel with the wind caressing their feathers in flight.

"Thank you." This time, she managed to get out the words in a small voice. Continuing with that frail voice she asked, "Shower?"

"Of course," Blake reassured her in an easy and comforting tone. He stood up and held his hand out, offering his assistance to help steady her if she needed it.

She placed her feet on the soft carpet, gripped the blanket with one of her hands, took his hand with the other, and stood up. She felt a little stiff and sore. It was similar to the feeling she got the day after crushing a gym workout.

"I'm okay," she said to Blake as she let go of his hand. She took a step but when she went to put her full weight on her right ankle, she almost fell. With shifter speed, Blake caught her and helped her balance. For whatever reason, the soreness was extremely intense in her right ankle and it caught her off guard. A memory flashed through her mind and she remembered when The Ghost broke her ankle.

No. I am safe. I am safe. I am safe. She kept repeating that in her mind as she gripped onto Blake's arm a little harder to feel his presence, making sure he was still there. She took a deep breath ready to move forward, but then a thought stuck in her mind.

How long have I been out? Long enough for the injuries to heal, including my ankle. Stop.

She commanded a cease and desist with her thoughts. She couldn't go there right now. No. She refocused on her mission.

Phoenix Shower.

She didn't know why that phrase popped into her mind but the more she thought about it, the more it grew on her. She was going to shower and scrub herself so fucking clean that when she emerged from the bathroom, she would be like a Phoenix rebirthing as it rose from the ashes.

I am safe. I am the fucking Phoenix.

Prepared for the intense stiffness and soreness in her ankle this time, she took careful slow steps toward the bathroom with Blake's support. She probably could have gone faster than her steady turtle pace but slow and steady felt sturdy and solid. And that was what she needed right now.

"Where am I?" she asked Blake as she took in the room for the first time.

"My bedroom. In our secure house. You're safe here," Blake reassured her again.

Knowing it was his room, she suddenly got more curious

and looked around the space to take in a bit more detail. It looked simple, clean, and casual. The room itself was very large, at least in comparison to her shoebox of an apartment. She turned her head slightly and noticed the sliding glass wall to the forested scenery.

Beautiful.

She paused on the forest for a moment before continuing with her curiosity about the room. She noticed that his bed was massive. Then again, he was also massive. The only other things in the room were a dark leather couch, wooden coffee table, and large TV. They walked by what she suspected was a walk-in closet and then Blake opened the bathroom door. His bathroom was also themed: simple, casual, and clean. It had white floors and countertops with double sinks, a giant soaker tub, and a large white shower.

Okay. Really nice yet not over the top with the ego.

He paused in the doorway and she realized he was being a gentleman. Even though they had seen each other naked, this was in a completely different context. Again, she appreciated how he respected her privacy and boundaries and didn't assume anything. She took her first step without Blake's steady support into the bathroom. She froze when she caught her reflection in the mirror. In a swift movement, Blake was in front of her blocking her view. Though she only caught a quick glimpse of herself, it was enough for her to see what she looked like: the walking dead. She knew he was just trying to protect her but she needed to see.

"No. I—" She swallowed. "I need to see." She looked him straight in the eye, letting him know that she needed to do this. He looked back at her for the longest moment, no doubt thinking that wasn't a good idea.

"Caly—" he gently protested.

"No, Blake. I need to do this." She didn't know why this was suddenly so important. A part of her agreed with him that this was a bad idea but a stronger part of her mind was adamant about this.

He looked at her for another long moment.

As soon as he stepped aside, Caly became a statue once more. Because, yeah. It was just as bad as she had suspected. She kind of did look like a rotting corpse resurrected from the grave. It also looked like there was Halloween makeup smeared in a few places on her arms and face. She concluded that must've been where Blake tried to clean her up.

Phoenix Shower.

That thought suddenly popped into her mind again and she refocused on her mission. She turned, looked at the shower and slowly walked toward it.

In a fluid movement, Blake was at the shower and started the flow of water. Assuming Caly liked hot showers, he made sure to turn the knob to the hotter side. After all, he remembered how her skin was a little pink after the shower she took at her place.

He grabbed her a couple of towels and said, "I'll be just outside if you need me at all." They locked eyes for a beat before he closed the door behind him.

Caly could see the steam rising from the shower and tentatively stuck her hand under the water. It was just how she liked it: hot but not scorching. She let the sheet, that was wrapped around her body, fall to the ground as she slipped out of her underwear and bra. She had a random thought that she wanted to burn her clothes. Like in a bonfire. It must've been a continuation of the Phoenix theme.

Stepping under the warm spray, she closed her eyes. It felt like a heated slice of heaven. She stayed like that for a few moments, just breathing with the warm water flowing down her body. She appraised the soap situation and saw some generic men's body wash and an "all-in-one" shampoo and conditioner. In normal circumstances, she might have wrinkled her nose at the all-in-one shampoo and conditioner but these were not normal circumstances. Far from it. She had just about lost it and cried all over again as a swell of gratitude circulated her body. She was so incredibly grateful for being safe and in this shower that it was almost overwhelming.

She grabbed the body wash, squeezed a generous amount in her palm, and got to scrubbing her body with the soapy suds from top to bottom. She squeezed more soap in her palm and scrubbed again. She repeated the soapy scrub routine over and over until her skin was pink, not only from the heat of the water but also from scrubbing so damn hard. She was probably cleaned off with the first scrub session but on the inside, she just felt like she couldn't get clean enough.

Next was her hair. And she had a lot of hair. Again she squeezed a generous amount of the shampoo/conditioner concoction in her palm and worked the lather from her scalp to the ends of her hair. Her hair felt like one giant dreadlock and she wasn't sure how long it was going to take to de-tangle the monster. But, whatever. She would rise through that just like this shower because this was mission Phoenix Shower. She also washed her hair so many times that the bottle was almost empty and her arms were getting tired.

She realized she had to relieve herself, probably because she drank almost an entire water bottle. Maybe it was gross and she wasn't supposed to do what she was about to, but at the moment, she didn't care. So, yeah, she totally peed in the shower and something about that also felt strangely liberating. She took some of the fresh water in her mouth and swished it around a few times before spitting it out. She didn't even realize how badly she wanted to brush her teeth all of a sudden. So, she repeated the swish and spit several times until she figured that was probably as clean as her teeth were going to get.

Turning off the shower, she wrung out her long hair, just as she always did, before stepping out of the shower. She opened the shower and the bathroom was basically transformed into a steam room, with the mirrors completely fogged. Stepping out of the shower, she wrapped one of the towels around her head in an easy, practiced motion and then wrapped the other around her body, tucking the corner in between her breasts so it would stay up on its own. She used the small face towel to wipe the foggy mirror to reveal herself once more.

Is that me?

It was her but it wasn't. Even without the Halloween zombie costume look, she barely recognized herself. Physically, she still looked relatively the same but the woman staring back at her in the mirror was no longer the same Caly. It was not necessarily a bad thing. It just felt like her twenty-year-old self suddenly woke up and looked in the mirror, only to find her twenty-five-year-old self, staring back. It was still her... just a different version of herself.

She looked at the counter and saw mouthwash, toothpaste and his toothbrush. Okay, so she wasn't going to use his toothbrush but she was going to use the mouthwash and then just use her finger with the toothpaste. Because it was better than nothing. With that done, she untwisted the towel in her hair and used the towel to squeeze out as much remaining water as she could.

Toothbrush and hairbrush.

She made mental notes of what she was going to ask Blake for. It wasn't until she opened the door and looked at Blake's bedroom that she realized she didn't have any clothes to change into. She looked around for Blake and thought she heard his voice outside the door.

As soon as he saw her, Felix jumped off the bed and

was doing figure eights in between her legs. She smiled and wanted to cry at the thought that Blake was thoughtful enough to not only bring but also care for, Felix. He was her baby and she couldn't bear the thought of something happening to him.

She waited a few moments, not entirely sure she should be rifling through Blake's closet... but then she thought, *Fuck it.*

His closet was really organized and she easily found a hoodie sweater and a pair of sweatpants. They were XL and she was swimming in them but there was just something so comforting about wearing a man's oversized hoodie. And, yeah. Okay, so she looked like one of those women models in the Midol commercials on their periods. Oh well. She could give two fucks right now with everything that just happened to her. Just as she stepped out of his closet in his clothes, she heard a knock.

"Caly?" Blake called out on the other side of the door.

She thought it was sweet of him to knock even though it was his room. "Come in."

He walked in and closed the door behind him.

She exhaled a breath she didn't know she was holding and a sense of relief washed over as she noticed no one else entered behind Blake. She was not ready to see anyone else let alone speak to anyone else.

Blake saw Caly standing just in front of his closet in his clothes. She was so beautiful and both he and his wolf wanted to growl in approval of her being covered in his scent. He caught her relieved exhale when he shut the door behind him.

"It's just us right now. You don't have to see or speak to anyone until you're ready." He paused. "We do have the healer here to check up on you. That's who I was speaking with in the hall. But she can wait until you're ready."

Caly let Blake's words sink in for a moment. She thought about it and decided that she did want to speak with the doctor. She wanted to know where she was at with... well, everything really. And the doctor was probably a good place to start. Besides, it was a woman doctor and that, for whatever reason, had Caly a little more relaxed and open about seeing someone else.

"Thank you. I would like to see her. The doctor." She hesitated. "But... would you stay? Please?" She tried not to sound so fucking desperate but when she heard herself, that's exactly how she sounded. Not only did she feel so safe with Blake but she also had this completely irrational pull toward him. And the thought of doing this without him caused a twinge of anxiety to knot up her stomach.

Blake noticed Caly's reaction at the thought of him leaving her alone with the healer.

Caly, I will never leave you. You're mine, he wanted to tell her but, yeah, now was not the time. *You're safe from that fucking psychopath, who I am hunting and will kill for you. Oh, and by the way you're mine.* Yeah, now was definitely not the time.

"Caly, I will stay as long as you need." Blake tried to reassure her without going overboard and scaring her off with the whole "you're mine" thing.

With Blake's words, Caly exhaled and suddenly felt like crying a little. She took another breath and tried to hold back the unexpected tears. *You're just emotional because you went through something traumatic,* she rationalized.

"Blake?"

"Yeah, Caly?"

Please don't ever leave, she wanted to say.

"Do you have an extra toothbrush and hairbrush by chance?" she asked, locking up her emotions. She knew she couldn't stay here with him in his room forever. But for right now, she was here and she would deal with all of the logistics later.

Good job, Blake, he thought. *First, you forget clothes for her. Not complaining about your scent all over her or anything. And now, she doesn't even have a toothbrush.*

"I should've thought of that. Yeah, we have both. Well, I don't have a hairbrush but I have a comb."

He walked into the bathroom, opened the bottom drawer, and pulled out a brand new toothbrush from a multi-pack. Then, he opened the top drawer and placed the comb on the counter.

She looked at him in the reflection of the still slightly foggy mirror with a half-smile and said, "Thank you," as she reached for the toothbrush. For a second, she thought he might stay while she brushed her teeth. But when he walked back into the bedroom, she was glad because brushing her teeth in front of him felt a little intimate, like something that only bonafide couples did.

A few minutes later, Blake saw Caly emerge from the bathroom with the comb in hand as if she was a warrior princess holding her weapon and preparing for battle. Blake saw the thin small comb and then assessed the sheer amount of hair she had, which, again, both he and his wolf wanted to growl in approval of because they both really liked the length.

Caly walked over to the bed and started working the comb through her hair starting from the bottom. She noticed Blake watching her and wondered what he was thinking. *Probably that you look like the Midol period model who decided to go hippie and stop brushing her hair.*

She saw Blake walk into the bathroom and come out with another comb in his hand.

"May I?" he asked.

"Honestly? I would love the help," she said with a smile.

"Sometimes randoms see my long hair and tell me they wish they had hair like me. I try to let them know that it's not always a walk in the park." She held up a massive knot and let out a little laugh. That was the first time she attempted a joke and a laugh. It wasn't her best work but it was a start.

He chuckled. "I never really thought about that." He sat on the bed next to her and grabbed a section of her hair. He was trying to mimic what she was doing.

"I have to confess, I've never combed hair this long before." He smiled.

"You're actually doing a really good job. Better than some women even," Caly chortled but hesitated when she noticed a slight pause in Blake's stroke when she said that.

"Blake?"

"Yeah, Caly?"

Okay, isn't this kind of like déjà vu... she thought, realizing that was exactly the same exchange they had a few minutes ago.

"I... I didn't mean that like you're feminine or anything."

His deep laughter caressed her skin at her response.

"I know, Caly. I didn't take it like that at all."

"Then..." She paused and bit her lip. "What did I say? I know I said something."

He hesitated. He was not sure if now was the right time. But he figured there probably wasn't ever going to be a right time for this conversation.

"Women. You said, 'women.' "

Her brows furrowed at his response. She was so confused. "I thought you said you didn't take offense to that though?"

"Yes, you're right I don't take offense to that. What I mean is we say *'females'* not women."

This time, she slightly hesitated, mid comb stroke, as a memory flashed through her mind of He-Who-Must-Not-

Be-Named shifting into a wolf before her eyes. And, yeah, she guessed she was going with the whole Harry Potter theme of do-not-speak-his-name, even in her thoughts.

"So, that wasn't a dream? I really saw him change into a wolf?" She swallowed as the nightmare crept back in.

"Maybe we should talk about this later," Blake prompted, smelling the subtle undertone of fear in her emotional layers.

"No. I want to know." Just like with the reflection thing, a part of her knew she should probably talk about it later. Yet, some other part of her wouldn't let this go. She turned her head to look at him once more to let her expression show him that she needed to do this.

He gave her an appraising look for a long moment before speaking. "No, that wasn't a dream. He's a wolf shifter," he answered her, keeping an attentive eye on her reaction. He was going to stop the conversation if either he or his wolf detected any distress at all.

She broke the gaze at his response and got back with the detangling of her rats' nest. This was going to take forever without a detangling product. Good. Because it gave her hands something to do while her mind was ruminating on the information that shattered the very nature of her existence—as if it wasn't already in tiny fragments at her feet.

"Like... you. You're a wolf too?"

"Yeah. I'm a wolf."

She paused for a heartbeat, working the comb through her hair.

"*What species are you, Caly?*" she heard *his* evil, psychotic voice ask in her mind.

"What... What am I? Am I human?" she dared to ask.

They were playing a game of Red Light, Green Light and this time, it was Blake's turn with the slight halt in the conversation.

"No, you're not human. You're species, Caly."

Species? "*What species are you, Caly?*" Again, she heard *his* voice in her mind and caught the same word: species.

"Species?" she asked while shyly hiding behind the blanket her tangled hair created. It gave her some sort of comfort to not be looking directly into Blake's eyes for this conversation.

"There are humans and then there are species," Blake answered.

Even though she wasn't looking directly at him she knew he was watching her closely.

"So, I'm... a wolf?" she asked, still confused.

"No, you're not a wolf," he said warmly with an amused, one-sided smile. She furrowed her brow in thought but before she could ask another question, he continued, "There are many different species that exist, Caly. Wolf shifters are one of them." He paused, unsure how to say that most of the monsters and myths in human culture were real. Well, to a certain extent.

"Like the whole 'aliens live among us' conspiracy theory?" she asked only half-joking because, at this point, anything was possible. Again, he had an amused curve of his lips.

"Species are not aliens from other planets. We have always lived here just like humans."

A million questions suddenly flooded her mind but she needed to refocus her thoughts and circle back to the questions that truly mattered in this moment.

"*What species are you, Caly?*" Again, she heard his evil voice in her mind.

"So, if I'm not human then what *species* am I?"

Never in a million years would she have ever thought she would be asking that question.

"You're a traveler."

"I'm a what?"

He chuckled. "You're a dream traveler. And a powerful one at that. I've known since you first pulled me into your dreams on the beach. Only powerful travelers have that ability, Caly." He paused and sharpened his senses to see how she was reacting to all of this.

She was quiet for a few long moments as she recalled the dreams with Blake, the dreams with GQ, and some other strange dreams she had experienced before. She knew everyone had weird dreams and she always thought hers were no different but now she wondered if her dreams actually were, in fact, different.

"How... How?" She couldn't seem to get out anything else other than the one-worded question.

"You're born this way. It's who you are. Just like humans are born humans. Species are born species." He wanted to reassure her that this was a normal part of biology.

She let that thought sink in for a moment. On some level, it made sense to her because there were so many different species of animals and plants in the world, so why couldn't there be other more sentient and intelligent species other than humans that existed too? She thought it was pretty arrogant of humans to cling to the belief that they were the most powerful; that they were the only ones.

"And we... I mean... humans don't know species exist?"

"No, humans don't know. And we keep it that way for our own safety and to maintain peace between us."

Unfortunately, that also made sense because she knew humans feared not only what was different but also, what threatened their power and status. She knew that they would probably experiment on species for their own advancement of science, technology, and power. It was no secret how they cruelly abused, treated, and tested on animals. She didn't have to stray too far in her imagination to see what would happen if humans knew that species existed. Her thoughts were cut off with his voice.

"Caly, the healer is here. Would you still like to see her?"

That flipped her thoughts to the present moment and Caly furrowed her brow. She didn't hear a knock at the door. But then again, her thoughts were so loud it probably just didn't register.

"Yes. Please."

Healer. He keeps using that word. It's probably just like how they don't say "women" but rather "females." So, they probably just say "healer" instead of "doctor," she thought, as Blake got up and opened the door a crack. She heard his voice and knew they exchanged a few words but she couldn't hear what was said.

Caly wasn't sure what she was expecting but it wasn't who walked in the room. First, she was expecting someone older. But the female was young and looked to be Caly's age. She had a professional yet cordial smile and she didn't seem to be anything like the fake LA women. She was naturally beautiful with blue eyes and blonde hair. She also came off as genuinely sweet and caring which matched her simple yet elegant style. Caly was also expecting someone in a white coat with their doctor's name sewn above the pocket and a stethoscope around their neck. But the doctor was wearing a loose white sweater, dark-wash skinny jeans, and stylish, black motorcycle boots that opened up above her ankle. Caly actually really liked her style and then remembered she looked like the Midol period model. Yup. She was really going to get Blake's attention looking like this. Though, it wasn't like she was trying to get his attention or anything. Okay fine, yes she was.

Stop, she told herself.

"Hi, Caly. I'm Aleia." Aleia's voice was calm and inviting as she sat in the chair Blake pulled up for her.

Again, Caly was expecting a formal "Hi. I'm Doctor

So-and-So." But she really liked Aleia's casual and calm approach. It was less intimidating than a formal doctor's visit.

"Hi." Caly smiled, putting down the comb on the bedside table. She would get back to the detangling of both her hair and her thoughts later.

"Blake, I'm sorry. I forgot my bag in the room. Would you mind grabbing it for me please?" Aleia asked with an apologetic look.

Blake looked at Aleia, then to Caly, and back to Aleia.

I mean, if this is a doctor that makes house calls, she is probably expecting a certain level of service, Caly thought to herself.

As soon as Blake shut the door behind him, Caly felt a little nervous about being alone with the doctor.

"Caly, Blake tells me that you would like him to stay in the room during the exam. I just want to make sure that's what you want and it's most comfortable for you."

Caly let out an exhale when she realized Aleia was just being a very thorough doctor. She could definitely see it from Aleia's perspective and how some women may be too scared to ask for what they need, including a private exam. Caly, really respected Aleia's call on this.

Points to Aleia, she thought.

"Yes, I want Blake here. I... I feel safe with him," Caly confessed, knowing how stupid she probably sounded.

"Okay. If at any time you want to be alone, just subtly pull on your right earlobe twice. And I will send Blake away without him knowing it was you." Aleia gave her a reassuring smile.

"Thanks." Caly returned the smile.

"You know, he never left your side since you were brought here."

Caly let that soak in for a moment. But before she could think too much into that (because, yeah, she would be thinking way too far into that), the door opened with Blake carrying a large black tote bag.

"Ah, thank you." Aleia smiled at Blake as he handed her the bag and then sat down next to Caly.

"Caly, are you okay with me checking your body to see how your healing is progressing?"

"Yes."

"Okay." Aleia nodded. "Please lie back on the bed and get comfortable."

Caly did as she was told and Aleia repositioned herself so that she was standing next to the bed.

"Don't you need me to…" Caly hesitated because she didn't want to but she knew it was probably coming next anyway. "Take these off to examine me?" Caly asked tugging on Blake's massive hoodie and sweats.

"Caly, have you ever had a session with a healer before?" Aleia asked with her professional smile.

"Umm… No, I haven't."

Sure, she had been to the doctor before but technically not a species healer. And technically both Blake and Aleia weren't human. Well, technically she wasn't either.

"Okay, not to worry. I will walk you through it, every step of the way." Aleia smiled at Caly and continued, "I am going to scan your body now, starting with your head down to your feet. It's really quick and you won't feel a thing."

Caly was half expecting to see Aleia pull out some sort of sci-fi futuristic device from her bag. Except Aleia simply hovered her right hand just above the crown of Caly's head.

"You are welcome to keep your eyes open or closed the entire time. Whatever is most comfortable for you," Aleia said, as her focus shifted slightly to the left in concentration.

Aleia's hovering hand traveled over Caly's body toward her feet. That was the moment when Caly knew that this was no ordinary doctor's exam and that the word *healer* did not mean doctor. Regardless, Aleia was right. Caly didn't feel a thing and it lasted only a matter of seconds as Aleia's hand scanned her body, slightly pausing at various points. Watching Aleia pause on her ankle, Caly winced at the horrific memory of how it broke. Both Blake and Aleia looked at Caly's reaction as if they could read her thoughts.

"Caly, is everything okay?" Aleia asked.

Caly's eyebrows raised a little in surprise and replied, "Yeah. I, umm, I just remembered..."

Blake gently touched Caly's shoulder to comfort her.

She exhaled and visibly relaxed with this warm touch.

"Your injuries are healing quite well and as expected. I picked up on some soreness. How is your body feeling?"

She picked up on my soreness? Nope. This isn't weird at all.

"Yes, I do feel really sore and stiff. Not painful but more like, you know, kind of like when you work out really hard and then you're really sore the next day."

"Mmhmm. Anything else?"

"No. My body feels... normal."

Normal for not being human, Caly thought.

"Good. I would like to do one more healing on you. It's not necessary but it will significantly speed up the final stretch of the recovery and relieve your body of the soreness and stiffness."

Caly had no idea what she was agreeing to but she trusted Blake and, so far, Aleia had been nothing but professional.

"Yes. I would like the healing please."

"Okay, Caly. Just like with the scanning it will not hurt at all. But this time, you may feel a little sensation. It's a little different for everyone but most often it's reported to feel slightly warm or tingly. Again, you are able to keep your eyes open or closed—whatever is most comfortable for you. And this will only take a couple of minutes. Did you have any questions before we begin?"

"Umm. No. I'm ready."

Ready for what? She didn't know. But she trusted Blake and, by extension, Aleia. Besides, Aleia was a healer. Caly wondered if healers also had a code of morals and ethics like human doctors did and also abided by the whole "do no harm" thing.

"Is it okay if I touch your arm?"

"Yes." Caly gave her consent.

Aleia lifted her hand, placed it on Caly's forearm over the thick fabric of the sweatshirt, and then, once again, gazed off to the left as she concentrated. This was something Caly had witnessed many nurses do over the years: redirect their focus as they concentrated.

Caly couldn't believe what she was looking at. She blinked. Yup. It was still there. Concentrated under Aleia's hand, was a glowing white light that had a hint of an aqua blue color. And Aleia was right. Caly felt a slight warming sensation flow through her body. It felt similar to how a bowl of hot soup on a cold day could warm up the body from the inside out. Caly was completely mesmerized and just stared, almost not believing what she was seeing and feeling. A few minutes went by quickly because before she knew it, the glowing was gone and Aleia refocused her eyes on Caly.

"That should do the trick." Aleia's hand reached behind Caly's shoulder to help her sit back up. "Please take it easy and rest to allow your body to recover fully. Caly, I'd like to check back in with you in the next couple of days just to make sure everything is going well. Will that be okay with you?"

"Yes. Thank you." Caly had no idea what had just happened. But she did know that so far, she liked Aleia.

"Sounds good."

Caly noticed Aleia looking at the comb on the bedside table.

"Female to female," Aleia began with a smile. "If you want, I always keep some hair oil and a brush on me. My hair is not as long as yours but I know that if I was just using that comb, it would take forever and be quite a battle."

"That would honestly be really helpful," Caly said with a slight chuckle.

Aleia reached in her bag and pulled out a travel-sized container of hair oil and a small brush. She placed them on the bedside table and then said, "Keep them. I have a whole stash at home because I travel a lot."

"Thanks, Aleia."

Yeah, so she really did like Aleia. And it wasn't just because of the hair oil. There was something about Aleia that just seemed genuine and caring to her core. It was refreshing to Caly after being surrounded by a sea of fake LA egos.

"You're welcome, Caly."

Shit! How are you going to pay for this?! House visits are not cheap. There's a reason why only the rich have concierge doctors, Caly thought, a little panicked.

"I... Umm..." Caly bit her lip. "How much do I owe you?"

Please don't be expensive. Please don't be expensive, Caly repeated as if she could chant the thought into reality.

"There's no charge."

"Wait, no charge? As in *nothing*?"

"Yes, as in nothing." Aleia smiled.

"No, I must repay you in some way. It's only... fair. I don't have a lot of money but—"

Aleia's smile softened a bit at Caly's consideration. "Caly, you're very nice and I truly appreciate your acknowledgment of the service exchange. But in this case, even if I wasn't Riordan's healer, I still wouldn't charge you. Speaking of,

I know Riordan would like to speak with you. But I will leave you two alone for now."

What Aleia didn't say was that she couldn't find it in her heart to charge Caly, considering everything that she went through and now knowing that Caly didn't have a lot of money. And not only that but helping Caly in this way was exactly what she always wanted to do: to use her healing gifts to make a difference and help those who were truly in need. Besides, as Riordan's healer, Aleia was financially secure and very well off. This didn't mean Aleia always gave free healings. No. It actually was very rare and she only offered it to those who were truly in need. The exchange for healing services, typically money for healing, was very important and considered sacred in the world of species. So, even when she did offer a free healing to someone in need, they would always find a way to repay the kindness and service in some way.

One time, Aleia healed a young boy and the family didn't have money, so the mother asked Aleia to stay for dinner. The mother prepared a warm, home-cooked meal that tasted of love in every bite. It was one of Aleia's cherished memories because she didn't have that growing up. Sure, she had a family and always had food on the table (their oversized table that always felt empty), but it was not the same. So, not only was experiencing a loving meal truly a fair trade in her eyes but also, she knew that by healing their son, she had given them the gift of his continued presence at the dinner table for an eternity of loving meals.

At the dinner, the boy shared how his mom told stories of their restaurant that was burned down in a fire and they didn't have enough money to start over. Aleia later found out that the family was screwed over by some wealthy bastard who loaned them the money to get the restaurant started. Even though the fire was not their fault and truly was a tragedy, that rich fucker ended the business deal and left them with nothing so they were barely scraping by. After finding that out, Aleia anonymously gifted the family some money to help get their restaurant back up and running. Every so often, Aleia visited their popular restaurant, Taste of Love, and checked up on the family. The family didn't know it was Aleia but the name of the restaurant and the warm welcome she always received when she stopped by, told her that they suspected that she was the anonymous donor. Aleia didn't care about taking the credit. The sheer love and joy this family spread to the world, through more than just their food, was what Aleia cared about.

Closing the door on those memories, Aleia brought her attention back to the present. Aleia would let Caly integrate for a couple of days and then bring up the option for the mind healer. She clicked the bedroom door behind her as she left.

Riordan's healer? Caly thought while exploring a way to express her gratitude for Aleia's help and generosity. Caly picked up the bottle of hair oil and examined it. It looked expensive and had a really pleasant naturally scented floral aroma.

Okay, so that was like incredibly nice of her, Caly thought as she worked the oil into the ends of her hair.

"I really like Aleia," Caly said to Blake, brushing out her hair. "And not just because of the hair gifts. She seems so genuine and caring. Like, you know when she asked you to get her bag?"

"Yeah," Blake said with a curiously amused look.

"I think she left her bag on purpose. After you left, she asked me if I wanted you to be present during the healing. That was when I knew she was no ordinary doctor... er, 'healer' ...because no ordinary doctor would be that attentive and caring. Well, that and the fact that she is no

ordinary human doctor with her hands glowing at all."
Caly attempted for another joke as she tried to wrap her
mind around all of this.

Blake chuckled. "I knew something was up when she
asked but she played that off very well."

"So, I'm just going to say this. A doctor is not the same
as a healer." She laughed a little.

"No, not in the human sense." Blake chuckled. "Although, species healers do go through medical training and
schooling and some like to be addressed formally as doctor."

"Do you know her very well?" Okay. Caly was fishing a
little to know about what his relationship was with Aleia.
But she also wanted to know more about her so she could
get an idea of how to get a thank you gift that Aleia would
like.

"No, not really. I just met her a couple days ago with
Riordan." Blake smiled inwardly as he caught the scent of
Caly's bait, fishing for his status with Aleia. And both he
and his wolf liked it.

"Hmmm…" Caly pursed her lips, trying to play it cool as
if she wasn't relieved to hear that.

Blake's inward smile widened because he could read his
Caly like a book. And she was *his*.

"I'd like to gift Aleia something to express my gratitude
for her healing me. I know she said I don't owe her anything
but I just have to say thank you in some way. It wouldn't
feel right otherwise."

Okay, maybe he couldn't read her as well as he thought
because he wasn't expecting that. But both he and his wolf
approved of her kind heart.

"I think that Aleia would appreciate that. Ask Riordan
when you speak with him."

Before she could ask who Riordan was, her stomach
growled so loud she knew Blake heard it. She was about to

apologize but Blake spoke in a matter of fact tone that she just knew he wouldn't budge on.

Your female is hungry, Blake thought as he heard Caly's stomach growl. *Way to go Blake. You're racking up quite a score. No clothes, toothbrush, hairbrush, hair oil—whatever the fuck that is—and no food. Male of the year over here.*

"I'll bring you some food. You can finish up your hair and rest. No one will come in here except me."

Caly exhaled. "Blake?"

"Yeah, Caly?"

This call and response apparently was kind of their thing.

"Thank you... for... everything."

Oh god. Do not cry again, she commanded her body to dry up the teary wells.

Blake wrapped his arms around her in a warm embrace. "You're welcome. Rest. I'll be right back with some food. What do you feel like?"

"Anything is fine," she said. And at this moment? It was the honest truth. Because in Blake's arms, she just knew that everything was going to be okay.

Chapter 23

Blake saw an orange nerf football spiral through the air. In a very practiced motion, the twins were throwing the ball back and forth with Felix coaching on the sidelines, or rather, next to Rhyker on their shared couch. Rhyland leaned farther back in the La-Z-Boy leather chair and the angle almost had his feet propped up higher than heart level. The orange football was on a sudden surprise trajectory straight for Deacon, who was currently preoccupied with Riordan, as they reviewed something on one of his projected imaging screens.

They were probably trying to gather any and all information and possibilities regarding Caly's unknown ability, The Ghost's possible whereabouts, The Mastermind, or even what the hell the dark liquid portal could be. Unfortunately, they were running into a whole lotta nothing new. Double unfortunately, knowing what they all knew about The Ghost's carefully calculating MO, plus the fact that The Ghost was severely injured by Blake, it was unlikely that he would strike again so soon.

The males of The Order learned long ago, two important things. First, they each played their part in a hunt and, right now, it was a time for Deacon to work his computer magic to see if he could gather anything else on The Ghost. Second, there were almost always inevitable lulls in the hunt. And during those lulls, it was important to continue to live life even when loose ends were yet to be tied. So, it wasn't that they were dismissing the very real threat of The Ghost by appearing to casually lounge around. No. Not even close. It was that they were celebrating their safe capture of Caly and continuing to live life even while still in pursuit of their target. And, right now, their money was on The Ghost licking his wounds in the defeat of this round. All the while, they figured he would be watching and planning from the shadows, just waiting for the perfect time to strike... And when that time occurred? All of the males would be more than ready to end this, once and for all.

Aleia, who was curled up on the other recliner with a blanket and a pillow, gasped at the inevitable "Deacon's head meets football" action that was about to happen. In a blur of movement, Nico intercepted the football just before impact.

Maybe Nico was enjoying Aleia's shocked reaction a little too much. And the way she was looking at him, as if he was a star NFL running back, wasn't helping calm his ego. In fact, it seemed to have the opposite effect and his chest may have puffed out a bit as he threw the ball at Rhyland.

"Didn't know you were the type of male to stash away your female," Rhyland quipped, passing the ball to Blake. Rhyland was only teasing because he knew that Caly needed time to integrate her entire world flipping on its axis.

Without missing a beat, Blake caught the football and had it sailing through the air so fast back at Rhyland that the orange blur made a high pitched whistle sound.

Rhyland caught the damn thing but the sheer force of the impact sent him and the chair over backward. Several laughs peeled out, with Rhyland leading the laugh parade, as he remained tumbled-over on the ground.

With the sudden cacophony of noise between the nerf missile, couch crash, and boom of laughter, Felix's ears were turned back on high alert, making him look like a horned owl.

Rhyker scooped Felix up in his arms to offer comfort.

Being a true healer, Aleia noticed Felix's reaction. It was like a homing beacon to her healer soul to offer comfort and aid. She got up, sat down on the couch next to Rhyker and pet Felix with her fingertips glowing a soft red. Felix would soon get used to all of the noises this pack of unconventional and rowdy males inevitably brought but she could at least offer him some temporary relief.

"Seriously though, how is she?" Rhyland asked Blake, as he righted the recliner.

Although Aleia had told everyone that Caly would make a full recovery, she didn't discuss anything more due to patient confidentiality.

Blake blew out a breath. "She's taking it surprisingly well, considering everything." Blake looked at Nico as they both thought about the first time they attempted to let Caly know she wasn't human. "But she's not ready to see anyone just yet," Blake said, glancing over at Riordan who nodded. "And she's hungry."

"That's my kind of female." Rhyland winked.

"Order pizza," Blake dished out the order to Rhyland, who decided to volunteer for the task by opening his trap. Blake decided on pizza because he remembered Rhyland telling him that Caly ordered pizza during his watch.

"Pizza." Rhyland's expression emulated the heart-eyed emoji. "Good call." He proceeded to take orders.

With that taken care of, Blake opened the fridge and saw the leftover sandwich stuff. He and his wolf decided that would be good for now until the pizza arrived. He didn't know what Caly liked so he just loaded a plate with everything and grabbed the condiments.

"Don't forget the chips," Rhyker called out.

"And an extra plate with napkins," Rhyland added.

"And a knife," Rhyker concluded.

It was definitely not their first bedroom sandwich rodeo by far and Blake was glad for their input because he wouldn't have thought of those things.

As Blake walked down the hall, with his hands full of a promise for an epic sandwich picnic, Felix jumped off of the couch and joined him to check on Caly. Blake went to knock, only to realize he couldn't because his hands were full. When he was about to use his foot to tap on the door, Felix meowed, waited for a beat, and then meowed again.

Clever cat, Blake thought, suppressing a grin. He decided not to announce his presence to surprise Caly. It was his playful wolf nature. He couldn't help it.

Caly was just working out the last of the knots in her hair when she thought she heard Felix meow. She paused because she always knew he meowed twice when he wanted to be let in her room. This wasn't her room but she figured the same principle applied. And apparently, she was right because then she heard his second meow. Smiling, she got up and opened the door only to stiffen for a beat before laughing at the sight of Blake with a playful grin and his arms full of food. Felix padded past her as if he didn't just partake in the mini surprise. She had a feeling she had to keep an eye on these two.

Shutting the door behind Blake, they made their way to the dark leather couch where he set out all of the food on the wooden coffee table. He arranged it like he was making her an offering as if he was trying to impress her. It kind of reminded her of that one time she binge-watched Animal

Planet all day and saw those male birds that would attract females by building a nest full of elaborate offerings. Except no. This was not that. Even though she secretly admitted wanting it to be. Okay, they may have slept together but that didn't mean Blake was building her a fucking nest of offerings for crying out loud.

Hell, he may not even be interested in you. He's just being nice and helping you because of everything that happened.

Her stomach growled, as if in protest of her thoughts, and she got back with the program.

"Thank you." She smiled and grabbed the plate, examining the robust array of sandwich makings. *Avocado? Yum!* She loved avocado on sandwiches. Well, truthfully she loved avocado on just about anything really. "Are you going to eat too?"

"I may have some but we're also ordering pizza. What kind of pizza do you like?" he asked, trying not to make it obvious that he was noting everything she put on her sandwich, including that she was a fan of both mayo and mustard.

"I'm good with anything really." She didn't want to be a nuisance and she was honestly grateful for just about everything at this point.

"No. Tell me. I want to know what your favorite pizza is," Blake said in a tone that was nice but firm, indicating that he wasn't going to let this go.

"Okay," she chortled out. "I like meat lovers' with extra olives." She paused. "I know it's kind of weird but really anything is fine. You can't really go wrong with pizza... Except for pineapples." She wrinkled her nose and Blake smirked. "I don't know how anyone likes that on their pizza. Oh, and anchovies." She made a slightly playful face of disgust and he chuckled. "Oh god, don't tell me you're a 'Hawaiian pizza with extra pineapple' kinda man?" she teased.

Both he and his wolf enjoyed her teasing and it told him she was a strong female for being able to handle everything with a playful smile.

"No, I'm a meat lovers' kind of male too. I haven't had it with olives before though. So, I'll give that a try."

While she was building her sandwich, he discreetly took out his phone and texted the order to Rhyland.

Male. Not "man," Caly corrected herself. *He's not human. Hell, you're not human.*

With that thought, her mind was once again flooded with so many questions. She took a glorious bite of sandwich and savored the flavors. It was the first time she ate since...

"Blake?"

"Yeah, Caly?"

"Why am I here?"

Blake blew out a breath and put his phone back in his pocket. "I'll start at the beginning. And maybe you can fill in the parts we don't know."

Caly nodded.

Felix jumped up on the couch, looking like he was going to curl up on her lap but plotted a new course when he saw the open real estate of Blake's lap.

"Before you say anything," she cut in with a smile as she watched Blake pet Felix. "Thanks for taking care of Felix. It—" She paused trying to swallow back the emotions and the sandwich. "He means the world to me. So, thank you."

"Of course. You might be interested to know that he didn't waste any time staking his claim on Rhyker's couch," he said with a half-smile.

"That sounds like him. There's a reason why I had to buy another sofa chair. He decided to claim my chair as his... which quickly became known as the 'hair chair,' " she chortled, figuring she would find out who Rhyker was soon enough. There was a slightly awkward silence when their chuckles subsided. She was waiting for Blake to explain everything.

"Eat," Blake said and didn't start talking until she started eating her sandwich. "As you know, I'm with Orion's Order. The Order is my pack. We are hunters." He hesitated. "We hunt the evil in the world."

A flash of Caly's horror went through her mind and she swallowed. Suddenly, her throat was dry.

As if Blake knew the desert ecosystem in her throat, he grabbed the water bottle, twisted the cap off and handed it to her.

"We were hired by SILE or Species Intelligence and Law Enforcement, for..." He hesitated as if calculating what to say.

"Tell me. I need to know, Blake. I need to know why I'm here." It was the same thing as with the mirror reflection. A part of her thought this was a bad idea but a stronger part of her mind was now adamant about knowing everything.

After a long appraising look, Blake continued, "We were hired to hunt James Barker AKA The Ghost."

Images of the horrific nightmare filled her mind as if she was a projector playing a silent film.

No, she commanded her mind to stop the film. *I will not let him win. I am safe. I am the fucking Phoenix.*

Blake brought Caly up to speed on everything. He shared how they found The Ghost in LA and that he was stalking her, which was why Nico was in her room that night. He shared about how they kept watch over her and by the time they got back from investigating The Ghost's most recent murder, she was taken.

"I knew something was wrong the second I was at your

place… and then I scented another shifter and I knew you were taken."

Finally, he let her know about Riordan's vision leading them to her, getting her out, how The Ghost escaped, and Aleia healing her.

Statue. Caly was a statue and she needed a moment to let all of this soak in. She let the cool water slide down her throat as she hit the pause button on her life.

When she resumed, she filled in her side of the story. She shared with Blake about the first dream, with who she guessed must've been Riordan, and how she crashed into The Ghost's car. She shared about how she saw him at The Drip and that he asked her out.

How could I have gone out with a psychopathic killer?

Caly's stomach lurched at the thought, putting up a good fight to eject the sandwich. She managed to keep it down though. Even though she was embarrassed and ashamed, she let Blake know that she willingly got into the car with him and how he drugged her. She only hesitated when it came to her torturous nightmare.

"You don't have to share anything you don't want to, Caly," Blake reassured her.

"I know. I want to share this with you."

For whatever reason, she felt safe with Blake and she trusted him. She shared what she remembered, even the horrific torture.

"I don't remember everything. I think that the drugs messed with my memories and… Well, let's just say I'm glad I don't remember everything."

Blake's wolf was pacing, with his lips curled back, baring his fangs at what The Ghost did to Caly. He was barely keeping it together and vowed he would fucking kill that evil bastard and avenge Caly.

"I do remember one time when he went to hit me," Caly confessed.

Blake bit back a growl as his face darkened impossibly more.

"At the time, I could have sworn there was some sort of energetic field around me blocking his punches. But it didn't last long."

Now she knew that was real because of what Blake told her about the force field in the car during her rescue.

"After that he... he was manic and demanded to know what species I was. I was so messed up on the drugs that I didn't know what was real and what wasn't. He was so convinced that I wasn't human. And then there was the force field and the dreams... So, there was a part of me that thought maybe he was right. But then another part of me just thought I was hallucinating everything from the drugs. Towards the end though, I... I thought that you weren't real and you were something my mind subconsciously made up as a coping mechanism. And right as I heard the cement door opening for that final time, I thought that was him and I..." Her voice cracked and her eyes began to water. "I knew I couldn't go on any longer. I thought I was about to die," she confessed in a wavering whisper.

"I'm here," Blake said, pulling her close to his chest and that was all it took for the floodgates to open once more. "You're safe."

And she believed him down to the very core of her soul.

When her tears were dry and she could once again breathe in a slow and steady rhythm, she asked, "Blake?"

"Yeah, Caly?"

Her head was still pressed against his chest and she liked the sound and feel of the deep vibrations in his chest when he spoke. It was soothing.

Please don't ask me to leave, she thought.

"I don't want to go back to my apartment," she confessed, praying that there was some sort of witness protection or something.

Blake blew out a breath in preparation for dropping another bomb on Caly. He wanted to say, *"You're not going anywhere because you're mine."*

"You're not going back," he said, feeling her let out a shaky breath in response. "The human police were called by your neighbor to report that your door looked like it was broken into. They showed up at your work and confirmed that you didn't show. In the eyes of the humans, you're a 'missing persons' case. And it will stay that way. Caly, you can't go back to the human world probably for at least fifty to a hundred years. You can't have the risk of being seen and identified."

"Wait, what? Human world? Fifty to a hundred *years*?!"

She pushed away from his chest and looked into his golden eyes to see if he was joking. Nope. His expression told her that he was dead serious.

"I promise it will go by quicker than you think," he chuckled.

She shot up and started pacing.

"That's my whole life! And what do you mean by *human* world? I thought you said species live among humans without them knowing?"

Blake's lips curved and then he started laughing. It was the first time she heard him laugh like this and she liked it. Except for the part where she didn't find this funny at all.

"You think this is funny?!" she said incredulously.

"I'm sorry, Caly," he said, still slightly amused. "There is something else important you need to know. Species are immortal. You're immortal."

She froze mid-step and almost fell over with that news.

"I'm... what?"

"You're immortal. Well, you will be. You haven't gone through your change yet."

"My what?"

"Your change. The time in all species' lives when their immortality sets in. It's different for everyone but it's around twenty-five to thirty years old. You will be going through your change soon."

"What do you mean by immortal?" She wanted to make sure she had the same definition and understood things correctly. After all, the last time she made an assumption, the "doctor" wound up having glowing hands.

"Species do not age. We can still be killed but we can potentially live forever," he said matter of factly, as though it was just another fact about biology. Because, to him, it was just another fact about biology.

She stood there in the middle of the room still as a statue, looking at her arms as if she had never seen them before.

Live forever? she thought, almost unable to comprehend the reality.

"Wait. What's the change?"

"It's a little different for everyone but I'm going to be honest and let you know it's intense and during the peak it's..." He paused. "Painful. Your body chemistry is changing on a cellular level. But healers can ease the pain and you can even choose to sleep through it if you want. Aleia has already agreed to assist you during your change if you'd like."

"She has?"

"Yeah. She's the one who discovered that you haven't been through your change yet when she was healing you initially. It's actually why you needed a couple healing sessions from her. Some subspecies, like me, have fast, natural healing abilities and only rarely need a healer. Other subspecies, like you, will still heal but at a slower rate and will, more often than not, seek out healers. Well, at least once you go through your change. Before the change, species haven't fully matured, which includes their species healing and so you have a really slow healing rate that's about the same as humans." There was a pregnant pause. "And to answer your question about species living among humans without them knowing? Yeah, that's true. Humans don't know about us and one big reason is because of The Barrier."

He explained what The Barrier was, why it was created, and how humans were unable to cross it unless accompanied by species.

Caly let all of this soak in and was sad to find out that her previous thoughts about humans turning on species were true.

"You said I'm a traveler? What does that even mean?"

"A traveler, or dream traveler, is a part of a subset of seers. Seers have the ability of foresight. And some have other additional rare abilities like backsight."

"So, I'm not a seer?" Caly asked, trying to grasp what this all meant.

"Not unless you have the ability to see the future or see in the past... and it would be extremely rare to have strong abilities of both seer and traveler. However, not impossible. There are some seers who may have small scale traveler abilities and vice versa. But usually, the non-primary ability is so minuscule that it doesn't really do much."

"Okay, that kinda makes sense," Caly said, feeling like she was actually kind of following along. "And no, I don't have that ability that I know of, and I would presume I would know if I was seeing the future." She managed a little laugh. "But what about the force field?"

"That we don't know. Caly, that's not an ability of a traveler... that we know of at least." He didn't want to scare her but she needed to know what he was about to say. "You must protect that secret with your life and be extremely careful who you wish to share that ability with. Even in the species world, there are those who would use your abilities for their own gain without regard for your life, especially if they knew you had a rare and unknown ability. My pack, Riordan, and Aleia have all sworn an oath of secrecy to guard your ability."

He left off the reminder about how The Ghost knew of her ability because that conversation could wait until she had a good grasp on everything. He didn't want to scare her, on top of everything else he was dumping on her.

"I understand." She nodded, wanting to continue this conversation but she had to pee from all of the water she was drinking to wash down the information overload. "I want to know more about... everything, really, but I'm going to use the bathroom first." She shot him a sheepish smile.

"Of course. Are you ready to speak with Riordan?" Blake asked, lifting Felix off of his lap and relocating him to the couch. "No rush. I just know he has more information to share with you."

"Actually, yes, I think I am. I want to know if Riordan is the man... I mean, male..." Caly corrected herself and he smirked. "I need to get used to saying that. Anyways, the male of my dreams." She blushed. "Wait. That came out wrong." She laughed awkwardly and tried to recall that embarrassing mistake but it was too late. The verbal email had been sent and delivered with no option to recall the thing—not like the recall button ever worked anyway... "*From* my dream."

Way to go, Caly. Number one flirt right here, she internally chided on a sarcastic beat.

"I'll go get Riordan." Blake chuckled.

"Okay," Caly said, opening the bathroom door. All

thoughts of embarrassment vanished and she froze as soon as she saw the pile of dirty and bloody fabric.

Seeing her stiffen, Blake appeared right behind her to see what caused her reaction. He saw the bloody pile and inwardly cursed.

"I'll take care of that," he said in a reassuring tone.

"No." Caly's tone was firm.

I am the fucking Phoenix, she thought.

"I want to... burn them."

It didn't really register how that might sound until after it came out of her mouth. Well, wasn't she a catch? The Midol period girl with a pyro fetish searching for the male of her dreams.

"Tomorrow we'll build a fire and you can burn them," he said without hesitation or even a trace of judgment.

Caly wanted to cry all over again. Not because of the pile of bloody nightmare that lay in front of her. No. It was because Blake not only didn't question her crazy but offered unwavering support to partake in the crazy.

As if he could read her thoughts, he wrapped his arms around her from behind and pulled her close to his body.

"Tomorrow," he reassured her. He walked into the bathroom, grabbed the pile, and walked out.

Clicking the bathroom door shut behind her, she reassured herself with a single thought. *Tomorrow.*

Chapter 24

Sinking into Blake's leather couch cushion, Caly noticed Blake had cleared away the food when she was in the bathroom. He had also moved the chair that Aleia used earlier so it was facing the couch.

Probably for Riordan, she concluded, since it would have been kind of awkward to try and have a conversation while sitting side by side on the couch. The corner of her mouth curved when she heard Felix snoring on the cushion next to her.

"Hey, panther boy," she said, running her fingers through his black silk. "How are you doing with all of this?"

Felix yawned and kick-started his purring motor in response.

Well, I'll take that as you approve of Blake, she thought with a smile.

Her head swiveled to the door when a gentle knock sounded. She made like one of those statue street performers and froze mid-stroke down Felix's back. Why she always acted like she was wanted for murder when someone knocked at her door unexpectedly? She didn't know.

"Caly?" She heard Blake's voice accompanied by another gentle knock.

"Come in," she called out in a tentative voice, shaking out of the statue performance. The door opened to reveal Blake and GQ.

It was surreal to finally be standing face to face with the other male in her dreams. And she had to admit, even with the slight heads up, she was still a little surprised that he looked just as he did in her dreams. But considering that Blake looked the same as he did in her dreams, why wouldn't GQ also look the same?

He was tall, she guessed just over six feet but her perceptual scale was skewed with Blake's NBA player stature in comparison. Riordan had this air of sophistication and strength. And not the macho, muscled kind of strength like the alpha wolf standing next to him. He certainly had a toned physique, just not bulked-up Brawny lumberjack status. His strength was twofold. A part of it was in the way he held himself in those expensive black slacks and fine-threaded, dark blue button-up that was rolled up the forearms. But mainly, the strength was in his jade green eyes. Looking into those eyes felt like looking into the starry night sky: full of depth, mystery, and all of the secrets of the Universe.

"I just know he has more information to share with you." Caly recalled Blake's previous words. *I bet he does,* Caly thought, unable to help stargazing into those orbs of wisdom.

"Hello, Caly. I'm Riordan Knight," he said, breaking the silence with his soothing Irish accent that wrapped around her in a gentle welcome.

"Hi." Caly smiled and stuck her hand out for a formal shake.

Riordan's eyes softened a touch and his lips curved in amusement at the gesture.

Recognizing the awkward moment, Caly went to pull her

hand away, slightly embarrassed at what appeared to be a species social faux pas, but before she could glue the thing to her side, Riordan's palm met hers. And just like that, handshakes were added to her ever-growing mental list of questions she was going to ask Blake.

"Umm..." Her go-to filler word naturally took center stage as she tried to understand why they were all standing as if waiting for something.

Handshakes and greetings, she thought, amending the mental list.

"Should we sit?" she asked, not really sure what else to say or do.

"Please," Riordan said, maintaining his amused expression.

The second Caly's backside met the couch cushion, the males joined in with the sitting situation. Riordan sat in the chair while Blake parked it on the cushion next to her.

Were they waiting for you to sit? she thought, bumping the handshakes and greetings up a few spots. If so, this was a little more formal of a meeting than she was expecting. *Then again, Riordan doesn't really seem like the type to do anything informal,* she internally guessed based on Riordan's suave demeanor. *Still, a heads up would've been nice, Blake,* she thought, noticing how even he seemed to be playing along with the formalities.

"Caly, I have some matters I wish to discuss that are private in nature," Riordan prompted.

She could read between the lines and the subtext clearly stated that Blake was the elephant in the room, and it had nothing to do with his size. Well, Blake was staying. So, anything GQ had to say he could say.

"Please share," Caly said, reaching over and giving Blake's hand a quick squeeze in silent confirmation she wanted him to stay. Just as quick as her hand made contact with his, it was back on her lap.

Okay, so that was incredibly bold of her and she didn't know where that came from. Hell, she didn't even know if it was okay to grab Blake's hand like that. But whatever, it was already done.

Blake was already mentally preparing to be excused from the room when Riordan made the subtle hint about Blake's presence for this discussion. Both he and his wolf didn't want to leave but he had no official claim on Caly. And even if he did, whatever Riordan was going to share was still her personal information and he would respect her privacy. When Caly suddenly squeezed his hand and announced she wanted him to stay, both he and his wolf wanted to howl in approval of her display of trust in him. Despite not knowing what Riordan was about to share, she chose to learn about it with him.

Without hesitation, he slid his hand into Caly's and echoed her gentle squeeze. But instead of pulling back as she did, he kept their palms pressed together. In his peripheral vision, he caught Caly's closed-lipped smile at his unexpected gesture.

Holding hands. They were holding hands. Caly suddenly had a million thoughts in her mind and none of them were regarding Riordan. No. Not even close. Her mind was hyper-focused on Blake's warm palm against hers. Later. She would think about all this later. And maybe she wasn't as skilled with reading between the lines as she thought because her mind was desperately grasping at a correct translation as to what holding hands with Blake meant.

She noticed Riordan's eyes flick to their clasped hands momentarily before refocusing on Caly. She swore she saw the barest hint of amusement in his green globes. God, she could only imagine how teenage they must've looked, sitting there holding hands for the first time.

"Caly, are you able to tell me about your parents?" Riordan spoke into the silence… the silence that seemed to be speaking a whole lot.

She swallowed. Okay, so she was not expecting the conversation to take a sudden sharp turn down the road she tried to never go down. A road that had big, red warning signs like "Danger," "Do Not Enter," and "Turn Back."

As if Blake could read her thoughts, he gave her hand a supportive squeeze.

"Umm, yes, of course," Caly answered, drawing strength from Blake's hand in order to continue the conversation. She took a breath and said, "My parents were Aaron and Irene Smith. They passed away four years ago in a freak car accident."

God, how she missed her parents. She missed the way her father used to pull her in for his hugs that would give a bear a run for his money. She missed the way her mother used to tuck her hair behind her ear, as she gazed into Caly's eyes with such adoration and love in a way only a mother could. She allowed herself to surf the wave of a memory that picked that moment to surface.

"You look so much like both of your parents. Like you know how I look like my mom but got my coloring from my dad? You look like a blend of both. Except, your eyes of course. Which are so cool BT-dubs." Rachel, her chatty high school friend, who was desperate to be noticed by the popular crowd, said to her when they were working on a biology class project about genotypes and phenotypes. *"Ginny, you know, skinny Ginny from third period? She swears that you wear contacts. She's just jealous in my opinion and—"*

For whatever reason, it never really dawned on Caly before that moment just how much she really did look like a blend of her parents—other than her eye and hair color.

When she asked her parents about the color discrepancy, she found out that her mother actually had dark hair like Caly's but she chose to dye it blonde. She never understood why her mom preferred it blonde but whatever, to each their own. And as far as her eye color? No, her parents didn't wear colored contacts or anything. Instead, her parents said her gray eyes were unique and that they shined bright just like the beautiful diamond she was.

Blinking. She was blinking back tears while she surfed the last of the memory wave to shore when a question popped into her mind.

"Is it common for humans to have species... children?" she asked Riordan, unsure if "children" was even the right word. She also wasn't sure if she would ever get used to the fact that she was no longer included in the human category.

Both Blake and Riordan stiffened in response.

Okay, if they didn't already have her attention then, that certainly would've done it. She shifted slightly at the depth of Riordan's gaze. She couldn't even imagine what it would be like to see into the future. To see things that should only be recalled as memories. Yeah, good thing she didn't inherit the seer part of her family tree or she might have gone crazy. Well, crazier than the crazy Caly she already was at least.

"No, Caly. It isn't," Riordan answered, leaving off the part about how species beget species young. Well, except for the extremely rare case of a successful, full-term pregnancy between a human and specian. The genetics between the two just weren't all that compatible. So, although it was possible that Caly was of mixed heritage, it was extremely unlikely. Especially when Riordan considered two additional factors. The first factor was the sheer strength of Caly's abilities. The strength, traveling, and force field did not coincide with the diluted, and often weakened, abilities of a human halfling. Second, she reminded him of someone, which was one reason why he wanted to find out more about her parents. He decided not to divulge on the details of that whole topic since now was the time for a different conversation entirely.

"Do you have any legal guardians?" Riordan inquired, steering the conversation back on course.

Legal guardians? I'm an adult, right? Caly thought, only to remember what Blake said about how the change was the time when immortality set in. She wondered if that was the equivalent to species reaching full maturity, cellularly speaking at least.

"Umm, no. It's just me," Caly said tentatively, unsure where he was going with this exactly.

Riordan nodded. "Since you do not have any parents or legal guardians, I have been charged by the Seer Council as your Primary to teach you the ways of species and the seers, including being a traveler."

She and Blake suddenly were twinning on the frozen ice sculpture front. And, yeah, they were still holding hands.

Okay, so apparently Blake wasn't expecting this bomb to drop either, she thought, not knowing what a Primary was but the gist was formulating in her mind from the legal guardian prompting. But she wasn't about to make another rookie mistake by assuming something meant one thing when in reality it had glowing hands and was healing her like she was in a sci-fi movie. Because, yeah, apparently that was her life now too. But before she could clarify, Riordan continued on.

"You have the choice to accept this or not. However, you should know that if you do not accept, then you will fall in the hands of the Seer Council and at that point, your future will be completely up to them, where you will not have a choice in the matter, including who will be your Primary. And there are those who would like nothing more than to have you under their control."

A minute. She needed a hot minute to think. She tried to think through the situation but no matter how she looked at it, it was still like dry swallowing a giant horse pill that had a bitter aftertaste of something that Blake said to her, not even a half-hour ago. *"You must protect that secret with your life and be extremely careful who you wish to share that ability with."*

Apparently, Riordan didn't hear the timeout whistle because he kept on going, "Caly, if you accept my offer, then know I will treat you fair and with respect, just as I would my own young. But you also must know that it will not be easy. There will be extensive training and schooling in order to give you the best chance of survival in the world of species. I will test your limits and then push you past them. Aleia and I will be leaving soon but you have three days to make a decision as I must report back to the Seer Council by then."

Finally, Riordan seemed to be done with his mini monologue that had her mind reeling. Forget the horse pill because her throat suddenly felt as if she swallowed cinnamon powder. And, hey, Blake's must've felt the same too because he grabbed the bottle of water from the table and took a pull. Which was a good idea. So, Caly followed suit with sipping some water, hoping that would help clear her thoughts somehow. It didn't. But one thing did manage to filter through.

"Are you Aleia's Primary as well?" Caly asked.

From what she saw, Aleia seemed happy and well taken care of. So, maybe she could ask Aleia what it would be like.

"No, I am not her Primary. Aleia is my healer. Although, I do care for her as one of my own." He smiled fondly at the thought. "If you were to accept, you would become a part of the Knight bloodline and be under my legal guardianship.

As your Primary, I would also be responsible for your basic learning and development. A Primary typically functions as a mentor or teacher to help younger species learn and train as they grow into their abilities. They can also act as a legal guardian figure. Although, that function of a Primary is a bit more rare in modern times."

Caly was beginning to see the picture more clearly. In the eyes of species, she was like a child in the sense of not knowing anything about her heritage, abilities, and the world she belonged in. Riordan was effectively offering to take her under his wing. And, yeah, what did that say about him? A whole lot. Because she couldn't even imagine if the roles were reversed. It was essentially like adopting a full-grown adult who had been living under a rock her whole life. So, she did not take what Riordan was offering lightly by any means. But at the moment, she felt as if there was a hose in her mouth and someone turned the water flow on full blast. She was officially on information overload and her brain was starting to shut down.

"I… I'm not sure what to say." Caly chose to be candid.

Riordan smiled. "There's no need to say anything. I understand this is a lot to take in and I want to make sure you have time to think through all of this. This is a big decision, Caly."

"Thank you, Mr. Knight." Caly went with the formal name because this whole conversation seemed formal and she didn't want to offend him.

"Please, call me Riordan," he said with a softness in his eyes at her formality. "There is something else I would like to discuss with you."

"Umm, sure," Caly said, wondering what else in the world needed to be discussed because, as far as she knew, the whole "Primary" thing pretty much took the cake and then some.

"I would like to teach you something about dream traveling. Blake tells me that you're able to pull him into your dreams?"

"Yes, the beach with the cave. It's always the same," she responded curiously.

"This is your *soul sanctuary* or your inner safe place. Every traveler has their own unique dream space that serves as a sanctuary. Only those that you specifically bring there are allowed to travel there. For you, it appears to be a beach with a cave."

My own cave. Caly's Cave. Oh, I like that. It has a nice ring to it.

"How was I able to pull Blake into my dreams if I didn't even know him?" Caly asked with a furrowed brow.

"Very keen of you." Riordan gave an approving smile. "Let's just say I may have gently *nudged* you in the right direction."

Again, Riordan chose not to divulge the details on this subject. There were things that he wasn't sharing, including that he had a vision of Caly and Blake together. But he had secrets of his own that he wished to remain as secrets.

Okay. Clearly, that's all you're getting on that subject for now, Caly thought, and then wondered if Aleia also got cryptic answers from Riordan, which reminded her...

"Riordan?"

"Yes, Caly."

"Blake told me about how your vision helped find me. Thank you."

He nodded in that warm way of his.

"I would also like to thank Aleia and give her a gift to show my gratitude for healing me. She said I don't owe her anything and it was already taken care of as your healer but I still want to say thank you in some way. Are you able to tell me about what she likes or if she has any hobbies? I'd like my gift to be meaningful."

Riordan's eyes softened once more as he looked at Caly. There was a subtle hint of a smile that said he knew something. Well, wasn't that his freaking theme song.

"What would you like if it were you?" Riordan inquired.

Okay. Not what she was expecting but she would play along.

"Umm… Well, some of my favorite gifts are herbal teas and books. But—" Caly stopped mid-sentence, seeing his knowing smile and realizing that was all she was getting on the subject.

So, teas and books, she thought. Again, definitely not what she was expecting but then again, what did she know? If anyone knew what Aleia would like, it would be Riordan.

Immediately, a gift for Aleia was formulating in her mind—which included some really nice, high quality, floral tea. She guessed she would like it because of the naturally scented floral hair oil.

Oh, and maybe a tea mug too, Caly thought, concluding that if Aleia liked tea, then she probably felt the same way that Caly did about not ever having too many tea mugs. Caly needed to think about which books to gift. Books were such a personal thing and as such, they could be a hit or miss gift, especially if you didn't know the recipient all that well. Well, she had some time to think about this at least. Besides, she would need to ask Blake how to arrange for all of this exactly.

Does my credit card even work over here? Hell, do they even use human money?

Caly suddenly had a strange thought of a male shop clerk with blue skin behind the shop counter giving her a weird look when she tried to hand him some green bills with pictures of old dead guys on the front. Okay, yeah, she seriously needed to tap out and—

"Caly." Riordan's voice thankfully shook her out of that weird scene playing in her mind. "If there's nothing else right now, then Aleia and I will be leaving shortly. But I will be in touch with you soon. Blake has my contact information if you would like to speak with me sooner though."

With that, Riordan rose from the chair. When Blake also stood, Caly followed suit, thinking it was some sort of formal meeting dismissal or something.

"Caly," Riordan said, with a single nod of his head and then repeated the motion with Blake before he walked out and shut the door behind him.

Mush. Her brain was officially mush and went on an automatic shutdown. She looked at Blake, thinking she would say something. Anything. But nothing came out. She wasn't sure what to say, especially about the fact that her hand was still warm from the heat of his and what the hell that even meant. So, yeah, she was done for the day... or night, rather, because she could see the sun was starting to set.

"I'll go grab us some pizza," Blake said.

She figured her expression must've told him that she was benching herself for the time being.

"Thanks." She thought a mind-numbing food coma sounded perfect.

As Blake turned to leave, Felix let out the laziest feline yawn and stretch, oblivious to the fact that Caly's reality was scrambled like someone's breakfast. With silent grace, he jumped off the couch and padded off with his new partner in crime. Watching those two males leave together, she smiled. Yeah, she definitely would have to keep a close eye on those two.

Closing the bedroom door behind him, Blake heard Riordan in the small spare bedroom. He didn't want to leave Caly so quickly after that life-altering conversation, well, after her hundredth life-altering conversation that day, but he needed to speak with Riordan, face to face, before he left. And he didn't lie about the pizza thing. He could smell the pizza's greasy promise from down the hall and he was going to make damn sure Caly was well fed.

"Riordan, a word," Blake said from the doorway of the spare bedroom.

Riordan responded with a single nod of his head.

Closing the door behind him, Blake decided to cut through all of the bullshit and get straight to the point. "She stays with me. She will be my responsibility."

Riordan's eyes danced with ancient amusement in Blake's subtle claim over Caly. "It is beyond both of our hands as I have been charged as her Primary by the Seer Council themselves. And if she does not accept my offer, then she will be assigned another Primary. It is her birthright to learn the ways of the travelers and her abilities. And it is too much of a risk for the council if they did nothing, knowing that one of their own could cause disruption or damage because she did not learn the ways of our world and how to control her abilities."

Shit, Blake thought, knowing the damn seer was right. If the Seer Council did make the official rule on this, then there was nothing they could do unless the council changed their mind. And he knew they wouldn't. Especially if any of them found out about Caly being a powerful traveler, not to mention whatever the hell her force field was exactly. On top of that, the council wouldn't risk having an untrained traveler meandering around because any mistakes she made, would fall back on them since they would have been the ones to release her without any training into their world. And surely they would have to speak to the higher Species Council at that point. Council politics aside, he agreed it was Caly's birthright to learn about who she was, the world she belonged in, and her abilities. Blake couldn't imagine what it would've been like to not know he was a wolf his whole life. Granted, that was a totally different situation since his wolf would've come out to play and it probably would not have been to play fetch. Blake rubbed the trimmed whiskers on his chin in a frustrated motion.

"Blake, if she chooses me then rest assured that she will be safe and protected on my watch. After all, her safety and protection would be my responsibility as her Primary."

No. Her safety and protection are my responsibility, Blake internally growled with an emphasis on the "my" part.

"I know that as her Primary, you have her safety and protection at heart and that she is your responsibility. But... She is *mine*."

Christ. It was the first time he had spoken his claim on Caly out loud. He didn't originally intend to go there but he needed to lay the cards on the table to see if that might sway the council enough. Although, he already knew that announcing his claim was not enough and the only way it would be is if they were officially mated.

So, Caly, you're mine and you're never leaving. Oh, and, by the way, we're getting mated... today. Yeah, that's going to go over so well, Blake thought dryly, suddenly wanting to punch something. Then he caught Riordan's amused expression that clearly told him the damn seer already knew she was his. Yeah, now he really wanted to punch something... or rather someone with an Irish accent.

"You already know a verbal claim will not be sufficient in the eyes of the council." There was a pause. "Blake, as she is yours, it looks like you're going to be... *busy*."

Riordan's half-smile, accompanied by that damn twinkle in his eye, was really not helping his chances of not getting punched. Blake put a lid on his punching fantasy to attempt to decipher what the seer was saying. He knew Riordan's word choice was specific. But he didn't know what the fuck the code was to crack his cryptic messages.

"I will see you very soon," Riordan said, walking toward the door. Just before he walked out, he turned his head and spoke over his shoulder. "Oh, and does she know?"

Riordan actually full-on smiled before slipping out of the room.

Goddamn fucking seers. Always enigmatic and know too much for their own good.

Walking out of the bedroom, Riordan's smile faded when another memory pushed its way to the surface…

The council chamber looked as if it was a mix between a sacred temple and a throne room, elegantly designed in the traditional colors of the seers, white and silver. There were a few steps leading up to the slightly elevated platform where the seven council members sat before Riordan. The elaborately hand-carved silver council chairs were side by side in a straight line facing the entrance. Behind the council members was a magnificent mural, painted long ago at the birth of the Seer Council. The mural depicted three scenes, representing the past, present, and future. The past portrayed chaos amongst the species, including between seers themselves. The present portrayed what was considered one of the species' greatest moments in history, The Declaration of Peace Species Treaty, where every subspecies representative sat around a table and signed the peace treaty. The third and final scene showed a glimpse of a peaceful future where all species lived and worked harmoniously amongst one another. The breathtaking three-part mural had always been in the council chambers to serve as a powerful reminder to the birth of all of the Species Councils, including the creation of the Seer Council.

"Council, I stand before you today to report a vision,"
Riordan began.

It was a part of standard protocol and not unusual for
seers to report various types of visions. Seers, just like healers,
had a sacred code they followed. One part of the seer code
explicitly stated they were not to consciously breach an in-
dividual's privacy without consent or otherwise authorized
by order of the Seer Council. That last clause allowed for
SILE to use seers for investigations. Another part of the seer
code addressed the fact that seers may be able to act as an
alert system of a danger to someone or something or be able
to provide information that could protect an individual or
situation from a threat.

"There is a female traveler who is unclaimed." Riordan
calculated his word choice carefully because he needed to
ensure this went his way.

All seers, and travelers were a subset of seers, were doc-
umented at birth in order to ensure their safety since seers
had a risk of losing touch with reality and potentially going
mad.

Riordan also intentionally withheld information from
the vision of the female, like just how powerful a traveler
she was, as well as, what he saw in that final image with
her arms outstretched to the sky, eyes glowing gray, hair
defying gravity and the shimmering vibration gathering at
her hands. Not everyone on the council was corrupt but
there were some who Riordan didn't trust and their motives
were questionable. He knew that if they were to know ev-
erything in his vision, at least one of those corrupt council
members would do everything in their power to claim the
female under their control. And like hell if he was going to
let that happen.

"Riordan... You must protect her... Protect Caly..."

Riordan recalled the distant angelic female voice from the vision.

"Unclaimed you say?" Deloreia spoke in a curious yet calm voice.

Deloreia was an ancient seer and had been on the council for centuries. In fact, all of the seers on the council were ancients. Her chestnut eyes matched the color of her sleek, shoulder-length bob. She wore a simple and elegant, floor-length, silver dress on her small frame. The high neck and long sleeves were made of delicate silver mesh that shimmered over her porcelain skin. While in session, it was a tradition for the Seer Council to wear one or both of the seer colors.

"Yes." Riordan didn't know for sure that the female was unclaimed but he learned from his research that there was no documented seer or traveler matching the description of the female from his vision. These were not public records but, being an ancient, Riordan had his ways. Besides, he knew that if he was wrong and the female turned out to be claimed then he would just report that back to the council as such. There would be no negative repercussions brought upon him as he would have just been acting on the seer code out of the safety and protection of someone or something, and an unclaimed seer, or in this case, traveler, fell into that category. So, if he was wrong, it was a loophole that fell into his favor.

But he was fairly certain he wasn't wrong. Although, he had no idea how there could be an unclaimed female traveler. A traveler was a highly revered subset of seers because of their rarity and ability. Bloodlines with a traveler tended to make it known, in order to gain status and power. So, an unclaimed traveler was unheard of.

And the two council members, with expressions of fascination flirting with possessiveness over the unclaimed *traveler, were exactly why Riordan was there. He was there to protect the female. And little did they know, he was also protecting her from the council themselves.*

In an attempt to cut off any further conversation and make this as quick and concise as possible, Riordan said, "Council, I bring this before you as I feel it is my sacred right as a seer to see this spontaneous vision through. In the vision, I was charged with a specific purpose. I trust there is a reason this vision came to me and, as such, I am requesting to be her Primary."

Several pairs of brows rose in surprise at Riordan's unexpected statement and request. In preparation for this meeting with the council, Riordan consulted with a species lawyer who was proficient with the ancient texts of species law. The motion to be a Primary had not happened for some time but it was still recognized as a legal part of the species law.

With this motion, Riordan was also consciously appealing to emotions by non-verbally alluding to the tragedy of the Knight family bloodline. It was the first time he had ever used the tragedy in such a deliberate power play and a part of him rejected the thought when he was initially strategizing. But, as if in protest, the angelic voice from his vision replayed in his mind. "Riordan... You must protect her... Protect Caly..." So, he knew he needed to use everything he could to leverage the outcome to his favor.

Riordan's purposeful word choice was also playing to another ancient and sacred way of the seers, spontaneous visions. There were reasons the seer code specifically stated to not consciously breach an individual's privacy. First, young seers who were just learning how to control their abilities may inadvertently and accidentally see something about someone they shouldn't. Second, some visions were completely out of the individual's control and came of their own volition. These were known as "spontaneous visions" and were taken very seriously because they usually contained important information.

The most commonly reported spontaneous visions only originated from powerful seers and were personal to the seer in some way, like a vision of a significant life event for either them or a loved one. Of course, life events could potentially be seen in a seer session but the significant difference was the spontaneous nature coming of its own accord. So, spontaneous visions were considered to be one of the most sacred visions a seer could experience as it was said to tap into the true essence of the seer itself. Every seer knew of the legends that spoke of the extraordinary spontaneous visions that were equated to fate or destiny. Some seers waited their whole lives for visions like these, only to never experience it.

"I had no idea you so deeply believed in the ancient ways, Riordan." Anguis' suspicious dark eyes and slicked back raven hair were in sharp contrast to his custom-tailored, ice gray suit.

He was questioning Riordan's motives and alluding to the fact that Riordan's request was based purely on blind faith and a spontaneous vision. Of course, there were some specians that deeply believed in the mystery and magic of life. Usually, these were more often seers and steorrians since, in their relative abilities, they saw things that others did not and would make choices based on the faith of what they saw, even when there was no proof.

Riordan knew this bold motion of faith was out of character for him but in a sense, it was true. He was taking bold actions solely based on his spontaneous vision, which some may have categorized as an extraordinary spontaneous vision. So, he appealed to the sacred seer ways, knowing that he had to use everything he could to his advantage to protect the female. And Anguis was one of the individuals Riordan was trying to protect this female from. There were no direct implications of Anguis, hence why he was still on the council, but that didn't mean anything in Riordan's eyes. When you have as much power and money as a member of the council, then there was a way to get your hands dirty without actually touching anything.

"One does not need to deeply believe in the ancient ways for centuries, Anguis. We all know it only takes one vision to change the very course of a life," Deloreia chimed in with a voice that appeared as soft as her gown. If someone were simply listening to the sound of the voices, they would not have known that Deloreia just shut down Anguis.

"I approve." Zahara spoke clearly from her regal position, with her long legs crossed at the knee and both arms resting on the chair on either side of her body. Her midnight hair flowed over the slim-fitting, elbow-length-sleeved, silver dress. Her hazel eyes popped against her dark golden skin, looking as if she had already mentally moved on from the request now that her decision was made.

One by one, each of the seven Seer Council members spoke their decision as Riordan stood in silence. The outcome was five approvals and two denials, one of which was Anguis.

"Riordan Knight, of the Knight seer bloodline, your request to be the unclaimed female traveler's Primary has been approved on the condition that you bring the female here before us along with a copy of the signed Primary papers," Deloreia concluded.

"Yes, council." Riordan bowed his head slightly.

Chapter 25

Sitting cross-legged on the floor in front of the magnificent glass wall in Blake's room, Caly silently watched one of the most beautiful sunsets she had ever witnessed. The forested skyline was glowing with various shades of gold, pink, orange, red, and even purple. She wondered what it would have been like to have witnessed the Universe's artwork with a higher vantage point, allowing an uninterrupted view of the canvas.

There was a knock at the door. She knew it was Blake. Because, yeah. Who else would it be?

"Come in," she said in a distracted voice, not bothering to turn around when the door opened. She didn't want to miss one moment of the sunset that had her in its thrall.

Blake stood in the doorway taking in the unexpected scene before him. Instead of sitting on the couch, Caly was taking full advantage of the floor-to-ceiling, glass wall, soaking in the sunset. Both he and his wolf suddenly wanted to take her to this secluded peak in the forest that he thought of his. It was where he often ended up after a run and he knew from experience that the view of the sunset from that spot was unparalleled. Making a mental note to take her there one day, he refocused on Caly. She seemed as serene as the silky length that cascaded down her back and flirted with the floorboards.

Christ, he thought, remembering what it was like to have her straddle him with that blanket of hair all around him trapping in her sweet scent as her lips pressed to his. Trying to recover from the seductive memory, he managed to make his way over to Caly, with a quick pizza delivery at the coffee table, before settling on the floor next to her. His wolf was begging for him to sit closer to her. To press his body up against hers. To drape his arm over her shoulder. To nuzzle in the crook of her neck. To lick...

No. He cut off those thoughts.

Gentlemale. He needed to be a gentlemale and give her space after the hell she went through, not to mention the whole reorientation of her reality thing. He settled for looking over at his beautiful female with the wonders of the sunset dancing in her eyes. Yeah, he was so going to take her to his peak.

They remained sitting in comfortable silence until twilight started to surrender to the starry night sky.

"Blake?"

"Yeah, Caly?"

"Thanks for staying earlier."

"Of course. I'll stay as long as you want," Blake echoed his earlier words, trying to reassure her without going overboard and scaring her off with the whole "you're mine" thing.

Can we stay in this room forever? she wished.

"Do you want to watch a movie? Or if you're tired and want to be alone, just let me know," Blake asked, not really sure what Caly was thinking or wanting to do. He figured a movie was a safe choice because it would give her mind a brief respite from all of the heavy conversations.

"Actually, I would love to," Caly answered.

Blake sharpened his senses and sniffed the air. He wanted to make sure Caly wasn't just being polite by not sending him away. Good. Her scent told him that she did want him to stay. Blake stood up and stuck out his hands with a smile. She accepted it without pause and he pulled her to her feet effortlessly.

"Oh jeez. I guess I was sitting longer than I thought," she said with a chuckling groan, bending her legs at the knees a couple of times to get the blood flowing.

"Go ahead and get settled on the couch. I'll get everything all ready," he said with a smile.

Blake's dark leather sectional couch was crafted with a contemporary and modern design complete with two, extra-wide, reclining chaise lounges. Caly considered the chaise but she ended up parking it in the center cushion so she had the perfect centered view of the screen. Yeah, she was one of those people sitting in the exact center of a movie theater.

Felix made his presence known at the door with his meow and Blake opened the door letting him in. Felix padded across the room, jumped up on the couch, and lazily laid out as if he owned the thing.

Blake noticed the way Caly looked at Felix, with such loving affection, and wondered if she would ever look at him like that. He also noticed what Caly did by sitting directly in the middle of the couch. He casually walked to the side of the couch, not doing anything to hide his wolfish grin. Caly let out a little yelp of surprise when the couch slid over a few feet without warning. Felix's head popped up with ears on high alert, looking around in an attempt to solve the mystery of the sudden earthquake. Blake saw the moment when Caly's surprised expression bloomed into understanding that he effortlessly moved the massive couch over several feet so that one of the extra-wide, reclining chaises was perfectly centered.

"Thank you. Honestly, you didn't have to do that." She smiled, scooting over to the newly centered chaise.

"I wanted to. Besides, why not have the best seat in the house?" He gave her a sly one-sided smile and settled on the couch with a respectably wide buffer between them. It took everything in him not to sidle up next to her and pull her in close to his body. *Gentlemale plan,* he reminded himself.

Why is he sitting so far away again? Maybe he doesn't want me to get any wrong ideas about the whole hand-holding thing? Caly contemplated.

"Blake?"

"Yeah, Caly?"

"There's plenty of room over here for you to put your feet up too if you want."

Okay, so it had nothing to do with putting his feet up and everything to do with the fact that she wanted to cuddle up close to Blake.

Both Blake and his wolf wanted to growl in approval at her invitation but he held back the growl for obvious reasons. Grabbing the pizza box, a stack of napkins, and two water bottles, he resettled next to Caly, while still leaving a couple of inches between them in order to maintain the gentlemale plan. Setting the extra-large pizza box on his lap, he did a one-eighty with the lid so it was lying flat on her lap as a makeshift plate. He tucked his water bottle on the seat next to him for easy access and Caly did the same on the opposite side. Yup. It was movie time.

"What movie do you want to watch? D has it rigged up so when I say we have every movie, I mean we have *every* movie."

Caly chortled. She didn't know who Dee was but she wasn't about to ask because she literally couldn't carry a conversation at the moment. And as far as the movie selection went, she didn't want to make him sit through a total sappy girl movie but, she couldn't handle anything that required an iota of brainpower or, God forbid, anything that ventured into the intense Scaryville.

As if he could read her mind, he said, "Don't worry about if the movie is something you think I may not like. Choose whatever you want. I'm happy if you're happy."

He's just being nice because of… everything, she internally rationalized.

For whatever reason, the movie *How to Train Your Dragon* popped into her head. Okay, so what if it was an animated family movie? She really liked that movie and it would be perfect for her escape of choice at the moment. Not scary? Check. Not intense? Check. Cute, funny, and lighthearted? Check.

Half expecting Blake to make fun of her or revoke his previous statement, she dared to ask, "Can we watch *How To Train Your Dragon*?"

"Of course. Tiffany, play the movie *How To Train Your Dragon*. Volume fifty," Blake responded without any hint of regret or mockery.

He must not know what the movie is. And Tiffany? Weird name for a TV but then again, so were Siri and Alexa.

Instantly, the large screen TV turned on and *How To Train Your Dragon* started playing. Caly held her breath waiting for some subtle joking comment from Blake. But it never came.

Instead, he said, "Oh, this movie. I've never seen it but I've heard it's good." Stacking two slices of pizza on top of each other, he took a huge bite. "Not bad with the olives." His voice was a little muffled as he chewed.

Okayyy, she thought, not anticipating that reaction for the movie or the pizza.

"I really like this movie," she sheepishly confessed, taking a bite of pizza herself.

"Good." He gave her a quick side smile before taking another bite of his pizza tower.

About twenty minutes later, the pizza was completely demolished. Blake ate most of it but Caly put in some work too. Putting the pizza box on the coffee table, he resettled back on the chaise. His arm naturally rose to drape across her shoulders so he could tuck her in closer to his side but he halted mid-air just before contact.

Gentlemale plan, he reminded himself, trying to play it off like he was scratching his head. *Good one. Real smooth. But she is the one who offered for you to sit next to her. That has to mean something, right?*

Why is he still sitting just far enough away so we are not touching? Caly wondered. *Again, probably because he doesn't want you to get the wrong idea about this. Whatever "this" is.*

About an hour into the movie, Blake saw Caly's eyelids become heavy until she succumbed to slumber completely. Turning off the movie, he scooped Caly up in his arms and walked to his bed to gently lay her down.

"Sleep, Caly," he coaxed in a low, calm voice when she stirred awake. Continuing with his gentlemale plan, he decided to give her his bedroom and he would sleep in the spare room. Even though they had slept together, he didn't want to be a bastard and assume that she wanted to sleep in the same bed. Especially because they slept together before she was taken and he didn't know how she even felt about him, if anything at all. She didn't make any moves to cuddle with him during the movie. And, yeah, normally he wouldn't wait for the female to make the move but this was different. Then there was the whole hand-holding thing which was still an unsolved mystery. It could have easily just meant that she needed a support system during the conversation with Riordan. So, yeah, he would be a gentlemale and give her space and privacy.

"Blake?" she said in a sleepy voice when he started for the door.

"Shhh. Sleep, Caly. I'll be in the spare room just down the hall."

Wait, he's leaving? Her mind started to come back online with that thought. *Well, duh, Caly. What did you think? He was going to stay with you in his bed and cuddle?*

She exhaled because, yeah, a part of her did think that. She got so caught up in how normal it felt to spend time with him. It was as if they had done the movie night thing a million times before.

Not only did he not make a move on the couch but also you're not together. And let's not forget that maybe he doesn't even have feelings for you like that. Sure we've slept together but people have meaningless sex all of the time. Maybe it didn't mean anything to him. Maybe sex doesn't even have the same intimate meaning for species. But maybe he was just being a gentleman?

Okay. She knew she was being a bit desperate and grasping at straws with that last thought. *Stop*, she commanded her mush of a mind, knowing her body wasn't fairing much better. So, yeah, maybe it was best to just go to sleep and try to integrate all of the information.

"Okay," Caly responded to Blake, trying to play it off like she wasn't about to be a full-on, stage five clinger. "Umm… I'll walk you out. I'm going to use the restroom and brush my teeth anyways." She just threw in that last part for believability points because what she really wanted to see was which room Blake was staying in. *Yup. Caly the Clinger.*

See, he told himself when he scented a slew of emotions coming from Caly. Confusion and sadness were competing for the top spot on the emotional charts. *She has a lot on her mind and she needs time to think about it all. Not only that but she just survived a fucking horrific nightmare, found out she's not human, can never go back to her home, and is about to have a Primary she doesn't even know. She probably needs to grieve too. And she can't do that when you're smothering her. Be the gentlemale and give her some space.*

Blake wanted to stay to comfort Caly and his wolf whined in protest of leaving her. But his thoughts reasoned with his emotions.

Gentlemale plan. Gentlemale plan, he repeated in his mind as he forced his feet to step one after another right out of the room.

Peering through a crack in the door, Caly watched Blake walk a few steps down the hall and enter the second room on the left. Her heart sank a little when the door closed.

Stop. Stop being Caly the Clinger. You're the fucking Phoenix. Act like it. With that mini pep talk—and good thing she never took up motivational speaking as a career—she walked into his closet and decided that her best bet for sleepwear was one of his white T-shirts.

Finishing up with the scrub job on her teeth, she hesitated with her hand hovering over the light switch. The nightmare decided for an encore, reminding her of the last time she was in total darkness.

Nope. Not going there. I'm safe. I am the fucking Phoenix. Even though she was apparently calling herself the Phoenix, she decided it wasn't against the mythical creature rules to keep the bathroom light on and leave the bathroom door slightly ajar so that she didn't sleep in total darkness. Pulling the covers over her, she let out a breath that she didn't know her stomach was clinging onto for dear life. She jumped out of her skin when Felix pounced on the bed.

"Jesus, Felix, you scared me," she said, placing her hand over her racing heart.

Felix curled up on the bed next to her and cranked his purring motor into full gear.

Thank God I'm not alone.

"Good night, Felix," she said, inhaling deeply.

Blake. She smelled Blake's earthy and masculine scent. She inhaled again.

So what if I'm being a stage five clinger smelling his pillow?

His scent, well actually that male in totality, was the only thing that had her feeling safe and normal, which in itself didn't make much sense, considering she barely even knew him. For whatever reason, he was the sturdy rock grounding her amidst the crazy chaos swirling around her. So she clung to that shit. She knew she couldn't hold onto it forever but she would deal with that when the time came. And, yeah, she would channel that Phoenix energy and rise out of that situation too. Breathing in Blake's scent lulled Caly to sleep.

Chapter 26

Darkness. Caly was in total darkness. She was catapulted back to the nightmare when the cement scraping sound scoured her eardrums.

"What species are you, Caly?"

The cement scraping sound amplified to torturous levels.

"You have secrets that I can't wait to break from your mind."

The chilling cold blade of The Ghost's large hunting knife slid against her bare skin. Then everything fell deadly still. All she could hear was her heart hammering in her chest. She blinked her eyes several times to make sure they were actually open, since all she could see was darkness. On a sudden woosh, the fiery torch was lit and The Ghost's sinister eyes and vicious grin appeared just inches from her face.

"Boo."

She screamed.

Caly shot upright in the bed on a frightened gasp. Her heart was pumping so hard she wouldn't be surprised if the thing broke right through her chest cavity. She frantically looked around the room and thank God she left the bathroom light on or else she may have been screaming in full panic mode. Instead, she was just freaking out internally.

Dream. Just a dream. Not real, she tried to reason with her body to level it down while her fear response was coursing through her body.

"You're safe." She heard Blake's voice in her mind and internally repeated the mantra. *I'm safe. I'm safe. I'm safe.*

It wasn't helping. Her heart was still pumping fast and the nightmare triggered something deep within her. All she could think about was being back in the safety of Blake's arms. Her body must've taken control of the reins because before she knew it, she was standing in front of the bedroom door. She didn't know what time it was but she did know she was going to be as quiet as a fucking mouse. Slowly turning the knob, she opened the door a crack and waited a beat. The coast was clear. Her heart was pounding but it was far too late to abort the mission now. She silently tiptoed past the first door until she stood in front of the door she saw Blake go in earlier. With her hand hovering over the door handle, her mind was flooded with thoughts of how she hadn't really thought this through. She jumped ten feet up in the air when the door suddenly swung wide open.

Blake. Blake was standing there... in nothing but red boxer briefs. She swallowed at the unexpected male underwear model scene. Meanwhile, she was only adding to the scene by standing there in nothing but his white T-shirt which barely covered her butt. Nope. Not awkward at all.

He inhaled and immediately said, "Caly, what's wrong?" His voice was low, morning gravel.

"I... I had a nightmare," she admitted on a shy whisper.

Both Blake and his wolf liked that she ran to him when she was scared. He would protect her from anything and anyone. But he didn't like that she was scared to begin with.

Still half asleep and on autopilot, he picked her up and

held her close to his chest.

"You're safe, Caly," he reassured her and felt her body relax as she curled in closer. It wasn't until he was a few steps into his current mission that it hit him. Walking Caly to his room in nothing but his boxers while all she wore was his T-shirt, which he most definitely approved of, was so not a part of the gentlemale plan. Fuck it. She needed him. Quietly shutting the door behind him, he made his way to his bed and gently laid her down.

Now what, genius? he thought, as his sleepy state faded away a bit more. He was just standing over her in nothing but his boxer briefs. *Yeah, real gentlemale of you.*

"Blake?"

"Yeah, Caly?"

Christ. He wanted to punch himself. Maybe that would knock some sense into him instead of standing there basically naked.

"Will you... Will you stay? Please?"

Okay... So, he wasn't expecting that. But then again, she did come to him for comfort. He wanted to say, *Caly, I will never leave you.* But that probably wasn't the brightest idea at the moment, considering the boxer brief situation.

"Of course," he said as his eyes automatically flicked toward the couch. Before he could command his feet to move, she peeled back the covers next to her and looked at him in question.

Gentlemale. Remember your gentlemale plan, he thought, sliding into the bed next to her and keeping a respectable distance.

That was when he noticed the light coming from the bathroom. Remembering what Caly said about it being complete darkness where she was held, he wanted to go round two with the punches. He was so used to being able to see in the dark that it didn't register how dark his room was at night. He inwardly cursed. He should've thought of that. He decided he was going to rectify the situation and get her a night light. Actually, make that plural: night lights. Yeah, he was going to light up his room like it was a Christmas tree.

What are you doing? Caly thought. *You're now in bed next to him practically naked. Again, notice how he is keeping his distance? Congratulations. You've just breached the clinger scale and are now off the charts.*

Laying on their backs, with eyes glued to the ceiling, they both stayed silent for several minutes.

"Blake?"

"Yeah, Caly?"

"I'm sorry. I don't mean to make you uncomfortable. I..."

Just come out and say it, McClinger Queen.

"I just feel safe with you." She paused. "I had a nightmare about..." Suddenly, she had a lump in her throat. She swallowed. "When I was in there, the only thing that kept me going was... you. Every time I felt like I couldn't go on, I would hear your voice in my mind saying, 'Keep fighting. I will find you. Caly, I will find you.' " Her voice trailed off and she could feel fresh tears pooling in her eyes.

Shit. Don't cry. Don't cry, she tried to command herself.

"So, when I woke up from the nightmare, I heard your voice in my mind and I just ran to you."

Fuck the keeping the distance gentlemale plan. She needed him. And he wanted to boldly answer how he wasn't uncomfortable in the least. Turning onto his side, he wrapped his arm around her and pulled her close to his body. Her face nuzzled into his chest seeking comfort and safety. Christ. He wanted to nuzzle her neck. He wanted to lick her face. And most of all he wanted to mark her with his scent. His wolf protested when he fought back the instinct but it was not the time to go wolf on her.

"Caly, I'm not going anywhere. I was keeping my distance because I wanted to respect your space and privacy."

That did it. Blake's words officially broke the dam and her tears were flowing out of her at an impossible rate. *God, if I could just never leave his arms then I would be okay.*

"Everything is just... complete chaos in my mind," she managed to choke out. "Is it crazy for me to think about how I miss waking up in the morning looking forward to my morning drink ritual of coffee and listening to music?"

There was a pause as her mind recalled when she was sitting at her work desk thinking about how there had to be more to life and daydreaming about moving away from LA. Well, in some crazy ass way, she manifested that in a sense. She thought about how there was just something special about her morning drink rituals and music playlists.

"I know it's totally stupid but I had playlists for everything. Music is therapeutic to me. And when I wasn't in the mood for music, I would curl up on the couch with Felix, a hot drink and—" She abruptly cut herself off.

Oh my god! she thought, almost letting it slip that she was a romance novel junkie. *Em-fucking-barrassing!*

"And?" he prompted genuinely curious about Caly's life before the horror.

"Nothing," she said, trying to play it off all cool.

"Oh, come on. You can't just leave me hanging like that," he teased a little, trying to lighten the mood.

Caly laughed. "It's embarrassing."

"Well, I'll share something about me if you share."

"Fine." Her cheeks heated. "*And* I would read romance novels." She held her breath waiting for his reaction.

Blake's brows furrowed slightly in confusion. "I'm going to go off on a limb here and say romance novels are about falling in love. So, what's embarrassing about that?"

"You're right. Not embarrassing at all. Your turn," Caly said, eager to change the subject.

He sniffed the air and gave her a look that said *"Spill."*

"You're not going to let this go, are you?"

"Nope."

"Okay. Fine." Her words came out on an exhale. "I like the romance novels with…" She hesitated. "…Hot, steamy sex scenes. Happy now?"

"Oh, do you now?" he drawled.

"Okay, your turn. Tell me something embarrassing about you."

"I said I would share something about myself. I didn't say something embarrassing." He gave her a wolfish grin.

"You sly wolf."

"I can't help it."

"Okay, fine. So share something about yourself with me, wolf." Her mouth turned up at the corners at their playful game.

"Well, how about I share how I am suddenly thinking about wanting to show up all those hot steamy romance novels you've read."

Way to go with the gentlemale plan, he thought, wanting to kick himself. He was so caught up in the playful banter with his female tucked close against his body that he forgot all about how he was going to keep his distance.

"Oh, come on," she said with a laugh. "That doesn't count. Share something else about yourself." Caly looked up slightly only to see he had his wolfy grin. So, she quickly added, "Something that is comparable."

He chuckled. "Well, I had long hair once. When I was younger. It did not suit me. At all. Which also reminds me, I look weird without facial hair."

Caly laughed at the unexpected confession. She was suddenly trying to picture what Blake would look like with long hair and clean-shaven. "I wanna see a picture. Please tell me you have one."

"Now that would be the embarrassing part." His smile widened. "Maybe one day I'll show you."

Yeah, one day, she thought, remembering how she had to leave soon. Like, as in a couple of days or less if she accepted Riordan's offer to be her Primary. Well, if that didn't put a sudden halt to the game.

"Blake?"

"Yeah, Caly?"

"What do you know about Riordan?"

Okay. Not what he was expecting. He cleared his throat. "You know, I have only known him for a few days now. I checked with my contact at SILE, whom I trust and have worked with for decades. He has known Riordan for a long time and trusts him. He said that Riordan is a well-respected ancient male with integrity. Word on the street is he turned down a seat on the Seer Council. And from what I've seen over the past few days, he is not like most ancients and so far, he has lived up to his respectful and trustworthy reputation. I also have nothing negative to report. I know he is not sharing everything he knows, but then again, we all, especially ancients, have our secrets. I mean, who wouldn't after living as long a life as them?" There was a pause. "Caly, I wish I knew more to help you but what I can share is that my instincts tell me to trust him and they do not give off any warnings."

She took a moment to let it sink in. "Is an ancient someone who has lived a long time? Like elders?"

"Yeah. And you can always see it in their eyes."

Caly remembered how Riordan's eyes held this depth of wisdom and flicker of something she couldn't quite place. Like a puzzle piece fitting into place, Caly mentally checked that question off her ever-growing list.

Now for the million other pieces to this infinite puzzle, she thought.

God, her brain was tired and still on DND mode. After a brief lull in the conversation, she pried a couple of inches off of Blake's chest so she could look into his eyes. When her eyes met his, she silently gazed into his golden galaxies. It reminded her of when she first saw him in her dreams except, with their closeness, it was way more intense and she could see every colored nuance.

The song lyrics from "Such Great Heights" popped into her head. It was the part about how the colored flecks in two lovers' eyes mirrored one another when they kissed. It was describing intimacy on a level that was beyond skin. The poetic words were an ode to that special soul connection that few ever dared to dream of.

Her body heated and she wanted him. There was just something about Blake that had her body respond on some deep unconscious primal levels. Then Caly did the third boldest thing ever in her life with a male. The first being that first time with Blake in her bed. The second being when she grabbed his hand during the conversation with Riordan. And the third? She kissed him.

Blake returned her kiss with an added layer of slow sensual passion. Their kiss was gentle and tender. Caly could feel every nerve ending light up with the slow pace. She felt as if she could kiss his soft lips forever. She gently bit his bottom lip in a tease and his lips curved slightly before he bit her lip in return. They continued with the slow playful exploration of their lips for what seemed like an eternity. She wanted more. Needed more. Licking his lips, she coaxed him to deepen the kiss. He obliged and their tongues were in the most sensual of duels. The kiss they shared was nothing like she'd ever experienced. She didn't know how a kiss could ever be so slow, deep, and intimately soul-shattering.

Sure, she had kissed males before, and she had even kissed Blake before, but this was different in the best way possible. She wondered if she would ever experience another kiss like this again.

Her body clenched in the most feminine of places, asking to continue the deep intimacy. Rolling on top of him, she straddled him and could feel his hard length at her core with nothing but the thin fabric of boxer briefs between them. With his hands on her hips, she broke the kiss to sit up straight. Gripping the bottom of the white T-shirt, she peeled it over her head while maintaining eye contact. There was a low rumble in his chest as he slid his hands up her waist, cupped her breasts, and traced her nipples with his thumbs. She tilted her head back and moaned at the little shocks of pleasure. Her feminine body was blooming for him and she rocked her hips slightly to work her sensitive spot over his hard length. They both groaned.

Taste. Blake needed to taste, lick, suck, and mark every inch of her with his scent.

No, he commanded his body to hold off on the pheromone scent factory. As much as he wanted to, he would not mark her with his mating scent until she knew and accepted the fact that she was his.

In a fluid motion, he rolled her onto her back and nestled between her thighs. Claiming her mouth once more, he gripped one of her legs at the knee and bent it so he could get even closer to her. He rocked his hard length and pelvis into her core. The thin fabric did nothing to mute the pleasurable sensations. She broke the kiss with a moan. He loved the sounds she made and it turned up the heat impossibly more. With her breasts flush against his chest, he kissed across her jaw until he was kissing her neck.

"Blake," she said in a breathy voice.

He continued to rock slowly into her core. Kissing his way

down her neck, past her collarbone, he swirled his tongue around her tight, pink nipple. She arched into him, pressing their bodies impossibly closer. Pleasure licked through her body as both of her breasts received the most tender touches. Looking into her eyes, he broke the kiss of her breast only to flick his tongue over her nipple. Recognizing her pleasured response, he did it again and then repeated it on her other nipple. As the pleasurable tide rose ever higher, he slid his fingers down toward her sex. He paused to make sure she was with him.

"Yes," she moaned.

He slipped his fingers into her silken flesh and groaned with how wet she was for him. His fingers teased her core and the scent of her arousal grew even thicker in the air. Christ, he needed to taste her silken honey. Parting her legs even wider for him, he kissed a slow path from her inner thigh to her sex. When he pulled away his fingers, she moaned in protest but it was quickly silenced by the slowest upstroke of his tongue on her core. He felt her quiver and smiled in wicked delight. Lapping up her sweet ambrosia, he teased her core with his tongue while she moved her hips in rhythm. He was licking and sucking in an impossibly sensual rhythm that was driving her wild. Sliding one hand up her body, he teased her nipple with his thumb and forefinger and cupped her breast using his thumb and forefinger to play with her nipple. He placed his free hand on her lower belly and stretched the skin toward her belly button, exposing more of her sensitive spot to his tongue.

"Blake!" she moaned.

"Come for me, Caly," he commanded and put his mouth on her core once more. Swirling his tongue around her sensitive spot, he felt her shatter.

"Blake!" she cried out as her head threw back into the pillows. His tongue continued to lap her up and ride her

308

through the orgasmic waves of pleasure.

"Inside me. Blake, I need you inside me."

She didn't have to ask twice. With a quick motion, his red boxers flew off of his body and landed somewhere. He didn't care where. He was transfixed on his female and her sensual demand. He rose over her and guided his hard length to her entrance.

"You're so wet." His voice was hoarse.

Inch by slow inch, he teased his rod into her until he was fully inside her. She wrapped her legs around his waist and he rocked into her, slow and deep, allowing full friction of her sensitive spot against his flesh. She moaned and he growled.

In a swift motion, he repositioned them so he was sitting on the edge of the bed and she was on top with him still inside her. He wrapped his arms around her waist while hers were around his neck. They stared into each other's eyes for the longest moment before their lips claimed one another's in a passionate kiss.

Breaking the kiss, she began to ride him in a slow steady rhythm. Moaning, she picked up the pace as the pleasurable wave began to crest.

"Caly," he growled.

"Blake," she cried out.

A moment later they fell together with pure pleasure pulsing through their bodies. Her sex was milking him and working his hot seed into her. She rested her forehead onto his and they stayed like that until their breathing started to slow to a natural rhythm.

Not wanting to let her go, he kissed her tenderly and she slid her hands into his hair. The intimate experience they shared started and ended with the best kiss of her life. When the kiss naturally came to a close, they just stared into each other's eyes for another long moment. There were no words that could come close to possibly describing one of the most intimate experiences of her life.

As if they had done this a million times, he laid back, slid out of her, and tucked her in close to his body so her back was to his chest. Moving one leg between hers, he gently kissed her neck until sleep claimed them both.

Chapter 27

Caly woke up with the warmth of the sun on her face as two birds sang a beautiful duet. She sighed. For the first time since she was taken, she slept deep and restful. Looking over her shoulder, she expected to see Blake. Except the bed was empty. She pulled the covers closer to her very naked body in a very empty bed.

What did you think was going to happen, Caly? You're not with him and this situation keeps getting way more complicated by you coming on to him. And remember you've initiated the intimacy not just last night but has it been every other time? God. But he wanted me too. I am just the one to have taken the first step. And that level of deepness last night, that was more than just casual sex, right? He had to have felt that too? And what about how he held me and said, "Caly, I'm not going anywhere. I was keeping my distance because I wanted to respect your space and privacy."

Her thoughts were suddenly a mile a minute on the over-analyze express. All aboard!

Exhaling, she decided it was time to face the music. She couldn't be cooped up in a cave her whole life out of fear. Fear for what was on the other side of the door. And fear for the reality of what the hell was actually going on between her and Blake.

I am the fucking Phoenix.

With that powerful affirmation, she rolled over to her side of the bed and stilled. There was a thermos and a blueberry muffin on the bedside table. Smiling, she reached a curious hand to the thermos and opened the lid. Coffee. It was steaming hot coffee. And just like that, all of the other thoughts crowding her head abruptly got off the overanalyze express and boarded the crying express. Crying again? Yep. She was crying for the hundredth time in Blake's bed.

Damn if this wasn't the most thoughtful thing anyone has ever done for me.

She recalled how last night she mentioned her morning drink ritual. It was as a total side comment but he had listened.

And not only did he listen but then he did this.

She didn't even care that it was straight-up black coffee either. At this point, the hot cup of coffee, plus feeling safe, shot straight to her soul.

Inhaling the steamy dark liquid, she took that first glorious sip. She felt the warmth slide down her throat and spread to the rest of her body.

"Ahhhhhh." She let out one of the biggest and most satisfying sighs of her life.

Curling in closer to the covers, she polished off the coffee and muffin. She savored all of the flavors and Blake's thoughtfulness sweetened every bite.

Caly took another steaming hot shower and, once again, realized she still didn't have anything to wear. So, yeah. She got back with the Midol period girl program. It was either that or the white T-shirt because apparently, he didn't wear anything else. And considering the fact that white was kind of see-through, she decided to play it safe with the not-showing-off-the-goods oversized hoodie and sweats.

Yup. Real hot, Caly. But oh well. I could honestly give two fucks right now with everything that just happened to me.

She was safe. She was warm. And that was all that mattered.

Looking at the bedroom door, she bit her bottom lip contemplating if she was brave enough to explore. As if the thing could read her mind, a knock sounded out and she jumped.

Yeah, real brave of you, Phoenix. Jumping at a knock.

Thinking it must be Blake, because, again, who else would it be? She walked to the door and opened it without pause.

Statue. She was suddenly a statue. Not only was it not Blake but she was standing in the presence of a real-life giant. He was so tall, she wondered if her head could even tilt far enough back to see all the way up to his face.

Oh my god. He's even taller than Blake and... She swallowed and let that thought drift off because she couldn't open that fucked up box of horrors.

This giant had piercing, electric blue eyes and obsidian, black hair poking out of a backwards baseball cap. He looked casual in a faded blue T-shirt and jeans.

What is up with all these giants? Are all species males giants? Wait, no because Riordan was definitely not in the giant range.

Refocusing her thoughts to the giant in front of her, something about him seemed familiar.

"Hey, Caly."

His deep voice sent a jolt of recognition through her and a memory flashed before her eyes. *"Caly, you're safe. I'm Rhyland. Blake and I are here for you."*

"Rhyland?" she cautiously asked.

"Yup. The one and only. But you can call me Rhy." He winked and gave her a half-smile.

Caly's throat was suddenly dry. Her memory was hazy at best but she knew what this male did for her because of what Blake shared.

"Thank you..." She couldn't get the rest out because she was holding back an unexpected wave of emotion. She wanted to thank him for rescuing her and carrying her to safety.

He inhaled in a way that reminded her of Blake but before she could process it, he did the unexpected. He pulled her in for a hug. When his scent wafted into her nose, another memory surfaced.

She was being carried in Rhyland's arms and the wind was rushing by as if she stuck her head out of a car window on the freeway.

As if he knew what she meant to say and that she didn't want to cry for the millionth time today, and it was still morning for God's sake, he pulled back from the hug and changed the subject.

"Blake sent me because he is stuck on the phone with SILE. I'm gonna give you the grand tour of our humble abode. And the first stop is the kitchen because, duh, food. Always food." He shot her a playful wink.

Caly laughed a little and appreciated the change in conversation.

"Ready?" he asked.

"Yeah," she said in a timid yet curious voice. Looking past the giant into the hall, she noticed it looked different in the daylight.

Funny how that happens when you're not scared shitless from a nightmare, she thought wryly. Following his lead, she walked past the threshold of her little bubble of safety.

"So, this is the hall of truth," he said in a very official

tone, only to chuckle a moment later. "Just kidding. It's just a boring old hall but I thought I might make it seem more epic, being this is the *grand* tour and all." Looking over his shoulder at her, he grinned wider when she laughed.

Caly really liked Rhyland's sense of humor and a deep part of her was relieved to be laughing casually again.

She didn't even notice it last night when she went to Blake but there were several doors on either side of the hallway. She also didn't see that the wood flooring was various shades of walnut brown.

"And this is the heart of the home," he said as the hall opened up into a large kitchen and living area. It was an open floor plan with a dark and handsome modern design. The wooden floors continued throughout the entire space and there was a seating area with several dark leather couches and chairs.

"And that is the stomach of the home," he joked, pointing toward the kitchen.

Smiling, she followed him to the kitchen. It was a mix between rustic and industrial with low-key modern features—without overdoing it with the ego effect. The cabinets were a deeper shade of brown than the floor, which contrasted nicely against the white-marble countertops and stainless-steel, Viking range and sub-zero refrigerator. There was a large island with a wooden finish on top and storage underneath. Separating the kitchen and living room, was a large, dark wood dining table. As they walked further into the kitchen, she realized that everything must've been custom made for giants because everything was scaled to size.

"You hungry?" Rhyland asked, opening up the fridge.

Okayyy, she thought, seeing that the massive fridge was full to the brim with tons of food. She was totally stereotyping and half expecting to see leftover pizza and beer.

Nope. Not even close.

"Actually, yeah I could eat something." And it was the truth. She was suddenly hungry looking at all of the food.

"Great." He started handing her food to set on the counter.

They were like a mini assembly line with the eggs, bacon, cheese, onions, frozen Potatoes O'Brien, butter, and milk. He opened some of the cabinets and she didn't know why she was still surprised to see they were also stuffed full with all sorts of snacks. He handed her a loaf of bread and then opened a few other cabinets bringing out the pans, cooking utensils, and a cutting board.

"Wow. Your kitchen is... well-stocked," she said, feeling like she was suddenly on set of one of those cooking shows on TV.

"Hell yeah it is. What a complete nightmare to be hungry and not have any food." Rhyland shuddered audibly as if that was a horrific thought.

They tag teamed for breakfast and Caly could not stop laughing at Rhyland's silly jokes. Which only seemed to encourage him to continue. She may have possibly laughed away her caloric intake for the next week.

"How many are we cooking for?" she asked when he kept handing her eggs to crack as he simultaneously threw strip after strip of bacon on the griddle. Caly swallowed, not sure that she was ready to actually meet an entire army.

"Oh, there's only a couple of us. But don't worry, nothing goes to waste around here." He winked and flashed his winning smile.

Well, she certainly wasn't worried about food waste at the moment.

I am the fucking Phoenix. I can do this. Besides, these males helped rescue you.

With another great mini pep talk under her belt, she

continued with her egg-cracking task.

Soon the smell of a promising hearty breakfast filled the kitchen and her mouth was watering in anticipation of the epic meal. Apparently, she wasn't the only one. Because another giant walked into the room.

He was absentmindedly sniffing the air in a way that actually reminded her of Felix and patting his stomach as if the smell of breakfast was like a sweet siren's song. Hesitating mid bacon flip, she looked at the male, looked at Rhyland, and back at the male. He looked like Rhyland... yet he didn't. They had the same strong jaw, giant brawny body, piercing blue eyes, and obsidian hair. But this male was drastically different as he had detailed tattoos weaving up his right arm to his neck and he was wearing all black including black stud earrings. So, yeah, black was his thing apparently.

They both let out deep chuckles.

Okayyy. They also sound the same too.

"You noticed did you? Some never even put it together. We still have no idea how that's even possible but it's the truth." Rhyland broke the bacon-sizzling silence. "That's my brother, Rhyker."

"Older brother," Rhyker added, with a feline grin that looked similar, but not an exact replica, to Rhyland's.

"By one fucking minute," Rhyland said in a tone that said they had had this same conversation for years.

Twins. They're giant twins.

"And never forget it," Rhyker shot back. "Now that that's established..." He focused his attention on Caly. "Hey, Caly." His gaze drifted to the piles of food. "Fuck yeah. You can stay as long as you want," Rhyker playfully exclaimed, loading up a plate without pause.

Just as they all sat down at the table, another male entered. She was actually half surprised that he wasn't a giant like the twins and Blake. She guessed he was just over six feet tall, but she wasn't sure because everything seemed out of scale in a kitchen full of giants that was also made for giants. The male was wearing deceptively casual, form-fitting black slacks and a dark blue sweater with the sleeves pulled up to the elbows. His short, sandy blonde hair and baby blue eyes were accentuated by bold, black frames that completed his whole "sophisticated hot surfer nerd" vibe.

"Hello, Caly. I'm Deacon. It's nice to finally meet you. Welcome to our home." His words were enunciated clearly and he addressed her politely.

"And that's Deac the geek. Gentlemale to his core. But there's no need for all that, D. She isn't one of those stuck up aristocrats," Rhyland teased.

"Thank fuck." Rhyker tacked on, shoveling a heaping forkful of food into his mouth.

"Hi, Deacon. Nice to meet you too. And no, I'm not a stuck up aristocrat by far... Thank fuck," Caly quipped.

Male laughter filled the room at her unexpected playfully cussing response.

"I repeat what I said earlier. You can stay as long as you want," Rhyker concluded, taking a huge bite of food.

Nico stalked in the room and she froze. Because, yeah. He was a scary male that could drop a room's temperature about ten degrees with one glare.

When Blake filled her in on their side of the story, she recalled that Blake told her he was a vampire. Caly frantically looked at the windows where sunlight was creeping in. Everyone noticed her reaction of fear paired with concern, as she glanced at the windows with the killing sun rays. One could've sworn Nico had a hint of amusement under the layer of ice. The twins chuckled and Deacon smiled.

"Oh, don't mind him. Mr. Freeze is always like that. If it was a couple of weeks ago, I would have made our next stop on the grand tour to be his room because you should've seen his recent redecoration." Rhyland paused, grinning from ear to ear. "It was decked out in all pink, complete with pink hearts on the ceiling and everything. We may even have a picture," he jested with a wink.

"Oh, we have pictures," Rhyker said with a wicked smile and then whispered to Caly, "Remind me to show you later." He winked.

Caly noticed how the gesture was just like Rhyland's except it was somehow different.

Low rolling laughter filled the room and the tension eased a little. Meanwhile, Nico was still channeling the arctic.

"And who knew our breakfast table discussion was going to be all about Nico? Nico is going to just *love* all of the attention," Rhyland joked sarcastically. He was grinning wide, as if amused to be able to toy with Nico in this way, knowing Nico wouldn't do anything because he would never go out of line, well without a damn good reason, in front of a female like Caly. He may be a lethal vampire but he wasn't a feral, ferocious beast.

Rhyker had a mischievous feline look in his eyes with a low laugh rumbling in his chest. The twins were always up for roasting Nico. It was a little cat game that the twins couldn't help but paw at when the opportunity presented itself.

Rhyland cleared his throat in a very audible and theatrical way. In an epic storytelling voice, he spoke the famous opening line to Star Wars about the story taking place in the past and being in a far, far away, distant galaxy.

Deacon laughed, choking on his bite of eggs.

Caly let out a laugh as well. She knew Rhyland was just trying to ease her tension after Nico came in the room. And it was working.

Satisfied by Caly's returned relaxed state, Rhyland continued, "The whole vampires can't go in the sun thing is an old human wives' tale that actually originated from vampires themselves. Same thing with the holy water, crosses, and mirror reflections." There was a pause. "Species used to live openly among humans."

Her eyebrows popped to her forehead in complete surprise.

"Yup. Where do you think all those human mythologies originated from? They usually have some sort of truth behind them once you factor out things like mistranslations, story inflations—which are mainly because a human wanted to be a hero or some shit and that was usually to impress females or gain status and power—and then let's not forget the age-old pitfalls of telephone. Oh, come on," he said, reacting to Caly's confused expression. "You've never played the game telephone before?"

"Ohhh." She laughed. "Yeah, I see what you mean."

He winked and continued, "The first subspecies the humans turned on, out of their own dumb fear, were vampires. Humans branded them as demons and would go "demon hunting" to wipe them out." Rhyland winced and his face went slightly grim because he was talking about genocide and war. "I know Nico does an *excellent* job of portraying this—" he said sarcastically. "But vampires are not evil, cold bastards. Sure, there are always bad apples but that goes for any species, including humans. I mean, look at all of the fucking psycho—" He cut his words off and wanted to headbutt himself hard because Caly was just rescued from one of those evil psychotic killers who was still out there.

Nico shot him a glare that said, *"Nice job, fucker."*

Rhyland cleared his throat and continued, "Yeah, so, the vampires were the first to hide their existence from humans and retreat to the shadows, naturally. A part of their strategy was to plant seeds in human minds so the rumors could take off. The humans' natural gossip tendencies and fear allowed them to construct the whole evil blood-sucking demon thing." He paused to shovel food into his mouth and wash it down with coffee.

Without pause, Rhyker picked up where Rhyland left off and continued the conversation, "But there is some truth to a few of the things in the human-vampire concept. Probably just remnants of stories of real vampires, like mesmerizing. Anyways, it's theorized that some subspecies are actually sort of cousins of shifters and just evolved into their own subspecies. Vampires are lumped into that theory and believed to have evolved into, sort of like, a nocturnal shifter somewhat."

"What up cuz?" Rhyland teased Nico with a cat-like grin.

Nico had the most unamused look.

Meanwhile, a laugh managed to escape Caly.

Rhyland continued without pause, "Think about it like this: Vampires are nocturnal creatures. So, you know how nocturnal animals can go out in the day but they just don't?"

"Their adapted abilities are honed for the hunt of night," Rhyker tacked on and continued, "Their pupils dilate fully..."

"Hence the black vamp eyes," Rhyland added.

"They also have similar characteristics of shifters like heightened strength, speed, hearing, and smell." Rhyker continued talking as if they weren't being all twin and talking in perfect sync with one another.

"Although, my sense of smell and Rhyker's hearing is far better than Nico's," Rhyland said, winking at Caly because no, he couldn't pass up an opportunity in the age-old male competition of "me-better-and-stronger." *Males.*

"So, yeah, they can go out in the day. They won't burst into flames and die. But they just prefer the night."

What about blood? Caly wondered to herself, noticing Nico filling up a plate with food while simultaneously doing an excellent job of ignoring the fact that he was the topic of conversation.

Her thoughts must've betrayed her because Rhyland said, "Yeah, he drinks blood but they also like to eat just like the rest of us. Well maybe not just like the rest of us," he teased, tapping his belly. Both him and Rhyker were in the midst of plowing through their second, giant pile of food.

A few minutes later, Blake walked into the dining room with the sound of laughter and he saw her smile. Jesus, her smile did things to him and his wolf. His female's smile could light up the room.

When their eyes met, her smile changed slightly as if it was just for him. He noticed she was still wearing his clothes. Blake knew he was going to immediately rectify that for her. But, damn if he didn't want to growl in approval with his scent all over her. Well, as if it wasn't already all over her after last night.

He wanted to sit next to her but the twins were on either side of her and she seemed content sandwiched between the towers.

Seeing Blake standing in the kitchen, Caly smiled. God, he was gorgeous. Without warning, a flashback of them together last night played in her mind and her body clenched in low feminine places.

"Yo, B-dawg! Guess what? SoCal can *eat!*" Rhyland playfully nudged her with his elbow.

Rhyker nodded in approval.

SoCal? Caly thought, liking that she already had a nickname. Smiling, she sipped her coffee.

"She almost out-ate us," Rhyland said with a grin.

Caly coughed out the coffee on a laugh with that remark. She knew Rhyland was just teasing her because holy shit,

Rhyker and Rhyland were already conquering their third mountain of food each. Deacon and Nico ate large portions but nothing in comparison to the twins. And, he was right, it looked like there wouldn't be any leftovers. It also was no wonder why they had their kitchen stocked piled as if they were hoarders prepping for a nuclear war.

"We don't know where it all goes either. My kind of female." Rhyland winked.

She knew he wasn't coming onto her. No. The more time she spent with Rhyland, the more she realized he was playful, funny, and easy-going. And his brother, although on the outside he was a total bad boy badass, also had some underlying hints of similar characteristics but just in his own way. She liked the twins and wondered if this was what it would feel like to have older brothers.

Grabbing a plate, Blake scooped up a bite of eggs.

Nico looked at Blake, wanting an update on the call with SILE.

Blake sent Nico a look that said, *"Not now."*

Rhyland spoke, "Well, I believe my tour duties are officially relieved." He gave an acknowledging head nod to Blake. "You know the bedroom and the kitchen. Basically, the only two rooms that matter." He shot Caly a quick wink before standing up.

He went to stack Caly's empty plate on top of his but she said, "Oh, no. Let me get them."

"No, my lady. You're our guest," Rhyland teased in a fancy English butler voice.

She laughed. "No, Rhy, please. It's the least I can do. I'll do the dishes." On that note, Caly got up, started collecting empty dishes, and got to work at the sink.

"Yeah, we like her…" Rhyland said to Blake, loud enough so everyone could hear.

"And she can stay however long she wants." Always

on that twin vibe, Rhyker finished his brother's thought without missing a beat. They both shot Caly their winning smiles.

The twins are certainly handsome with great personalities. I'm sure they have no problem with the women—er, females.

But right now there was only one male who had her attention in that way. She looked at Blake and he was looking back at her as if he read her thoughts. With a smile, she subtly bit her bottom lip before getting back to the soapy suds.

Completely satiated from the food, the twins sauntered off to their usual lounging places. Rhyker was on his couch and Rhyland was on the other large sectional. Rhyland wasn't as picky. Soft and somewhat fit him? Purr-fect. That was all he needed for a cat nap.

Deacon walked over to the sink with his dish.

"Thanks for breakfast, Caly. It was really good. Don't worry about mine. I'll wash it," he said in a polite tone.

"No, no. I totally got this," Caly insisted with a smile. She gestured for him to hand over the plate.

"Thank you," Deacon said, giving up the plate.

Caly was arms deep in dishes but she didn't mind. She noticed that Nico repositioned himself so he was sitting next to Blake as they both finished their breakfast. She wondered what they were talking about. Whatever it was, it looked serious. She guessed it probably had to do with the SILE call Rhyland said Blake was on earlier.

Nico stood up from the breakfast table and relocated to the seat next to Blake. He didn't need to say anything because Blake already knew Nico wanted the update with Blake's meeting with Bartell.

Blake took a sip of his black coffee before speaking in a

low voice, "Even though Marie's partner, Greg, was cleared to return home after his injury, he still wasn't cleared to return to work. But apparently that didn't stop him from continuing the hunt. Bartell found a file, which was an entire recap of what they knew, including all of the details from the last assignment where Marie was taken." Blake paused to take a bite of bacon. He casually glanced over at Caly before refocusing back to the conversation. "Bartell thinks Greg's memory must've been slowly returning because the last entry had something new that the official records didn't have. *"Predatory shifter. Tattoo. Disappeared."* No other details, just those words."

"Tattoo?" Nico questioned.

"Yeah. That stood out to me too," Blake agreed before continuing. "I filled in Bartell on The Ghost being a wolf shifter and Caly's rescue."

Blake didn't divulge any details more than needed to Bartell. Especially anything that had to do with force fields or portals. Blake knew that Bartell suspected he was withholding information but he had a solid relationship with Bartell and the detective was smart enough not to ask. Bartell knew that if Blake wanted him to know, then he would know.

Nico cursed under his breath, which echoed Blake's own thoughts.

"Fill the others in," Blake ordered.

Nico nodded.

With that, they both stood up and concluded the mini breakfast meeting.

Caly figured that the short meeting between Blake and Nico appeared to be over because they both stood up. Blake offered to take Nico's plate and Nico gave a head nod that translated to a *"Thank you"* as he stalked out of the room.

Blake walked over to Caly who was still playing dish-washer at the kitchen sink. His body was just inches away from pressing up close behind her when he reached around either side of her body to place the dishes in the warm and soapy sink. With his hands tangled with hers in the sudsy water, he pressed in close to her backside and kissed her neck. He didn't care if anyone saw. Hell, it was good if they did see because he was publicly claiming her (as if it wasn't clear enough already).

"I like how you look in my clothes," he whispered in her ear.

God, she suddenly remembered that she was the Midol period model. Hot. And it was literally starting to get hot with him behind her all close like that.

"Thank you for the coffee and muffin this morning. It honestly was—"

The most thoughtful thing anyone has ever done for me and I cried.

"Really thoughtful."

"My pleasure," he said in a low voice only meant for her.

She shuddered at the vibrations coming from his chest. It felt as if she was pressed up to a bass speaker. The source of vibrating heat at her back disappeared when Blake rolled away and leaned against the counter in a smooth motion.

As if he didn't just tease her, he casually continued the conversation, "I intended to have Felix stay in the room with you when you woke but he was hell-bent on following me around."

Damn if that wasn't the icing on the cake to her already melting heart.

Speaking of which, where is Felix? she wondered.

As if he read her mind, he gestured with his head to where the twins were sprawled out on the massive couches. And, yeah, Felix was there curled up on Rhyker's chest. It was a cat nap triad.

See, Caly thought with a smile. She knew Rhyker was a big ol' softy under that bad boy facade.

"Who usually cleans up around here?" she asked, placing another dish in the dishwasher.

"The general rule is clean up after yourself. And, well, we haven't all sat down and had a meal together like that in…" He paused in thought. "Ever."

"Ever?" Caly said with brows popped.

"Sure, sometimes we eat at the same time but it's more like someone will grab something quick, like a bowl of cereal or a muffin. Or we'll just order pizza like last night. Usually, the only ones cooking meals are the twins and they tag team and have their own system down. And, yeah, the twins do the shopping and everyone just pitches in for groceries. Once we tried to take turns on the shopping task but that turned out into a brawl when the bacon was forgotten."

She laug]|[[hed as he helped her load the last couple of dishes.

"By the way, breakfast was good. Thank you." He kissed her on the cheek and she blushed.

As if he liked her reaction, he turned her chin toward him with the crook of his finger and kissed her. It was slow as if savoring his favorite dessert. He wanted to take her right there. He imagined lifting her to the edge of the counter, settling between her thighs, slipping his hoodie over her head, leaning down to taste…

Later, he commanded his mind to cut off the fantasy. But that didn't mean he couldn't deepen the kiss. When his tongue slid in to dance with hers, a wolf whistle sounded from the twins' direction. Blake sent them the middle finger while his attention remained on Caly. He playfully nipped at her lower lip and the corners of his lips turned up in a closed-lipped smile. He took a step back leaving some space between them.

"Come on. I'll show you around the rest of the house." He tried to sound casual as if that kiss did not just make him want to only show her his bedroom.

Putty. Her legs were putty. It took a moment for them to receive the command from her brain that told them to move. The things this male did to her. Yeah, she was screwed. She recalled the tender moments and deep intimacy they shared last night. She remembered feeling safe while sleeping peacefully and when she blinked her eyes open, she was greeted with hot coffee and a muffin. And, yeah, now the PDA. She felt her mind hop back on the overanalyze express.

Stop, she commanded the railroad conductor. She had to get off that train, and fast... because it was so not the time for that merry go round.

Caly walked with Blake as he finished the tour of the house. It was unassumingly large and spacious, including the high ceilings in every room, which made sense with a bunch of giants living there. The whole "dark and handsome" theme carried on throughout the ranch-style home. The kitchen and living space were the focal points that separated the house into two halves. One side of the house was for the six bedrooms. The end of the hall was Blake's bedroom, or the master suite. One side of the hall was Rhyker's room, then a bathroom, hall closet, and Rhyland's room. On the other side, was Nico's room and then a small spare bedroom. Blake said that it used to be a full-sized bedroom but they cut the room in half and converted it into a bathroom because one bathroom between four males would have been a daily brawl waiting to happen. When Caly peered into the small bedroom, she was surprised at the size because it actually wasn't all that small for being cut in half. But then again, she was comparing it to what she was used to in LA. On the other side of the second bathroom was Deacon's room. The entire other side of the house was renovated into a large workout space. There was even a room that was apparently dubbed the "fight room." Blake said he would explain that to her later but she had a pretty good idea at what the room with the wrestling mats on the floor was all about.

"Blake?"

"Yeah, Caly?"

"Can we see the outside too?" She had been wanting to go outside since witnessing the sunset yesterday.

"Of course," he said, leading her through the sliding glass door in the living space.

She stepped outside for the first time since she was taken. The clean forest air washed over her body and soul. At the edge of the short, grassy clearing was the forest of massive trees with the iconic brown trunks and thick, dark greenery. It was like looking at a wall of noble giants standing guard to the world within.

Breathtaking, Caly thought, while Blake's arm wrapped around her and tucked her close to his side. Leaning into him, she took a deep breath of the crisp air and sighed.

God. I could get used to this. Except... No. I am leaving. And what was this even? Maybe he just wanted to keep it casual because he hasn't said anything otherwise. But then what about the whole PDA in the kitchen? Stop.

She had to stop herself from getting back on the over-analyze train. But damn those thoughts. The air suddenly seemed cooler than a moment ago. It also didn't help that while she was in the shower this morning, she decided that she was going to accept Riordan's offer to be her Primary. She had intended to ask Blake if she could call him today. She knew that meant she would probably be leaving in a few hours because... Why would she stay here otherwise?

Where does Riordan even live? she thought. And, *yeah,* Caly the Clinger hoped it would be close to Blake. *But what if it wasn't? What if he didn't even want to see you? What if I won't ever see him again?*

Out of nowhere, Blake scented a fresh hint of sadness in the air. Before he could ask Caly what was wrong, she broke the silence.

"Blake?"

"Yeah, Caly?"

"I've decided to accept Riordan's offer... for him to be my Primary."

He stiffened at her words that were like a dose of cold reality to his senses. Suddenly, he was in a bad mood and his wolf was pacing at the thought of her leaving him.

Say something you bastard, he commanded his brain to get with the program.

"Good," he somehow managed to get out without growling.

Good?! he thought, wanting to punch himself.

Good?! she thought, feeling like she got punched.

"Good?..." she managed to choke out, visibly recoiling.

Nice fucking job, Blake. You're handling this so well.

"I mean, good because I honestly think that is your best choice considering your options."

But you can't leave because you're mine, he silently tacked on.

Caly suddenly felt a pang in her heart at Blake's response. *God, Caly what did you think he was going to say? For you to stay? And then what? You move in? No. You can't stay. Stop being Caly the Clinger and start being the fucking Phoenix.*

They stayed silent for several minutes just looking at the trees. Blake and his wolf could not take the slight scent of despair in the air. But he couldn't keep her with him because, Seer Council or not, it was her birthright to learn about herself as Riordan said. And he couldn't just leave to go with her. As alpha, his first priority was his pack. Besides, she didn't even know that she was his life mate. But no. He couldn't let his female be sad at the moment.

"Caly?"

"Yeah, Blake?"

"My wolf wants to meet you." Technically, he already had when he went wolf and Caly was out cold. But this was different.

She stilled when a memory of the nightmare suddenly surfaced in her mind. It was when she first witnessed The Ghost shift into a wolf and tormented her.

No. This is different. This is Blake. And she knew she was right.

She cautiously responded, "Okay."

In a swift movement, he stepped away from her and stripped off his shirt.

"What? Like right now?!"

"Yeah. Like right now," he echoed with a grin, peeling off his jeans and boxers.

My god, how this male did things to her. He was gorgeous.

"You're just getting naked right now out in the open?" she said, unsure why she was protesting exactly.

"Not like you haven't seen me." He sent her a wolfish smile and she blushed.

Almost before she could blink, a massive grey wolf was in front of her.

"Beautiful..." Caly said on a surreal whisper that was hardly more than exhalation of air.

She almost couldn't believe what she just saw. It was, in one small sense, similar to what she witnessed with The Ghost yet it was wholeheartedly not the same in almost every other way.

He was beautiful in wolf form too. His wolf must've stood closer to six feet tall and was like a heavy draft horse: thick and muscular. He had those same impossibly beautiful golden eyes and she could see flecks of the same brown color of his human hair woven in with different shades of gray in his fur. It was him but it wasn't. She just stood there staring at his wolf in complete awe of this beautiful creature.

After what seemed like a lifetime, Caly saw Blake's wolf sniffing the air. She didn't move, not from fear but she wasn't sure what to do exactly. As if he was satisfied with something, he took one slow step toward her. He kept sniffing the air and she wondered what he could smell. He took another cautious step toward her and then paused with his gaze on hers. God, his gaze was so intense. It always was intense but there was something about looking into his eyes in his wolf form. It almost had her looking down at the ground in a knee-jerk reaction but she held it.

"Blake? Can you hear me?"

With a chuff she got her answer.

Okayyy. This isn't weird at all. Nope, she thought with a good dose of sarcasm.

"It's okay. You can come closer. I'm not scared."

And it was the truth. She wasn't scared of him at all. She felt completely safe with Blake's wolf just like she did with his human form. He continued with the sniff and step routine while she apparently decided to see if she could become one with the forest and stand still like a tree. As Blake closed the final step between them, his wolf sniffed her hand and rubbed his head into it. In a natural reaction, she went to pet him and then froze with her hand in the air.

What if it's rude to pet him? What if there is some sort of wolf etiquette I don't know about?

As if reading her thoughts, he pressed his head into her

hand and took two steps forward rubbing against her body. With that swift motion, his fur slid between her fingers.

"So soft," she said on a half-whisper.

He looked at her with a slight gleam in his wolf eyes and she laughed softly.

This is probably going right to his head. Whatever. He has to know he's beautiful and he probably gets this reaction from females a lot.

And with that thought, she suddenly didn't want any other females petting him. Like ever. But that wasn't fair of her. She had no claim on him.

Besides you're leaving. Like probably today. Like in a few hours.

With another wave of despair in the air, Blake had a feeling he knew what it was. Caly must've been thinking about her impossible decision about her future that she was practically forced into. He cursed because there was nothing he could do.

And what? Tell her she's my mate when she's about to leave? What the hell would that accomplish? Except maybe more things to add to her plate. Not to mention it most likely would scare her off. It wouldn't be fair to her. But then what? I'm just supposed to let my life mate go?

Forcing those thoughts to the back burner, he refocused on Caly. Caly, who was his priority at the moment. Caly, who was in distress, which was unacceptable. At least, there was something he could do about that.

He looked into her stunning gray eyes. Jesus, her eyes were captivating and it felt as if he was staring into the eye of a hurricane. They held this quiet strength like the way storm clouds were both beautiful and ominous. And the way she could hold his alpha gaze? Yeah, both he and his wolf would never tire of getting sucked into the silent staring vortex with her.

When Blake started to walk away from her toward the trees, Caly figured he was going to go do what wolves do, whatever that was. Before she turned back to the house, he stopped and looked back at her, as if waiting for her. Understanding dawned. He wanted her to go with him.

Smiling. She was smiling ear to ear at the alpha wolf who had somehow managed to transform her previous thoughts of hopelessness about the future into curiosity about the present.

Is he going to show me something? Or are we just going for a walk? Or—

Her thoughts were cut off when Blake's body was pressed close to hers as they walked side by side. She wondered if it was a wolf thing to walk like they were literally attached at the hip. But she didn't mind. In fact, she rather liked it.

Caly lost track of time and didn't know how long they walked. But all she saw were trees in every direction. In fact...

"What's that?" she asked, looking at the trunk of what must've been a very old tree considering its massive size.

The tree was just far enough ahead that she couldn't quite make it out but something definitely happened to the trunk of that tree.

"Oh, sorry." She laughed a little, realizing she just asked Blake a question in his wolf form. Yeah, like he could answer. Well, maybe with a chuff.

Even though Blake was in his wolf form, it was still Blake. Clearly, because she just asked him a question as if he was walking next to her in his "human" form. In either form, she felt as if some deep part of her knew that golden gaze and alpha presence. As if she had known him her entire life and gone on a thousand forest walks with him.

As they approached the gigantic, old tree, she saw that one side of the trunk was covered with deep grooves.

Claw marks, she thought as her eyes widened a touch.

That was the moment of dawning realization. She was in the middle of a forest on the species side of The Barrier.

Lions, tigers, bears, and an unknown, clawed creature with a bone to pick with Mr. Tree? Oh my.

She knew she was safe with Blake. But, yeah, the Freddy Krueger inspired tree attack may have given her a slight pause. And she may have stepped just a little closer to Blake. He noticed. Of course he noticed because nothing got past that alpha wolf. His smooth pink tongue licked the palm of her hand as if reassuring her that she was safe and he wouldn't let anything happen to her. She welcomed the touch and unconsciously stroked his fur as they continued walking. With each step they took, she could feel his powerful muscles flex underneath the thick layer of soft fur. The close contact helped soothe her irrational fears about clawed creatures with a thirst for tree bark.

No one would dare mess with an alpha wolf... right?

On the heels of that thought, two wolves appeared up ahead. She froze and looked around to see if there was anything she could use to defend herself. Perhaps a rock or a fallen tree branch.

God, why was the forest floor so damn tidy? Who knew forest fairies had OCD.

Blake's wet tongue against her hand brought her out of her ridiculous thoughts. Ridiculous because it didn't take a wolf expert to see there were no signs of aggression from either Blake or the wolves up ahead. Instead, it almost seemed like they knew each other. It was as if the two wolves were waiting for Blake's command.

Are these shifters too? No. They must be wild wolves, she concluded, noting the significant size difference in comparison to Blake and The Ghost's wolf forms.

Blake's wolf took one step forward. His head and tail

were held high while his eyes were trained on the wolves ahead. She noted how they averted their eyes and bowed their heads. Blake was clearly the alpha here. The two wolves cautiously approached, keeping an attentive eye on Blake for his direction.

At the sound of Blake's low, short woof, the two wolves immediately halted in their tracks. Caly translated that as, *"Stop. That's close enough."*

When he looked over his shoulder and met her eyes, she got the feeling he was communicating to her that it was her choice if she wanted to meet these two wolves up close or not. Going with her gut, she nodded at Blake. Again, it was clear that Blake was the alpha in charge in this situation and she wasn't in any danger. Also, now that the two wolves were closer, she could only see curiosity in their yellow, wolf eyes.

Blake motioned for her to sit down by echoing the movement in his own body. When her butt planted on the forest floor, he looked at one of the wolves and must've given a silent command to approach. The slightly larger wolf, with wild markings of gray, white, and black, took a cautious step closer. The head was lowered but ears were pricked up in interest. Caly remained completely still. Yes, she was a little scared but she didn't dare move. She didn't want to inadvertently spook the wolves out of her own ignorance of not knowing wolf etiquette. Blake's body was right next to hers the entire time as the wild wolf continued to take cautious steps toward her until his snout was just close enough to sniff Caly.

With his head still lowered, the wolf looked at Blake, then Caly, and circled back to Blake, as if in silent inquiry. Blake must have given a silent command of approval because the wild wolf closed the distance and began sniffing Caly. As if she passed some sort of inspection, the wolf's tail began wagging and then he started licking her face. She couldn't help the toothy grin that took over her face. She remained still and let the wolf do all of the exploring.

After a few minutes, she gave another approving nod of her head to Blake at his silent question. With another alpha wolf A-Okay signal, the other wolf came over and joined the sniff and lick party as well. This wolf was slightly smaller and had light gray and white markings. Due to the smaller size, Caly guessed this wolf was female. Within minutes, Caly found herself in the middle of the best therapy session of her life. It wasn't like she had other therapy sessions to compare it to but she was certain that the wolf nuzzle-party beat laying on a therapist's couch any day.

Once Caly was completely covered in wolf hair, and she couldn't wipe that damn toothy grin off her face even if she wanted to, she looked over at Blake with a sheen of tears powered by pure unbelievable joy. Never had she ever imagined she would be sitting in a forest next to a gorgeous alpha wolf shifter while being greeted by two wild wolves. She didn't even know that she craved this experience somewhere deep in her soul until it was happening before her eyes.

In response to her sheer joy, Blake's wolf was playfully licking and nuzzling her face until she was laying on the forest floor, laughing with him standing over her. There was a natural pause in the play and she grew still when he leaned down and touched his nose to hers while looking into her eyes. She smiled up at him.

Blake nudged her body and then motioned with his head to the forest as if to say, *"Come on. Get up. Let's continue walking."*

She shot him a playful frown in protest but he insisted.

"Okay, fine," she said with a smile, brushing off some dirt on the hoodie and sweatpants. She felt like she could've stayed like that all day with the wolves… with her wolf.

No. He is not yours. You're leaving, like in a few hours, remember?

That thought was the bucket of cold ice water she needed to jolt her back into reality. After this—whatever this was—she was going to call Riordan and accept his offer to be her Primary. Which meant she was going to be leaving Blake. Not to mention the fact that she still didn't understand what was even going on between them, if anything.

Stop, she told herself, putting a lid on that emotional merry go round.

Focusing on putting one foot in front of the other, she walked with Blake, who was once again pressed close to her side.

No, you're not going to read into that body language either. Again, with the cease and desist order.

To her pleasant surprise, the wolf party wasn't quite over because the two wild wolves joined in for the walk. After their mini wolf pack walked a good distance, she was about to call a timeout. She was shoeless after all. And, damn, if she wasn't getting a little hot in his hoodie and sweats, despite the cool forest air. She figured Blake must've given some sort of silent signal because the wolves took a final glimpse at Caly before bounding off into the forest. Following Blake, she ducked behind a couple of thick, tree branches toward the sound of running water.

"Woah," she said, stopping short after clearing the final branch.

She was looking at a breathtaking scene of lush greenery, enormous rocks, and mini waterfalls all flowing into a natural pool of clear blue water that was shining in the sunlight. It felt like she stepped straight into a Bob Ross painting. Without warning, a gorgeous and very naked Blake stood in front of her. He shot her a wicked smile and then jumped into the water.

"Oh my god! It must be freezing!" she called out when his head surfaced out of the water.

"It's not too bad. Besides, I'll keep you warm," he said, still sporting his wolfish grin.

God. Was she really about to be naked in the middle of the forest with Blake like a bunch of hippies? Yup, she apparently was. She stripped out the clothes and heard a low approving growl from Blake.

"Caly, you're so beautiful."

With a blushing smile, she walked up to the water and jumped in on a shout of joy. To her surprise, the water wasn't freezing. It was refreshingly cool and perfect after the long walk.

As soon as she broke the surface, Blake pulled her in close so her legs and arms were wrapped around him and the only thing keeping them afloat was his powerful body treading water. And it felt like she sidled up to a portable water heater.

Is that a wolf thing? Or does he just run at a hotter temperature? she wondered.

"Are wolves hotter?"

"Yes. But the twins might disagree," he said with a wolfish grin.

She laughed. "No. You know what I mean. Like temperature-wise. You're so warm."

"Yeah, shifters naturally run at higher temperatures than humans and other species. Oh, and that tree you saw. That's Rhy's favorite tree."

Of course, she thought, unsure why she didn't put two and two together herself. This territory was not only home to a predatory alpha wolf but also two jaguars and a vampire. She internally gave herself a face palm, realizing how silly her reaction was earlier. Because, yeah, only someone with a death wish would dare encroach on these males territory in such a blatant declaration.

He nipped her earlobe and she melted into his warm, powerful body. She felt his hard length making its presence known between them. Her body responded with a wave of warmth settling in her most feminine of places. His lips pressed against hers and she sank into the kiss. From one heartbeat to the next, he playfully dunked them both under the water while still lip locked. When they surfaced, she was laughing and he seemed all too amused with his playful antics.

"So, you like it when I howl?" he drawled.

She blushed at the memory of her bold request for him to howl when they here having hot cave sex in her dream. Before she could answer, he threw his head back and howled. It was just as hauntingly beautiful as the other times she heard it. It sent a shiver of pleasure down her spine and, as soon as his wolf song ended, she pressed her lips to his with a chorus of responding wild wolf howls, as if it were their make out-session, background music.

He licked his way inside her mouth and their tongues were dancing with one another in a slow and sensual rhythm. He teased her lower lip with quick nips and sucks and she retaliated by creating friction between their bodies. He growled in approval and migrated the kiss to her neck just below her ear.

"Blake," she moaned at the sensation.

With his name on Caly's lips, Blake responded by swimming to shore, carrying her out of the water, and laying her onto the soft grass. Settling between her thighs with his hard length on her belly, he leaned down and claimed her mouth in a demanding kiss.

He was desperate to also claim her with his mating scent.

She was his and his wolf was pacing at being denied the pleasure to mark what was his. But he wasn't an animal and would never mark her unless she accepted him as her mate.

Sliding his palm up her waist, he cupped her full breast and teased her nipple with his thumb. She moaned into the kiss while arching into him. Her sweet scent was flooding his senses and his cock twitched in response, demanding to be inside her. He kissed his way down to her breasts, cupped the full peaks, and took turns worshipping her nipples with his wicked tongue. She arched her chest into him on a begging moan and widened her legs for him in invitation. Sliding his fingers down her core, he began to stroke her sensitive spot. Christ, she was so wet for him and his fingers felt slick across her wet folds. He penetrated her slit with two fingers while using the heel of his palm to stimulate her erotic bundle of nerves.

"You're so tight and wet for me," he growled.

"Oh god... Blake, don't stop," she pleaded on an exhale as he worked her into a frenzy.

"Never," he vowed, picking up the sensual rhythm with his fingers. He felt her tightening around him and knew she was close.

"Come for me, Caly," he commanded.

A moment later, she succumbed to the wave of ecstasy erupting through her. Her sex squeezed around his fingers with pulsing waves of pleasure and he kept working her so she could ride out the waves.

When she came back to reality, he locked eyes with her, pulled his fingers out of her tight sheath and sucked off her sweet nectar. He groaned. He loved the taste of her.

With the desire to claim his female from behind, he flipped her over so she was on all fours and spread her legs wide for him. Her sex was glistening and he growled in anticipation at the sight of her.

She shot him a sensual smile over her shoulder and teased her hips in invitation.

He sent her a grin full of erotic promises, gripped his throbbing length in one hand, and brought his tip to her slick entrance. He slid into her to the hilt and they both moaned. With his hands firmly at her hips, he began pistoning into her hard and fast. Leaning forward, he planted one hand on the ground and reached around with his other to tease her sensitive spot as he thrust deep. He loved the way his female sounded in the heat of the moment and each throaty moan that escaped her kiss swollen lips drove him wilder and wilder.

"Blake!" she cried out.

He was just as close, with the intense tightening and tingling sensation at the base of his spine.

"Come for me Caly!" he growled in a loud demand.

As if waiting for his command, she came with powerful contractions triggering his own release on a triumphant shout. Her sex was milking every last drop out of him.

Both breathing heavy and coming down from the heavens, he pulled out of her and maneuvered them so their sticky, hot bodies were spooning. Her backside was tucked close to his front and she fit so perfectly next to his. She curled impossibly closer into him and sighed.

Fuck his previous thoughts. He was going to tell her. She needed to know she was his. He inhaled and opened his mouth to tell her.

"Blake?"

"Yeah, Caly?"

Screw it, Caly thought. She needed to lay it all out there. She was about to leave and maybe wouldn't see Blake again. She took a deep breath like she was taking a drag on a joint rolled with leaves of courage.

"I... umm... Everything is so jumbled right now. My whole life is literally crazy... it's as if I jumped into the pages of the books I read. Sometimes I think maybe I will wake up and find out I was in a coma or something and this was all just a weird dream. But I know that's not true because it feels so right being here... with you."

That was the crack in the dam and there was no stopping the water of words flowing from her mouth.

"Since the moment I saw you in my dream, I felt a pull. I know it's crazy and makes no sense. You've somehow become this steady pulse in my heart. But I can't stay here and, even if I could stay, then what? I live here with you? That seems crazy and way too soon. Not to mention I don't have any money, a job, or a place to stay. And there is this gnawing fear in the back of my mind torturing me with thoughts of how the hell did I go out with..."

She swallowed back the bile rising in her throat.

"You know... and not only once but two times. God, we even kissed. Granted, it was like ice." Her stomach lurched. "And I was going to break it off that third date because I didn't like him at all but..." She paused briefly. "How did I even go out with a psychopathic killer in the first place? What is wrong with me?" Her voice trailed off and she closed her eyes for a moment. "But what I feel for you is completely different and can't even be compared at all. What I feel for you scares me in a totally different way because I've never felt like this with anyone."

Well good job, Caly. Caly heard internal clapping in her mind. *You are officially Clinger Crazy Caly Condition at the worst stage: Infatuation and borderline obsession. You've professed your deep feelings for your rescuer. How original. And you don't even know how he feels. What if I am just a good lay and he was having fun with me especially knowing I would be leaving? Sure, he rescued you and saved you but that was a part of his job for the case he is working on.*

She felt insanely vulnerable all of a sudden and, no, it did not help that she was naked in the afterglow of sex.

And BTW nice timing for this conversation, Caly.

She needed to pull away from his body and start the awkward back peddling. As if he could hear her thoughts, his grip tightened on her so she couldn't pull away.

"Caly, there's something you need to know."

Here it is. Your heart is about to be crushed, Caly. Brace for impact and pretend like everything is fine and that you were just confused. There's so much going on and I am confused is all. Yeah, that's it.

"I—" she started to make the back-peddling escape.

"No. You need to hear this," Blake said, cutting her off for the first time ever. It was enough to keep her trap shut momentarily. "Wolves mate for life."

Oh god. Here it comes. I was just a play thing. A distraction until he finds his wolf mate. I'm such an idiot. Just keep it together, Caly. You can keep it together for a few hours until you leave and never have to see him again.

Blake scented the sudden sting of heartbreak in the air.

Shit. This wasn't going how he thought. He hugged her closer to try and comfort her.

"What I mean is—"

"Blake. It's fine. I'm just confused and like I said, everything is a total mess in my head right now. Just forget it."

She tried to break free of his grip but he held her tighter.

Do not cry. Do not cry. Do not cry, she kept telling herself.

"Caly, listen to me. I didn't know how to tell you this."

Oh god. Here it comes.

"You're my life mate."

"Like I said it's fine. I'm just confused," she said, trying to peel away from him.

Why is he gripping me so tight? she thought, desperately trying to escape because she was about to lose it.

Why can't he just let it go?! And let me go! Tears were pricking her eyes. *God, I have to get the fuck out of here!*

"Caly! You're not listening. You're my mate. You're *mine* and I'm *yours.*"

He rolled on top of her to cage her in because clearly she was a flight risk and he needed to stare into her eyes to make sure she understood. "I'm *yours,*" he repeated, looking directly into her stormy eyes.

She froze as the words finally started to sink in.

"Wh-What? But... but I'm not a wolf."

He smiled. "I know."

"But don't only wolves, umm, mate with wolves?" she said in a shaky, confused voice.

"Not always. There are interspecies mates. It's not as common but not unheard of."

"Wait, how can you be sure? We don't even know each other."

He smirked. "It's instinct. My wolf has always known since the first dream. It just took me a little longer to understand.

"Okay... hold on... I need to think." She pushed on his arms that were still caged around her.

She couldn't have a conversation like this: naked with him above her.

He hesitated, trying to determine if she was going to bolt before rolling off.

She shot to her feet a little too quickly and had to take a breath to let the lightheaded sensation pass. Slipping back into his hoodie and sweatpants, she realized that he didn't have any clothes to put on. So, yeah, this wasn't awkward or anything. Plus, she had so many questions. This was like déjà vu and her brain was back to being on freeze mode.

"Okay. So you think I'm your... life mate?" she finally began, pacing a bit and trying to ignore all of his nakedness.

"I *know* you're my life mate," he said definitively.

"How can you be so sure? We don't even know each other!" she exclaimed.

Why are you arguing this? Weren't you just heartbroken because you thought he was about to break your heart because he has another wolf mate? And now you're freaked out because he says you're his mate? WTF is wrong with you, Caly?!

"Instinct. The male just knows," he said clearly and cautiously, sensing her conflicting confusion.

"Okay, but what if you're wrong? I mean—"

"Do you not want me?" he cut her off for the second time ever.

"What? Of course I want you. So much so that it scares me. But I don't know you and you don't know me. And what if this doesn't work out? And what is *this* even?" she gestured between them. "And... god. I am leaving to go with Riordan." Her thoughts were like the scrambled eggs she made for breakfast.

"We'll make it work," Blake reassured her.

She could tell he was serious.

Memories started to surface of the few friends she had growing up being all googly-eyed over a boyfriend one month and then the next time she saw them, they looked as if they threw said googly-eyed boyfriend's clothes out a window, kicking them out of their life.

"How? I mean, okay, let's say poof," she gestured with her hands like a magician. "We magically are life mates. Then what? I'm still leaving. And your life is here." Her arms were spread wide indicating the picturesque forest scenery around them.

Blake blew out a breath and ran his hand through his hair.

"I don't know, Caly... But I do know in here." he pounded his fist onto his chest over his heart. "That you're my life mate."

A wave of chills rushed over her because, yeah, deep down she knew it too. She exhaled on that soul-shattering acceptance.

As if he knew that acceptance, he approached her, cupped her face, and kissed her long and slow.

Yeah, deep down she knew. When the slow declaration naturally died out, Caly said in a soft voice, "So, what does this mean exactly?"

"It means you're mine and I'm yours. Caly, there is only one life mate for me. And you're my one and only. I have waited for over a century for you and will wait forever until you accept me as yours."

Suddenly, she wanted to cry because his words shot straight to her soul and ignited a fire somewhere deep within her.

Breathe. Just breathe, she commanded herself to take in what all of this meant.

"What do you mean by life mate? Is it like... marriage?"

Oh god, not the "m" word. She wasn't opposed to marriage. In fact, she always wanted to get married one day with the love of her life. But all of this seemed so sudden and she barely even knew him. And it didn't help that her mind was like a photo album flipping through pictures of friends that went from madly in love, to divorced in like two years or less.

I just found out I'm immortal and now I suddenly have a mate for eternity?

"I think it would be similar to the concept of twin flames the humans have. But it is far more meaningful amongst species. 'Life mates' is one of the most sacred and powerful bonds that exists in our world. It is said to be so powerful that it extends beyond our physical reality into the very fabric of the magic of life itself. It is how I *know* deep down in every fiber of my being that you're mine," Blake declared while looking deep into her gray eyes.

Caly exhaled acceptance because, again, she knew it too. "Somewhere deep inside me knows this truth. And I think on some subconscious level, I've always known since the moment I first saw you in my dream. It's always felt... magnetic... between us. Like an invisible force I can't help but gravitate toward." There was a pause. "But I have doubts and fears. What if this doesn't work out? What if we get annoyed with each other and want nothing to do with each other in like a month or a year? What if long-distance doesn't work? How long will I even be living with Riordan? I don't even know how I can possibly be in a relationship when I don't even know who I am really. How is that fair to either of us? What if I turn out to be some crazy immortal? Or, hell, for all you know, I am crazy and you don't even know—"

He kissed her hard and the impact was just what she needed to get kicked off the overanalyze express.

"*That's* how I know this will work out," he said, knowing full well that she felt the undeniable soul-deep chemistry they had between them.

"You're right," she said on an exhale. "But I still have doubts and it just seems so soon."

"We'll figure this out *together*," he reassured her, emphasizing the last word.

"Do I have to go with Riordan? What if..." She hesitated but decided to just say it because they needed to be open with each other, "What if I just stay here?" She held her breath, waiting for his response.

"I thought of that too and I already asked Riordan. He confirmed that a verbal claim of us being mates is not enough to sway the council."

"You already asked Riordan?" she said, feeling an unexpected emotion rise within her.

"Yeah. Last night before he left."

It looked like he was about to say something else but then she turned into a whole new layer of crazy Caly and pushed away from his embrace.

"Let me get this straight. You asked Riordan if I could stay with you?" she said in a tone that sliced the air.

Wait, what just happened? Blake thought as both he and his wolf suddenly pricked their ears on high alert trying to solve the mysterious one-eighty of Caly.

"Yes," he said cautiously, not knowing what set her off.

"Wow." She felt like she was a bull seeing red. "Blake, did it ever occur to you to come to me *first*? You know, *before* you ask my surrogate father about where I should live *my* life?"

Okay. "Surrogate father" is a bold word choice and I probably could tone it down on the slicing tone, she thought. But apparently her point hit home by the way Blake recoiled.

Shit, Blake thought as a wave of realization washed over him.

"Caly—" he started to explain.

"No." She cut him off and apparently there was no stopping this crazy Caly train because it was running on pure emotional full steam ahead. "Did your *alpha-ness* decide what my future would be without my input? Blake, I need to let you know something right now. I am not going to be your submissive, wolfy bitch doing whatever the fuck you say. I am my own god damn woman... female... whatever!" she huffed out a frustrated breath before continuing. "...

and *I* am the only one who decides how *I* am going to live my life. Even if some of the options are fucking shitty, like with this whole Primary thing, *I* am still the one making the choices about *my* life."

Yup. Full-on cursing crazy Caly at your service, she thought. *And fat chance you're going to get a word in edgewise. See how it feels to not even be considered in the conversation?*

Feeling like she was about to explode, she stormed off. She didn't know exactly where to go but she guessed it was the direction of the house. And it didn't seem to matter at the moment.

"Caly, wait! Let me explain!"

She heard Blake call out after her.

"No. Let's see how you like it when you're not given a chance to speak for yourself. And don't even *think* about following me!" she yelled, not even bothering to turn around to look at him. Instead, she charged off even faster.

Several minutes later, she heard a noise behind her.

"Blake, I swear to God—" She whirled around and her angry voice was abruptly cut off. She froze when she saw the two wolves. It was fine earlier because Blake was there and he was in charge.

But what happens when he's not here? They aren't being aggressive but still, they are wild wolves.

"Hi." She tried to sound calm but it came out shaky. "I'm just going to walk back to the house now. Everything is fine," she said in a tremulous, sing-song voice.

As if noticing her tension, both of the wolves lowered their heads, bowed down a little, and looked up at her with huge puppy dog eyes.

Clearly, they aren't here to attack you and they're giving you the puppy dog eyes.

"Okay, come here," she said with a smile as she plopped

down on the ground just like before. The wolves cautiously approached and got back with the sniffing, nuzzling, and licking routine. A moment later, she burst into tears.

"I know I overreacted a little… okay, maybe a lot. And he didn't mean to steamroll me but that's what it felt like," she choked out as if the wolves could understand her. Wiping her eyes, she continued, "Like, it was as if my life was being decided without me. And how is it that Blake tells Riordan before me? I mean, I'm his mate but he didn't go to me?" She tried to suck in even breaths of air in an effort to calm the turbulent sea of emotions.

"I mean, all of a sudden I'm not human, I'm forced to have a Primary, and I've found my life mate. Granted, two of those things I'm not complaining about by any means but I'm just sick of feeling completely helpless and out of control of my own life."

A memory of being chained in the darkness flashed across her mind.

"No." She opened her eyes and wiped the new wave of tears away. "Not anymore. I am *done* with being the help-less chained Caly in the darkness. I survived. I am safe. I am the fucking Phoenix." Again, she tried with the slow calm even breaths while the wolves comforted her.

She didn't know how long Caly Cry Fest number three hundred and twenty-eight lasted and when she was feeling somewhat back to herself, she slowly got up and looked around. Yup. There were trees everywhere.

"Do you know the way back to the house?" she asked the wolves with a slight laugh and began walking in the di-rection she thought was toward the house. The two wolves walked with her, one on either side and she smiled. "I'm so glad you've decided to join me."

Eventually, she got to a point where she wasn't quite sure where she was going and being lost was a valid possibility.

She remembered this patch of trees because there was a large branch that was half hanging and earlier she thought about what it would've been like to climb it. But she couldn't remember if she should go right or left. When the male wolf took the lead, Caly followed, hoping he was leading her back to the house.

I'm sure they are. I mean, where else would they take me? They can probably see I'm a lost pup just trying to get back to the den.

Thanks to a couple more course corrections from her fury tour guides, Caly saw the house up ahead through the clearing of the trees. It was a good thing too because she was starting to get tired and hungry. Kneeling down, Caly offered her gratitude to the wolves and welcomed the nose-nuzzling sendoff of affection.

"Thank you both. I probably would have been lost without you."

Smiling, she watched the two wolves pad off into the forest. Heading toward the house, Caly made a mental plan.

I'll stop by the kitchen, grab something to eat really quick, and then go to the small spare bedroom.

Caly chose the spare bedroom instead of Blake's room because it just seemed weird to use his room with the way things were left between them. She knew they were going to talk but she still needed some time to think.

Chapter 28

From the forest, Blake watched Caly enter the house. Caly didn't know that he followed her and the two wolves the entire way home. Caly also didn't know that he ran off to get the two wolves to escort her back home. He needed to make sure that she got home safely. It's not like anything would happen in these woods but he couldn't help it. She was his and he wouldn't just leave her.

He heard what Caly confessed to the wolves and the walk home gave him plenty of time to digest it. He knew she was right. He should've spoken with her first before going to Riordan. Of course, he didn't mean for it to seem like he was going behind her back or dominating her life. From what she said to the wolves, she knew he didn't mean it like that either. Clearly this ran far deeper than just going to Riordan. Caly was triggered about feeling out of control and helpless. Which was a part of the reason he didn't go to her to begin with because he didn't want to add to the weight that she was suddenly carrying on her shoulders. He decided to give her some space and let her cool off before explaining everything.

Blake saw that Caly was in the kitchen and it looked like she was making some food. Good. He also made a mental note to have Rhyland bring her some food just to make sure she wasn't hungry. He would've liked to do it himself but, yeah, he was probably the last male she wanted to see right now.

Blake shrugged into his jeans and white shirt (the same ones he stripped out of before shifting into his wolf) and made a mental plan that he figured was probably similar to Caly's: food and being alone. Oh, and he had one more thing to do but that could wait until a little bit later. Executing his plan, he stalked into the house.

In the kitchen, he smelled peanut butter and jelly and presumed Caly made a PB&J sandwich. He liked where her mind was at. It was efficient and easy which was good so he could get to sulking in the spare room. Hell, he may even just go for another run and—

Shit, he thought, sensing Rhyland and Nico approaching. He looked at the door to make a quick escape. Suddenly, the run sounded like the best plan.

"Blake," Nico said in his cool tone.

"Not now," Blake growled out.

"Meeting in the fight room," Nico sliced back.

What the hell? They need to meet right now? Blake thought, realizing it must be important or they would no doubt leave him alone when he was in this kind of a mood. That, and the fact that it was in the fight room, meant that they didn't want Caly to hear. So, it was probably an update with the case.

Just fucking great.

"What crawled up your ass?" Rhyland theatrically sniffed the air, half curious about what caused Blake's dark mood. When his feline grin spread across his face, it said all that needed to be said. But no, Rhyland just couldn't let it go with a non-verbal acknowledgment. "I mean, we all heard your howl earlier and I would've put my money on you being in a better mood," he teased with a waggle of his eyebrows.

Blake let out a low growl that let him know he was in no mood for Rhyland's jokes right now.

"Alright. Message received," Rhyland said, putting his hands up to signal that he would back off. "But we still need to meet," he concluded, strolling to the fight room.

Blake and Nico followed suit, both silently stalking into the room after Rhyland.

Being Blake's second, Nico was the one who spoke. "Blake, we've all talked."

Okay, you have my attention, Blake thought, his wolf's ears pricking up.

"Is the female your life mate?" Nico cut right to the chase in his typical, concise, and "no bullshit" way of communicating.

Blake cursed. This was so not the time. His pack brothers did have a right to know and he was going to tell them but just not right now. Especially with the fight between him and Caly.

"Yeah. She's my life mate." Blake spoke in a direct tone that would shred any doubt. His pack brothers would never question his claim but Blake spoke with certitude and clarity regardless. "But it's fine. She's still leaving, probably tomorrow. And, yeah, she knows… as of an hour ago. Look, if that was it then I'm gonna go."

Blake was met with a long stretch of silence. He narrowed his eyes slightly when he noticed all of the males look at each other in agreement. Clearly, there was a silent conversation going on that he wasn't clued in on. And, as alpha, he didn't like not knowing what was going on with his pack. Because whatever this was, it was important by the look on their faces.

"What?" Blake barked out, holding back a growl because

he knew it wasn't fair for him to take out his frustration on them.

Nico was about to speak but Rhyland interjected and gave Nico this look that said, "*Yeah, second or not, this conversation is not your strong suit.*" Nico crossed his arms over his chest because he knew Rhyland was right.

"Blake, we suspected she was your life mate really since you went wolf. Look, you're our alpha and brother. And she's your mate. Your fucking *life mate*. You need to be with her. And... we follow you." Rhyland paused and then a slight feline grin came over his face. "And I'm so down for some foreign females. Nico, maybe you won't have to use your vamp charm on these females. Oh, which is a good reminder, maybe you also want to cool it on the pink when you decorate your new room?" Rhyland quipped.

Nico's eyes narrowed to lethal slits.

It took Blake a moment to register what Rhyland said.

In a sudden swift movement, all of the males were standing in a semicircle around Blake. As second, Nico locked eyes with Blake and spoke first. "I follow you." He pounded his dominant hand over his heart, warrior to warrior. Second to alpha. Brother to brother.

One by one, they each re-pledged their unwavering allegiance to Blake. They knew that as alpha, Blake not only looked out for each of them but also, without hesitation, he would put every single one of them and the pack before himself. And, in this case, they knew that Blake would even put the pack before being with his life mate, without any animosity or grudges. They knew that just as they pledged their loyalty to Blake, he pledged his loyalty to them. But now, it was their turn to put their alpha first before each of them. Because they knew that Blake needed to be with his life mate. It was one of the most sacred bonds and some specians waited their entire existence to be with their life mate. So, it would kill them to know that they were the reason that was keeping him from his life mate.

Blake's heart swelled with pride and love for his pack brothers.

His mind was racing a mile and minute. Glancing up at his pack mates, he concluded, "I need to talk to Caly."

...*First*, Blake mentally noted. He was not going to repeat what got him into the situation he was currently in with Caly.

"We'll keep this home as a backup location. And, of course, we have enough pack funds to invest in a second location. We can work for SILE cases anywhere. That's never been an issue..."

Yup. Blake's brain was kicking into full alpha gear as the tasks were churning out and calculating what it all meant.

They hashed out a proposed plan and Blake ended the meeting with, "Nothing leaves this room until I speak with Caly."

Blake wasn't going to let Caly go without a fight, a damn good fight, but he also knew it was her choice as to whether or not she wanted to be with him and whether or not she potentially wanted to live with them. A part of their plan was to find a second location close to where Riordan lived. If Caly accepted the invitation to live with them, then she would still be close to Riordan for training. And if Caly didn't want to live with them, then that would be okay too because, again, they would at least be near each other and he would court the fuck out of his female—not like he wasn't going to already. And, well, that would be okay for right now, but, truthfully, Blake did intend to live with Caly eventually.

With the meeting concluded, they all walked out of the training room.

"D," Blake added.

Turning, Deacon looked at Blake.

"I need a favor."

* * *

Caly hadn't seen Blake for the rest of the day. In fact, she really hadn't heard one peep from any of the males, including Felix.

Traitor.

Okay, fine. It was a big house but she just figured she would hear something, like even footsteps or doors opening at the very least. But it was as if everyone suddenly had everywhere else to be except on this side of the house. Although, there had been that single knock at the door a while ago but by the time she answered the door, all that was there was a sandwich and a bag of chips on the floor. Blake probably warned everyone to give her some space. She knew she was the one isolated in the room by choice and she was kind of hoping that Blake would come and talk to her. But that probably wasn't the best idea. If she was being honest with herself, she would have to admit that she was still a little upset.

How could he have not talked to me first?

Yet at the same time, she also knew she overreacted and went from zero to batshit crazy Caly in three seconds flat. So, yeah. She needed to apologize too. Caly blew out a breath and was going a little stir crazy in this room. It was strange how she went from never wanting to leave his room to now feeling cooped up. Granted, it wasn't his room she was in, but still. Keeping her thoughts and emotions occupied thus far were movies and food. Always a good combo. She was going to watch one of her favorite go-to movies, *Twilight*, but that hit a little too close to home at the moment. So, she opted for *Kung Fu Panda*.

Because a chubby panda eating his body weight in food and rolling around isn't something you can relate to at all, Caly thought dryly, looking over at the small mountain of empty bags of chips, candy, and crumbs that she had conquered. Oh, and that was crumbs from not one, but two PB&J sandwiches, not to mention the additional mystery sandwich which just so happened to be prepared exactly as she liked it. So, nope. She couldn't relate to that panda at all.

With that, she decided that she needed to get out of this room. Peering through the sliding glass door, she saw the sun was just starting its descent. When she entered the room earlier, she was somewhat surprised to see there was a sliding glass door to the outside, even in the small spare room but she figured it was probably just a standard among species houses with shifters to have rooms with outdoor access. Looking at the sunset as it unabashedly showed off its beauty, she recalled the stunning sunset yesterday and wanted to watch the replay. Pushing the sliding glass door open, she plopped down on the cement steps and wondered what everyone was doing—especially Blake.

"*That's* how I know this will work out... We'll figure this out *together*..." She heard Blake's words replay in her mind.

Okay, Caly thought, with a hint of sarcasm. Then, Master Oogway's voice from *Kung Fu Panda* unexpectedly appeared in her head. It was the part where the wise, old turtle was giving the clumsy panda sage advice about how one must relinquish the illusion of control in order to fulfill their destiny. *Who knew you could relate to more than just being a chubby panda?* Caly thought wryly. The talk of destiny was a bit much for Caly but the part about letting go of the illusion of control hit home. She did feel like her life was spinning out of control in a storm of chaos. She knew it was actually the underlying reason for the complete freak out on Blake.

I think it's time to raise the white flag and talk this through with Blake, Caly thought on an exhale.

A knock sounded at the door.

He has some timing...

"Bla—" She halted mid-word, surprised to see Rhyland when she swung open the door. Okay. Not who she was expecting. And wasn't this déjà vu all of a sudden?

"Hey, Caly," Rhyland greeted. "So, this isn't awkward or anything," he joked with a chuckle. "But, yeah, Blake wants to see you."

Apparently, crazy Caly was back up to bat because suddenly, the white flag was on the ground and she felt another wave of emotion rise in its place.

Blake wants to see me but he sends someone else to bring me to him? Like I'm being summoned while he is sitting there in all his alpha-ness waiting for me to come to him? Caly wondered if she just totally misread this male altogether. *Well, it wouldn't be the first time you misjudged a male... No. Not going there right now.* She shut the lid and locked that vault real quick. *Besides, there's no way I could be that wrong about Blake, right?*

She tried to contain her swirling storm of emotions because it wasn't Rhyland's fault that he got stuck in the middle of this and she wasn't going to shoot the messenger.

Rhyland inhaled and, as if he could tell she was in a lethal mood all of a sudden, he cut right to the chase, "Uh, he's this way."

Instead of walking toward Blake's room, as she was expecting, he walked right past her, into the room toward the sliding glass door. And she swore she caught the faintest grin from him as if he was amused at the catfight between her and Blake. When he paused, she felt a wave of embarrassment wash over the anger and confusion. Because she knew Rhyland saw the mini-mountain of food remains. Again, to her surprise, all he did was give her a side smirk of approval, with a bit of mischief in his eyes, and then proceeded to walk outside. Caly followed Rhyland and was debating how she should approach this exactly.

Cool, calculated distance or just full-on crazy Caly Jerry Springer style? she thought as they cleared the corner of the house.

A statue. She turned into a statue, for the seven hundredth time in the past week. She was staring at Blake's shirtless torso gorgeously glistening with sweat as he stacked firewood in a makeshift bonfire pit.

Oh. My. God. He remembered.

Caly's jaw literally dropped open in disbelief of what she was seeing. She surveyed the scene and saw a shovel, wheelbarrow, an axe next to a pile of dirt.

Not only did he remember but he dug the pit and cut the firewood himself.

In a split second, it felt as if the swirling storm of emotional chaos drained out through the soles of her feet into the earth. She was so wrapped up in her emotional drama that she forgot all about her Phoenix pyro request. But he remembered. Crap. Was she about to cry for the seven hundredth time too? Yeah. When her vision blurred, she stared unblinking into Blake's eyes. An apologetic smile touched his lips and she responded with her own.

"Go easy on him. He means well," Rhyland said in a low voice meant for only her to hear. "Besides, he can't help that he's a wolf." He winked with a playful elbow to her arm and she let out a little laugh. No doubt Blake heard what Rhyland said with his shifter hearing but his focus remained completely on Caly. And, yeah, Rhyland knew when he was a third wheel and, right now, he was a major fucking third wheel. So, he walked back to the house and left them alone.

"You remembered," she said in a soft voice as a tear escaped. Before the tear finished its descent down her cheek, Blake was in front of her in the blink of an eye. He cupped her face and gently pressed his lips to her cheek kissing away the tear.

"I'm sorry, Caly. I should've spoken with you first. I didn't mean for it to seem as if I was going behind your back or trying to dominate your life. I didn't plan on telling Riordan but it just kind of happened. I know there's so much going on that's out of your control. And that's part of the reason I hesitated telling you. I didn't want to add to the overwhelming mess on your shoulders. And I didn't want to scare you away." He kissed away another tear. "From this moment on, I will always go to you first and we can talk about things together. Caly, will you forgive me?"

Speechless. She was literally speechless. Damn, if that shouldn't receive the number one apology award of the century. And now that he explained his side, it actually did make sense. It also didn't help that he was kinda, sorta right about the overwhelm and the scaring her off thing. Because, yeah. She knew right before this blow-up, she had the gear shift in reverse at the cross streets of fear and doubt and she was about to back the fuck out.

"Of course I forgive you. And I'm sorry too. I overreacted and unfairly unleashed everything on you. I mean, yeah, I'm a little hurt that we didn't talk about it together first but I understand why. And you're right about your fear of being overwhelming and scaring me off. I guess everything was just kind of snowballing and that was the thing that set me off. And I shouldn't have taken it all out on you like that. I'm sorry, Blake."

He kissed her, slow and deep, and when he pulled away, he was sporting one of his wolfish grins.

"Submissive wolfy bitch?" he teased.

She laughed. "Yeah, I don't know where that came from. Sorry about that... My words tend to get a little colorful when I'm mad," she confessed with a chortle.

"So I've noticed," he chuckled. "Oh, and you should also know that you're not a submissive by far and my *alpha-ness* wouldn't have it any other way," he drawled, claiming her mouth in a playful kiss until she was laughing.

"Speaking of going to you first and talking about things together, there is something else," he prompted in a somewhat serious tone that caught her attention.

"Okay," she said in a cautious yet curious voice.

"Probably best if we sit down," Blake suggested, walking them over to a couple of chairs set up around the fire pit.

"When I got back from the forest earlier, the pack called me into an unexpected meeting. They asked me if you were my life mate and I confirmed." He paused, not entirely sure how to say this. "Do you remember how I said that life mates are considered one of the most sacred bonds recognized among species?"

"Yeah," she said cautiously, unsure where this was all going exactly.

"Caly, I want to be with you and only you."

"I only want to be with you too, Blake," Caly said, furrowing her brows a little because she could feel a "but" coming on.

"But—" he prompted.

Yup. There's that big fat but.

"My wolf and I can't stand the thought of you moving away."

She exhaled. "I know, Blake. I don't want to leave either. But—"

Oh god, now I'm the one passing the "big fat but" ball back in his court.

"I don't have a choice. I have to go with Riordan."

"And I would never want to get in the way of that. It's your birthright to learn about who you are and the world you belong in."

"And *you* don't have a choice. Your commitment is to your pack. And your pack is here," she concluded. And, yup. They were back at square one.

"Well, actually, I do have a choice now." Blake offered up that mini morsel of new information.

Wait, what? Caly thought, furrowing her brow in confusion.

"They called the meeting to tell me that they all unanimously agreed that if you were my life mate, they would follow me wherever I go... and I would like to follow you wherever you go. That is, if you would have me," he said, looking into her stormy gray eyes.

Okay. So, she was back to the speechless thing.

"Blake, are... are you saying that you want to move to wherever Riordan lives so we can be together?" Caly held her breath.

"Yeah," Blake said, sharpening his senses in anticipation of her reaction.

Caly shot up out of the chair and practically jumped into Blake's lap. She didn't have shifter speed but it was pretty damn fast and even Blake seemed pleasantly surprised.

"Blake, this is..." Words. She was trying to find words. "This is amazing news!" she exclaimed, smiling at the unexpected turn of events.

"Caly, there's one more thing too."

"Yeah?" she asked with a curious smile.

"Caly, I want to be with you and live our lives together. I want to welcome you as the first female to live within our pack." Blake said, laying it all out there.

Caly's heart and soul lit up and, in a knee-jerk reaction,

she almost immediately exclaimed, *"Yes!"* But on the coat-tails of the affirmation, insidious fear and doubt crept its way into her mind. *No,* she commanded an excision of that demon. *Stop being scared of the future. You want this so why let doubts and fear dictate your life?*

Then that effing song "Call Me Maybe" by Carly Rae Jepsen, with its catchy chorus, decided to play in her head at that very moment. Except, there was some additional ad-libbing with the lyrics. Caly internally sang along with the chorus but, instead of giving her number away, she ad-libbed in, *But I'm moving in with you. Call me crazy.* Great. Now that song was suddenly stuck in her head.

"Okay," she accepted with a smile.

"Yeah?" He returned her smile.

"Yeah. I mean, it's crazy and I'm scared... I've never done anything like this but, hell, *all* of this is crazy and so outside the bounds of anything I've ever known." She laughed a little as she said that but it didn't dim her huge smile. "And like you said, we'll navigate through all of this crazy *together*."

She touched her heart and used her other hand to touch his. They stared into each other's eyes for a moment before he claimed her mouth once more as if pulled together by a magnetic force that was impossible to resist.

The kiss was hot and possessive in the sexiest way and her body was heating for him. Their mouths were dancing a sensual duet to the pounding rhythm of their hearts. His hands caressed her breasts while she tunneled her fingers through his hair. Yup. They were totally making out like straight-up teenagers, until a loud wolf whistle called out along with a male voice, "Get a room!"

Suddenly, they looked like a pair of hormonal teenagers who were caught red-handed in a hot and heavy make-out sesh behind the bleachers. She knew it was the twins but she wasn't sure which one whistled and which one called out.

"Get used to it!" she retorted in a lighthearted laugh.

Blake chuckled, amused with her playful side.

"Now, where were we?" he drawled, nipping at her lower lip before sucking at it. Way too soon, he broke the kiss and she let out a protesting moan. "If I don't stop this now, then I won't stop."

"So let's not stop," she proposed with a wicked smile.

"Because I'm going to keep my promise to you and light this fire."

"I still can't believe you remembered," she said on an exhale full of affection for her gorgeous, golden-eyed male.

"How could I forget a request like this?" he quipped with a smirk and she chortled. "You ready, Caly?"

"Yeah," she said and turned toward the pile of wood that was soon to be an inferno of flames.

Blake got up with Caly in his arms effortlessly. Why? Just because he could. He also liked her little squeal of surprise in response. And fine, maybe he wanted to show off his strength for her just a little bit. Blake set her gently back in the chair and kissed her again with his arms planted on both armrests. *Later*, he promised, forcing himself to break the kiss. His eyes landed on her swollen lips and a fantasy started to formulate in his mind. He was going to pick her up and... *Focus*, he ordered his mind into obedience and got with the fire starting program.

Caly felt as if she was in some sort of a trance watching the fire. The flickering flames brought flashes of memories of the torch *he* used.

No... James, she thought, internally speaking his name for the first time.

That was the moment she decided she was going to start calling him by his real name. She was not going to give James Barker power by cowering away from the mere thought of his name. When her gaze fell on the deceptively placid pile of bloody and dirty fabric, her mind was somewhere else from one flicker of flame to the next.

Darkness. Caly was in total darkness. She was catapulted back to the nightmare when the cement scraping sound scoured her eardrums.

"What species are you, Caly?"

The cement scraping sound amplified to torturous levels.

"You have secrets that I can't wait to break from your mind."

The chilling cold blade of The Ghost's large hunting knife slid against her bare skin. The pain of slicing skin, broken bones, and a bruised body jolted through every tortured nerve ending. Her heart was kicking in her chest and pumping pure terror into her veins. She was frozen in fear, desperately trying to lock the lid to the vault of her nightmares but it wouldn't close. The darkness was oozing out of it and into her mind.

"Caly! Caly!" She could hear Blake's voice yet she couldn't. It sounded so distant as if it were a faint echo on the wind miles and miles away.

"Caly... Caly..." It was as if Blake's voice warped into The Ghost's dark psychotic taunts in an evil melody. The Ghost's cold, dark brown eyes were staring at her from the black hole of nightmares. She heard the rhythmic clattering sound of metal caused by her body trembling and saw The Ghost's evil expression of pure dark fascination flickering in the firelight. His fist raised in preparation for a strike and she instinctively curled into the fetal position.

"Keep fighting! I will find you! Caly, I will find you!"

With her eyes shut tight, all Caly heard were the repetitive booming sounds and felt the force field weaken with each pounding strike of The Ghost's fists.

"Keep fighting! I will find you! Caly, I will find you!"

There was a sudden, ear piercingly loud noise and, from one heartbeat to the next, a blanket of sweet silent stillness enveloped her.

Blake started the fire and worked it attentively until the flames were full of vibrant thick colors of gold, orange, and red. Caly's mirror-like eyes captured the fire dancing in their gray depths.

Jesus, she's beautiful, he thought, turning away to add one more log to the fire for good measure. His wolf suddenly bared his teeth and the smell of stabbing fear and pure terror stung his senses. He whipped around so fast and saw Caly's gaze on the pile of bloody and dirty fabric.

"Caly?" Blake's hands were on her shoulders and when his eyes met hers, he was not greeted with Caly's quiet strength. He was looking into the eyes of a distant storm, unfocused by a thrashing wind.

"Caly! Caly!" Blake increased the volume of his voice and gently shook her shoulders in an attempt to reach her.

"What's going on?!" The twins yelled in confusion as they, and Nico, appeared on the scene with supernatural speed.

"I don't know," Blake growled back. "She's not here."

"But she's not a seer," Rhyland bit out.

"How can this be?" Rhyker finished.

Deacon burst out of the house running at his slow-paced, non-shifter speed toward them.

As if triggered by his pounding rhythmic footsteps, Caly belted out an ear-splitting scream of bloody murder. A sudden blast of energy shot out of her and knocked all of them on their asses. Recovering a moment later, Blake's heart froze in his chest at the sight of Caly curled in a lifeless ball on the grass.

"Caly, come back to me!"

Caly felt, more than she heard, Blake's voice vibrate through her body. Holding her. Blake was holding her close to his chest. Opening her eyes, she immediately met Blake's golden galaxies that were like a beacon to her soul.

"B-Blake?" She tried to speak but, god, her throat was killing her and she felt so weak.

"Caly." The desperation in his voice transformed into relief.

"Wh—" She coughed and tried to clear her throat. "What happened?" she rasped out. A bottle of water appeared in front of her and she drank. Hearing the snap of the fire, her nightmare flashed before her eyes as if it were commanded by the crack of a whip.

"I'm taking you inside," Blake said, standing with her in his arms.

She blinked a couple of times trying to regain her bearings. The twins, Nico, and Deacon were all there staring at her with an intense expression of concern but also something else she couldn't quite translate.

"No," she said to Blake while looking at the fire.

"Caly, you need to rest."

"No." This time, she spoke in an adamant tone. "I'm not leaving until..." Her eyes fell on the sheet covered in dirt and blood. As if the sight of it gave her a shot of strength, she continued, "Blake, put me down. I'm not leaving until it's in fucking flames." She looked straight into his eyes. God, she didn't know why she was so hell-bent on this but, exhausted or not, she was damn determined to see it burn to ash.

As if he could see the unflinching resolve in her eyes, Blake gently set her on her feet and helped steady her.

Bambi. She was Bambi all of a sudden, with unsteady wobbly legs, and she didn't know what the hell was going on. But she did know one thing: Operation burn-the-fucking-pile-to-ash was in full effect. She took a step forward and tested her balance. Good. She didn't fall flat on her face. On her second slow step, she swayed a little but Blake was there to steady her. And, no, she wasn't too prideful to reject his help. She loomed over the pile of physical remains of her nightmare.

I am the fucking Phoenix. Watch me rise.

She called on all her power reserves, snatched the pile, and threw it with such strength it catapulted into the fire and spit out a gust of flying embers. She didn't care. Okay, maybe she should tone it down because it wasn't like she was The Unburnt, AKA Daenerys Targaryen from *Game of Thrones.*

Caly turned around with the inferno blazing at her back and looked at Blake. There was no need for words. And, it appeared everyone was rendered speechless. Good. She was so not in the mood for words. She pushed one of the chairs to the exact spot where she became an Olympian, clothing-destroying, shot putter and parked it. It was nothing but her, the fire, and the sweet smell of smoke as she watched her nightmare burn. It took the males a good, long minute to comprehend what they had just witnessed and get with the fire-watching program. Starting with Blake, they all pulled up chairs on either side of Caly, including the cold and distant Nico. In fact, Nico pulled up his chair to the right of Caly, in a silent statement of his approval of this female.

Minutes? Hours? Maybe even days passed by as the flames burned into the night.

"Damn, SoCal... Damn." Rhyland was the first to break the silence, naturally.

Caly let out a little laugh. As if the laugh slid that final piece of normalcy back into place, she crawled into Blake's lap, who was still gloriously half-naked.

"If you two start making out again, I'm leaving," Rhyland quipped and a few chuckles filled the fire pit.

Before any comebacks could shoot back, Caly's stomach growled. And fat chance the three shifters and a vampire didn't hear it.

"Good point," Rhyland said, patting his belly. "Hot dogs and s'mores?"

Nico stacked more wood on the fire and the twins were back in a flash with all of the fixin's: graham crackers, chocolate, marshmallows, hot dogs, buns, condiments, chips, plates, napkins, and long metal skewers. This clearly wasn't their first campfire BBQ sesh either apparently. Everyone knew they needed to talk about the giant elephant in the room as to what the hell happened but now was not the time. They roasted hot dogs and stacked up mountains of s'mores while shooting the breeze as the campfire smoke rose into the starry night sky. And when Caly shared a bite of her half severely burnt hot dog with Blake, not only did he not complain but he ate it like it was the best damn hot dog of his life. With his cheekful of burnt hot dog, she kissed Blake and knew without a doubt, it was the best hot dog of her life too.

With bellies full of campfire food and the fire dying out, Blake nibbled on Caly's earlobe and she smiled.

"Are you up for a little stroll?" he whispered in her ear.

She wasn't at full strength by far but the food and fire brought some life back into her. And, apparently, Blake also brought life back into *other* places. So, yeah, she was up for a "little stroll." Caly got off of Blake's lap, he clasped his hand into hers, and they started to walk off toward the trees. When deep laughter rolled out behind them from back at the fire pit, Blake flipped off his pack brothers without even bothering to turn around.

Males, Caly thought with a twitch of her lips. *I wonder*

how far— Her thoughts were cut off when Blake lifted her with shifter speed.

She was suddenly straddling him with her back pressed up against the trunk of the tree. Growling, he gave her a wicked, wolfish grin that promised all sorts of things. Her body heated and clenched in low feminine places. Their kiss was hot and wet.

Blake's instinct to mark his female blazed to the surface.

"Caly," he said in a gruff voice breaking the kiss. "Caly, I want to mark you. Will you let me mark you as mine?"

"Mark me?" she asked on a breath.

"With my scent... my mating scent."

"Mating scent?" Her brain was struggling to keep up amidst the sensual fire burning between them.

"It's my own unique scent. And it's only for my mate... only for you." He growled with his eyes starting to glow in anticipation of the alluring act.

"Yes," she agreed, recognizing that some part of her deeply desired the possessive claim by Blake.

"Yeah?" he asked roughly, wanting to make sure.

"Yeah, mark me... mark me, Blake."

The fire burning in his golden eyes ignited into an inferno. When his lips found home against hers, he let his marking scent fly.

A delicious, earthy fragrance drifted to Caly's senses. A hint of spice. Rich chocolate. Amber. Fresh cut pine wood. It was dark, sensual, and whispered seductive temptations to her senses.

"Blake, it... God, it smells so good." She breathed in the aphrodisiac and her body reacted to his scent like she was one of those women in the Axe commercials, irresistible to deny the lure of the cologned man.

"Good," he growled, salaciously sucking in her lower

lip. "Because it's going to cover every inch of you. Inside and out."

She shuddered in anticipation of the seductive promise as her feet met the soft earth.

"Off," Blake commanded, tugging at his hoodie she wore.

In one fell swoop, she slipped it over her head and bared her creamy breasts. Heat snapped between them and she knew there would be no slow eye-gazing tease this time. This was going to be hot and heavy and one hell of a ride. Their bodies collided as if they were both magnets for one another pulled together by the sheer force of the desire pulsing between them. Their lips claimed each other in a sensual battle of licks, nips, and sucks. Their hands were at each other's pants, frantically trying to get them off while keeping the lip lock. Caly couldn't free the button on his jeans and she broke the kiss.

"Off," she demanded, breathing heavily while indicating that he needed to remove the jean barrier.

He chuckled and stripped off his jeans while she easily slipped right out of the oversized sweats.

Their bare bodies were pressed skin to skin as they fell back into the kiss. While still lip-locked, he guided her backward until her body was sandwiched between him and the tree trunk. And Caly liked the slightly scratchy sensation of the bark against her back. Blake broke the kiss and titillated her nerve endings as he licked and caressed his way down her body, pausing for some play at her tight, pink nipples, until he was kneeling in front of her. He swung her right leg over his shoulder so her sex was bare to him. His eyes feasted on her glistening folds.

"Caly, you're so beautiful," he groaned, looking into her eyes. His hand traveled up her inner thigh until he slid two fingers into her silken heat.

"Blake!" she moaned as her eyes closed and head tilted back into the tree.

The heated slickness of her arousal on his fingers mixing with the erotic sounds and his mating scent was driving Blake wild. He feverishly worked her wet core with his fingers until her breath quickened into a begging rhythm. Her feminine musk was dripping down his hand and his tongue salivated. He needed to taste. Sliding his fingers out, Caly looked down in protest but before she could react, he met her eyes and sucked up her sweet honey on his fingers. Her pupils dilated even further at the sensuous sight. Without delay, his tongue lapped up her liquid ambrosia straight from the source. Her head threw back into the trunk with the sensations of his wicked tongue on her throbbing sex.

"Blake!" she exclaimed on a breathy moan.

He was ruthless in the devouring licks and sucks. He could feel the waves of pleasure rising within her with every breathy moan and squeeze of her sex.

"Oh god. Don't stop. Blake, don't stop. I'm going to come."

Obeying her command, he kept the erotic rhythm until she exclaimed, "I'm coming! Blake!"

Blake growled, knowing he brought his female to ecstasy. He could almost feel the orgasmic jolts shooting through her body as he worked her with his tongue coaxing out every last drop of pleasure.

"Inside me. Blake, I need you inside me."

She didn't have to command him twice. Putting her leg down, he flared his delicious, earthy mating scent and made sure to slide up her body, skin to skin, to thoroughly cover her. When he stood at his full height, his mouth claimed hers in a very hot and possessive kiss.

"Turn around," he ordered.

She smiled and did as she was told, bracing her hands on

the trunk exposing her backside to him.

"Spread your legs."

Listening, she widened her stance.

"Bend over," he barked out another order and she obeyed.

He growled loudly as her glistening sex was bare to his viewing pleasure once more. Gripping his hard length with one hand and placing his free hand firmly on her waist, he slammed into her, balls deep. He groaned with her tight, wet heat wrapped around him and he began thrusting into her hard and deep, using his grip on her waist as leverage. Skin was slapping and pleasured sounds filled the forest night.

"Fuck. That's so hot, Caly," Blake grunted out when Caly's hand slid to her sensitive spot and she began working herself.

"Come with me, Caly."

A moment later, they both cried out as exquisite ecstasy ripped through their bodies. Her sex was milking his in pulsing waves of pleasure and his hot seed was pumping into her.

They came back to consciousness with their chests heaving and subtle waves of pleasure still coursing through their bodies. He slid out of her and spun her around to kiss her soft and slow, letting her know how he felt with no words. And then he spoke those words he felt.

"You're so beautiful, Caly." His tone was of utter adoration. "Every inch of your body is so fucking beautiful." He stared into her eyes. "Your stunning stormy eyes." He softly kissed her luscious lips. "These." He firmly grasped her curvy ass. "This." He sensually slid his hands up her waist and cupped her full breasts that spilled out even around his massive hands. "These." He knelt and kissed her flat stomach. "This." He savored a quick taste on both of her inner thighs. "These." His kiss made its final stop just above her sex and growled in reverence. "You're beautiful and drive me wild."

Caly had always been a bit self-conscious of her curves, especially her slightly thicker thighs and belly. Sure, her stomach was flat but she still had a thermal layer. As her male worshipped every single peak and valley of her body, the self-consciousness melted away and she never felt so beautiful in her entire life.

Staring into his gorgeous golden eyes, she reached down to his face and he let her lift him until he was gloriously standing before her at his full height. Never breaking eye contact, she brought his lips to hers and poured her adoration into the slow kiss.

"Blake," she said on a soft exhale.

"Caly." He tilted his head down so their foreheads were touching.

Her hands wrapped around his neck as his circled her waist. Their eyes were closed and they both felt something deep inside them as if their very souls were synchronizing to each other's essence.

Chapter 29

"Eggs," Rhyland requested.

The twins did the breakfast plate exchange, Rhyker passed the eggs and Rhyland sent back the potatoes. Blake was sitting at the head of the table, Caly was to his right, followed by Deacon, Nico at the other end, and the twins were on the remaining side of the table.

Last night after the "little stroll" in the woods, Blake carried Caly in his arms all of the way to his room. She didn't protest at all, especially because her body felt like a pool of melted chocolate. Also, she loved being in his half-naked arms, feeling his strength effortlessly carry her. And she had the feeling he liked showing off his strength to her. Total win-win. When they got into his room, they both stripped out of their clothes and may have had another little stroll in the shower before getting into bed. And she may have shown him just how much she worshiped his body in return. She didn't mind the slight bruises on her knees one bit. Nope. Not at all.

She slept deep and peaceful and woke up this morning tangled with Blake's warm body. And, yeah, they may have had a third little stroll in his bed. Her body was melted chocolate once more and she knew she was still glowing from the intimate after effects. Not to mention she was covered in Blake's mating scent which, of course, Nico and the twins detected the second she walked into the kitchen.

She had never had, let alone desired, so much sex in her life. It was as if her body was making up for being on vacation all this time. Caly pushed the erotic memories of her and Blake aside. Damn, if it wasn't hot all of a sudden. And, no, it was not because she was in another pair of Blake's sweats and hoodie. And, yeah, he gladly growled in approval of her wearing his clothes with his scent all over her. In fact, it almost made them skip breakfast altogether.

"Last night..." she said, breaking the normal breakfast table noises and conversation. Suddenly, everyone was all ears.

After their morning "stroll," Blake filled Caly in on what happened and Caly shared her side. "Blake told me about how some seers go mad and lose touch with reality, some even get lost in a vision."

Blake had explained to her that this was why the Seer Council kept a close watch on seers and he guessed that was also why she was assigned a Primary. Although, Blake had his suspicions that some of the council kept watch over seers for more than just the welfare of their own subspecies. Because with most ancients, there was always some sort of strategic power play in motion like chess pieces sliding into place.

"Even though I'm not a seer," Caly looked at Blake and he nodded in agreement with her to continue, "We think that because I'm a traveler and my ability is in my mind, that when I was... triggered... it somehow set off the... episode." She hesitated. "It was as if someone pushed play and then I was experiencing... it... all over again."

Blake grabbed her hand in reassurance and support.

"Nothing even close to any of this has ever happened

before." She paused and took a breath. "We're going to talk with Riordan and Aleia after breakfast. Blake told me Aleia mentioned a mind healer and I'd like to make an appointment."

All of the males were speechless and several moments went by without so much as a bite of food.

"Holy shit, SoCal. I don't know the last time anyone has been able to render us all speechless. And you've managed to do it twice... actually, three times, counting the car episode," Rhyland said with a chuckle, lightening up the heavy conversation load. "I think I can speak for all of us and say that whatever the fuck that was, we're just glad you're okay."

Everyone nodded in agreement.

With a mischievous expression, Rhyland added, "And your grand finale fire stunt was epic."

"Fucking badass, female." Rhyker gave her a grin and held up his full fork in a mini salute before shoveling it into his mouth.

"We *were* going to give you a good old-fashioned initiation into our clubhouse, but, shit." Rhyland drew out that last word with his own grin.

Caly chortled and warmth spread through her chest.

"Thank you." She spoke in a soft, heartfelt tone and looked into each of the males' eyes, even Nico's.

The two words were easily translated as the bi-layered gratitude she intended. It was a thank you for caring for their brother and alpha by sticking by his side and moving so he could be with his mate... with her. And it was a thank you for welcoming her into their pack and not treating her like a freak of nature when she went for round two of the mysterious ability or *"whatever the fuck that was"* as Rhyland so eloquently put it.

She could feel the emotions swelling in her and ordered it

to simmer the hell down before she started crying... again.

As if Rhyland knew how she was feeling and that she didn't want to go there, he took a bite of his toast and, before she could blink, it flew through the air like a Frisbee straight for Nico's face.

Nico caught it midair, only a centimeter before the facial collision, and shot icicles at Rhyland. But they weren't Nico's usual lethal kind, because he knew what Rhyland was trying to do and, yeah, Caly was growing on him. So, Nico decided Rhyland would get a pass... for now.

The twins bumped fists and were sporting their feline grins.

Nico gave them a cool and calculated smile that had the twin's narrow their eyes in suspicion.

Just wait, Nico thought. *Fucker 1 and Fucker 2 were going to get what they deserved... very soon.*

No one else at the table seemed to notice the silent war going on. Caly was too busy laughing and Blake was bewitched by her laugh. Deacon was chuckling but also trying to play it off by avoiding eye contact and focusing on his plate of food. No doubt he was keeping true with his MO by staying out of whatever shit show was going down between the triad. Well, most of the time at least.

Breakfast was over too soon and Caly sank into Blake's chair in the living room which faced the gigantic TV that, apparently, moonlighted as the communication system.

Is technology in the species world more advanced than the human world? If something as simple as a TV is this advanced (and a bit foreign), then I can only imagine what else might exist, Caly pondered, figuring she would find out soon enough.

When Blake pulled up a chair next to Caly in preparation for the meeting with Riordan, she suddenly felt a bit nervous. She wasn't nervous in a bad way but she was experiencing a slight flutter of butterflies in her stomach as if they knew their world was about to uproot and settle in a new location… once again.

Only after a couple of short days, Caly was growing attached to the house with the males and the forest. And, apparently, Felix was in the same boat.

Her gaze shifted to the snoozing mound of black fur sprawled out on Rhyker's couch. A small stream of sadness trickled through her mind with the thoughts of leaving, especially because she wasn't sure where they would land or what lay on the other side.

As if Blake knew that her thoughts were starting to get sucked into the black hole of worry and fear of the unknown, he kneeled in front of her, held her hands, and focused his eyes on her. At that moment, Blake was her anchor. The warmth of his gaze and hands radiated through her, soothing the mini flurry of butterflies back to the earth.

"We'll figure this out together." She thought of Blake's previous promise and took a grounding breath, knowing it was going to be okay with Blake by her side.

"Ready?" Blake asked with a gauging expression.

"Yes," Caly answered, her confidence fueled by Blake's unwavering support.

After Blake keyed in the call code, he took his place next to her, reached over, and held her hand in his. It was a total flashback to that first time they spoke with Riordan and brought a smile to her face.

Yeah, everything is going to be okay, she thought, as Riordan and Aleia appeared on the screen.

"Riordan. Aleia." Blake greeted them with a welcoming single word and head nod.

Both Riordan and Aleia immediately noticed the teenage hand-holding session between her and Blake.

"Blake," Riordan echoed and then turned his attention

to Caly, with the faintest smile. "Caly."

"Umm, Riordan. Aleia. " Caly smiled, following suit with the single-word greeting. She made a mental note to ask if this was some sort of a standard species greeting or just male efficiency at its finest.

"How are you feeling, Caly?" Aleia asked with one of her warm, healer smiles.

Blake gently squeezed her hand in reassurance to begin. Caly relayed what happened and Blake filled in his side. When they were done speaking and silence stretched out, both Riordan and Aleia's brows furrowed in thought.

"Riordan, what do you make of this?" Blake prompted.

"I will need to sit with this," Riordan responded with that somewhat distant look in his eyes that said he was sifting through his vast database of memories and knowledge. "I do follow the logic of your theory though. It's possible that, being a traveler, this could be connected through seer ancestry which was triggered by the circumstances."

But, with that thought, Riordan recalled the final image of Caly from his vision and, again, wondered about her heritage. It was true that she had powerful traveler abilities but there was something else that had been puzzling Riordan ever since that vision. And he was still mulling over his seemingly impossible theory. Even though his discreet research hadn't yielded any proof yet, he would argue that nothing truly was impossible in the species world. Those thoughts prompted his next question. "Has Deacon come across anything?"

"No," Blake responded, making a mental note to follow up with Deacon. He was so caught up with everything else (okay, really he was just consumed with Caly) that he forgot to check in about the searches. But he knew that if Deacon did find anything then he would've let Blake know immediately.

As if knowing that was the end of that conversation for now, Aleia chimed in. "Caly, I'm glad to hear that physically you're feeling fully recovered. And I agree with Riordan. The connection between the episodes and the circumstances cannot be ignored." She paused briefly, letting that speak for itself. "Now, I'm not a mind healer but it certainly does seem very similar to seer episodes." Aleia's voice trailed off as if chasing a thought before continuing. "Caly, have you considered the possibility of consulting with a mind healer?"

"Actually, I have. Blake said that you know of a mind healer?"

"Yes." Aleia nodded her head. "I work very closely with Dr. Oliver and we often team up for clients that benefit from both of our respective healing specialties. Dr. Oliver is a very skilled mind healer whom I trust and know will maintain confidentiality and the utmost secrecy. With your consent, I would like to consult with Dr. Oliver and put you both in contact to set up a session."

"Yes, please," Caly answered almost before Aleia was done speaking. She was eager to know what the hell was going on with her and, hopefully, how to prevent another episode.

"Of course. Either Dr. Oliver or I will be in touch soon. If you need anything else or if anything changes at all then just reach out," Aleia concluded with one of her warm smiles.

"Thank you." Caly returned the smile.

Aleia gave a final head nod to Blake and then walked out of the room.

Riordan's jade eyes refocused on Caly and a slight smile tugged at the corner of his lips. He stayed silent as if he was patiently waiting for her to speak. Caly was expecting him to say something or ask her about the Primary thing but all she saw was a subtle glint in his eyes.

Is it possible he already knows? Caly wondered. *He is a seer after all. Didn't Blake say, "They know too much for their own good?"*

"So, Riordan. I've thought a lot about, well, everything," Caly said with a bit of an all-of-this-is-batshit-crazy, laughing exhale, "And I would like to accept your offer to be my Primary."

Riordan's face softened. "Caly, I'm truly honored. As your Primary, I vow to support and protect you in every way I'm able to."

An unexpected wave of emotion crested inside Caly. It was as if Riordan's vow struck somewhere deep in her soul. She believed him and this felt right.

Not going to cry. Not going to cry. Not going to cry.

She saw Riordan's focus briefly fall on the teenage hand-holding part two before his eyes met hers once more. Again, all he did was wait with a smile that said he knew too much.

Yes, seers apparently do know too much for their own good. I'd like to see how someone would go about surprising a seer.

"I'm still not sure what this whole Primary thing means exactly but, yes, Blake and I are together. And..." She paused, not really sure how to say her next statement. "...Blake and I are going to live together."

"Myself and The Order will be moving to a second location near you so Caly will still be able to train with you as her Primary," Blake added, giving her hand a little squeeze of reassurance.

"I see," Riordan began. "Considering the recent events, I believe it is in your best interest to start training with me and Dr. Oliver immediately." There was a pregnant pause. "Caly, I vowed to support you in every way I'm able to." Riordan refocused on Blake. "Blake, I welcome you and The Order into my home. It is, of course, your choice if you would like to still find a second location but this will allow Caly to start training without delay."

Wait, did he just offer...?

"Riordan, are you sure? I mean, this is so kind of you and totally unexpected in an amazing way but I don't want to impose... and there's like seven of us, including Felix." Caly wanted to jump at the chance but she truly didn't want to be a burden. *I mean, he is already taking me under his wing and now I come with baggage, in the form of five large males. Well, six if you count how big Felix believes himself to be.*

"Yes, I'm sure, Caly. It's no imposition," Riordan said with an amused quirk of his lips. "Besides," he began with another soft knowing glint in his eyes. "I think we can make it work."

Okay, what's up with the twinkle in his eyes? He totally knows something. I'm starting to see why Blake says they know too much for their own good.

Blake gave another gentle squeeze to Caly's hand before speaking.

"Thank you, Riordan. I agree that Caly should start training immediately. How soon are you able to accommodate us?"

"Why don't you all stay with me for the next few days. I'll show you around and it will give you all a chance to get a feel for the arrangement," Riordan offered.

"Agreed. Thank you," Blake said and gave an alpha nod of his head concluding this verbal agreement.

"It looks like you're going to be *busy*." Riordan smirked as he spoke in a casual tone.

With that statement, Blake recalled when Riordan spoke those same words to him when he told Riordan Caly was his.

Damn seers, he thought, realizing that Riordan knew this

whole time that they would be *busy* moving. Blake originally thought Riordan was referring to being busy with Caly as a new mate but he was starting to see that the seer's words had a double meaning.

"It appears so," Blake said in a subtle, flat tone, letting Riordan know he understood damn well what was going on with the wordplay.

"I will see you all very soon," Riordan said with a smile, repeating the same words from that first conversation with Blake.

"Yes, that also appears so," Blake echoed in his unamused tone with a slight smirk of his own. He knew Riordan was playing in his own, very understated, way.

He's no ordinary ancient, Blake thought. This playful interlude with the seer had both him and his wolf curious to get to know this male more.

The conversation ended with a confirmation for dinner tomorrow night and staying at Riordan's for a few days.

Males, Caly thought with an inward shrug. She did not even try to understand what that whole "being busy" exchange between Blake and Riordan was all about.

Chapter 30

A crack sounded as Rhyland's jaw opened wide in a lazy morning feline yawn. He rolled out of bed with one thing on his mind. Okay, well, maybe two.

"Coffee... Food..." he mumbled to himself, opening his bedroom door.

Only moments after he began his sleepy pursuit down the hall toward his morning fix, he heard his brother following suit behind him. It was a twin thing that became their morning routine since, well, forever ago. The unspoken golden rule was: *no speaking until coffee happened.* So, they were silently shuffling down the hall. On some subconscious level, they sensed something seemed a little off but it wasn't until they finally made it to home base when the subconscious alarm bell pushed to the front of their minds.

"The fuck?" they both growled out in their groggy gravel morning voice.

They had a coffee machine that was automatically set to brew the steamy deliciousness every morning because they liked their coffee like their females: hot, ready, and waiting for them. But this morning? It was nowhere to be found. Well, not only was the coffee not waiting for them but the entire machine was gone.

Nico coolly stepped into the kitchen with an icy grin and a steaming mug of the dark deliciousness in his hand. It was too early for words, especially pre-coffee, and Nico jumped at the opportunity to speak first... for once.

"Cat got your tongue?" His cool and calculated grin widened a fraction before he took a sip of the coffee and continued. "Maybe it's in the fridge?" he suggested wickedly, enjoying this entirely too much.

Rhyker almost tore the refrigerator door off the hinges as he angrily opened it.

The twins froze. The thought of cold coffee alone almost set them off but there was another unexpected surprise waiting for them.

Gone. All of the food was gone. It was an empty sub-zero igloo. Low twin growls sounded out as the fridge door slammed shut, shaking the empty shell. Just before the twins pounced on Nico's face, his next words stopped them in their tracks.

"Scaring Caly probably isn't a good idea. But then again, go ahead. I'd enjoy Blake kicking your asses. After I already did," Nico taunted. He knew that if that didn't push them over the edge then what he said next would. "Oh." He pursed his lips as if in thought but he knew damn well what he was doing, "Maybe it's in the cabinets." He wasn't one for theatrics or words usually but this was too fucking good not to rub in their faces. Payback's a bitch after all.

This time, it was Rhyland with the aggressive maneuver to open the cabinet in front of him.

Empty. The cabinets were a barren wasteland. And, yup, that did it. The twins pounced at the same time. But Nico was already anticipating the twin attack. In a blink of an eye, he was already at the entrance to the hallway while the twins bumped into each other.

Classic, Nico thought with a dark chuckle as he made his

way down the hall with vampire speed. He knew those two against him wasn't a fair fight unless he got to his dungeon, AKA his room, where it was already pre-programmed for pitch darkness. His battle strategy was to fade and have the advantage. His room was also close to Blake's room, so they would have an audience soon enough. It was all a part of the payback plan.

He made it to his room and faded into the darkness, making his body no longer physical matter and no longer visible to the physical eye. Sure, there was still a trail of light from the open door but the rest of the room was consumed in shadows. Yeah, now, it was a fair fight against the well-trained twins.

Not even a second later, the twins were in his room ready for a fight with dilated pupils.

"Fucking Nico!" Rhyland growled out loudly into the silent darkness and Rhyker followed up with, "Running like a female!"

Initiate phase two, Nico thought as he went back into physical form for just a second, grabbing the two mugs he strategically placed next to the door. Before the twins could even react to his physical presence, a rush of room-temperature coffee waterfalled over the twins from above just as Nico faded once more. Taking advantage of the momentary surprise of the coffee wake up, Nico's physical body reappeared in front of them and swung two booming punches that hit home on the twin targets before going back non-corporeal.

"NICO!" the twins yelled out in frustration, sharpening their senses.

Phase three. The strategy? Block. Punch. Fade. This really was a fair fight not only because of the two against one but also, the twins were well-trained in fighting fading vampires. After all, Nico was the one who trained them in that arena.

And the two keys with fighting vampires? First, get into the light and second, know thy enemy to anticipate their attacks. Since they were like brothers and fought together for years, Nico knew that the twins would eventually anticipate his fading attacks. But Nico was counting on the emotions of the twins to give him just a little bit of an edge. Well, at least until phase four when Blake broke up the fight while Nico was still ahead. Yeah, he planned this out to a T.

Going in for another fading punch attack, Nico appeared to the left of Rhyker and swung a fist. Anticipating Nico's punch correctly, he blocked Nico and went in for the tackle. Their bodies flew across the room and landed with a boom as something broke. With dust particles still showering the air, Rhyland pounced into the brawl. Fists were flying with bone-cracking contact. But Nico was holding his own. He took a few hits, sure, but he also did some damage and was using his fading ability to his advantage. And it was working.

With a well-practiced block and fade maneuver, Nico appeared some feet behind them so he could gain momentum for his grand finale. With swift vampire speed, he tackled both of them at once and all three of them went flying through the air until their momentum was halted with a crash into the wall and the pulverized nightstand became a shower of splintering dust.

"ENOUGH!" Blake's booming alpha voice vibrated through the room like an earthquake.

Blake, Caly, and Deacon were in the doorway. Caly was completely nonplussed, standing there wide-eyed and mouth open in disbelief at what she just witnessed. Unlike Caly, Deacon wasn't surprised at all and, instead, he looked somewhat amused because he knew damn well what it was like to be the one in the brawl aftermath. He wasn't above it by any means but it was just that the trio got into it nine times out of ten and the few times he got into it was usually due to a Starr-induced fight mood.

"Oh my god!" Caly exclaimed, seeing the three males with chests heaving and bloodied and bruised bodies. Rhyland's arm looked like it was unnaturally bent in the forearm. She immediately ran over to him and, upon further examination, realized not only was his arm broken but all of the males had broken bones.

"Oh. My. God!" Caly's tone reflected the bloody aftermath she was staring at. She frantically turned back to Blake. "Call Aleia!" she called out in a distraught voice.

Blake appeared beside Caly in the blink of an eye just as Rhyland smirked and spoke with a slight lisp from his fat lip, "Caly, give us some credit. We're tougher than that." He ended with a wink and winced a little at his black eye.

"Caly, they'll be fine. Shifters and vampires have fast healing abilities," Blake reminded her in a reassuring tone as he put his arm around Caly to try and comfort her. He shot a glare at the three stooges who thought it would be a good idea to scare the shit out of his female.

Caly swallowed, trying to compute the new information. *Remember, they're not human. They're species. And with fast healing abilities.* She pulled the reins to a halt of the mini panic carriage that was running rampant in her mind. Then, she witnessed the impossible. The gash above Rhyland's black eye was healing before her eyes. She then observed the incredibly fast healing happening for both Rhyker and Nico.

"Oh my god..." She exhaled out on a long breath. Apparently, her brain was reduced to a three-worded vocabulary bank.

"Let's get some breakfast," Blake reassured her, directing

her away from the bloody mess and toward the door.

"Yeah, how are we going to eat breakfast, Nico?" Rhyland bit out in a tone that still stung but was dialed way back because of Caly's presence.

"The food's in the training room," Nico replied with a little verbal stinger of his own, completely satisfied that the twins got paid back in full for their recent bullshit antics.

With that remark, Blake halted, turned around, and focused on Nico. "Explain," he ordered. Although, he already had an idea of what the fuck happened.

"Payback's a bitch," Nico replied. It was, again, all that needed to be said. Because, truthfully, everyone knew the twins had it coming. Well, everyone except Caly.

"What happened?" Caly tentatively asked, while also mentally checking off that this confirmed her suspicion of what the fight room was all about.

This time, Blake was the one who blew out an exhausted breath.

"We're males," Rhyker started.

"We brawl... and Nico gets his *pink* panties in a wad when we win. Which reminds me to show you a picture of his pink fetish," Rhyland finished.

With that, the twins were sporting their usual feline twin grins and dusting themselves off.

"My final tackle speaks for itself." Nico shot frosty glares at the twins but also dialed down the testosterone tone in his voice.

Ignoring the trio, Blake spoke to Caly as they walked out of the room. "I should've warned you about the fighting."

"It's okay. I, uh, kinda had an idea with the whole... 'fight room.'" She laughed a little and tried to speak in a reassuring tone. She knew that men wrestled but this was another reminder that these were not human men. They were species males who also happened to be trained fighters from what Blake told her. So, she guessed that she should probably get used to this since she was going to be living with them. "Does this sort of thing happen often?"

"Often enough for us to build the fight room..." Blake tried to bite back his growl. He went to switch subjects but Caly spoke first.

"Blake, this doesn't change anything. I get it. I mean, human men wrestle all of the time. I just wasn't expecting the extreme level of *wrestling* that species males do."

She laughed a little in another effort to let Blake know she was truly okay. Playfully pushing Blake's back into the hallway, she gave him a quick kiss. Then, with a wicked smile she said, "Besides, I wouldn't mind wrestling a bit." Before he could respond, she was already walking down the hall as if she didn't just tease him.

When his low playful growl sounded out behind her, she smiled.

With shifter speed, Blake had her gently pinned to the wall with her arms above her head. "You want to wrestle?" he drawled with a wolfish grin and pressed his lips to hers, nipping at her lower lip.

"Get a room," one of the twins called out.

Probably Rhyland, Caly thought.

A wolf whistle promptly followed.

Probably Rhyker.

Blake broke the kiss and his eyes were full of promises for the wrestling matches yet to come. This time, Blake pulled away and walked down the hall as if nothing happened.

Walk, Caly tried to command her legs to get with the program but her knees almost buckled from the sensual promises and the lingering sensations of that hot, dominating kiss. Oh, the things this male did to her was unlike anything she ever experienced.

On somewhat wobbly legs, Caly finally made it to the

kitchen, thinking she was about to suggest that they take the wrestling to the bedroom but then, her stomach growled in protest.

Opening the fridge to get breakfast started, she froze as she stared at a whole lot of nothing.

"What a complete nightmare to be hungry and not have any food." She thought of what Rhyland said to her that first morning when he gave her the grand tour. Then, she burst out laughing when she realized what Nico did to get back at the twins. Blake was beside her chuckling as well.

"Oh my god," she said as her laughter died down. "What exactly did the twins do to Nico?" she asked Blake.

"They're always doing something. The twins recently redecorated Nico's room in all pink." He chuckled. "I'll let the twins show you the picture."

Caly was thankful for the unexpected species smackdown because it provided somewhat of a comedic respite with everything that was going on. After the conversation with Riordan and Aleia yesterday, the rest of the day went by in a blur. Everyone was busy packing not only getting ready for the mini getaway but also for the big move. Although, Caly discovered rather quickly that the only things the males were really packing were their weapons and clothes. Fitting.

Caly thought about how she didn't really have anything to pack, except cat food. Oh, and the brush and hair oil Aleia gifted her. Which reminded her that she still wanted to do something to show her appreciation for Aleia. Blake said he already packed some extra sweats and hoodies in his bag for her. Which also reminded her that she really was going to have to get real clothes soon. Although the past few days as the Midol period girl have been nice and comfortable, she was starting to miss her clothes.

Caly's thoughts traveled to her apartment in LA and all of the things she would never see again. Sure, she had some favorite things that she would miss, like clothes and books, but those were all replaceable and she would find new favorites. No big deal. But the things she kept getting hung up on were her phone and laptop. Well, really it wasn't those devices themselves. It was really the pictures and the playlists that were on those devices that she truly cared about. Yeah, she would start over with the playlists but she spent countless hours over the years collecting songs and creating various playlists. As far as the pictures went, there were some that held fun memories but those weren't even the ones that felt like a pang in her heart. No. It was the pictures of her parents and their family trips together.

Nope. Not going there. You're safe. You're alive. That's what really matters, Caly told herself and tried to slam the door shut on those thoughts along with the accompanying swell of emotions.

"Caly?" Blake asked, walking out of the bedroom closet.

She saw his concerned look, appraising her as she sat on the reclining chaise in his room.

"Yeah?" She tried to play it off like the floodgates of emotions weren't about to crack open with the thought of her parents and losing those pictures forever. Apparently, she wasn't as good of an actress as she once thought because Blake walked over to her and wrapped her in his arms.

"Talk to me," he ordered in one of his gentle commands and she felt the deep soothing vibrations in his chest as he spoke.

I'm sad that some pictures are lost to me forever. And, fine, I'm also mourning my music playlists. That didn't make her sound a tad ungrateful for the fact that she was alive and healthy or anything. Oh, and immortal.

"It's nothing." So, she decided to go with the totally B.S. cliché "it's nothing" line.

Classic, Caly, she internally mocked.

Blake glanced down at her with his look that said, *"I'm not buying it."*

Okay, yeah. Good thing I didn't go into acting. Not like any of that even matters now. She let out a breath and let the thought go with it.

"I was just thinking about... my parents." She swallowed back the emotions. "I've just seen everyone packing and it made me realize the things from my apartment that truly mean the most to me... and they're gone. It's the pictures of my parents." She blinked back a few tears and continued. "Sometimes I would curl up in my reading chair and go through my favorite pictures of us while listening to the playlist I made that reminded me of them. It was a mix of their favorite songs and some I threw in just because it reminded me of them for one reason or another. And don't get me wrong. I'm truly grateful to be here, happy and healthy, but... yeah." She didn't know what she was expecting Blake to say or do but it wasn't anything remotely close to what he did.

"Caly." He kissed the top of her head as he held her close to his chest.

I understand more than you know, he thought.

"I was going to wait to give it to you until tonight when we're at Riordan's. But..." He got up and walked over to the closet. Turning his head over his shoulder to look back at her, he said with a sly one-sided smile, "Close your eyes."

Caly obeyed. She heard him unzip his packed bag along with some ruffling and then his footsteps were approaching once more.

"I'm not... well, I haven't wrapped it or anything," he confessed.

She smiled while keeping her eyes closed. "Blake, I honestly don't care about stuff like that. The thought alone is what really matters."

And it was the truth. She never really understood how some people would sometimes spend more than the gift itself on elegant wrapping paper, bows, ribbons, tissue paper, and an overpriced generic card. In fact, she always felt a little bad throwing the card away and tearing into the expensive gift wrapping. So, she would try and gently open the gifts, just to salvage what she could. But all that left her with was a craft container in the back of her closet full of what looked like The Ghost of Gifts' Past, reject pile. Sure, opening gifts were fun, along with the anticipation of what it could be. But she preferred something simple and practical that she didn't feel bad ripping into, like recycled newspaper or even her favorite go-to method of just resealing the Amazon box and writing her mom or dad's name on it.

She felt the slight weight and shape of a box placed on her lap.

"Open your eyes," Blake coaxed.

Caly followed suit.

It was not one but two boxes stacked neatly on top of each other. The top box was smaller at about six inches. It was matte black except for the soft white font of *Light Up The Night*.

She furrowed her brow, not entirely sure what she was looking at.

"Open it," Blake urged with eyes fixed on her as if wanting to gauge her reaction.

"Okay." She drew out the word with a little smile, amused with the mystery of the gift.

She lifted the lid and was looking at a set of two night-lights. They were rather fancy night-lights with what appeared to be different colors and brightness settings from light reading all of the way to dim sleep.

Oh my god. How did he know?

Caly, of course, noticed that Blake continually left the

bathroom light on at night and she didn't question it be-cause, hell, it was exactly what she needed. She felt safe in Blake's arms at night but the chilling total darkness still haunted her. It wasn't until this moment that she realized he did that for her. And just like that, the floodgates were offi-cially opened and she was the goddess of tears once more.

"Blake, this is so thoughtful," she choked out.

He cupped her face, wiped her tears from her cheeks with his thumbs, and gave her a quick kiss on the lips.

"Open the next one," he coaxed once more with a hint of gratification in his smile for getting that first gift right.

Caly set the box of night-lights aside and was looking at a generic white box that was a little less than two-feet long and only a couple of inches in height. She opened the lid and saw black material. Picking it up in her hands—and wow, the material was soft, thick, and great quality—she outstretched her arms in front of her to see what it was.

Yoga pants. Again, how did he know that's what I basi-cally live in?

The box contained nice yoga pants, sports bras, panties, tank tops and a pair of generic black slide sandals. There were two pairs of everything and it was all black.

And, again, how did he know about black being my thing?

It wasn't because she was an undercover Goth, but rather, black was not only flattering for her curves but also it was simple, never went out of style, and covered up sweat marks nicely when she would work out (on those very random occasions). Okay, and, yeah, it also covered up coffee and tea stains when she would spill because sometimes she just had those days where her clothes were like a magnet for stains. Of course, she had other colors too but black was a majority of her closet color of choice.

"I know you wore black yoga pants and tank tops

around your house from when we watched over you those few days," Blake divulged with a brief pause. "And this is just to get you started. If you don't like them then you never have to wear them." He suddenly was sporting a wolfish smirk and continued, "You know how I like it with my scent all over you in my clothes anyways." He playfully growled and she let out a little laugh.

I'm keeping his hoodie, she made a mental plan. *Because, yeah, what is it about the male hoodie that is so magical?*

"Blake, thank you so much. Seriously, this is so thoughtful."

Goodbye Midol period girl. Hello, black pants. Black shirts. All black everything, Caly thought as she made a mental ode to Jay-Z's album.

She made a motion to get up so she could try on the new clothes but Blake rested his hand on her thigh and said, "There's more."

More?

"Okay." She, once again, drew out the word with her amused smile for the mystery of the surprise multi-layered gift.

"Close your eyes." He echoed his previous teasing command.

She did.

Once more, she felt a box placed on her lap. But this time, it was small and had almost no weight. Caly opened her eyes and was looking at a slender box, similar to the size one would gift jewelry. It was all white with an embossed symbol of what looked like a dragon.

Jewelry? she thought as her brows furrowed slightly. She lifted the lid and saw a small square of sleek, metallic material.

"What is this?" she curiously asked, looking up at Blake.

"Your new phone or CCD, Computer Communication

Device. Species have a bit more advanced technology than humans," Blake explained, sitting down next to her. He picked the sleek square up and placed it in her palm.

It felt as light as a feather.

"We'll bring you up to speed on basic species technology another day but I know you'll catch on quick," he said, turning it on with a quick motion she didn't catch.

A moment later, a small looking computer screen lit up and then Blake did the impossible. He stretched the square apart until it was about the size of a cell phone.

"This can go to about twenty inches. You can wear it as a watch, necklace, belt, or just the classic: in your pocket or purse. Just like the large screen we use to watch TV, it's really just a screen because the computer aspect of it is actually stored in your own private secure virtual vault, or PSV. D can explain all of that way better if you're interested. Speaking of..." He paused and looked at her with the corner of his mouth curved. "D has it all set up for you to make calls, load any books, music, movies, and shop for just about anything."

Speechless. She was completely speechless staring at an impossibly stretchy computer phone.

"Blake... How?... What?..." It was like her brain was Windows 95 and stuck on single-word mode.

He chuckled. "Like I said, our technology is a bit more advanced. Here," he reached over to the screen and stretched it so it was the size of an iPad, "I want to show you a couple things." He pushed the icon that looked like a shopping cart.

Okay, so that certainly seems intuitive enough.

"Again, I ordered these clothes just to get you started but while we finish packing, you can order whatever you want," he said matter of factly.

Wait, order whatever I want? And how much is this...

What did he call it again? PCD?

"Blake, thank you but this looks expensive and I... I don't have any money," she managed to get out.

"We have money." He smirked amusedly.

"Blake, I can't spend your money. It's yours. It doesn't feel right," she protested.

"Caly." His golden eyes locked directly on hers. "You're my mate. *We* have money. Let me provide for you." He spoke in his alpha tone, letting her know he wasn't budging on this.

What Blake didn't say was how his wealth did not solely accrue from his SILE cases, and they were compensated quite well for the high profile VIP cases they worked. But now was not the time for any of that.

"But—" She kept up with the protest because she didn't want to be featured in Real Housewives: Species Edition.

"Caly," he cut her off. "You will always be taken care of now. If not by me then by Riordan as your Primary. You never have to worry about money ever again."

Never again? She let that thought sink in for several moments and tried to wrap her mind around her new financial reality.

"Blake, I... I don't even know what to say," she confessed.

"You don't have to say anything." He kissed her on the lips. "Caly, there's something else."

She noticed his playful tone was gone and it was replaced with his intense focus on her, again, as if to gauge her reaction. His eyes refocused on the CCD screen in her palm. He touched the music note icon—again, pretty intuitive—and she blinked almost not believing what she was seeing.

No... It can't be... Can it?

She used her finger to scroll through the screen to confirm what she was seeing. It was all of her playlists.

Before she could react, he revealed, "D, hacked into your human account and transferred your music..." He paused with a calculating look before continuing on. "And all of your photos that you had uploaded. We haven't opened it for your privacy but they're all there too." He closed the music menu and indicated to the photos icon.

They're all there?

"Blake..." Her lip quivered as tears pooled in her eyes. She wanted to open the photos but she knew she couldn't go there right now.

"There's one more thing," he said, bringing back his slightly playful tone.

More? I don't know how much more I can take.

"I took the liberty to load some *romance* books to start you off." He opened the book icon and there were several preloaded books.

Caly wiped the tears from her eyes commanding her brain to switch gears once again with the surprise gift that just kept on giving. She took a closer look.

Oh. My. God.

All of the books were about wolf shifters. Caly burst out laughing and didn't stop until there was a stitch in her side. She had to take several calming breaths to come down from the laughing high.

"Blake," she said in a tone of deep appreciation. "You have no idea how much this means to me. This is the best gift anyone has ever given me." She wrapped her arms around his neck and pulled him in for a quick kiss. "Thank you," she said with a smile, gazing deep into his impossibly golden eyes.

Their eyes were locked for a brief moment, silently saying all that needed to be said.

"We still have some time before we leave. I need to check on a few things and continue with the preparations. Why don't you do some shopping?" He eyed the CCD and his lips curved.

Caly bit her lower lip as she tried to, once again, fully grasp her new financial reality.

"Order whatever you want," Blake reassured her with a slight hint of his alpha tone. He abruptly inhaled and said, "The pizza's here." A wolfish grin spread across his face as he continued, "You're only getting some if you start shopping." He gave her a quick kiss before he stood up and walked out.

Even though it was still early morning, they all opted to order a breakfast pizza—well, actually, several breakfast pizzas—instead of cooking breakfast due to the unexpected eventful morning and the whole packing thing. Caly had never heard of a breakfast pizza before and when she asked the twins what it was, their eyes lit up as if they were thinking of a long lost love. The way the twins talked about food, with eye-twinkling descriptions, always made Caly laugh. She was definitely game to try it out.

"We have money... You never have to worry about money ever again." Blake's words echoed in her mind.

Yeah, that might take some time before it truly sinks in.

Getting up from the couch, she walked into the closet to try on her new clothes. She slipped into the clothes and they fit, miraculously enough. New yoga pants were always kind of a hit or miss with her curves and "thermal layer." But the ones Blake bought, fit her nicely and she made a mental note to order some more from this company.

Hello, new lounging around the house clothes.

She slowly turned to thoroughly inspect the outfit in the mirror. Satisfied, she pulled on Blake's hoodie (because, duh) and then found her spot on the reclining chaise once more. She palmed the CCD and gripped the sides like Blake did when he did the impossible stretch stunt. She echoed the movement and pulled it apart.

Incredible, she thought, resizing it back to fit in her palm comfortably. She looked at the box it came in and saw two earplug-looking things that she didn't notice before.

Nice!

She put the earbuds in and opened the music menu.

Hmmm... what to play?

Scrolling through her playlists, she selected her *Random Chill Oldies* mix. Because, yeah. Those were the types of playlists she had. She pushed shuffle.

Okay, she thought with a slight smile as "Bills, Bills, Bills" by Destiny's Child started playing. *The Universe apparently has a sense of humor today. And, bonus! Complete noise cancellation without the bulky, construction worker, ear protector look. I could so get used to this.*

On that note, Blake came back in with the pizza and appraised her new outfit. He gave an approving smirk at her still being in his hoodie and using the CCD.

Pausing the music, Caly asked, "Can I order something for Aleia too?"

It felt weird asking for permission but then again, it really was his money and she didn't want to cross any lines or anything.

"Caly, you don't have to ever ask me to order anything. Just order it," he said with a smile, setting down the pizza.

How can any of this be real?

"Thanks." She smiled back. "I'm not entirely sure what to get her. I mean, I kind of have an idea from Riordan's riddle but I still am not sure what she really likes," Caly said, half speaking out loud and half pondering about her previous decision to gift Aleia some high-quality, floral tea, a tea mug, and books.

"She likes cats," Blake offered.

Caly gave him this look that said, *"And how would you know that?"*

Chuckling, he gave a one-word explanation, "Felix."

At the sound of his name, Felix lazily blinked one eye open at Blake in inquiry of being summoned. He was sprawled out on the other end of the couch in a patch of sun shining through the window. Concluding there were no treats or head scratches being offered, he went back to his afternoon agenda: a cat nap.

Catching the momentary rise from Felix, Caly smiled. Oh, how she loved Felix and hoped he wouldn't mind another move.

He's a tough male and will be fine. I mean, look how he's doing in this pack of males.

"Cats, huh?" Caly spoke, still looking at Felix and wondered about getting Aleia a cute cat tea mug. Again, if Aleia liked tea and books, then maybe she felt the same way as Caly about having a favorite mug for reading. *I mean, you really can't have too many tea mugs.*

Caly's mind drifted to her favorite tea mug that she would never see again. It wasn't that fancy or anything by far. In fact, it was just a simple white mug with cartoon cat outlines on it and on the inside of the rim, it said, "You've cat to be kitten me right meow." She found it on a fifty-percent-off discount at Marshalls and couldn't pass it up. Who knew it would become her new favorite?

I'll get myself a new mug too. And maybe I'll also order some tea for myself, she decided. *Hmm... What about books?*

Again, books were such a personal thing, and it could either just be another book on the shelf collecting dust or a book with the binding worn from use. Yeah, books were a little tricky, especially if you didn't know the recipient all that well.

Her thoughts were temporarily distracted by Blake with his double stack pizza slice eating method. She picked up a slice and they finished the breakfast triangles together. Blake reloaded with a new double stack and gave her a quick, greasy kiss on the lips.

"We'll just be out there packing," he indicated with his head toward the heart of the home.

"Okay." She responded with a close-lipped smile and a cheekful of breakfast pizza.

When Blake left the room, she got back with the mission: music and shopping. Yeah, she could get used to this.

It didn't take long for Caly to figure out how to order from the CCD. Blake was right. She really was able to catch on quickly to how it worked.

First, she wanted to get Aleia's gift taken care of. After scrolling through what felt like hundreds of different cat mugs, and even through some unexpected humorous species ones, like "Shift Happens," she finally found one for Aleia. It was white with a cute, cartoon cat that was curled up sleeping and had "Just what the doctor ordered," in black, feminine font.

Purrrfect, she thought and began the hunt for her new mug. Caly was going to get a cat mug for herself too but then a thought popped into her head. *Wolf mug.* So, she decided she would surprise Blake with a playful wolf mug.

Again, there was more incessant scrolling until she found two contenders. The first was a mug that said, "Once you go alpha..." with an outline of sexy, red lips as if someone kissed the mug. The second said, "I'm with the wolf" with an iconic outline of a wolf howling.

Which one? Hmmm... Wait. Why not both?

"We have money... You never have to worry about money ever again... Order whatever you want..." Blake's words echoed in her mind.

Okay, she thought, with her finger hesitating over the "Add to Cart" option. *Screw it. Two mugs are not a big deal.*

It was as if the act of adding both items to the cart cut her a little more free from the financial ties of her past.

Another thought popped into her mind and she let out a wicked smile. It was an image of her in sexy lingerie seductively sitting in Blake's chair, blowing hot steam over the rim of the "Once you go alpha…" mug. Riding on the wave of inspiration from that little fantasy, she swiftly shifted gears and was on the hunt for sexy lingerie to surprise Blake with. She had never worn lingerie for anyone before but she was practically buzzing with excited anticipation at the thought of surprising Blake.

As if heated by her fantasy, the cheesy breakfast pizza had a melty mishap, resulting in a landslide of sausage scramble on her new black yoga pants.

Yup. This is why it's all black everything for me, she thought, picking up the melted pile and bringing it to her mouth. Using a napkin, she tried to wipe up the remaining grease.

Wow. If Blake only knew what a greasy slob I looked like when I ordered the sexy lingerie. She looked down at the grease stain. *Yeah, real hot.*

Caly didn't know how long she went on her shopping spree but it was as if the music and the magic of the male hoodie sucked her into a shopping vortex where time didn't exist. It reminded Caly of when she would go to Target. She would walk in to buy one thing and then, two hours later, she'd leave slightly dazed and confused, hauling ten bags of who knows what into her car. Caly's cart was full with the basics like pants, panties, bras, socks, and some practical shoes.

Okay, do I really need all of these? she thought, biting

her lower lip as she scrolled through a few little extra things, like the lingerie, makeup, and what she hoped would be her new favorite black dress.

Maybe I've gone a little overboard with the lingerie? But now that I'm living with Blake, I have to step my game up. I mean, all he really knows of me is either the Midol period girl or skyclad... whatever. It's not like he is going to mind the new sexy surprises.

Continuing with the review of her cart, Caly came across Aleia's gift and she was excited at the solution she came up with for the book gift conundrum. She would give Aleia a book gift card and on the card, she would include some of her favorite books as suggestions for different categories like "light weekend binge read," "inspiration," and, yeah, she would even write a suggestion for a romance novel or two. Because, why not? Aleia was a female after all and all of the women Caly knew who went romance never went back. Granted, they were human women, not species females, but she figured it couldn't be that different. Regardless, she would just subtly add the romance category sandwiched between other ones so it wasn't awkward or anything.

Caly scrolled across the herbal teas in the cart. When she was on the hunt for tea blends, one thing Caly quickly discovered was that the species world had plants, spices, and herbs she had never even heard of. Her mouth was salivating at all of the new taste bud possibilities for her drink rituals and meals. She was a little scared of some, like a tea blend called *Species Spellbound* by Dr. Amare because the description said it was "enhanced with the purest potent love allowable on the market," in combination with ancient herbal formulations with the eye-rolling promise to "have him obsessed with you and only you." So, yeah, Caly stayed away from Dr. Amare and anything weird like that. She also made a mental note to ask Blake if witches and wizards were real.

She ended up deciding on a tea blend that looked safe on the witch front and intriguing to the point where she may be like an eager child checking the mailbox every day until it arrived. It was an assorted mix of wild-harvested, high-quality, specialty, floral teas. She couldn't wait to taste them all but she was especially looking forward to the *Rare Rainbow Rose* tea, which apparently only grew in the high mountain altitude of a secret location in the Sacred Summit. She didn't know where the hell that was but with one glance at the picture of the flower with the impossible kaleidoscopic petals, her hand moved of its own volition and added it to the cart for both her and Aleia. The multi-colored beauty also shed a little more light of realization on the fact that she was living in a whole new world: full of its own wonders that she couldn't wait to explore.

Chapter 31

"Wait, what?" Caly said, pausing mid-stroke down Felix's fur.

A few chuckles rippled through the living room at her reaction.

Blake, Nico, Deacon, and the twins were in their usual spots with the new addition of Caly on Blake's lap and Felix on the chair's armrest, doing his best impression of a loaf of bread with his paws and tail tucked beneath him.

Okay. First, it was the whole Nico mesmerizing Felix. Now, it's teleporting?!

"Oh come on, SoCal," Rhyland said with an amused smile. "How primitive do you think we are?"

"Teleportation. Like…" Her voice trailed off because, yeah, she didn't have any real-life examples of teleportation for crying out loud.

"Like beam me up!" Rhyland quipped and popped a few peanut M&M's into his mouth.

"Teleportation is the most common way to travel," Blake added and then he briefly brought Caly up to speed on MEs and teleportation stations.

"So, we're teleporting to Riordan's…" Caly spoke in a voice of curious wonder.

Truthfully, she was a little wigged out by the idea of teleportation but they already assured her it's completely safe. Although, the first few times she may feel a little disoriented.

"Imagine if you've never been in a car before and then go for a ride. You may get car sickness or feel a little weird but you get used to it." That was how Rhyland explained it and on some level that made sense to Caly.

"We leave for Riordan's in five minutes. Pack up the vehicles." Blake's voice cut through her thoughts.

Okay. Five minutes. No, I don't suddenly need to nervous pee or anything.

Caly looked at Blake. "I'm just going to use the restroom real quick. Are you able to see if Felix wants any food or water before we leave?"

Blake nodded and walked over to Felix as she made her way down the hall to Blake's room.

Can I be mesmerized for the teleporting too? Caly thought, feeling butterflies in her stomach take flight in anticipation of teleporting. It wasn't just the act of teleporting that made her nervous. She was also feeling anxiety around the thoughts of seeing more of the species world for the first time and staying at Riordan's.

Finishing her business in the bathroom, Caly looked at herself in the mirror while washing her hands.

I can do this. I am the fucking Phoenix.

Why the whole Phoenix thing stuck with her and became her new mantra? She didn't know. But that didn't matter to her because it seemed to work amongst all this influx of impossible information that made up the species world, as well as, all of the storm of chaotic change that she seemed to be in the middle of.

Taking one last look at herself in the mirror, Caly felt her shoulders relax when she saw Blake's oversized hoodie. Even though all of this was slightly overwhelming and the thought of teleporting kind of freaked her out, the hoodie reminded her that Blake was going to be with her and they would do this together. Taking a final deep breath, she walked out of the bathroom and back into the living room.

She noticed that Blake had set out a few treats next to Felix's bowl of water and it looked like Felix took him up on the fishy morsels and was currently washing them down with some water. Good. She wanted to make sure Felix had a full belly and was as comfortable as possible.

Kneeling down next to Felix, she tunneled her fingers through his fur in an effort to comfort him. Although, it really was Felix who was comforting her.

"Hey, Felix. We're going to go on a little adventure. But don't worry, you'll be in a deep sleep the whole time."

"Meow," Felix responded, quickly gobbling up the last of the treats.

"Caly?"

All it took was one glance at Blake for her to see his one-word question actually asked, *"How are you doing with all of this?"*

"I'm good... a little nervous to leave the house and have my molecules scrambled and then put back together after thousands of miles traveled but, you know, other than that I'm good." She smiled at her feeble attempt at a joke.

When Blake pulled her in for a hug, she exhaled and visibly relaxed.

The twins strode in grinning and Rhyland said, "Felix's carriage awaits," in an English accent as if he was Felix's chauffeur. He was holding a medium-sized cardboard box that was lined with a soft blanket.

"This is perfect. Thank you both so much," Caly said, giving an appreciative look at the twins and then looked at Nico. "So, how does this work exactly?"

"Direct eye contact," Nico replied, closing the short distance between them.

"And his vampy charm," Rhyland tacked on with a wink.

Caly chortled.

Yes, clearly he is quite the charmer with his iciness and few words. She was starting to see that Nico was just being Nico and he was like that with everyone—well, everyone so far.

Caly picked up Felix, who looked a bit suspicious with all of the attention on him all of a sudden, and it only took a moment of Nico's gaze for Felix to fall asleep.

Suddenly, the memory of the first time she met Nico, and him mesmerizing her, flashed through her mind. Tucking that happy memory back into its box, she carefully placed Felix in his carriage.

Rhyland handed the box to his brother and as soon as the handoff was executed, he exclaimed, "Shotgun!" as he ran out the door.

Caly laughed and Blake swung his arm around her shoulders to pull her in for a quick side hug. They walked out into the early afternoon toward the two, blacked-out SUV pack vehicles. Each of the males had their own vehicles but they decided to take the two SUVs for this excursion.

Blake helped Caly into the SUV with the unoccupied front seat.

Rhyker placed the box with Felix on her lap and got settled into the backseat.

Blake turned on the SUV and suddenly, "California Love" by Tupac was blasting on the speakers. Caly jumped at the unexpected sound and Blake immediately turned down the music to a reasonable level. Blake gave Rhyker an accusatory side-eye, only to be met with an all too familiar mischievous twin grin. Before Blake could question what the twins were up to, "California Girls" by Katy Perry began booming from the other SUV.

Immediately turning off the blaring pop music that was assaulting the speakers, Nico glared daggers at Rhyland in a way that said he wanted to make a quick pit stop to the fight room. Sporting his feline grin, Rhyland soaked up the fact that he annoyed Nico and playfully winked at Caly. Caly was laughing so hard she almost cried because it didn't take a genius to put together the California reference between where she's from, the twins calling her SoCal, and of course, her name. She could totally get used to the twins' jokes and laughing until she cried. And on that note, Blake put the vehicle in gear and they were off.

Caly wasn't sure what she was expecting to see but the drive to the SILE station seemed relatively normal, at least in comparison to her human experiences.

Rhyker was the DJ and bumped mainly old-school hip hop, mixed with a few good rock songs.

They drove on a small two-lane highway with large forest trees and greenery on either side. It kind of seemed like they were on a mini road trip. Not too long later, they came upon the local town which, again, looked normal to Caly. But she made her assessment based on what it looked like from a distance because they actually didn't drive through the town since one of the first turn offs was the SILE station.

With both vehicles parked, they all got out of the SUVs and the males grabbed their bags while Caly held Felix. Blake reached out in offer to hold Felix but Caly shook her head. For whatever reason, she wanted to hold Felix for this mini-adventure. Not only was he her fur baby but also, holding Felix helped keep her grounded because, even in his sleep, his presence was comforting.

The SILE station looked like a large, generic, and nondescript gray, square, two-story building with blacked-out windows. It was not what she was expecting but then again, she didn't know what she was expecting really. They walked up to the building and the sleek, dark and tinted glass door slid open. Blake led the way inside with Caly right behind him and the rest following suit. The inside of the station was lit up with white walls, which contrasted the gray and black exterior. Just inside the doors, there was a security check-in area.

"Hey, Blake." The male security guard at the check-in station smiled. "I see you got the whole gang with you today." He paused, looking at Caly and Felix. "And a few additions." He smiled at Caly and, with a single head nod, said, "Name's Sirlei."

"Hi. I'm Caly." She smiled at Sirlei. "And this is Felix." She gestured to the box with her head.

Sirlei certainly had that whole *"I'm a cop"* look about him in his black sunglasses and all black SILE uniform of pants, a T-shirt with the white, bold lettering of S-I-L-E across his chest, and a weapons' belt—complete with a gun strapped to his hip. Although you could tell he worked out, he wasn't nearly as large as Blake and the twins, both in the height and weight department. In fact, if Caly didn't know he was species then she would have thought he was human because nothing really gave away the fact that he was species.

Sirlei slid off his black shades and gave her an appraising look.

Scratch that thought. He definitely couldn't pass as human, she thought, noticing that his eyes were bright shades of amber with a thin, black, vertical-lined pupil.

"You have beautiful eyes, Caly. I don't think I've ever seen anything quite like them before."

"Thanks." She spoke in a shy voice with a slight smile.

She broke eye contact by looking at Felix as if she wasn't that confident in owning the compliment. If Caly wasn't holding Felix, she probably would have tucked her hair behind her ear in a knee-jerk reaction. Even though Caly was used to compliments and comments about her gray eyes, there was just something about it that still had her retreat to her inner shy girl.

Blake wrapped his arm around her shoulders in a very silent command that said, *"Back off. She's mine."*

Sirlei received the message loud and clear and gave a look to Blake that said, *"Duly noted."*

The twins chuckled and both Deacon and Nico smirked in amusement at the dominant display.

"Boss male isn't here. You just missed him actually," Sirlei said to Blake.

"We're just passing through today, Sirlei," Blake responded.

Sirlei nodded. "Nice to meet you, Caly. And you know where to find me if you ever run into trouble." He smiled.

Past the security check-in, there was a large staircase leading to the second floor. To the right of the staircase, there was a hall with several doors that eventually curved to the left. There was also a small waiting area of sorts with chairs and a TV on mute with the news. To the left, there was a similar setup, minus the waiting area.

Blake turned left down the hall and they walked past several closed doors.

Continuing down the hallway, they walked past a few other SILE cops who gave acknowledging head nods to everyone. Their casual (not casual) cop gaze seemed to linger on Caly in calculated curiosity before continuing their conversations. A couple of the cops were on the taller side of the scale. This triggered Caly to remember what Blake said about it being easy to distinguish predatory shifter males with large animals. Concluding that's what those taller males were, she wondered what animal they shifted into.

Turning around the corner, the hall looked as if it came to a blank-walled dead end but as soon as Blake got close enough, a large door in the wall slid open. There was a small hallway that, again, looked like another dead end. They halted about halfway down the short hallway because there was a small security room to the right with large glass windows. There was a hefty security guard standing at the doorway. Just like Sirlei, he was also wearing the black SILE uniform. Unlike Sirlei, this male looked dark and dangerous. His tattoos brought out his tan skin and his no-nonsense, buzz cut spoke volumes. This male competed in the height department with Blake—although Blake was still slightly taller—and Caly had a feeling this male must also be a predatory shifter with a large animal.

Maybe he's a wolf too? she thought, looking at him a bit closer while he gave a quick once over at the group.

No... doesn't seem like a wolf... Lion? Are there even lion shifters? she wondered and again, she looked at him while thinking of him shifting into a lion.

No... that doesn't fit either...

As if he knew she was trying to figure out what subspecies he was, he looked at her for the longest moment before turning his attention back to Blake.

"Blake." The guard gave a single head nod.

"Drex," Blake responded, echoing the movement.

"Whad'ya do this time to get stuck with port duty, Sexy Drexy?" Rhyland said, interjecting into the seemingly civil interaction.

Rhyker chuckled and fist-bumped his twin for the crack.

There was a glint of amusement amongst all of the males, except Drex. Caly may have stepped a bit closer to Blake as Drex crossed his arms over his chest with a look that said he wanted to take Rhyland for a round in the fight room.

"Oh, come on. We all know you probably colored outside the lines again," Rhyland quipped.

Drex's lips curved in dark amusement. He may have been notorious for "coloring outside the lines" on cases when it came to teaching a fucker a lesson or two… off the record of course.

"Then don't ask stupid questions, Tweedle Dum," Drex responded with a satisfactory smirk of his retort. His gaze flicked back to Caly and then Felix.

"This is Caly." Blake answered the unspoken question and this time, he may have taken a step closer to Caly with another unspoken directive.

"Caly." Drex nodded his head in acknowledgment, amused at Blake's subtle reaction.

"Drex." Caly followed the lead with the one-word introduction and smiled.

"Don't know how you got caught up in this group of males but you're in good hands… minus those two." Drex's eyes flicked to the twins and his lips twitched. "I'd be happy to *color outside the lines* when it comes to these two for you." Drex actually cracked a full-on smile at that and Caly saw a split-second glimpse under his dangerous cop exterior.

"Oh, there would be colors alright," Rhyland started.

"Black and blue," Rhyker finished.

There was a round of chuckles and Drex even fist-bumped the twins. It was just male banter at its finest and all in good fun.

Clearly, they know each other well… probably worked on cases before, Caly thought, seeing Drex walk into the security room. A second later, a door appeared at the end of the hallway and slid open. They walked through the door and into an open space. Directly in front of them, up against the back wall, was a large platform that was slightly raised off the ground by only a couple of inches. To the left was a small operating panel.

"You ready, SoCal?" Rhyland playfully nudged her with his elbow before making his way on the platform.

This is the teleporting room? she thought, looking at the room once more. Again, she didn't know what she was expecting but the simplicity and unassuming nature of this room certainly did surprise her.

"Ready as I'll ever be," she responded, letting out a tremulous laugh.

"You'll be fine." Blake looked into her eyes with reassuring strength.

"Thanks," she said.

Blake indicated with his head to get on the platform like the other males were doing. The platform was large and looked like everyone would fit relatively comfortably. He gave her a quick kiss and then walked over to the panel.

She made her way next to Rhyland.

"I can hold Felix for this part." Rhyland reached out his hands in offering.

Remembering his analogy about being in the car for the first time and there being a possible "getting used to this" period, she agreed.

"Thanks." She handed Felix over to Rhyland.

Looking over at Blake, she noticed the number 314 in white bold characters above the door they came through. She watched Blake make a few quick movements on a small screen before making his way to the platform next to her.

The butterflies in Caly's stomach were fluttering with a combination of nervous excitement and, yes, a little fear... and maybe more than just a little. Now that her hands were free of Felix, she almost didn't know what to do with herself because at least that had given her hands a concrete task.

Blake pulled Caly in for a hug and then whispered in her ear, "You're safe. I promise." She saw a strip of light appear around the edge of the platform. Closing her eyes, she clung to Blake's body and listened intently to the steady rhythm of his heartbeat as the butterflies became a fluttering storm of nervous chaos in her stomach. Blake's arm left her body for a moment to initiate the port and then resettled back home around her waist.

"I got you," his steady voice trailed into her ear.

She held on tighter.

A moment later, there was a flash of bright light that forced her eyes closed from the sheer brightness.

Between one breath and the next, she felt a little light-headed and disoriented, like her stomach had turned upside down and then back right again.

She dared a peek.

To her surprise, they looked like they were in the same room. But then she noticed the number above the door now showed 458.

Was that it? she thought, braving more of a look around at the other males.

"See, that wasn't so bad, huh?" Rhyland winked.

The strip of light around the edge of the platform disappeared and the males made their way off of it.

"How do you feel?" Blake asked with eyes focused on her and her alone.

"I..." She looked up into Blake's eyes and paused as she did a quick self-assessment. "A little lightheaded and kind of like I just rode a roller coaster actually. And I'm not really a fan of roller coasters. So, don't expect us to go to an amusement park for date night." She smiled and peeled away from Blake.

That wasn't so bad. I mean, good thing you didn't do the panda food buffet part two right before... because that could have been a different outcome.

"Good to know. I was never really into them either." He held her hand as they walked off the platform.

Her legs felt a little shaky and her body felt light.

"Here. Eat this." Surprisingly enough, Nico was actually the one to speak, and his arm was outstretched offering her an energy bar.

"Good idea… for once," Rhyker added with a feline grin.

Nico shot him a side-eyed glare.

"Thanks," she said, accepting the offering. Peeling open the wrapper, she took a bite. It was actually really tasty. "This is good." She inspected the wrapper and then gave a smile to Nico. Nico gave her a head nod in response and she did the chew and swallow thing a few more times. It did actually feel like it was helping as if each bite was a weight-grounding and centering her body.

"Better?" Blake asked with a careful watch on her.

"Yeah." She exhaled and then squeezed his hand reassuring him she really was fine.

And with that, their tight-knit group made their way out the door marked 458.

Chapter 32

Caly was a little surprised at how the theme song kept ringing the tune that everything seemed relatively normal. Well, considering the fact that she was in a magical world, teleporting thousands of miles, and traveling with a crew of species males that only just days ago she found out existed. So, yeah, relatively normal.

The SILE station they landed at was nothing like the first. This building seemed more grand, with high ceilings and endless rooms. It was also similarly scattered with tight herds of cops, conversing about who knew what, some of which were the easy-to-spot, predatory, large-animal, male shifters. And that made sense because who would make for better cops? Caly conjured up an image in her mind of a pack of wolves hunting down their prey in the wild.

She was also somewhat surprised to witness that even at this station, thousands of miles away, the cops silently acknowledged Blake and their pack while, of course, doing the cop "once over glance" at Caly and Felix. It was as if they knew of Blake and the males but not necessarily knew them on a personal level. That got her thinking about just how well-known The Order actually was, either publicly or privately in the SILE hierarchy, or if she was just misinterpreting the whole thing due to her lack of experience with species social situations.

They walked outside and it seemed to be early evening with the fading remnants of what looked like a colorful sunset. The air seemed thick with the promise of rain and there were a few fat, gray clouds in the sky. The time of day and the weather were the first things that physically clued Caly into the reality of how far they had traveled in virtually a blink of an eye.

The other thing she noticed was the single-stone building for the gatekeeper, which had a gate made of black iron spikes that wrapped around the property. It was odd though because it was just the spikes standing by themselves without anything connecting them. *Maybe they are still installing them.* That thought faded away as soon as she saw the faintest shimmer between the spikes. *Maybe it actually is finished and it's some sort of electrical barrier?* she wondered as her gaze followed the spikes until it landed on the SILE building that they had just walked out of.

As she suspected, the building was not anything like the small, nondescript SILE station they came from. This building was regal with its older style and gray, stone composition. It reminded her of an elite private college with lots of windows and a large, old-school clock above the entrance. Even with the large, stone building, there was greenery everywhere in the form of trees, shrubs, and grass. In fact, beyond the gates, that theme continued with what appeared to be a large park. But she was guessing about the park because the trees were so large and thick, hugging the roads close, that she couldn't see far beyond them.

Turning back in a full circle to the gate guard building, her eyebrows raised in surprise. Instead of two large SUVs, Riordan had arranged what looked like a solid black, SUV limo waiting for them. It wasn't one of those obnoxiously large limos Caly was used to seeing in LA, that came fully-loaded with an equally loaded ego. Rather, it was just as if the pack's SUV was stretched just enough to accommodate everyone comfortably but not to be an impractical nuisance on the road.

The driver must've spotted them too because the limo pulled up to meet them.

The driver's door swung open and a young male with light brown hair, light skin the color of cream, and honey brown eyes hopped out of the limo and was smiling ear to ear as he walked up to them. He had a youthful air about him like he must've been in his early twenties and was wearing black slacks and a white button-down with one side slightly untucked.

"Name's Nate." He spoke with an Irish accent but it seemed more casual and modern than Riordan's. He bowed his head at Blake in a respectful greeting.

"Nate," Blake acknowledged and his eyes seemed to dance with amusement for the energetic youth beaming off this young male.

"I still can't believe I won the raffle of who got to pick you all up... This is officially my first task as a full-fledged castellan and—" Nate cut himself off and blushed a little. "Sorry... Let me get your bags." He rushed over and scooped up one of the bags. As he carefully placed it in the back of the limo he called out, "Feel free to get settled in the vehi—" and then he turned white as a sheet. "Sorry, I forgot to open the doors."

"Chill, Nate." Rhyker was smiling to help comfort Nate as he proceeded to open the limo door himself.

Rhyland hopped on that train and finished with, "Yeah, we're not some stuck up aristocrats with egos shoved up our asses."

The twins chuckled and Rhyker said, "By the way, I'm Rhyker."

Rhyland finished with, "And I'm Rhyland."

Rhyland, who was still carrying the sleeping Felix, passed him off to Caly.

"Oh, I know who you are. Believe me, we all know who you are back at home." Nate smiled sheepishly.

"Well, that's good because if something gets broken then we all know it's Rhyker's fault." Rhyland inserted the joke, trying to ease the tension again for the young male.

"Fuck you," Rhyker retorted in a playful tone as they both hauled their bags in the back.

Rhyland winked at Nate, who was just standing there trying to comprehend what to do since the twins and Nico started to load the bags themselves, which went against all of his training.

To Nate's utter surprise, the twins held out a fist and, still a little stunned, Nate fist-bumped the twins. He was left staring at his fist for a moment before refocusing on the males who were grinning as they filed into the limo.

"You're doing fine." Blake gave a quick reassuring squeeze to Nate's shoulder as he proceeded to load his and Caly's bag in the back.

"Hi, Nate. I'm Caly. And this is Felix. It's nice to meet you." She smiled at Nate and, as if for the first time, he really focused on her. He visibly swallowed.

"Wow, your eyes are beautiful." He blushed. "I... uh... sorry... I..." Nate was backpedaling because he couldn't believe he said that out loud.

Caly laughed a little and gave him a smile. "Thanks."

Even though Caly wasn't usually one to accept compliments, the Sirlei interaction being the most recent example, in this case with Nate, it seemed different because it felt sweet and innocent. It was the difference between someone simply complimenting a beautiful bouquet of roses versus someone complimenting them with the underlying intention to have the petals spread on the bed with some other ideas in mind. Besides, Nate just seemed so young to Caly. From his appearance alone, he looked to be a decade younger than her.

Coming back from around the limo, Blake kissed Caly on the lips and grabbed Felix from her arms.

She smiled at the surprise, quick kiss.

Nate's face paled for the second time. But before Nate could recover enough to speak, Blake did.

"I'm just glad your eyes fell on me first because I see I would've had some competition here." Blake's mouth turned up at the corners.

Suddenly, old-school hip hop started bumping in the limo and then Rhyland called out, "Blake stop stealing kisses like you're in a rom-com and get your ass in here so we can be on our merry way."

"I... uh... I didn't..." Nate was visibly distressed at unknowingly and unintentionally hitting on, what he understood now as, Blake's female.

"Relax, son. I know," Blake reassured Nate.

It would be a very different conversation otherwise, Blake thought.

Caly climbed into the limo and saw they left the back bench-style seat for her and Blake. As soon as she got settled in, Blake set Felix on her lap before sitting next to her with his arm over her shoulder.

She looked down at Felix and, even though he was in a deep sleep, she pet him. When they were walking through the SILE building after they arrived, she felt Felix stirring a little and Nico added just a touch more mesmerization for the rest of the trip to Riordan's.

"I like Nate," Caly said to Blake.

"Do you now?" Blake teased.

She laughed. "Come on. You know what I mean." She paused. "He seems sweet and innocent... and young?" She looked at Blake in question to see if she gauged that right. Blake nodded.

"He said this is his first task as a..." Caly paused, trying to remember the word. "Castellan. What is that?"

"A castellan is a subspecies," Blake began.

Caly's eyebrows shot up because that was not what she was expecting. She thought it was a job title or something like that, not a subspecies. Of course, she knew Nate was species but from what she saw, he could totally pass off as being human.

"Castellans are true caretakers to their very core," Blake continued.

Her eyebrows furrowed, not really knowing where this was going.

"They live for taking care of a family and a home," Blake explained.

"What do you mean 'taking care of'?" Caly asked, not understanding.

"Maintaining the home. Cooking, cleaning, and house repairs," Blake answered matter of factly.

"Wait, what are you saying? Because that sounds..." Caly let her voice trail off. She didn't want to finish her sentence as it sounded like castellans were getting the short end of the very unfair 1950's housewife role. Caly's inner feminist was suddenly ready to start a revolution on behalf of the castellans.

"No, nothing like that." Blake shook his head with a smirk, catching her protectiveness and proud of her reaction to a situation like that. "Castellans are truly happy when they have a family and home to care for. It's just their nature." He paused and then repeated his first statement, hoping for her to see what he meant in this new context. "They are true caretakers down to their core. They are often the glue that keeps a strong house going." He paused again to see how else he could explain this. "Castellans often bond with a prominent family and they have a mutually beneficial relationship of not only love and loyalty but also, they are provided for on other levels, including financially."

Caly's inner feminist relaxed a bit as she started to understand. "Oh okay. I think I get it."

Blake nodded and then added, "Just as it's natural instinct for me to live in a pack, it's also their natural instinct as well. Except the difference is that their instinct is to maintain the homefront while mine is to hunt and protect. And we respectively have abilities that compliment those instincts. Castellans have more strength and speed than a human, but not as much as vampires or shifters. This plays to their advantage around the house."

Caly thought about that one time when she was inspired to spring clean her entire apartment, which included a whole new layout plan to rearrange the furniture. After only moving the table and her reading chair, she quickly realized she was a tad overly ambitious.

Yeah, some extra strength and speed would certainly have made that whole adventure easier.

"They also have a knack with cooking chemistry and architecture. In fact, to them, those are considered both a sacred art and science. And many castellans that don't choose to bond with a family, often wind up opening restaurants or working with buildings in some manner," Blake finished.

"*I still can't believe I won the raffle of who got to pick you all up.*" Caly remembered what Nate said with his genuine youthful eagerness.

"It makes sense. Like how whales have those smaller fish that clean them of parasites but on the flip side those smaller fish are well fed from the parasites and protected because no other fish would dare get close to the whale." She paused and then said, "Okay, wait that's a terrible analogy." She laughed a little and made a mental note to stop bingeing Animal Planet when she was sick. "I didn't mean like bigger as in the whale is better than the fish. Because without the small fish then the whale wouldn't thrive and may even die from the parasites and the diseases they bring." She stopped talking and then looked at Blake for a second before they both just started laughing at the ridiculousness.

"And what does the cute couple find so funny?" Rhyland almost couldn't believe he passed up on a joke, or hell, wasn't the epicenter of it.

"Whales," Caly said, still laughing a little while glancing at a smiling Blake.

The twins let out a girly sigh and theatrically looked at each other batting their googly-eyed eyelashes.

Blake gave an unamused look at the twins while all of the other males laughed.

They had been driving for a while and the males, including Nate, were in some sort of heated discussion about what Caly deduced was a sports team rivalry about a big game coming up. She didn't know and she didn't even try to follow along. Instead, what had her attention was the scenery. They drove out of the city, which continued with the lush greenery, and she wondered what LA would have looked like if humans didn't bulldoze everything for concrete and metal. The further away they drove from the city, the less homes and buildings there were and, instead, the more rolling hills of green. She imagined this must've been what Ireland looked like or at least this was what she pictured when she read all of those romance novels based in Ireland. Besides, she figured she couldn't be that far off with Riordan and Nate's accents.

Even with the light of the day fading into early evening, she could still see how each home they drove past started to get bigger and fancier. And even bigger and fancier until she was literally gawking at the homes—if you could even call them that. The last one they drove by, which was several miles back, was a legitimate mini-mansion.

No. There's no way... Caly thought, almost unable to comprehend that Riordan may live in something like that.

They kept on driving for what seemed like miles and miles without a home in sight.

See. He doesn't live in one of those. We were just passing through a wealthy neighborhood, she told herself.

But then she saw it. She blinked in complete shock at what she was looking at.

"Is that...?" Caly let the words trail out of her mouth in disbelief of what she was looking at.

"Well holy fucking shit... Welcome to Riordan's humble abode." Rhyland broke the silence.

A castle? Riordan lives in a fucking castle?! Caly thought with her brain cramping at the idea of actually staying here.

Chapter 33

"Welcome to the Knight bloodline manor," Nate called out over his shoulder from the driver's seat.

As they drove up the lane to Riordan's home, AKA the castle, Caly wished it was earlier in the day so she could see it in full daylight. But even without the daylight, it was surreal and felt like she was, once again, plopped right into an Irish romance novel. The grandiose and regal elegance of the estate became quickly apparent. Yet, to Caly's eyes, there only appeared to be two stories. So, it seemed grand yet intimate at the same time. If the pristine green grass and tree-covered landscape was any indication, then the castle was probably just as well-maintained throughout, both inside and out. The forested backdrop was a beautiful touch, making it feel secluded.

Caly noticed Deacon's expression change, interest piqued, as he motioned for Rhyker to move down so he could sit closest to Nate.

"Deacon who's always geekin'." Rhyland couldn't help but insert a joke whenever possible. "Are you sure ICIS won't be jealous over you ogling whatever tech caught your eye?"

A round of male chuckles reverberated in the vehicle.

Deacon was too busy, wrapped up in conversation, to

even bother to send an annoyed look to Rhyland.

"From what I can tell, although, I don't speak computer nerd," Rhyland continued and, to his satisfaction, that did get Deacon to send him a side look. "This place is decked out to the nines in security."

Caly looked around with a furrowed brow in confusion. "But it just looks like an open landscape?"

"Oh, there is so much for you to learn, little Padawan," Rhyland quipped with a grin.

"Look over there." Blake pointed behind them.

Caly twisted her upper body to look out the back window.

"I don't see anything," she said, squinting her eyes in confusion. Then she saw a quick shimmer. "Wait. Are my eyes playing tricks on me or did I just see a *shimmer*?"

Blake smirked. "That *shimmer* is, what I'm guessing, a full perimeter security boundary. And from Deacon's reaction and enthusiastic conversation," Blake paused, glancing over at Deacon who was still engrossed in conversation with Nate. "I would agree with Rhy. This place is highly secure."

"But... I don't get it. I mean, sure a little ADT home security makes sense. But why would you need your home to be like Fort Knox?" Caly asked.

"SoCal, Riordan is a fucking *ancient*. He hasn't become an ancient by trusting in 'the magical powers that be' to be his sole security guard," Rhyland said with a smirk. "Don't tell me we have to start calling you SoCal The Sheltered."

"I thought you were from LA, SoCal," Rhyker tacked on in jest.

"Okay, true. But I didn't live in the hood," she added with a laugh.

Nate parked their mini SUV limo right in front of the castle, or rather, "the fortress," as Caly dubbed it. Almost before Caly realized, Nate was out of the driver's side and opening up the side door for them to get out.

"I'll get your things to your rooms," Nate said, shutting the side vehicle door.

There was a round of thanks and fist-bumps for Nate.

With Caly's close view of the fortress, she could see the floor-to-ceiling windows on both levels of the gray stone castle.

When the massive, dark-wood, double-door entrance opened, as if on cue, Riordan and another male were standing in the entrance doorway in greeting.

"Welcome," Riordan said as everyone walked up the few entrance steps. "I'd like to introduce Jax Knight, our head castellan." Riordan indicated to the male standing next to him.

Jax was dressed in a formal black coat, white dress shirt, black tie, and matching gray vest and trousers. His brown eyes matched his hair which was neatly trimmed and styled against his light complexion.

It was traditional for castellans to take on the blooded name of the family they were bonded to. His castellan family had been with the Knight bloodline for centuries. Jax had been the head castellan since the tragedy of the Knight family. The devastating event was merciless and had the heartbreaking result of a very empty homefront, except for Riordan and the remaining castellans. The castellans had been faithfully maintaining the castle but they craved for a home bursting with life once again. For a castellan, there was a deep level of joy and a fulfilled sense of purpose to care for a thriving homefront.

"Jax." Blake gave an alpha head nod in greeting.

Jax bowed his head. "Blake Stone of Orion's Order. It is an honor." He spoke in an Irish accent that had a more similar lilt to Riordan's. To Caly's ear, it sounded like an older origin in comparison to Nate's. When his warm, brown, smiling eyes fell on Caly, he said, "Ms. Calypso," with another dip of his head.

"Hi, Jax. And it's just Caly, please," she said with a smile.

Jax's face softened as he continued with the rest of the greetings with the males.

Caly's breath caught when they all walked inside. The two-story, elegant entryway featured a double grand stairway, each equipped with a half-landing and bordered by a detailed, bespoke, wrought-iron balustrade. The walls were made out of a smooth, light stone that naturally faded from light to dark gray, making each stone unique and bringing a hint of desirable texture and contrast. The white marble floors sang in perfect harmony with the light and bright theme and were designed with large, light-gray diamonds. There were three grand-arches with columns that were carved with intricate designs. Beyond the archways were wide-open living spaces. The entrance view was breathtaking. At the top of the stairs, the entire second-floor landing was bordered with the same iron balustrade and detailed archways, which allowed glimpses of the hallways and rooms beyond. The custom detailing fell in sync with the designs of the crown molding on the ceilings, which displayed a bright chandelier in the center.

"Is this real?" Caly said in disbelief, under her breath to Blake.

"Don't wake me if it isn't," Blake whispered in her ear, sliding his arm around her waist and stealing a quick kiss.

"Agreed." She smiled.

"Really? Can't even wait until we get to our rooms?" Rhyland's purposefully loud, stage whisper interrupted their romantic moment.

Caly playfully elbowed Rhyland's side and his lips curved.

Felix, who Blake was currently holding, started to stir.

"Hi, Felix," Caly said, petting her purring and utterly relaxed fur baby. "How did you sleep?"

Caly kneeled down on the floor and Blake crouched down beside her, setting down the box with Felix between them.

Felix lazily started sniffing the air. As if in curiosity for the scents around him, he blinked one eye open and then the other. With nonchalant feline grace, he hopped out of the box and succumbed to a glorious, good-morning stretch followed by a wide yawn. His golden eyes, with that splash of viper green, looked at Caly.

"Meow."

"We're going to stay here for a while, Felix," she said with a quiet voice, continuing to pet him. Although, she had a feeling that everyone's attention was on the crazy cat lady talking to her cat.

A bowl of water and Felix's cat treats appeared in front of them by a female wearing a long, lavender dress and white apron. Her dark blonde hair was pulled back in a loose bun at her nape. She smiled at Felix as he sniffed the treats. Warm, blue-green eyes met Caly's.

"Thank you, Meri," Riordan said fondly. "Meri is in charge of the kitchen and the genius behind the creations, which we will have the honor of tasting at dinner."

Meri smiled at Riordan's compliment and made her way next to Jax's side.

Caly noticed that Jax slid his arm around her waist and, at the same time, she leaned her head on his shoulder. The little moment between them warmed her heart.

Caly refocused on Felix as he took a couple sips of water. He sniffed the treats again but seemed to be more interested in the change of scenery. Being an ever-curious cat, Felix proceeded with his investigative sniff routine, starting with smelling every single one of them, as if to put his stamp of approval on them. When that was done, he moved to the two new scents, Jax and Meri, but it appeared as though they passed the sniff test too.

"I'm going to get back to dinner preparations." Meri's voice was light and soft, like a tinkling bell. "I will set up his food and water in the dining area though. It was nice to meet you all." Her warm smile wrapped around Caly like a hug.

Walking up the staircase to the right, with Felix keeping up at his own pace, Riordan and Jax proceeded to show them to their rooms so they could freshen up and get settled in a bit before dinner. Turning right down the hall, Caly was looking at the various artwork and statues as they passed several, dark-wood, floor-to-ceiling, arched doors. The hallway curved left and they stopped at the first door.

"Deacon, we hope you find this suitable," Jax said, opening the door.

"Thank you." Deacon nodded at Jax and Riordan.

With their curiosity taking the lead, the twins entered the room with shifter speed right after Deacon.

"Suitable is one way to put it," Rhyland said on an impressed note.

With that, Caly's curiosity peaked, and apparently, so did everyone else's, because soon they were all in Deacon's room checking it out.

The room was practically the same size as Caly's entire LA apartment (if not bigger) with sky-high ceilings. It was fully furnished and had a sleek, modern male theme. From the little Caly knew about Deacon, she figured it fit him very well. There was a massive, curved computer desk off to one side with a painting of a starry night sky behind it. The couch and coffee table combo faced a blank wall that Caly figured probably had some sort of projection screen setup. The massive bed was facing the floor-to-ceiling, French doors that led to the large balcony with a view of a courtyard. The balcony was set up for stargazing and was complete with lounge chairs and a telescope.

One by one, they were shown their bedrooms and each was individualized down to the last detail. Nico's room had this dark and masculine look about it. There was also a large balcony with private roof access. Rhyland's room had a more handsomely simple and relaxed theme with comfy, leather chairs and a sofa that looked lounge-worthy. Rhyker's room was a blend between Nico's dark-colored theme and his brother's comfy, relaxed elements. Blake's room was very similarly themed and furnished similar to his room back at their pack home. Caly's room was bright, warm, and cozy featuring a reading chair and sofa with fluffy pillows and fuzzy blankets. There were even fresh flowers and chocolates set on the table. The bonus, and best surprise of all, was that Caly's closet wasn't empty. There were various clothes and shoes, from workout casual to even a couple of fancy dresses. One of the dresses was made of a long, black, soft, and silky material. It was styled with a reverse-racerback, high neckline.

Where I will wear this? I don't know, Caly thought, kind of hoping for an excuse one day. Being an introvert, she wasn't one for big, fancy parties by far. But every once in a while, it felt nice to get dressed up.

What each room had in common were massive beds, spacious walk-in closets, fireplaces, and spa-like, marble-finished en suites with walk-in showers and deep-soaker tubs. The soaker tubs were actually like mini Jacuzzis because they were big enough for two, even with the size of the twins.

Other than the obvious personalized differences between each room, there were also differences in the locations. Deacon and Nico's rooms were on the second level while the rest were on the floor level. Caly figured it was because shifter animals would like to have indoor and outdoor access, just like how the pack's home was set up. And she presumed that she ended up on that level by default of Blake's room being right next door. This was something she didn't mind because she was obsessed with the floor-to-ceiling, sliding-glass wall in each of the ground level rooms.

Blake's conversation with Riordan, when he first spoke his claim on Caly, came to the forefront of his mind once again.

"It looks like you're going to be busy."

Damn seers, Blake thought, realizing that Riordan probably had been preparing for their arrival since then. Because these rooms were far too personalized to have been thrown together in the short time they made the plans.

"Riordan, it looks like you've been *busy*." Blake emphasized the last word and quirked his brow.

"So it would seem." Riordan's lips curved in amusement.

"This is our fitness facility," Riordan, AKA the fortress tour guide, indicated as they entered the wide-open space. As they continued the walkthrough, it looked like there was every machine, weight, and gym situation you could imagine. And it all looked brand new. It was also very well laid out. There were designated workout areas and, because of that, nothing felt crowded despite all of the equipment.

"Through that door, you will find our aquatic center. It has a pool, sauna, Jacuzzi, and steam room." Riordan pointed toward the left.

I wonder just how big each of those really is, Caly wondered, conjuring an image of a small-sized lake as the pool.

Riordan's focus shifted to a door on the right. "These are our fitness rooms. Down this hall, you will find our heated salt room as well as the igloo."

Heated salt room? Igloo? Caly made a mental note to come back and check out whatever those were. She smiled as she caught the faces of the males because they looked like they had fallen in love with the fitness facility.

"Caly, after you move in, you may, of course, have a couple days off to get acclimated. But we will begin training after that." Riordan paused to look at Caly and she nodded.

"You will start taking self-defense classes. Blake, I presume you got that covered?" Riordan inquired.

"Yes," Blake said with a head nod, pausing briefly in thought. "Caly can train with each of us on a rotating schedule. This way she can get exposed to hand-to-hand defense techniques with different species."

The idea was for Caly to start with self-defense and then, once she had a solid foundation, they would start teaching her offensive moves. Blake knew that she would be getting the best training with them because they were hired for the VIP SILE cases for a reason after all.

Riordan nodded and then continued, "We will also have sessions, which will include traveler training and texts for you to read for your education of species and our world."

Okay. So, I'm in like full-blown school all over again. Except, sub PE for what feels like is going to be some serious ass-kicking, Caly thought. Not that she wasn't honestly eager to get into a little better shape and read all about this whole new world or anything. But there was something about being assigned texts to read that made her inner school rebel want to groan a little.

"Finally, you will be meeting with Dr. Oliver regularly. In fact, I have arranged for your first session tomorrow. I figured, considering everything, you wouldn't have a problem with getting started on those sessions immediately."

"Yes, thank you," she said, trying not to remember the nightmare that unleashed out of the box of her mind at the bonfire.

Riordan nodded. "We can work out the fine details later. For now, let me finish showing you around."

Chapter 34

"Riordan was right," Caly began. "Meri's a genius in the kitchen. I mean, that was seriously like the best dinner ever."

Blake gave a satisfied, full-bellied grunt in agreement.

Deciding to take an after-dinner stroll around the courtyard, their hands were clasped and swinging in rhythm with their slow pace.

"It was also really nice for all of us to sit and eat together." Caly recalled how it was kind of cool to see a slightly more relaxed side of Riordan and Aleia. She internally smiled at the memory of even Felix enjoying himself in the dining room too. Just as Meri said, she set out Felix's dinner and, when he was done with that, he seemed to be saying hello to everyone's legs under the table.

Her thoughts were interrupted by the sound of water.

"Is that water?" she asked.

Blake nodded. "I believe it's a lake. Here." He tugged at her hand and they turned down another pathway. "It's this way."

"And how would you know?" she teased him.

He gave her an instinctual look.

He's a wolf. Duh, Caly, she reminded herself with a laugh.

"Okay, well you have to remember I am still trying to get used to all of this."

His lips curved as they turned another corner on the path until it was parallel to a large lake. Since the sky was lit up by moonlight, the lake looked like a black, glass mirror reflecting back the moon and stars. They continued to walk with the gentle, rhythmic sound of small waves kissing the shoreline.

This is really nice, Caly thought. *Surreal as all hell but still really nice. I wonder if, in a few years from now, we'll still be taking night strolls after dinner?* Then a familiar feeling started to creep into Caly's gut. Fear. Specifically, fear of the future. *A few years? What about a decade? Oh god, a century? No. Stop. You're being ridiculous and getting way ahead of yourself.*

"Blake?" Caly broke the silence between them.

"Yeah, Caly?" Blake said, sharpening his senses because he scented a subtle shift in her emotions.

"Can we just take it one day at a time?" She paused briefly. "It's just the 'forever thing' is kind of freakin' me out. I only want to be with you but is it okay if we take it one day at a time?"

He cupped her face and looked into her eyes for a moment before he stole a kiss. "One day at a time, Caly." And his next kiss was slow and deep. Too soon, way too soon, he broke the kiss and was sporting a wolfish grin.

"What?" she asked in a playfully skeptical tone because she was starting to know that grin of his.

"I want to show you something."

"Okay." She drew out the word, still a little skeptical but with a hint of curiosity. She remembered how he said that he needed to grab something from his room before they left on the walk. She presumed it was his phone but now she was thinking otherwise.

Still grinning, he handed her a photograph. Her brow furrowed as she looked at a picture of three people—er, specians, posing for a nice picture. They were wearing clothes that looked to be styled from at least a hundred years ago. Her focus fell to the male in the middle, who appeared to be the youngest.

"Oh my god! Is that you?!" She pointed to the male in the middle.

When he nodded, she started laughing. She couldn't stop staring at young Blake. He looked like a young male, clean-shaven with shoulder-length hair.

"How old were you?" she asked with her eyes still glued to the picture of him and smiling ear to ear.

"Early twenties."

"Wait…" With her brain catching up with that thought and the old-style clothes, she looked up from the photo and directly at Blake. "How old *are* you?"

He paused for a moment. "About one hundred and fifty."

Her eyes bugged.

"Years?! You're one hundred and fifty years old?!"

He chuckled. "Yeah. I'm actually not that old for species."

She tried to let that sink in for a moment. She accepted that species were immortals and some were hundreds (maybe even millennia?) years old but that was in theory. Realizing that, until this moment, she never really thought this through with Blake or the others because, well, they seemed so normal, relatively speaking of course.

"But how can this photograph seem so… modern?"

"Species have always been ahead of the curve when it comes to technology."

"But not clothing?"

"There was no need for species to advance clothing. Besides, we try and blend in."

"Wait. Hold on. What about the others? How old...?" Her voice trailed off as possibilities swam through her mind.

His lips curved in amusement. "Nico is the oldest at three hundred, give or take."

"Three hundred?!" Her eyes widened.

He chuckled. "I thought that might blow your mind. The twins are around my age and Deacon is a little older than us but still hasn't quite hit the big two."

Blown. Her mind was literally blown.

"And I saved the best for last. We don't know how old Riordan is. It's, well... it's not socially acceptable to ask someone how old they are. But I'm giving you the scoop." He winked. "We actually have a running bet of how old Riordan is... but they're all in the ballpark of one to two thousand."

"One to two *thousand?!*" Since her mind had already blown off a few minutes ago, she now felt like a volcano, erupting in shock.

She turned her attention back to her hands. Oh, yeah, she was holding a photograph of Blake only a couple of years younger than she was now. As in, like a century younger. God, if that didn't put some things into perspective. For the longest moment, she just stared at the picture, fixated on young Blake with long hair and clean-shaven, smiling from ear to ear.

"See. I told you it doesn't suit me," Blake interrupted her thoughts. "And now I've shared something embarrassing about me too."

Screwing her head back on and getting back with the program, she replied, "It's not *that* bad," she teased. "But, I mean, your short hair and scruff is..." She bit her bottom lip. "Hot."

"Hot, huh?" He gave a wickedly playful grin and acted like he was going in for a kiss but then purposefully rubbed his scruff on her neck.

She laughed and then he stole a kiss.

Looking at the photograph once more, she intentionally focused on the other two specians and saw a resemblance.

"Blake?"

"Yeah, Caly?"

"Who are the two other specians in the photograph? Are they your... parents?"

His grin faded slightly for a split second but she caught it.

"It's okay if you don't want to talk about it. I don't mind talking about something else."

"No, it's okay. Yeah. Those are my parents."

She was about to switch the subject because clearly there was something about them that changed the mood slightly. And she knew all about that didn't she?

"They've passed on."

Blake turned toward the lake and looked out at the water. And she did the same. Blake could smell the sting of heart-break and sorrow in the air. He wrapped his arm around her shoulder and pulled her in for a side hug.

"Caly... I'm sorry."

"What? Why?"

"I didn't mean to make you sad."

"How do you know I'm sad?"

"I can smell it."

Okay déjà vu anyone? Caly thought. *I've heard that before when he said he could smell when I was fertile. And that, ironically, was the thing that, at the time, tipped the scale into Crazyville.*

"You can *smell* it?"

"My wolf's nose can scent emotions. I can smell your

heartbreak and sorrow," he said with a concerned look in his eye.

Okay, first, I find out he's one hundred and fifty. Now, I find out he can scent my emotions. Yeah, so, I will need to process what all this means later. And suddenly, all of those subtle, air-sniffing moments made sense. It also made sense how he could read her so well. But, again, now was not the time.

"Blake, my heartbreak and sorrow are for you and your parents..." She paused. "Because I know how it feels."

She leaned her head on his shoulder and they stood like that for several moments in silence, looking at the lake.

"This is nice." Blake broke into the peaceful quiet between them.

She nodded her head in agreement because she understood. She always knew when someone would find out about her parents because they would give her *the look*. The "full of sadness for her loss, helpless because they couldn't fix it, and guilt for their blessings" look. There was nothing wrong with that and she understood what she was reflecting back to the person. But sometimes, she just wanted to be treated like before the accident. Also, the conversations would get inherently awkward. She recalled how she drastically grew apart from the few friends she had because of this. So, yeah. She got it and he knew that. It was nice to have someone who truly understood.

"My mother loved my long hair. I kept it long for her. I haven't had it long since it happened." He paused for a moment. "They were killed by a specian. A fire elemental. They were in the wrong place at the wrong time. My parents got trapped in the building and were knocked unconscious when the building fell. Shifters are strong, with fast healing abilities, but there are things we can't come back from. There were three other species that were claimed by the flames."

There was another pause. "The elemental was a criminal who was wanted for murder even before this attack. That's how I became a bounty hunter… A damn good hunter. And eventually, SILE started to hire me for high profile cases."

She stayed silent for a moment to see if there was anything else he wanted to share. When there was only silence, she said in a gentle voice, "Thank you for sharing and letting me in."

He turned to face her and their eyes met for the longest moment. Caly saw the heartbreak and pain in the golden depths, at the loss of his parents. She also saw his strength, determination, and fire. He leaned down and kissed her. It was the kind of kiss that spoke from the soul and communicated without words. Their lips spoke of empathy, tenderness, warmth, and a shared scar they both bore in their souls. She hugged him with her head on his chest while his warm arms wrapped around her. They remained in a silent embrace for several heartbeats. Without words, they walked back toward their new house, hand in hand.

"Will you light the fire?" Caly asked, curling up on the couch in Blake's room. She could still feel the warmth of his hand in hers from their walk back. The memory of the last time he lit a fire for her, hung between them and he gave her an appraising look for a long moment.

"I'm fine. I promise. I just…" She bit her lower lip. "I thought it would be romantic."

There was another calculated pause before he walked over to the fireplace.

Just as he finished lighting the fire, Caly walked up and hugged him. He leaned his head down and gently kissed her on the lips. The kiss naturally deepened, becoming hot and sparking with desire. His arm snaked around her waist and pulled her close to his body. The fingertips of his free hand traveled across her shoulder and up her neck until they wove through her hair and gently tugged. The sensation sent a tiny shock of pleasure down her body and she tightened in the most feminine of places.

Without warning, he lifted her up, with his hands under her thighs, and carried her toward his bed. Gently laying her out on the soft sheets, he settled between her thighs and closed the distance with his mouth once more. Sliding his hand underneath her shirt and gripping her waist, he nipped at her lower lip in a playful demand for her to open. Caly obeyed and her lips parted for the promise of a deeper kiss. Their tongues were in the most sensual of dances while his hand traced the curve of her breast still trapped by her sports bra.

With the scent of her arousal tantalizing the air and enticing his senses, he needed skin to skin. He broke the kiss and when she was about to protest he commanded, "Off." And tugged at her shirt.

"Off," she said, echoing the command while tugging at his shirt.

They both smiled at their secret, sensual, Simon Says game.

Looking into his golden eyes, she lifted her torso off the mattress, gripped the bottom of her shirt, and teased it off inch by slow inch. He growled at the slow tease and she smiled. When the shirt was stripped off, it revealed her full breasts, gift-wrapped by her black sports bra.

"Off," he commanded in a rough voice, looking at her trapped breasts.

Undoing the front zipper of the bra, one metal tooth at a time, she watched in devilish delight as his eyes tracked every single movement until her breasts were free.

"Caly," he groaned out with hooded eyes.

She boldly slid her hands up her waist and cupped her own breasts in a teasing display. His responding growl was so loud and deep, she felt the vibration dance across her skin and awaken her nerve endings. Her reward was his own slow striptease, revealing his hard chiseled abs. With his broad chest pressed to hers, they fell into a possessive kiss full of need. She basked in the feeling of his body on top of hers with his hard length pressing into her core. On a moan, one of his hands slid underneath her and gripped her ass, pulling her impossibly closer to him. He broke the kiss to lick his tongue over her pulse and blow a teasing breath over the wetness. She shuddered at the tantalizing sensation and he continued to kiss her neck just the way she liked it. His thumb teased the curve of her breast and brushed over her nipple.

"Blake," she moaned in pleasure.

His response was to kiss his way across her collar bone, past the hollow of her throat, and tease her nipples with seductive sucks and licks. His other hand slid down to her core and stroked her.

Feeling everything through her yoga pants, she let out a moan and moved her hips against his fingers in rhythm.

He gently scraped his teeth over her nipple in a new sensation that sent a wave of pleasure through her. With her encouraging moan, he repeated the motion and another wave of pleasure cascaded through her. He kissed a path down her stomach and slowly brushed one finger along the seam of her pants, just barely touching the skin of her waist.

She shuddered as her nerve endings were firing with pleasuring pulses of sensation.

He kissed right along the seam of her pants and looked up into her eyes in inquiry.

"Oh god... Yes," she begged on a breath.

Gripping both sides of her pants, he slid them off of her body in one fluid motion. The enticing scent of her arousal was filling his senses and he couldn't wait any longer. His hot mouth kissed her core through her wet panties and he got a teasing taste of her. But he needed more.

With his patience gone, he flared his seductive mating scent and used a claw to slice her panties off. Her beautifully glistening sex was bare to him and she moaned in the pleasure of his scent that was like an aphrodisiac to her. Sliding his tongue up her sex, he tasted her sweet honey and growled in pleasure.

"Blake, oh god. Do that again." Her voice was husky and full of desire. His tongue slid up her sex once more. "Growl... do that with a growl again," she begged.

He understood. Growling so low and deep, he could feel the vibrations dance across his tongue as he lapped at her sensitive spot.

"Oh god, yes. Blake, that feels so good," she moaned in response to the added an erotic sensation on her core.

He found a rhythm with growling, licking, and sucking over her wet heat which drove her wild with erotic pleasure.

"Blake! I'm going to—"

"Not yet," he cut her off, pulling back on the growls and teasing his tongue around her sensitive spot, careful not to push her over the edge. He wanted to take his female even higher.

"Blake!" she protested.

"Caly, trust me." He chuckled, sliding two fingers into her tight, wet heat. "You're so tight and wet," he grunted out. He worked her core with thrusting fingers and laving tongue, in just the right motions and rhythms.

"Oh god, Blake!"

Feeling her core start to tighten around his fingers, he pulled back once again.

"Blake!"

He looked up into her eyes with a wicked smile at the teasing withhold of her release.

"I'm going to seek my revenge," she said with her own sinful smile.

His response was to start moving his fingers inside her while stroking her with his tongue once more. He worked her core until she was even more wild with pleasure.

"Come for me, Caly," he commanded and, knowing it would push her over the edge, he growled low and deep, as his tongue seductively swirled around her sensitive spot.

Caly let out the throatiest moan and the orgasm of all orgasms ripped through her. She saw stars as her sex sent pulsing waves of pleasure through her. His fingers stayed inside her, gently stroking every last drop of pleasure out of her.

When she slowly came back to consciousness, Blake's eyes met hers as he pulled his fingers out of her and licked up her sweet honey.

She shuddered. "God. It's so hot when you do that."

"You're so hot when you come for me."

"Speaking of which…" She smiled, sinfully nudging him to his back and gripping his hard length in her hands.

"Caly," he groaned out.

She slowly licked the full length of his shaft. He shuddered. She repeated the motion with the added tease of her tongue over his sensitive tip. He groaned and reached down to sweep her hair away from her face so he could watch. Taking him into her hot, wet mouth, she looked up to meet eyes that were glowing and glazing over with pleasure. Sucking him in even deeper, her fisted hand slid to his base only to ascend back to his tip. He tightened his grip on her hair and growled in approval. She swirled her tongue around his tip and then took him back into her mouth as deep as she could. He was too big to fully fit but her tightly fisted hands more than made up for it.

"Caly," he groaned, eyes rolling back.

She was worshiping him with her mouth and she loved the pleasure it brought him. In fact, it gave her pleasure knowing she could give him such pleasure and her core started to bloom for him once more. She allowed his hand in her hair to guide her head in an erotic "up and down" motion, just the way he liked. Teasing his balls, she could feel them tighten in preparation for a release. Knowing he was close, she backed off and he immediately growled in frustration.

"Revenge," she said with a sinful smile.

With shifter speed, Blake flipped her on her stomach and was behind her.

"I'm going to fuck you from behind, Caly. Then you're going to ride me."

He gripped her hips, pulled her up on all fours, spread her legs wide, and thrust into her, balls deep. She gasped with pleasure. He pulled out to the tip and slammed back into her. She let out a throaty moan. With all control lost, he thrust into her hard, fast, and wild. And his seductive mating scent mixed with her sweet arousal, created an intoxicating combination in the air. He used his grip on her waist for even deeper penetration. Skin was slapping on skin in an erotic rhythm and he smacked her ass just hard enough for a titillating sensation. She moaned in response. Feeling her tighten around his shaft, he reached around and teased her sensitive spot with his fingers.

"Come for me, Caly!" he growled out the command and a moment later she did, on a throaty cry of pleasure. He felt her sex milking him in with pulsing pleasure and he almost let it take him over the edge but he wanted her on top. He pulled out, flipped on his back, and guided her on top of him.

"Fuck me, Caly."

With his hands on her waist, she rode him, grinding

her hips on his hard length. Finding a fast pace, he felt her core squeeze around him and he growled loudly. When she leaned forward onto her hands, he took one of her nipples into his mouth and sucked hard.

"Blake!" she moaned out and quickened the pace.

He felt her core tightening once more in preparation for another release.

"I'm going to come."

"Come with me, Caly."

They both cried out, falling over the edge and plunging into the pools of pure pleasure. Her sex milked his seed out of him and he filled her up in hot pulses. She collapsed on top of him and their chests were breathing heavily.

Sometime later, she rolled off of him and he tucked her close, with his chest to her back and one leg in between hers. Then they both fell into a blissful sleep.

Chapter 35

"Caly, this is Dr. Oliver," Aleia proceeded with the introduction.

Okay, so not what I was expecting. Starting with Dr. Oliver being a female.

Caly wondered if it was some messed-up, human social thing that was ingrained in her brain to automatically think that Dr. Oliver was a male.

Hi, Dr. Oliver. Yeah, so, I thought you were going to be a male. Why? I don't know. Doc, why don't we start there because clearly I have a lot of shit to work through.

With Caly's inner feminist ready for an internal battle, the other thing Caly was still getting used to in the species world was how everyone was frozen in time and would look around thirty years old for the rest of their existence.

With no exception to that biological fact, Dr. Oliver looked to be around thirty years old. She was only slightly taller than Caly and her frame was long and lean. Similar to Aleia, she had a sweet and innocent girl next door vibe about her that was slightly different than Aleia's.

More relaxed? Maybe. But there's something else too, Caly thought, trying to put her finger on what exactly was different.

Dr. Oliver was wearing tight, blue jeans, a snug, white, scoop-neck T-shirt, and a simple, small-chained, golden, upside-down, crescent-moon necklace resting on her upper chest. She had long, copper, wavy hair with natural highlights of gold. Her emerald-green eyes popped against her alabaster skin as she smiled at Caly.

"Hi, Dr. Oliver." Caly smiled, relieved that Dr. Oliver was, in fact, a female who appeared to be someone Caly may be able to relate to—relatively speaking of course.

"Hi, Caly. It's nice to meet you. And please, call me Keena." Dr. Oliver's voice had a gentle and soothing quality.

"Why don't I leave so you both can get started? You know where to find me if you need me." Aleia smiled and walked out the door.

Instead of being in an office, they were actually in one of the fitness rooms that was attached to the fully equipped gym. The fitness room had all of the bells and whistles, including exercise balls, weights, bands, straps, yoga mats, bolsters, blankets, and blocks. The floors were glossy, light tan wood and the floor-to-ceiling mirrors on the walls had curtains that could be closed if one was not feeling the mirrors that day. In the middle of the room, there were two BackJacks with a couple of blankets and bolsters set up for their session.

"Would you like to begin or is there something else you would like in order to be more comfortable?" Keena asked calmly.

"I'm ready and this is fine. Thanks."

They got settled into the two floor chairs, which were surprisingly more comfortable than Caly thought they would be.

"Caly, have you ever had a session with a mind healer before?"

"Umm, no, I haven't."

Keena nodded and smiled. "Are you familiar with mind healers?"

"No, not really," Caly admitted. She did ask Blake about it and he said it was a little *therapisty*, to use Caly's word, but there were also some species elements to it, like Aleia's healer session. Since he hadn't had a mind-healing session before, he couldn't really speak from experience and said it was a little hard to describe.

"This gives us a nice place to start," Keena said with a warm smile. "Mind-healer sessions can vary depending on the healer, their training, and their healing ability or abilities, plural. I'm a healer of the mind and also a healer of the spirit. As such, my training and background reflect my passion for how I help others with my innate abilities. It involves psychology, counseling, psychotherapy, spirit medicine, and some other things I won't bore you with. Basically, when it comes to anything to do with the mind and spirit, I'm afraid I'm a bit of a nerd."

Her smile widened, producing a relaxing effect on Caly.

"Also, from what I understand, our species' way of thinking can sometimes be vastly different from humans in many respects, one being that our primary approach is an integrative, holistic perspective of both the mind and spirit. And, well, that's where my secondary passion comes into play. I also incorporate the physical body through mindful movement as well, even though I'm not a healer of the body, like Aleia. So, in a nutshell, my style is an integrative and comprehensive mind, spirit, and body approach."

Okay, again, so not what I was expecting at all. As if the fitness room with BackJack seating wasn't your first clue. Or the fact that you're so not in Kansas anymore. But, yeah, unexpected in a good way.

"As you have probably noticed," Keena continued, "In combination with my approach, I also have a bit of a relaxed style which is pretty unique among my colleagues. So, our sessions may include both, some, or all, of the following depending on what comes up: mind-healing, spirit-healing, and yoga."

Yoga? Caly thought as her eyebrows shot up in surprise.

"Where do you think humans got yoga from originally?" Keena's lips curved with amusement. "From species. Well, specifically it's from spirit healers. Did you know that yoga originally wasn't a physical practice?"

Caly shook her head side to side at the unexpected origins of yoga.

"Instead, it was a very conscious practice of the spirit. It's a practice for us to connect with the magic of life and heal from the core of our soul. The physical practice became a component later on when it became clear that the mind, body, and soul are all connected and cannot be treated as anything else."

Makes sense, Caly thought. She did like yoga... at least when she could get herself on the mat. Sometimes that seemed to be the hardest part of yoga: to actually get to class. Truthfully, it really depended on what yoga class, teacher, and studio she went to as well. She had been to a couple of yoga studios that were so LA that she wanted to gag at all of the botoxed women, decked-out in Lululemon, Manduka, and Spiritual Gangster attire.

Keena finished laying out the foundation for what Caly could expect in their sessions. She concluded that this first session would be the longest and, in fact, she had cleared her schedule for the rest of the day. Caly had a feeling that Riordan may have had something to do with that. Caly felt a little nervous about spending several hours with a mind and spirit healer but Keena reassured her that the session would be solely guided by her and have lots of breaks. She also indicated that it might not even take the entire time she had set aside.

"*We'll know when the first session comes to a natural end.*" Caly recalled Keena's words and thought it was a little weird but, hey, Keena was the expert after all.

"So, Caly, are you comfortable with sharing a little bit about why you're here?" Keena gently asked.

Caly took a deep breath and then laid it all out there. Everything. Her parents, being raised as human and thinking she was human until she wasn't, the nightmare she just survived, her and Blake starting a new relationship, Riordan as her Primary, and, of course, the fire incident. She almost couldn't believe she was pouring all of this out there. But there was something about Keena that made her feel safe, understood, heard, and not judged at all.

In fact, Keena didn't interrupt once and she didn't really speak at all, yet she was fully present the entire time. Caly was the one who did most of the talking and she didn't know even for how long but, hell, it felt like a long time. And yes, she cried a few times too. But, overall, it felt really good. Thinking back, Caly realized when the emotions started to swell and rise like a tsunami, she didn't drown in it. Instead, it felt as if there was a lighthouse guiding her and she not only got through it but also felt empowered and liberated.

Could that have been some sort of mind or spirit healing? Caly wondered, washing her hands in the bathroom.

Just as Keena had said, that part of the session did come to a natural stopping point. So, they took a little break and Caly was back in her room to change into clothes for yoga. Caly had let Keena know that she had some yoga experience but admitted it had been a hot minute and she was really rusty.

Caly opened the fitness room door and paused.

Woah, Caly thought. The room felt so different than

before. The lights were down low and there were tea light candles that created a large circle around both Keena's and Caly's mats. There was soft, serene, and soothing music playing. The curtains were drawn over the mirrors and the room was slightly heated to the perfect temperature. It was not too hot but not so cold that it would be hard to relax. The porridge was just right.

Is that? Caly sniffed the air. There was a natural floral scent dancing in the air.

All of her senses were bathed in relaxation as she was lulled deeper with each passing moment.

Caly noticed that Keena also changed. Keena's white T-shirt was now knotted at the waist which allowed full effect for her high-waisted, black yoga pants and her hair was in a messy bun with a few strands that had fallen loose.

That looked suited her, Caly thought, walking in. *And, damn. How come some women—er, females, could pull off that messy bun so well? Whenever I do it I look like I am concealing a small doorknob with all these extra flyaways. So, really a doorknob with a lion's mane.* With that (totally zen) thought, Caly got settled on her mat.

"We'll begin in Child's Pose. Bring your knees as wide as the mat. Touch your big toes together. Outstretch your arms in front of you. Rest your forehead on the mat. Good. Take a deep breath in. Allow your belly to sink toward the earth. Audible open-mouth exhale out. Nice breath, Caly. Again. Deep breath in. And exhale out like you're fogging up a mirror. One more time. Deep breath in. And this time, on your exhale, seal your lips and engage your oceanic breath as it sounds like the waves of the ocean. Allow this breath to lull your mind, body, and spirit throughout your practice today."

There was a brief pause before Keena spoke in her warm voice into the realm of relaxation.

"Healing is nonlinear. Sometimes going from point A to point B is a journey full of unexpected twists and turns. How are you able to honor the unexpected? How are you able to let go of how you thought things should go and, instead, trust in the flow and magic of life? You are exactly where you're meant to be on your journey, in this moment."

Caly felt a wave of *something* flow through her body. It felt as if the wave washed the tension, that she didn't even realize she was holding, right out of her body.

"Good, Caly. Just breathe."

A few breaths later, everything else seemed to fall away in her mind until it was only her and her mat.

Sixty minutes went by in the blink of an eye and before she knew it, she heard Keena's voice closing the class.

"Namaste." Keena spoke the final word of practice, bowing her head.

"Namaste." Caly echoed both the word and movement. It felt like she was in a slight daze. "Woah. That was... hands down *the best* yoga class I've ever taken. Like nothing even comes close to that."

"Thank you. You're a natural." Keena smiled.

"What... What was that I felt in the beginning?"

"That is what makes mind and spirit healer yoga classes so popular," Keena said with a playful smile, casually switching subjects. "To start, I recommend we meet three times a week. Two of those sessions will be two hours in length, one hour for discussion and one hour for yoga. And just like with today, we may go deep but we will never go anywhere you're not comfortable or ready to. The third session will be one hour just for yoga. What do you think of that?"

"Sounds great. If I wasn't already going to be training in self-defense with the males then I would've said that we can meet for yoga *every* day."

They both laughed.

"Self-defense training?" Keena asked in a curious tone.

"Yeah. Riordan and Blake want to make sure I'm trained so I can protect myself. I've always been curious to learn about it but never really got myself to take a class."

"You know what? Me too. Maybe one day I will also take some self-defense classes."

Chapter 36

The castle. The fortress. My new home? Caly thought as
she reflected on the past couple of days. Even though
it's a freaking castle for crying out loud and it makes my LA
apartment look like a shoebox, it still feels... homey.

The fortress just felt like one of those homes, no matter
the size, that had this aura of invitation and warmth. Caly
had been to some fancy LA parties through her paralegal
job and, even though the houses were beautiful, and had all
of the elements of a home, they felt cold and uninviting. It
almost felt like she had to ask permission to sit on the couch
or breathe.

Okay, sure, there was definitely an adjustment period to
living in a castle on so many levels but it wasn't uncomfortable. It was more of a curious exploration. In fact, on one
of her walks around the castle, she ran into Nate and he
showed her a hidden hallway, or a shortcut, to save time by
bypassing through a couple of rooms. She almost squealed
with delight when she learned that there were secret passages. And, okay, so they weren't really secret because all of
the castellans, and Riordan, knew of their existence. Also,
it was clear that they functioned as a sort of superhighway
to get from point A to point B faster. Nate offered to show

Caly some more but she declined because she wanted to discover the passages in her free time. She was so going to get her Harry Potter on and hopefully stumble across something as awesome as the Room of Requirement.

The fortress also seemed to be bursting with life and love. Caly caught Jax and Meri having another moment, this time in the kitchen. The interaction had both her and her heart smiling wide. Meri must've been baking something because she was elbow deep in white flour. Jax came up behind her and surprised her. In her playfully spooked reaction, flour went everywhere. Everyone in the kitchen laughed at the flour cloud dust that settled on a grinning Jax. Caly also noticed that the castellans were often in pairs or groups and were almost always laughing and smiling with whatever they were doing. Caly couldn't even imagine what the upkeep and maintenance must be like for a castle but it seemed like they genuinely enjoyed the task of keeping the place thriving and in tip-top shape. Whenever Caly saw the castellans, they cheerfully greeted her as she walked around and explored. Caly knew it may take time but she wanted to meet them all and get to know them a bit more.

This morning "the crew," a term Caly recently coined for her pack of males, went back to the bachelor pad, AKA the pack's house in the forest. Again, this was something else she dubbed and the males seemed to be humoring her by going along with her weird habit of giving nicknames. They went back to tie up any loose ends, bring anything else they wanted and make the move to the fortress official. Blake said that they would be back later tonight and that he would have his phone on him in case she needed to reach him. Not five minutes after they left, Caly may have sent a playful text to Blake.

Caly: *I have a surprise for you later tonight when*

you get back... I think you're going to like it. She included the emoji that smiled wickedly and had horns.

Blake immediately texted back.

Blake: *Damn. All I'm going to be thinking about is you and what this surprise is.* He included the wolf and smirking emoji.

Caly replied with the innocent angel emoji that was smiling with a halo. Her phone immediately chimed. Except this text wasn't from Blake. It was a group text message from Rhyland to the crew.

Rhyland: *Caly, we are having one hell of a time giving Blake shit and guessing what you just sent him... because we know with his wolfy expression it was you.*

Rhyker: *Yeah, that fucker deleted it too.*

Rhyland: *Smart move because no one's safe with Deac the geek.*

Deacon liked the last comment.
Nico was silent, per usual.

Caly: She inserted the LOL emoji. *Thank God I didn't send him anything inappropriate... or did I?* She included the winky emoji.

That was when Blake entered the conversation.

Blake: *Alright. That's enough. And don't encourage them Caly... You're not the one who has to deal with them right now.* He inserted the facepalm emoji. *I'll get you back for this later.*

Rhyland chimed in before Caly could respond.

Rhyland: *Yeah you will.* He included the high five and winky emojis.

Rhyker, Deacon, and Nico liked that message. Caly just sent three LOL emojis in response.

Laughing, Caly refocused on the packages from her shopping spree that had been delivered, thanks to Deacon rerouting the shipping to the fortress. She was waiting until Blake was gone to unpack the clothes so there was no chance of him seeing. She was going to bring to life that vision she had of wearing lingerie and casually sipping tea out of the "Once you go alpha..." wolf mug.

Getting out of a hot shower after an early session with Keena, Caly looked over at all of the packages in her room by the door. It was like waiting to unwrap Christmas presents and she couldn't wait to start the glorious unpacking once she got back later. Riordan was taking her to see the Seer Council and, although the early yoga session helped, her stomach was tight with nervousness.

Caly hung up the wet towel and then walked into her closet. Jax had already picked her outfit out. It was a long sleeve, knee-length dress which hugged her curves. Caly questioned the color choice of white with an elegant silver pattern when Jax brought it in. But Riordan explained that the seer colors were silver and white and wearing the colors was a sign of respect, especially for the first meeting. That was when Caly found out that Riordan would be wearing the colors too. She was actually looking forward to seeing exactly what Riordan wore because she couldn't quite picture it.

Would it be a shiny silver suit? That can't possibly look good. But then again, if anyone could pull that off, it would be GQ.

Even though the dress was probably the nicest one she had ever worn, Riordan said this wasn't a formal event but rather a meeting. So, they would not be in formal attire. She looked at what she would've categorized as a fancy dress.

So, what is formal attire then?

She guessed she would find out at some point because that was when Jax had mentioned that the designer would be stopping by next week to take her measurements. For what exactly? She didn't know, but again, she figured she would find out.

As Caly applied her makeup with her go-to look, she thought about the conversation she had with Riordan yesterday.

"Caly, you are new to our world and do not yet know all of the layers at play. I vowed to protect and keep you safe and that I will do. Follow my lead and remember to only share what we talked about if asked. My belief is that this will be a short meeting."

Earlier in that conversation with Riordan, they practiced how Caly should answer questions that he anticipated the Seer Council may ask. She thought some of the answers and phrases were weird, especially with the whole "where does she come from" question. That question they practiced again, and again, and again to really instill it in her mind so it became second nature and she wouldn't stumble.

"Once more, Caly. Where do you come from?"

"Council, I do not know my true origins. Those whom I called mother and father raised me as human and have passed away," she recited and then paused. "Riordan?"

"Yes, Caly."

"I do not know my true origins? And why..." She just couldn't seem to say it out loud because she couldn't believe it was true.

Why is the phrasing sounding like my mom and dad aren't my mom and dad? she thought as the words seemed to get stuck in her throat.

Riordan knew what the silence was asking and spoke gently. "Caly, you once asked me if it is common for species children to be born of human parents." Riordan paused.

She nodded with a sudden knot in her chest.

"I answered truthfully that it is not common. What I didn't say at the time, is that species history shows that only species can have species young. I didn't share that at the time because I did not think it was the right time to have that conversation."

Again, he paused and silence stretched through the room, giving Caly space to think.

She was trying to grasp what he was saying but she refused to believe otherwise. At first, she felt anger rise... because how could Riordan not tell her? Then her memory flashed to that former moment. She was just rescued from the nightmare of hell and, yeah, she knew she wasn't in a place to have her very foundation of love and family potentially shatter beneath her. But, no, it wouldn't shatter because it wasn't true. She looked too much like a blend of her parents for them not to be her parents.

"Riordan, I understand what you're saying but I do not accept it. And I'm not being stubborn or closed-minded."

Suddenly, an image of her psychology professor lecturing about cognitive dissonance scrolled across her mind.

Damn it.

"Okay, maybe I am but I just know they are my parents and they always will be." Fresh tears started to pool in her eyes but she needed to get out the rest. *"I will play along with the council games and recite the phrasing as you taught me... but I want you to know that I do not believe the words."* Then a thought flashed into her mind. *"Wait, isn't it possible that my parents were not human either then? What if they didn't even know?"*

Riordan was proud of this young traveler for her courage and strength in this conversation. It was a conversation he wished upon no young specian, especially Caly.

"It is possible they were species and I have been searching for answers along that route. However, due to the change, it is unlikely that they did not know they were species."

Riordan didn't want to give her false hope. He felt that would be irresponsible since her heart was so fragile at the moment. But that was his theory as well. That her parents were actually species and living among humans. But if that were true, then the only possible explanation of living among humans was to hide from the species world.

Why? he wondered.

He was still pulling at threads of memories and strands of possibilities. Caly reminded him of someone—or rather, two someones—more than ever in this moment of strength and courage. But, again, that would be impossible considering her age and how those someones died before she was born.

Unless...?

But no... because when he looked at her parents' human identification driver licenses, he noted some vague similarities but also differences. He couldn't be sure especially because the hair and eye color were wrong. Unless they were like that by design? And editing photos to pass human *detection was easy enough, of course. Which would make sense if they were species covering their tracks. But, again, Riordan kept asking the question of why and nothing seemed to be adding up.*

"Riordan, I must believe that my parents were my parents... and that they must've been species too. They have to be." *Caly's voice cracked and the tears flowed down her cheeks like rain falling from stormy gray clouds.*

"Caly." *Riordan got up and didn't hesitate to wrap her in a hug.*

It was the first time they ever made physical contact (other than that one handshake when they first met) and it seemed fitting that it would be a hug of comfort and support.

"We will search for the answers together," *Riordan vowed.*

* * *

"Young child, what is your name?" Deloreia spoke in her soft and gentle feminine voice. Yet, Caly could still feel the notes of power in it.

Take a breath. Smile. Don't stutter. Caly gave herself mental commands so she didn't look like an idiot and, in turn, make Riordan look bad.

Speaking of which, that may not be possible. Riordan was wearing a custom, tailored gray and white suit. It was definitely not the shiny '80s flashback situation she was originally envisioning. She also made a mental note to thank Jax for the outfit because she almost felt underdressed, looking at all of the elegant, ancient, council members.

"Calypso," she answered Deloriea's question and intentionally didn't give her human last name, remembering that Riordan said it was irrelevant.

"Ah. What a lovely name," Deloreia continued with a

slight smile. "Of whom do you come from, young Calypso?"

Caly's throat felt dry with all of those attentive, ancient eyes on her.

"Council, I do not know my true origins. Those whom I called mother and father raised me as human and have passed away."

A few eyebrows raised at her unexpected response.

Caly sent a silent prayer over to Riordan for the previous practice session. And, yeah, in front of all these ancients, in this place that looked like a temple for gods and goddesses, she was grateful for the phrasing as it led to no further questions. She made another mental note to thank Riordan again and give him a hug for this.

"Human you say?" Deloreia was apparently the first to recover from the unexpected answer.

"Yes, council," Caly replied.

A long and uncomfortable silence stretched through the space and all eyes were fixed on Caly with unwavering focus.

"An unclaimed traveler hidden away by humans. This is a *council* matter."

Caly knew that was councilmale Anguis from Riordan's brief description during their prep conversation. It was the first time he spoke and his voice felt like snakes slithering up her spine as it sliced through the silence. His eyes sharpened on her even more with that news and it sent another cold shiver up her spine. She made yet a third mental note to profusely thank Riordan for offering to be her Primary because she couldn't even imagine being in the hands of someone like Anguis. Especially because he was looking at her like she was a prize waiting to be claimed. She swallowed.

"True enough, Anguis. And she stands before us as such." Zahara spoke for the first time.

"Female." Anguis didn't use Caly's name. "*Humans*

raised you in their world." She could tell how he felt about humans from the disgust in his voice. "Do you know nothing of our world?"

Caly internally panicked. That was not one of the questions they practiced as it was presumed.

Take a breath. Just say, "No, council." Caly mentally coached herself through it.

"No, council."

His expression told her that seemed to be the answer he was anticipating and wanting her to say. She internally shuddered.

"The female is too much of a risk to be left at the supervision of a non-council member," Anguis argued.

Oh my god. No. No. No. Caly's internal panic drums were beating louder, realizing Anguis was trying to separate her from Riordan.

"Council—" Riordan spoke in defense.

Deloreia held up a hand to silence Riordan. "You are correct, Anguis. With her upbringing, or lack thereof as it concerns our world, she is a risk that we cannot ignore. And you have already made your stance on the matter clear in our previous meeting. However, we have already voted and granted Riordan to be her Primary." She paused and then continued, "Does anyone wish to propose a change of vote?"

Silence filled the room and all Caly heard was the pounding of her heart as her very future was being decided. Anguis looked like he was about to retort but a deep male voice spoke first.

"Let us be done with this."

Caly guessed that was Aetius, from his short, military-style haircut. His tone gave away the fact that he was preemptively ceasing a long, drawn-out discussion, which

Caly guessed was a moot point due to what Deloreia said about their previous vote.

"Agreed, Aetius," Zahara spoke. "Riordan, do you still pledge as Primary to this young traveler?"

"Yes, council." Riordan spoke clearly.

"Present the papers," Zahara said.

Riordan walked up to the council stairs but didn't ascend. Zahara rose from her chair like the regal goddess she looked like and accepted the electronic document. The document was previously signed and fingerprinted by Caly and Riordan, with Riordan's lawyer as legal witness.

They waited in silence as each council member looked over the electronic document until it made its way back to Deloreia.

"By the powers of the Seer Council, we hereby acknowledge you, Riordan Knight of the Knight bloodline, as the Primary of this young traveler, Calypso, who shall henceforth be known as Calypso Knight of the Knight bloodline." There was a pregnant pause. "Riordan, bring young Calypso to our next gathering. I look forward to seeing her growth and development under your care."

"Yes, council." Riordan bowed his head and Caly copied the motion.

"Thank you." Caly wrapped Riordan in a fierce hug as soon as they were out of the eyes and ears of the council. These were the first real words she had spoken since the council meeting. She wanted to immediately hug Riordan as soon as the words were spoken, making it official, but she didn't dare move, let alone breathe, because she wasn't sure what was socially acceptable behavior in those situations and she didn't want to take any chances and inadvertently jinx herself.

Anguis' eyes and words appeared in her mind at that

moment and she internally shuddered at his cold possessiveness.

"I don't even want to think about where I might be if it weren't for you." She pulled away from the hug and looked into Riordan's wise gaze. "I promise to do my best to honor the gift you've given me."

Chapter 37

"Point to Caly." Rhyker's voice cut into the self-defense match between Caly and Rhyland. And, Caly knew he was being a little more lax with the point giving on her side. It had only been three months since they moved in and started training, so she was still very much a newbie.

"I know—" Caly gritted out, blocking a gentle punch from Rhyland before continuing. "...what you're doing." She managed to huff out the rest of her thought.

"I don't know what you're talking about," Rhyker feigned innocence with a slight smirk.

She jumped over Rhyland's swinging kick, which was an attempt to knock her on her ass like last time.

"Good. You're learning." Rhyland added, feeling like a proud older brother.

"Point to Caly," Rhyker called out once more, assessing her jump maneuver as he ticked another point on the scoreboard.

She looked over at Rhyker and rolled her eyes.

Okay, maybe I did deserve that point though because it was kind of badass of me to jump and not get tripped up like last time.

Her eyes flicked to the scoreboard and she smiled. The

score was ten to two, with Caly in the lead. Which was ridiculous because she knew Rhyland was not going full strength and that Rhyker was bulking up her points to boost her confidence.

Okay, so sue me, she thought because it totally worked and made her feel better, especially in comparison to her sessions with sergeant Nico. Nico would kick her ass in every session which may or may not have prompted Caly's creatively violent fantasies of revenge and payback. But even though he was tough, he never crossed the line or went past her breaking point. Ever. Caly didn't know how but he just knew when to push her and when to scale it back. She also thanked him after the sessions, usually the next day, when the urge to stab him died down a bit. She knew his sessions were definitely a part of the reason she was stronger, faster, and felt like she could hold her own in a hand-to-hand fight. Well, at least, not with an expert trained fighter... yet.

The one thing to her advantage, that may one day seriously tip the scale in her favor, was her blocking ability. Riordan believed that it was still in its infancy stages, assuming it would continue to grow with her just as she did. His theory was that, on some instinctive level, her ability was triggered by the innate wiring to survive. Although, it was evident that some part of her blocking ability had been in place and protected her even before that, due to being able to block herself from seers and even from Blake's view when they first met in her dreams. Regardless, when she was in her hellish nightmare of torture at the hands of James Barker, her survival instincts kicked in and some other dormant part of her blocking ability was activated. Riordan also believed this survival instinct gave a natural boost to her traveling ability. Kind of like how adrenaline can pump through a mother's heart so she can lift a car to save her child. He said this was a part of the reason why she was able to travel to Blake even when heavily drugged and almost unconscious.

"On some level, your soul recognized Blake as your life mate and instinctively knew to reach out to him."

Consequently, Riordan believed this was how she was able to pull Blake into her soul sanctuary, or "Caly's Cave" as she called it, before they ever met in person. Although he didn't explain exactly how, he did share that he played his part in that first soul meeting.

"I may have played my part in the introduction, but you, your soul, Caly, is the only one who could have brought Blake to your cave."

That thought always sent a wave of emotion through her. Because she still was head over heels crazy about that male... *her* male. They had been taking it one day at a time, just as they promised on that moonlit night walk along the lake, and so far it had been going really well. Too well. Sometimes she caught herself internally holding her breath as if waiting for the other shoe to drop. Okay, it hadn't been all butterflies and rainbows but nothing bad though. It was just like a settling in of sorts. Caly went from living alone in a pretty solitary lifestyle for years to suddenly sharing a space and being in a serious relationship. She wasn't complaining in the least, but yeah, there were definitely some kinks that she and Blake worked through. Like their ongoing playful argument about how no matter how big the bed was and how many damn covers there were, Blake swore that she somehow ended up with them all on her side by morning. She denied everything, of course. But she may secretly have woken up a time or two and noticed them all bunched on her side. Or like how often his socks were somehow "mysteriously" in the middle of the floor as if they crawled around when no one was looking. Or even how they both realized that although living together and sharing their bedroom together was truly great, they still needed their own separate spaces. Caly ended up reclaiming her room that just kind of sat there for a few weeks. Blake's male cave ended up in the empty room next to Caly's. So, essentially they carved out a mini, three-room space just for themselves.

"Umph," Caly grunted as her ass hit the ground in a hard thump.

"Point to Rhy," Rhyker called out.

"Damn it," Caly said in a breath of defeat.

"Don't be hard on yourself, SoCal." Rhyland reached out a hand to help her up. "It was a new move you haven't seen before." He grinned. "I was testing you."

"Thanks," she said, getting to her feet. "And it looks like I failed that test." She tried to laugh a little to make light of the situation but inside she was a little disappointed in herself.

Scratch that whole being able to hold your own, she thought, rubbing her lower back. Yeah, she was going to feel that later for sure.

"Hey."

Before she blinked, Rhyland was at her side and Rhyker on the other side with a gentle elbow nudge.

"You would think after three months I would be able to hold my own," she said in defeat.

"SoCal," Rhyker began and then they both spoke in unison. "We know you can hold your own."

Rhyker continued, "We've seen countless bar fights that we know you would *totally win, Caly Girl.*" He said that last part like a California Valley Girl. Caly Girl was a play on words due to the similarity to Valley Girl. This was another nickname they liked to call her, even though she had said multiple times that she was not from the valley.

Rhyland added, "Yeah. And you have two things going

for you automatically. One." He held up his index finger. "You look sweet and innocent, not saying you're not..." He winked. "But that will be a grave mistake on your opponent's part."

It was true that even though Caly had been training almost every day, she didn't look cut like a female UFC fighter by far. She still held her curves. They were now just slightly more toned curves. So, yeah, he did have a point there.

"And two." He held up another finger. "Your blocking ability."

"But my blocking ability is a joke. It comes of its own volition and I have no control over it. I mean, you've seen it. The days it cooperates, it's like really weak. And, well, the other days, I swear it laughs at me and says, 'Not today, B.' "

The twins chuckled and she grinned.

"True enough... for *now*," Rhyker responded.

"Yeah, SoCal. Besides, it's only been three-fucking-months. *Three,*" Rhyland said, emphasizing that last word. "We've had *decades* of training and practice."

"I know. But I just feel like I'm just so behind. Like I am a lamb among a pack of..." She paused. She was going to say wolves but realized her audience. "Jaguars." She smiled slightly but it faded quickly. "Which brings me to my last point. I don't have superhuman strength, heightened senses, fast healing abilities, or the ability to shift into a massive animal with razor-sharp teeth." She sighed.

"But you've had more training these past few months than some specians ever have," Rhyland retorted.

"Hell, some specians have never even fought against jaguars or wolves before. And you do it on the reg," Rhyker tacked on.

Okay, sure she didn't actually *fight* them but she was learning first-hand techniques and tactics to use to her advantage when the males were in animal form.

"Besides, like hell any of us would ever let anyone hurt you." This time, Rhyland had a growl to his voice and Rhyker's growl chimed in agreement.

"Okay, don't go cat on me." She smiled at these two males with whom she was becoming close. Sometimes, like in these moments, she swore this was what it must've felt like to have protective older brothers. "And thank you. Sorry for getting all Debbie Downer. I just..." She exhaled. "If I'm ever alone in this crazy species world, I just... I just want to feel safe." She swallowed but before she could say anything else, the twins spoke in unison once more.

"You will."

"Just keep training with us," Rhyland added, pulling her in for a side hug.

"Besides, who says you can't carry a weapon?" Rhyker grinned and Rhyland fist-bumped him with that response.

"Fuck yeah. Make that a minimum of two weapons," Rhyland continued and Rhyker grunted in agreement.

"True." Caly paused, considering that suggestion. "I guess I never really thought about carrying a weapon before. But you're right."

The twins exchanged a quick glance over Caly's head. Yup. They were both thinking the same thing. Naturally. They were going to talk with Nico and Blake about a knife for Caly. Then they would talk to Deacon for some sort of techy thing that would be reasonable for her to carry and conceal.

"Hey, totally random question," Caly said as her mind suddenly switched gears.

The twins grinned at each other and then said, "Like totally rando?" in their Valley Girl impression.

"Oh, come on. I don't even sound like that." She rolled her eyes smiling. "What I was going to say is that I don't know why I never thought of this before now and why now? I don't know... but how come both your names start with Rhy but only you're called Rhy?" She looked at Rhyland.

"Does Rhyker look like he would respond to Rhy?" Rhyland quipped.

She looked at Rhyker and tried to imagine calling him Rhy.

"Good point," she chortled.

"Up for another round?" Rhyker checked in with Caly.

"Yeah. And, hey, thank you both again," she said with a hint of sincerity for their support and patience with her.

"Are you sure you want to thank us before the session is even done? What if we decide to become the ruthless Rhy twin trainers?" Rhyland quipped.

She laughed. She loved how, no matter what, she knew that laughs were always accompanied by these two males.

"How was training today?" Blake asked Caly as she walked into their room. He wanted to growl because she looked hot when she was all sweaty, post-workout. Admittedly, she just looked hot to him all of the time. He was off of the couch and behind her with his hands on her waist before she could blink.

"Blake." She laughed. "I'm all sweaty."

He just growled in response.

"I also have a session with Riordan soon."

"How soon?" he drawled.

"Thirty minutes," she playfully argued as she took a step away from him. Just as he was about to close the distance, she looked over her shoulder and gave him a sinful smile. She slowly peeled her white T-shirt over her head and dropped it to the floor. Then she proceeded to the bathroom as if she didn't just provoke an alpha wolf with her suggestive striptease.

One step onto the tile floor was as far as she got before he was right behind her once more kissing her neck and caressing her breasts in just the way she liked. Since they were now so familiar with each other's bodies and unique pleasures, it was tantalizing to tease her in the exact ways he knew she liked.

"Blake," she said with a husky voice.

"Shower." Blake delivered his one-word command.

They both stripped and got under the warm water. The large walk-in shower had three rainfall showerheads and four wall jets. With shifter speed, he had her back up against the wall and her legs straddling him. Their kiss was hot, wet, and demanding. She broke the kiss to playfully nip at his lower lip, ear lobe, and jaw. Again, his female knew it drove him and his wolf crazy when she played with her teeth on him like that. He growled in approval. He wanted to take his sweet time to play and lick his female all over but he wouldn't make her late for her training session with Riordan.

"I want to lick and suck every inch of your body," he whispered in her ear. Before she could protest, although it looked like she wouldn't, he added, "But consider this just the appetizer." He slid his hard cock into her to the hilt. She moaned and her head went back in pleasure. He started to move inside her in a hard and fast rhythm.

"Oh god, Blake." Her voice was thick with pleasure.

He suddenly pulled out and set her down. He knew his female and wanted to play with her as he thrust inside.

"Turn around," he commanded.

She smiled wickedly and obeyed, opening her legs to display her sex to him.

His growl was so loud this time that it reverberated inside the shower walls. In an instant, he plunged his cock back into her and found another fast-paced rhythm, gripping her hips. His arm slid around her so his fingers could play with the most sensitive flesh on her body.

"Don't stop," she pleaded.

"Never," he promised.

A moment later and they both fell over the blissful edge.

Breathing heavily, they tried to get back with the program.

Oh yeah. Shower, she thought, as the warm spray kissed her body. *Wash your hair.* Her brain was only firing in short commands at the moment as it came back online.

They finished the shower and got dressed. Blake was in his typical jeans and white T and Caly was in her black yoga pants, tank top and, of course, his hoodie.

"Okay, I'm off to see Riordan," Caly announced casually over her shoulder, walking toward the bedroom door.

With shifter speed, Blake's arms circled Caly from behind pressing her in close to his body.

"See you at dinner, my sexy goddess," he whispered in her ear, alluding to the meaning of her name, Calypso—being the sea goddess.

When he began worshipping her neck with a kiss, she attempted a protest by saying, "I'm going to be late, wolf." Except, the tone of her voice and the way she smiled and sunk back into his embrace, said otherwise. Allowing her to pull away from his hug, she gave him a quick kiss before she was out the door.

God, he loved his female. He would do anything for her. Starting with making sure she was safe. His thoughts drifted to The Ghost. Frustratingly, there was nothing new to go off of. It was as if The Ghost disappeared and went underground. Well, for all they knew with the black portal that was exactly what he did. Initially, they knew he needed time to recover from his injuries. But since he was a shifter, he would have far been healed by now. So, they all believed he was plotting his revenge in the shadows. Blake growled and bared his teeth. Fat fucking chance he, or his pack, was going to let that happen. Once again, they were doing everything they could to try and find the fucker but they were back to square one with The Ghost going off the grid and out of sight for seers.

A knock at the door thankfully interrupted his thoughts. Scenting his entire pack on the other side of the door, he opened it.

"Yo, B-dawg," Rhyland acknowledged.

Blake motioned with his head toward the room next door which was his male cave. It became their new meeting room and their main hangout. It had two large dark leather couches along with a matching set of four recliner chairs. For entertainment, there was a pool table, dartboard, and a gigantic screen for TV and movies. There was also a small fridge and wet bar, both were fully stocked with drinks and snacks.

"Beer?" Rhyland called out, walking over to the wet bar with Deacon.

Meanwhile, Rhyker grabbed some chips from their snack stash.

"Yeah," Rhyker and Blake both answered.

"Hey, grab me a bag," Rhyland said to his brother.

While the twins did the chips and beer exchange, Deacon poured himself a whiskey neat and then looked over at Nico. "Nico?"

With Nico's silent nod, Deacon found a spot next to Blake at the dark wooden table between the dartboard and pool table and set down a glass of chilled tequila for Nico.

"Thanks, D," Nico said as a dart left his hand and flew through the air straight for the bullseye.

"So, Blake," Rhyland began and a crack sounded out as his twin took his shot in the pool game. Rhyland frowned slightly when Rhyker sunk two striped balls. Then he continued with the conversation. "We had our session with Caly and something came up."

Both Blake and his wolf were all ears with that kind of an opening for a conversation.

"Caly needs weapons." Rhyker cut right to the chase as he hit another striped ball into the corner pocket.

"Yeah. We're thinkin' a knife," Rhyland began.

"And some sort of tech gadget." Rhyker finished.

The twins looked over at Deacon.

Deacon's brain was automatically thinking of ideas and he immediately pulled up one of his imaging screens to explore possibilities.

"How'd this come up?" Blake needed to know because from what he knew of his female, she wasn't that into weapons and this had never come up in conversation before.

"She said she wouldn't feel safe if she were alone in public," Rhyland responded in a way that clearly communicated the underlying message of *we better fix this shit now because we won't stand for that.*

Blake growled in agreement and suddenly the room was full of protective testosterone.

"Small knife. Thigh holster." For once, Nico's cool edge was not out of place.

"Agreed." Blake nodded and then looked at Deacon. "D?"

"Give me some time to design and test it. But I have a couple ideas involving a stun gun," Deacon said with his attention scrolling through the screen.

"Too bulky." Blake immediately ruled that option out.

"Already on it. A small stun gun..." Deacon half-mumbled, shaking his head side to side as if non-verbally dismissing that incorrect label. "...small electrical weapon...." he muttered to himself with his attention still on the screen.

"Small electrical weapon?" Rhyland asked with his feline curiosity coming to the fore.

Deacon nodded. "Like the size of..." Deacon's gaze fell on Rhyker's earrings and a light bulb went off.

"What?" Blake asked, knowing that eureka gleam in Deacon's eyes well.

"Earrings... Jewelry..." Deacon mumbled, his fingers tunneling through his hair as the wheels turned inside his mind.

Everyone's eyes locked onto Rhyker's black diamond studs.

"Woah, D. That's genius. Blake, maybe you can give her your *stunning*, protective heart on a chain," Rhyland quipped, taking full advantage of the double meaning of the word "stunning" in this case. He took a pull on his beer as if in celebratory salute to his clever joke.

Even though it was meant as a joke, Deacon paused and looked at Blake as if in inquiry of the idea.

"Actually." Blake drew out the word in consideration. "D, can it, you know, look nice?"

"On it. I'll still make the small electrical weapons I was originally thinking because, well, now I'm just curious. But I'll work on the heart too. And—" Deacon started muttering as he cataloged ideas and designs.

"What about one of the small electrical weapons—Jesus, let's just call it SEW—on the knife holster?" Blake looked at Deacon to see if that was a possibility.

"Good idea," Rhyland followed up.

Deacon nodded. "Let me work on this and I should have designs to show you shortly." He sat down in one of the recliner chairs surrounded by screens.

"Nico," Blake began but Nico answered his question before he even had to ask.

"Yeah. Tomorrow."

Blake nodded.

Nico was a master of blades, particularly knives, and had his own personal collection, amongst other things, that Blake suspected he used for more than just fighting. So, it went unsaid that he would bring Nico as an expert to weigh in on the knife and holster design. They would both go to the SILE station that was located close to the bachelor pad to see the weapons master, Gunner. Sure, there would be a weapons master at the SILE station closest to the fortress, but, over the years and after many cases, they knew Gunner and their personal weapons were designed and made by Gunner. Pulling out his phone, he texted Jax for Caly's measurements so Gunner could custom design it just for Caly.

With the text sent, Blake looked around the room at his pack and reflected on how they were thriving here at the fortress. The extra space and fitness facility had given them additional breathing room, which was never a bad idea for a pack of hot-blooded males. Also, the rotating training schedule with Caly was helping to keep them preoccupied with the frustrating dead ends they kept running into with their hunt for The Ghost.

A couple of weeks after moving in, they had a pack meeting and, with a unanimous decision, they decided to stay at the fortress for the foreseeable future. Deacon still had an alert set up for any real estate that went for sale in the area just in case. But they decided this would be their new home and the news practically had the castellans jumping for joy.

Damn seers, Blake thought after seeing Riordan's unsurprised reaction to the news that the pack was staying.

Blake and his pack fit really well with Riordan and Aleia and seemed to grow closer as each day passed. It wasn't beyond Blake's alpha eye that Caly was the epicenter of that particular pack bonding and the growth he witnessed over the past few months. And he guessed she didn't even realize it. Because as he got to know his female more, he understood it was just who she was. She naturally built strong relationships with everyone in the fortress, including the castellans. She had even become good friends with Aleia and Keena. So, yeah, his chest may have swelled with pride when he thought of his kindhearted female. His *alpha* female. Because that was what she was, even though she didn't know it yet.

His mind traveled to that night with Caly at the bonfire. Much to everyone's relief, she hadn't had any further episodes, which they all contributed to the mind-healing sessions with Keena, the traveler training with Riordan, and the self-defense training with the pack. Both Keena and Riordan remained confident that what happened with Caly at the bonfire was a severe episode of PTSD and that the best preventative measure was for Caly to continue her training on all fronts, including learning about herself and the world she belonged in.

Blake's lips curved at a memory of Caly's reaction to one of the many books Riordan assigned her.

"Mermaids, Blake... Mermaids!"

He loved how enchanted she was about their world. In fact, her energetic reactions, often at the discovery of learning about a new subspecies, had him realizing just how much he took for granted because it had always just been a fact of his reality. His beautiful Caly, with her curious heart, allowed him to see the world of species with a new sense of wonder. He recalled more of the memory when she also discovered that angels were real. Except, of course, they weren't really angels in the sense that humans made them out to be. Not to mention, they weren't even called angels and mermaids but rather alisaerians and syrenians.

Similar to vampires, it was theorized that both alisaerians and syrenians were distant relatives of shifters in their evolution. However, they both were ancient subspecies, all their own with unique abilities. His smile deepened as the memory continued to play out in his mind.

Caly was turning through pages in the textbook only to frantically flip back several pages and pause with frozen wide eyes.

"What is it, Caly?" Blake asked, a little concerned at her reaction. But she just kept staring at the page with wide eyes. He walked over to see that she stumbled upon the chapter on dragons.

She was sad to learn that, according to ancient legend, all of the dragons were said to have gone into a slumber, in the Earth, only to awaken once more with the rise of the blue. It had been an ongoing debate of what that truly meant. The most commonly backed and accepted theory was that the rise of the blue meant the rise of the sea.

Rhyker's loud crack of the pool ball snapped Blake out of his thoughts and back to the present. With another look around at his pack, he smirked and took a sip of his beer.

Chapter 38

"For three months, our focus has been on the basic mind-body relaxation techniques," Riordan began. "Dr. Oliver has been incorporating this in her sessions with you as well. As you know, this is by design."

Here we go, Caly thought. *Another "You must have a solid foundation" speech.* Caly internally sighed. It wasn't that she didn't understand, because she did and it made sense. It was the whole "you have to learn how to walk first before you can run" thing. And she was basically starting with learning how to crawl since she was three decades late to the race. All species young had some level of training when growing into and learning to control, or rather be in harmonious balance, with their abilities and specian nature. Specifically for seers and dream travelers, this training included basic mind-body relaxation techniques because the ability to induce a vision or dream travel on command required a certain level of calmness and clarity of mind. So, she had been practicing these techniques every day and felt like she had mastered both crawling and walking, and was ready to learn how to jog at least.

While mentally preparing for *the speech*, she looked around Riordan's office which was where they had all of their sessions. She often admired his office during their sessions because it reflected his humility. From what she understood of most ancients and aristocrats, it was basically one big ego contest after another with power plays. Of course, his office was decorated to match his suave GQ style and consisted of two large rooms. But it was like the perfect blend of style and grace. Although, the meeting room, where he conducted his video meetings and calls, was a bit more polished. But she believed that was a strategic move on his part to portray a certain image to everyone in the outside world. Meanwhile, the office room, and where he spent most of his time, was simple and elegant. The feature wall was made up of a floor-to-ceiling window, where you could sit in one of the two dark leather chairs to take in the view of the courtyard and lake. She wondered if, when no one was looking, he would spend his time looking out the window and thinking about... well, who knew what an ancient thought about?

At that moment, Caly sat in one of the two matching chairs that faced the deep mahogany desk. Riordan sat in his chair on the other side of the desk with a backdrop of floor-to-ceiling shelving. It was full of books and various items on display that doubled as bookends.

Caly's gaze flicked to something she often looked at on Riordan's desk, a palm-sized, gold, geometric shape. It was always on his desk in the same spot but she noticed that it would often be rearranged into different shapes. She wondered if it was like a puzzle, like a species Rubik's cube, or if it was just Riordan rearranging it to give his hands something to do while in thought about something else. Today, there was also something new on his desk, a book titled, *The Traveler's Techniques.*

"It's now time for you to learn your first traveler technique, the *sleep state.*"

Caly's eyebrows shot up.

Okay, that was an unexpected plot twist.

"Really?" she asked with her eyes full of youthful anticipation.

Riordan's expression warmed. "Yes. Your dedication and commitment to the techniques show and it's the reason we're having this conversation." He paused briefly. "Caly, you've done well."

"Thanks." His words went right to her heart.

As if he knew she didn't want to get all sappy, he continued, "The sleep state is one of the most powerful techniques for a traveler."

As Riordan continued, Caly listened attentively just like she did for all their sessions together. It was not just because this was finally something new and exciting. Rather, it was a combination of the fact that she was a good student at heart, as well as, being genuinely curious to learn about this new world, especially with the opportunity of an ancient. She adjusted her position in the roomy chair by tucking in her knees and leaning over to one side of the armrest.

"It allows a traveler to induce a state similar to our natural sleep in order to travel at will. In certain situations, this technique has also been used to facilitate healing. Sleep is one of the most ancient healing aids of our natural world. Our mind, body, and spirit heal on deeper levels in our sleep. Although travelers do not have fast healing abilities, they do have access to tap into their innate ability to heal through sleep."

Riordan paused as he opened the book, flipped to a chapter, and slid it over to her.

She saw that the page outlined the sleep state technique in detail.

"We will review the two stages of the technique and then practice. Just like with the other techniques, it takes time and practice, so be patient with yourself." His eyes softened and lips curved slightly in a way that she knew he was re-ferring to the fact that she could be really hard on herself.

The memory of Nico mesmerizing Felix to sleep came to the forefront of her mind.

"How is this different than when a vampire mesmerizes someone into a trance or to sleep?" Caly asked.

"Good question. Although, I should expect that from you by now." He smirked in approval. "It is similar to that because the end goal is being in a sleep state. A vampire is able to access that part of your mind-body control center and, for lack of a better analogy, command the brain to flip a switch. Whereas a seer or traveler must learn to locate the switch, walk over to it, and then flip it. Eventually, you will be able to quickly induce, as well as, come out of the sleep state."

"Makes sense. Thanks." She nodded.

"This process is split into two stages, with the one ca-veat being that there is a pre-stage of the basic mind-body relaxation techniques that we've been working on. Once you're in the state of mind-body relaxation, then you can proceed with the first stage, or the *transition*. The *transition* is so named because it is the transition between waking and sleeping by bringing the mind from active and awake to slightly drowsy to then, a full-on sleep state. This is done by building onto the mind-body relaxation techniques. This stage is the most challenging of the stages as you are manually turning down the dial on your active brain. In this stage, the physical body will visibly relax to stillness, just like in sleep. The muscles will grow heavy, the heart rate slows, and the breath cycle elongates and evens out. The second stage, or the *activation*, is where the seer or traveler activates their ability to either induce a vision or dream travel. A seer or traveler is most vulnerable during this time because their body is completely asleep and they are not aware of the world around them."

Riordan proceeded to walk Caly through the two stages and go into further details. At the end of the lecture part of the lesson, he asked, "Any questions before you try it out?"

"No," Caly replied on an excited breath. So far, the only dream traveling she did was to her cave and most often, it was involuntary. And, more often than not, she would pull Blake into the dream, which may or may not lead to some fun times in the cave. But Caly was eager to learn more about her ability and to be able to dream travel on command.

Caly closed her eyes and began the mind-body relaxation techniques by tuning into her breath, calming her mind, and allowing her body to sink into the soft cushions of the sofa. Since Riordan thought it was best to start out practicing by laying down, as that was what the body was already accustomed to, he already had her relocate to the sofa. Once she was ready to try stage one of the sleep state, she took a breath and walked through the steps. She approached the internal door of her mind. It was a large, wooden, arched door with a gold handle that was embedded in large gray stone. She turned the knob and pushed the door open. Walking through the doorway, she began to descend the seemingly never-ending, spiraling, stone staircase. There were torches with firelight lighting the way.

I don't think this is working, she thought but she continued on down the stairs for what felt like forever anyway.

"Riordan," she said, keeping her eyes closed. "I don't think it's working."

"Why is that?"

She heard the amusement in his voice and opened her eyes to see his lips curved.

"What?" she asked, unsure what was so amusing.

"You fell asleep for—" He looked at his watch. "Almost two minutes."

"Really?" She smiled a little and he nodded. "But I didn't travel anywhere."

"That will come in time. For now, the first part is to train your mind and body to go into stage one at will. Then we will practice stage two: activating your traveling ability."

Chapter 39

"Meow." The sound of Felix's meow and purr in Caly's ear summoned her from the world of dreams. Even though it had been two weeks of solid practice, she still hadn't been able to induce her dream traveling ability as of yet.

"Good morning, Felix," Caly lazily said, stretching her arms over her head.

Is that...? Caly smiled, smelling a fresh-baked blueberry muffin along with her newest drink obsession, a caramel hazelnut macchiato. She rolled over toward the smell and blinked her eyes open to see Blake looking at her with a wolfish grin.

"Morning, wolf." She playfully responded to his expression. "Is that the good-morning smile I think it is?"

"No, but it can be," he drawled out on a low growl.

Her laugh was husky. As she propped her head on her hand, she noticed that he had brought her more than her morning drink. Sitting on Blake's lap was a rectangular black box. Her brow furrowed in curiosity. "What's that?"

"For you," he teased.

"Is that a weird, kinky sex toy which explains that wolfy grin on your face?" she teased back.

His lips twitched. "No, but now I'm wishing it was."

She shot him a promising smile before rolling out of bed and walking to the bathroom in nothing but black panties and his white T.

"We could just pretend it is," he drawled.

"We certainly could," she said in a sultry voice and looked over her shoulder playfully before closing herself in the bathroom.

A couple of minutes later, she walked back into the room with a freshly washed face and brushed teeth. She plopped onto the couch next to Blake and took that first sweet sip of caramel hazelnut macchiato, closely followed by a bite of the warm blueberry muffin.

"Mmmm." She closed her eyes as the flavors burst into her mouth.

This is so much better than The Drip, she thought and made a mental reminder to thank Meri, the genius of the kitchen.

Suddenly, the memory of The Drip and her first conversation with James Barker came to the forefront of her mind. She wanted to internally throw up at even the thought of a mocha latte now. She shut the door on those thoughts and allowed the promising scent of coffee, muffin, and Blake to refocus her attention.

"Thanks for breakfast in bed. So, what's with the black box?" she asked curiously, noticing his still, very present wolfy grin.

"I thought you would never ask," he teased and handed her the box. "Open it."

"Okay." She playfully drew out the word because she wasn't sure where this was going exactly. "Woah. It's a lot heavier than I was expecting. Are you sure you don't have some sort of kink chains or something in here?" She gave him a wicked smile.

"Why do you keep bringing up kinky sex toys?" His lips curved.

She laughed. "I don't know. Maybe because I have a hot wolf waking me up with—" Her playful banter cut off as she looked into the box.

Blake took the liberty of freeing Caly's hand of the lid which she was still holding out to the side as if she was a statue.

Oh. My. God. Those were the only words that came to her mind as she remained frozen in time, staring at a knife handle peeking out the top of a black holster. Carefully gripping the handle, she held down the holster with her other hand in order to slide the blade out. The motion was smooth and deathly silent. The shiny silver knife, of about six inches, looked lethally sharp.

Blake wasn't sure how to read her reaction. Her scent was all over the place in a cocktail of curiosity, confusion, excitement, and fear.

"If you don't like it—"

"Oh my god," Caly cut off Blake. "Blake, no. I love it!" She paused. "How did you know?" And as soon as the words came out, she remembered that conversation with the twins. "The twins?"

Blake nodded. "It was a pack effort." Blake picked up the holstered knife. "And these..." He pointed to the two small metal pieces on the holster. "These are D's upgrades. Small electrical weapons, or SEWs... his invention." He smirked because Deacon was a techy genius. "One of those will momentarily incapacitate an opponent, even a large shifter animal. They won't kill but it will give you time for your next move or escape. They are each good for one charge and D can recharge it once it's been used."

"Blake... This..." She couldn't find the words. "This is

so… *thoughtful.*" She hugged him and pulled away to look at it once more.

He kneeled down and looked up at her in a silent question if he could put it on her.

"Yes." She shot to her feet in an excited blur of movement sending blueberry muffin crumbs flying. He snapped the knife holster in place. It looked like a sexy, strappy garter belt of sorts.

"Oh my god! I seriously love it! The design… I mean, it's like a sexy spy!"

He chuckled. "The design has Nico's influence."

"Really?" She took a couple of testing steps forward. "I mean, I can't even feel it. And it fits perfectly."

Blake made a mental note to let Nico and Gunner know about her positive reaction. "It was custom made just for you. This is the first piece of what the twins are calling the Calyp-So Gonna Kill You Collection."

"Really?!" she laughed. "Okay, now I really feel like a special agent or something." Smiling, she started walking around the room. "I just can't believe how it's like it's not even there."

He followed her as she walked into the walk-in closet. Blake's lips curved at his female strutting around the room like it was her catwalk. She probably didn't even notice Blake because she was so busy looking at it in the mirrors with a wide smile.

"We'll start incorporating this into your training so it will become second nature to you."

She walked over to him and looked into his eyes.

"Thank you. This means so much." She pulled his face to hers and pressed her lips to his. When she pulled back, she saw his wolfy grin back on his face.

"What?" she asked with a skeptical smirk.

"There's more."

"More?" She paused. "Although, I should've known there'd be more considering that last gift that kept on giving."

They both smiled at the memory of his gift of clothes, night lights, and her CCD, fully loaded with her pictures, playlists, and wolf-shifter romance books. And Blake was all too pleased to hear that one of the books he selected became her newest obsession.

In the blink of an eye and a whoosh of air, Blake was in front of her and presenting her with a long, thin, black, velvet jewelry box. She looked up at him in surprise. With his gaze solely focused on her to capture her reaction, he slowly opened the lid and revealed a thin titanium heart on a slim chain. Before she could speak, he turned the heart over.

With a curious expression, she leaned closer to get a better look.

Speechless. She was completely speechless. The curved arch of the heart had an elegant engraving with the letters "B+C" and the year.

This is the year my heart was no longer my own, Blake thought but didn't say it out loud because he knew sometimes she still got in her head about the "together forever" thing. He made a promise to take it one day at a time and so he would.

"Blake." Tears pooled in her eyes as she looked into his.

He set the box down on one of the dressers and stood behind her. Brushing her hair aside, he carefully clasped the necklace in place and kissed the curve of her neck while keeping eye contact with her.

"There's more," he said with a sly smirk back on his face.

She laughed as a tear escaped the pool of her eyes and fell down her cheek.

"Blake you shouldn't spoil me with these gifts that keep

on giving and giving," she teased, wiping the tear away.

"It's my style. So, looks like you will have to find a way to get used to that," he drawled. "This necklace is actually another SEW."

Oh my god. She reached up and placed a hand over the titanium heart which laid over her own heart. *I will always feel safe with you close to my heart,* she thought.

"Blake, I love it. *All* of it... Thank you." With blurred vision, she turned around and jumped into his arms. Wrapping her arms around his neck, she kissed him in expression of the deep emotions she felt for him.

* * *

"That's so thoughtful," Keena said with her gaze flipping between the necklace and the thigh holster over Caly's yoga pants.

And, yeah, Caly may have been proudly showing off her new spy gear all day. The crew was loving that she was loving it. She made sure that each of the males got a big hug and thank you from her. Yes, even Nico.

"And really cool," Aleia added.

"I know right? I told Blake I feel like a sexy, secret spy or something," Caly admitted, eliciting a round of laughs from the trio.

"Caly, you're so lucky to have found your life mate so early," Keena said on an envious exhale.

"Seriously," Aleia added.

"And lucky he is not only gorgeous but also kind and good-hearted," Keena chimed in.

"And loves you to pieces," Aleia concluded.

Caly couldn't help but grin because she knew she was lucky. There was a quiet pause before Keena spoke again.

"God, I'm so done with males."

"Does that mean...?" Aleia asked gently.

"Yes, it does. I broke it off with Liam. And, no, I don't want to talk about it."

"Fair enough. And I'm proud of you. That's all I'll say." Aleia wanted to say, *Good fucking riddance because that male was a self-absorbed ass and you deserve so much better.* Not only would that not be appropriate but also she knew that on some level, Keena already knew that.

"And, yeah, I'm so done with males too, Kee." Aleia smirked.

Both Caly and Keena looked at her with an eyebrow raised, calling bullshit. Aleia was always sexually satisfied but she would never divulge any of the details of who the male was, what he looked like, or even how they met.

"Okay, what I mean is relationship-wise," Aleia clarified with a look that said, "*you know what I meant.*"

They all laughed.

"Yeah. Well, be careful about saying that. Because when I swore off guys, all of a sudden I woke up species and mated for eternity," Caly quipped. "Granted, I'm not complaining about either."

There was another round of laughter.

"But, still. Need we remind you that we've had like centuries more experience in the dating pool?" Aleia countered, reminding Caly something she often forgot. Keena and Aleia were actually much, much older than she was and had already hit the big two. In fact, Aleia was the oldest at around two hundred and fifty years old.

"Okay, true enough. But what you both don't know is that I had my fair share of asshole males." Caly meant that to be a joke but then, as if all their thoughts were synced, they thought of the nightmare Caly went through, which, of course, started out as someone Caly dated.

"Caly, I'm sorry... I didn't mean—"

Cutting off Aleia's apology, Caly tried to fix her joke that had gone so terribly wrong. "No, *I'm* sorry. That's not even what I was talking about." She let out a breath and laughed a little. "Honestly, don't even think twice about it..." She paused but it was still a little awkward. "Okay, yes, that certainly was the most fucked up situation like *ever.*" It was Caly's feeble attempt at another joke and to hopefully lighten the mood. "But I choose to believe, perhaps on some crazy, fucked-up level and some sort of love destiny path, it brought me to Blake." She looked at Keena. "And don't psychoanalyze that."

They all laughed at that last remark.

"Anyways, if we all want to swap bad date stories then I'm down for some good laughs. I may not have centuries of being in the species dating pool but I'm guessing that you'll laugh at some of the human males I've gone out with."

"Deal," Aleia agreed.

"And I do have some funny stories for you both. Although, Aleia, you've heard some of them before," Keena added while mentally tucking away the memory of her recent ex. She couldn't go there. Not now. Not ever.

"Likewise. But it will be so fun to bring Caly up to speed on the species dating scene and the massive bullet she dodged," Aleia quipped.

"Yes. Okay. But right now we do need to start yoga practice. We can chat about males after."

"Agreed," Aleia and Caly both said as they all looked at each other and exchanged friendly smiles.

Caly felt so lucky to have these two strong and intelligent females as friends. When she could, Aleia joined in Caly's one-hour yoga sessions with Keena. And Aleia's presence didn't take away from Caly's healing and training at all. If anything, it only added to Caly's healing path because it kind of became like their weekly female hangout session.

And, being the only female in the crew of males, Caly felt that their mini female retreats provided some much-needed balance.

Caly's friendship with Aleia really started when Caly gave her the thank you gift. It turned out, Aleia not only was a bookworm at heart but she was also a romance book enthusiast, which was a pleasant surprise for both of them. Their friendship naturally blossomed from their mutual love of romance books where they often had mini, book discussions over tea about book characters or where they thought a book series was going. Keena overheard them in one of their conversations one day and they managed to convince her to read one of the books. In fact, both Caly and Aleia decided to read it all over again too. Keena ended up loving the book and so their mini book club was born.

They would often block off a whole afternoon just for yoga, book discussion over yummy foods, and all things feminine, like mani-pedis, facials, and even massages by none other than a few of the multi-talented castellans. And occasionally, some of those castellans even joined them for yoga beforehand too. Caly playfully deemed it as a female-only zone and her crew of males respected that, even if they were curious as to what exactly went on.

Chapter 40

Maybe I should take today off? Caly thought to herself because she woke up sore and tired this morning. But it honestly was to be expected because of all of the training she had been doing for the past week, especially with the addition of training with her secret spy gadgets. Well, that was what she was calling the knife and SEWs.

No. Just power through, Caly. You need to get stronger and faster. Besides, the soreness just means the training is working and your muscles are toning. Or was that just something she remembered from one of Jackie Warner's workout videos?

The memories of working out with her neighbor Megan came to mind as she touched the light switch panel to turn off the lights in her room before heading over to the gym for her training session with Rhyland. The lights flickered before turning off.

Weird, she thought and went to text Jax that the wiring in her room may need to be checked.

What the…?

Her phone was dead.

But it was on the charger all night. How…? Oh, the electricity must be faulty in the room. Makes sense with the lights and now the charger. Especially since my phone has been dying impossibly fast lately. She made a mental note to let Jax know and in the interim, she doubled back, down one of the hallways and up the stairs, so she could swing by Deacon's room. She knocked on the door and Deacon opened it.

"Hi, D," Caly said.

"Hey, Caly."

"Do you have an extra battery for my phone?" She handed him the phone.

"Why do you need an extra battery?" he asked, a bit puzzled because Caly's CCD was only a couple of months old and shouldn't have any issues.

"Oh, I think the wiring in my room needs to be checked. I thought it was charging all night but it wasn't because as you can see it's dead. I was about to go work out a little before my session with Rhy and wanted to listen to some music."

"Well, if you wait three minutes I can fast-charge it to a decent percentage, which should be plenty for your pre-workout," Deacon proposed.

"That would be awesome. Thank you!"

Looking over at Deacon's desk, she noticed it looked like there was some serious technology puzzle going on with little pieces splayed all over it. But then again, when wasn't he working on some sort of techy thing?

"What are you working on?" she asked curiously. Although, there was a good chance she wasn't going to understand any of it.

"Oh, just playing around with some ideas. One of them is expanding on the SEWs to see about using them for when we are out in the field on cases. But the thing that I'm working around is the obvious obstacle of everyone but Nico having paws. But, for right now, I'm working on upgrading all of our weapons with SEWs."

"Makes sense." Caly nodded. "I know I've said this like a million times but, seriously, thank you." She touched her hand at her heart and could feel the outline of the heart necklace that she always wore under her shirt.

His mouth turned up at the corners. "I'm just glad you like it."

"I really do. And I'm getting better at using the ones on my holster too. I'm still slow but I know the males will fix that soon enough."

"True enough."

She didn't get too much one-on-one time with Deacon because they all usually hung out together. But when she did, she enjoyed the time together with him. She knew she only got glimpses of his level of genius in their previous conversations and wondered what it must be like in his brain full of secrets to the computer world. She also wondered if it was lonely because, as she understood it, there were only a known handful of others with abilities similar to Deacon but he didn't identify with any of them. Blake didn't divulge any details because it wasn't his place to share but he did say that Deacon wasn't always accepted into society or even accepted by his own subspecies. Whenever Caly thought of that, it made her heart hurt. She couldn't imagine why steorrians would not accept their own kind. She didn't know any of the details as to why but she didn't need to know because what she did know, first hand, was that he was a good male.

Her gaze fell on the painting of the starry night sky behind his desk, as it often did when she was in his room.

"Beautiful isn't it?" He broke the mini respite in their conversation.

She nodded.

"Did you know it was painted by a steorrian?"

She shook her head.

"Stella Nightingale. She is known for her talent of capturing the stories told by our night sky."

Caly continued to take in the painting and let his words soak in. If Caly stared long enough, she swore she sometimes saw shapes in the stars. It was kind of like when she was young and would stare up at the puffy white clouds that resembled things. In this painting, she most often saw what looked like a female crying. But it didn't feel sad, rather more like abundance—if that even made any sense. She just brushed it off as some weird subconscious psychology thing of her mind similar to those pictures therapists used where the patient was supposed to share what they see.

"This is titled *The Tears of Life*."

Her head snapped toward Deacon, who was still looking at the painting. "I swear, I often see a female crying in the painting."

Meeting her gaze, his lips curved into a half-smile. "You have an eye for Ms. Nightingale's work then."

"What does it mean? You know, the painting?"

"That's the other layer of beauty to her work. Ms. Nightingale believes she is just the messenger and that her art will be, and mean, whatever it is that it needs to be for the observer."

Caly was never really into art but with this piece, she could see how some people were fascinated and practically spent their entire lives in museums.

"Your CCD is probably charged enough by now." He walked over to the charger and then handed it to her.

"Thanks."

"You're welcome."

There was a pause.

"How come you call it a CCD and not a phone?" she asked.

"Well, technically, it's a CCD. And if it were a sentient being, she may have words as to why everyone is short-changing her."

She laughed at the unexpected joke from Deacon. She didn't realize he had a sense of humor and wondered if it was because of the twins' massive personalities and endless supply of playful jokes that were always at the forefront in conversations.

"So, I guess it's probably just a habit from my 'computer-speak side,' as the twins would say."

She laughed again. "I don't know if I've ever heard you joke before." She shot him a fun smile. "Keep doing it."

"Well, to be honest, I just filled my joke quota for the next month. So, don't expect any encores anytime soon." He smirked.

Yes, there's certainly a lot more to him beneath the surface, Caly thought.

"Thanks again."

"Anytime."

With her somewhat charged phone, she replotted her course to the fitness facility.

God, I'm so tired. Why does it feel like just walking to the gym is a mission in itself right now? Stop complaining. Besides, you will feel better once you get moving. In fact...

On the heels of that thought, she decided to pick up her walking pace and get like a pre-pre-workout walk in. The facility wasn't miles away but it was on the other side of the fortress.

Putting in her earbuds, she scrolled to her new workout playlist and pushed shuffle. "High Hopes," from Panic! At the Disco, played.

Perfect! she thought. That song always got her pumped up.

Just as the song ended, she walked into the gym and

onto the treadmill. "Rise" by Jonas Blue was up next on the shuffle.

Fitting, Caly thought. *Rise above this sore, achy funk I appear to be in.* And she needed to because she had her sparring session with Rhyland in about twenty minutes. *Thank God the session is with Rhy. Because I don't think I'd survive today if it was with No-Mercy Nico.*

"You sure you're okay, SoCal?" Rhyland checked in again after noticing that she was moving slower and seemed to be breathing a lot heavier than usual. They were only about halfway through their session.

"Yeah. I'm fine. Just tired is all."

"Okay." Rhyland decided to scale it back a little because there was no reason to run Caly into the ground. "Again."

They started circling each other. He went in for the attack. She blocked his right punch and then his left punch. But when she went to jump over his swinging kick, she didn't jump high enough and, instead, tripped and landed on the mat.

Rhyland had seen Caly master that move tons of times before. He could tell she was tired and he didn't want Caly to get hurt by trying to push her too hard. So, he decided to end the session.

"SoCal," Rhyland reached a hand out to help her up. "I'm going to c—"

A loud snap sounded as a tiny, static shock shot through his hand the instant their hands met. She pulled back her hand in a knee-jerk reaction and they both laughed.

"Anyways, before I was so rudely interrupted by static electricity, I was going to say I'm calling it."

"Okay. Yeah, you're right. And to be honest, I'm so exhausted right now. I think I'm just going to shower and then take a nap."

"Next time, make sure to tell your male not to keep you up all night if you have a session in the morning." He winked.

She laughed. *If that was only it,* she thought. She actually got plenty of sleep last night.

"I'm going to stay and workout for a bit."

"Sounds good." She grabbed her water bottle, towel, and workout waist pouch that carried her phone and earbuds. "Bye Rhy," she called out over her shoulder as she walked out of the gym.

She was so exhausted and the trek back to her and Blake's room seemed like she was running a marathon. The door to their room didn't come soon enough, but she finally made it. Walking into their room, a tired, hot, sweaty mess, she touched the light panel to turn on the lights and one of the lights blew out completely.

"Oh, well, hell," she said out loud with an exasperated breath.

She decided to text Jax before she forgot again.

"Oh, are you kidding me?" Her phone was dead once again. "Okay." She threw her hands up in proverbial surrender to the Universe. "I'm taking this as a sign that I need to just *unplug* from life and sleep for a year."

On that note, she put her phone on the charger, even though she knew that it probably didn't matter, and then took a quick shower. As if the heat of the shower turned up the dial of her exhaustion, she curled up in bed and fell into a deep, immediate and restorative sleep.

* * *

"Where's Caly?" Blake asked Rhyland, who was entering the male cave.

Usually, after their training sessions together, Caly and

Rhy would meet up with Blake and the others.

"She said she was tired and was gonna take a nap." Rhyland shot Blake a feline grin. "At least let her get some sleep the night before if she has a training session in the morning, you dog."

Blake let the twins have a good laugh over that before giving him a look that said, *"Not one more word, cat."*

Meanwhile, internally Blake's wolf seemed to be on alert because Caly actually fell asleep early last night on the couch, not even ten minutes into the movie. So, she actually got more sleep last night than she usually did. Blake got up with the intention to go check on her.

"Dude, chill. Let her sleep," Rhyland said. "Besides, from what I hear, D has an update from Starr." Rhyland grinned.

Suddenly, Blake understood Deacon's frustrated mood. He should have known it was Starr related.

Deacon, who apparently was taking a lesson from Nico, shot a glare over at Rhyland with a look that said, *"How in the fuck did you know that?"* and then gave an accusatory look to Rhyker who was also grinning.

"Someone's in a bad mood," Rhyland muttered under his breath.

"Hey, I can't help it. I'm curious and have excellent hearing." Rhyker's grin matched his twin's for a split second but when he saw the kind of mood Deacon was in, he clarified. "Don't worry. I tuned it out as soon as I heard you answer the call."

Deacon knew that Rhyker wasn't an eavesdropper, well without good reason. And he did answer the call in the courtyard so Rhyker was probably just nearby and didn't mean to pick up on it. It didn't matter anyway because Starr was keeping him at a frustrating distance per usual.

"Hi, Deacon," Starr said in that voice that made Deacon's

body become alert. Well, actually anything to do with this female had his full attention.

"Hey, Starr," Deacon replied, trying to keep it cool like he wouldn't drop everything to get a chance to interact with her.

"I heard you moved."

"Keeping tabs on me, Starr? Be careful or I might get the wrong idea," he drawled.

"And what idea would that be?" she asked in her sinfully playful tone.

"You tell me." He smiled.

"Hmmmm…" she purred. "I'm not sure. I'll have to get back to you on that."

"Please do."

When the sound of her laugh came through the speaker, he closed his eyes briefly to take it in fully.

"Anyways, I'm calling because I wanted to pass on an update… well, sort of an update, from the one and only Whisper." When he didn't say anything, she continued. "She told me that the dark fog she sees around The Ghost is stirring and that it's similar to the last time before she saw the LA vision. She can't guarantee that she will see another vision but she wanted me to pass the info on."

"Thank you. I'll be sure to let Blake know."

"By the way, I heard what you all did for the female that's now under Riordan's care." The playful banter in Starr's voice was gone. "I…" There was a pregnant pause.

Strange. She is not usually one to get hung up on words, Deacon thought.

"Well, yeah, I'm just really happy she was rescued and is safe."

"I feel the same."

There was another slight pause.

"Is she the reason you moved to Riordan's?"

517

Odd, he thought, again picking up on something in the tone of her voice that he couldn't quite place.

"Yes." It wasn't Deacon's place to publicly air out Blake and Caly's relationship. They weren't keeping it a secret by far but they hadn't made any public announcements or anything. In fact, he knew Blake and Riordan were trying to give Caly as much time as possible to get acclimated to their world before doing so. After all, with Riordan as Caly's primary, there would certainly be gossip and speculation. It was just how the aristocrats rolled. That was another reason why Deacon couldn't stand them.

"Oh, I see."

Again, there was something in Starr's voice that had his brow furrowing.

"Starr?"

"Yeah?"

"Is everything okay?" Deacon dropped all of the flirty banter because something felt off.

"Why wouldn't it be?" There was a brief pause. "And be careful Deacon, or I might get the wrong idea." And just like that, her flirty purr was back in place.

He wasn't convinced but there was nothing else he could do.

"And what idea would that be?" he echoed the beginning of their conversation.

"You tell me," she echoed right back and he could hear the smile in her voice.

"How about the idea that you come see our new home." He tried to play it cool.

"Ah, so you're the type of male that makes the female come to you on your command?" she wickedly teased, emphasizing the word "come." Before he could respond, she said, "And what if I'm the type of female who likes the male to... come to me?"

Was that a double entendre? Better yet, was that an invitation? Deacon wondered. "Well, invite me over and I guess you'll find out."

Okay, so it was a bold move but his thread seemed to be getting shorter and shorter when it came to this female.

"So, demanding." *She laughed.* "But I like to get to know males before I invite them over." *Before he could respond, and maybe it was a good thing because he was losing patience with this game, she spoke in a suddenly hushed voice, as if she didn't want to be overheard,* "Deacon, I gotta go. I'll keep you posted if I hear anything else." *And then she ended the call.*

God damn it. This female was frustrating as hell. But that was classic Starr at her finest. She could have easily texted you the update but, no, she called. So, did she actually want to hear your voice as much as you wanted to hear hers?

Shaking off the frustration, Deacon focused his attention on Blake.

"Yes, I do have an update from Starr. But all she said is that The Whisper is once again starting to see the dark fog stirring like she did the last time, right before she had that LA vision. She doesn't know what it means or if it means she will see anything. But it's an update."

Blake nodded and was suddenly in just as bad of a mood as Deacon. Blake's wolf snarled in frustration at not being able to rip The Ghost's throat out.

Patience, Blake ordered his wolf. *We will avenge our mate. It's only a matter of time.*

Low, twin growls sounded out and Nico threw a dart so hard it actually went right through the board in a perfect bullseye. Apparently, they were all thinking the same thing: The Ghost was a walking dead male.

When Caly never came to the male cave to hang out after her post-training nap, Blake made it a point to check on her. In fact, Blake quietly walked into their room to check on Caly for the second time in the past couple of hours. He knew he was probably just being paranoid but he couldn't help it. He knew it wasn't a bad thing to take a nap and it was probably just her body tapping out for a mini-break because she had been training really hard lately.

Confirming that Caly was still fast asleep, he gently tucked a loose hair behind her ear and kissed her on her forehead before silently leaving the room once more.

Chapter 41

"Caly." Blake kept his voice relaxed and gentle, trying not to give away his concern. "Caly." He brushed her hair away from her face and kissed her forehead.

She stirred and mumbled a little. "Mmmm?"

"Caly, are you okay?"

"Yeah... Why?" she asked in her morning sleepy voice.

He twisted off the cap of a bottle of water and offered it to her.

She accepted it and took a sip, letting the cool liquid coat her throat.

"You've been asleep for fifteen hours." His concern showed in his voice and facial expression.

"What? Fifteen *hours*?" she replied, completely non-plussed. Her brain was starting to come back online a little more after her long sleep. She went to roll out of bed and then groaned.

"What is it? Are you okay?" Blake reached out a hand and touched her shoulder.

"Yeah. I'm just really sore and achy. I think I've just pushed myself too hard in training lately." This time, she pushed through the achy discomfort and began to shuffle to the bathroom. Blake was right by her side and she could tell he was thinking about carrying her. "Blake, I'm fine."

He just gave her *"the look"* and then, after the longest moment of appraisal, he said, "I'm calling Aleia."

"No, don't bother her." But there he was with that *look* once more and she knew she wasn't going to win this. Raising the white flag, she said, "Okay, fine. You can call Aleia."

"And I'm calling up some food from the kitchen," he added.

She didn't argue with that because she actually was kind of hungry.

"That actually does sound good." Lips curving ever so slightly, she shut the bathroom door to take a quick shower and freshen up.

When she emerged from the bathroom in a fresh pair of sleep pants and a T-shirt, which Blake set out for her while she was in the shower, Aleia was standing next to a concerned Blake. Caly shuffled over to the couch and plopped down.

"How are you feeling, Caly?" Aleia asked in her healer mode.

"Just sore and achy. I'm sure I just have been training too hard lately."

"Mmhmm." Aleia nodded but it was easy to see she wasn't taking Caly's word at face value. "May I?" She lifted her hand in question to complete a scan.

"Yeah."

Aleia finished the preliminary scan and then asked, "Can you lay down on the couch so I can complete the full-body scan?" Her healer voice was calm, collected, and didn't give anything away. Aleia completed the scan two more times in silence.

Both Blake and his wolf were about ready to explode

because he wanted to demand why Aleia was scanning so many times.

"Caly, you can sit up now. Thanks." Aleia paused until Caly was back upright. "Caly," Aleia began, looking directly into Caly's eyes. "Your cells are showing signs of preparation for your change."

There was a pause and Caly's surprised expression seemed to fill the silence. "What? Really?"

"Yes," Aleia said.

"How soon?" Blake asked, still brimming with concern.

"I can't pinpoint it exactly but my guess is very soon. Probably within the next day or so."

"What?! What do I do?" Caly asked, suddenly hopping on that concerned train.

"Rest, relax, and refuel your body," Aleia said with a smile, indicating to the food Blake brought her.

Caly nodded.

"Call me as soon as anything changes and I'll be here. I'll reschedule my appointments tomorrow—" She looked at her watch. It was about two in the morning. "Or rather, today."

"Thanks, Aleia."

"Of course, Caly. And don't be nervous. Remember, we've all gone through it and I'll be here to help ease the process." Aleia sent Caly a reassuring smile.

Caly should've known Aleia would have picked up on her nervousness.

"Thanks." Caly returned her smile.

"Make sure she rests and eats, okay?" Aleia gave Blake her healer's order. She knew Blake was also concerned for his female and, sometimes, in times like these, males just needed to have a succinct and simple plan for them to execute. It helped them by giving them a task to focus on to best support their female. Total win-win.

Blake nodded accepting her healer's order and, while walking Aleia toward their door, he already began mentally putting plans in place so that Caly wouldn't have to lift a finger and had a full belly.

"Thanks, Aleia," Blake said in a quieter tone, purposefully staying out of earshot of Caly.

"Of course." Aleia also spoke in a lower volume. "And you did the right thing by getting me. Be sure to let me know the moment anything changes so I can soothe the pain of the change."

Blake nodded and Aleia left.

"Want to watch a movie?" Blake asked, trying not to be obvious with the fact that he was on full watchdog mode. But, yeah, it was obvious.

"That sounds good." Caly served herself some of the lasagna and side salad on one of the two plates. "Wow, this looks and smells so good. Is this leftover from dinner?"

"Yeah. I'm surprised there was any left over from the way the twins were shoveling it down."

Caly burst out laughing. "Please tell me you all know about the lasagna-loving cartoon cat, Garfield."

Blake chuckled. "Of course. And I'll leave that fine joke for you to greet them with in the morning when you see them."

Thinking ahead, Blake grabbed Caly's favorite fuzzy blanket so that she could curl up when she was done eating. Settling on the couch next to her, he began making up his own plate when he asked, "What movie do you want to watch?"

"Hmmm... Why is it always so hard to choose a movie? Like I swear there are tons of movies I want to see or wouldn't mind seeing again but it's like as soon as I sit down in front of the TV then my mind goes blank."

"Let's just scroll through the comedy section?" Blake suggested.

"Okay, that works."

"Tiff—" Before Blake could summon the TV, the lights in the room flickered and then completely burned out. Blake's brow furrowed.

"Oh, jeez. I forgot about that. I meant to text Jax when this happened earlier. I think there's faulty wiring or something."

"Hmmm..." Blake wasn't satisfied but he wasn't going to wake the castellans in the middle of the night. Getting up, he walked over to light the fireplace instead.

They finished their leftover, late-night meal and talked about nothing in particular. It was so simple yet, it was everything. Caly loved those moments with Blake where they would sometimes even be in silence for several minutes with her curled into his side, just enjoying each other's company. Plus, the glowing ambiance and light crackling of the fire added a romantic layer.

Caly slightly adjusted her position so she could playfully scratch her nails at the nape of Blake's neck just the way he liked. A low, pleasured growl hummed out of him. Lips curving, she repeated the motion a few more times until her body suddenly started to heat with need for him. In a swift motion, she was straddling him and she realized she caught him off guard. Smiling, she continued with the scratching pets which quickly became a full-blown scalp massage. Blake's low pleasured growl had her most feminine of places clenching in response. Because she loved that growl.

Especially when... she thought of how his growling added a deliciously sensual layer to their intimate play. Her body was blooming for him and she could feel her panties dampen at the thought.

At the scent of her arousal, Blake's growl shifted from a

low hum to a deep resonant vibration. "Caly." His voice was rough.

"Blake, I want you so bad right now."

God, she thought and was on the verge of an orgasm with just the sound of his growl and her name on his lips. She wanted those lips on hers and his cock deep inside her.

"Blake," she said with a breathy moan of need, closing her eyes and tilting her head back in pleasure.

"Jesus, Caly."

In response to his beautiful female, his body hardened, golden eyes began their seductive glow, and his deliciously dark and earthy mating scent mixed with her sweet arousal in the air. He let out a low and deep chuckle.

"What?" she asked, a little breathy.

"It's the change. Hormones are intensified and adjusting to the preparation of the change... But I'm not complaining," he said with a wolfish smirk.

She let out a husky laugh. "Me neither."

Her mouth claimed his in a possessive kiss. This was not going to be slow and drawn out. No, this was pure, hot need. His hand slid up her neck and with a fistful of hair, he gently tugged and forced her head to the side so their kiss could deepen. She moaned and all she wanted was to be taken. She broke the kiss to speak her desire.

"Claim me, Blake."

In an instant, they were on the bed with her underneath him. He gripped his shirt by the hem and pulled it over his head. She copied the motion and took it a step farther by slipping out of her damp panties.

"Caly, my sexy goddess, you're so beautiful... and mine." He smiled wickedly.

Her laugh was husky.

Getting with the program, he lost his jeans and boxers and settled back into place between her thighs. Feeling her slick, wet heat on his throbbing cock, he groaned in pleasure. Leaning down, he took her nipple into his mouth and she let out a pleasured sound. His hand caressed her toned curves as it made its journey down to her center. Cupping her core, he teased two fingers deep into the slickness and pressed the heel of his hand in just the right spot.

"Oh, god. Blake, I want your growling lips on me," she pleaded with a moan.

With the scent of her intoxicating arousal luring him closer, he kissed his way down her body until her glistening sex was mere inches from his mouth.

"Blake, please," she begged on a desperate breath.

His lips curved sinfully before his tongue tasted her sex with a long, upward stroke.

Her head threw back into the pillow and she let out a throaty pleasured sound. His growling licks and sucks at the most sensitive of places sent waves and waves of pleasure through her. Only moments later, ecstasy exploded through her entire being on a cry.

"Inside me. Blake, inside me," she demanded with her heart still beating rapidly and a slight gleam of sweat on her body.

He slammed his cock into her to the hilt and groaned.

"You're so wet," he said in a thick, strained voice.

He began pumping in a hard and fast rhythm and she crested once more, clenching his cock in pleasured pulses. He growled at the sensations that shot through his own body and kept with the rhythm.

"Deeper," she moaned out as her body was preparing for yet another release.

Placing his hand under her thigh, he bent it up into her side and went deeper.

She let out a throaty moan and he returned with his own pleasured groan.

"Blake, come with me," she ordered.

With three final powerful thrusts, the orgasms ripped through them as they fell together.

A heartbeat later, Caly let out a sound of pain that cut into the aftermath of ecstasy.

"What is it? Are you okay?" Blake's expression instantly shifted to concern.

"I—" Her words were cut off by another pained sound coming out of her. Closing her eyes, she curled into herself.

When her eyes flicked open, Blake saw the depth of her pain.

"Caly, I'm calling Aleia." With shifter speed, Blake was digging through his pants pocket for his phone. "Aleia, the change. Caly's in pain," he said with anxious urgency and hung up the phone without waiting for a response. A second later, he was back at Caly's side.

"Blake." She winced as another wave of pain washed over her. "Clothes."

He knew exactly what she meant and grabbed one of his white T-shirts for her and helped her into it. Just as he was sliding into his jeans, a knock sounded at the door.

"Aleia, come in."

Without pause, Aleia rushed in and started scanning Caly. Seconds later, she announced, "Caly, you're going through your change. I'm going to—"

Suddenly, a loud snap broke into the air with a flash of light.

Aleia was catapulted backward on a collision course with the stone wall.

With shifter speed, Blake caught Aleia just before her body introduced itself to the very unforgiving stone. They both rushed back over to Caly who was moaning in pain.

Aleia let out a little yelp as another snap and flash of light broke into the space once more. Caly's force field was like an electrically charged wall and neither of them could get near her. Blake needed to be with Caly. Aleia needed to ease her pain but her healing energy was being rejected by the force field.

The entire room shook when Blake belted out a loud roar of pained frustration.

"Blake, what's going on?! I'm scared!" Caly cried out and tears of confusion, fear, and pain were falling down her face.

The twins appeared in the doorway in only sweatpants.

"What's going on?!" They both growled out at the sight and sounds of Caly in pain and the stricken look on Blake and Aleia's faces.

"She's going through her change but we can't get near her!" Aleia exclaimed and before she could warn them about the shock factor of Caly's force field, they both slammed into the energetic wall and found out first-hand.

"What the fuck?!" Nico's lethal voice sliced through the air as he witnessed the twins get a shocking rejection from Caly's force field.

Caly was now curled into her side, crying in pain, with her eyes squeezed shut.

Blake suddenly shifted into his wolf and was growling and pacing around the force field.

"Fuck!" the twins bit out in response to Blake going wolf and losing himself to the instinct of the wild predator within.

Riordan and Deacon came running into the room with their chests heaving. Before they could speak, Aleia gave the update.

"Caly's going through her change. Blake's gone wolf. We can't get near her because of her shocking force field."

Riordan was about to ask about what she meant by "shocking force field" but then, he saw Blake's wolf get zapped as he tried, yet again, to get to Caly. His brows furrowed as he tried to collect his thoughts. "Nico, can you mesmerize?"

"Not unless I can see into her eyes. Even then I don't fucking know with the force field."

Caly's back was currently facing all of them and she was curled into a painful ball. Trying not to set off Blake's wolf, Riordan calmly walked over to Caly and, when he knew Blake's wolf wasn't going to attack him, he refocused on Caly.

"Caly, induce the sleep state." Riordan spoke with booming clarity that cut through the confusion of Caly's mind. He noticed her reaction and he repeated it. "Induce the sleep state."

Induce the sleep state, Caly tried to command her brain but instead, a jolt of pain shot through her once more and she cried out.

"Breathe, Caly. Breathe." Riordan's voice was like a life raft.

Sleep state. Breathe, she told herself, trying to breathe through the pain. Her breaths were shaky and shallow and it felt like she was getting stabbed with scalding hot knives and needles all over her body from the inside out.

"Good, Caly. Breathe." Riordan kept up with the coaching, encouraging her to continue. "Keep breathing. See the door of your mind."

Another pained scream escaped her. *No, damn it. You can do this. Breathe. See the door of your mind.*

"Good, Caly," Riordan said, remaining her anchor. "Breathe and see the door of your mind. You know what to do. Walk through the door of your mind."

Just as she was about to walk through the door, her steps faltered and the image wavered by another eruption of stabbing pain.

"I can't do it!" she yelled out with a scream of painful frustration.

"Yes you can, Caly. Start over. Breathe." Riordan continued to coach her through it.

It took several attempts but she was finally able to surrender to the sleep state and escape the pain of this reality. The moment Caly succumbed to the sleep state, silence stretched through the room.

"What. The. Fuck," Rhyland bit out.

"I don't know," Aleia said with an exhausted breath. "I don't fucking know." There was almost nothing more painful to a healer than to be so close to someone in need but to not be able to do anything. "The first time this happened in the car, I got a tiny shock but I thought it was just static electricity." Aleia wanted to kick herself for being so stupid and brushing that off. "Nothing like this though."

"Caly shocked me during our training yesterday. We both thought it was static electricity too," Rhyland added.

"The electricity..." Deacon muttered under his breath and attempted to turn the lights on to no avail. Deacon's eyes ended up on Caly's force field for a beat before going back to the light switch.

"Yes," Riordan said, following Deacon's thoughts, as if they were spoken out loud.

"Yesterday morning Caly asked me to charge her CCD because she said the wiring in her room was faulty..."

Riordan broke the silence, "So far, the force field has come at a time when Caly is in survival mode. Even though the change is a natural part of our existence, I believe Caly's fear and confusion triggered, on some subconscious level, that she is fighting for her life." He paused briefly. "Aleia, suggestions?"

Aleia blew out a breath. "Monitor her. Unless anyone else has any other suggestions?"

The room fell silent.

Riordan nodded. "So, we monitor her." And Riordan was going to need to think about this too.

"What about wolfy?" Rhyland looked over at Blake who was still in wolf form and pacing but not as frantically as he was before.

Blake's wolf wasn't paying them any mind because the wolf knew they were his pack and were no threat.

"Wait," Nico ground out.

"I agree," Aleia concurred. "His wolf is already starting to calm down a little now that she is sleeping and not in pain or distressed."

With that, they all looked over at Caly laying in the bed, sound asleep.

Chapter 42

"Caly... Caly..."

A compelling voice with the barest English accent called to Caly in the depths of her mind. There was some distant aspect about the hypnotic voice that made her blood run cold. In her dreams, a dark mist appeared to be slithering toward her. Caly stirred in her sleep. Just as quickly as the voice and the mist appeared, they were gone. It was as if it were swept away by some unknown force.

A pair of glowing, red eyes with two vertical slits from the depths of hell itself, reflected in a pool of black liquid. Violently, the male sent the obsidian bowl, containing the black pool, splattering to the ground. The room was shrouded in a dense, dark fog.

"How?!" The voice was now almost completely absent of its bewitching charm. It was dark with a distorted element, born from the depths of the underworld. And it was seething on a hiss of anger. He lashed out again with a venomous sting at the truth of this female evading him even in her sleep. The momentary eerie silence was suddenly consumed with his maniacal demonic laugh.

* * *

Blinking open his eyes, Blake reached his hand out, only to get shocked. At the place of impact, it sent a slight ripple out into Caly's invisible force field.

Fuck! Blake wanted to roar in frustration but his thoughts were cut off.

"Here." Aleia threw a towel over Blake's naked body and then refocused on Caly.

Getting with the program, he got up with the towel covering his waist. He looked at Caly who was sleeping in the bed. It only took a moment for him to dress in jeans and a white T before he repositioned himself next to Aleia, at Caly's bedside, just outside the force field.

"Talk to me, Aleia." His voice was gravel. He grabbed one of the water bottles on the nightstand, hoping that would help.

Aleia blew out a breath. "What do you remember?"

Although shifters were conscious and aware when in animal form, when it came to losing themselves completely to the instincts of their animal, memory gaps were common.

"Just that Caly was in pain and we couldn't get to her."

Aleia nodded. "Yes. Riordan was able to verbally guide Caly into the sleep state that travelers use and she has been asleep since. She does not appear to be in any pain, at least that I can see. And I believe her subconscious mind took her deep under for, what appears to be, the duration of the change."

She paused and then proceeded to fill Blake in on Riordan's theory, the strange events regarding electricity, and both her and Rhyland getting shocked. Blake's brow furrowed but before he could ask, she added, "We don't know. Riordan and Deacon are researching to see if there are any records."

"How long?" Blake asked with his gaze still fixed on Caly.

"It's been a few hours. You were only asleep for about an hour."

Blake nodded. "How much longer?"

Aleia blew out another breath. "I don't know. On top of the fact that everyone's change is slightly different, I can't get near her to even scan to see how far along her cells have progressed. But, as I'm sure you know, the change is typically between four to twenty-four hours."

Blake nodded and went to reach for his phone in his pocket only to realize he didn't know where it was.

"Deacon has it," Aleia informed him. "He said something happened to it during your shift and he is trying to see if he can even repair it." She pulled out her phone. "Here." She handed her phone to him.

"Thanks." He dialed Deacon, who picked up on the first ring.

"Aleia?" Deacon answered.

"It's me," Blake said.

"On my way," Deacon replied without pause.

Blake hung up the phone and handed it back to Aleia. Seconds later, the twins and Nico appeared in the room. And a few moments later, Riordan and Deacon walked in. Everyone looked to be in about as good of shape as him right now... which wasn't good at all.

"Aleia brought me up to speed. Have you found anything?" Blake's gaze only flicked to Deacon's for a moment before returning to Caly.

"No." Deacon ran his hand through his hair in a frustrated motion. "I'm still searching but there is nothing to explain the electrical force field."

Blake nodded and then looked at Riordan who shook his head.

The final image in Riordan's previous vision of Caly had been replaying in his mind for hours now. Caly was standing with her legs hip-width distance, arms outstretched to the sky, eyes glowing gray, hair floating around and defying gravity. Along with the shimmering vibration gathering all around her and concentrating in her hands. But he still didn't know what he was seeing. When, or if, the time came to share the vision, he would share it with Caly alone. Unless, of course, she consented otherwise. And he would put his money on her wanting Blake by her side for that discussion.

Blake rubbed the scruff of his jaw in frustration. "I'm calling Alexina."

Normally, Blake would call her in private, as he knew she was very much a solitude ancient, but he couldn't wait. He walked over to the panel on the wall and it appeared that the electricity was back online. Good. He punched in the code and moments later Alexina's warm smiling face appeared on the TV screen. Her smile immediately faded to a furrowed brow of concern.

"Blake?"

"Alexina. Caly's going through her change," Blake began, cutting right to the chase.

Alexina was already aware of Caly and his relationship with her. Blake filled her in after Caly's rescue and she was still searching archives and records but nothing had come of it so far. Caly was aware of the ancient who knew of her, although Caly hadn't met the ancient yet. Caly trusted Blake who trusted the ancient, so she was okay with her unknown ability being known by the ancient.

"But there's a new development." Instead of telling her, Blake decided to show her. He walked over to Caly and when he got shocked, Alexina's eyebrows shot up and she pressed her face closer to the screen.

"Does it hurt?" she asked with concerned curiosity.

"No," Blake answered. Okay, it stung a little but it wasn't painful and he sure as hell wasn't going to disclose that and lose his alpha card to static electricity.

"Will you please do it one more time?" Her brow furrowed with eyes solely concentrated on the connection. When Blake got shocked once more, Alexina drew a pencil out of her hair. The brown waves pooled down past her shoulders as she bit on the eraser end of the pencil in contemplative thought.

Everyone was so concentrated on Alexina that no one noticed that Riordan was staring at Alexina, for reasons other than the obvious. There was something about the ancient female that caught his eye. As if she could read his thoughts, her gaze fell on his for the longest moment before she refocused back on Blake.

"Blake, I need to look into the texts about this new development." There was something in the far corners of her mind that seemed to spark a distant thought but it was gone before she could unravel it. She was biting on the tip of her pencil with her gaze focused elsewhere once more.

Blake nodded. "Oh, Alexina, this is Riordan and Aleia."

Alexina's eyes landed on Aleia and she smiled. "Aleia," she said and then refocused on Riordan. Her smile changed slightly, indicating shyness. "Riordan. It's a pleasure to meet you both."

"Alexina." His deep Irish accent seemed to wrap around her.

Being ancients, they, of course, knew of each other and had even been to the same social gatherings but they had never met or really noticed one another before. Especially since they both tended to keep to themselves.

"Blake, I will let you know if I find anything."

"Thanks." Blake nodded and Alexina ended the call.

Chapter 43

Caly blinked and waited for her eyes to adjust to the bright sunlight. She heard ocean waves kissing the shoreline. Slightly squinting, she looked around and upon recognition, her eyes instantly became blurry with emotion.

She was dreaming of one of her favorite memories with her parents.

The crystal clear, saltwater was lapping up against her thighs. Looking down at herself, she thought she might see herself at ten years old, just as she was on that day. Instead, she stood as the female she had grown into. Her gaze fell upon the light, tan beach with shimmering flecks of gold. She saw her mother under the white and blue umbrella reading a book. Her mother was smiling and slid her sunglasses to the top of her head. Instead of her mother's hair being the blonde color she was used to, it actually was like Caly's: dark brown and almost black. The beach was completely empty except for her mother. When Caly felt a warm, wet hand on her shoulder, her head turned to see her father smiling at her. Caly's tears were falling down her cheeks. She knew this was just a dream but it felt so real.

God, I miss you both so much, she thought, as the deep core of her heart and soul ached with emotion.

Her father pulled her into a warm embrace. "Shhh. My sweet Caly Lilly. Don't cry."

That was the nickname her father called her and also the reason why her favorite flowers were calla lilies. She closed her eyes and let her tears flow. She felt her mother's arms wrap around her and it was just like when she was a young girl—she was sandwiched between their loving arms once more.

So what if this is a dream? Maybe she could finally say the heartbreaking goodbye that she never got the chance to.

"Mom... Dad... I miss you both so much," she choked out.

"My sweet baby, we are so proud of you. We are sorry that we can't be there with you for your change and to see you become who you are meant to be." Her mother's sweet angelic voice seemed to fill her with loving warmth. It sounded so real. It all felt so real.

"Is this real or just my imagination?" Caly asked, pulling away from the embrace to look into her parents' eyes and take it all in.

"Who says reality and imagination are not fabrics woven together to form the whole?" her father answered. When she was about to ask what he meant, her father said, "My curious Caly Lilly, maybe we can go down that road one day but for now, we are here to share who you are and who we are."

There was a pregnant pause and Caly was confused at where this strange dream/non-dream was going.

"In the species world, your mother and I were Isadora and Alistaire Eliades. Your mother was a seer and I, an elemental. Water was my specialty. We both worked for SILE and met on an assignment for SILE. She was the seer on the case." He paused to smile at his beautiful life mate and then refocused back on Caly. "As you know, we fell in love and soon after, your mother was with young. We couldn't have been happier. In the very beginning, your mother had visions of you, naturally. But then, she started to see that you would be hunted for what you are. For you are not just born of a seer and elemental. You are both: a cross-species with rare abilities from both. You're a traveler and a magnetic."

"Caly, my beautiful baby," her mother said and her father wiped tears from his mate's face. "When I started having the visions that you would be hunted and taken from us, we decided to fake our death and hide in the human world. We decided to live as humans to protect you. The farther along I got in the pregnancy, the more difficult it became to see into the future. And once you were born, your future was completely blocked from my visions."

"You see, sometimes when species young are born of two species parents, the young doesn't come into their abilities until after their change. Your mother saw what may be and we decided to wait to tell you until you started to show your abilities. We wanted for you to have a normal life as much as possible and not live in fear of being hunted or taken. And we thought that if you knew the truth, then you would want to be with species. But we couldn't allow that without really knowing what you were, how to teach you to control your abilities, and knowing that you would be hunted. It's easier to hunt species on the species side of The Barrier because the rules are different there."

"My sweet baby, we were just trying to protect you. All we wanted for you was to live a normal youth and life as much as possible."

"The night we were taken from you." Her father paused, not sure how to say this. "It wasn't just any car accident. We were murdered... It must've been a last-minute decision because your mother didn't see it coming until it was too late. We believe he was hiding in the human world and recognized us, just as we recognized him. He was a criminal in one of our biggest cases and we got very close several times but never caught him." There was a hesitant pause. "Caly, it was The Ghost. It was James Barker."

Caly was trying to process all of this impossible information but that last part put her right into frozen shock.

"One more thing you need to know," her father added. "We sent Riordan to you. We met on a case and kept in touch over the decades. He has suspected but there was no way for him to confirm. You can trust him."

"My sweet Caly." Tears were streaming down her mother's face. "We wish we had more time with you then... and now. We are so proud of you and love you so very much."

"We love you, Caly Lilly."

"I—" Caly was feeling the entire spectrum of emotions. The pain of it all at once had her paralyzed... except for the tears which were flowing as if making up for the rest of her being frozen. "I love you." That was all her brain managed to process.

She was sandwiched in another warm embrace a moment later. She felt her father kiss the top of her head and her mother kiss her cheek. The dream started to fade into bright white light.

"Mom... Dad... Wait! No, don't go! I need you! I can't lose you again!" Caly was desperately trying to cling to their fading figures. But they were slipping right through her hands.

"You never lost us, sweet baby." She barely heard her mother's angelic voice as if it was caught in a gentle breeze.

"We're always with you. We love you." Her father's fading voice was the last thing she heard.

Crying. She was crying. It was the kind where breathing was impossible. It felt like being stabbed straight in the heart of your soul. Then, the dream faded completely to bright white light.

Chapter 44

The second her breathing pattern changed, Blake was right by her side... an inch from the force field. She was crying. His female was crying. The sting of heartache and the unmistakable scent of pure love filled Blake's nose. Both he and his wolf were pacing once again in frustration for being kept from his female when she was in need of comfort and support. In need of him.

It had been one week since Caly started her change and still no one could get near her. But Blake never left her side. He knew that he probably looked as hellish as he felt but he didn't care. The only thing he cared about at that moment was his female. Aleia and Riordan believed that Caly was in a self-induced coma state but, again, no one knew for sure because of the force field. The one thing that didn't have him going wolf every five seconds was the fact that, until this moment, Caly appeared to be without pain and sleeping peacefully.

In aggravating frustration, he went to pound a fist on the force field except he almost fell over because there was no force field. Recovering quickly with shifter speed, Blake sent the emergency text that everyone had been on standby for this exact situation. Aleia and the entire crew, including

Riordan, would get the text that Caly was waking. He immediately was on the bed next to her, pulling her close to his chest. Without pause, he was kissing and nuzzling her face, letting her know he was there for her.

"Caly?!" He kissed her tears away.

Caly cracked open her eyelids that were wet with tears. It took several moments for her eyes to focus and, when they did, she was staring into those impossibly beautiful, golden eyes that belonged to her wolf.

"Caly, you're awake!" He kissed her lips in pure relief and joy.

Her throat was like the Sahara desert. Caly tried to speak but it just came out a raspy noise. He grabbed the bottle of water next to her on the nightstand, twisted off the cap, and gently put it to her lips. The room temperature liquid slowly slid down her throat in a refreshing wave.

"Blake–" She coughed up the sandy desert and her voice was like that of a thousand-year-old mummy.

God, how long was I asleep? she thought, taking another drink of water while clearing her throat.

"I saw my parents. Blake, I saw my parents." The deep pain in her heart registered as tears pooled in her eyes once more.

The twins and Nico suddenly appeared in the room. Moments later, Aleia, Riordan, and Deacon ran in, chests heaving from bolting at full speed. Aleia immediately scanned Caly and gave her healing energy as a preemptive measure just in case. The twins didn't wait for Aleia to be done because Caly looked fine... except for the unmistakable sting of heartbreak. Rhyland gave her a massive bear hug followed by Rhyker.

"You're not allowed to scare us like that," Rhyland said and then both he and his brother added in unison, "Ever. Again." They were only half-joking.

Caly laughed a little.

As soon as the twins were out of the way, Nico was there and gave her his version of a hug: a quick squeeze, welcoming her back in his own wordless way. It was actually the first time Nico had ever hugged Caly. And even though his hug didn't compare to the bear hugs of the twins and wasn't going to win any hugging contests, it didn't matter because it meant just as much to her heart and soul.

"Congratulations on your change, Caly," Riordan said, leaning in for his own hug.

Deacon quickly replaced Riordan's hug with his own and said, "Welcome back, Caly."

Finally, Aleia pulled Caly in for a hug.

Caly had never been hugged so many times in a row, but she didn't mind it one bit.

"I was so worried. Are you okay? Why am I picking up on distress?" Aleia finished up her scan and gave Caly healing energy.

"I'm fine. I..." She didn't know how to say this without sounding crazy.

Screw it.

"I saw my parents."

She shared her dream-like experience and the room fell silent with furrowed brows.

"Is this even possible?" she asked, suddenly unsure and questioning her sanity.

"Yes, it is. I believe you did see your parents." Riordan paused briefly. "And, they were right. I did suspect them from the moment I saw you in the first vision. You do remind me of them." He smiled warmly.

Blake wiped a tear from her cheek.

"Well holy shit! Cross-species with rare abilities from both sides?" Rhyland playfully broke the emotional state of the room. He knew everyone was trying not to go *there* right now with the whole other layer as to why that fucker, The Ghost, needed to die. Caly just went through a lot and it was compounded, considering everything she had gone through over the past few months. So they would have plenty of time to address that but now was not the time.

"Badass," Rhyker added, knowing exactly what his brother was doing.

She let out a little laugh.

"And that explains why your scent has never quite fit in with your seer half-siblings." Rhyland commented, putting a puzzle piece into place that had them all wondering about that seemingly subtle note to her scent that hinted at something different from the very beginning.

"Magnetic?" Blake asked Riordan.

Riordan paused for the longest moment. He was sifting through the knowledge in his ancient mind. Riordan's brow furrowed slightly and then he shook his head when the fragment of a thought didn't come to fruition.

"There may be something... but I will need to sit with this. Perhaps Alexina?" Riordan suggested. From what he knew, because, yeah he did follow up on who she was after that last call, she was an ancient steorrian and this could be more her area of expertise with the knowledge the ancients texts held.

Blake nodded before refocusing his full attention back on Caly.

It was clear that the conversation with Alexina would happen later. And it was also clear that Blake wanted to be alone with his female.

"I'll have Jax bring up some food. For now, I'll leave you two be. Caly, again, welcome back." With that, Riordan left.

The others took the unsaid cue and did the same.

"I need to shower," Caly said with an exhale.

"Me too," Blake agreed and stole another quick kiss.

She got out of bed slowly with Blake by her side. Her body was a little stiff but not too bad, thanks to Aleia.

"Why does everyone keep saying welcome back? Is that like a species change thing or something?"

"Caly."

She looked over at Blake with that unexpected serious tone from him.

"You've been out for a week."

"A week?!" she said in disbelief with wide eyes. From what she knew of the change, it lasted a day at most.

He nodded and pulled her in for another hug. He knew he would never let go of his female.

* * *

Alexina greeted Blake and Riordan on the call screen with one of her warm yet tentative smiles. She knew their call must be about Caly.

"Alexina." Blake and Riordan both greeted her.

"Caly is awake and has gone through her change," Blake began and then outlined the details of Caly seeing her parents and her being a cross-species.

Silence stretched on the call and Alexina had that distant look in her eyes. She was summoning and sifting through the Rolodex of memories.

"Magnetic..." she spoke partially out loud, echoing her thoughts.

She bit the eraser side of a pencil and kept filtering through the thoughts. A thread of memory that had been elusive to her finally came to the forefront of her mind. It was the memory of an ancient text. Her gaze refocused on Blake in what seemed like a moment of clarity.

"Magneticus or The Earth's Light. Legends of the ancient

texts say that during the battle of The Ancient Ones, he called forth the light of the Earth..." Her voice trailed off, as if trying to tease out more threads from the thought. "It could be unrelated. But the name..." Her voice trailed off once more. "Blake, I will research this more."

Her gaze started to go distant again as if she was already standing in her private library and searching for the ancient text.

"Thank you."

"Of course," she said but her brain was already on auto-pilot as she ended the call.

Chapter 45

"Caly... Caly..."

The hauntingly hypnotic voice called to her in the depths of her mind while she slept. Simultaneously, the ominous dark fog crept in the corners of her mind carrying the sinuous voice in its midst. Caly stirred in her sleep. But, just as before, the charmingly chilling voice and mist were gone as if repelled away by the bright light of her mind.

Caly blinked her eyes open and felt a chill in her bones. And, no, it was not just because the weather was getting colder as winter approached. She was trying to shake off the dream with the icy fog and the beguiling voice. Since she awoke from her change-induced coma three weeks ago, she had been on a mission. And that mission was to avenge her parents. She was one hundred percent focused on this mission, which was fueled by her determination to succeed. *Mission: Avenge,* she thought, as she did almost every morning when she woke up. It had become like her rocket fuel for getting out of bed and getting her ass into the gym to train.

She rolled out of bed and got ready quietly, not wanting to wake Blake. Yes, quietly because she wanted to be courteous to Blake sleeping but also because she didn't want any distractions.

Felix lazily yawned and just repositioned himself to continue sleeping next to Bake.

Thankfully, her abilities blossomed after her change, as if the whole magnetic force field during her change coma wasn't a sign of that. Although she wasn't able to call on anything that strong or powerful herself yet, she was able to hold the force field with only a barrier of a couple of inches around her. It was nothing like the massive bubble that formed several feet around her during the change coma. And the only shock value she could summon was like the smallest static shock. So, no, it wasn't anything like they all knew was inside of her but it was still something. Because now, she actually stood somewhat of a chance when sparring with Blake, Nico, and the twins. Even if the twins definitely thought that her little static electricity "attack" was cute. And unfortunately, she couldn't hold her force field forever. But when she could, it was an incredible advantage.

Her self-defense strategy was to incapacitate her opponent in the time she could hold her force field. To everyone's surprise, her force field would allow her to throw things, like her knife or SEW, outside of the force field without her having to take it down. It just slid through the force field like liquid and sent ripples out of the exit point. They were still training with her on defensive skills but they had finally decided to also incorporate offensive techniques. Another part of her ability that came out of the change was that she was now able to activate her dream-traveling ability while in the sleep state. Riordan was still working with her on the basics of traveling but again, it was a solid foundation for her to continue training.

She washed down the nutritional breakfast bar with a protein shake, that Jax now kept stocked in the gym for her.

Not only did she not have time for morning macchiatos and muffins anymore, but also that wasn't exactly fueling her body for success... for her mission to get stronger so she could avenge her parents.

* * *

Blake heard Caly get up and leave quietly and it stung a little more each morning she did that. He and his wolf could feel Caly pulling away from him. She was consumed by revenge and it was creating this gap between them that grew bigger with every passing moment. At first, he wanted to give her space because he, out of anyone, could understand what it would be like to see your parents after losing them tragically. Especially, with the added, fucked-up layer that they were murdered by none other than the evil bastard that tortured her. And, yeah, Blake was so on board with sinking his teeth into that fucker's throat once more and this time, he wouldn't give the bastard a chance to run away. So, he got it. And he was trying to be respectful of Caly's space, that she was clearly, non-verbally, asking for. However, he and his wolf wouldn't just stand by and do nothing as his female pulled away and left a hole in his heart, where she was meant to be.

"I'll talk to her again," Blake said to Felix as his hand stroked the feline's midnight fur. The last couple of times Blake attempted to bring this up with Caly, she flipped out. She said he didn't understand and that she wasn't pulling away. Instead, she was just focused on actually doing something with her life that had meaning and could bring justice to her parents. Blake understood all of that but she just crossed that thin line of revenge that was hard to come back from. She was unknowingly isolating herself. Really the only times he would see her was when they sparred or ate during meals, and even then that was hit or miss. They hadn't been intimate in a couple of weeks because she said she just wasn't in the mood or that she needed to train or study. And the last time they had sex, Blake ended up pulling out halfway through because he could tell she wasn't into it. It felt like mercy sex on her end, which just drove a knife through his heart. With an exhale, Blake rolled out of bed to get ready and go down for breakfast. Afterward, he planned on coming up to their room to see if he could catch Caly after her sparring session with Rhyland so he could try and reach her again.

* * *

"Stop holding back, Rhy!" Caly bit out.

"SoCal, maybe we should take a break?" Rhyland suggested with a concerned look.

"No, not yet," she gritted out, throwing another punch.

Rhyland blocked it with ease but she knew she just exposed her side and he didn't even try to take advantage of that.

"What the fuck, Rhy? Stop holding back!" This time, her voice was just tip-toeing into the angry yelling zone. "I'm sick of being treated like I'm fragile!" She attacked again and he blocked her once more.

"Caly, it's time for a break. I'm calling it," he said firmly, which was absent of his usual hint of playfulness.

"No! I won't stop until he is *dead*!" She attacked again but this time, he not only blocked her but also pinned her to the mat. Seeing red, Caly tried to break free from his grip but he was so much bigger and stronger.

"Caly—"

"No! Fuck you, Rhyland! Maybe you get *pleasure* out of pinning weaker females and being the strong dominant savior. But no more. I'm done!"

He looked at her for a long, hard moment with steel in his piercing blue eyes. Everyone had noticed Caly's behavior since her change. She had been progressively getting more acquainted with her inner bitch and teetering toward complete isolation. Rhyland could empathize because he had practically been in her shoes once upon a time. At one point, both his and Rhyker's sole mission in life was hunting a sadistic fucker with the intention to give him a taste of his own murderous medicine. But at this moment, Caly had crossed the line. With shifter speed, Rhyland got up and stormed out.

"ARGH!" Caly yelled out in anger. Maybe she was a little harsh but whatever. He deserved it.

Why can't he see that all I'm trying to do is avenge my parents and make things right? And that can't happen if he holds back! Whatever.

She blew out a breath. It was like she was a fire-breathing dragon that was ready to burn down a village. Putting on her angry music playlist, she pushed shuffle. NF's "Therapy Session" started playing. Fitting. She probably needed a therapy session, except not with Keena. Lately, she felt those were just a waste of time. So, she let the sparring mat be her therapist instead.

Caly stayed and practiced both defensive and offensive moves by herself until her body almost gave out. She was still pissed off from what happened with Rhyland earlier. With a slam of the door, as if it was her evil Ice Queen's epic entrance, she stormed out of the sparring room and into the gym only to see Rhyker, Deacon, and Nico.

Why the fuck is everyone in here all of a sudden? Out of the whole damn castle and everyone decides to work out?

She gave everyone a frosty glare as she stomped past with her villainous exit.

When the gym doors closed, Rhyker looked at Nico and Deacon with a questioning raise of his brow. They both shrugged their shoulders with equaled puzzled looks and then just kept working out. No one dared to approach a female in this kind of a mood. And they knew she had been in somewhat of a mood lately.

* * *

Entering their room on the coattails of her anger and frustration, Caly saw Blake. She closed her eyes and internally exhaled. She knew they were on weird grounds right now. And, yeah, that last time they had sex was so bad and she knew it was her doing but she just couldn't turn her brain off and get into it. She did feel bad about that but he just didn't understand what she was going through. He didn't get where she was at. And every time he said that she was "consumed by revenge," it seriously just pissed her the fuck off. Because no she wasn't. She was just focused on her mission.

Besides, excuse me for wanting to kill the bastard who not only tortured me but also murdered my fucking parents.

And that thought just added to her frustration since there were no updates. Actually, that wasn't true. There was an update but just not about The Ghost. The update Blake recently shared with her was that the ancient steorrian that he trusted had been looking into the ancient texts and found something out about Magneticus.

Magneticus was said to be born of the first elementals, Ignis and Terra, or Fire and Earth. During the days when The Ancient Ones walked the Earth, it was said that Magneticus' son of three generations, Fulgur, took after him. It was written that while traveling the world, Fulgur saved a village from a terrible storm. No one knew how but it was as if the storm simply passed over the entire village. She also found one or two sentences here or there that alluded to a subspecies born of Magneticus but she was unable to find any further information on any of it.

"But as you know there is much that has been lost and still yet to be recovered, if it was not destroyed." That was what Alexina said to Blake before ending the conversation on the note that she would keep searching.

Caly attempted another calming breath so she wouldn't attack Blake for her frustrations with everything, including what happened with Rhyland.

"Hey," she managed to awkwardly say.

"Hey," he echoed. It looked like he was about to say something but she spoke first.

"I'm gonna take a shower." Again, she tried not to sound like a fucking fire-breathing dragon. And why she decided to announce her shower? She didn't know.

Blake looked away with a long exhale as she walked into the bathroom, shut the door, and blew out her own breath. She didn't want it to be awkward with Blake but right now was so not the time. She was still fuming from Rhyland and it took everything for her not to take it out on Blake. Besides, she knew that look of his because it was the same look he had before he tried to talk to her about how she was "consumed with revenge." God, just the thought of that last conversation they had annoyed her. So, yeah, now was so not the time.

Blake was still there after Caly emerged from the bathroom.

Okay, she thought, with the feeling of the hot shower draining out of her and being replaced with annoyance. *Why hasn't he moved? And why is he still giving me the "we have to talk" look?*

Silently avoiding him, she just walked into the closet and

proceeded to get dressed. And yup. He was still there when she came out of the closet. And, hey, wasn't that symbolic? Because maybe she needed to come out and let Blake know he needed to just leave her alone right now. Hashtag Flipp Dinero.

"Caly," Blake began, in a cautious but firm tone.

This time, she audibly exhaled and waited for him to speak.

"I—" He blew out a breath and along with it went his mini-speech he had prepared. "I miss you."

"I haven't gone anywhere." Her tone was caustic.

God. Why am I being such a bitch right now? She tried to scale it back because beneath everything, she did miss him too but there was just no time for them right now. And back to Flipp Dinero because didn't he say that perfectly?

"I just... Hell, I don't know," she said with an exasperated breath. "I miss you too but I just need some space to work this out for myself."

"I've given you space but it's driving a wedge between us. Space is not the answer."

"Oh? And what is the answer?"

So much for not being a bitch. But what? Like he has all of the answers to my situation?

He exhaled and rubbed his hand over his jaw in frustration. "Taking a break with training."

"Oh Jesus fucking Christ! Did Rhyland put you up to this?!"

"What? No. What are you talking about?"

She narrowed her eyes to furious suspicious slits.

"Caly..."

"No, Blake! No, I'm not fucking taking a break. And, in fact, how *dare* you for even suggesting to take a break. If your parents' *murderer* and the sole being that created a living *torture hell* for you was still out there, would you fucking take a break?! No, I don't think you would!"

And with that, she stormed out and slammed the door behind her. Seconds later, she heard Blake's angered roar but he didn't go after her.

* * *

"Riordan, I'm worried about Caly." Blake cut out all of the bullshit and got right to the point.

After the fight with Caly, Rhyland ended up coming to talk with Blake and, surprise (not surprise), Rhyland had the same concerns. He also said that he would not be sparring with Caly until *"she stops turning into Darth Vader."* And he didn't say it in the playful way he normally would. But rather, he growled it out angrily. Blake didn't know what exactly went down between Caly and Rhyland but he knew it took a lot to get Rhyland in that kind of a mood.

After that conversation with Rhyland, Blake went for a long run to try and clear his head. He came to the conclusion to talk with Riordan to see if he had any suggestions. He was an ancient after all. So, Blake was betting on the fact that he had to have had some sort of experience with someone getting lost to the Dark Side, to continue with Rhyland's earlier Star Wars reference.

"I, too, have noticed her behavior and it is starting to concern me as well," Riordan agreed. "I actually was going to suggest that we meet. I'm glad you beat me to it."

Blake nodded and expressed his concern that Caly was being consumed by revenge. He also shared what Rhyland said, that *"she won't stop until The Ghost is dead."*

"I've tried to talk to her several times. But whenever I bring it up, she gets mad and doesn't hear me. And when I tried again this morning, it ended up just being a big blow up."

Yeah, like the entire castle didn't hear him roar.

Riordan nodded. "I have a session with her shortly. I'll see if I can get through. And, whether she likes it or not, I will cancel our session. She is also getting the next few days off. And that won't be optional."

Blake nodded in agreement.

* * *

"Caly." Riordan's tone had Caly suddenly on alert. Of course, he was more on the serious side of the scale but there was something about his tone that had her wondering what exactly he was about to say.

I've been doing all my homework and reading assignments, she thought, a little panicked. *I've even gone above and beyond and have been reading extra texts and practicing more frequently and for longer.* She racked her brain to see if she forgot something.

"Revenge is a serpent that slithers into your mind and can take the reins without you realizing it." He paused with his eyes locked on hers.

What the fuck?! she thought as a surge of anger rose within her. *Did Blake and Rhyland fucking tattle on me?! Doesn't fucking matter. I haven't done anything wrong. Besides, he may be my primary but he is not my father.*

"It's a dangerous road to go down, especially as a specian... when time is all you have. I've seen it more times than I would like in my existence."

There was a pause and Caly was just biting her tongue. Riordan had been nothing less than supportive and, hell, amazing to her. She may not like this but she would not lash out at Riordan.

"Caly, we will find him. But don't lose touch with who you are and where you come from."

Caly bit her tongue but her thoughts were loud and clear. *Who I am? Where I come from? THAT'S the whole point! He fucking killed where I come from and forever changed who I was.*

"You have the rest of the day plus the next two days off."

"Wait, what?" she blurted out in surprise. "But—"

"Rest of the day plus the next two days," Riordan repeated himself in a tone that said the conversation was over.

You've got to be fucking kidding me! Caly stormed out of Riordan's office. *I have to get out,* she thought desperately, bolting out of the nearest exit. Even though the sun was high in the early afternoon sky, the weather was still a little on the chilly side. But with Caly heated by her rage, she blazed into the woods and forged her own path. She didn't know how long she walked but eventually, her angry, fast pace had slowed down. She had a million thoughts going through her mind and even more emotions.

She wanted to scream.

Walking through a clearing in the trees, she froze, almost not believing what she was looking at. It was the magically exotic garden where she first saw Riordan in her dream. Walking up to the garden just as she did in that first dream, what felt like lifetimes ago, she saw a butterfly that wasn't a butterfly. She didn't know why but she held her hand out as if she could touch it. To her surprise, it landed on her finger. She swore it was staring at her just as she was staring at it.

Full circle, Caly thought, as she was reminded about who she was when she first saw this place and this creature. A wave of emotion swelled in Caly as memories of her parents began to play through her mind. Tears were now flowing down her cheeks. It was the first time she had cried since seeing her parents in the dream. It was the first time she had allowed herself to feel the pain of losing them all over again. Caly thought about how her parents left everything they knew to protect her. Then, new memories started to stream through her mind. Of her new family. Of Blake. God, Blake. And how he had been this steady rock in her life and had treated her like a queen. Like his mate. She felt another stabbing pain in her heart next to the constant one that lingered at the thought of how much she missed her parents. How could she have been so mean to Blake lately? The memory scrollathon wasn't done yet apparently because then, she was thinking about Riordan and how he had been like an uncle of sorts. Finally, she thought of her brothers, because, yeah, that was what they were to her.

God. Who am I? Who have I become? Caly didn't even recognize herself. *I am not someone who is consumed by revenge and rage. No. I am Caly, lover of morning drink rituals, Felix, epic playlists, romance novels… and, yes now a badass magnetic traveler, if I do say so myself.*

And then a mantra that she all but forgot popped into her mind.

I am the fucking Phoenix.

Her lips curved and, at the same moment, the butterfly creature flew off, fluttering it's brilliantly delicate wings. She made her way through the garden and sat on the bench overlooking the lake, finally feeling a level of peace she hadn't felt in weeks.

Chapter 46

Caly knew that she needed to do some major damage control. On the walk back toward home, Caly hashed out a plan to do just that. First stop on the apology express? Riordan.

She knocked on Riordan's office door and waited. She didn't know if he was there but it was a good place to start at least. Right before she was going to knock again, he opened the door and seemed a bit surprised to see her.

"Umm, can I come in?" she asked with an apologetic tone and tilt of her lips.

"Of course." Riordan gave her an appraising look while stepping aside and inviting her inside. "Would you like to sit down?" Riordan offered, as he closed the door.

"No, that's okay. Umm. I'm hoping this won't take long."

He nodded and just waited in that way ancients did.

Well, spit it out, Caly. We have a lot of stops on this train ride before nightfall.

"I'm sorry and… Thank you."

Riordan's face softened.

"I know you were just looking out for me and you were right. Also, I found the garden with the bench overlooking the lake. I hope you don't mind that I sat on your bench."

He smiled warmly. "Ah, yes. I have had many thoughtful breakthroughs on that bench myself."

"If I didn't know better, I would've sworn that the whole place is enchanted or something." Caly was only half-joking and was curious if there actually was some sort of species magical thing going on there.

This time. he smiled wide in amusement. "You know, I wouldn't doubt it."

She wanted to unravel more of that but not right now. Right now, she had to move on to her next stop: Aleia.

"Anyways, again, I'm sorry for acting the way I did and thank you for helping to keep me in check."

He simply nodded.

"Well, I hate to apologize and run but there are others that I owe an apology to as well."

Riordan nodded again.

She smiled and was out the door.

The apology with Aleia went basically the same as Riordan's. Although Caly didn't do anything specifically to Aleia, she was kind of a crappy friend lately by being distant. Aleia accepted her apology without pause.

Okay, next stop: the kitchen.

In the dining room, Caly saw Rhyker with a pile of food on his plate, naturally. He gave her a cautious side glance as if trying not to set her off unintentionally.

Cute, she thought as she walked up to him.

"Hey… yeah, sorry about earlier. I was in a bad mood."

He chuckled. "Yeah, we didn't notice… at all. Nope." He winked. "It's all good, Ms. Frost."

She laughed and gave him a hug. "Thanks."

She walked into the kitchen. "Hey, Meri."

"Hi, Caly," Meri said with her warm smile and tinkle voice but it was clear that she was trying to hide her concern.

"I, umm, I'm sorry about being distant and, well, weird lately. And, umm... I'm wondering, you know, only if you have the time... Well, I miss your amazing macchiatos and muffins in the morning." Caly tentatively smiled.

Meri's eyes lit up in delight. "Of course, Caly. Of course." And Meri hugged Caly.

"Ummm." Caly bit her lower lip. "I know it's a little late but do you think you could do me a favor?"

"Yes, of course. What is it?" Meri said with her joyful expression.

Feeling pretty good about how this apology assembly line of sorts was going, Caly made her way to her next stop. She knocked on Rhyland's door and waited. There was no answer.

He probably smells you and is ignoring you, she thought, as she summoned the courage to knock once more. Still no answer.

"Rhy? It's me. Umm, can I come in?" she asked in a tremulous voice. This time, there was an answer but it was just his voice through the door.

"Why? So I can get *pleasure* out of dominating you?"

His words cut like knives.

Rightfully so. You were the evil Ice Queen the last time you spoke.

"Rhy, I'm really sorry... Please, will you let me in so we can talk?"

She was met with silence for several long moments. Right when she was about to speak once more, the door unlocked. Without looking at her, he opened the door, walked back over to the couch, and proceeded to watch TV.

Okay. So, yeah. Maybe you do deserve this...

"I, umm, brought you your favorite snack?" She held out the peace offering but he didn't even look at her. Instead, he acted like she wasn't even there.

Shit, she thought, setting one of his favorite go-to meals on the table. It was a turkey, bacon, and avocado sandwich with extra bacon, barbeque potato chips, and three thin and crispy chocolate chip cookies. Yes, thin and crispy—just as he liked. It was almost blasphemous to Caly since, hands down, she loved chewy and thick chocolate chip cookies. But apparently, for Rhyland, it was all about the thin and crispy.

"Look, Rhy. I am really sorry."

"Yeah, you've said that," he bit out. "If there is nothing else, then you know the way out."

"I... god." She blew out a breath. "I really fucked this up, didn't I? I'll leave after this because... I get it. What I did and said was completely uncalled for. I took out my anger and frustration on you. I didn't mean what I said. Everything that I was bottling up about my parents, myself, and everything that is out of my control... Well, I unfairly unleashed that on you and it wasn't right. I wasn't myself and I know that's no excuse but I want you to know that I really am truly sorry. And I hope that one day you can forgive me and we can start over because—" She swallowed a sudden lump in her throat. "Losing you would be like losing a brother and I—" Tears started to pool in her eyes and her throat grew thick with emotion. "I can't bear the thought. But I get it. Honestly, I really do. And I'm sorry, Rhyland."

Caly was walking to the door in defeat. She knew she fucked up and she said her piece so now it was time for her to go.

With shifter speed, Rhyland was in front of her and pulled her in for a hug.

"Shit, Caly. Blake is screwed if those are the epic apologies you give." He grinned and she laughed but it was one of those laugh-cries where she was laughing but also crying. "Glad to have you back, SoCal."

"Well, I actually owe him an apology too. So, hopefully, you're right and he forgives me because I really was the evil Ice Queen lately."

He chuckled and gave her a little squeeze. "I have full confidence in you. And, hell, I may need to consult with you in the future if I need to apologize to someone."

Her lips twitched.

"Oh, and the food was a nice touch. Speaking of..." He walked over to the food and took a giant bite of the sandwich. "Extra bacon too?!" he said with a mouthful of sandwich. "Shit. Yeah, Blake doesn't stand a chance." He winked, taking another huge bite.

Still laughing as she left Rhyland's room, she saw Nico walking toward her in the hallway. She noticed him giving her an appraising look. No doubt, to see if she was still giving him a run for his money in the frost department. She offered an apologetic look.

"Ummm... sorry about earlier... in the gym."

Like he doesn't know you're talking about being the Ice Queen in the gym.

A one-sided smile appeared on his face as if in slight amusement of the memory.

"Forget it."

And just like that, in Nico's minimalist anti-word way, they were okay and back to normal.

There was one more stop on the apology express before the final destination.

She knocked on Deacon's door.

Deacon opened the door a moment later. As soon as he saw it was her, he went still with caution.

Caly had to hold back a laugh at his reaction.

"Hey, Caly." He spoke in a tentative tone, testing the

waters to see if he was about to get blasted with a freeze gun.

"Hi, Deacon. I'm sorry about earlier. I was in a bad mood and it wasn't about you or the others."

"It's okay. We all know how it is." His mouth turned up at the corners. "Hell, I mean, Blake told you about the fight room in the old house, right?"

"Yeah, he did."

They both chuckled.

"Come here." He gave her a quick hug. "We're good."

God. How did I get so lucky with all these brothers?

* * *

Walking up to their room, Blake was sweaty from a session with the weights at the gym as he tried to work off his emotional cocktail full of frustration, anger, and a stabbing pinch of heartache. It didn't work. His thoughts were full of the growing chasm between him and Caly. He was trying to figure out what his next move would be. There was no way in hell he would give up on her. On them. He would keep fighting.

He hadn't seen Caly since their fight earlier and he could smell that she wasn't in their room. Entering the room, he walked straight to the bathroom to shower. He froze. There was a note taped to the bathroom mirror.

7:30 pm. Our spot.

He blew out a breath.

Fuck, he thought as fear and anger started to swell within him. *Am I too late?* No. He wasn't losing her. Not like this. Not ever.

Wet from the warm shower, he toweled off and pulled on his blue jeans and white T. He had no idea what he was about to walk into. But he refused to let Caly end it like this.

He walked out of their room and started to make his way to a secluded part of the castle. As far as both Caly and he knew, no else really ventured this way often. Shortly after they moved in, they both discovered a room tucked away with a cozy balcony that overlooked the lake. They used to sneak away to this room together and it would be like their little secret getaway. Sure, anyone could have followed their scent to find them but it kind of felt like when a child created a makeshift fort and as soon as they were inside, they were transported to another place.

His nose twitched as he turned the corner. But it was not only Caly's scent that he smelled.

Food?

His brow furrowed. Not wanting to waste time sifting through the scents and deciphering what exactly he was smelling, he pushed open the door and blinked. He was looking at a romantic indoor picnic scene. A very comfy and cozy indoor picnic. The candlelight danced across the pillows, blankets, and picnic basket. The balcony's French doors were wide open and the warm glow of the candlelight mingled with the silver luminescence of the moonlit night sky. His gaze landed on Caly's captivating stormy eyes and a nervous smile spread across her face. And just like when they first met, they silently stared into each other's eyes.

"Blake," Caly said, biting her lower lip and feeling a wave of emotion. "I'm sorry. God, I'm so sorry for everything. For what I said and how I've been acting. You were right. I was consumed by revenge, hate, and anger. Thank you for calling me out and being there even when I wasn't myself. And even when I lashed out at you. And even when I was pushing you away."

There was a pregnant pause and her throat grew thick with another wave of emotion.

"After Riordan canceled my session, I spent some time by

myself in the secret garden. It really put things into perspective. And I finally grieved for losing my parents, what felt like, all over again. Anyways, I really am sorry, Blake. And I hope that I haven't messed things up too badly between us… Can you forgive me?"

He stood there for a moment almost thinking he was imagining this. When he finally allowed himself to accept this as reality, he silently closed the distance between them, wrapped his arms around her, and held her close to his chest.

Tears began their downward descent along her cheeks.

"Caly, I will always forgive you. I love you."

It was the first time he said those words out loud to her. He had said it plenty of times to himself, just never out loud. He knew she was a flight risk with the "life mate for eternity" thing and he didn't want to push her away by declaring his love too soon. It finally felt like the right time so he didn't hesitate to speak the words of his heart and soul.

Caly stiffened for a second at those three words.

Stop being afraid of the future. Live in the present, she told herself.

"I… I love you too."

She looked up into those impossibly beautiful, golden eyes as they kissed, long and slow. When the kiss naturally ended, he leaned his forehead onto hers, closed his eyes, and breathed deeply. She brushed her lips across his once more before leaning her head on his chest. She heard his heartbeat that pumped love for her, just as hers did for him.

"Caly?"

"Yeah?"

"I have to ask." There was a brief pause. "What's the secret garden?"

Caly chortled. "Oh, it's a special place that I didn't even know was real until today. The first time I met Riordan, when this all started, was in this magical garden overlooking a lake. It was in a dream. It really was the first species experience I've had."

There was another moment of silence.

When Caly caught a whiff of the food, she asked, "Are you hungry?"

She got her response in the form of a growling kiss. Her laugh was husky.

"I meant for food." With a smile, she pointed to the picnic setting.

"Yes. But I already know what I want for dessert," he drawled, kissing and rubbing his scruff over her neck in just the way she liked. If they didn't move to the blanket now then they never would eat.

She bit his lower lip. "Deal."

"So, what's on the menu?" he asked, sniffing the air and settling onto the pillows.

"Your favorite. Italian." She beamed and started pulling out the food-warming containers from the picnic basket. "Bread, butter, spaghetti with meatballs, and gelato for dessert."

His lips curved at how well his female knew him.

"Can you pour the wine while I get the rest set up?" She smiled and stole another quick kiss while handing him the wine and glasses.

Thank you, Meri, she thought, seeing breath mints. She made a mental note to give Meri and Jax a huge hug each and make sure they knew that they were the best for helping her to pull this off on such short notice.

"I'm stuffed," Caly announced and patted her full belly.

"I could go for dessert," Blake drawled.

Her laugh was husky because she knew what he meant since they already polished off the gelato. She leaned over and pressed her lips to his.

"Balcony," she said, smiling against his lips.

She planned on walking out to the balcony but in the blink of an eye, Blake already had her laying on top of him under the night sky. They were both grinning and their kiss became this sort of smiling kiss.

Rolling over on top of her, he settled between her thighs. The slightest hint of her arousal teased his senses and that was all it took to drive him wild with need.

"Caly," he groaned out, pushing his hard length against her core through their clothes.

"Blake," she moaned and saw his eyes went wolf, glowing an inhuman shade of bright gold.

"Caly..." He spoke with a wondrous expression.

"What?" she asked with a slightly concerned breath.

"Your eyes. They're glowing." He stared at her beautiful gray eyes that were now glowing as if lit up by a lightning storm.

"So are yours," she teased playfully.

But she noticed his eyes were actually glowing a lighter shade of gold—a shade she had not yet seen before. And she felt it. Something deep inside of her. It was as if the heart-breaking space between them had not only healed closed but it was put back together by an unbreakable bond that made them stronger together.

On a more heartfelt note, she said, "I love you, Blake."

And her heart ached at those words; a deep ache of love.

"I love you, Caly."

He kissed her soft, full lips, long and slow, until the kiss naturally deepened. His deliciously dark and earthy mating scent wildly permeated the space around them as their tongues stroked one another with passion as if making up for lost time. He slid his hand up her shirt and cupped her breast through her bra. He needed skin. He lifted her shirt to expose her cupped breasts, on beautiful display by her black bra, as if in offering to him.

He growled.

She lifted the shirt up and slipped it easily over her head. As she worked on removing her bra, he got with the program and lost his shirt. Taking one of her nipples into his mouth, his hand caressed her neglected breast. Breaking the contact with his mouth, he gently grazed his teeth across her nipple before blowing a cool breath over it for added sensations. He kissed his way back to her lips and nipped playfully at them. She responded by gently biting his lower lip and tugging. She wrapped her arms around him and was sensually scratching his back in long, slow strokes. It was just the way he liked. His erection was bulging in his jeans and straining to get free.

"Blake," she said with a breathy moan. "I need you."

His low, deep growl was all she heard in response.

In a swift motion, he tugged her yoga pants off and did the same with his jeans and boxer briefs. He bent down and playfully kissed her sex through her wet panties.

"Blake," she pleaded.

Losing all patience, he used a claw to slice her panties right off of her body, careful not to leave a single scratch on her.

"You're so beautiful, Caly," he said, looking deep into her glowing gray eyes.

"You are too," she said with a slight curve of her lips.

He shot her a wicked smile and, without warning, began lapping up her sweet nectar.

She moaned and her head threw back into the pillows. He was licking and sucking and driving her wild.

"Blake. Oh god. I'm going to come."

A moment later, he felt her shatter on his lips. He slowed the rhythm and worked every last wave of pleasure out of her.

Caly reached down and brought his face to hers for a long, slow kiss. She could taste herself on his lips and it added to the eroticism of the moment. Pushing him onto his back, she gripped his length in her hands and he groaned. She licked his shaft from the base to the tip on a sinfully slow journey. He grabbed a fistful of her hair and she moaned, liking it when he slightly tugged at her hair. She repeated the motion with her tongue a couple of times before taking his sensitive tip into her mouth. She began sensually sucking and licking while working his shaft with her hands. His eyes closed and his head went back, drowning in pleasure.

"I want my cock in you, Caly," he growled out his desire.

Her core clenched in response and she crawled on top of him. She guided his hard length to her opening and slowly lowered. He groaned in pleasure at the tight wetness of her around him. He filled her completely and she gave her body a moment to adjust before grinding in a slow sensual rhythm. His hands were on her hips as they danced an erotically intimate duet.

"I want you from behind," he said in a rough voice, thick with need.

Seconds later, she was on all fours with her glistening sex bare for his viewing pleasure.

"Fuck, Caly," he groaned out, grabbed her hips, and slammed into her, balls deep.

"Blake," she moaned out, sliding her hand to her sensitive spot.

"That's so hot, Caly."

Skin was slapping and he could feel her tighten around him. She reached her hand back farther and played with his balls. He cursed out a pleasured groan. She slid her fingers back to her sex and he could feel her body preparing for a release just as he was.

"Come with me, Caly."

Erotic ecstasy claimed them on cresting wave and he spilled into her with wave after wave of pleasure. They both were breathing heavily as the pleasure continued to pulse through them. She laid flat on her stomach while he remained on top, semi-hard and still inside her.

Coming back to consciousness and not wanting to squish her, Blake repositioned himself so he was laying on his back with her pressed close to his chest as his arm draped around her. They both gazed up at the starry night sky, under the light of the full moon.

"Did you see that?" Caly asked excitedly, as the bright trail of a shooting star waned into midnight.

"Yeah." He kissed the top of her head.

"Make a wish," she said.

Blake chuckled. *I wish for us to be like this forever,* he thought.

I wish for us to have endless nights like this together, Caly thought.

"Done," he announced with a contented smile.

"What did you wish for?" she asked.

"Don't you know that I can't tell you or it won't come true?" he teased with that wolf grin of his.

"Oh, come on. That's not real."

"Well, you should ask Deacon about that sometime…"

"What do you mean?"

"Well, you know he's a steorrian."

"Yeah, but I thought his ability was with computers."

"It is but from what I hear, he has a special way with stargazing."

That would explain the telescope and starry night sky painting in his room, Caly thought.

"Okay, but what do you mean?"

"Like I said, maybe you can ask him sometime."

She laughed because she knew he was playing with her and he wasn't going to give away any more clues to this little game he started.

"Fine, wolf."

He chuckled and stole a kiss under the midnight sky that was colored with bursts of silver light that would forever remind him of his female.

Chapter 47

As soon as Caly entered the fitness room, Keena got up from her yoga mat and walked over to Caly to greet her. Caly was a little surprised to see Keena in a full-sleeved, tight, black, crop top with a slight turtleneck, wearing makeup. It looked good but she was just so used to seeing Keena au naturel and in her cute sports bras during their sessions, especially since their yoga sessions were slightly heated. Caly may have even started to cop Keena's style and bought some of those cute sports bras for herself.

"Hey, Keena."

Just as with Aleia, Caly had been distant and not really a great friend lately. She didn't do anything specific but she knew the distance was palpable. So, she wanted to rectify that immediately.

"I'm sorry for being distant and a crappy friend lately."

"Water under the bridge." Keena smiled.

Being a mind healer, Keena understood the complicated inner workings of relationships, both external and internal, far better than most. She knew everyone was on their own unique healing path. In fact, it was this deep understanding that actually sometimes made her easy to take advantage of. Because, how could she not forgive someone who was just trying to navigate this thing called life? She knew that everyone made mistakes and figured it was how they healed through those mistakes that truly mattered.

Right? she thought, attempting to justify her painful past.

Keena thought about another apology she had received recently from Liam, her ex. Keena had received a hand-written letter and a single yellow rose. In the letter, he said he was seeing a mind healer, which was something she practically begged him to do at the end. He owned up to his faults and said that he never meant to hurt her. He knew he messed up and he didn't expect her to forgive him. But he wanted her to know that he was sorry and that he would always regret how he treated her toward the end. He said he would always love her and that she would forever be the one that got away. He didn't ask for her forgiveness, a response, or even to get back together. It was him trying to make amends and bring closure to a terrible ending of what was a fairy-tale beginning. She loved Liam and she thought that some part of her might always have love for that male.

One week after receiving the letter, Keena couldn't stop thinking about Liam and she reached out to him. They started talking just as friends but their feelings for one another were so deep and strong that it quickly transitioned into dating once more. And, it was going so well... until it wasn't. It was just like it was in the beginning when they first met. Actually, it was even better than she could have ever imagined. She saw and witnessed the changes in him. Then, it took a sudden sharp turn and she found herself on a familiar dark street on memory lane that she swore she would never go down ever again. Yet, there she was.

"Thanks for being so understanding and patient with me lately." Caly hugged Keena.

"Of course. What are friends for?" Keena hugged her back, allowing the friendly embrace to anchor her to the present and away from her thoughts of Liam. "Okay, ready to get started?"

"Yes, *please*," Caly playfully begged, totally craving one of Keena's magical yoga classes.

It had been three days since Caly's "consumed with revenge," Ice Queen fiasco. The first two days were her and Blake practically never getting out of bed. They flip-flopped between movies, conversation, and intimate moments between the sheets. Then, she decided to take an extra day to just chill and binge on Meri's cooking and one of her favorite romance novels. So, yeah, although the past three days had been nothing less than amazing, she really was looking forward to yoga with Keena. She had grown accustomed to their sessions and her mind, body, and spirit craved the special moments on the mat.

"Breathe Caly... Breathe..." Keena gently guided Caly through the emotions that were swelling inside of her.

Caly was crying and her muscles were shaking in the stillness of the challenging pose.

"Remember, you can breathe through anything. Breathe through the emotion..."

Memories of Caly's parents burst to the forefront of her mind and the tsunami of emotions rose to a storm inside her. At the same instant, her muscles began shaking even more intensely and the stream of tears flowed stronger.

"Keep breathing, Caly. Let go... It's okay to let go..."

Caly let out a loud guttural cry. The lights flickered and, finally, the floodgates opened. The emotional storm burst free of the dam that she didn't even realize was previously containing them. She felt Keena's presence, strength, and supportive energy assisting in the moving of the emotions so they would not get "stuck" in the body as Keena taught her.

"Good, Caly. Good... Breathe and let go... Let go of what no longer serves you... It's time..."

The loving memories of her parents suddenly flashed to her nightmare of torture and The Ghost. She thought of what he did to her parents and screamed in tortured pain of the loss of them by his malicious hands. Several of the flickering lights abruptly burned out in a snap of sound. The screaming wave of pain, hurt, and heartache naturally subsided until the waves calmed. With her next exhale, she collapsed to her knees and closed her eyes, just breathing in stillness. Keena was right there with her and held her like the friend she was. They stayed like that, in a kneeling hug, heart to heart, for several moments. It was exactly what Caly needed.

"Thank you," Caly managed to choke out, releasing the hug.

"Of course. That was an amazing breakthrough, Caly. To witness your strength, courage, and growth is truly an honor."

"I wouldn't be here without you. Thank you, Keena."

"What are friends for, huh?"

They both smiled.

"As you know, I haven't been myself lately. I was consumed with revenge and rage. I was pushing away everyone that I love and care about." Caly paused. "The other day it all caught up to me and I... let's just say I am not proud of how I've been acting, especially that day. Then I... I cried for the first time since seeing my parents again. I found myself full circle, literally and figuratively. I was at this place where I had first seen Riordan, in my dreams. I didn't even know the place existed in real life and yet, there I was, grieving for my parents all over again. I was experiencing the hardest thing I ever had to go through all over again." There was a silent pause. "I realized how far I've come and how I have a new family and friends that truly care about me and I truly care about them. I thought I got past that and then, during our session, it's like it all came crashing back—the rage, the revenge, the sadness. It was so unexpected."

"You said you came full circle," Keena began. "And that's truly how healing works. It's nonlinear. It's cyclical. Each time you come full circle, there are deeper layers. Healing is a lifelong journey." And Keena couldn't help but take a dose of her own medicine with what she was going through as well.

"You know, that actually was the first thing you taught me. That healing is nonlinear. So, it's interesting that this has also come full circle."

They both smiled at that realization.

Caly blew out a final breath, nonverbally signifying that the session was done.

"So." She laughed a little as if that intense healing didn't just happen. "Do you want to stay for dinner? You know Meri always has plenty of food."

"Oh, I would love to but I have an errand to run and I'm kind of tired so I will probably get to bed early."

Ah, an errand to run. That must be why she is wearing makeup, Caly thought.

What Keena didn't say was that she was not in a place to see anyone right now because of her recent relationship status change… again. Keena only realized too late just how much of a mistake it was getting back together with Liam. Especially, when she barely had the strength to leave the first time.

After a late session with Caly recently, Keena ended up expressing her concerns about Caly to Aleia. It turned out that Aleia had the same concerns because she had also been observing Caly's concerning behavior around the castle. The conversation went on a lot longer than Keena expected and she ended up staying for a cup of tea. When she left, she saw that she had five missed calls and several texts from Liam demanding to know where she was. She immediately texted back and apologized for worrying him, stating that her phone was turned off as a standard protocol during her sessions. She explained that she had stayed late for a consultation with Aleia and that she had forgotten to turn her phone back on so she didn't see his messages until after.

As soon as she walked in the door of his place, she experienced a level of fear she had never experienced before. She had never seen that look in his eyes before, not even in the worst moments of their relationship. She tried to explain once more, in hopes of calming him down, but it was no use. He was infuriated with her and accused her of lying and cheating. He lost his temper and crossed a line he never had before. He smacked her hard across her face and, being a fire elemental, he left burn marks on her arms where he gripped her. Up until that point, the abuse she had experienced was verbal and somehow, she could always justify it and see his side of what she believed he was trying to express. She knew it just came out wrong. She was so ashamed and embarrassed. She also felt like a failure and a fraud. She was an intelligent female and an educated mind healer, after all.

So, how did this happen? How can you claim to help others when... look at what a mess you've gotten yourself into? No one forced you to reach out to Liam. No one forced you to get back together with him. That was all you.

So, no, Keena didn't lie to Caly. She did have somewhere to be. But she just didn't want anyone to know that she was going to see a healer to get rid of the marks on her body—and there was no way she was going to go to Aleia with this. The long sleeves and makeup were doing their cover-up job but she knew she would be so relieved after tonight's session with the healer when all of the marks would be gone.

Walking back to her and Blake's room after the session with Keena, Caly furrowed her brow when she noticed a sign taped to their door.

Don't come in or you'll ruin the surprise.

Okay, she thought, curious what her wolf was cooking up. *Good thing there's a shower in my room and I keep extra clothes in the closet too.* Overhearing the males and the TV in Blake's male cave, she decided to casually stop by after she had showered and changed. She wanted to see if she could squeeze out any of the details for the surprise. And she knew the twins would be her best bet for that. She opened the door and blinked in surprise.

Frozen. Everywhere. Like *Frozen* as in the Disney movie. As if Snow Queen Elsa had a tantrum in her room. The lights in her room were replaced with blue bulbs which gave it a snowy glow. There were fake icicles hanging from the ceiling, filling the entire room. The floor was completely covered in ice blue satin. The bedsheets were switched out to the same ice blue satin, with a stuffed Olaf the snowman plush toy in the middle of her bed... No. Wait. That wasn't a stuffed Olaf, it was Felix dressed up as Olaf. Right next to Olaf—er, Felix—was even a Snow Queen Elsa costume laying on the bed. And, to top it all off, there were ice castle-themed backdrops on each of the walls, making it feel like she was standing inside of Elsa's ice castle.

"Oh. My. God..."

On the heels of her disbelief, a boom of laughter sounded out behind her and she jumped. all of the males were suddenly behind her, dying of laughter. Even Riordan, Aleia, and Jax were there too.

Caly burst out laughing.

"Oh Ice Queen Caly, hopefully, this pleases you," Rhyland teased.

"Ice Queen Caly, you have the frostiest glare in the kingdom. It even silenced Nico," Rhyker tacked on.

Suddenly, her TV turned on to Snow Queen Elsa singing "Let It Go" from the movie *Frozen*.

"Oh my god! Is that... surround sound?!"

Deacon's smile widened. "I hope it pleases you, Ice Queen."

Caly started laughing so hard she cried and rolled onto the oversized, blue bean bag chair. Okay, so she liked the bean bag chair. Maybe she would keep it. When her laughter finally subsided, a new song started playing.

Is that...?

It was "Castle" by Halsey.

"Oh my god!" she exclaimed, inducing a whole new round of crying laughter.

And she wasn't surprised at how they knew of the human pop culture references. She had learned it was somewhat of the norm for specians to make conscious strides to keep up with the modern times. Some specians, more than others, paid close attention to the human world, including vernacular, fashion, and current events, which sometimes led to a blending of both worlds. It was a practice that was adopted long ago, so their kind could blend in more easily when venturing across The Barrier and into the human world.

When her stomach started to cramp from laughing so hard, Caly tried to take slow breaths to stop the cramping laughter.

Blake scooped her up in his arms and kissed her. "Are you hungry, my Ice Queen? Your dinner awaits," he drawled with a wolfish grin, giving her another kiss. He set Caly's feet down on the ground and she walked over to a dressed-up Felix.

"I don't know how you got him to go along with this…" Caly said, scooping up Felix who was still impersonating the *Frozen* snowman character.

"Meow." It was as if Felix said, *"Mom, can you take this off now?"* He looked like a kid on picture day, grumpily accepting their fate for an unacceptable outfit.

Chortling, Caly freed Felix of the costume and kissed his furry nose. As he began purring up a storm, they all made their way to the kitchen, with Jax in the lead.

"I still can't believe what just happened. Or where you even found an Olaf cat costume? I mean, who's idea was it?"

"Rhyland started it off by wanting to get you the Queen Elsa costume," Rhyker started. "And then everyone pitched in ideas and it snowballed from there. Pun intended," Rhyland finished.

The twins were sporting their matching grins.

"This is hands down one of the best moments of my life… and… I love you all."

A few overly emphasized "ahhhs" echoed out in the male's pretend "female" voices.

"My Snow Queen, with declarations like that, if you're not careful, you might lose your ice crown," Rhyland said with a wink, pulling her in for a side hug.

The contact was too much for Felix, who was probably still disgruntled with Rhyland for putting that costume on him, and he gracefully leaped out of Caly's arms.

They all marched along to the kitchen, including Felix. Because, costume or not, that cat never missed a party and he always knew when it was dinner time.

"You know what this reminded me of?" Caly said to the crew.

"That, Ice Queen or not, you are subject to our pack antics just like the rest of us?" Rhyland quipped.

Laughing, she said, "No. That we need to have more fun. Like, you know, we should all go out or something."

"I like where your mind's at," Rhyland agreed and offered, "Let's go to the local species bar to blow off some steam."

"Agreed," Rhyker added and fist-bumped his twin in approval of the idea.

"Yes, exactly! Who else is in?" Caly asked and looked around.

"I'm in," Blake said.

"Me too," Deacon followed up.

Nico nodded.

"Riordan, you have to come too," Caly said.

Riordan chuckled. "Alright."

"Aleia? Come on. You can't leave me alone with this bunch," Caly said with a grin. "We'll invite Keena too."

"Count me in," Aleia agreed.

"Yay! When?" Caly asked.

"Now?" Rhyland proposed, only half-joking.

"Not now," Caly laughed. "What about in a couple days... like Saturday?"

Caly received a round of agreeing head nods.

"Ah, shoot," Aleia said with a frown, looking at her calendar on her phone. "I'm busy Saturday." Aleia opened up the calendar appointment to see what it was. "Wait! Nevermind, I can reschedule this."

Aleia would be gone, all night, usually a couple of times per week. Everyone presumed it was for her standing VIP night patient, who wanted to keep things discreet. Little did everyone know the secret she was hiding.

Nico may have been keeping an eye on her, from a distance, of course. He didn't know why it mattered but he couldn't seem to let it go. To Nico, Aleia's VIP patient scenario just didn't add up. Why did her patient only have night visits?

And why did they need so many healings every week? Nico figured no one else questioned her because of healer-patient confidentiality and they appreciated her secrecy with them. But Nico just couldn't let it go with this female for some reason. He knew she was hiding something. And, yeah, he should know when one had a secret to hide because he had a few secrets tucked away in his deep, dark closet too.

"Oh my god. I'm so excited! My first species bar!" Caly did a little celebratory happy dance. Again, she wasn't normally so excited about being in a crowd of people but these weren't people, they were specians. It would be her first experience in a social setting with specians and she was curious to see how it compared to humans. And, yeah, of course, she was mainly excited to go out with her crew and have some fun.

"I got twenty on Blake knocking out some dumb male," Rhyland quipped.

"Thirty that male will be you," Rhyker retorted.

"Fifty on Caly doing the honors," Nico added a rare verbal comment and it resulted in another round of laughter.

"I would have to agree with Nico. My female is more than capable of handling herself." Blake pulled her in for a side hug. But everyone knew that Blake would be watching her. They almost felt sorry for the poor bastard who so much as breathed wrong around Caly. And, yeah, that bastard would be answering to more than just Blake.

Chapter 48

Keena walked into Spiked, the local species bar, and was confronted with a sea of specians dressed in casual yet sexy attire, grinding to the heavy beat of the speakers. She headed straight for the back since Aleia and Caly had previously texted her and told her that was where their table was. Keena's heart started to beat faster when she walked by a male at the bar. There was something about him and she just couldn't take her eyes off of him.

God, what is wrong with me? Like a bad boy is really what I need right now. Well, like any of that even matters. Just look at how your situation with the opposite sex has been going. Actually, no. Don't think of that. Remember, tonight is about having fun and hanging out with Aleia and Caly.

She may have stolen one more glance at Mr. Tall Dark and Handsome with the tattoos once more as she walked by.

Yeah, probably better if you just let that be. Besides, like you're even in a place for any of that right now.

"One bottle of *sex magic* and two pitchers of *rugged* for our table in the back," Rhyker ordered from the male bartender and pointed to their table in the VIP section. He inwardly smirked. Since the whole point of the night was to blow off some steam, he was just going to help that along a little with the *sex magic*. His nose twitched suddenly at what seemed like a faintly familiar smell but he couldn't quite place it. He turned his head but didn't see anything other than a sea of specians, all sexed-up on their spiked drinks. He did another glance and sniffed but there were too many sweaty bodies. He concluded it was nothing, but both his and his cat's curiosity were caught by something.

"Trixie, the waitress, will bring it to your table. She'll also be your server for the rest of the night," the male bartender said.

Rhyker nodded and headed back toward their table.

"Keena! Yay! I'm so glad you're here!" Caly greeted Keena with an enthusiastic hug.

"Hey, Kee," Aleia followed up with her own greeting and hug.

"Keena, this is Deacon, Rhyland, Blake, Riordan, and Nico." There was a round of male nods while Caly smiled. "Everyone, this is Keena."

"Hey, everyone." Keena smiled and laughed a little.

Of course, everyone knew of Keena but this was the first time they actually met her because whenever she was at the fortress, they knew it was their "female time" and Caly made it very clear that no males were allowed.

"Rhyker just left to get us all drinks. We decided to get a bottle and a couple pitchers, so we got you covered, Kee," Aleia said.

"Thanks."

"How come I didn't know about the dress code?" Rhyland interjected with a feline grin.

Aleia, Caly, and Keena had a group text going earlier

that day to figure out what each other was wearing. Caly initiated the group text because she wasn't sure what was normal to wear for species bars. It turned out, just like human establishments, the attire was really just dependent on the venue. There were upscale lounges, where everyone was dressed "sexy classy." Then there were relaxed bars with dance floors, where everyone was dressed "casual sexy." Then there were more racy and theme-based clubs, some of which were super elite, where you needed a membership to even get in. For those? The dress code was really just dependent upon what their club scene was all about. The common underlying thread for all bars though? Sexy. Just like with human clubs and bars, it was about getting dressed up in sexy clothes, getting tipsy, and then flirting, dancing or, in some cases, grinding on someone, or many someones, you found attractive. Since they were going to a casual bar, they all decided on dark-wash, skinny jeans and black shirts. Why not match and have some fun? Caly paired her jeans with a black, low-cut tank top and comfy, black heels. Aleia was wearing a loose-fitting, long-sleeve, black shirt and stylish, gray combat boots with black soles and laces. Keena was sporting her tight, scoop-neck, black T-shirt and cute peep-toe, black wedges.

"Next time we're wearing dresses, so I'll be sure to have Jax order one for you, Rhy," Caly retorted playfully.

When the round of chuckles died down, Keena pointed with her hand toward the back corner of the bar. "I'm going to the bathroom."

"Good idea. I'll come with," Caly said.

"Me too," Aleia added.

Sitting down at the table, Rhyker asked, "Where are the females?" And his nose twitched once more. He casually looked around and sniffed.

Nothing. No, wait...

He thought there was something but it was in some part of his distant mind and he couldn't quite place it. Whatever it was, it definitely caught his cat's attention too. He sniffed again and, when he didn't get anything further, he internally shrugged it off.

"Keena arrived and they went to the bathroom," Rhyland answered. "Why they all congregate in the bathroom may forever be a mystery to the male species."

Two waitresses walked up to their table, holding their drink order.

"Hi, I'm Trixie. I'll be your waitress tonight." Trixie's dusky skin was highlighted with her very heavy eye makeup and red lipstick. She was wearing a revealing, red corset tube top which showed off her perky breasts and slim waist.

"Thanks, Kat," Trixie said to the other waitress who set the bottle of *sex magic* and glasses on the table.

Kat was also rocking the smoky eye look, which contrasted against her light skin and light brown hair. Also similar to Trixie, Kat was showing a lot of skin in her revealing, red, crop top tank and low-rise, skin-tight, black jeans.

Riordan nodded at the waitresses and tipped them generously.

"Thanks, handsome," Trixie all but purred in Riordan's ear while Kat was on the other side of Riordan.

"We'll let you know if we need anything else," Riordan politely dismissed the females to their visible disappointment.

"Anything you say, handsome," Trixie said in a silken voice, full of promises, before they both left.

"Oh, come on Riordan." Rhyland poured both himself and his brother a glass of *rugged*, a brand of species beer. "When was the last time you had some fun with the females?"

Rhyker added, "And my money is on Trixie being a fire elemental..." He took a pull of his drink. "And that can be *hot* in bed... if you know what I mean." He winked and then looked at the waitresses who were now being super flirty with the other table they were servicing.

"When you get to be my age then we can have this conversation," Riordan said and took a sip of his drink.

"And how old would that be?" Rhyland pounced at the chance for the opportunity to conclude the bet they had ongoing about Riordan's age.

Riordan's lips twitched and they all knew that was all they were getting out of him.

"Boys." Rhyker tipped his glass in salute. "It's time to hunt." With that, he was off. He was going to stop by the bathroom, take a leak, and then go out on the hunt for a female. And maybe sniff out what that scent was that he couldn't quite place.

Caly, Aleia, and Keena walked up to the table and Rhyland poured them all a drink. Almost instantaneously after swallowing, Caly felt warmth spread through her like wildfire. She was suddenly in the mood to let loose and dance. Maybe she could even talk Blake into dancing with her and perhaps even sneak off to the bathroo—

Wait. What?! Did I just think about having sex with Blake in the bathroom?

"What is this?" she asked, glancing suspiciously at the glass in her hand as if it was suddenly on trial.

"You must be a lightweight." Rhyland winked and tipped his glass in salute. "That's a drink of *sex magic*. Welcome to the world of species, Caly."

"*Sex magic?*" Caly asked with a raised eyebrow.

"Species specialty drinks are spiked with emotions," Aleia clarified.

"Spiked with *emotions*?" Then Caly remembered that tea by Dr. Amare, Species Spellbound, and how it was *"enhanced with the purest potent love allowable on the market."*

Oh my god. That's right.

"Wait, are witches real?" Caly didn't remember reading about witches in any of the species books but maybe that was because they had a different name.

There was a round of chuckling.

"No. Not unless you call myself or Aleia a witch," Keena said. "Humans' imaginations really took our healing abilities to a crazy extreme. I mean, how in the hell did we become long-wart-nosed, old hags with cackling laughs who ride brooms? Brooms for heaven's sake!"

There were a few laughs at that remark.

Keena continued, "Anyways, Caly, mind healers have the ability to infuse emotions into certain things including drinks. A lot of mind healers that don't necessarily have strong abilities or a desire to pursue healer training often become bartenders. And I knew some of my fellow classmates who would bartend at night as a side hustle to help pay for training too. Anyways, part of our specialty lies in emotions."

"I knew that mind healers' specialties were emotions but I had no idea about the whole infusion thing." Caly looked at her drink. "Crazy..."

"It doesn't last long in inanimate objects, hence the temporary drink buzz. And there are legal limitations," Keena added.

"Makes sense. I mean, I can also see how addicting that probably could be too, right?"

"Exactly." Keena nodded, taking a drink. "Enough with that, let's take advantage of this nice buzz and have some fun, shall we?" She smiled and looked at the dance floor.

"Agreed," Aleia chimed in.

"I'm so down!" Caly exclaimed in a sing-song voice.

As they walked away, Caly looked over her shoulder at Blake. He did an obvious up and down with his eyes, stopping on her backside before giving her a wicked smile. She bit her lip in sinful consideration. She really wanted to take a sudden detour to the bathroom with her male because if he didn't look hot as hell sitting there checking her out.

"Come on Caly!" Aleia tugged at her arm and all three of them laughed. "You can spend time with him later. Now, it's time for us to cause a little sensual chaos." Aleia caught a glimpse of Nico looking directly at her for a split second before she turned around.

They made their way to the middle of the dance floor and started dancing. Everything really did seem very similar to the human bars Caly had been to. Loud music and lots of bodies dancing in groups. Some of which were the small female groups, like they were in, but the others were just sweaty bodies grinding up on one another all sexed-up on what Caly presumed was *sex magic*.

And, wow, Caly thought, looking at Keena.

Keena had some serious dance moves of her own. She was an undercover sensual goddess. Of course, that should have been expected because Caly knew that Keena was into yoga and dance in her spare time. But Caly didn't realize just how much rhythm or how many moves Keena had.

And then there was Aleia who was surprisingly confident and feminine in her own way. Caly swore she just looked at a male and, as if he was at her beck and call, the male walked over and danced with her for a song. When the song was over and she was done with the male, she just gave him a smile and said, "Thanks for the dance" in a way that made it clear that was all there was going to be. The one-dance male left with a bit of pleading look at Aleia, wanting it to go further.

"Wow. That's impressive." Caly was grinning at Aleia's skills.

"What?" Aleia answered casually.

"What do you mean, 'what'? Umm your confidence with that male! I *never* would have been able to do what you just did. Hell, I never would have even been able to approach someone like Blake." Caly looked over at her male and, yup, even through the crowd he was still watching her. She smiled at him and he gave her one of his wolfish smiles, full of promises. She noticed Nico was also watching them with blackened eyes.

Okay, he can calm down on the big brother routine. It's not like I was the one dancing with another male, Caly thought.

Aleia laughed. "Oh, that?" She signaled with her eyes to the male who was still looking puppy-dog-eyed at her, hoping she would call him back over.

"Yeah, *that!*"

Their little trio laughed.

"Oh, come on, that wasn't hard. He was practically begging for it and he's a good looking male. So, why not? I mean, we gotta do something with this buzz we got going on," Aleia joked, casually shrugging her shoulders.

"Maybe I will try that then," Keena said half-joking.

"Yes! You so deserve it!" Aleia took a sip of her drink and was glad that Keena was getting back out there. She knew Keena got back together with Liam and that it ended almost as abruptly as it began. Keena didn't give her any details but she just said it was over for good. Again, Aleia didn't know the details but she got a strong sense of resolution from Keena. And Aleia was glad because she didn't like that male. She just got a bad vibe about him and she didn't like how Keena wasn't really herself when she was with him.

"Do it!" Caly coaxed playfully.

"I'll think about it," Keena said with a smile and took another sip of her drink.

They danced and laughed for several songs until eventually, Caly said, "I have to pee."

"Yeah, me too," Aleia agreed.

"I'm good. You two go." Keena took the last sip of her drink and smiled.

"Are you sure?" Caly asked.

"Go!" Keena spoke loudly over the thumping music. "I'm having fun dancing. I'll be fine! Besides, your male and his crew have been keeping an eye on us. Nothing will happen to me."

Caly and Aleia looked over at their table and, yup, they weren't even trying to hide their watchful eyes on them.

"Are you sure, Kee?" Aleia asked one more time.

"Yeah, I don't want to leave you alone. It seems like it goes against the female, 'friend rules' or something," Caly joked with a smile.

"Female friend rules?" Keena chuckled and Aleia coughed on her drink from laughing.

"Yeah, like the unwritten girl code. Oh please, you both know what I mean," Caly said with a roll of her eyes. "And now we're getting off-topic and I still have to pee. And if the lines for the bathroom are anything like the human bars, then my bladder may explode by the time I actually get to a stall."

"Unfortunately, it sounds like the bathroom dilemma extends to both worlds," Aleia said on a consolatory note.

"It's not breaking any girl code," Keena laughed. "I'll be fine. Don't worry about me. I just want to dance a little longer."

"Okay," Caly agreed but with a little hesitation.

"Go. Before your bladder explodes," Keena teased.

"I want to stop by our table really quick first," Caly said to Aleia as they made their way off the dance floor.

Aleia nodded.

"So, how was it?" Rhyland waggled his brows.

Caly laughed as she sidled up next to Blake. He put an arm around her and pulled her close.

"Fun! We're taking a quick bathroom break." She looked over at Keena who was dancing and enjoying herself. "Keena wanted to continue dancing though. Can you guys keep an eye on her?"

They all gave her this look that said, *"Female, like we would let anything happen to any of you?"*

Both Aleia and Caly laughed in response.

"Thank you," Caly said in Blake's ear and stole a quick kiss.

"When do I get to dance with my sexy Ice Queen?" he drawled and playfully grabbed her ass.

"Whenever you want," she promised.

Without warning, he spun her around so her back was pressed against his front and began swaying their bodies in a sensual rhythm.

"Blake," Caly giggled in a pathetic protest as his arms snaked around her front side and he kissed her neck.

"Save it for the dance floor you two," Rhyland said with a smirk.

"When you get back from the bathroom, I'm taking you out on that dance floor and we're finishing what we started," Blake promised in her ear before releasing her.

"Count on it, wolf," she teased, biting his lower lip in that way she knew he liked. He growled and she saw his eyes started to glow with desire. She knew those eyes were fixed on her as she walked away to the bathroom with Aleia.

Rhyker halted and inhaled. Yup. There was that same subtle scent that he kept picking up on and this time, it was strong. He followed the scent trail as if it was a homing beacon. Turning his body around toward the dance floor, his gaze landed on a beautiful female dancing. He knew it was her scent. Both he and his jaguar were practically mesmerized by the way the female moved. Without hesitation, he made his way toward her.

Keena's heart fluttered.

Omg. It's that male, she thought, catching a glimpse of Mr. Tall Dark and Handsome with the tattoos at the bar. *Stop. He looks like the bad boy type and you don't need any bad boy anything right now. Remember what you just survived.*

She looked at the male again.

Okay, not only is it unfair of me to judge someone by their looks but also, I'm not going to live my life afraid. Besides, I can do what Aleia did. I am here to let off steam and have fun. That's all. Just like Aleia. One dance and then send him away.

Attempting to channel her best friend Aleia, she silently looked at the male and invited him in with her body language. To make sure her non-verbal invite was clear, she also took a step closer to him and smiled. He closed the remaining distance and their bodies were pressed close together as they danced.

There was something about the combination of her scent and the way her body moved on Rhyker's that had both his and his jaguar's complete attention. His hands were on her hips and they guided him as they danced in a sensual rhythm to the heavy beat of the song. She leaned into him even closer and her body fit snug against his. The song was over too soon but they continued dancing through the next song. They both didn't want the second song to end, thereby breaking the connection, but it eventually did.

"Can I buy you a drink?" Rhyker asked.

Keena bit her lower lip. *This isn't a part of the Aleia "one-dance plan." Not like dancing with him for more than one song was a part of that plan either.* But she couldn't seem to stop herself. *One drink. One.*

"Sure." She smiled.

They walked off the dance floor and made their way to the bar.

"What are you drinking?" he asked.

"Sex magic."

Do you really need another one of those, Keena?

"Two sex magics," Rhyker said to the male bartender.

Okay. So, he is having one too.

A moment later, the bartender came back with the drinks.

"Wanna go outside and cool off?" Rhyker proposed.

"Sounds good."

Cooling off did sound like a good idea and maybe the cool air would knock some sense into her. She wasn't usually one to go off with a male at a bar. Okay, she wasn't usually one to be at a bar, period.

One drink.

Making their way through the crowd, they walked outside on the patio. It appeared that they weren't the only ones with the idea to cool off outside, seeming as there were other smaller groups scattered around. A quick scan of the patio revealed a nice quiet spot in the corner. With his head, he indicated to the corner spot and she followed behind him.

"So, do you come out here a lot?" she asked, casually trying to stir up conversation and took a sip of her drink.

"I've been here a couple times with my brother," he said, also taking a sip. "You?"

"I've been a couple times, like a long time ago... It's

actually been a while since I've been out. My girlfriends invited me."

"Does this bother you?" he asked, pulling out a hand-rolled indie.

Of course he smokes. Because how else could he be hotter?

"No, I don't mind."

He nodded and held it in between his lips to light it.

Keena may have lingered a little too long on his lips with her gaze. She hadn't kissed another male since Liam.

One drink Keena and then say goodbye and go find Caly and Aleia.

But then, her gaze went from his piercing blue eyes to his lips once more. She didn't mean to but she bit her lower lip in response. Holy hell this male was so hot and she wanted to know what kissing his lips would be like.

Screw it. You played it safe with Liam and look how that turned out? How about you stop playing it safe and start just having fun and loosen up? Just kiss the male and have some fun making out for a minute and then go on your merry way.

She took a breath and when he blew out a puff of smoke she made a confident move out of Aleia's playbook and leaned in for a kiss.

Kissing. This beautiful female was kissing him. Rhyker quickly got with the program and kissed her back. Her lips were so soft and he wanted more but he kept it light and playful. But with his free hand, he pulled her close to his body. Just before he was going to deepen the kiss, she broke the connection and took a step back.

Okay. Well if that wasn't going down as one of the hottest kisses of your life, Keena thought, a little breathless. Which was why she had to stop it. Because instead of kissing him and then checking that off of her girls-night, post-break-up list, she was feeling more drawn to this male. Which was dangerous. She just got out of a fucked up situation and she didn't need to add to that pile of emotions with regret tomorrow.

"I... uh... I never do this," she confessed with a shy smile.

"I don't mind." He gave her a playful smirk.

She laughed a little. "I mean, I don't even know your name."

"Rhyker." He took a drag and blew out blue-gray smoke.

Rhyker?! As in... she thought. Swallowing, she set her drink on the table. Her look must've given her thoughts away because he looked at her and furrowed his brows.

"I'm... Keena. I'm here with Caly and Aleia."

"Unexpected," he chuckled. "But that doesn't change anything for me. You intrigue me, Keena." He took a sip of his drink and she blushed.

You intrigue me too, she thought as warning bells went off in her brain. Apparently, the drink went straight to her head because she was ignoring those signals. She looked at his lips once more and bit her lower lip. He caught the motion and set both his drink and hand-rolled down. This time, he went in for the kiss. It was round two of the hottest kiss of her life. His hands were on her waist and hers around his neck. Again, with the warning bells. This time, she heeded their advice and pulled back.

"This really isn't a good idea," she said, picking up her drink to give her mouth something to do before it somehow ended up back on his.

"You're probably right... but I don't seem to care about good ideas all of a sudden," Rhyker teased.

She laughed.

"So." He drew out the word with a smirk. "You were saying you never do this. And what is this exactly?" he continued with the teasing.

Chuckling, she took a sip of her drink. "Make out with strangers who end up being like a brother to my friend." She offered a flirty smile.

"We have that in common. I've never made out with my friend's brother either."

"You're funny, Rhyker," she said with a laugh.

"Well, you are talking with one of the class clowns."

"Ahh, let me guess, your brother is the other class clown?" He winked and took a sip of his drink.

"Maybe we should get back to the group," she said, despite that being the last thing she wanted to do. Then again, that also meant it probably was the best idea because this was going to get sticky fast if they stayed out here alone any longer.

"Yeah, probably should…" he drew out that last word and gave her a look full of feline mischief in his eyes that said he clearly had other things on his mind.

She laughed and then said, "Let's just forget about our little rendezvous and get back to the group."

Yeah, like you can forget about that kiss, she thought, stealing one last look at his lips and piercing blue eyes. And, damn, he blew out another sexy cloud of smoke.

He nodded but had no intention to let this female go at all. *Let the hunt begin.*

Walking out of the bar, the males broke off from the females to get their rides situated. They were going to call Ethan, the male castellan who dropped them off and insisted that they call him when they were ready for a pickup.

"So," Rhyland teased out the word and cut into the silence as soon as he knew the females were out of earshot.

There was an immediate round of male chuckles in response.

"Keena," Rhyland added, slugging his brother in the

arm. "This should be fun to watch."

Rhyker shot a side glare at his brother.

"What? Like we didn't see you two canoodling on the dance floor and then sneak away?" Rhyland was all too cheery with his needling.

"Canoodling? What in the actual fuck kind of a word is that?" Rhyker bit out, inspiring another chorus of deep chuckles.

"Don't make it awkward for Caly. That's her friend," Blake cut in on a more serious note.

"Always thinking about your female, Blake... just like Rhyker over here. Hey, I have an idea. Maybe you should take one of her yoga classes so you have an excuse to ogle her for an hour. In fact, I would pay money to see that." Rhyland couldn't help but continue the playful roasting of his brother.

"Fuck you." Rhyker ended the conversation, secretly thinking that actually wasn't such a bad idea.

Sparing a quick look over at the group of their crew's three females in the short distance, Rhyker sharpened his hearing.

"Yeah, you're right too. But just jumping the first male that I find sexy as hell is not a good idea. No matter how hot and irresistible his blue eyes and bad boy looks are..."

Sexy as hell? Hot? Irresistible? Rhyker was suddenly all ears but kept his gaze focused on the males and smirked to himself. Yeah, the hunt was so on and this female didn't even know it.

"Rhyker! Earth to fucking Rhyker," Rhyland broke his brother's former concentration on Keena's conversation. "As I was saying before, you did your eavesdropping thing. And don't think I don't know that's what you were doing because we've only known each other our whole lives."

"Real subtle." Nico sliced his joke into the conversation

and punched Rhyker in the shoulder.

All of the males laughed.

"So..." Aleia started and gave Keena a mischievous look.

"What?" Keena asked innocently.

"Oh don't what me."

"Yeah, you know exactly what we're talking about," Caly chimed in.

They were all a little tipsy and a little giggly. All three of them looked over at the males who were far enough away, getting the rides sorted out, where they could have this conversation quietly.

"Like we didn't see Rhyker staring at you all night," Caly noted with a knowing curve of her lips.

"Was he? I didn't notice..." Keena smiled a little, trying to play it off.

"Oh, please, Kee. And like we didn't notice you side glancing at him too," Aleia added with the same expression that Caly had plastered on her face.

"Great... was it really that obvious?" Keena sighed.

"Maybe..." Caly said with a wicked smile.

"Yeah, it really was, Kee," Aleia added. "So, what's wrong with that? He's a good male and clearly interested in you as well."

Keena let out a breath. "I just need some time alone for now... and besides, he's like a brother to you." She looked at Caly. "Isn't that weird? And what if it doesn't work out? Then that can get complicated and super messy really fast."

"Okay, first of all. No, it isn't weird," Caly said.

"And," Aleia interjected. "Who said it has to get all complicated and weird? I have successfully had fun with males and it didn't get weird or complicated after the fun time was over."

"Okay, but that's you, Aleia. I don't work that way and

you know it," Keena pointed out.

"Yeah, you're right. But there's no harm in flirting a little," Aleia responded.

"Yeah, you're right too. But just jumping the first male that I find sexy as hell is not a good idea. No matter how hot and irresistible his blue eyes and bad boy looks are."

Caly and Aleia shot playful smiles at her. Then they all looked over at the group of males.

Keena saw that Rhyker wasn't looking at her but had a satisfied, smug look on his face. She wondered what it was the males were talking about exactly. "I mean, that alone should be enough for me to not make the same mistake again."

Because that was how it began with Liam. She found him really attractive. Except, Liam wasn't anything like the bad boy exterior Rhyker had going on. Liam was refined in his expensive taste and style.

"Okay, but Kee, he is *not* Liam and you know it. Hell, we *know* that. Rhyker is a good male," Aleia made her point clear.

"You're right. He isn't Liam." Keena blew out a breath. "Okay, can we not talk about this right now?" Keena knew that even though they weren't going to talk about it, she damn well was going to be thinking about it.

"Yes, of course. Sorry. I don't know why I pushed. I guess, I just want to see you happy and with someone who treats you like the female you are." Little did Aleia know just how much her statement went straight to the fresh, gaping wound in Keena's heart.

"Thanks, Aleia. I know. I want that too. But it's too soon and I need to heal."

"I know." Aleia let out a breath and hugged Keena.

"But it doesn't hurt to look," Caly said with a playful smile.

And they all giggled as they looked over at the males once more. Caly's eyes met Blake's. Keena's eyes met Rhyker's. And Aleia's eyes met Nico's.

No, it certainly doesn't hurt to look... even if it won't ever work out, Aleia thought to herself.

Chapter 49

The crew was lounging in Blake's male cave, and Caly spoke over the noise of the sports game on the TV.

"Am I the only one who feels like it's too quiet?"

"Tiffany, turn up the vol—"

"No, that's not what I meant." Caly cut Rhyland off and laughed a little. "I mean, with... *Barker.*"

Low male growls filled the room as a loud crack of a pool ball slammed home into a side pocket. Three darts sliced through the air out of Nico's hand like bullets. Blake pulled Caly in for a side hug and Deacon lowered the volume on the TV anyway.

"Like what?" she continued, "We're just supposed to wait and hope we get a lead from The Whisper or Riordan? I mean, that could be months or even years, right?" She paused before continuing. "And what? I'm just supposed to go on my merry way and live my life as if this isn't hanging over my head?" Caly let out a frustrated breath. "Sorry. I don't mean to be Debbie Downer. And, no, I'm not turning into the evil Ice Queen again. I just... I don't know..."

Blake pulled her in even closer to his chest.

"I know. Our world runs on different timelines than you're used to. And, you're right, some cases can go on for years. Speaking of..." Blake turned his gaze to the rest of the group. "SILE reached out with another case. Nico and D, this one's yours with the twins as back up."

Nico and Deacon nodded.

"Caly, you know we won't stop until we find him." Blake thought it was better that he didn't say, *I won't stop until my fangs rip out his throat.* "Focus on you and what's in your control for now."

She knew Blake was right. She still couldn't really understand the whole "potentially live forever" thing. Let alone how that rippled out into every area of her life. Besides, she did have a lot to focus on and be grateful for. And she had never really been happier.

I mean, I can't walk through life and just keep waiting for the other shoe to drop because that's no way to live life. Especially since that could be decades and decades of life wasted on the what if's. So, yeah, we'll keep searching but we'll also keep on living. Like that night out two weekends ago was fun, so maybe I'll propose a second round.

Caly thought about how she had another one of those weird dreams with her name being called in the fog. She knew it was just that dream that had her on edge.

"Hey, Rhy. I know our session isn't until later but would you mind if we pushed it up?" Caly asked.

"Not at all," Rhyland answered and stretched out on the couch in a way that reminded her of Felix after he would take a catnap.

Speaking of which, she looked over at her midnight fur-baby in the exact same position as Rhyland but he was located in a patch of sunlight that was shining through the sliding glass door.

"I'll come too," Rhyker added.

"Okay. Meet up in ten?" Caly asked.

"Roger that," the twins said in unison and sauntered out.

"Nico and D," Blake began. "I'll fill you in on the details of the case in a minute."

They nodded.

"Caly?" Blake asked in a low voice that was meant just for her. His eyes were fixed on hers because he knew there was something else she wasn't saying.

"Yeah?"

He just gave her the *look*.

She exhaled. "I had another one of those dreams. And I guess it just put me on edge. It feels like something is coming... but maybe I'm just paranoid? And if it is coming, then am I even ready? A few months of training versus Barker's, what, like centuries of experience?"

He cupped her face. "*We* are ready and will face this *together* and as a pack. Besides, you will have the element of surprise with your training and abilities." He paused and then vowed, "Together, Caly."

"Together," she echoed and pressed her lips to his.

Breathing hard, Caly blocked Rhyland's punch and kick maneuver with her magnetic force field ability. She quickly dropped and swung out her leg in an attempt to knock him over but he was too fast. She rolled while keeping her force field in place but she knew she couldn't keep it up forever. She had to find a way to incapacitate Rhyland before her force field ran out of gas. She was able to hold it for much longer than she ever had. It was kind of like a muscle, the more she practiced, the longer she could hold it and the stronger it became. And good thing she threw up her force field because she felt Rhyland's sneak attack blocked as she rolled.

"Point to Caly," Rhyker called out at the block.

"You're getting good, SoCal."

She could always count on the twins to not only be her

cheerleaders but also, to keep it real so she truly did get better.

"I'd like to see one of the stuck up aristocrats just try and lay a paw on you, so we can see you kick their asses," Rhyland quipped.

"Okay, that is if Blake isn't there first. Besides, I highly doubt we would ever be invited to a fancy-schmancy aristocrat party."

"You haven't heard?" Rhyland's feline ears perked up.

"Heard what?" Caly smiled suspiciously.

The twins were suddenly sporting their wide feline grins.

"Spill it," Caly demanded playfully.

"You have been cordially invited to the Gallagher gathering." Rhyland was speaking in a prissy English accent. "It's only the party of the season and only someone who is someone is invited."

Laughing, Caly managed to get out, "Okay, but why am I invited?"

"You, my dear Calypso Knight, are now a part of the Knight bloodline."

"Cut it out with that accent. I can't take you seriously." She laughed and looked at Rhyker. "Is he just messing with me?"

"'fraid not, Ms. Knight." Now Rhyker spoke in an English accent.

"Oh god. Not you too." She laughed and knew they were having fun playing with her.

"Actually, yes. Us too. In fact, we've all been invited, Caly Girl," Rhyland said.

"Enough with the accents. I can't take you both seriously right now." She smiled as she took a sip from her water bottle. "So, have we really been invited to some fancy party or not?"

"Yup," the twins replied in unison, dropping the English accent.

"When is this party?"

"One month," Rhyker answered.

"And when was I going to be told about this party?"

"You just were," Rhyland said with a grin.

Caly jokingly rolled her eyes. "Is The Order usually invited to these kinds of things?"

She knew they worked high profile VIP cases, sometimes directly for the aristocrats themselves. So it would make sense that The Order would be invited to the elite social gatherings. The Order represented status and power without even trying and because Caly heard so much about aristocrats valuing those two things so much, she assumed the aristocrats would leap at an opportunity to put them on display. Who better to have on your side in your social chess match than The Order?

"Yup," the twins said at the same time.

"But why do I get the feeling that you all never go?"

"Your feeling would be correct," Rhyland answered.

"Then why...?"

"Because like hell if we would miss your big debut." Rhyker playfully elbowed her shoulder.

"And like I said, we have bets on if you or Blake will be kicking some aristocrat ass that night." Rhyland grinned and fist-bumped his twin.

"Oh god. Let me be clear: there will be *no* aristocrat ass kicking. Even if I was a more violent female, I couldn't do that to Riordan. Being featured on the front page of the Species Gazette? For that? No way."

"Oh, he could use a little spice in his ancient routine. Speaking of." Rhyland drew out the last word. "Will *someone* have the balls to invite—"

He was cut off by a sudden tackle by his brother.

When the brotherly brawl was dying down a few minutes later, Caly casually said, "That actually would be great. Because then Aleia, Keena, and I would all be together." She flashed a teasing smile at Rhyker.

Rhyker froze, surprised at Caly's acute feminine perceptiveness.

"Oh please," Caly continued with a dramatic eye roll. "Like I didn't notice you both looking at each other at the bar. And don't act like I haven't seen you casually sniffing around the gym at the exact same time when I have yoga sessions with Keena."

"Oh shit." Rhyland's feline grin widened. "How in the hell have I missed the sniffing around?" Rhyland burst out laughing and literally started rolling on the floor.

"Don't hate me." Caly was smiling and patted Rhyker's shoulder.

He was giving her a side-eye for ratting him out.

"Especially because I *may* have seen her checking you out on the bench press more than once. Besides, I think it might be good for her to get out." Caly paused and then, on a more serious note, said, "Rhyker?"

"Yeah." He was now slightly easing up on the side-eye, feeling triumphant knowing that she was checking him out too.

"Just don't hurt her, please. She—" Caly cut herself off because it was none of her, or anyone else's, business. "Not like you would but... you know what I mean."

"Hmmm. Doesn't that sound familiar?" Rhyland chimed in. "Your male said something very similar. Are you both going to turn into *that* couple where you start finishing each other's sentences?"

"Well, wouldn't you two really be the ones to know all about that?" Caly teased with a smile.

Chapter 50

"Bring her to me," demanded the male with his cunning yet chilling charm.

"Yes." Barker bowed his head, all but heeling to his master.

"I know you will not fail me, James."

"No, I will not." Barker's determination to succeed surged at the confident words.

* * *

"Wow," both Keena and Caly said at the same time.

"If I didn't know you were a healer under oath, I would swear you sneak off to makeup artist school at night or something," Caly said, only half-kidding while admiring her makeup in the mirror.

It was flawless. Beyond flawless. It was this perfect blend between natural and elegant. Her eyes were enhanced with a soft and sparkly, silver, smokey situation, complete with a thin layer of obsidian eyeliner. She also naturally had thick and long eyelashes, so all Aleia did was curl them and apply jet black mascara. And as far as her cheeks went, it was just a simple blush and highlighter. The final touch was that of a neutral shade of lipstick with just a hint of color.

"Wow." Caly let out another admiring exhale. "I mean, seriously. I have all of the same shades and palettes yet my makeup never turns out like this."

"I know right. She just has that magic makeup touch," Keena said, a bit envious. She then enthusiastically added, "My turn!"

And the three of them laughed.

"I seriously can't wait to see how yours turns out," Caly followed up and looked at her nails. Caly, Keena and Aleia had a mini spa day yesterday. On top of getting her eyebrows shaped and waxed—and holy crap did they need it—Caly also got a mani-pedi. Her nails were painted in all white except the ring finger which had a subtle ombre layer of silver sparkles.

"Wow," all three of them said, completing their final check in the full-length mirror in Caly's room.

Caly was wearing a stunning dress which featured long and slim sleeves, an open dipped back, high neckline, and a floor-length hem. The fabric was her favorite part because it subtly danced between black and silver, depending on how the light hit the fabric. Azaeleia, the artist behind the dress, truly outdid herself with the custom design just for Caly. In fact, she outdid herself with Aleia and Keena's dresses as well. Aleia was in a gorgeous dark navy, sleeveless, mermaid-shaped dress which featured a modest neckline, low open back, and fine tonal sequins that shimmered across the full-length hem. Keena was in a simple yet stunning burgundy gown that featured a plunging neckline with delicate nude mesh, a side slit, and low back. Although Aleia and Keena's were not custom made (which was the only way that could have worked out because Azaeleia was already huffy with Riordan for giving her such short notice), they certainly could have fooled anyone. However, Riordan did insist upon a custom original for Caly's first official gathering. At first, Caly thought it was a bit much. Actually, she thought it was a bit much until this very moment, when she saw the final, finished look.

Her focus shifted slightly when she caught the glimmer of their earrings, which were all approved by Azaeleia, of course. Caly's were a sleek, three-tiered display of black and silver diamonds. Dangled at Aleia's ears were a pair of large two-tiered blue sapphires surrounded in white diamonds. And Keena's earrings were also three-tiered but with an elegant display of rubies and chocolate diamonds.

"I still can't believe our earrings. I feel like a secret spy or something." Caly smiled, touching the one hanging from her right ear gently.

"I know, right," Keena agreed.

"It's honestly genius," Aleia followed up.

The males surprised them earlier today with the upgrades that Deacon had made to their earrings. He managed to conceal an SEW on each earring. It's not like they would need it with all of the males with them but, with all that power in one place, they couldn't be too careful. Caly placed a hand on her heart and smiled when her fingertips outlined the thin titanium heart over her own.

"Let's take a picture," Keena suggested.

"Yes, totally! I want something to remember this moment," Caly said on an excited beat.

Aleia nodded, already setting up the camera on Caly's CCD. They took a couple of pictures, both selfie-style and full-length, because, duh, options and angles. Satisfied, they all looked at each other and smiled as they made their way to the door.

* * *

"Females," Rhyland said with amusement as he theatrically looked at the imaginary watch on his wrist once more. "And I don't even have a date."

It was currently ten minutes past the time they were instructed to meet in the lobby and all of the males were waiting in the grand foyer, dressed to the nines in their expensive suits. Even Felix was there, curious as ever to discover what the mini gathering was all about and secretly hoping some sort of treats were involved.

"And who's fault is that?" Rhyker retorted, amused with one-upping his brother in this case.

"Fuck you, Mr. Wanna-go-to-the-school-dance-with-me-Keena?" Rhyland shot back playfully with just a hint of bite.

"Fuck you. And you can hang out with Nico and Deacon all night and sulk for all I fucking care."

A growl started to rumble from Rhyland in protest when suddenly everyone stilled at the sound of female laughter down the hall. Seconds later, the three females appeared at the top of the staircase.

Blake's eyes locked on Caly and both he and his wolf knew they were completely and utterly lost in the beauty of their female.

Caly smiled shyly back at him as if trying to gauge his reaction.

Although they were certainly beautiful females, Rhyland just didn't think of them in any romantic sort of way. Instead, he noticed that his brother seemed to be in a similar trance Blake was in. Then his gaze landed on Nico, who also appeared to be enthralled by the three descending goddesses.

"Now would be a good time to close your drooling snouts and comment on how utterly beautiful your females look." Rhyland broke the silence with his humor and it seemed to snap the males out of it.

"You look beautiful, Caly." Blake walked up to Caly and gave her a quick kiss on the lips before offering his arm.

"You look stunning, Keena." Rhyker walked up to Keena, who was blushing. He kissed her on the cheek before offering his arm.

"Meh. You both get a six out of ten for originality and execution. But Rhyker, maybe you get a half point more for the different adjective," Rhyland quipped and a round of laughter sounded out through the room.

Rhyland, and some of the others, noticed Nico and Aleia staring at each other like the first time they met.

"Nico, stop staring at Aleia or she may turn into an ice sculpture from your frostiness." Rhyland playfully slugged Nico in the shoulder which seemed to snap him out of the thrall. Nico was about to stalk off but Jax called out, "Picture. Everyone gather in for a group picture."

Nate, who was previously gawking a little at the females, managed to pull it together to get everyone in the picture.

"One... two... three..." Nate said and several flashes went off, indicating that multiple pictures were being taken.

"Couples next," Jax ordered and a few groans sounded out.

After the couples—and, Caly may have insisted on having a picture with her, Blake *and* Felix—it was a group photo of all of the males. Then, all of the females. By the time the photo op was done, everyone was shuffling toward the exit.

Caly smiled and walked up to Nate. "Nate, would you be so kind as to take a photo with me?"

"Of course, Caly." Nate held up the camera as if to take another picture of her and Blake.

"Nate?" Caly asked as her lips curved.

He peered over the camera.

"I meant, will you be in the picture with me?" she asked.

His eyes widened in disbelief.

"Blake, will you take the picture for us?" Caly asked with a smile to her male who gave her an approving nod.

A couple of flashes later and Nate was beaming from ear to ear.

"You realize you just made that young male's bragging rights go through the roof for the foreseeable future?" Blake teased in her ear as they made their way to the black SUV limo. This time, it was a full-sized limo with all of the bells and whistles. He kissed her cheek as she laughed.

"What can I say? I have a soft spot for young Nate." She paused briefly to look back at Nate who was still beaming. "You know I asked Jax to keep an extra eye on him and he said that he already was."

"I see a bright future in that young male as well, Caly," Blake replied and was proud of his alpha female for keeping tabs on their extended pack mates. After all, that was what she was unknowingly doing. Whether she acknowledged it or not, she subconsciously saw everyone under Riordan's roof as exactly that: an extension of her pack.

At the Gallagher's massively modern mansion, everything looked like something out of a VIP, Hollywood, red-carpet event, paparazzi and all. Although, Blake explained it really wasn't paparazzi but rather the Gallagher castellan staff, who offered professional photography throughout the event. Everything seemed so extra and elegant with a mix between ancient and modern art, two topics that appeared to be the center of conversation—or at least these were excuses for what aristocrats called "conversations."

"Woah," Caly whispered under her breath while still gawking at the entire scene.

Blake chuckled and pulled her in for a side hug.

Suddenly, Caly felt nervous.

"I feel so out of place." She paused briefly. "Promise you won't leave my side?" She was only half-joking as she nervously laughed.

A sudden social nightmare for an introvert crept into her mind: being alone in a corner, socially shell-shocked into awkward stillness, while swarms of people gossip and laugh. And no, not people but rather specians for the extra layer of social fuckery.

Blake gave her this look that said, *"Female, do you really have to ask that question?"*

Both of their lips curved.

"Besides, I'm just as out of place as you are. If anything, the twins and Deacon have more experience with this level of social shit than I do."

Caly's eyebrows raised. "I thought you all opted out of this type of stuff?"

"We do. What I meant was because of their bloodlines."

Caly's eyes furrowed in confusion.

"They are from prestigious bloodlines and were raised among this," Blake clarified.

Her eyebrows shot up in surprise. "Deacon, okay, yeah I can see that. But the twins?"

She laughed as plenty of memories of their twin antics played through her mind. But then she remembered that first time she met these males at the breakfast table what felt like eons ago.

"And that's Deac the geek. Gentlemale to his core. But there's no need for all that, D. She isn't one of those stuck up aristocrats," Rhyland teased.

"Thank fuck," Rhyker tacked on and shoveled a heaping forkful of food into his mouth.

"Hi, Deacon. Nice to meet you too. And no, I'm not a stuck up aristocrat by far... Thank fuck," Caly quipped and

male laughter filled the room at her unexpected playfully cussing response.

Caly smiled as she recounted the memory, suddenly realizing why the twins had that noticeable prickle in their tone regarding aristocrats.

"What?" Blake asked, seeing her smile.

"Oh, I just remembered when I first met Deacon and the twins."

"It was that bad, huh?" Blake teased.

She laughed. "No, not like that. It just made sense why we established early on how I wasn't a stuck up, fake, LA ego."

Caly looked around the room for the rest of their crew. This place was so big, with so many grand rooms and so many specians, she didn't see anyone from their group at first glance. But she soon saw Riordan and Aleia chatting with another male along with a third male joining their conversation. Continuing the scan of the room, which was one of the main gathering rooms, she then saw Keena and Rhyker in one corner, casually chatting.

"I think they both look so cute together." She indicated toward them with her eyes and Blake nodded.

At that same moment, Keena laughed at something Rhyker said and Caly smiled.

"This is between us, like couple confidentiality, okay?" Caly looked at Blake and she could tell his ears pricked up. She internally smiled at his response. "She just got out of a bad relationship. I don't know the details really because she doesn't talk about it but, from what Aleia says, that male was a complete self-centered ass and he really hurt Keena."

Blake stiffened.

"I know," Caly agreed. "And, no, I don't know who the male is. And even if I did, like I would tell you with that kind of reaction?" she teased but truthfully, she was proud of this male, her male, for his knee-jerk reaction to stick up for Keena. "I won't lie. It makes me want to get in a good punch too because Keena is so sweet." She exhaled. "Anyways, I think she is a little wary to just jump into something else so soon. I mean, it's obvious she is attracted to him and vice versa… but, yeah."

Blake nodded. "Makes sense. And if I ever find out who this male is that hurt her, I will have *words* with him."

She laughed and elbowed him.

"What?" he said with innocent puppy dog eyes. "I said *words*. You're the one who said you wanted to punch him." Blake's lips curved into a wolfish grin.

"Touché, wolf." She smiled.

"I haven't seen Rhyker look at a female the way he does Keena. She has appeared to have caught his attention."

Blake decided to leave out that Rhyker was known, as Rhyland so eloquently put it, for the one-night, faceless fuck routine. He paused and they both looked over at Rhyker and Keena at the same time. Yes, Rhyker had his full focus on her despite other females in the area that were clearly sending glances at Rhyker, trying to catch his attention. Meanwhile, Keena blushed, looked at her drink and smiled at something Rhyker must've just said.

"And I think both he and his cat know she is a cautious deer," he added, making a mental note to keep an eye on this.

He wouldn't interfere or anything. But just like with Deacon and Starr, it was his job, and natural instinct, to look out for his pack. However, in this case, there was the extra layer of Keena being Caly's friend. So, he would definitely keep an eye on this. And as far as Deacon and Starr went, Blake knew that she was keeping him at a frustrating distance. He didn't know if Deacon had any or much interaction with Starr lately. But if there wasn't any contact between them then that was probably by design... on her part at least.

"Look at us talking about another couple at the party. If we're not careful we might turn into one of these social vipers," Caly quipped and Blake smirked.

Caly didn't know how long they had been at the gathering, but her cheeks hurt from continuously holding her Academy Award-winning smile like she was in a Miss America pageant. Oh, and her head was spinning—and it had nothing to do with the drinks. She couldn't possibly remember all of the my-bank-accounts-are-bigger-than-yours aristocrats that she had met or what their meaningless two-minute conversations had been about. Especially because Caly was too busy seeing her reflection in the ridiculously sized diamonds on the other females—females who were pinned to the sides of their males like priceless jeweled brooches. Some of the aristocrats that she did remember briefly speaking with were a few of the ancients on the Seer Council, like Deloreia and, unfortunately, the creepster, Anguis. But it wasn't too bad since Blake was with her and basically gave Anguis the alpha stare down without actually crossing into the offensive or rude territory. Anguis was an ancient aristocrat seer, after all. And how Blake managed that was beyond her. She was actually kind of jealous of his alpha skills in those cases. The point was that she was hitting her introvert limit and her "social situations gas tank" was close to empty.

Riordan casually walked up to Blake and Caly with one of the males that Caly had seen him conversing with earlier—or at least that's who she thought it was. The male had cream-colored skin, short and dark, rust-colored hair, and green eyes that were lighter than Riordan's.

"Blake." The unknown male spoke in an Irish accent

that had just a slightly different lilt and higher tone than Riordan's. Caly preferred Riordan's lower and rich tone.

"Sean," Blake said in greeting.

"What a pleasure to see you. I hope you're enjoying yourselves." Sean smiled a perfectly gleaming white smile at Blake and then Caly.

Ugh, Caly thought, immediately thinking that Sean's smile reminded her of Brett, the fake frat fucker. And Caly realized how it felt like that whole chapter of her life was lifetimes ago.

"Sean, may I have the honor of introducing Calypso Knight?" Riordan's words were refined and smooth. Yet, she had a feeling his method acting skills were far more advanced than her own.

He has had hundreds of years, if not millennia, of practice after all.

"Calypso. What a beautiful name that suits the female and her extraordinary eyes. It is a pleasure." Sean flashed another one of his smiles that she knew probably caught females' eyes. But, having lived in LA, Caly was a pro by now in seeing right through phony smiles.

"Caly. Please." Caly amped up her own, rusty as hell, acting skills and smiled.

"Caly, this is Sean Gallagher, our gracious host," Riordan continued.

Of course. Gallagher. I should've known.

"Exquisite party. Thank you for the invite," Caly added.

Exquisite? What the hell kind of a word is that? Why couldn't you just say lovely? Lovely party. See? That's normal. Maybe I'm really rusty, like straight-up, a broken down car in the middle of the desert for years disintegrating from rust, rusty.

"I wouldn't dare think to not invite the Knight bloodline." Sean paused to take a sip of his drink. "I'm glad you find the party suitable for your taste. Speaking of," Sean glanced over her dress. "Is that Azaeleia's fine work?"

"Yes. It is." Caly smiled.

"I see you have a high taste. Of course, I would expect no less from a Knight… blooded or *not*." Sean flashed his "all looks but no depth" smile.

Oh no you fucking didn't. Caly internally narrowed her eyes at his insinuating remark at how she became a Knight and how she wasn't blooded. But she kept her outward Academy Award-winning smile in place.

"I believe some of us are just born with a fine finish and an innate perception for the truly desired flavors of life, just like wine," Caly retorted with her own sophisticated and sneaky jab but again, all she was sporting was her own classy smile.

Sean laughed. "True enough, Caly." Then he looked at Riordan. "I can certainly see how this female caught your attention. I only regret that I didn't see her first."

Riordan smiled but it actually was more in amusement and support of Caly than at what Sean said.

Caly's anger rose to the forefront. *See me first? What? Like I'm some prize to claim and you can call dibs?*

Blake placed his hand on her exposed lower back which snapped her out of that train of thought.

"Speaking of fine taste. Caly, weren't you wondering if there were any courtyard pieces that we should make it a point to see?" Blake cut into the conversation and it was clear with his hand placement that Sean was treading on thin ice.

"Of course," Sean said with his eyes flicking to Blake's hand for a quick second before refocusing back on Caly. "My newest collection piece is by Alexandre Donnadieu," Sean said with a hint of boredom at the rarity of the collection. "If you would excuse me. I must make my rounds." He nodded at Riordan and Blake. "Caly, it was truly a pleasure to meet you. Please enjoy your evening."

As if I need your permission to enjoy the evening? Caly thought with an internal eye roll.

"Exquisite?" Blake teased with a raised brow as soon as Sean was out of earshot.

Riordan smirked.

"I know. God, I didn't realize how rusty I am at all of this fake BS," Caly bit out with a smile of her own.

"I think you did just *fine*, Caly." Riordan emphasized the word "fine" in a way that alluded to the obvious retort she made to Sean about fine wine.

Each of their lips curved until Caly laughed again.

"Well, I couldn't just let that slide," she said in her defense.

"And I'm glad you didn't. I was actually about to step in but you caught Sean off guard as he would have expected me to step in," Riordan added.

"Ugh. I hate these dumb social politics. It's like being in a pit of vipers." Caly finished off her drink.

"Why don't we both get refills so we can survive the viper pit." Blake squeezed her hip and then looked at Riordan in silent question if he wanted to join them.

"I wish. But, unfortunately, as an ancient, there are certain social expectations I must fulfill," Riordan said, also unimpressed by the aristocratic games.

"Hey, where's Aleia? Should we try and save her from the pit too?" Caly was only partially joking.

"She is used to this viper pit and has many secret passages of escape. I am sure she has already used one of them by now," Riordan remarked with lips curved.

"Secret passages of escape? Okay, well, I see I'm going to have to have a conversation with her to let me in on that for the future," Caly quipped.

"Riordan Knight," said one of the female vipers slithering toward them. She was dripping in diamonds with her eyes on her next victim.

"Better get out while we can," Blake said under his breath and caught Riordan's amusement just before he turned to greet the female.

Leading Caly toward one of the drink stations, he smiled when he saw a familiar face. "Come on. I actually want to introduce you to someone."

Caly gave him this look that said, *"but we just got away from the vipers."*

He chuckled. "Trust me on this."

"Okay," she said suspiciously as they walked over to a female who appeared to be studiously contemplating the choices laid out on the fancy "food and drink" display in front of her.

She had thick, wavy, chestnut brown hair, highlighted with natural gold, that pooled down past her shoulders. She was wearing an elegant, midnight navy dress, shimmering with the finest diamonds. It reminded Caly of the starry night sky.

"Alexina," Blake said and Caly noted he openly showed his smile.

Why does that name sound familiar? Caly thought, trying to rack her brain. There were so many names going through her mind. *Was it one of the specian bloodlines Riordan briefed her on before the party? Or maybe she was in something I read?*

"Blake. What a pleasant surprise," Alexina greeted him with her warm, welcoming smile. With one glance at Caly she said, "Ah, so this must be the lovely Caly." She smiled at Caly and it felt like a breath of fresh air from the viper pit.

Caly immediately noticed the female's big brown eyes

with a star-burst of hazel, as if it held an old flame of knowledge. It reminded her of how she felt when she looked into Riordan's eyes.

Ancient? Caly wondered, still taking in the utter natural beauty this female illuminated as if it shone straight through her sun-kissed, light gold complexion.

Chuckling warmly, Blake replied in his usual fashion with her, "Sharp as ever, Alexina. Caly, this is Alexina Astéri Diamánti."

"Oh, Blake. You humor me. You know we are far past formal introductions." Alexina smiled and then decisively plucked a piece of gourmet hors d'oeuvre from the elegant table setting that they were all standing in front of.

"I didn't know you would be coming or I would've extended an invite to join us at Riordan's," Blake said, handing Caly a drink.

Her eyes danced with warm fondness at Blake. "Alas. There are certain functions that someone, even as old as myself, has not yet quite mastered how to evade."

Blake chuckled.

"Ah, yes, and Riordan. Do you know where he might be by chance?" Alexina inquired casually.

Both Blake and Caly looked over toward Riordan and the female who was clearly trying to win his attention. Yet, it appeared the piece of art on the wall was suddenly the most fascinating thing to Riordan.

"I'm sure Riordan would appreciate the rescue." Blake chuckled as he took in the scene.

"You know, maybe I will indulge myself and do just that." Alexina smiled faintly as she looked at Riordan and then refocused on Caly. "Caly, it really was nice to meet you and I hope to see or at least hear from you both more often." And with that, Alexina glided over to Riordan like the ancient Greek goddess she so resembled.

"Okay. You were right. She was a breath of fresh air and I actually like her," Caly admitted. "And extra points for her gallant attempt to rescue Riordan."

Blake's lips curved.

"Why does her name sound so familiar? Should I know who she is?"

"Yes, but not in the way that you're thinking. Alexina is the ancient steorrian I told you about."

"Of course."

It all clicked back into place. That was during her evil Ice Queen stage and she was so consumed with revenge, she didn't even really pay much attention to anything if it didn't have to do with Barker. She, of course, remembered the update about Magneticus (duh) but she forgot the steorrian's name.

"How do you know her?" Caly asked, wondering if she forgot that too.

"Alexina knew my parents," Blake said and took a sip of his drink as if to clear his throat for this conversation.

And, no, even as the evil Ice Queen version of herself, Caly would not have forgotten about the connection with his parents. This was the first time Blake was sharing this with her.

"Is she an ancient?" At Blake's nod, Caly continued, "So, were your parents' ancients as well?"

"No. They were relatively young for species. In fact, not much older than I am now. My parents lived in the Stonebrook wolf pack. My father was a sentinel and my mother, well let's just say her bakery had a local fan base." His lips curved as if he was recounting a memory. "Alexina says she was gifted an apple pie from Anna's Bakery one day. After the first bite, she knew she had to make a trip to the village to meet this Anna." He paused with a half-smirk. "I became closer to Alexina when my parents passed away." Caly slid her hand into his and squeezed.

He gave her a quick kiss for her support.

"Anna. Is that your mother's name?" Caly asked gently, unsure how far down this road he wanted to go.

"Yeah. Annalisse. But she went by Anna." Blake had a distant look in his eye and she knew that look well. He was no doubt recounting a memory of his parents. A long moment of silence passed before Caly spoke.

"Alexina seems really nice and I honestly would love to get to know her more. Maybe we could take a trip and visit her or she can come over and visit us sometime?" Caly asked softly.

"I think she would really like that," Blake concluded, pressing his lips to hers.

They both looked over at Alexina and, what do you know? She not only managed to rescue Riordan but it also appeared that she managed to induce a genuine smile from him. This was the first real smile Riordan had given all night.

"You're so bad," Keena managed to get out in between her laughs.

"So I've heard." Rhyker had a playfully wicked expression on his face and took a sip of his drink.

Keena smiled and there was a brief pause before she spoke on a more real note. "Thank you for inviting me tonight. I can't remember the last time I've had this much fun."

Okay, yes you can. It was the night you met this male and made out with his oh-so-kissable lips, Keena thought, looking at said lips. *No. What if it doesn't work out? Or if it's just a quick fling? Not only do you know that you can't do quick flings because you get too emotionally attached but also, it would just get messy and super awkward for everyone. Besides, it's too soon after Liam. Okay, but then why did you say yes to go out with him and in this very public way? Because I am really attracted to him and find myself looking forward to those fleeting moments, walking through the gym with Caly to see if he will be there working out.*

Her thoughts were like an indecisive scale, frantically flipping between one extreme to the next. It was just one of the joys of being an overthinking mind healer with various degrees in psychology, therapy, mental health, and counseling.

"That's funny because I can remember the last time I had fun," Rhyker teased.

"Oh really?" Keena played along, curious where he was going with this exactly.

"Yeah. It was a little over a month ago. You see, my friends and I went out, you know to blow off some steam, and then this beautiful female caught my eye on the dance floor. Well, actually her scent is what caught my attention first." He paused to pretend like he was taking a sip but he added the calculated pause for effect. "And before you know it we were kissing in a dark corner. Haven't been able to stop thinking about it since." Rhyker sharpened his senses and both he and his jaguar were completely focused on Keena and her reaction.

Blushing, Keena looked down at her drink. It was suddenly ten degrees hotter in the room.

Say something. All those mind-healing degrees and you can't even formulate a short sentence?

"I, umm..." she managed to say.

Okay, two words. It's a start. How about, "I haven't been able to stop thinking about it either?" But is that sending the wrong message? What is the right message even? What is wrong with my brain? Is there a dial so I can turn down the crazy?

"I can almost see the steam coming out of your ears with

your brain working so hard." He chuckled. "It's okay. You don't have to say anything. The fact that you said yes to join me tonight is good enough for me."

Oh, hell. Since when did you become tongue-tied? Since him. Duh.

"I was going to say that I've been thinking about that night as well," Keena said, stripping away all of the baggage to speak from the core of her attraction to this male.

But we can't go any further than that.

He inhaled and then looked at her. "Why do I smell a 'but' coming on?" His lips curved in his playful response.

She laughed a little. "But it's like I said before. This could get awkward quickly."

"And yet here we are. And it's not awkward," Rhyker drawled.

"Point taken." Keena tipped her glass in his direction with a smile. She took a sip and then exhaled. "I want to be honest with you."

"I want that too," Rhyker retorted.

She laughed. "How am I supposed to have a serious conversation with you if you keep making me laugh?"

"Laughing of course." He continued to play with this female.

"Alright. You win." She smiled. "What I'm trying to say is that yes, I'm attracted to you. But I just got out of a relationship and am not really in a place for anything. I wanted to come with you tonight—"

"I want that too," Rhyker quickly inserted and she laughed. He liked it when this female laughed and planned to make her laugh a lot in the foreseeable future.

"You're so bad." Keena laughed with a slight blush on her cheeks.

"Yes, we've covered this before." Rhyker also liked pawing at this female.

"I came—wait no, that's not what I meant." And this time, they both laughed. "What I mean is, I really am enjoying spending time with you. But I also don't want to lead you on when I'm not really in an emotional place for anything right now."

Both he and his jaguar came to full alert. He knew a hurt female when he heard it and the slight hint in her voice confirmed it. He bit back a growl and suddenly he wanted to know who the male was that hurt her.

Focus, he commanded his brain.

"I'd be lying if I said I wasn't thinking about tasting your lips again," he began with his eyes falling to her lips. "But why don't we take the pressure off and just play in the moment?" Rhyker proposed with keen focus on her.

Play in the moment, Keena mentally repeated his words. *Play. Yes, why not play and have fun and keep things light? It doesn't have to be all serious and heavy. Who says that healing after a bad relationship has to be a solitary journey? You want to spend time with this male so why not spend time with him and enjoy it?*

"To playing in the moment." Keena reached her drink toward his.

"To playing in the moment," Rhyker echoed the toast and clinked his drink with hers.

"Blake Stone."

A silken female voice, dripping with class, had Caly's people-watching, or rather specian-watching, suddenly halt.

"Imagine my surprise when Selene spotted you and I just knew I *had* to stop by for old times' sake. How long has it been?" She pursed her perfectly plump, red lips against her perfect porcelain skin, pretending to be in thought.

Caly's female instincts were suddenly on full alert at this female with her perfectly-styled, natural blonde hair, blue eyes, and designer outfit that looked like it cost two of these mansions.

Thank you Riordan and Azaeleia, Caly mentally sent them another prayer of gratitude for her custom designer outfit.

"A long time, Liviana," Blake said and internally, his wolf bristled. He very publicly slid his hand to Caly's lower back and gently squeezed to send a clear message. "Have you met, Caly?"

He already knew she hadn't but he had to play by the aristocratic culture full of meaningless conversations on the surface and ego backstabbing underneath.

Liviana's gaze finally acknowledged Caly's presence.

Bitch, like you didn't see me before? Caly thought, gritting her teeth internally but suddenly finding herself dusting off her old acting skills once again. Caly had the urge to bare her teeth and do the punch and swinging kick combo on this female.

Okay. So, maybe Rhyland wasn't too far off with the Species Gazette front page fight news. Out of the corner of her eye, Caly saw Blake's lips slightly curve in amusement before he took a sip of his drink as if he heard her thoughts.

"No, I don't believe I've had the pleasure as of yet," Liviana all but purred.

"Caly, this is Liviana De Fiore of the De Fiore bloodline," Blake proceeded with the stale, formal introduction.

"Pleasure to meet you, Liviana," Caly continued with the nauseating, aristocratic introduction that Riordan taught her.

"Liviana, this is Caly Knight of the Knight bloodline," Blake said, once again moving the introduction along.

Liviana's expression changed with the slightest fraction at the realization of Caly's connection to the Knight bloodline. "Pleasure to meet you, Caly. Imagine being surprised two times by Blake this evening? I find myself standing before, none other than, the elusive Calypso Knight... that I see has caught more than just Riordan's eye." Liviana smiled lethally and took a sip of her martini, which, wouldn't you know, appeared to have as much depth as her. "I wonder if you will surprise me a third time this evening, to complete the saying that it comes in threes," she purred at Blake.

I'll show you what comes in threes. Right hook. Left hook. And uppercut. Caly internally shook her head at that thought. *God, since when did I become so violent? Probably since spending all your time training to fight and living with a pack of hot-blooded males who often resolved things with their fists. And since this predator was clearly encroaching on your territory...*

"I guess we'll just have to see. Excuse us. I promised Caly I would show her the work of Alexandre."

Caly swore she saw a slight tick under Liviana's right eye at Blake's dismissal of the conversation.

"How's that for a third surprise?" Blake whispered in Caly's ear as they walked outside.

She laughed. "My sly wolf." Caly brought Blake's face to hers to steal a quick kiss under the full moon. "Why do I feel like if I was a wolf shifter, I would have torn out that female's throat?" She smiled innocently as if the question wasn't talking about straight-up wild ferocity.

Blake laughed. And, god, it was one of his laughs where his head tilted back a little and the corner of his eyes formed into tiny creases. She loved when he laughed freely like that.

"I would say that my female's senses were very acute."

Caly blew out a breath. "Look, I know you obviously weren't celibate when we met and neither was I. I just didn't expect to run into... your past. And now that I think about it, it's probably a small world... a *very* small world when it comes to species since everyone plays in the same sandbox for literally eternity. But I don't want to know. I mean, a heads up would have been nice. But then again, I don't know because then all I would want to do is rip out females' throats apparently."

He chuckled. "Caly, you're my mate. And I love you and only you." He kissed her and continued, "Yes, I have a past. And let's just say it's probably a good idea that I don't know about your past either or else more throats would be ripped out."

They both smiled.

"What if I only tell you about my past if I think it might get awkward or leave you caught off guard to where someone like Liviana can dangle that in your face and try to get a shocked reaction out of you?"

Caly had to think about that for a moment. "Okay. Deal. But if someone winds up throatless... then don't say I didn't warn you," she quipped.

His lips twitched. "Have I told you that I love you?" He teased his scruff over her neck and it sent a shiver of pleasure through her.

"Blake." She let out a breathy sound.

He growled. "Caly," he said in a low, rough voice in her ear that was only meant for her to hear.

"So, where is this magnificent art of Alexandre I keep hearing so much about?" She was desperately trying to switch subjects because the way this was going, they wouldn't last the whole party.

He chuckled and pulled away from her body. "I'll show you," he said with a wolfish grin.

"Blake—" she began but her words were cut off.

"Oh, thank fuck," Rhyland bit out with Deacon by his side. "We're so ready to blow this joint. Literally blow up this mansion of fakeness, just to get some realness kick-started up in this Stepford housewife hell."

Both Caly and Blake laughed.

"There aren't any females that caught your eye?" Caly asked, a little curious to hear because she knew that females would certainly have their eyes on these two handsome males.

Both Rhyland and Deacon just gave her this look that said, *"Really? Have you seen the females here?"*

"Okay, good point," Caly said with a laugh. "I was actually just about to ask Blake how much longer we have to stay until it won't be rude for us to leave."

"See? My kind of female. I knew I liked you, SoCal." He winked and took a sip of his drink.

"Wanna go secretly spy on Keena and Rhyker?" Caly asked with a wicked smile.

"Blake. Seriously, I never thought I would be jealous of you but, damn," Rhyland teased.

"Where's Nico?" Caly asked Rhyland after her laughter died down.

"Who knows but when we passed him earlier, his eyes were black and he was stalking out of the gathering and into the shadows of the courtyard. My guess is the fake-ass specians are driving him just as crazy as us."

"Yeah, I can actually see that. Have you seen Aleia or Riordan at all?" Caly was taking tabs on their crew.

"Last I saw Ale—" Rhyland stopped speaking mid-sentence and then smiled. "Why don't we ask her ourselves?" With shifter speed, he was gone.

Caly looked to Deacon and Blake and they just rolled their eyes. At this point, they were used to Rhyland's playful quirks. Then a minute later he strolled up with none other than Aleia.

"Oh, thank God Rhyland found me. Please tell me this is a plot for us to leave unnoticed." Aleia half-smiled but was seriously waiting to see what everyone else said.

"What do you know? Another female who is smart, beautiful, and sees right through this fucking facade." Rhyland purred out a seductive yet playful growl.

Suddenly, Nico appeared beside Blake with black eyes staring daggers at Rhyland.

"Sir Iciness, how nice of you to join us," Rhyland began. "You know, I never realized how your ability to fade could come in so handy in situations like this."

In response, Nico crossed his arms over his chest and narrowed his eyes.

"More touchy than usual. Or is it that you're not being touched by females as usual?" Rhyland said in jest.

A low growl came out of Nico.

"Alright boys," Aleia cut in a split second before Blake did, as they all knew this was escalating quickly. "It's clear that we all want to leave. Thank God. What about Rhyker and Keena? And I know Riordan. He doesn't like these parties either. We will have to rescue him."

"We actually were making plans to secretly spy on—" Caly was interrupted by a phone pinging which signified that a text came through.

"It's Keena," Aleia said, looking at her phone and then smirked. "They want to know where I am and if I know where the others are." Aleia sent a quick text back with their location. "Okay, so Riordan. This can get tricky because he is an ancient and is expected to converse with at least the most prominent bloodlines here." She paused and looked at the time. "This is good because I would say that enough time has passed for him to have made the most important rounds and then some."

Aleia paused as Keena and Rhyker joined the group.

"So, I take it this group huddle means we all have the same idea?" Keena asked and there was a round of head nods.

"Thank fuck," Rhyker bit out, lighting up a hand-rolled indie.

"So, what's the plan?" Keena asked, slightly mesmerized by how extra hot Rhyker was when he smoked.

"We were just getting to the good part. And apparently, Aleia has been dubbed the leader of this operation due to her previous experience. No offense, Blake." Rhyland grinned.

"None taken," Blake said with an amused smirk.

"So, this is my Hail Mary, go-to move if all else fails. I pull the whole, *I'm a healer, 'Excuse me, Riordan, may I have a word?'* thing. I then whisper a made-up patient situation and a yes or no question in his ear. From there he either nods in agreement or shakes his head in disagreement. That is how I know if we can leave or not. If he indicates he can't leave as of yet then he gives me a number which I know means how many minutes until I can come back and rescue him again."

Caly's laughter suddenly burst into the silent circle of serious faces. They all looked at her, wondering what the hell was wrong with her. Sometimes, she wondered the same thing.

"I'm sorry," she managed to get out in between laughing fits. "I just find it hilarious that we are literally plotting our escape like it's our sole mission."

"Caly, it is our sole mission," Rhyland deadpanned.

There was a heartbeat of silence as everyone looked at each other. They all busted up laughing once Caly brought to light the true hilarity of the situation.

"I'm suddenly feeling like I've missed the best part of the evening." Riordan's voice broke into the dying laughter.

"I would agree with you, Riordan," Alexina added with a faint smile.

"I was just letting them in on our standard operating procedure," Aleia said with her lips curved.

"Oh, yes. Riordan let me in on that. I may want to adopt it myself." Alexina's smile deepened.

"So, are we all in agreement then?" Riordan asked.

A round of emphatic "yeses" called out.

"Who's up for stopping at that fast-food burger joint that we passed on our way?" Rhyland asked but he wasn't joking, for once.

Caly's stomach growled at the thought of burgers and fries.

"My female is hungry, so I second the motion," Blake added as Rhyland fist-bumped Caly at her body's support of his proposal.

And that was how they all ended up at Brett's Burgers in the middle of the night in outfits that probably could have bought the entire franchise multiple times over. Caly figured Connor, Brett's nephew, was going to tell that story for years and years to come. And yeah, they may have all lined up for a group picture with Connor too.

Chapter 51

Despite the cool winter air and light blanket of snow on the ground, the sun was out for the first time since the first snowfall, about a week ago. Caly knew she had to take advantage of the brief respite. Not that she hadn't loved the whole winter thing so far with lots of curling up by the fire next to Blake or to read. Or even on that first day when she was so excited about a snow day she managed to get everyone rounded up for a good old fashioned snowball fight. Living in LA, she never really got a chance to experience snow days. So, yeah, she enjoyed the snow but she also wouldn't waste the gift the sun gave today.

Wrapped in a winter coat and boots and with a fresh-baked, blueberry muffin and caramel hazelnut macchiato in hand—thank you Meri—she was out the door. She didn't know why but she felt called to go to the secret garden. She was feeling nostalgic today for some reason. It was probably just that dream she had last night. Well, the *first* part of the dream she had. She dreamt that she was back in LA curled up on her reading chair with Felix on her lap as she devoured a coffee and pastry from The Drip and the latest romance novel in the series she loved.

Then, the dream suddenly went into Scaryville.

Dark fog crept in through the cracks of the doors and windows. The words on the page of the book morphed into *"Soon, Caly... Soon..."* in black oily font, which looked like it was dripping the darkest blood. Screaming, she threw the book and woke up sweating with her heart beating and an evil laugh resounding in her mind. She, of course, told Blake of the dream and he agreed she should let Riordan know in her session with him later today. So, she would. But for now, she wanted to get in a little solo practice-session of the sleep state and soak up the sun. Besides, she didn't know if the dream was just her own subconscious paranoia, fears, or what exactly. And she reminded herself that she couldn't live her life based on her own fears or plans of revenge. Hello, evil Ice Queen.

Lost in her thoughts and feet crunching through the light layer of snow, she walked through the forest toward the secret garden. She liked how it was a bit of a hike through the trees and, unlike the well-kept and decorated paths in the courtyard, there was not a well-established path to it. Even though she knew everyone knew about it, the off-the-beaten-path vibe it had just added to its secrecy, serenity, and seclusion that made up the beauty of the garden. Well, that and the exotic nature of the plants of course. She took in a deep breath of fresh and crisp, winter air, exhaled a puff of white steam, and sighed with content.

An icy chill crept up her spine and it wasn't the cool winter air. The hairs on the back of her neck rose and she felt her body stiffen in response. She turned around but saw nothing.

Paranoia, Caly. She laughed a little to herself. *It's just that creepy-ass dream that has you on edge. Stop waiting for the other shoe to drop.*

She took another deep and clarifying, winter breath and continued walking. But she couldn't shake the feeling like she was being watched. Looking around through the trees, she saw nothing.

See? Paranoia. Stop being ridiculous. And, remember, there's a reason this place is called the fortress.

Minutes of her snow-crunching footsteps passed and she allowed her thoughts to get lost once more. Breaking through the treeline, she saw the secret garden and smiled. She, of course, knew there would be snow.

I mean, hello, I just walked through it for like forever.

But for whatever reason, it didn't really register that she would be seeing the delicate, white snow over the garden. It took her breath away. The sun was already melting some of it but it was as if everything was in a peaceful slumber. She walked through the garden and up to the bench overlooking the lake with a surface like calm glass. Brushing off some of the snow to clear a spot for her on the bench, she sat down and took a sip of warm macchiato. She spent several minutes in silence looking at the lake and enjoying the rest of her morning drink ritual.

Sleep state, she thought and took a deep breath. Closing her eyes, she breathed and walked herself through the stages of the sleep state. She was getting much faster and could induce it in just under a couple of minutes now. She exhaled in preparation to succumb to the deep state altogether.

"Caly, did you think you could get away from me?"

All of the blood drained out of her.

It's not real. You're just paranoid and imagined it, she told herself.

But she knew she wasn't imagining it and as soon as she turned around, she would see James Barker. She swallowed and somehow managed to command her frozen body to stand up and turn around.

His possessive smile shot her straight back to the dark horror of torture and the version of herself curled up shaking in fear on the cold cement. Before she could blink, he was gone. She almost thought she imagined the whole thing but the adrenaline pumping through her veins and her body frozen in horror told her otherwise.

"Boo."

She jumped as she heard his taunting voice behind her, mere inches from her ear. A memory shoved to the forefront of her mind of the first time he did that to her. Like a scared animal, she whipped around fast to face the predator. She saw his satisfied smirk at her reaction.

Frozen. She was frozen once more with pure, ice-cold terror pumping through her veins as the remaining blood drained out of her. She couldn't move. She couldn't think. She couldn't breathe.

"Imagine my surprise to see you at the Gallagher gathering with another wolf."

Her eyes went wide at the realization he had been watching her the whole time.

"Yes. How dare you cheat on me. And not just with any wolf. But I have something special in mind for it being the same wolf who attacked me in my own home. First, the special surprise will start with you and then it ends with him." His predatory grin widened with madness and his eyes danced with evil thoughts of torture and death.

"H-h—" She was shaking so badly, she couldn't even speak.

He laughed in pleasure at her fear and inhaled.

"Oh, how I have missed that sweet scent of your fear. And how? Well, I can't give you all my secrets. Just as you haven't given me yours... yet." Another sinister smile flashed across his face, pleased with the taunting game. "In fact, I'm eager to hear about those." He gripped her arm firmly.

She didn't know what came over her. But it was as if the instant his hand gripped her arm, her body took over in muscle memory of the self-defense training. She lifted her arm up and came down hard with her elbow bending his arm at the hinge and breaking his grip. At the same time, she punched out with her other hand and she felt and heard the crack as his nose broke.

His grin widened and his eyes were shining with a new level of crazy as the blood gushed down his face. His expression told her that he loved her blood-spurting rule change of their predator vs. prey game.

She swallowed.

With shifter speed, he spun her around with one hand holding both her hands behind her back and the other around her mouth so she couldn't scream.

"So many secrets I can't wait to tease out of you," he continued with the bone-chilling taunt in her ear, so close she could feel the warmth of his breath.

Sheer panic laced with terror made it impossible to think. Her heart was beating so fast and it pounded like a drum in her ears.

My heart, she thought, remembering her heart necklace. But she couldn't get to it. Her arms were pinned to her back. And now he was too close to throw up her force field.

"As I've said, I have plans to make our reunion very special." His voice was like poisonous snakes slithering under her skin.

A pool of black oily liquid started to rise out of the ground in front of them. She struggled and tried to scream but it was useless. He was too strong. The pool continued its ominous ascent and she continued to struggle for her life. She knew if she went into that dark hell she wouldn't survive. She knew he would torture her worse than before and this time, kill her.

NO! NO! NO! She panicked like a rabbit caught in the

sharp jaws of a predator with the impending promise of death.

"Keep struggling. I like this new side of you. It's going to be fun," he said with his grip tightening on her.

Her instinct to survive took over and with everything she had, she threw up her force field in a final effort to get free. She knew she only had seconds before the dark hell was big enough for them both to fit through. She gritted her teeth, exerting all her power into the force field.

With a slam, it pushed him back several feet and the black wall collapsed at the interruption.

She took advantage of his stunned surprise. Holding the force field in place, she fumbled with her gloves and pulled the chain to reveal her heart necklace. He was pounding on her force field and his pleasured psychotic laughter at the game she played rippled through her just as her force field did with the force of his punches. Slipping the back half of the heart off of the necklace, which activated the SEW, she threw it at him through the force field. It was the first time she ever actually used an activated SEW on a live body and she held her breath.

She was so shaky and everything was in a blur of movement. For a frozen heartbeat, she thought she almost missed him but then, his right arm threw another punch and that was where it landed. As soon as the contact was made, she knew the SEW's tiny barbs clung to his skin. In an instant, his body hit the ground on a convulsing boom. She flew and didn't look back. She just ran toward home and screamed like she never screamed before in her life. It was the unmistakable, high pitch of pure terror.

Racing. Heart beating. Muscles cramping. Tears flowing. *RUN! RUN! RUN!*

Every fiber of her being was screaming for her to run. She heard the angered roar behind her and stumbled.

NO!

In slow motion, she felt herself falling to the ground. She knew she wouldn't make it home in time. She saw Barker's wolf with teeth bared, closing the distance between them effortlessly. Hitting the icy ground on a hard slam, the wind was knocked out of her and she was frozen in place, just the snow beneath her. She tried to throw up a force field but it was so weak and she knew she was just delaying the inevitable. Curling into a tight ball, she heard and felt him growling and snapping his teeth against her force field. Any second her force field was about to give out completely.

She screamed as unbearable pain seared through her when his teeth sank into her shoulder and his claws scraped her legs. He was making sure she couldn't run from him. He growled in satisfaction and his jaws clamped harder on her shoulder.

This was it. She knew she was about to lose consciousness from the pain. She knew he was going to take her and torture her. She knew she was going to die.

A booming roar broke through her spiraling thoughts of panic, fear, and death.

Blake.

It was the first time tears pricked her eyes and she felt something in her heart at the sound of his roar. For her. He heard her and was coming for her. It was as if that roar of the male she loved sent a jolt of power through her. No. There was suddenly a literal jolt of electricity running through every cell of her being. It felt as though she was drinking in the energy from the Earth itself. Memories of the past six months flashed through her mind. Of Blake, her heart. Of her parents. Of her family. Of her friends.

No. He will not hurt anyone else. This is not how it ends.

Then something that she had long forgotten came to the forefront of her mind.

I am the fucking Phoenix.

A loud snap, like the crack of an electric whip, sounded out, followed by the yelp of a wolf. Her shoulder was suddenly free from his grip. She blinked open her eyes to see Barker's wolf, stained and dripping with her blood. He shook his head as if trying to reorient himself. She began to rise from the Earth. She didn't know how but it was as if the Earth itself was lifting her up. Face to face with the wolf of her nightmares once more, she saw the sick gleam in his eye for her secrets and the continued, unexpected extension of his game of torture and death.

"I am not yours!" she declared, feeling another surge of power flow up from her feet through her entire body. Her entire being was tingling with energy. She vaguely heard a crackling sound but all she saw was James Barker.

Then she saw it. She saw a flicker of fear flash across his eyes. An instant later, he bared his teeth and attacked.

With a flash of bright light and a thunderous snap, Barker made contact with a solid shield of pure power. His body flew back several feet and landed with a deafening boom. Upon impact, he shifted out of his wolf form and had smoke rising from his blackened and charred chest as if it was burned. With blood pouring out of his mouth, he looked up at her with gasping breaths in evil fascination. His sudden manic laughter, while spewing blood, broke the deathly silence.

"He..." Blood spattered as he coughed. "Comes..." There were more blood-gurgling coughs before his last two words were spoken on a faint breath. "For you..."

Caly saw the life leave Barker's eyes as his body fell limp on the crimson-stained snow.

His charred chest started to glow. No, the tattoo of the strange, spiraling symbols were glowing a deep purple, almost black, color.

Caly jumped back as black, oily liquid pooled beneath his body and seconds later, his body was pulled into the abyss. The black liquid rose higher and higher as thick, hazy darkness fell all around. She thought she heard a faint roar but her head was suddenly humming with a loud frequency. She looked around and saw that she was still protected by her dome-shaped force field of pure power. In fact, the force field was sending the dark fog back with loud electric snaps each time the fog tried to penetrate it.

"Caly," a charismatic male voice, with a subtle note of chilling wrongness, called out. The voice seemed to slither down her spine and had her blood run cold.

And she knew that voice. It was the hypnotically haunting voice from her dreams. She was trying to focus her eyes but all she could see was the thick, black fog swarming around the liquid wall. As if she willed it so, part of the fog cleared and, in the liquid wall, she saw a nightmare she could never unsee. She saw a pair of blood-red, ruby eyes, each with two black vertical pupils, as if they belonged to a serpent from hell. Looking into those eyes felt like confronting black holes that could suck the light out of the sun itself. The dark liquid wall suddenly collapsed into itself and disappeared.

As the fog began to dissipate, she saw him. Blake. Her Blake. Her heart. His wolf was frantically pacing in frustration with bared teeth. Her thoughts were becoming hazy and her body light. She vaguely wondered why Blake, and the others for that matter, were acting as if there was an invisible barrier between them. Something seemed off but she couldn't quite make it out because it felt like her brain was swimming through molasses.

Tired. So tired...

That was the last thought she had before she collapsed and gave into the deep sleep that was calling to her soul.

As soon as the second shield was down, Blake was by Caly's side and shifted out of his wolf form.

"Caly!" He cradled her in his arms and felt her faint heartbeat.

"Out of the way!" Aleia commanded as her potent cocktail of healing energy flew out of her hands into Caly. "We need to get her inside!"

With shifter speed, Blake had Caly inside and cradled against his chest on one of the chairs in the living space, just past the grand entrance.

Without hesitation, Nico picked up Aleia and they were next to Blake and Caly seconds after. It was the first time they had ever had such close contact. They only looked at each other for a half a second while Aleia tried to reorient herself from the unexpected transport at warp speed. A heartbeat later, she was back at Caly's side giving her healing energy.

"I don't know how long we have before she goes into her induced cocoon coma," Aleia said in frantic frustration. Aleia wasn't sure that Caly would go into a coma-like state but if the past was any indication, then it was almost certain Caly would. And with Caly's current condition, she guessed she had minutes at best. Caly's pulse was so weak.

"Damn it!" Aleia yelled, feeling Caly slipping away.

Tears were streaming down Aleia's face which mixed with the sheen of sweat from the sheer amount of healing she tried to exert in such a short time. Too soon and, just as she predicted, Caly's force field shot into place and catapulted Aleia away from Caly's body. Nico was there and caught Aleia before she landed on a crash. Everyone blinked as Blake held Caly's limp body close to his chest on the inside of the force field.

Chapter 52

Caly blinked and waited for her eyes to adjust to the bright sunlight. She heard ocean waves kissing the shoreline. Slightly squinting, she looked around. Upon recognition, her eyes instantly became blurry with emotion. She was once again at the beach with her parents.

"Mom! Dad!" Her tears were blurring her vision as she ran to her parents' open arms.

"My sweet baby." Her mother was combing her fingers through Caly's hair in that soothing way mothers do.

"We're here, our brave Caly Lilly." Her father spoke, kissing the top of her head.

Caly cried in her parents loving embrace until the tears naturally slowed.

She inhaled a shaky breath. "I—I have avenged you... You may now be at peace."

"You have avenged yourself," her father began. "And we hope you accept peace."

I killed someone. Caly recalled the electrical bolt and charred mark on Barker's chest as she watched the life leave his body. Even though it was self-defense and he was an evil male, who more than had it coming to him, taking a life and watching that life drain away left its mark somewhere deep.

Maybe that is what dad means by accepting peace? she wondered, taking another shaky breath.

"How…?" She replayed the scene in her mind. None of what happened really made any sense.

"We're all born of the Earth, and you, my dear Caly Lilly, are more of the Earth than some. Just as the Earth has a magnetic field, so do you. You are able to connect with her magnetic and electrical currents deep in her core. This is what you felt."

Even though she knew time didn't exist here in this place, it suddenly felt like they were out of time. At that exact moment, she saw a bright white light as if a white sun was rising above the horizon of the sea.

"Am I to go with you?" Caly moved her gaze from the white sunrise to her parents.

"That, my sweet angel, is up to you." Her mother smiled.

In response, Caly clung to her parents and vowed, "I'm never letting go of you."

"Caly Lilly, we are never apart. So, it is impossible to even let go." Her father's eyes shone with love.

Caly looked at the horizon with the gentle white rays that were extending farther and growing brighter. But she felt an ache so deep that it hurt down to the core of her very soul.

"Why does my heart still hurt when I am with you now?"

"Because we are not the only ones you carry in your heart now," her mother answered with eyes full of a mother's love.

Memories of Blake started scrolling through her mind so fast. The first time they met in her dreams. The first time they made love. The first time she saw his wolf. The first time they said, "*I love you.*" Memories of them laughing and playing. Memories of countless conversations. And the final memory was of her, Felix, and Blake curled up in bed watching a movie. Her throat was thick and the tears were flowing like rushing rivers.

"Blake," she whispered out on hardly more than an exhalation of air.

"Yes, Caly Lilly."

"But how can I go through losing you all over again?" Caly choked out with a wave of deep emotion.

"Who says it is a loss? Haven't we seen each other twice now?" her father retorted with an amused philosophical smile.

She managed to crack a small smile through the tears. "I wish you could meet him."

"My sweet angel, we already have. Through here." Her mother touched Caly's heart. "We love you both so much."

"You're stronger together. Never forget that." Her father looked deep into Caly's eyes for emphasis.

"Please pass our love along to him too."

Her parents pulled her into a warm embrace once more, as the dream-like experience started to fade. Caly tried to hold on tighter but everything was fading into bright white light.

"I love you, mom and dad."

"We love you, Caly."

Caly felt that deep pain of heartache once again as her parents' voices and forms faded. She had to close her eyes from the growing bright white lights all around. She couldn't see but she could feel... pure love.

✳ ✳ ✳

The fresh scent of tears, the sting of heartache, and the unmistakable scent of pure love filled Blake's nose.

"Caly?" Blake was on the bed with Caly in his arms within the blink of an eye, holding her close to his chest.

Unlike during Caly's change, Blake was able to leave

and re-enter her force field. Blake was also able to carry Caly to their room and the force field simply just stayed around them like a protective bubble. He carefully washed her body of the bloody battle before laying her in their bed. He tended to her wounds with Aleia's direction outside of the force field. One week had passed and he never left her side once. No one knew how long she would sleep or if she would ever wake. Her pulse got stronger as the days passed and when Blake slept, he waited and called to her to pull him into her dreams. But she never did. Oftentimes, the others found Blake's wolf curled up next to Caly, nuzzling her gently and licking her. They would also hear his wolf howl as if attempting to coax her awake. And today, right now, her body stirred and he knew his female was waking.

"Caly, come back to me." He was kissing and nuzzling her face.

Without pause, he sent the emergency text on standby, notifying their crew that Caly was waking up.

With her eyes still closed, Caly made a sleepy sound in her throat and took the first deep breath after what felt like a long, long sleep. She slowly blinked her eyes open. It felt as if her soul sighed when she met the eyes of impossible gold that became her heart. As if their eyes spoke the language of their soul, they stayed there, silently gazing upon one another for the longest moment.

"B—" Caly tried to speak his name but, god, her throat was like the Sahara desert. Blake immediately had a water bottle at her mouth and slowly let the liquid slide down her throat as she swallowed.

"SoCal!" the twins called out in unison as they appeared by the bed with shifter speed. They looked as if they wanted to pounce for a big feline pile up but Blake gave them a look that made them pull the reins back on that idea.

Then Caly noticed Nico.

Wait, am I seeing this right?

Nico was setting down Aleia who was holding Felix. Caly blinked. Yup. She didn't make that up.

"Caly!" Aleia blurted out, as Felix hopped onto the bed next to Caly, purring and rubbing his face on Caly's. Aleia automatically went into full healer mode, not only scanning Caly but also sending healing energy into her.

Nico gently squeezed her forearm with one of his side smiles in his silent way of greeting.

"Caly." Riordan gave her a warm smile and gently brought his fist over his heart in the way that warriors acknowledge one another.

Caly returned the smile and a whole new, fresh set of tears were flowing at his proud and loving gesture.

"Caly, your starlight has been missed dearly." Deacon spoke his poetic words. His pack brothers had only seen that side of him on the rarest of occasions.

Caly took another sip of water and cleared her throat. "I don't think I've ever heard my name spoken so many times in a row." She coughed out a laugh. On a more calm note, she refocused her gaze on Blake. "I saw my parents again. They—" She had to swallow. "They said they love you too." She was smiling at the memory.

Or was that a dream?

Blake may have blinked a couple of times before pressing his lips to hers. A wolf whistle called out, probably one of the twins, and the kiss was broken with laughter.

"Caly," Riordan began with a look in his eye that Caly couldn't quite translate, but that was often the way of ancients. "Some travelers evolve with the ability to travel to the realm of The Ancient Ones. I believe one day, you will." He had been mulling this over since she saw her parents during her change and with this second incident, he felt that she had a right to know. He also wanted to add additional training to help build a strong foundation for this ability to naturally grow.

Silence stretched through the room as she caught up to what he said.

"What do you mean, 'travel to the realm of The Ancient Ones'?" She knew what it sounded like but Caly had lived long enough in this world of species to know that assuming anything was a rookie mistake.

"It's the ability to dream-travel to the ancestors. To those that have passed on," Riordan explained.

What he didn't say was that, even though it was out of her control at this point, the fact that she had even connected with her parents twice showed that the strength and degree of this ability would one day be incredibly strong.

Caly noted the stunned silence in the room.

Out of all of the crazy-ass shit that has happened and this has everyone stunned and staring?

"Ummm..." She tried to find her voice. "You all are freaking me out a little." The corners of her lips lifted in a tremulous smile. Everyone was awkwardly recovering from the freeze-frame. "Is this a bad thing or something?" she asked, not wanting to know the answer if it was.

"No, Caly. It's not bad." Blake gently squeezed her for reassurance.

"It's typically an evolved ability for an ancient traveler," Riordan offered with a warm comforting smile.

"But why not add on an ancient ability to your badass magnetic arsenal?" Rhyland quipped, trying to make light of the news and mask his own emotions trying to claw out. "Besides, the few ancients who are known to have the ability... well, let's just say they are ancients and don't usually go around offering their services out of the goodness of their hearts."

Of course. That's why everyone looked at me like that,

she realized, thinking she heard a faint growl from Rhyker.

"Look, you all are my family and I know first-hand what seeing my parents again has done for me." She paused. "*If I do have this ability and one day I can control it, then, of course, it goes without saying, that all you have to do is ask.*" She made eye contact with each of them on that vow.

"Bold move," Rhyland continued with his playful tone. Again, he kept a lockdown on his own emotions for what Caly was offering. "What if our ancestors are like bat shit crazy? Or in Nico's case, an actual vampire bat?"

His humor thawed the heavy emotion in the room.

Caly burst out laughing.

Nico shot a side glare at Rhyland with a look that said, *"I'll let that one slide this one time."*

Rhyland returned Nico's look with a sly, one-sided smile.

Epilogue

"Wow. It feels kind of surreal being back here," Caly said, walking into what Caly dubbed to be the bachelor pad. She knew she only spent a couple of days there but it would forever be the safe haven to her heart. It would forever remind her of Blake.

Blake set their bags down and shut the door to keep cool evening air out. Even though they technically just transitioned into spring, there was still a fading chill in the air. And, Blake agreed. It did feel strange being back at the house. He wasn't entirely sure what he was going to feel walking back into the place he called home with his pack for so long. Oddly enough, it wasn't how he thought it would feel. Of course, this place, and the forest itself, would always have a spot in his heart but he didn't long for it or miss it in the way he thought that he might. Because, his home was wherever his beautiful, strong, and courageous alpha female was.

It had been almost two months since Caly woke from the coma after battling Barker. Last week, The Order finally closed out the other case and, now, it was time for a much-needed break. Caly and Blake decided to get away and spend a few days at the bachelor pad. It would be the first time they would be spending time alone with each other and they were so looking forward to it. It's not like they both didn't love their pack and living in the fortress, but sometimes, time alone was necessary.

Besides, Blake had a special surprise for Caly. It was hard to keep a secret from Caly on principal but he was sure this secret was okay to keep. He thought the secret was blown after the twins sniffed it out and spilled it to the rest of the pack. Naturally, almost anything was impossible to keep a secret among the pack. But everyone was on board and liked the secret game. And the best part of all? To everyone's knowledge, Caly still had no idea nor did she even suspect anything.

Caly and Blake spent the evening relaxing and eating one of the several packed meals Meri prepared, and watched a movie. On the surface, it appeared like it was nothing special but it was everything. For those were the moments, the moments from light laughter to minutes of sweet silence, that truly meant the most. The movie may have had an encore of their own intimate scene on the couch. And, they may have also had a sequel in the kitchen while playing a sinful game with the whipped, strawberry dessert. Okay, so they may have been taking advantage of the fact that they were alone and had the entire house to themselves. When they finally made it to the bed, Caly fell asleep in Blake's warm arms on a contented sigh.

Caly was walking in the lush forest, as the warmth of the sun peeked through the canopy of the trees. She halted when she saw two grey wolves up ahead. She knew they were shifters from their large size. And she knew which one was the male since he was slightly larger. She didn't feel threatened, instead, she felt… love?

The wolves approached and shifted before her. She

blinked and furrowed her brow.

How could they shift into clothes?

They were smiling with fondness as if they knew her. They looked familiar.

Why do they look so familiar and yet...

Her heart stopped at the moment of recognition. She was face to face with Blake's parents. Their smiles deepened the moment they caught Caly's recognition.

"Caly," Blake's father greeted her with a warm smile. She saw so much of Blake in that smile.

"We are so pleased to meet you," his mother said.

His mother's eyes. Blake had his mother's golden eyes.

"H-hi," Caly managed to get out and they pulled her into a loving embrace as if she was their own.

"We are so proud of the male that he has become and the fine pack he leads," his father said with pure love in his eyes.

"Please let him know we didn't suffer." Tears were pooling in his mother's eyes, triggering Caly's own set of tears.

"We couldn't have imagined a more suitable alpha female for our Blake." His father added and this time, the love was directed at her.

Caly's tears freely flowed down her cheeks at the purest love she felt from his parents.

"Oh, and let him know that we approve of the color design and choice." His father had the same sly, one-sided, wolf smile that Blake did when he was playing a game with her. And then she saw that same playful look in his mother's eyes that she knew too well.

Caly smiled.

"We love you both very much." His mother's words were the last thing she heard as everything faded to warm bright white light.

"Caly?" Blake gently held her close as the unmistakable scent of fresh tears, full of pure love, filled his senses.

"Blake..." Her throat was thick. She was still processing the lingering love she felt from his parents.

"Did you see your parents again?" he concluded. That was the only time he scented that on her.

"No, I—" She swallowed. "Blake, I saw *your* parents."

He stilled and his golden eyes met hers.

She smiled. "You have your mother's eyes and your father's smile." She saw a sheen to his eyes and continued, "Their love for you is... pure love." She paused, trying to remember everything. "They said they are proud of you, the male you have become and the pack you lead. They wanted you to know that they didn't suffer."

With her words, it felt as if a great weight was lifted off of his heart. He never mentioned this to Caly, or to anyone, but the thought of them suffering in the fire, haunted the back corners of his mind.

"They said they couldn't have imagined a more suitable alpha female for you. And that they love us both very much." She paused. "There's one more thing." She had a more curious tone to her voice now. "They approve of the color choice and design?" Caly was surprised at Blake's sudden stiffness to that last part. Especially because that was the one thing she didn't understand.

"Did they say anything else?" Blake asked with an expression that had Caly concerned.

"No, I'm sorry. Honestly, I have no idea what it means. I just figured it was something only for you. Your father said it with that sly, wolfy smile that you do with me when we're playing. I'm sorry... I should have asked them what they meant."

"No, Caly." He blew out a breath and visibly relaxed.

"I'm sorry. I know what they mean. It just caught me off guard, that's all."

She was curious what it meant. But she of all specians knew that some things between a parent and their child were sacred and not meant for others.

"Thank you, Caly." He looked into her eyes for the gift she just gave him. Pressing his lips to hers, he heard her stomach growl and smiled. "Let's eat breakfast."

They ate breakfast and Caly noticed something about Blake seemed a little... off. She wondered if she did something wrong or maybe should have waited to let Blake know about his parents. But no. She wouldn't keep that from him. Whatever it was, she knew Blake was trying not to show it, but she knew her male too well not to catch the little nuances. She almost brought it up to him but then she figured she'd give him more time to process.

They had another slow, lazy start to the day and may have walked around the house naked, you know, just because they could. It wasn't until about midday, when Blake suggested for a hike, that they put on clothes and went outside for the first time. Okay, well, their nude lunch on the back porch, which quickly escalated to a sinfully sensual dessert, didn't really count for going outside. Or did it?

Caly's heart just about burst when she saw the wild wolves. This time, Blake brought her to their den. She went through a sniffing welcome and her heart overflowed when she saw that the same two wolves she previously met were accompanied by four little wolf pups. The pups nipped and played with her and eventually she was surrounded by almost ten wolf pups. She was rolling in the grass, laughing, and playing. She caught Blake looking at her with this expression she almost couldn't read. There was love, yes, but something else. Then, she whispered to the wolf pups, as if in playful conspiracy, and led the crawling charge to ambush Blake. He allowed Caly's tackle to take him down and the wolf pups pounced and joined in.

Their time with the wolves ended too soon but Blake said they would visit again tomorrow. He wanted to show her something. She wanted to protest so she could stay with the wolves but, again, she saw the look in his eyes. He was trying to cover it up but it was there.

They hiked through the lush forest and Caly was about to say she needed a break when he announced, "We're here." She followed him past a few trees and through a gap between two boulders. On the other side, there was an incredible view of the forest below. The sky was blushing it's brushstrokes of golds, pinks, and purples, as the sun started its descent.

"Wow. It's so beautiful," she said with an awed breath.

Blake pulled her in for a side hug. "This is one of my favorite spots to watch the sunset."

It brought her back to that first species sunset she watched in Blake's room.

Looking up at him, she smiled. "Thank you."

He leaned down and pressed his lips to hers. He had to force himself to pull away to get their mini picnic set up so they could enjoy it as the sun set.

"Okay, but this is the last one," she said with a smile and a full belly as he fed her another sweet, juicy strawberry.

He licked the light red juice that dripped down her chin and then kissed her.

She gave him a protesting moan as he pulled away.

He chuckled.

She was about to take matters into her own hands when he stood up and offered his hand to help her up. Giving her wolf a curious look, she got to her feet and they walked away from the picnic, closer to the view. He looked at her and it sent this strange, warm feeling throughout her entire body.

Then, he knelt down on one knee and looked up at her.

"Blake?" she whispered.

"Caly. You are my heart. You are my soul. Will you be my forever?"

Blake uncurled his fist to reveal a breathtaking, heart-cut, bright, golden citrine surrounded by gray moonstone on a white gold band. It was them. His impossibly golden eyes and her stormy, gray eyes.

Caly's eyes shot up to Blake's and she smiled so wide with the waterworks that came as if on cue.

"Yes. Blake, yes!"

With shifter speed, she was in his arms, heart to heart, and he kissed her. He slid the ring on her ring finger.

They both looked at her hand as she held it out, gazing at the ring that represented them as it shone brightly against the magical, twilight sky.

Mom and dad, do you see this ring?

As if in answer, two white doves flew across the sky.

She wrapped her arms around his neck and gazed into his golden eyes.

"I love you, Blake."

"I love you, Caly."

Turn the page for a preview of

RHYKER'S KEY

The next novel in the Orion's Order series.

Book 2 Sneak Peek

Here's a sneak peek at:

RHYKER'S KEY

The next novel in the Orion's Order series.

Chapter 1

"Why do you think that's the case, Tom?" Keena asked in a gentle, calm voice.

Tom's dark brown eyes shifted to something over her left shoulder. He was probably looking at the geometric abstract art piece, made up of different shades of gray again.

Keena simply waited.

"It was just how she looked at me." Tom's eyes only focused on hers for a split second before they were glued back on the geometric art.

"And how did she look at you?" Keena probed again in a soft voice.

"Like as if I didn't exist."

"And how would it have felt if she did look at you as if you did exist?"

Tom's blue jeans, that were worn out at the knees, and his clean white T-shirt were soundless as he fidgeted in his seat a little. "I—" He cleared his throat. "I would have felt scared."

Keena felt Tom's fear but it wasn't into unproductive or dangerous territory, so there was no need for her to intervene. Instead, she asked, "What could have been one thing that might have helped you move toward your goal of complimenting this female when you felt scared?"

Tom's eyes were back on the art piece over her shoulder.

Keena felt Tom's fear subside somewhat as he was more focused on something other than the fear itself.

"Getting curious," he answered after a moment.

"And what would getting curious look like?"

"I could... I could focus on something specific about her."

"What could you have focused on about her?"

"The pastry she was eating?" he asked, slightly unsure.

"So, by getting curious and focusing on something specific about her, the pastry she was eating for example, then that could've been one thing that might have helped you move toward your goal of complimenting her. Do I understand that right?"

A faint line appeared in his russet skin between his dark brows as he considered what she said. Somehow after hearing it out loud with phrasing it like that, Tom realized that it seemed so simple and obvious to him.

"Yes." He spoke confidently.

"So, let's say you're focusing on the pastry. What could be one possible next step?"

There was a pause.

"I could ask her where she got the pastry?"

"And if you did ask her where she got the pastry, and let's say she answered, then what might be one thing that would bring you closer toward your goal of complimenting her?"

"I could... Well, I could compliment her," he said as if it was an easy and natural next step in the hypothetical conversation.

"And how would you compliment her?"

He was back to staring over her shoulder and he ran his hand through his short, dark brown hair.

She felt a slight rise of his anxiety at the question. No doubt, it was because he was imagining himself back in front of the female and playing this scenario out in his head.

But, again, the anxiety she felt wasn't overwhelming and she did not need to step in.

"I could say she has lovely eyes."

"And do you feel that would accomplish your goal?"

"Yes." He smiled, realizing how simple it all was when it was broken down in this way. "Thank you, Dr. Oliver." He looked into her eyes with gratitude. "That was... Thank you."

Tom now preferred to call her Dr. Oliver even though she had a rather relaxed style to her healing sessions and most of her patients called her by her first name. She knew that it helped him to address her as Dr. Oliver because of his recent development of social anxiety with females. She had been working with Tom before this, so he did not feel the anxiety with her. But rather, his anxiety was more with the prospect of potentially dating a new female.

"You're welcome, Tom. But that was all you. Such great progress."

His smile widened. "Thank you. And I'm going to try this before our next session."

She returned his smile like a proud mama bear. "I look forward to hearing how it goes." She looked at the clock on the wall. They were out of time. "Will I see you in class?"

"Of course. You know I wouldn't miss it. Again, thank you, Dr. Oliver."

"You're very welcome, Tom. And I'll see you in class in a bit."

Locking the door to her office after Tom left, Keena opened the door to the side room, which she used as a mini closet and changing room. Her simple and small office was a part of Inner Serenity, the local and quaint species healing center. As she walked into the side room, she thought of Tom. Tom had been her patient for years and she had a soft spot in her heart for that male. She had watched him rise above the difficult hand he was dealt.

Although, truthfully, she had a soft spot in her heart for a lot of her patients. It was just her nature being a mind and spirit healer. And, well, it also was how she chose to use her natural-born gifts and abilities. Since mind healer's specialties were with the internal workings of the mind, including emotions, it was not uncommon for middle to lower class mind healers, who couldn't afford the extensive healer training, to become bartenders. But not just any bartenders. They usually became successful and often highly sought after bartenders because of their ability to spike drinks with emotions.

But, no. Keena's parents sacrificed so much to help pay for her healer trainings. Since she was gifted with strong abilities for both mind and spirit, it was like putting two young through specialized medical school at the same time. And it was their sacrifices that ultimately resulted in Keena now being alone in the world. So, she built her entire practice to be of service to others who experienced tragic and traumatic events. It was an ode to her parents. It was an ode to her younger self. It was an ode to the vow she made on that terrible day to help others who were going through what she went through. Every time she walked over the threshold into her sacred office space or whenever she helped a patient, it was one more loving, gold flower placed at the altar to that vow she made so long ago.

She stripped out of her jeans and replaced it with her high-waisted, black yoga pants. Instead of changing out of her white T-shirt, she simply knotted it at the waist and then threw her long and wavy, golden-copper hair in a messy bun, allowing a few strands to escape. She really embraced her whole "Namaste meets sweet girl next door" vibe and didn't fuss with a lot of makeup or fancy clothes. She did a quick check in the tall mirror that fully captured her long and lean, 5'10" frame. Her emerald green eyes, which popped against her alabaster skin, landed on the simple small-chained, golden, upside-down crescent moon necklace resting on her upper chest.

The crescent moon was a little thicker than it was when she originally bought it. And it wasn't because the necklace changed with the phases of the moon—although, that certainly did exist in the species world. Keena liked the crescent moon in stasis because every time she looked at it, it was as if the moon was smiling at her. But the crescent moon's smile was now wider because it was recently upgraded and secretly fully-loaded with an SEW, or small electrical weapon, invented by none other than Deacon, the computer-genius steorrian and brother of everything but blood to a rowdy unconventional pack of five hot-blooded males.

After the terrifying incident between Caly and James Barker, AKA The Ghost, during this past winter, both Orion's Order, which was the rowdy pack of hot-blooded males, and Riordan Knight, would not accept anything less than both Aleia and Keena wearing a hidden SEW at all times, just as Caly did. Okay, so she wasn't a part of The Order or anything but she was very close friends with both Aleia, Riordan's healer, and Caly, who was now mated to Blake Stone, alpha wolf shifter and leader of Orion's Order, AKA the lethally-skilled hunters that often took on the most VIP cases for SILE, Species Intelligence and Law Enforcement.

Caly and Blake recently had their mating ceremony at "the fortress," an affectionate name Caly gave to the castle with which the pack now called home. It was a small ceremony consisting mainly of the crew, or The Order, along with Riordan, Aleia, and Keena. The only others present at the mating ceremony were the castellans bonded to the Knight bloodline and Alexina, the ancient steorrian that Blake had developed a special relationship with after his parents passed away in a tragic fire.

At the ceremony, Keena spent a considerable amount of time with one of the five males, Rhyker. Nothing happened, of course, because of the vow they made together at the Gallagher gathering, *"To playing in the moment."* Sure, she was incredibly attracted to this male and oftentimes found herself feeling like a schoolgirl with a major crush as she reminisced about their sexy kiss, stolen in a dark corner the first time they met. But she wasn't in a place to start a new relationship, no matter how badly she wanted to. She was still healing from her previous relationship that had gone so terribly wrong.

After a few years, she found the strength and courage to break up with Liam Carter, her ex, because the relationship turned toxic on many levels and she knew she couldn't save it or, rather, save him. And nor was it her responsibility to. That was a very hard lesson for her first-hand, especially as a mind and spirit healer. Then, out of the blue, Liam sent her a handwritten letter and a single yellow rose.

In the letter, he said he was seeing a mind healer, which was something she practically begged for him to do at the end of their relationship. He owned up to his faults and said that he never meant to hurt her. He knew he messed up and he didn't expect her to forgive him. But he wanted her to know that he was sorry and that he would always regret how he treated her towards the end. He said he would always love her and that she would forever be the one that got away. He didn't ask for her forgiveness, a response, or even to get back together. It was him trying to make amends and bring closure to a terrible ending of what was a fairy-tale beginning.

One week after receiving the letter, she reached out to Liam. They started talking just as friends but their feelings for one another were so deep and strong that it quickly transitioned into dating once more. Yeah, even though it was hard to admit, a part of her may have still loved Liam. And their second time around was going so well... until it wasn't. It was just like it was in the beginning when they first met. Actually, it was even better than she could have ever imagined. She saw and witnessed the changes in him. But she only realized too late just how much of a mistake it was getting back together with Liam, especially when she barely had the strength to leave the first time.

One night, their relationship took a sudden sharp turn and she found herself on a familiar dark street on memory lane that she swore she would never go down ever again. Yet, there she stood physically and emotionally bruised.

She was late getting home that night because, after her session with Caly, she met up with Aleia to express her concerns that she noticed in Caly. Caly was going through a really rough patch and they were all close to losing her to "the Dark Side." Well, that conversation went on a lot longer than Keena expected and when she left, she saw that she had multiple missed calls and several texts from Liam, demanding to know where she was. She apologized profusely and immediately explained that, not only did she keep her phone off during sessions but also, she was in a consultation with Aleia. But it didn't matter. He accused her of lying and cheating on him. She had never seen that look in his eyes before, not even in the worst moments of their relationship. Infuriated, he lost his temper and crossed a line he never had before. He smacked her hard across her face and, being a fire elemental, left burn marks on her arms where he gripped her.

Up until that point, the abuse she experienced was verbal and somehow she could always justify it, seeing his side of what she had believed he was trying to express. She knew it just came out wrong.

She was still so ashamed and embarrassed and no one really truly knew what she went through. She also felt like a failure and a fraud. She was an intelligent female and an educated mind and spirit healer. So, she couldn't understand how any of that had happened. How she claimed to help others when she single-handedly got herself into that abusive situation not once but twice. No one forced her to reach out to Liam. No one forced her to get back together with him. It was all her. She knew all of the telltale signs and red flags and it was so classic, almost textbook, and yet there she was, healing from an abusive relationship.

Closing the lid to that box of wounds, Keena's mind shifted gears and she thought about something she often did... Rhyker. Naturally, because she couldn't seem to stop thinking about that sexy bad boy. This time, her mind conjured up the memory with Rhyker as the two of them clinked their glasses together and made the friendly vow, *"To playing in the moment."* She remembered that moment clearly as if it just happened a few minutes ago. She remembered their conversation and she remembered thinking about why couldn't she play and have fun? Why couldn't she keep things light? Why did it all have to be so serious and heavy? And who the hell said that healing after a bad relationship had to be a solitary journey? She wanted to spend time with Rhyker, so she did. And, to his credit, he had kept his word by honoring and respecting the boundaries she set.

"I'd be lying if I said I wasn't thinking about tasting your lips again. But why don't we take the pressure off and just play in the moment?" That was what Rhyker proposed and that was what they had been doing.

The crew all hung out a lot at the fortress and she usually joined them after her sessions with Caly a few times a week. So, yeah, they had been spending a lot of time together but it was always in a group setting, never one on one. And, other than that first time they met with the hottest kiss of her life, they had not crossed the friendship line drawn in the sand. Although, the line didn't really matter because everyone knew that they both had their eyes on each other. Especially since his gorgeous, piercingly blue, feline eyes practically devoured her in a single glance. He was a predator, prowling and watching his prey, just waiting to pounce. She knew the moment they both hung out together alone, that line would no longer exist because their magnetic attraction for each other was palpable and their chemistry was off the charts. And it was all confirmed by that first kiss of course.

Keena walked into the slightly heated yoga room and froze. In the back right corner of the room, she saw Rhyker. It was as if she manifested him into existence from her all-consuming thoughts of that sexy male. Either her fantasies of him took an unexpected turn or he was actually there on one of the spare blue, studio yoga mats. The mat looked absolutely ridiculous in comparison to his giant, almost seven-foot tall, muscular body of sigh-worthy cut muscle.

God, just one look at that male had her body reacting in a very feminine way.

Together. She needed to pull herself together from being a melting pool of desire on the honey-colored, wooden floor. She pumped the brakes on her hormones and recovered quickly. But it didn't matter. She knew he caught her re-action from his satisfied smug feline expression. And, holy hell, that sexy smirk of his almost had her as the melted pool once more.

His gorgeous blue eyes met hers for a split second before he proceeded to lay down on the mat and close his eyes, as if he was leisurely taking a cat nap.

Apparently, she wasn't the only one who noticed his presence, because, yup, every single female, and male for that matter, was subtly (not so subtly) gawking at him. Her lips twitched when she saw a few of the females adjust their hair and bras to perk up their attributes a little.

Swallowing, she tried to get back with the program.

Turn down the lights. Put on the pre-class playlist. Diffuse the blended floral scent of relaxation. Turn up the heat. Although, that male seemed to have accomplished that last part, purely with his presence, Keena thought, giving her mind simple commands to not make it seem so obvious how much he affected her.

Her eyes flicked to the time on her phone. *Okay, I have fifteen minutes to dunk my head in cold water and prepare for class. You know, because you have to teach right now.* If that thought didn't knock some sense into her all of a sudden...

Being a strong healer of both the mind and spirit, her training and background was extensive and included things like psychology, counseling, psychotherapy, and various components of spirit medicine. Basically, anything to do with the mind and spirit, she soaked it up like the curious sponge she was. The healing world of species was vastly different than the healing world of humans in many respects, one being that it was well-known and accepted that healing was an integrative holistic approach of the mind, body, and spirit. Even though Keena was a spirit and mind healer, she was also naturally passionate about the third part of that healing triad, the physical body. That was why she incorporated mindful movement, such as yoga and dance, into her personal and professional practice. It was also why her style was a bit unique because she not only had an integrative and comprehensive mind, spirit, and body approach but also, she was humble and down to Earth.

Humans adopted yoga from species, specifically spirit healers. Because yoga originally wasn't a physical practice.

In fact, it was a very conscious practice of the spirit. Spirit healers considered it a practice to connect with the magic of life and heal from the core of the soul. The physical practice of yoga didn't become a component until later on when it became clear that the mind, body, and spirit were all connected and couldn't be treated as anything else.

Before walking back into the yoga room, she took a deep, centering breath. On her exhale, she set her feelings for Rhyker aside. Right now, she was Keena, the mind and spirit healer and she was about to lead the class. With that, she walked in. Slowly phasing out the song that was playing, she put on the playlist for the class.

"Hello, my name is Keena and I'm honored to guide you through your practice today," she began in her "yoga teacher voice" which was slow and soothing. "Remember, that I'm just a guide and this practice is for you. Honor your unique body and mold each pose to best suit your body and your practice. We'll begin in Child's pose. Bring your knees wide apart. Encourage your big toes towards one another. Outstretch your arms in front of you. Rest your forehead on the mat or a block. Good. Take a deep breath in. Allow your belly to sink towards the earth. Audible open-mouth exhale out. Nice breath everyone. Again. Deep breath in. And open-mouth exhale like you're fogging up a mirror. One more time. Deep breath in. And this time, on your exhale, seal your lips and engage your oceanic breath as it sounds like the waves of the ocean. Allow this breath to lull your mind, body, and spirit throughout your practice today."

She paused briefly, allowing her students to sink into the space further.

"Focus on the four corners of your mat. Know that anything beyond that sacred space does not exist. Yoga is a personal practice to heal from our core, from our soul. It is a practice to acknowledge the challenges we experience and feel. It is an opportunity for us to practice how we move through them. So, for the next hour, I encourage you to close your eyes as much as possible and focus inward. Focus on your intention for being on your mat today. On your next inhale, call in that intention. Why are you here?"

As the students silently called in their intentions, she energetically carved out their own individual sacred space around each of their mats. This was for support and encouragement for them to connect with their spirit as they moved throughout their practice. She also opened her mind-healing abilities and sent out a touch of relaxation into the space to ease any physical or emotional tension. With her senses now open, she would also be able to help guide students through any challenging emotions that arose. Emotions could get "stuck" in the energetic body and Keena's ability allowed her to help a student let go of the emotions and heal from their core wounds.

Keena spared a glance at Rhyker and internally smiled. She knew, no matter who you were, it took a level of courage and vulnerability to walk into a yoga class by yourself, especially at a new studio you've never been to before. Let alone that being your first ever yoga class. She knew this was his first class too because he told her he'd never done yoga before. And, yet, he casually sauntered into her class and was in his version of child's pose. Of course, there was no right or wrong way for any of the poses, for everyone was unique and each pose was unique to them. But she did secretly admit to herself he looked extra cute with his butt up in the air. His body and muscles were so large, there was absolutely no way his butt would get any closer than the few feet off the ground it currently was. And throw out the fact that it would be impossible for his toes to touch. And he owned it. She could feel his easy confidence and comfort in his own body. And that was so hot.

Well then, Rhyker thought, a bit surprised as he felt waves of relaxation and what he presumed was some sort of spirit-healing thing. He knew that Caly not only raved about Keena's classes but also tried many times to get the males to join in with her. Fat chance that was going to happen. Yet, here he was at yoga class. If this was the only way he could be with Keena without everyone else in the crew watching them like they were a personal daytime soap opera, then so be it. His ass would be at yoga once a week.

He knew this was a big surprise and an even bigger step for them. He had been respecting the boundaries she set initially, but plenty of time had passed. The only thing that changed was that he was more interested in her than ever. This female fascinated him. She was not only beautiful but also intelligent. And he knew she was interested in him as well. So, he figured it wouldn't hurt to play a bit more and test the waters so to speak. Besides, he liked playing with her and had so many fun games in mind for them both.

But he also knew why she set those boundaries. He knew she was really hurt from her last relationship. He didn't know any specifics because she never spoke about them but he could scent the change in her emotions, including the doubt in herself, whenever it was brought up. He wanted to find whoever the male was who hurt her and made her feel anything less than the strong and smart female she was and... have *words* with him.

"On your next inhale, call in that intention. Why are you here?" Keena guided the class in a voice that had his other half practically purring.

If she only knew why I was here, he thought with an inward feline grin. Because he was here for a specific reason and it was not just to take her yoga class.

Chapter 2

"Great class, Keena!" a female called out over her shoulder as she walked out.

"Amazing! Thank you!" another female followed up.

"Thank you," a male said.

It was Tom. He was just shy of six feet with dark brown hair and shy eyes. He looked like he could have been a brother to one of the Native American wolf shifters in *Twilight*—just a more introverted and timid brother, with the testosterone dial turned way down. Keena noted that Tom dared a quick look at the massive male that was towering over everyone.

At one glance, everyone knew the massive male, AKA Rhyker, was a predatory shifter with a large animal because they were notoriously tall—it was just how they were built. Rhyker stood back a couple of feet behind Keena and she could practically feel the intensity of his piercing blue eyes fixed on her.

She saw Tom swallow and felt a hint of fear. Because her mind-healing abilities were on the stronger side of the scale, she was able to pick up on hints of emotions without completely "turning on" her ability. For some healers, their abilities were not strong enough to pick up on emotions or bodily injuries without being in a healer session and fully opening up their abilities. That was not the case for Keena. So, picking up on subtle hints of emotions was as natural to her as breathing. In conversation, she once explained, *"Everyone breathes and we are all constantly smelling things in the air, literally all of the time, whether we are conscious of it or not. Sometimes when the scent is strong, you immediately notice, like an aromatic perfume or a delicious-smelling meal. But sometimes it's not as obvious unless you specifically close your eyes and consciously focus on what you're smelling."* For Keena, it was just as if her dial to pick up on emotions was a touch more sensitive. It was similar to the naturally-heightened senses of the shifters and vampires—they weren't trying to pry or cross an ethical line by eavesdropping, they simply couldn't help it. It was just who they were.

She internally closed her eyes, knowing that Rhyker's presence was extremely intimidating to Tom. It no doubt just highlighted his social anxiety around females, especially considering the fact that all of the females were still attempting to get Rhyker's attention, which meant, just as Tom said earlier in their session, that the females were looking at him as if he didn't exist.

"You're welcome, Tom. See you next week." Keena smiled. She wanted to send Tom off with a little extra boost of confidence while at the same time easing his fear. Except, that would be completely unethical and against the healer's oath she took upon completion of her healer training. She would never use her ability and manipulate someone's emotions without their consent. During yoga class or patient sessions, she clearly outlined the context for which she would use her abilities. So, everyone knew what they were walking into when they stepped foot into her office or onto the yoga mat. But it would be completely inappropriate for her to use her abilities on Tom right now without his knowledge or consent, no matter how good and pure her intentions. Especially because it was possible that if she did ease his fear and send him a boost of confidence, it might actually hinder his progress. It would be far more beneficial for him to work through his emotions in a healthy way instead of putting a proverbial Band-Aid over them. Because at that point, she might as well be a walking pharmacy, dispensing emotional doses so her patients didn't have to deal with their emotions.

As Rhyker waited for everyone to leave—and Jesus, some of them were extra chatty—he thought about the class. It was nothing like he expected. And, yeah, he was sweating balls during it. In some of the poses, they had to hold still for several breaths. And why were the breaths like several seconds each? His original plan was to watch this beautiful female when she was in her element, doing what he knew she was so passionate about. And he did watch her. But he also found himself mysteriously, and repeatedly, getting sucked into some sort of vortex, where he forgot he was watching her and became so involved in the moment of the pose. Before he knew it, the class was over. It was all very curious.

Finally, the bell on the door chimed, signifying that the last student had left the studio. It was now just them.

Keena slowly turned around and looked at Rhyker with a curious smile. His black basketball shorts and black, muscle T clung close to his big body with sweat. He lit up a hand-rolled and the detailed tattoos weaving up his right arm and teasing above the neckline of his shirt, flexed with the motion. He was the ultimate bad boy with his strong jaw, light skin, black, diamond-stud earrings, obsidian black hair, and piercing, electric blue eyes. And she knew his hair matched the silky midnight fur of his jaguar form. Although, she had never seen him in animal form. And holy hell, she found it so hot when he lit up a smoke.

Rhyker smoked indigo, a plant with blue flowers that was said to have evolved from the tobacco plant species after The Barrier was put in place. The Barrier was a magical barrier that separated the human world from the world of species. Legend says, it was created as a final solution to bring peace to the world and end the ancient territorial world war where humans turned on the other species out of fear.

The indigo plant only grew on the magical side of The Barrier. Species were more relaxed about smoking than humans because they were not susceptible to the negative side effects of smoking, like cancer. And, yes, this also meant that it wasn't unusual to smoke indoors.

"Humans would seriously be freaking out about the indoor smoking situation of species," Caly said once when they were out at Spiked, the species bar. *"I mean, we probably would have a straight-up riot on our hands and the Surgeon General breathing down our backs—probably with an oxygen mask, of course. And thank God indie is nothing like human tobacco. I mean, that stuff smells like complete shit and it's no wonder with all of the chemical crap they stuff into it. Not to mention the second-hand smoke would have my lungs coughing in protest. But, yeah, indie smells nice. It has just a hint of something floral, like incense. And the smoke isn't heavy or anything at all. It's so light and dissipates quickly."*

"How are you feeling?" Keena teased with a smile as she watched Rhyker blow out a puff of blue-gray smoke. The pleasant aroma of the smoke wafted over to her and teased her senses.

"Relaxed," he said with a lazy smirk.

"Rhyker, why are you here?" she asked with a playfully curious smile.

"Because I wanted to take your class," he drawled and she laughed. He liked it when she laughed.

"Seriously. Not that you're not welcome because you are. Although, you certainly were distracting to some of the females… and males," she quipped.

"Was I distracting to you?" His lazy feline grin was full of amusement.

"Of course not," she teased sarcastically.

"Good. Because I plan on coming back next week." Smoke poured out of his mouth like a dragon as he spoke. When he saw her eyebrows quirk up in surprise, he added, "Do you think I should get a bigger mat?" And his grin widened.

She laughed, remembering how the mat almost looked like an elongated hand towel underneath his massive body. "Perhaps we should find one that's a little bigger," she managed to say in between her laughs.

"Wanna get some ice cream?" He casually slipped in the invitation but both he and his wild cat were anything but casual as he sharpened his senses and focused on her.

Being a black jaguar shifter, he not only had shifter strength and speed but he also had heightened senses of smell, hearing, and eyesight. In fact, his hearing far exceeded the standards for shifters. So, he definitely noticed her breath catch in surprise as she bit her lower lip. He knew this female well enough now to know that she, no doubt, had a million thoughts racing through her mind. So, he waited and watched with fixed focus.

Go get ice cream? Keena thought. *As in, just us two getting ice cream together? As in us hanging out alone for the first time? As in… a date? Would this be a date? He didn't say it was a date but it certainly seems like it would be a date.* She thought about the friendship line drawn in the sand between them. *Dare I cross the line?* She knew once she crossed the threshold, things would forever be changed—for better or for worse.

Friends or not, she knew she was already too emotionally invested in this male. It was how her heart sped up whenever he walked into the room. Or how she fussed with her hair or clothes in the mirror, knowing she was about to hang out with their crew and that he would be there. Or how she still fantasized about their one and only, hot as hell, kiss. Okay, well, it was technically two, mind-blowing kisses but they were only moments apart, so she kind of lumped it into one. So, yeah, despite her trying to keep him at a friendly distance, she was already way too emotionally invested in this male.

On top of that, she was not the type of female who could do one night stands, unlike her friend, Aleia, who appeared to be the master at that. She didn't understand how Aleia even did that. Sex to her was intimate on so many levels. To her, it was an impossibility to just have casual sex with no strings attached. And, yeah, Keena knew if she crossed the line in the sand, she would inevitably have sex with this male.

And she also knew that if it didn't work out between them, things would get really awkward and would change the dynamic of the tight-knit group, which had become her friends too. She knew, since she was the newest member of the crew, it would be the right thing for her to be the one to leave and keep a respectable distance. She would just have to hang out with Caly and Aleia separately. She knew that in the chance that things didn't work out, she wouldn't be able to be in the same room as this male once the line was crossed. No way.

But what if it did work? Okay. What would that even

mean? What is wrong with me? Is there a dial so I can turn down the crazy train of thoughts? Sometimes she swore all of those mind-healing degrees backfired in the form of being an overthinker and overanalyzing everything. *Stop. Do you want to get ice cream with him? Yes. Then what's stopping you?*

She blew out a breath because it was fear. Fear that this wouldn't work out and she would lose her friends, including her friendship with Rhyker. And fear that she couldn't trust her own self after Liam. Even though she knew with every cell in her body, Rhyker was nothing like Liam. In fact, Rhyker was a good, honorable, and trustworthy male who would never intentionally hurt a female. But if it didn't work out then she would inevitably be hurt, not by his intentions but simply because she would have put her heart on the line without it panning out. *Are you really going to let fear of the what-if and the unknown dictate your life? If you don't do this and let's say a decade or two passes, how would you feel? Regret,* she thought, her heart sinking at the thought of missing an opportunity because the overanalyze express train simply missed the stop. Then, an image of him going out with another female popped into her mind. No. She wouldn't let that happen. So, she decided to cross the line in the sand.

"Yes, I would love to get ice cream with you," she said with a smile.

She said yes. Say something, Rhyker thought, quickly getting into gear. He was almost preparing for her to say no. But she said yes. Both he and his jaguar were very pleased. The hunt had just become more interesting.

"Have you been to that new place, Swirlberry?" he asked, keeping his reaction cool and casual. He already checked ahead of time and knew that place had her favorite flavor. Yeah, this was his plan all along but just sped up on the timeline a bit. But, hey, he wasn't complaining about that.

"Actually, I haven't yet. But I've been wanting to try it. I've heard it's really good."

"Cool. Do you wanna change or anything?"

"No, I'm good. I'll just go grab my purse from my office real quick."

"No need. It's my treat." He gave her a smile that was deceptively lazy but because she knew this male, she noticed that look in his eyes that said he wasn't budging on that.

Okay. So, yeah. This is a date. Why else would he make it clear he was paying? "Thanks." She smiled and switched subjects. "So, seriously. What did you think?"

He held the door open for her. "Well, I'm coming back next week, aren't I?"

"True enough. Caly may be jealous that you came to class without her."

He chuckled. "She had training with Rhy today. Besides, she already has class with you a few times a week."

Little did Keena know, he intentionally planned this little outing exactly when Caly had self-defense training with Rhyland. Because he wanted this to be just him and Keena without any peanut gallery. And, yeah, if he knew his identical twin brother at all, Rhyland would be all too eager to pounce at the chance to watch him make a fool of himself in yoga class, all for a female. And his brother would definitely have plenty of words about that because this actually was his joking idea after all.

"Hey, I have an idea. Maybe you should take one of her yoga classes so you have an excuse to ogle her for an hour. In fact, I would pay money to see that."

Yeah. He didn't plan on letting anyone know about this. Ever.

Walking out of Inner Serenity, Keena took a deep breath and soaked up the early afternoon sun. Even though they technically just transitioned into fall, it was as if the summer sun decided for a warming encore before succumbing to its inevitable winter slumber. Keena's eyes fell on the large forest park across the street, Rutherford Falls.

The species world was extremely mindful of protecting the natural world and habitats as much as possible. They respected the world they lived in and because some subspecies abilities were so attuned to the Earth and nature, they understood the delicate balance of nature very well. They also understood that these places were home to so many different subspecies and creatures that sustained the natural balance of life. So, protecting the environment was just the way of species. This is also why there was always a lot of nature around wherever one was.

"Beautiful, huh?" Rhyker asked when he noticed her looking at the leaves that had begun their transformation to deep golds, scarlets, and purples, as if they were brush-stroked with watercolors. He may have also been secretly referring to the beautiful female by his side. Although, he kept that part to himself, for now. He didn't want to scare her off when they were only a couple of steps into their first date.

She nodded. "Caly tells me that LA and so much of the human world has been bulldozed and replaced with concrete and metal. It's such a shame and I can't even imagine." She had never been on the other side of The Barrier. Of course, she could go if she wanted but she never really felt called. Plus, the risk of being caught by humans was too great and not worth the mini-exploration.

"Yeah. It really is a whole other world on the other side." He shook his head in sad disapproval because he had seen the concrete jungle that the humans had created on the other side of The Barrier. It made the wild cat in him want to claw some of those humans to knock some sense into them. "It's nice out. Do you wanna get the ice cream to go and walk through the park?"

"Yeah. That sounds really nice."

He opened the door to Swirlberry and they walked inside. It was a charming, little, mom-and-pop ice cream shop. There were a few others in line so Keena had time to look around. It was bright, clean, and simple with the vivid colors of various ice cream flavors on display. She noticed a couple of females sitting down in one of the booths, perk up, whisper to themselves with smiles, and then giggle while looking at Rhyker. Yeah, Keena knew what that was all about because she practically had the same reaction to him too. On the wall behind the display case, the shop's name, "Swirlberry," was in a fun and inviting, flowy font of pastel pinks, purples, and blues. Swirlberry was an actual berry that grew on a plant exclusive to the species side of The Barrier.

The berry itself was similar to a blueberry in size, shape, and texture but they grew like grapes in a bunch. And, as both the berry and the ice cream shop's name alluded to, their color was what made them unique. The sweet and juicy berries were a swirl of varying pastel shades of light pinks, purples, and blues. It always made pastries and deserts look like they were full of fun and happy promises. And best of all, thanks to their vivid variety of colors, they were considered a nutritious superfood. It was just one of mother nature's gifts.

On the wall to the left, Keena saw a single picture. It was of a male and female couple in front of the shop, smiling wide, with a bold sign displaying the grand opening. Keena took a step closer and glanced at the short text under the picture. She was pleased to read that this shop was locally owned and run by a young castellan couple, Penny and Rowan.

Castellans were a subspecies and were true caretakers to their very core. They often bonded with a prominent family to form a mutually beneficial relationship of not only love and loyalty but also, the castellans were provided for on other levels, including financially. They were truly happy when being of service for their family or others. When they were bonded with a family, it translated to caring for and maintaining their homefront with things like cooking, cleaning, and house repairs. And their abilities complemented this with things like strength and speed—but not nearly as much as vampires or shifters had. When they didn't choose to bond with a family, they often owned restaurants or worked with buildings in some manner because they had a knack with cooking chemistry and architecture. In fact, castellans considered those to be a sacred art and science.

Keena refocused back behind the counter and now recognized that both Penny and Rowan were working. She caught their quick, smiling glance to one another and felt their loving affection pulse off of them as if it was a part of their beating hearts. Keena smiled and had to blink back tears because it reminded her of her parents.

Rhyker picked up on a subtle shift in Keena's scent. But almost as soon as it was there, it was gone. He gave her an appraising look but before he could question it his thoughts were cut off.

"What can I get you both?" Penny asked with a cheerful smile.

Neither of them knew. Keena was caught up with taking in the shop and then blinking back her emotions, she didn't even get to thinking about what she was going to order. And Rhyker was originally amused with her curiosity of the shop, only to be distracted with his attempt to decipher what that faintest scent of hers was before it was gone a heartbeat later.

"Can I try the—" he just said the first flavor that he saw. "Coffee Toffee Nut Crunch?"

Coffee Toffee Nut Crunch? What in the actual fuck? he thought, but tried to play it off cool. Because hey, he liked all of those things separately so why not mix it all together?

"Of course," Penny said with a bright smile. She scooped a little spoonful and handed it to him. "Here you go."

He shoved it into his mouth and—hey, what do you know? It actually was pretty damn good. He may even get a scoop of it.

"Did you see they have Dark Ambrosia?" Rhyker casually slipped that suggestion in because he knew that was Keena's favorite flavor. It was a dark and rich, velvety chocolate with swirls of salted caramel and chunks of chocolate fudge.

Keena's eyes lit up. "I didn't. Oh, I'm so getting some of that." But then her gaze fell on the Full Moon flavor. She bit her bottom lip, clearly torn between the two. The marbled white and light gray was another species flavor she really liked.

He caught the dilemma in her expression. "You know, you can have as many flavors as your heart desires, right?" He winked and gave her a side smirk.

She laughed a little. "I know. But I don't think I'd be able to finish it all."

"Female, you know you don't have to worry about that with me around. It would bring me pleasure to lap up anything of yours," he drawled, letting the sensual double entendre speak for itself. And, yeah, he noticed the tint of blush on her cheeks, as well as her parted lips and quickened pulse.

The visual image of Rhyker's tongue licking her and kissing her once more speared straight through her, right down to her most feminine of places.

Focus, Keena. She broke his eye contact to refocus on Penny, who was giving off the subtle hint of amusement at their playful banter, even though her outward smile was still perfectly cute and charming.

She cleared her throat. "I'd like two scoops of Dark Ambrosia and Full Moon please."

"Two scoops of each or just one of each?" Penny clarified.

"Oh, sorry." Keena laughed a little, trying to play it off but she knew that she needed to get the image of Rhyker's mouth on hers out of her mind so she could place an ice cream order for heaven's sake. "Just one scoop each."

While Penny scooped up her order, she caught the satisfied smug expression on Rhyker's face.

"Here you go." Penny handed Keena a gigantic waffle cone with two equally large scoops.

Keena's eyes widened. There was no way she was going to be able to finish that. "Wow, that's really big." She half-laughed with an exhale.

With shifter speed, Rhyker's mouth was suddenly brushing the softshell of her ear. He teased with the barest whisper of breath, "That's what she said."

It had nothing to do with what he said but it was more of how he said it, how his breath teased her neck, and how his earthy, sexy, and masculine scent wafted around her. And holy hell, she could feel the sensual desire pulsing off of him. Her own body responded with her inner muscles clenching as slick liquid started to pool between her thighs. She knew this time, her blush was deep and she would've dropped the damn cone if Rhyker's broad, and slightly calloused, hand didn't cup hers and steady it.

A heartbeat later, and as if he didn't just stir up a sensual storm, he casually put in his three-scooped order with that unassumingly lazy, feline tone of his. Keena didn't even know what he ordered because all she was trying to do was recover from the haze. When her mind finally came back online, she realized he had already ordered and paid, and now, he was holding the door open for her. Okay. If that was her reaction to a little innocent flirting, then, yeah, she was way too far gone when it came to this male.

"I'd like one scoop each of Snickering Surprise, I Keep It Vanilla, and Coffee Toffee Nut Crunch." Rhyker had to force himself to pull away from Keena and place his order. Yeah, so screw him. He decided to get the Coffee Toffee Nut Crunch.

"Toppings?" the female worker asked.

"Oh, definitely. Can you mix double gummy bears into the vanilla scoop and then top the entire thing off with brownie bites?" His eyes landed on the old fashioned Rolo candy. He didn't even know those were even still in existence. "And add the Rolos?"

"Absolutely," the female worker said with a perky smile and started preparing his order with quick, efficient hands.

He could smell the slightest scent of Keena's arousal and heard her pulse quicken. Ever since that first night when he caught her intoxicating feminine scent amidst the sea of specians at Spiked, the species bar, and tasted her sweet soft lips, he could not stop thinking about her. Both he and his jaguar were fascinated with wild interest with everything about Keena. He had been thoroughly enjoying prowling from a friendly distance with a predatory watchful gaze on his gorgeous prey. The past several months had been a torturous game of tease and a sheer show of his self-restraint. Oh, he played with her plenty up until this point. But now it was time to paw her in a bit more of obvious ways. Especially because his control was starting to tread a thin line and his sexual frustration did nothing but make matters worse.

He was known in his pack for his faceless fuck routine and, before meeting Keena, he indulged in that often. In fact, he had been happily doing that for decades. Sex was just a physical release. It was a way to play and blow off some steam. He rarely fucked the same female twice, not only on principal but also because it got quickly complicated on the females part. He wasn't a bastard about any of it either. In fact, it was cordial between him and the females afterward. He was one hundred percent upfront with every single female beforehand. They knew that it was just a quick, fun fuck and nothing else. And almost all of the females were on the same page, except there were a few who thought they'd be the exception. They weren't, of course. Not by far. He knew his heart was permanently closed. He once was young and dumb. He had been there and done that and vowed that would never happen—ever again. But that didn't mean that he couldn't date Keena. And, yeah, there was the added complication of her friendship with not only him but also Caly and his pack. But he wouldn't let that stop him from pursuing what had both his and his jaguar's rapt attention.

While they walked through the park, he kept the banter playful and light. His plan was to slowly tease this female and dance along the edge of the friends-not-friends barrier she had in place. It went without saying that he wouldn't cross any lines without her consent. But who said he couldn't have some fun while waiting for her to make the next big step? So, right now he was working on getting everything in place so that the bases were loaded and the baseball was resting on that tee, as if it were served up on a silver platter, just waiting for her to hit a home run.

"Okay, I did my best work but I'm tappin' out." She laughed a little as she held up the white flag, or in this case, the ice cream cone with less than a quarter of the Dark Ambrosia left on a partially eaten cone. At this point, it actually just looked like a mini ice cream cone of sorts.

"You did good, female," he grunted in approval and meant it. The damn cones were huge. Of course, it was nothing that his bottomless pit of a stomach couldn't handle. He took her sweet offering and with hooded eyes said, "I'll happily lick up the last of your ambrosia and savor every taste." With smoldering eye contact, his tongue licked the cone in the slowest ascent to only slightly suck at the top.

Her lips parted on a breathy exhale as the juncture between her thighs responded in the most feminine of ways. Suddenly, the memory of his mouth on hers slammed into her mind. The silky sensuality of his emotions rubbed up against her skin and it sent a shiver down her spine. She unknowingly licked her lips while staring deep into his piercing blue eyes. His deceptively lazy, feline smile was full of dark promises. A heartbeat later, he proceeded to walk down the path as if they did not just share the erotically electric moment.

Putty. Her legs were putty. And it was a miracle that she wasn't a melted pool of the dark ambrosia on the park path right now. For a moment, all she could do was watch that wicked male saunter down the path in that easy-going way he had of moving his big body.

Walk. Right foot. Left foot. Right foot. Left foot, she mentally commanded and—hey, what do you know? Her body seemed to be on board with following that male. It took her a few steps to catch up to his long, lazy strides and when she did, she looked over at him. He was already done with the mini cone and her eyes fell to the corner of his mouth.

Cute, she thought with curved lips, seeing that a smudge of chocolate ice cream had escaped and took up residence at the cross streets of his lips and chin. She could tell by that smug, satisfied expression on his face, he wasn't even aware of the offending sweetness. She looked at the chocolate smudge again. Was the Universe being cruel or giving her a gift, wrapped in chocolate?

Are you really going to do this? She bit her lip because she already knew the answer. And screw it. She already passed the line. So, why hold back now? Hell, the line was so far behind her that she didn't even see it anymore. She softly touched his strong arm and he looked at her in question, as if not expecting that.

Yeah, well, get in line, she thought, because she wasn't even expecting it either. It took everything in her to not look at the smudge or let her lips betray her in a playful smile. She simply tugged on his arm with the nonverbal motion for him to lean down. And this time, his reaction was the one that had her in unexpected territory. She caught his lips twitch in amusement and, as he leaned down, it was clear he thought she was going to whisper in his ear. He probably thought it would be like when he whispered in her ear earlier at the ice cream shop.

Again, cute, she thought, as her slight fingers landed on his chin and gently guided his face towards her. Without pause, she slowly licked the chocolate smudge off of the corner of his mouth. Instantly, a fire ignited in his eyes and the smoldering desire between them crackled with intensity. She brushed her lips on his in a teasing motion.

The unexpected teasing torture of witnessing her lick her ice cream cone during their entire walk, drove both him and his jaguar wild and had him on the knife-edge of his control. And when she slowly licked the corner of his mouth and kissed him? Yeah, well, that control snapped.

With shifter speed, he was in front of her and pressed her body into his as he kissed her soft lips. One of his hands gripped her waist and the other was at the crook of her neck with his fingers tangled in her hair. Their kiss quickly escalated into a hot and demanding territory. To his sensual satisfaction, she playfully nipped at his lower lip and he growled in approval before nipping at hers. He slightly tugged at the grip he had in her hair and tilted her head so he could deepen their kiss. Her lips parted for him and he slid his tongue inside. Their tongues were in the most sensual of duels. The moment he caught the scent of her arousal, he growled into the kiss.

Too soon. She pulled away from the kiss way too soon. Their chests were heaving and pupils were dilated with desire—his piercing blue eyes also held a slight glow of erotic promises. It took him a minute to remember where they were. Oh, yeah, they were in the middle of a public park. And, hey, it looked like their teenage, lip-lock sesh caught some attention of a few onlookers. His chuckle was low even for his already naturally deep vocal range.

"What?" she asked with notes of breathy curiosity, wondering why he was chuckling.

He indicated with his eyes and a slight nod of his head toward a couple of the onlookers.

She chortled. "I see."

"I don't mind voyeurs if you don't." His voice was rough as he waggled his brows.

"I prefer intimate privacy," she replied in a husky tone.

"Hold on to my back and I could have us up that tree in a few seconds." He shot her a feline grin full of intimate promises.

She laughed but she got the feeling he was only half-joking about that. "Maybe another time," she teased.

"Duly noted." He grinned and then stole a quick kiss while playfully squeezing her ass.

She snorted in delight as he kept both his hands firmly on her ass. "You're so bad." She laughed a little but it was hardly more than an exhalation of air.

"Haven't we covered that before?" He shot her a mischievous grin accompanied by another gentle squeeze of her ass, as if in emphasis. They both knew what he was referring to, of course. That was what she had said to him a couple of times now, including the first time they met at Spiked and then again when she went as his date to the Gallagher gathering.

"I believe we have," she purred back, hearing and feeling the low rumble in his chest in response. Something about that growl was so sexy and safe. Yes, she felt safe in his arms. She leaned her head on his chest and slid her arms around him in their first-ever embrace. She breathed deep and exhaled a contented sigh.

"I probably should warn you against deep breathing," he drawled.

"Why?" Her lips curved in curiosity.

"You didn't know?"

She looked up to see him flash her his heart-stopping smile. "Know what?" This time, her curiosity was mixed with a hint of suspicion. She knew he was playing with her but she wasn't quite sure what the endgame was.

"Well, I got my ass kicked in yoga and haven't showered yet."

She laughed openly and her joy was palpable. She loved how this male could make her laugh until her side hurt and then make her laugh some more. This time, she added a little theatrics to her deep inhale. "I didn't even notice."

One of his hands slid up her back and cupped the nape of her neck. He leaned down and pressed his lips to hers.

* * *

What is taking her so long? Liam Carter thought as annoyed anger started to bubble within him.

While in his luxury sports car, he took a couple of conscious breaths just the way Keena had taught him once. The breathing didn't help but the memory of her did. The bubbling emotion simmered slightly. His eyes flicked to the time displayed on the dash before refocusing back on the building. He became too antsy to sit patiently in the car. Patience was never his strong suit after all. Closing the car door, he leaned up against the side of his car. To anyone who noticed him, he appeared as he always did: cool, calm, collected, and quite charming. It wasn't hard to master that over the centuries, especially in all of those important aristocratic business meetings.

"Oh, how sweet. Gerry, why don't you do things like that for me anymore?" A female on the arm of a male gave Liam a sweet smile with fond memories swimming in her eyes. He returned her smile with his own as the couple walked past.

Across the street, the door to Inner Serenity opened. Just as Liam was about to walk toward it, he saw Keena smiling and walking out with another male. No, not just any other male. It was the same male she was with at the Gallagher gathering. He knew because he saw them there together. And not only that, but there was irrefutable evidence of that in the form of a picture. The picture captured exactly what he witnessed at the gathering: Keena being too damn close to that male and laughing openly, while the male's eyes did nothing to hide his intense focus on her. It had taken every ounce of his self-control to keep it together. If he was in any other place, and not among peers and business associates, then he probably would have lost it. But he knew all too well not to show his hand when in the middle of a sea of ancients and aristocrats, who wouldn't blink an eye to use his weakness to their strategic advantage in order to further advance their own position, both politically and socially.

Because for almost all ancients and aristocrats, it was all about money and power.

How dare Keena embarrass him like that. How dare she make him look bad. Starting with the fact that his own damn assistant was the one who showed him the photograph of Keena and the male featured in the Species Gazette.

Rhyker, he thought, as the muscle in his jaw clenched. It took almost no effort to find out that male's identity because it turned out that was Rhyker Kingsley of the prestigious Kingsley bloodline of jaguar shifters. He was also a part of Orion's Order, which Liam found amusing, of course. Because what a disgrace for the two Kingsley sons to go off and play cops and robbers instead of following in their father's footsteps and honoring their bloodline.

After further digging, he discovered that last year, The Order moved in with the ancient, Riordan Knight. And he knew all too well of Dr. Aleia Reaux of the Knight bloodline because that was Keena's best friend. It didn't take a genius to put all of the pieces together. He had finally caught her red-handed at her own lies and deceit. A memory flashed through his mind. It was the last night he touched her. Granted, it was not in the way he intended to touch her and he did regret that. But this just confirmed she did, in fact, lie straight to his face. He now knew that night she came home late from a supposed "healer consult" was just a cover for her cheating on him with none other than Rhyker.

From one moment to the next, the simmering anger transformed into an erupting volcano of fury. As he watched them walk into the ice cream shop, the dozen yellow roses he held suddenly burst into flames. The gray ashes blew to the ground on a light breeze.

How dare you, Keena. You said you were mine and I do not share what is mine.

Sign up for the newsletter at www.mcsolaris.com to be the first to grab your copy of Rhyker's Key (Book 2 in Orion's Order series)! See the next page for a special note from Caly to *you!*

A Special Note From Caly To You

Hello, fellow lover of all things PNR, HEA, and my crew of specian friends!

Oh, and PS, in case you're wondering, PNR means "Paranormal Romance" and HEA means "Happy Ever After." I know, right? Who knew that there was a whole "secret language" just for romance book nerds like us?

Anywho, would you mind doing me like a humongously huge favor? Pretty please with a cherry on top? *Insert my cheesy smile here*

It's super simple and easy and it can take like five seconds... And, okay, I know that's like five seconds of your time that you would have spent swooning over my mouth-watering alpha wolf, Blake. Or maybe you have your eye on our resident, tattooed bad boy, Rhyker? Or his hilarious twin, Rhy? Or maybe you're into Deac the Geek? Or maybe you have a thing for an older male who has some serious GQ swag? Wait, don't tell me you're secretly swooning over Mr. Dark and Deadly himself?

Well, how about we make a deal?

If you do this super easy favor for me then I promise I'll put in a good word about you to that sexy specian pack mate of mine... Oh, and if you also share my story with your friends, then I will do my best to get said sexy specian male to open up and share his story with you one day.

What do you say?!

All I'm asking is if you would pretty please leave a review on Amazon. Yup. That's it! I know super simple, right? And once you're done you can totally go back to swooning over one of my pack brothers... I promise I won't tell. ;)

Okay, sorry I have to run but I am meeting up with M.C. Solaris for tea so I can share more stories about my crew of specian friends. Oh, which reminds me, totally stalk her by joining our newsletter on www.mcsolaris.com so you can hear more about my crazy life and crew!

XO
Caly

www.mcsolaris.com
www.instagram.com/mcsolarisauthor
www.facebook.com/mcsolarisauthorofficial

About the Author

M.C. Solaris's life took an unexpected turn during the super blood moon eclipse on January 20, 2019. She woke up and began writing bios for her imaginary friends that she met that day. As soon as the pen hit the paper (or fingertips to the iPhone), she couldn't stop. It was kind of like one of those fire hydrants, spewing copious amounts of water all over the place. The characters and their stories just flowed out of her. She is honored to be the scribe, getting to share her friends' stories. You can read all about her gifted friends in the Orion's Order series (Book 1 is *Calypso's Heart*).

On a personal note, M.C. Solaris is actually the pseudonym of Marina Schroeder, women's health enthusiast and lover of all things paranormal romance (PNR) and happily ever after (HEA). When she is not curled up on the sofa with her partner's oversized hoodie, a PNR novel, peppermint tea, and one of her three cats, you will find her either at the ocean with her toes in the sand or in a forest hugging a tree. Well truthfully? There is one more place you might find her: trolling the aisles of Whole Foods for a satisfying combination of salty and sweet while hiding in her partner's hoodie… like any proper PNR-writing introvert.

Want to get the latest scoop, sneak peeks, and short shares all about her imaginary friends? Go to www.mcsolaris.com and sign up for the newsletter.

Welcome to The Order!
www.instagram.com/mcsolarisauthor
www.facebook.com/mcsolarisauthorofficial
www.mcsolaris.com

.

a **LANGE** medical book

CURRENT

Medical Diagnosis & Treatment 1995

Thirty-fourth Edition

Edited By

Lawrence M. Tierney, Jr., MD
Professor of Medicine
University of California, San Francisco
Associate Chief of Medical Services
Veterans Affairs Medical Center, San Francisco

Stephen J. McPhee, MD
Professor of Medicine
Division of General Internal Medicine
University of California, San Francisco

Maxine A. Papadakis, MD
Professor of Clinical Medicine and Epidemiology
Director of Student Programs, Medicine
University of California, San Francisco

With Associate Authors

Prentice-Hall International, Inc.

This edition may be sold only in those countries to which it is
consigned by Prentice Hall International. It is not to be re-exported
and it is not for sale in the USA, Mexico, or Canada.

Notice: The authors and the publisher of this volume have taken care to
make certain that the doses of drugs and schedules of treatment are correct
and compatible with the standards generally accepted at the time of
publication. Nevertheless, as new information becomes available, changes in
treatment and in the use of drugs become necessary. The reader is advised to
carefully consult the instruction and information material included in the
package insert of each drug or therapeutic agent before administration.
This advice is especially important when using new or infrequently used drugs.
The author and publisher disclaims any liability, loss, injury, or damage incurred as
a consequence, directly or indirectly, or the use and application of any of
the contents of the volume.

95 96 97 98 99 / 10 9 8 7 6 5 4 3 2 1

Prentice-Hall International (UK) Limited, *London*
Prentice-Hall of Australia, Pty. Limited, *Sydney*
Prentice-Hall Canada, Inc. *Toronto*
Prentice-Hall Hispanoamericana, S.A., *Mexico*
Prentice-Hall of India Private Limited, *New Delhi*
Prentice-Hall of Japan, Inc., *Tokyo*
Simon & Schuster Asia Pte. Ltd., *Singapore*
Editora Prentice-Hall do Brasil Ltda., *Rio de Janeiro*
Prentice-Hall, *Englewood Cliffs, New Jersey*

ISBN: 0–8385–1460–X.
ISSN: 0092–8682

Production Editor: Christine Langan
Acquisitions Editor: Shelley Reinhardt

PRINTED IN THE UNITED STATES OF AMERICA